STEELHEART

STEELHEART

BRANDON SANDERSON

DELACORTE PRESS

Text copyright © 2013 by Dragonsteel Entertainment, LLC
Jacket art copyright © 2013 by Mike Bryan

Visit us on the Web! randomhouse.com/teens

Educators and librarians, for a variety of teaching tools, visit us at RHTeachersLibrarians.com

Library of Congress Cataloging-in-Publication Data
Sanderson, Brandon.
Steelheart / Brandon Sanderson. — First edition.
pages cm
Summary: At age eight, David watched as his father was killed by an Epic, a human with superhuman powers, and now, ten years later, he joins the Reckoners—the only people who are trying to kill the Epics and end their tyranny.
ISBN 978-0-385-74356-3 (hc) — ISBN 978-0-449-81839-8 (ebook) —
ISBN 978-0-375-99121-9 (glb) — ISBN 978-0-385-37493-4 (intl. tr. pbk.)
[1. Supervillains—Fiction. 2. Guerrilla warfare—Fiction. 3. Science fiction.] I. Title.
PZ7.S19797Ste 2013
[Fic]—dc23
2012045751

The text of this book is set in 11.5-point Apollo MT.
Book design by Angela Carlino

Printed in the United States of America

10 9 8 7 6 5 4 3 2 1

First Edition

Random House Children's Books supports the First Amendment
and celebrates the right to read.

For Dallin Sanderson,

who fights evil each day with his smile

Prologue

I'VE seen Steelheart bleed.

It happened ten years ago; I was eight. My father and I were at the First Union Bank on Adams Street. We used the old street names back then, before the Annexation.

The bank was enormous. A single open chamber with white pillars surrounding a tile mosaic floor, broad doors that led deeper into the building. Two large revolving doors opened onto the street, with a set of conventional doors to the sides. Men and women streamed in and out, as if the room were the heart of some enormous beast, pulsing with a lifeblood of people and cash.

I knelt backward on a chair that was too big for me, watching the flow of people. I liked to watch people. The different shapes of faces, the hairstyles, the clothing, the expressions. Everyone showed so much *variety* back then. It was exciting.

"David, turn around, please," my father said. He had a soft voice. I'd never heard it raised, save for that one time at my mother's funeral. Thinking of his agony on that day still makes me shiver.

I turned around, sullen. We were to the side of the main bank chamber in one of the cubicles where the mortgage men worked. Our cubicle had glass sides, which made it less confining, but it still felt fake. There were little wood-framed pictures of family members on the walls, a cup of cheap candy with a glass lid on the desk, and a vase with faded plastic flowers on the filing cabinet.

It was an imitation of a comfortable home. Much like the man in front of us wore an imitation of a smile.

"If we had more collateral . . . ," the mortgage man said, showing teeth.

"Everything I own is on there," my father said, indicating the paper on the desk in front of us. His hands were thick with calluses, his skin tan from days spent working in the sun. My mother would have winced if she'd seen him go to a fancy appointment like this wearing his work jeans and an old T-shirt with a comic book character on it.

At least he'd combed his hair, though it was starting to thin. He didn't care about that as much as other men seemed to. "Just means fewer haircuts, Dave," he'd tell me, laughing as he ran his fingers through his wispy hair. I didn't point out that he was wrong. He would still have to get the same number of haircuts, at least until all of his hair fell out.

"I just don't think I can do anything about this," the mortgage man said. "You've been told before."

"The other man said it would be enough," my father replied, his large hands clasped before him. He looked concerned. Very concerned.

The mortgage man just continued to smile. He tapped the stack of papers on his desk. "The world is a much more dangerous place now, Mr. Charleston. The bank has decided against taking risks."

"Dangerous?" my father asked.

"Well, you know, the Epics . . ."

"But they *aren't* dangerous," my father said passionately. "The Epics are here to help."

Not this again, I thought.

The mortgage man's smile finally broke, as if he was taken aback by my father's tone.

"Don't you see?" my father said, leaning forward. "This isn't a dangerous time. It's a wonderful time!"

The mortgage man cocked his head. "Didn't your previous home get *destroyed* by an Epic?"

"Where there are villains, there will be heroes," my father said. "Just wait. They *will* come."

I believed him. A lot of people thought like he did, back then. It had only been two years since Calamity appeared in the sky. One year since ordinary men started changing. Turning into Epics—almost like superheroes from the stories.

We were still hopeful then. And ignorant.

"Well," the mortgage man said, clasping his hands on the table right beside a picture frame displaying a stock photo of smiling ethnic children. "Unfortunately, our underwriters don't agree with your assessment. You'll have to . . ."

They kept talking, but I stopped paying attention. I let my eyes wander back toward the crowds, then turned around again, kneeling on the chair. My father was too engrossed in the conversation to scold me.

So I was actually watching when the Epic strolled into the bank. I noticed him immediately, though nobody else seemed to pay him much heed. Most people say you can't tell an Epic from an ordinary man unless he starts using his powers, but they're wrong. Epics carry themselves differently. That sense of confidence, that subtle self-satisfaction. I've always been able to spot them.

Even as a kid I knew there was something different about that man. He wore a relaxed-fitting black business suit with a light tan shirt underneath, no tie. He was tall and lean, but *solid,* like a lot of Epics are. Muscled and toned in a way that you could see even through the loose clothing.

He strode to the center of the room. Sunglasses hung from his breast pocket, and he smiled as he put them on. Then he raised a finger and pointed with a casual tapping motion at a passing woman.

She vaporized to dust, clothing burning away, skeleton falling forward and clattering to the floor. Her earrings and wedding ring didn't dissolve, though. They hit the floor with distinct *ping*s I could hear even over the noise in the room.

The room fell still. People froze, horrified. Conversations stopped, though the mortgage man kept right on rambling, lecturing my father.

He finally choked off as the screaming began.

I don't remember how I felt. Isn't that odd? I can remember the lighting—those magnificent chandeliers up above, sprinkling the room with bits of refracted light. I can remember the lemon-ammonia scent of the recently cleaned floor. I can remember all too well the piercing shouts of terror, the mad cacophony as people scrambled for doors.

Most clearly, I remember the Epic smiling broadly—almost leering—as he pointed at people passing, reducing them to ash and bones with a mere gesture.

I was transfixed. Perhaps I was in shock. I clung to the back of my chair, watching the slaughter with wide eyes.

Some people near the doors escaped. Anyone who got too close to the Epic died. Several employees and customers huddled together on the ground or hid behind desks. Strangely, the room grew still. The Epic stood as if he were alone, bits of paper floating down through the air, bones and black ash scattered on the floor about him.

"I am called Deathpoint," he said. "It's not the cleverest of names,

I'll admit. But I find it memorable." His voice was eerily conversational, as if he were chatting with friends over drinks.

He began to stroll through the room. "A thought occurred to me this morning," he said. The room was large enough that his voice echoed. "I was showering, and it struck me. It asked . . . Deathpoint, why are you going to rob a bank today?"

He pointed lazily at a pair of security guards who had edged out of a side hallway just beside the mortgage cubicles. The guards turned to dust, their badges, belt buckles, guns, and bones hitting the floor. I could hear their bones knock against one another as they dropped. There are a lot of bones in a man's body, more than I'd realized, and they made a big mess when they scattered. An odd detail to notice about the horrible scene. But I remember it distinctly.

A hand clasped my shoulder. My father had crouched low before his chair and was trying to pull me down, to keep the Epic from seeing me. But I wouldn't move, and my father couldn't force me without making a scene.

"I've been planning this for weeks, you see," the Epic said. "But the thought only struck me this morning. Why? Why rob the bank? I can take anything I want anyway! It's ridiculous!" He leaped around the side of a counter, causing the teller cowering there to scream. I could just barely make her out, huddled on the floor.

"Money is worthless to me, you see," the Epic said. "*Completely* worthless." He pointed. The woman shriveled to ash and bone.

The Epic pivoted, pointing at several places around the room, killing people who were trying to flee. Last of all, he pointed directly at me.

Finally I felt an emotion. A spike of terror.

A skull hit the desk behind us, bouncing off and spraying ash as it clattered to the floor. The Epic had pointed not at me but at the mortgage man, who had been hiding by his desk behind me. Had the man tried to run?

The Epic turned back toward the tellers behind the counter. My father's hand still gripped my shoulder, tense. I could feel his worry for me almost as if it were a physical thing, running up his arm and into my own.

I felt terror then. Pure, immobilizing terror. I curled up on the chair, whimpering, shaking, trying to banish from my mind the images of the terrible deaths I'd just seen.

My father pulled his hand away. "Don't move," he mouthed.

I nodded, too scared to do anything else. My father glanced around his chair. Deathpoint was chatting with one of the tellers. Though I couldn't see them, I could hear when the bones fell. He was executing them one at a time.

My father's expression grew dark. Then he glanced toward a side hallway. Escape?

No. That was where the guards had fallen. I could see through the glass side of the cubicle to where a handgun lay on the ground, barrel buried in ash, part of the grip lying atop a rib bone. My father eyed it. He'd been in the National Guard when he was younger.

Don't do it! I thought, panicked. *Father, no!* I couldn't voice the words, though. My chin quivered as I tried to speak, like I was cold, and my teeth chattered. What if the Epic heard me?

I couldn't let my father do such a foolish thing! He was all I had. No home, no family, no mother. As he moved to go, I forced myself to reach out and grab his arm. I shook my head at him, trying to think of anything that would stop him. "Please," I managed to whisper. "The heroes. You said they'll come. Let them stop him!"

"Sometimes, son," my father said, prying my fingers free, "you have to help the heroes along."

He glanced at Deathpoint, then scrambled into the next cubicle. I held my breath and peeked very carefully around the side of the chair. I had to know. Even cowering and trembling, I had to see.

Deathpoint hopped over the counter and landed on the other side, our side. "And so, it doesn't matter," he said, still speaking in a conversational tone, strolling across the floor. "Robbing a bank would give me money, but I don't need to *buy* things." He raised a murderous finger. "A conundrum. Fortunately, while showering, I realized something else: killing people every time you want something can be extremely inconvenient. What I needed to do was *frighten* everyone, show them my power. That way, in the future, nobody would deny me the things I wanted to take."

He leaped around a pillar on the other side of the bank, surprising a woman holding her child. "Yes," he continued, "robbing a bank for the money would be pointless—but showing what I can do . . . that is still important. So I continued with my plan." He pointed, killing the child, leaving the horrified woman holding a pile of bones and ash. "Aren't you glad?"

I gaped at the sight, the terrified woman trying to hold the blanket tight, the infant's bones shifting and slipping free. In that moment it all became so much more *real* to me. Horribly real. I felt a sudden nausea.

Deathpoint's back was toward us.

My father scrambled out of the cubicle and grabbed the fallen gun. Two people hiding behind a nearby pillar made for the closest doorway and pushed past my father in their haste, nearly knocking him down.

Deathpoint turned. My father was still kneeling there, trying to get the pistol raised, fingers slipping on the ash-covered metal.

The Epic raised his hand.

"What are you doing here?" a voice boomed.

The Epic spun. So did I. I think everyone must have turned toward that deep, powerful voice.

A figure stood in the doorway to the street. He was backlit, little more than a silhouette because of the bright sunlight shining in behind him. An amazing, herculean, awe-inspiring silhouette.

You've probably seen pictures of Steelheart, but let me tell you that pictures are completely inadequate. No photograph, video, or painting could *ever* capture that man. He wore black. A shirt, tight across an inhumanly large and strong chest. Pants, loose but not baggy. He didn't wear a mask, like some of the early Epics did, but a magnificent silver cape fluttered out behind him.

He didn't *need* a mask. This man had no reason to hide. He spread his arms out from his sides, and wind blew the doors open around him. Ash scattered across the floor and papers fluttered. Steelheart rose into the air a few inches, cape flaring out. He began to glide forward into the room. Arms like steel girders, legs like mountains, neck like a tree stump. He wasn't bulky or awkward, though. He was *majestic,* with that jet-black hair, that square jaw, an impossible physique, and a frame of nearly seven feet.

And those eyes. Intense, demanding, *uncompromising* eyes.

As Steelheart flew gracefully into the room, Deathpoint hastily raised a finger and pointed at him. Steelheart's shirt sizzled in one little section, like a cigarette had been put out on the cloth, but he showed no reaction. He floated down the steps and landed gently on the floor a short distance from Deathpoint, his enormous cape settling around him.

Deathpoint pointed again, looking frantic. Another meager sizzle. Steelheart stepped up to the smaller Epic, towering over him.

I knew in that moment that this was what my father had been waiting for. This was the hero everyone had been hoping would come, the one who would compensate for the other Epics and their evil ways. This man was here to save us.

Steelheart reached out, grabbing Deathpoint as he belatedly tried to dash away. Deathpoint jerked to a halt, his sunglasses clattering to the ground, and gasped in pain.

"I asked you a question," Steelheart said in a voice like rumbling thunder. He spun Deathpoint around to look him in the eyes. "What are you doing here?"

Deathpoint twitched. He looked panicked. "I . . . I . . ."

Steelheart raised his other hand, lifting a finger. "I have claimed this city, little Epic. It is *mine*." He paused. "And it is *my* right to dominate the people here, not yours."

Deathpoint cocked his head.

What? I thought.

"You seem to have strength, little Epic," Steelheart said, glancing at the bones scattered around the room. "I will accept your subservience. Give me your loyalty or die."

I couldn't believe Steelheart's words. They stunned me as soundly as Deathpoint's murders had.

That concept—*serve me or die*—would become the foundation of his rule. He looked around the room and spoke in a booming voice. "I am emperor of this city now. You will obey me. I own this land. I own these buildings. When you pay taxes, they come to me. If you disobey, you will die."

Impossible, I thought. *Not him too.* I couldn't accept that this incredible being was just like all the others.

I wasn't the only one.

"It's not supposed to be this way," my father said.

Steelheart turned, apparently surprised to hear anything from one of the room's cowering, whimpering peons.

My father stepped forward, gun down at his side. "No," he said. "You aren't like the others. I can see it. You're better than they are." He walked forward, stopping only a few feet from the two Epics. "You're here to save us."

The room was silent save for the sobbing of the woman who still clutched the remains of her dead child. She was madly, vainly trying to gather the bones, to not leave a single tiny vertebra on the ground. Her dress was covered in ash.

Before either Epic could respond, the side doors burst open. Men in black armor with assault rifles piled into the bank and opened fire.

Back then, the government hadn't given up yet. They still tried to fight the Epics, to subject them to mortal laws. It was clear from the beginning that when it came to Epics, you didn't hesitate, you didn't negotiate. You came in with guns blazing and hoped that the Epic you were facing could be killed by ordinary bullets.

My father sprang away at a run, old battle instincts prompting him to put his back to a pillar nearer the front of the bank. Steelheart turned, a bemused look on his face, as a wave of bullets washed over him. They bounced off his skin, ripping his clothing but leaving him completely unscathed.

Epics like him are what forced the United States to pass the Capitulation Act that gave all Epics complete immunity from the law. Gunfire cannot harm Steelheart—rockets, tanks, the most advanced weapons of man don't even scratch him. Even if he could be captured, prisons couldn't hold him.

The government eventually declared men such as Steelheart to be natural forces, like hurricanes or earthquakes. Trying to tell Steelheart that he can't take what he wants would be as vain as trying to pass a bill that forbids the wind to blow.

In the bank that day, I saw with my own eyes why so many have decided not to fight back. Steelheart raised a hand, energy beginning to glow around it with a cool yellow light. Deathpoint hid behind him, sheltered from the bullets. Unlike Steelheart, he seemed to fear getting shot. Not all Epics are impervious to gunfire, just the most powerful ones.

Steelheart released a burst of yellow-white energy from his hand, vaporizing a group of the soldiers. Chaos followed. Soldiers ducked for cover wherever they could find it; smoke and chips of marble filled the air. One of the soldiers fired some kind of rocket from his gun, and it shot past Steelheart—who continued to blast his enemies with energy—to hit the back end of the bank, blowing open the vault.

Flaming bills exploded outward. Coins sprayed into the air and showered the ground.

Shouts. Screams. Insanity.

The soldiers died quickly. I continued to huddle on my chair, hands pressed against my ears. It was all so *loud*.

Deathpoint was still standing behind Steelheart. And as I watched, he smiled, then raised his hands, reaching for Steelheart's neck. I don't know what he was planning to do. Likely he had a second power. Most Epics as strong as he was possess more than one.

Maybe it would have been enough to kill Steelheart. I doubt it, but either way, we'll never know.

A single *pop* sounded in the air. The explosion had been so loud it left me deafened to the point that I barely recognized the sound as a gunshot. As the smoke from the explosion cleared, I could see my father. He stood a short distance in front of Steelheart with arms raised, his back to the pillar. He bore an expression of determination on his face and held the gun, pointing it at Steelheart.

No. Not at *Steelheart*. At Deathpoint, who stood just behind him.

Deathpoint collapsed, a bullet wound in his forehead. Dead. Steelheart turned sharply, looking at the lesser Epic. Then he looked back at my father and raised a hand to his face. There, on Steelheart's cheek just below his eye, was a line of blood.

At first I thought it must have come from Deathpoint. But when Steelheart wiped it away, it continued to bleed.

My father had shot at Deathpoint, but the bullet had passed by Steelheart first—and had grazed him on the way.

That bullet had *hurt* Steelheart, while the soldiers' bullets had bounced off.

"I'm sorry," my father said, sounding anxious. "He was reaching for you. I—"

Steelheart's eyes went wide, and he raised his hand before him, looking at his own blood. He seemed completely astounded. He glanced at the vault behind him, then looked at my father. In the settling smoke and dust, the two figures stood before each other— one a massive, regal Epic, the other a small homeless man with a silly T-shirt and worn jeans.

Steelheart jumped forward with blinding speed and slammed a hand against my father's chest, crushing him back against the white stone pillar. Bones shattered, and blood poured from my father's mouth.

"No!" I screamed. My own voice felt odd in my ears, like I was underwater. I wanted to run to him, but I was too frightened. I still think of my cowardice that day, and it sickens me.

Steelheart stepped to the side, picking up the gun my father had dropped. Fury burning in his eyes, Steelheart pointed the gun directly at my father's chest, then fired a single shot into the already-fallen man.

He does that. Steelheart likes to kill people with their own guns. It's become one of his hallmarks. He has incredible strength and can fire blasts of energy from his hands. But when it comes to killing someone he deems worth his special attention, he prefers to use their gun.

Steelheart left my father to slump down the pillar and tossed the handgun at his feet. Then he began to shoot blasts of energy in all directions, setting chairs, walls, counters, everything alight. I was thrown from my chair as one of the blasts struck nearby, and I rolled to the floor.

The explosions threw wood and glass into the air, shaking the room. In a few heartbeats, Steelheart caused enough destruction to make Deathpoint's murder spree seem tame. Steelheart laid waste to that room, knocking down pillars, killing anyone he saw. I'm not sure how I survived, crawling over the shards of glass and splinters of wood, plaster, and dust raining down around me.

Steelheart let out a scream of rage and indignation. I could barely hear it, but I could *feel* it shattering what windows remained, vibrating the walls. Then something spread out from him, a wave of energy. And the floor around him changed colors, transforming to metal.

The transformation spread, washing through the entire room at incredible speed. The floor beneath me, the wall beside me, the bits of glass on the ground—it all changed to steel. What we've learned now is that Steelheart's rage transforms inanimate objects around him into steel, though it leaves living things and anything close to them alone.

By the time his cry faded, most of the bank's interior had been changed completely to steel, though a large chunk of the ceiling was still wood and plaster, as was a section of one wall. Steelheart suddenly launched himself into the air, breaking through the ceiling and several stories to head into the sky.

I stumbled to my father, hoping he could do something, somehow stop the madness. When I got to him, he was spasming, blood covering his face, chest bleeding from the bullet wound. I clung to his arm, panicked.

Incredibly, he managed to speak, but I couldn't hear what he said. I was deafened completely by that point. My father reached out, a quivering hand touching my chin. He said something else, but I still couldn't hear him.

I wiped my eyes with my sleeve, then tried to pull his arm to get him to stand up and come with me. The entire building was shaking.

My father grabbed my shoulder, and I looked at him, tears in my eyes. He spoke a single word—one I could make out from the movement of his lips.

"Go."

I understood. Something huge had just happened, something that exposed Steelheart, something that terrified him. He was a new Epic back then, not very well known in town, but I'd heard of him. He was supposed to be invulnerable.

That gunshot had wounded him, and everyone there had seen him weak. There was no way he'd let us live—he had to preserve his secret.

Tears streaming down my cheeks, feeling like an utter coward for leaving my father, I turned and ran. The building continued to tremble with explosions; walls cracked, sections of the ceiling crumbled. Steelheart was trying to bring it down.

Some people ran out the front doors, but Steelheart killed them from above. Others ran out side doors, but those doorways only led deeper into the bank. Those people were crushed as most of the building collapsed.

I hid in the vault.

I wish I could claim that I was smart for making that choice, but I'd simply gotten turned around. I vaguely remember crawling into a dark corner and curling up into a ball, crying as the rest of the building fell apart. Since most of the main room had been turned to metal by Steelheart's rage, and the vault was steel in the first place, those areas didn't crumble as the rest of the building did.

Hours later, I was pulled out of the wreckage by a rescue worker. I was dazed, barely conscious, and the light blinded me as I was dug free. The room I had been in had sunk partially, lurched on its side, but it was still strangely intact, the walls and most of the ceiling now made of steel. The rest of the large building was rubble.

The rescue worker whispered something in my ear. "Pretend to be dead." Then she carried me to a line of corpses and put a blanket over me. She'd guessed what Steelheart might do to survivors.

Once she went back to look for other survivors, I panicked and crawled from beneath the blanket. It was dark outside, though it should have only been late afternoon. Nightwielder was upon us; Steelheart's reign had begun.

I stumbled away and limped into an alley. That saved my life a second time. Moments after I escaped, Steelheart returned, floating down past the rescue lights to land beside the wreckage. He carried someone with him, a thin woman with her hair in a bun. I would later learn she was an Epic named Faultline, who had the power to move earth. Though she would one day challenge Steelheart, at that point she served him.

She waved her hand and the ground began to shake.

I fled, confused, frightened, pained. Behind me, the ground opened up, swallowing the remnants of the bank—along with the corpses of the fallen, the survivors who were receiving medical attention, and the rescue workers themselves. Steelheart wanted to leave no evidence. He had Faultline bury all of them under hundreds of feet of earth, killing anyone who could possibly speak of what had happened in that bank.

Except me.

Later that night, he performed the Great Transfersion, an awesome display of power by which he transformed most of Chicago—buildings, vehicles, streets—into steel. That included a large portion of Lake Michigan, which became a glassy expanse of black metal. It was there that he built his palace.

I know, better than anyone else, that there are no heroes coming to save us. There are no good Epics. None of them protect us. Power corrupts, and absolute power corrupts absolutely.

We live with them. We try to exist *despite* them. Once the Capitulation Act was passed, most people stopped fighting. In some areas of what we now call the Fractured States, the old government is still marginally in control. They let the Epics do as they please, and try to continue as a broken society. Most places are chaos, though, with no law at all.

In a few places, like Newcago, a single godlike Epic rules as a tyrant. Steelheart has no rivals here. Everyone knows he's invulnerable. Nothing harms him: not bullets, not explosions, not electricity. In the early years, other Epics tried to take him down and claim his throne, as Faultline attempted.

They're all dead. Now it's very rare that any of them tries.

However, if there's one fact we can hold on to, it's this: *every* Epic has a weakness. Something that invalidates their powers, something that turns them back into an ordinary person, if only for a moment. Steelheart is no exception; the events on that day in the bank prove it.

My mind holds a clue to how Steelheart might be killed. Something about the bank, the situation, the gun, or my father himself was able to counteract Steelheart's invulnerability. Many of you probably know about that scar on Steelheart's cheek. Well, as far as I can determine, I'm the only living person who knows how he got it.

I've seen Steelheart bleed.

And I *will* see him bleed again.

PART ONE

1

I skidded down a stairwell and crunched against steel gravel at the bottom. Sucking in air, I dashed through one of the dark understreets of Newcago. Ten years had passed since my father's death. That fateful day had become known by most people as the Annexation.

I wore a loose leather jacket and jeans, and had my rifle slung over my shoulder. The street was dark, even though it was one of the shallow understreets with grates and holes looking up into the sky.

It's always dark in Newcago. Nightwielder was one of the first Epics to swear allegiance to Steelheart, and is a member of his inner circle. Because of Nightwielder there are no sunrises, and no moon to speak of, just pure darkness in the sky. All the time, every day. The only thing you can see up there is Calamity, which looks kind of like a bright red star or comet. Calamity began to shine one year before men started turning into Epics. Nobody knows why or how it still shines through the darkness. Of course, nobody knows why the Epics started appearing, or what their connection is to Calamity either.

I kept running, cursing myself for not leaving earlier. The lights along the ceiling of the understreet flickered, their coverings tinted blue. The understreet was littered with its typical losers: addicts at corners, dealers—or worse—in alleyways. There were some furtive groups of workers going to or from their jobs, thick coats and collars flipped up to hide their faces. They walked hunched over, eyes on the ground.

I'd spent most of the last decade among people like them, working at a place we simply called the Factory. Part orphanage, part school, it was mostly a way to exploit children for free labor. At least the Factory had given me a room and food for the better part of ten years. That had been way better than living on the street, and I hadn't minded for one moment working for my food. Child labor laws were relics of a time when people could care about such things.

I pushed my way past a pack of workers. One cursed at me in a language that sounded vaguely Spanish. I looked up to see where I was. Most intersections were marked by spray-painted street names on the gleaming metallic walls.

When the Great Transfersion caused the better part of the Old City to be turned into solid steel, that included the soil and rock, dozens—maybe hundreds—of feet down into the ground. During the early years of his reign, Steelheart pretended to be a benevolent—if ruthless—dictator. His Diggers had cut out several levels of understreets, complete with buildings, and people had flowed to Newcago for work.

Life had been difficult here, but it had been chaos everywhere else—Epics warring with one another over territory, various para-governmental or state military groups trying to claim land. Newcago was different. Here you could be casually murdered by an Epic who didn't like the way you looked at him, but at least there was electricity, water, and food. People adapt. That's what we do.

Except for the ones who refuse to.

Come on, I thought, checking the time on my mobile, which I wore in the forearm mount of my coat. *Blasted rail line outage.* I took another shortcut, barreling through an alleyway. It was dim, but after ten years of living in perpetual gloom, you got used to it.

I passed huddled forms of sleeping beggars, then leaped over one sprawled in the street at the end of the alleyway and burst out onto Siegel Street, a wider thoroughfare that was better lit than most. Here, one level underground, the Diggers had hollowed out rooms that people used as shops. They were closed up for the moment, though more than a few had someone watching out front with a shotgun. Steelheart's police theoretically patrolled the understreets, but they rarely came to help except in the worst cases.

Originally, Steelheart had spoken of a grand underground city that would stretch down dozens of levels. That was before the Diggers had gone mad, before Steelheart had given up the pretense of caring about the people in the understreets. Still, these upper levels weren't terrible. At least there was a sense of organization, and plenty of burrowed-out holes to use as homes.

The lights in the ceiling here were faintly green and yellow, alternating. If you knew the color patterns of the various streets, you could navigate pretty well through the understreets. The top levels, at least. Even veterans of the city tended to avoid the lower levels, called the steel catacombs, where it was too easy to get lost.

Two blocks to Schuster Street, I thought, glancing through a gap in the ceiling toward the better-lit, gleaming skyscrapers above. I jogged the two blocks, then swerved into a stairwell going up, feet falling on steel steps that reflected the dim, half-functional lights.

I scrambled out onto a metal street, then immediately ducked into an alleyway. A lot of people said that the overstreets weren't nearly as dangerous as the understreets, but I never felt comfortable on them. I never felt safe anywhere, to be honest, not even at the Factory with the other kids. But up here . . . up here there were Epics.

Carrying a rifle around the understreets was common practice, but up here it could draw attention from Steelheart's soldiers or a passing Epic. It was best to remain hidden. I crouched beside some boxes in the alleyway, catching my breath. I glanced at my mobile, tapping over to a basic map of the area, then looked up.

Directly across from me was a building with red neon lettering. The Reeve Playhouse. As I watched, people began pouring out the front, and I breathed a sigh of relief. I'd made it just as the play ended.

The people were all overstreeters, in dark suits and colorful dresses. Some would be Epics, but most would not. Instead they were those who had somehow gotten ahead in life. Perhaps Steelheart favored them for tasks they performed, or perhaps they had simply been born to rich parents. Steelheart could take anything he wanted, but to have an empire he needed people to help rule. Bureaucrats, officers in his army, accountants, trading gurus, diplomats. Like the upper crust of an old-school dictatorship, these people lived off the crumbs that Steelheart left behind.

That meant they were almost as culpable as the Epics in keeping the rest of us oppressed, but I didn't bear them much ill will. The way the world was these days, you did what you had to in order to survive.

They had an old-fashioned style—it was the current trend. The men wore hats, and the women's dresses looked like those from pictures I'd seen of old Prohibition days. It was a direct contrast to the modern steel buildings and the distant thumping of an advanced Enforcement copter.

The opulent people suddenly began moving out of the way,

making room for a man in a bright red pinstriped suit, a red fedora, and a deep red and black cape.

I ducked down a little lower. It was Fortuity. He was an Epic with precognition powers. He could guess the numbers that would come up on a dice roll, for instance, or foretell the weather. He could also sense danger, and that elevated him to High Epic status. You couldn't kill a man like him with a simple rifle shot. He would know the shot was coming and would dodge it before you pulled the trigger. His powers were so well attuned that he could avoid a machine-gun barrage, and he would also know if his food had been poisoned or if a building was rigged with explosives.

High Epics. They're blasted hard to kill.

Fortuity was a moderately high-ranking member of Steelheart's government. Not part of his innermost circle, like Nightwielder, Firefight, or Conflux, but powerful enough to be feared by most of the minor Epics in town. He had a long face and a hawkish nose. He strolled to the curb in front of the playhouse, lighting a cigarette as the other patrons spilled out behind him. Two women in sleek gowns hung on his elbows.

I itched to unsling my rifle and take a shot at him. He was a sadistic monster. He claimed his powers worked best when practicing an art called extispicy: the reading of the entrails of dead creatures to divine the future. Fortuity preferred to use human entrails, and he liked them fresh.

I held myself back. The moment I decided to try to shoot him, his powers would activate. Fortuity had nothing to fear from a lone sniper. He probably thought he didn't have anything to fear at all. If my information was right, the next hour would prove him very wrong on that count.

Come on, I thought. *This is the best time to move against him. I'm right. I've got to be.*

Fortuity took a drag on his cigarette, nodding to a few people who passed by. He had no bodyguards. Why would he need bodyguards? His fingers glittered with rings, though wealth was meaningless to him. Even without Steelheart's rules granting him the right to take what he wanted, Fortuity could win a fortune in any gambling house on any day he chose.

Nothing happened. Had I been wrong? I'd been so *sure*. Bilko's information was usually up to date. Word in the understreets was that the Reckoners were back in Newcago. Fortuity *was* the Epic they'd target. I knew this. I'd made a habit—maybe even a quest—of studying the Reckoners. I—

A woman walked past Fortuity. Tall, lithe, and golden-haired, and perhaps twenty years old, she wore a thin red dress with a plunging neckline. Even with two beauties on his arms, Fortuity turned and stared at her. She hesitated, glancing back at him. Then she smiled and walked up, hips undulating back and forth.

I couldn't hear what they said, but in the end, this newcomer displaced the other women. She led Fortuity down the road, whispering in his ear and laughing. The other two women waited behind, arms crossed, not daring to complain. Fortuity did *not* like his women to speak back to him.

This had to be it. I wanted to get ahead of them, but couldn't do so on the street itself. Instead I moved back through a few alleyways. I knew the area perfectly; studying maps of the theater district was what had almost made me late.

I hustled around the back of a building, sticking to the shadows, and arrived at another alleyway. From here I could peek out and see the same road, but from another angle. Fortuity ambled along the steel sidewalk outside.

The area was lit by lamps hanging from streetlights. The streetlights themselves had been turned to steel during the transfersion—electronics and bulbs included. They no longer worked, but they did provide a convenient place to hang lanterns.

Those lanterns left pools of light that the pair moved through, in and out. I held my breath, watching closely. Fortuity was packing a weapon for certain. The suit was tailored to hide the bulge under his arm, but I could still make out where his holster was.

Fortuity didn't have any directly offensive powers, but that didn't really matter. His precognition powers meant he never missed with a handgun, no matter how wild the shot seemed. If he decided to kill you, you had a couple of seconds to respond, or you'd be dead.

The woman didn't appear to be carrying a weapon, though I couldn't be certain. That dress showed plenty of curves. A gun strapped to her thigh, perhaps? I looked closer as she moved into another pool of light, though I found myself staring at her, rather than looking for weapons. She was gorgeous. Eyes that glittered, bright red lips, golden hair. And that low neckline . . .

I shook myself. *Idiot,* I thought. *You have a purpose. Women interfere with things like a purpose.*

But even a ninety-year-old blind priest would stop and stare at this woman. If he weren't blind, that is. *Dumb metaphor,* I thought. *I'll have to work on that one.* I have trouble with metaphors.

Focus. I raised my rifle, leaving on the safety and using the scope for its zoom. Where were they going to hit him? The street here ran through several blocks of gloomy darkness—broken only by the lanterns—before intersecting Burnley Street. That was a major hub of the local dance scene. Likely the woman had enticed Fortuity to join her at a club. The quickest route was through this dark, less-populated street.

The empty street was a very good sign. The Reckoners rarely struck at an Epic who was in too public an area. They didn't like innocent casualties. I tilted the rifle up and scanned the skyrise windows with my scope. Some of the glass-turned-steel windows had been cut out and replaced with glass again. Was anyone up there watching?

I'd been hunting the Reckoners for years. They were the only ones who still fought back, a shadowy group that stalked, entrapped, and assassinated powerful Epics. The Reckoners, *they* were the heroes. Not what my father had imagined—no Epic powers, no flashy costumes. They didn't stand for truth, the American ideal, or any such nonsense.

They just killed. One by one. Their goal was to eliminate each and every Epic who thought himself or herself above the law. And since that was pretty much *every* Epic, they had a lot of work to do.

I continued scanning windows. How would they try to kill Fortuity? There would only be a few ways to go about it. They might try to catch him in a situation impossible to escape. A precog's powers would lead him down the safest path of self-preservation, but if you set up a situation where *every* path led to death, you could kill him.

We call that a checkmate, but they're really hard to set up. More likely, the Reckoners knew Fortuity's weakness. Every Epic has at least one—an object, a state of mind, an action of some sort—that allows you to void their powers.

There, I thought, heart leaping as—through the scope—I spotted a dark figure huddled in a window on the third floor of a building across the street. I couldn't make out details, but he was probably tracking Fortuity with a rifle and scope of his own.

This was it. I smiled. I'd actually found them. After all of my practicing and searching, I'd *found* them.

I kept looking, even more eager. The sniper would just be one piece of the plot to kill the Epic. My hands began to sweat. Other people get excited by sporting events or action films, but I don't have time for prefabricated thrills. This, however . . . getting the chance to watch the Reckoners in action, seeing one of their traps firsthand . . . Well, it was literally the fulfillment of one of my grandest dreams, even if it was only the first step in my plans. I hadn't come just to watch an Epic be assassinated. Before the night's end, I intended to find a way to make the Reckoners let me join them.

"Fortuity!" yelled a nearby voice.

I quickly lowered my rifle, pulling back against the side of the alleyway. A figure ran past the opening a moment later. He was a stout man in a smoking jacket and slacks.

"Fortuity!" he yelled again. "Wait up!" I raised my weapon again, using the scope to inspect the newcomer. Was this part of the Reckoners' trap?

No. That was Donny "Curveball" Harrison, a minor Epic with only a single power, the ability to fire a handgun without ever running out of bullets. He was a bodyguard and hit man in Steelheart's organization. There was no way he was part of the Reckoners' plan—they didn't work with Epics. Ever. The Reckoners hated the Epics. They only killed the worst of them, but they would *never* let one join their team.

Cursing softly to myself, I watched Curveball confront Fortuity and the woman. She looked concerned, full lips pursed, gorgeous eyes narrowed. Yes, she was worried. She was one of the Reckoners for certain.

Curveball started talking, explaining something, and Fortuity frowned. What was going on?

I turned my attention back to the woman. *There's something about her . . .* , I thought, my eyes lingering. She was younger than I'd originally thought, probably eighteen or nineteen, but something in those eyes made her *seem* much older.

Her look of concern was gone in a moment, replaced by what I realized was intentional vapidity as she turned to Fortuity and gestured onward. Whatever the trap was, she needed him to be farther down the street. That made sense. Trapping a precog is *tough*. If his danger senses got even a faint whiff of a trap, he'd bolt. She *had* to know his weakness, but probably didn't want to try to exploit it until they were more isolated.

Even then, it might not work. Fortuity would still be an armed man, and many Epic weaknesses were notoriously tricky to exploit.

I kept watching. Whatever Curveball's problem was, it didn't seem to have anything to do with the woman. He kept gesturing back toward the playhouse. If he convinced Fortuity to return . . .

The trap would never be sprung. The Reckoners would pull out, vanish, pick a new target. I could spend years searching for another chance like this one.

I couldn't let that happen. Taking a deep breath, I lowered my rifle and slung it over my shoulder. Then I stepped out onto the street and took off toward Fortuity.

It was time to hand the Reckoners my résumé.

2

I hustled down the dark street on a steel sidewalk, passing in and out of pockets of light.

I might have just decided to do something very, very stupid. Like eating-meat-sold-by-shady-understreet-vendors stupid. Maybe even stupider. The Reckoners planned their assassinations with extreme care. It hadn't been my intention to interfere—only to watch, then try to get them to take me on. By stepping out of that alleyway, I changed things. Interfered with the plan, whatever it was. There was a chance that everything was going just as it was supposed to— that Curveball was accounted for.

But maybe not. No plan was perfect, and even the Reckoners failed. Sometimes they pulled out, their target left alive. It was better to retreat than risk capture.

I didn't know which situation this was, but I had to at least try to help. If I missed this opportunity, I'd curse myself for years.

All three people—Fortuity, Curveball, and the beauty with the dangerous air—turned toward me as I ran up. "Donny!" I said. "We need you back at the Reeve!"

Curveball frowned at me, eyeing my rifle. He reached under his jacket for his gun, but didn't pull it out. Fortuity, in his red suit and deep red cape, raised an eyebrow at me. If I'd been a danger, his powers would have warned him. I wasn't planning to do anything to him in the next few minutes, though, so he got no warning.

"Who are *you*?" Curveball demanded.

I stopped. "Who am I? Sparks, Donny! I've worked for Spritzer for three years now. Would it *kill* you to try remembering people's names once in a while?"

My heart was thumping, but I tried not to show it. Spritzer was the guy who ran the Reeve Playhouse. Spritz wasn't an Epic, but he was in Steelheart's pay—pretty much anyone with any influence in the city was.

Curveball studied me suspiciously, but I knew he didn't give much mind to the lowlife thugs around him. In fact, he probably would have been shocked by how much I knew about him, along with most of the Epics in Newcago.

"Well?" I demanded. "You coming?"

"You don't give lip to me, boy. What are you, a door guard?"

"I went on the Idolin raid last summer," I said, crossing my arms. "I'm moving up, Donny."

"You call me sir, idiot," Curveball snapped, lowering his hand from his jacket. "If you were 'moving up,' you wouldn't be running messages. What's this nonsense about going back? He said he needed Fortuity to run some odds for him."

I shrugged. "He didn't tell me *why;* he just sent me to get you. Said to say that he'd been wrong, and you weren't to bother Fortuity." I looked to Fortuity. "I don't think the Spritz knew about . . . er . . . that you had plans, sir." I nodded to the woman.

There was a long, uncomfortable pause. I was so nervous, you could have scratched off a lottery ticket by holding it against my knuckles. Finally, Fortuity sniffed. "Tell Spritz that he's forgiven, this time. He should know better—I'm not his personal calculator." He turned, sticking out his elbow to the woman and walking away, obviously assuming that she'd jump at his whim.

As she turned to follow, she glanced at me, long lashes fluttering above deep blue eyes. I found myself smiling.

Then I realized that if I'd fooled Fortuity, I'd probably fooled her too. That meant she—and the Reckoners—now thought I was one of Steelheart's lackeys. They were always careful not to endanger civilians, but they had nothing at all against taking out a few hit men or thugs.

Aw, sparks, I thought. *I should have winked at her! Why didn't I wink at her?*

Would that have looked stupid? I'd never really practiced winking. Could you do it the wrong way, though? It was a simple thing.

"Something wrong with your eye?" Curveball asked.

"Er, got a lash in it," I said. "Sir. Sorry. Um, we should get back." The thought of the Reckoners setting off their trap in time to take out Curveball—and me—as a nice side effect suddenly made me very, very nervous.

I hurried down the sidewalk, splashing through some puddles. Rain didn't evaporate quickly in the darkness, and with the steel ground, there wasn't anywhere for it to go. The Diggers had created some drainage, along with pipes to circulate air in the understreets, but their eventual madness had disrupted those plans and they'd never finished.

Curveball followed me at a moderate speed. I slowed down, matching his pace, worried he might come up with a reason to go back for Fortuity.

"What's your hurry, kid?" he growled.

In the distance, the woman and Fortuity had stopped beneath a streetlight, where they had taken to searching one another's mouths with their tongues.

"Stop staring," Curveball said, walking past. "He could gun us down without even looking and nobody would care."

It was true. Fortuity was a powerful enough Epic that—so long as he didn't interfere with one of Steelheart's plans—he could do whatever he pleased. Curveball himself didn't have that kind of immunity. You still had to be careful when you were at his level. Steelheart wouldn't care if a minor Epic like Curveball got himself stabbed in the back.

I tore my eyes away and joined Curveball. He lit up a cigarette as he walked, a flash of light in the dark, followed by the coal-red sizzle of the tip hanging in the air before him. "Sparks, Spritz," he said. "Could have sent one of you lackeys out after Fortuity in the first place. I hate looking like a slontze."

"You know how Spritz is," I said absently. "He figured that sending you would be less offensive to Fortuity, since you're an Epic."

"Suppose that's right." Curveball took a pull on his cigarette. "Whose team are you in?"

"Eddie Macano's," I said, naming one of the underlings in Spritz's organization. I glanced over my shoulder. They were *still* going at it. "He was the one who made me run after you. Didn't want to do it himself. Too busy trying to pick up one of those girls Fortuity left behind. Whatta slontze, eh?"

"Eddie Macano?" Curveball said, turning toward me. The red tip of his cigarette lit his perplexed face a scarlet orange. "He died in that skirmish with the underbloods two days back. I was there. . . ."

I froze. *Whoops.*

Curveball reached for his gun.

3

HANDGUNS have one distinct advantage over rifles—they're fast. I didn't even try to beat him to the draw. I ducked to the side, running as fast as I could toward an alleyway.

In the near distance, somebody screamed. *Fortuity,* I thought. *Did he see me run? But I'm not standing in the light, and he wasn't watching. This is something else. The trap must have—*

Curveball opened fire on me.

The thing about handguns is that they're blasted difficult to aim. Even trained, practiced professionals miss more often than they hit. And if you level the gun out in front of you sideways—like you think you're in some stupid action movie—you'll hit even *less* often.

That was exactly what Curveball did, flashes from the front of his gun lighting the darkness. A bullet hit the ground near me, spraying sparks as it ricocheted off the steel pavement. I skidded into an alleyway and pressed myself back against the wall, out of Curveball's direct line of sight.

Bullets continued to spray against the wall. I didn't dare look out, but I could hear Curveball cursing and yelling. I was too panicked to count shots. A magazine like his couldn't hold more than a dozen or so bullets—

Oh, right, I thought. *His Epic power.* The man could keep blasting away and never run out of bullets. Eventually he'd round the corner and get a direct shot.

Only one thing to do. I took a deep breath, letting my rifle slide off my shoulder and catching it with my hand. I dropped to one knee in the mouth of the alleyway, putting myself at risk, and raised the rifle. The burning cigarette gave me a sight on Curveball's face.

A bullet hit the wall above me. I prepared to squeeze the trigger. "Stop it, you slontze!" a voice called, interrupting Curveball. A figure moved between us in the dim light just as I fired. The shot missed. That was *Fortuity.*

I lowered my gun as another shot rang out from high above. The sniper. A bullet struck the ground nearby, almost hitting Fortuity—but he jerked sideways at just the right moment. His danger sense.

Fortuity ran awkwardly, and as he got closer to a lantern, I saw why. He was handcuffed. Still, he was escaping; whatever the Reckoners' plan was, it looked like it had fallen apart.

Curveball and I glanced at each other, then he took off following Fortuity, firing a few stray shots in my direction. Having infinite bullets didn't make him any better a shot, however, and they all went wide.

I climbed to my feet and looked the other direction, toward where the woman had been. Was she all right?

A loud *crack* sounded in the air, and Curveball screamed, dropping to the ground. I smiled, right until a second shot fired and a spray of sparks exploded from the wall beside me. I cursed, ducking back into my alleyway. A second later the woman in the sleek red dress spun into the alleyway, holding a tiny derringer pistol and pointing it directly at my face.

People firing handguns missed, on average, from over ten paces—but I wasn't sure of the statistics when the pistol was fifteen inches from your face. Probably not so good for the target.

"Wait!" I said, holding up my hands, letting my rifle fall in its strap on my shoulder. "I'm trying to help! Didn't you see Curveball firing at me?"

"Who do you work for?" the woman demanded.

"Havendark Factory," I said. "I used to drive a cab, though I—"

"Slontze," she said. Gun still trained on me, she raised her hand to her head, touching one finger to her ear. I could see an earring there that was probably tethered to her mobile. "Megan here. Tia. Blow it."

An explosion sounded nearby and I jumped. "What was that!"

"The Reeve Playhouse."

"You *blew up* the Reeve?" I said. "I thought the Reckoners didn't hurt innocents!"

That froze her, gun still pointed at me. "How do you know who we are?"

"You're hunting Epics. Who else would you be?"

"But—" She cut off, cursing softly, raising her finger again. "No time. Abraham. Where is the mark?"

I couldn't hear the reply, but it obviously satisfied her. A few more explosions sounded in the distance.

She eyed me, but my hands were still raised, and she *must* have seen Curveball firing on me. She apparently decided I wasn't a threat. She lowered her gun and hurriedly reached down, breaking the stiletto heels off her shoes. Then she grabbed the side of her dress and ripped it off.

I gaped.

I normally consider myself somewhat levelheaded, but it's not every day that you find yourself in a darkened alleyway with a gorgeous woman who rips off most of her clothing. Underneath she wore a low-cut tank top and a pair of spandex biker shorts. I was pleased to note that the gun holster was, indeed, strapped to her right thigh. Her mobile was hooked to the outside of the sheath.

She tossed the dress aside—it had been designed to come off easily. Her arms were lean and firm, and the wide-eyed naivety she'd shown earlier was completely gone, replaced with a hard edge and a determined expression.

I took a step, and in a heartbeat her pistol was trained on my forehead again. I froze.

"Out of the alleyway," she said, gesturing.

I nervously did as asked, walking back onto the street.

"On your knees, hands on head."

"I don't really—"

"Down!"

I got down on my knees, feeling stupid, raising my hands to my head.

"Hardman," she said, finger to her ear. "If Knees here so much as *sneezes*, put a slug through his neck."

"But—" I began.

She took off at a run down the street, moving much more quickly now that she'd removed the heels and the dress. That left me alone. I felt like an idiot kneeling there, hairs on my neck prickling as I thought of the sniper who had his weapon trained on me.

How many agents did the Reckoners have here? I couldn't imagine them trying anything like this without at least two dozen. Another explosion shook the ground. Why the blasts? They'd alert Enforcement, Steelheart's soldiers. Lackeys and thugs were bad enough; Enforcement wielded advanced guns and the occasional armor unit—twelve-foot-tall robotic suits of power armor.

The next explosion was closer, just down the block. Something must have gone wrong in their original plan, otherwise Fortuity wouldn't have gotten away from the woman in red. Megan? Was that what she'd said her name was?

This was one of their contingency plans. But what were they trying to do?

A figure burst out of an alleyway nearby, almost making me jump. I held still, cursing that sniper, but I did turn my head slightly to look. The figure wore red, and still had handcuffs on. Fortuity.

The explosions, I realized. *They were to scare him back this way!*

He crossed the street, then turned to run in my direction. Megan—if that was really her name—burst from the same road he'd appeared out of. She turned this way, trying to chase him down, but behind her—in the distance—another group of figures rushed out from a different street.

They were four of Spritz's thugs, in suits and carrying submachine guns. They pointed at Megan.

I watched from the other side of the street as Megan and Fortuity passed me. The thugs were approaching from my right, and Megan and Fortuity were running to my left, all of us on the same darkened street.

Come on! I thought at the sniper up above. *She doesn't see them! They'll gun her down. Take them out!*

Nothing. The thugs leveled their guns. I felt sweat trickle down the back of my neck. Then, teeth clenched, I rolled to the side, whipping my rifle out and drawing a bead on one of them.

I took a deep breath, concentrated, and squeezed the trigger, fully expecting to be shot in the head from above.

4

A handgun is like a firecracker—unpredictable. Light a firecracker, toss it, and you never really know where it's going to land or the damage it's going to do. The same's true when you shoot a handgun.

An Uzi is even worse—it's like a string of firecrackers. Much more likely to hurt something, but still awkward and unruly.

A rifle is elegant. It's an extension of your will. Take aim, squeeze the trigger, make things happen. In the hands of an expert with stillness inside of him, there's nothing more deadly than a good rifle.

The first thug fell to my shot. I inched the gun to the side, then squeezed again. The second went down. The other two lowered their weapons, dodging.

Look. Squeeze. Three down. The last one was full-out running by the time I focused on him, and he managed to get behind cover. I hesitated, spine itching—waiting to feel the bullet from the sniper hit my back. It didn't come. Hardman, it appeared, had realized that I was a good guy.

I stood up hesitantly. It wasn't the first time I'd killed, unfortunately. It didn't happen often, but once or twice, I'd had to protect myself in the understreets. This was different, but I didn't have time to think about it.

I shoved those emotions aside, and not knowing what else to do, I turned to the left and took off at a dead run down the street after Fortuity and the Reckoner woman. The Epic cursed and weaved toward a side street. The streets were all empty. Our explosions and gunfire had caused anyone nearby to clear out—this sort of thing wasn't uncommon in Newcago.

Megan dashed after Fortuity, and I was able to cut to the side and meet up with her. She glared at me as we barreled down the cross street, shoulder to shoulder, after the Epic.

"I told you to stay put, Knees!" she yelled.

"Good thing I ignored you! I just saved your life."

"That's why I haven't shot you. Get out of here."

I ignored her, aiming my rifle as I ran and taking a shot at the Epic. It went wide—it was too hard to run and fire at the same time. *He's fast!* I thought, annoyed.

"That's useless," the girl said. "You can't hit him."

"I can slow him down," I said, lowering the rifle, running past a pub with lights off and doors closed. A group of nervous patrons watched from one of the windows. "Dodging will throw him off balance."

"Not for long."

"We need to both fire at once," I said. "We can pin him between two bullets, so either way he dodges, he'll hit one of them. Checkmate."

"Are you insane?" she said, still running. "That would be near impossible."

She was right. "Well, let's use his weakness, then. I know you know what it is—otherwise you'd never have gotten those handcuffs on him."

"It won't help," she said, dodging around a lamppost.

"It worked for you. Tell me what it is. I'll use it."

"Slontze," she cursed at me. "His danger sense is weakened if he's attracted to you. So unless he finds you a *whole* lot prettier than I do, it's *not* going to help."

Oh, I thought. Well, that was a problem.

"We need to—" Megan began, but then cut off, raising her finger to her ear as we ran. "No! I can do this! I don't *care* how close they are!"

They're trying to get her to pull out, I realized. It wouldn't be long before Enforcement arrived.

Ahead of us an unfortunate driver, probably on the way to the club district, pulled around the corner. The car screeched to a halt, and Fortuity cut in front of it, heading to the right down another alleyway that would lead him toward more populated streets.

I got an idea.

"Take this," I said, tossing my rifle to Megan. I whipped out my extra magazine and tossed it to her as well. "Fire at him. Slow him down."

"What?" Megan demanded. "Who are you to give me—"

"Do it!" I said, skidding to a stop beside the car. I pulled open the passenger door. "Out," I said to the woman behind the wheel.

The bystander got out and scurried away, leaving the keys in the ignition. In a world full of Epics with the legal right to take any vehicle they want, few people ask questions. Steelheart is brutal with thieves who aren't Epics, so most would never try what I'd just done.

Outside the car, Megan cursed, then raised my rifle expertly and took a shot. She had good aim, and Fortuity—just a little ways down the alleyway—stumbled to the right, his danger sense prompting him to dodge out of the way. As I'd hoped, it slowed him considerably.

I gunned the engine. It was a nice sporty coupe, and it looked practically new. Pity, that.

I tore off down the street. I'd told Megan that I'd been a cab-driver. Which was true; I'd tried it a few months back, right after graduating from the Factory. I hadn't mentioned, however, that the job had lasted only one day; I'd proven terrible at it.

You never know how much you'll like something until you try it out. It had been one of my father's famous sayings. The cab company hadn't expected me to "try out" driving for the first time in one of their cars. But how else was a guy like me supposed to get behind a wheel? I was an orphan who had been owned by the Factory for most of my life. My type didn't exactly make big money, and the understreets don't have room for cars anyway.

Regardless, driving had proven a tad more difficult than I'd expected it to be. I screeched around the corner of the dark street, the gas pedal pressed to the floor, barely in control. I knocked down a stop sign and a street sign on my way, but I made it down the block in a matter of heartbeats and screeched around another corner. I hit a few trash cans as I went up over the curb, but managed to retain control as I turned and pulled the car to a stop facing south.

I was pointing it directly down the alleyway. Fortuity was still stumbling through it toward me, tripping on refuse and boxes as Megan slowed him.

There was a pop, Fortuity dodged, and my windshield suddenly cracked—a bullet blasting through it about an inch from my head. My heart leaped. Megan was still shooting.

You know, David, I thought to myself. *You really need to start thinking your plans through a little more carefully.*

I slammed the pedal down, roaring into the alleyway. It was just barely wide enough for the car, and sparks flew up on the left side as I veered a hair too far in that direction, shearing off the side mirror.

The headlights shone on a figure in a red leisure suit, hands cuffed together, cape flapping behind him. He'd lost his hat while running. His eyes were wide. There was nowhere for him to go in either direction.

Checkmate.

Or so I thought. As I got close, Fortuity leaped into the air and slammed his feet into the front of my windshield with superhuman dexterity.

That utterly shocked me. Fortuity wasn't supposed to have any enhanced physical abilities. Of course, for a man like him—who avoided danger so easily—there may not have been many opportunities to display such things. Either way, his feet hit my windshield in an expert maneuver only someone with super reflexes could have managed. He pushed off and jumped backward, the windshield shattering into pebbled glass, using the momentum of the car to throw himself into a backflip.

I slammed on the brakes and blinked as the glass sprayed my face. The car screeched to a halt in a shower of sparks. Fortuity landed his flip with poise.

I shook my head, dazed. *Yeah, super reflexes,* a piece of my mind thought. *I should have realized. Perfect complement to a precog portfolio.* Fortuity was wise to keep the secret. Many a powerful Epic had realized that hiding one or two abilities gave them an edge when another Epic tried to kill them.

Fortuity ran forward. I could see him glaring at me, lips curling up in a sneer. He was a monster—I'd documented over a hundred murders tied to him. And from the look in his eyes, he intended to add my name to that list.

He leaped into the air, toward the hood of the car.

Crack! Crack!

Fortuity's chest exploded.

5

FORTUITY'S corpse slammed down onto the hood of the car. Megan stood behind him, my rifle in one hand—held at the hip— her pistol in the other hand. The car's headlights bathed her in light. "Sparks!" she cursed. "I can't believe that actually worked."

She fired both at once, I realized. *She checkmated him in the air with two shots.* It had probably only worked because he'd been jumping—in midair it would have been harder for him to jerk out of the way. But still, shooting like that was incredible. A gun in each hand, one of them a rifle?

Sparks, I thought, echoing her. We'd actually won.

Megan pulled Fortuity's body off the hood and checked for a pulse. "Dead," she said. Then she shot the body twice in the head. "And double dead, to be certain."

At that moment about a dozen of Spritz's thugs appeared at the end of the alleyway, sporting Uzis.

I swore, scrambling into the back seat of the car. Megan jumped onto the hood and slid through the shattered windshield, ducking down in the passenger seat as a hailstorm of bullets slammed into the vehicle.

I tried to open the back door—but, of course, the walls of the alleyway were too close. The back window shattered and puffs of stuffing flew from the seats as they were shredded by Uzi fire.

"Calamity!" I said. "Glad it's not *my* car."

Megan rolled her eyes at me, then pulled something out of her top. A small cylinder, like a lipstick case. She twisted the bottom, waited for a lull in the bullets, then lobbed it out the front window.

"What was that?" I yelled over the shots.

I was answered by an explosion that shook the car, blowing scraps of trash from the alleyway across us. The bullets stopped for a moment, and I could hear men crying out in pain. Megan—still toting my rifle—hopped over the torn-up seat and lithely slipped through the broken back window, then ran for it.

"Hey!" I said, crawling out after her, bits of safety glass falling from my clothing. I jumped to the ground and dashed to the end of the alleyway, cutting to the side just as the survivors from the explosion started firing again.

She can shoot like a dream and she carries tiny grenades in her top, a bit of my addled mind thought. *I think I might be in love.*

I heard a low rumbling over the gunfire, and an armored truck pulled around the corner ahead, roaring toward Megan. It was huge and green, imposing, with enormous headlights. And it looked an awful lot like . . .

"A garbage truck?" I asked, running up to join Megan.

A tough-looking black man rode in the passenger seat. He pushed open the door for Megan. "Who's that?" the man asked, nodding to me. He spoke with a faint French accent.

"A slontze," she said, tossing my rifle back to me. "But a useful one. He knows about us, but I don't think he's a threat."

Not exactly a glowing recommendation, but good enough. I smiled as she climbed into the cab, pushing the man to the middle seat.

"Do we leave him?" asked the man with the French accent.

"No," said the driver. I couldn't make him out; he was just a shadow, but his voice was solid and resonant. "He comes with us."

I smiled, eagerly stepping up into the truck. Could the driver be Hardman, the sniper? He'd seen how helpful I'd been. The people inside reluctantly made room for me. Megan slipped into the back seat of the crew cab beside a wiry man wearing a leather camouflage jacket and holding a very nice-looking sniper rifle. *He* was probably Hardman. To his other side was a middle-aged woman with shoulder-length red hair. She wore spectacles and business attire.

The garbage truck pulled away, moving faster than I'd have thought possible. Behind us a group of the thugs came out of the alley, firing on the truck. It didn't do much good, though we weren't out of danger quite yet. Overhead I heard the distinctive sound of Enforcement copters. There would probably be a few high-level Epics on the way too.

"Fortuity?" the driver asked. He was an older man, perhaps in his fifties, and wore a long, thin black coat. Oddly, he had a pair of goggles tucked into the breast pocket of the coat.

"Dead," Megan said from behind.

"What went wrong?" the driver asked.

"Hidden power," she said. "Super reflexes. I got him cuffed, but he slipped away."

"There was also that one," the guy in the camo jacket—I was pretty sure that was Hardman—said. "He came up in the middle of it all, caused a wee bit of trouble." He had a distinctive Southern accent.

"We'll talk about him later," the driver said, taking a corner at high speed.

My heart started to beat more quickly, and I glanced out the window, searching the sky for copters. It wouldn't be long before Enforcement was told what to look for, and the truck was rather conspicuous.

"We should have just shot Fortuity in the first place," said the man with the French accent. "Derringer to the chest."

"Wouldn't have worked, Abraham," the driver said. "His abilities were too strong—even attraction could only do so much. We needed to do something nonlethal first—trap him, then shoot him. Precogs are tough."

He had that part right, probably. Fortuity had possessed a *very* strong danger sense. Likely the plan had been for Megan to cuff him and maybe lock him to the lamppost. Then, when he was partially immobilized, she could have rammed her derringer into his chest and fired. If she'd tried that first, his power might have warned him. It would have depended on how attracted he was to her.

"I wasn't expecting him to be so strong," Megan said, sounding disappointed with herself as she pulled on a brown leather jacket and a pair of cargo pants. "I'm sorry, Prof. I shouldn't have let him get away from me."

Prof. Something about that name struck me.

"It's done," the driver—Prof—said, pulling the garbage truck to a jarring halt. "We ditch the machine. It's been compromised."

Prof opened the door and we piled out.

"I—" I began to say, planning to introduce myself. The older man they called Prof, however, shot me a menacing glare over the hood of the garbage truck. I cut myself short, choking on my words. Standing in the shadows, with his long jacket and that grizzled face, hair peppered with grey, that man looked *dangerous*.

The Reckoners pulled a few packs of equipment out of the back of the garbage truck, including a massive machine gun that Abraham now toted. They led me down a set of steps into the understreets. From there the team hustled through a set of twists and turns. I did a pretty good job keeping track of where we were going until they led me down a long flight of stairs, several levels deep, into the steel catacombs.

Smart people stayed away from the catacombs. The Diggers had gone mad before the tunnels were finished. The ceiling lights rarely worked, and the square-shaped tunnels through the steel changed size as you progressed.

The team was silent as they continued down the passages, turning up the lights on their mobiles, which most wore strapped to the fronts of their jackets. I'd wondered if the Reckoners would carry mobiles, and the fact that they wore them made me feel better about mine. I mean, *everyone* knew that the Knighthawk Foundry was neutral, and that mobile connections were completely secure. The Reckoners' using the network was just another indication that Knighthawk was reliable.

We walked for a time, the Reckoners moving quietly, carefully. Several times Hardman went ahead to scout; Abraham watched our rear with that wicked-looking machine gun of his. It was hard to keep my bearings—down in the steel catacombs it felt like a subway system that halfway through development had turned into a rat's maze.

There were choke points, tunnels that went nowhere, and unnatural angles. In some places electrical cords jutted from the walls like those creepy arteries you find in the middle of a chunk of chicken. In other places the steel walls weren't solid, but instead had patches of paneling that had been ripped into by people searching for something worth selling. Scrap metal, however, was worthless in Newcago. There was more than enough of *that* lying around.

We passed groups of teenagers with dark expressions standing beside burning trash cans. They seemed displeased to have their solace invaded, but nobody interfered with us. Perhaps it was due to Abraham's enormous gun. The thing had gravatonics glowing blue on the bottom to help him lift it.

We worked our way through those tunnels for over an hour. Occasionally we passed vents blowing air. The Diggers had gotten some things working down here, but most of it made no sense. Still, there was fresh air. Sometimes.

Prof led the way in that long black coat. *It's a lab coat,* I realized as we turned another corner. *One that's been dyed black.* He wore a black buttoned shirt beneath it.

The Reckoners were obviously worried about being followed, but I felt they overdid it. I was hopelessly lost after fifteen minutes, and Enforcement *never* came down to this level. There was an unspoken agreement. Steelheart ignored those living in the steel catacombs, and they didn't do anything to bring his judgment down upon them.

Of course . . . the Reckoners changed that truce. An important Epic had been assassinated. How would Steelheart react to that?

Eventually the Reckoners led me around a corner that looked like every other one—only this time it led to a small room cut into the steel. There were a lot of these places in the catacombs. Places where the Diggers had planned to put a restroom, a small shop, or a dwelling.

Hardman the sniper took up position at the door. He'd taken out a camo ball cap and put it on his head, and there was an unfamiliar emblem on the front. It looked like some kind of royal crest or something. The other four Reckoners arranged themselves facing me. Abraham got out a large flashlight and clicked a button that lit up the sides, turning it into a lantern. He set it on the floor.

Prof crossed his arms, his face emotionless, inspecting me. The woman with the red hair stood beside him. She seemed more thoughtful. Abraham still carried his large gun, and Megan took off her leather jacket and strapped on an underarm gun holster. I tried not to stare, but that was like trying not to blink. Only . . . well, kind of the opposite.

I took a hesitant step backward, realizing I was cornered. I'd begun to think that I was on my way toward being accepted into their team. But looking into Prof's eyes, I realized that was *not* the case. He saw me as a threat. I hadn't been brought along because I'd been helpful; I'd been brought along because he hadn't wanted me wandering free.

I was a captive. And this deep in the steel catacombs, nobody would notice a scream or a gunshot.

6

"TEST him, Tia," Prof said.

I shied back, holding my rifle nervously. Behind Prof, Megan leaned against a wall, jacket back on, handgun strapped under her arm. She spun something in her hand. The extra magazine for my rifle. She'd never returned it.

Megan smiled. She'd tossed my rifle back to me up above, but I had a sinking suspicion that she'd emptied the chamber, leaving the gun unloaded. I started to panic.

The redhead—Tia—approached me, holding some kind of device. It was flat and round, the size of a plate, but had a screen on one side. She pointed it at me. "No reading."

"Blood test," Prof said, face hard.

Tia nodded. "Don't force us to hold you down," she said to me, removing a strap from the side of the device; it was connected to the disc by cords. "This will prick you, but it won't do you any harm."

"What is it?" I demanded.

"A dowser."

A dowser . . . a device that tested if one was an Epic or not. "I . . . thought those were just myths."

Abraham smiled, enormous gun held beside him. He was lean and muscled and seemed very calm, as opposed to the tension displayed by Tia and even Prof. "Then you won't mind, eh, my friend?" he asked with his French accent. "What does it matter if a *mythological* device pricks you?"

That didn't comfort me, but the Reckoners were a group of practiced assassins who killed High Epics for a living. There wasn't much I could do.

The woman wrapped my arm with a wide strap, a bit like what you use to measure blood pressure. Wires led from it to the device in her hand. There was a small box on the inside of the strap, and it pricked me.

Tia studied the screen. "He's clean for certain," she said, looking at Prof. "Nothing on the blood test either."

Prof nodded, seeming unsurprised. "All right, son. It's time for you to answer a few questions. Think very carefully before you reply."

"Okay," I said as Tia removed the strap. I rubbed my arm where I'd been pricked.

"How," Prof said, "did you find out where we were going to strike? Who told you that Fortuity was our target?"

"Nobody told me."

His expression grew dark. Beside him, Abraham raised an eyebrow and hefted his gun.

"No, really!" I said, sweating. "Okay, so I heard from some people on the street that you might be in town."

"We didn't tell anyone our mark," Abraham said. "Even if you knew we were here, how did you know the Epic we'd try to kill?"

"Well," I said, "who *else* would you hit?"

"There are thousands of Epics in the city, son," Prof said.

"Sure," I replied. "But most are beneath your notice. You target High Epics, and there are only a few hundred of those in Newcago. Among them, only a couple dozen have a prime invincibility—and you *always* pick someone with a prime invincibility.

"However, you also wouldn't go after anyone *too* powerful or *too* influential. You figure they'd be well protected. That rules out Nightwielder, Conflux, and Firefight—pretty much Steelheart's whole inner circle. It also rules out most of the burrow barons.

"That leaves about a dozen targets, and Fortuity was the worst of the lot. All Epics are murderers, but he'd killed the most innocents by a long shot. Plus, that twisted way he played with people's entrails is *exactly* the sort of atrocity the Reckoners would want to stop." I looked at them, nervous, then shrugged. "Like I said. Nobody had to tell me. It's obvious who you'd end up picking."

The small room grew silent.

"Ha!" said the sniper, who still stood by the doorway. "Lads and ladies, I think this means we might be getting a *tad* predictable."

"What's a prime invincibility?" Tia asked.

"Sorry," I said, realizing they wouldn't know my terms. "It's what I call an Epic power that renders conventional methods of assassination useless. You know, regeneration, impervious skin, precognition, self-reincarnation, that kind of thing." A High Epic was someone who had one of those. I'd never heard of one who had two, fortunately.

"Let us pretend," Prof said, "that you really did figure it out on your own. That still doesn't explain how you knew where we'd spring our trap."

"Fortuity always sees the plays at Spritz's place on the first Saturday of the month," I said. "And he always goes to look for amusement afterward. It's the only reliable time when you'd find him alone and in a mind-set where he could be baited into a trap."

Prof glanced at Abraham, then at Tia. She shrugged. "I don't know."

"I think he's telling the truth, Prof," Megan said, her arms crossed, jacket open at the front. *Don't . . . stare . . . ,* I had to remind myself.

Prof looked at her. "Why?"

"It makes sense," she said. "If Steelheart had known who we were going to hit, he'd have had something more elaborate planned for us than one boy with a rifle. Besides, Knees here *did* try to help. Kind of."

"I helped! You'd be dead if it weren't for me. Tell her, Hardman."

The Reckoners looked confused.

"Who?" Abraham asked.

"Hardman," I said, pointing at the sniper by the door.

"My name's Cody, kid," he said, amused.

"Then where's Hardman?" I asked. "Megan told me he was up above, watching with his rifle to . . ." I trailed off.

There never was a sniper up above, I realized. *At least, not one specifically told to watch me.* Megan had just said that to make me stay put.

Abraham laughed deeply. "Got caught by the old invisible sniper gag, eh? Had you kneeling there thinking you'd be shot any moment. Is that why she calls you Knees?"

I blushed.

"All right, son," Prof said. "I'm going to be nice to you and pretend none of this ever happened. Once we're out that door, I want you to count to a thousand really slowly. Then you can leave. If you try to follow us, I'll shoot you." He waved to the others.

"No, wait!" I said, reaching for him.

The other four each had a gun out in a flash, all pointed at my head.

I gulped, then lowered my hand. "Wait, please," I said a little more timidly. "I want to join you."

"You want to what?" Tia asked.

"Join you," I said. "That's why I came today. I didn't intend to get involved. I just wanted to apply."

"We don't exactly accept applications," Abraham said.

Prof studied me.

"He *was* somewhat helpful," Megan said. "And I . . . will admit that he is a decent shot. Maybe we should take him on, Prof."

Well, whatever else happened, I'd managed to impress her. That seemed almost as great a victory as taking down Fortuity.

Eventually Prof shook his head. "We aren't recruiting, son. Sorry. We're going to leave, and I don't want to *ever* see you anywhere near one of our operations again—I don't want to even get a hint of you being in the same town as us. Stay in Newcago. After today's mess, we won't be coming back here for a long while."

That seemed to settle it for all of them. Megan gave me a shrug, an almost apologetic one that seemed to indicate she'd said what she had as thanks for saving her from the thugs with the Uzis. The others gathered around Prof, joining him as he walked to the door.

I stood behind, feeling impotent and frustrated.

"You're failing," I said to them, my voice growing soft.

For some reason this made Prof hesitate. He glanced back at me, most of the others already out the door.

"You never go for the real targets," I said bitterly. "You always pick the safe ones, like Fortuity. Epics you can isolate and kill. Monsters, yes, but relatively unimportant ones. Never the *real* monsters, the Epics who broke us and turned our nation to rubble."

"We do what we can," Prof said. "Getting ourselves killed trying to take out an invincible Epic wouldn't serve anyone."

"Killing men like Fortuity won't do much either," I said. "There are too many of them, and if you keep picking targets like him, nobody's going to worry about you. You're only an annoyance. You can't change the world that way."

"We're not trying to," Prof said. "We're just killing Epics."

"What would you have us do, lad?" Hardman—I mean, Cody—said, amused. "Take on Steelheart himself?"

"Yes," I said fervently, stepping forward. "You want to change things, you want to make them afraid? He's the one to attack! Show them that nobody's above our vengeance!"

Prof shook his head. He continued on his way, black lab coat rustling. "I made this decision years ago, son. We have to fight the battles we have a chance of winning."

He walked out into the hallway. I was left alone in the small room, the flashlight they'd left behind giving a cold glow to the steel chamber.

I had failed.

7

I stood in the still, quiet box of a room lit by the abandoned flashlight. It appeared to be running low on charge, but the steel walls reflected the dim light well.

No, I thought.

I strode from the room, heedless of the warnings. *Let them shoot me.*

Their retreating figures were backlit by their mobiles, a group of dark forms in the cramped hallway.

"Nobody else fights," I called after them. "Nobody else even tries! You're the only ones left. If even *you're* scared of men like Steelheart, then how can anyone ever think any differently?"

The Reckoners continued walking.

"Your work means something!" I yelled. "But it's not enough! So long as the most powerful of the Epics consider themselves immune, nothing will change. So long as you leave them alone, you're essentially *proving* what they've always said! That if an Epic is strong enough, he can take what he wants, do what he wants. You're saying they deserve to rule."

The group kept walking, though Prof—toward the rear—seemed to hesitate. It was only for a moment.

I took a deep breath. There was only one thing left to try. "I've seen Steelheart bleed."

Prof stiffened.

That made the others pause. Prof looked over his shoulder at me. *"What?"*

"I've seen Steelheart bleed."

"Impossible," Abraham said. "The man is perfectly impervious."

"I've seen it," I said, heart thumping, face sweating. I'd never told anyone. The secret was too dangerous. If Steelheart knew that someone had survived the bank attack that day, he'd hunt me down. There would be no hiding, no running. Not if he thought I knew his weakness.

I didn't, not completely. But I had a clue, perhaps the only one anyone had.

"Making up lies won't get you on our team, son," Prof said slowly.

"I'm not lying," I said, meeting his eyes. "Not about this. Give me a few minutes to tell my story. At least listen."

"This is foolishness," Tia said, taking hold of Prof's arm. "Prof, let's go."

Prof didn't respond. He studied me, eyes searching my own, as if looking for something. I felt strangely exposed before him, naked. As if he could see my every wish and sin.

He walked slowly back to me. "All right, son," he said. "You've got fifteen minutes." He gestured back toward the room. "I'll listen to what you have to say."

We walked back into the small room amid a few grumbles from some of the others. I was beginning to place the members of the team. Abraham, with his large machine gun and beefy arms—he had to be the heavy-weapons man. He'd be around to lay down cover at Enforcement officers if something went wrong. He'd intimidate information out of people when needed, and would probably work the heavy machinery if the plan called for it.

Red-haired Tia, narrow-faced and articulate, was probably the team's scholar. Judging from her clothes, she wouldn't be involved in confrontations, and the Reckoners needed people like her—someone who knew exactly how Epic powers worked, and who could help decipher their targets' weaknesses.

Megan had to be point woman. She would be the one who went into danger, who moved the Epic into position. Cody, with his camo and sniper rifle, was most likely fire support. I was guessing that after Megan neutralized the Epic's powers in some way, Cody would pick them off or checkmate them with precision fire.

Which left Prof. Team leader, I supposed. Maybe a second point man, if they needed one? I hadn't quite placed him yet, though something itched at me regarding his name.

As we entered the room again, Abraham looked interested in what I was going to say. On the other hand, Tia looked annoyed, and Cody actually looked amused. The sniper leaned back against the wall and relaxed, crossing his arms to watch the hallway. The rest of them surrounded me, waiting.

I smiled at Megan, but her face had become impassive. Cold, even. What had changed?

I took a deep breath. "I've seen Steelheart bleed," I repeated. "It happened ten years ago, when I was eight. My father and I were at the First Union Bank on Adams Street. . . ."

I fell silent, story finished, my last words hanging in the air. *And I intend to see him bleed again.* It sounded like bravado to me now, standing before a group of people who had dedicated their lives to killing Epics.

My nervousness had evaporated while telling the story. It felt oddly relaxing to finally share it, giving voice to those terrible events. At last, someone else knew. If I were to die, there would be others who had the information I alone had carried. Even if the Reckoners decided not to go after Steelheart, the knowledge would exist, perhaps to be used someday. Assuming they believed me.

"Let's sit," Prof finally said, settling down. The others joined him, Tia and Megan reluctantly, but Abraham was still relaxed. Cody remained standing by the door, keeping guard.

I sat down, setting my rifle across my lap. I had the safety on, even though I was pretty sure it wasn't loaded.

"Well?" Prof asked of his team.

"I've heard of it," Tia admitted grudgingly. "Steelheart destroyed the bank on the Day of Annexation. The bank rented out some of the offices on the upper floor—nothing too important, some assessors and bookkeepers who did government work. Most lorists I've talked to assume that Steelheart hit the building because of those offices."

"Yes," Abraham agreed. "He attacked many city buildings that day."

Prof nodded thoughtfully.

"Sir—" I began.

He cut me off. "You've had your say, son. It's a show of respect that we're talking about this where you can hear. Don't make me regret it."

"Er, yes sir."

"I *have* always wondered why he attacked the bank first," Abraham continued.

"Yeah," Cody said from the doorway. "It was an odd choice. Why take out a bunch of accountants, *then* move on to the mayor?"

"But this is not a good enough reason to change our plans,"

Abraham added, shaking his head. He nodded to me, enormous gun over his shoulder. "I'm sure you're a wonderful person, my friend, but I do not think we should base decisions on information given by someone we only just met."

"Megan?" Prof asked. "What do you think?"

I glanced at her. Megan sat a little apart from the others. Prof and Tia seemed the most senior of this particular cell of the Reckoners. Abraham and Cody often chimed in their thoughts, as close friends would. But what of Megan?

"I think this is stupid," she said, her voice cold.

I frowned. *But . . . just a few minutes ago, she was the friendliest toward me!*

"You stood up for him before," Abraham said, as if voicing my own thoughts.

That made her scowl. "That was before I heard this wild story. He's lying, trying to get onto our team."

I opened my mouth to protest, but a glance from Prof made me bite off the comment.

"You sound like you're considering it," Cody said to Prof.

"Prof?" Tia said. "I know that look. Remember what happened with Duskwatch."

"I remember," he said. He studied me further.

"What?" Tia asked.

"He knows about the rescue workers," Prof said.

"The rescue workers?" Cody asked.

"Steelheart covered up that he killed the rescue workers," Prof said softly. "Few know of what he did to them and the survivors—of what happened at the First Union building. He didn't kill anyone who went to help at other city buildings he'd destroyed. He only killed the rescue workers at First Union.

"Something *is* different about his destruction of the bank," Prof continued. "We know he entered that one, and spoke to the people inside. He didn't do that elsewhere. They say he came out of First

Union enraged. Something happened inside. I've known that for a while. The other cell leaders know it as well. We assumed that whatever made him angry had to do with Deathpoint." Prof sat with one hand on his knee, and he tapped his finger in thought, studying me. "Steelheart got his scar that day. Nobody knows how."

"I do," I said.

"Perhaps," Prof said.

"*Perhaps*," Megan said. "Perhaps not. Prof, he could have heard of the murders and known of Steelheart's scar, then fabricated the rest! There'd be no way to prove it, because if he's right, then he and Steelheart are the only witnesses."

Prof nodded slowly.

"Hitting Steelheart would be near impossible," Abraham said. "Even if we *could* figure out his weakness, he's got guards. Strong ones."

"Firefight, Conflux, and Nightwielder," I said, nodding. "I've got a plan for dealing with each of them. I think I've figured out their weaknesses."

Tia frowned. "You have?"

"Ten years," I said softly. "For ten years, all I've done is plan how to get to him."

Prof still seemed thoughtful. "Son," he said to me. "What did you say your name was?"

"David."

"Well, David. You guessed we were going to hit Fortuity. What would you guess we'd do next?"

"You'll leave Newcago by nightfall," I said immediately. "That's always what a team does after springing a trap. Of course, there *is* no nightfall here. But you'll be gone in a few hours, then go rejoin the rest of the Reckoners."

"And what would be the next Epic we'd be planning to hit?" Prof asked.

"Well," I said, thinking quickly, remembering my lists and

projections. "None of your teams have been active in the Middle Grasslands or Caliph lately. I'd guess your next target would be either the Armsman in Omaha, or Lightning, one of the Epics in Snowfall's band out in Sacramento."

Cody whistled softly. Apparently I'd guessed pretty well—which was fortunate. I hadn't been too sure. I tended to be right about a quarter of the time lately, guessing where Reckoner cells would strike.

Prof suddenly moved to stand. "Abraham, prep Hole Fourteen. Cody, see if you can get a false trail set up that will lead to Caliph."

"Hole Fourteen?" Tia said. "We're staying in the city?"

"Yes," Prof said.

"Jon," Tia said, addressing Prof. His real name, probably. "I can't—"

"I'm not saying that we're going to hit Steelheart," he said, holding up a hand. He pointed at me. "But if the kid has figured out what we're going to do next, someone else might have too. That means we need to change. Immediately. We'll go to ground here for a few days." He looked at me. "As for Steelheart . . . we'll see. First I want to hear your story again. I want to hear it a dozen times. Then I'll decide what to do next."

He held out a hand to me. I took it hesitantly, letting him pull me to my feet. There was something in this man's eyes, something I didn't expect to see. A hatred of Steelheart nearly as deep as my own. It was manifest in the way he said the Epic's name, the way his lips turned down, the way his eyes narrowed and seemed to *burn* as he spoke the word.

It seemed like the two of us understood each other in that moment.

Prof, I thought. *Professor, PhD. The man who founded the Reckoners is named Jonathan Phaedrus. P-h . . . d.*

This wasn't just a team commander, a chief of one of the Reckoner cells. This was Jon Phaedrus himself. Their leader and founder.

8

"SO . . . ," I said as we left the room. "Where's this place we're going? Hole Fourteen?"

"You don't need to know that," Prof said.

"Can I have my rifle magazine back?"

"No."

"Do I need to know any . . . I don't know. Secret handshakes? Special identifiers? Codes so other Reckoners know I'm one of them?"

"Son," Prof said, "you're *not* one of us."

"I know, I know," I said quickly. "But I don't want anyone to surprise us and think I'm an enemy or something, and—"

"Megan," Prof said, jerking his thumb at me. "Entertain the kid. I need to think." He walked on ahead, joining Tia, and the two of them began speaking quietly.

Megan gave me a scowl. I probably deserved it, for yammering questions at Prof like that. I was just so nervous. Phaedrus himself, the founder of the Reckoners. Now that I knew what to look for, I recognized him from the descriptions—sparse though they were— that I'd read.

The man was a legend. A god among freedom fighters and assassins alike. I was starstruck, and the questions had just dribbled out. In truth I was proud of myself for not asking for an autograph on my gun.

My behavior hadn't earned me points with Megan, however, and she obviously didn't like being put on babysitting detail either. Cody and Abraham were talking ahead, which left Megan and me walking beside each other as we moved at a brisk pace down one of the darkened steel tunnels. She was silent.

She really was pretty. And she was probably around my age, maybe just a year or two older. I still wasn't certain why she'd turned cold toward me. Maybe some witty conversation would help with that. "So, uh," I said. "How long have you . . . you know, been with the Reckoners? And all?"

Smooth.

"Long enough," she said.

"Were you involved in any of the recent kills? Gyro? Shadow-blight? Earless?"

"Maybe. I doubt Prof would want me sharing specifics."

We walked in silence for a time longer.

"You know," I said, "you're not really very entertaining."

"What?"

"Prof told you to entertain me," I said.

"That was just to deflect your questions onto someone else. I doubt you'll find anything I do to be particularly entertaining."

"I wouldn't say that," I said. "I liked the striptease."

She glared at me. *"What?"*

"Out in the alley," I said. "When you . . ."

Her expression was so frigid you could have used it to liquid-cool a high-fire-rate stationary gun barrel. Or maybe some drinks. Chill drinks—that was a better metaphor.

I didn't think she'd appreciate me using it right then, though. "Never mind," I said.

"Good," she said, turning away from me and continuing on.

I breathed out, then chuckled. "For a moment there I thought you'd shoot me."

"I only shoot people when the job calls for it," she said. "You're trying to make small talk; you're simply not very good at it. That's not a shooting offense."

"Er, thanks."

She nodded, businesslike, which wasn't exactly the reaction I'd have hoped for from a pretty girl whose life I'd saved. Granted, she was the first girl—pretty or not—whose life I'd saved, so I didn't have much of a baseline.

Still, she'd been kind of warm to me before, hadn't she? Maybe I just needed to work a little harder. "So what *can* you tell me?" I asked. "About the team, or the other members."

"I'd prefer to discuss another topic," she said. "One that doesn't involve secrets about the Reckoners *or* my clothing, please."

I fell silent. Truth was, I didn't *know* about much other than the Reckoners and the Epics in town. Yes, I'd had some schooling at the Factory, but only basic kinds of stuff. And before that I'd lived a year scavenging on the streets, malnourished, barely avoiding death.

"I guess we could talk about the city," I said. "I know a lot about the understreets."

"How old are you?" Megan said.

"Eighteen," I said, defensive.

"And is anyone going to come looking for you? Are people going to wonder where you went?"

I shook my head. "I hit my majority two months ago. Got kicked out of the Factory where I worked."

That was the rule. You only worked there until you were eighteen; after that you found another job.

"You worked at a factory?" she asked. "For how long?"

"Nine years or so," I said. "Weapons factory, actually. Made guns for Enforcement." Some understreeters, particularly the older ones, grumbled about how the Factory exploited children for labor. That was a stupid complaint, made by old people who remembered a different world. A safer world.

In my world, people who gave you the chance to work in exchange for food were saints. Martha saw to it that her workers were fed, clothed, and protected, even from one another.

"Was it nice?"

"Kind of. It's not slave labor, like people think. We got paid." Kind of. Martha saved wages to give us when we were no longer owned by the Factory. Enough to establish ourselves, find a trade.

"It was a good place to grow up, all things considered," I said wistfully as we walked. "Without the Factory, I doubt I'd have ever learned to fire a gun. The kids aren't supposed to use the weapons, but if you're good, Martha—she ran the place—turns a blind eye." More than one of her kids had gone on to work for Enforcement.

"That's interesting," Megan said. "Tell me more."

"Well, it's . . ." I trailed off, looking at her. Only now did I realize she'd been walking along, eyes forward, barely paying attention. She was just asking things to keep me talking, maybe even to keep me from bothering her in more invasive ways.

"You're not even listening," I accused.

"You seemed like you wanted to talk," she said curtly. "I gave you the chance."

Sparks, I thought, feeling like a slontze. We fell silent as we walked, which seemed to suit Megan just fine.

"You don't know how aggravating this is," I finally said.

She gave me a glance, her emotions hidden. "Aggravating?"

"Yes, aggravating. I've spent the last ten years of my life studying the Reckoners and the Epics. Now that I'm with you, I'm told I'm not allowed to ask questions about important things. It's aggravating."

"Think about something else."

"There *is* nothing else. Not to me."

"Girls."

"None."

"Hobbies."

"None. Just you guys, Steelheart, and my notes."

"Wait," she said. "Notes?"

"Sure," I said. "I worked in the Factory during the days, always listening for rumors. I spent my free days spending what little money I had buying newspapers or stories off those who traveled abroad. I got to know a few information brokers. Each night I'd work on the notes, putting it all together. I knew I'd need to be an expert on Epics, so I became one."

She frowned deeply.

"I know," I said, grimacing. "It sounds like I don't have a life. You're not the first to tell me that. The others at the Factory—"

"Hush," she said. "You wrote about Epics, but what about us? What about the Reckoners?"

"Of course I wrote it down," I said. "What was I supposed to do? Keep it in my head? I filled a couple notebooks, and though most of it was guesswork, I'm pretty good at guessing. . . ." I trailed off, realizing why she looked so worried.

"Where is it all?" she asked softly.

"In my flat," I said. "Should be safe. I mean, none of those goons got close enough to see me clearly."

"And the woman you pulled out of her car?"

I hesitated. "Yeah, she saw my face. She *might* be able to describe me. But, I mean, that wouldn't be enough for them to track me, right?"

Megan was silent.

Yes, I thought. *Yes, it might be enough.* Enforcement was very good at its job. And unfortunately, I had a few incidents in my past, such as the taxi wreck. I was on file, and Steelheart would give Enforcement a great deal of motivation to follow every lead regarding Fortuity's death.

"We need to talk to Prof," Megan said, towing me by the arm toward where the others were walking ahead.

9

PROF listened to my explanation with thoughtful eyes. "Yes," he said as I finished. "I should have seen this. It makes sense."

I relaxed. I'd been afraid he'd be furious.

"What's the address, son?" Prof asked.

"Fifteen thirty-two Ditko Place," I said. It was carved into the steel around a park in one of the nicer areas of the understreets. "It's small, but I live alone. I keep it locked tight."

"Enforcement won't need a key," Prof said. "Cody, Abraham, go to this place. Set a firebomb, make sure nobody is inside, and blow the entire room."

I felt a sudden jolt of alarm, as if someone had hooked up my toes to a car battery. *"What?"*

"We can't have Steelheart getting that information, son," Prof said. "Not just the information about us, but the information on the other Epics you collected. If it's as detailed as you say, he could use it against the other powerful Epics in the region. Steelheart already has too much influence. We need to destroy that intel."

"You can't!" I exclaimed, my voice echoing in the narrow, steel-walled tunnel. Those notes were my life's work! Sure, I hadn't been around *that* long, but still . . . ten years of effort? Losing it would be like losing a hand. Given the option, I'd rather lose the hand.

"Son," Prof said, "don't push me. Your place here is fragile."

"You *need* that information," I said. "It's important, sir. Why would you burn hundreds of pages of information about the powers of Epics and their possible weaknesses?"

"You said you gathered it through hearsay," Tia said, her arms crossed. "I doubt there's anything in it that we don't know already."

"Do you know Nightwielder's weakness?" I asked, desperate.

Nightwielder. He was one of Steelheart's High Epic bodyguards, and his powers created the perpetual darkness over Newcago. He was a shadowy figure himself, completely incorporeal, immune to gunfire or weapons of any kind.

"No," Tia admitted. "And I doubt you do either."

"Sunlight," I said. "He becomes solid in sunlight. I've got pictures."

"You have *pictures* of Nightwielder in corporeal form?" Tia asked.

"I think so. The person I bought them from wasn't certain, but I'm reasonably sure."

"Hey, lad," Cody called. "You want to buy Loch Ness from me? I'll give you a good price."

I glared at him, and he just shrugged. Loch Ness was in Scotland, I knew that much, and it seemed that the crest on Cody's cap might be some kind of Scottish or English deal. But his accent didn't match.

"Prof," I said, turning back to him. "Phaedrus, sir, please. You have to see my plan."

"Your plan?" He didn't seem surprised that I'd worked out his name.

"For killing Steelheart."

"You have a plan?" Prof asked. "For killing the most powerful Epic in the country?"

"That's what I told you before."

"I thought you wanted to join us to get us to do it."

"I need help," I said. "But I didn't come empty-handed. I've got a detailed plan. I think it will work."

Prof just shook his head, looking bemused.

Suddenly, Abraham laughed. "I like him. He has . . . something. *Un homme téméraire*. You sure we aren't recruiting, Prof?"

"Yes," Prof said flatly.

"At least look at my plan before you burn it," I said. "Please."

"Jon," Tia said. "I'd like to see these pictures. They're likely fake, but even so . . ."

"Fine," Prof said, tossing something to me. The magazine for my rifle. "Change of plans. Cody, you take Megan and the boy and go to his place. If Enforcement is there and looks like they're going to take this information, destroy it. But if the site looks safe, bring it back." He eyed me. "Whatever you can't carry easily, destroy. Understood?"

"Sure," Cody said.

"Thank you," I said.

"It's not a favor, son," Prof said. "And I hope it's not a mistake either. Go on. We may not have much time before they track you."

It was getting quiet in the understreets by the time we neared Ditko Place. You'd think that, with the perpetual darkness, there wouldn't really be a "day" or a "night" in Newcago, but there is. People tend to want to sleep when everyone else sleeps, so we settle into routines.

Of course, there are a minority who don't like to do as told, even when it comes to something simple. I was one of those. Being up all night means being awake when everyone else is sleeping. It's quieter, more private.

The ceiling lights were set to a clock somewhere, and they colored to deeper shades when it was night. The change was subtle, but we learned to notice it. So, even though Ditko Place was near the surface, there wasn't much motion on the streets. People were sleeping.

We arrived at the park, a large underground chamber carved from the steel. It had numerous holes in the ceiling for fresh air, and blue-violet lights shone from spotlights around the rim. The center of the tall chamber was cluttered with rocks brought in from outside—real rocks, not ones that had been turned to steel. There was also wooden playground equipment, moderately well maintained, that had been scavenged from somewhere. In the daytime the place would fill with children—the ones too young to work, or the ones with families who could afford not to have them work. Old women and men would gather to knit socks or do other simple work.

Megan raised her hand to still us. "Mobiles?" she whispered.

Cody sniffed. "Do I look like some amateur?" he asked. "It's on silent."

I hesitated, then took mine off the place on my shoulder and double-checked. Fortunately it was on silent. I took out the battery anyway, just in case. Megan moved quietly out of the tunnel and across the park toward the shadow of a large rock. Cody went next, then I followed, keeping low and moving as quietly as I could, passing large stones growing lichen.

Up above a few cars rumbled by on the roadway that ran past the openings in the ceiling. Late-night commuters heading home. Sometimes they'd throw trash down on us. A surprising number of the rich still had ordinary jobs. Accountants, teachers, salesmen, computer technicians—though Steelheart's datanet was open only to his most trusted. I'd never seen a real computer, just my mobile.

It was a different world above, and jobs that had once been common were now held by only the privileged. The rest of us worked factories or sewed clothing in the park while watching children play.

I reached the rock and crouched beside Cody and Megan, who were stealthily inspecting the two far walls of the chamber, where the dwellings were cut. Dozens of holes in the steel provided homes of various sizes. Metal fire escapes had been harvested from unused buildings above and set up here to give access to the holes.

"So, which one is it?" Cody asked.

I pointed. "See that door on the second level, far right? That's it."

"Nice," Cody said. "How'd y'all afford a place like this?" He asked it casually, but I could tell that he was suspicious. They all were. Well, I suppose that was to be expected.

"I needed a room by myself for my research," I said. "The factory where I worked saves all of your wages when you're a kid, then gives them to you in four yearly chunks when you hit eighteen. It was enough to get me a year in my own room."

"Cool," Cody said. I wondered if my explanation passed his test or not. "It doesn't look like Enforcement has made it here yet. Maybe they couldn't match you from the description."

I nodded slowly, though beside me Megan was looking around, her eyes narrowed.

"What?" I asked.

"It looks too easy. I don't trust things that look too easy."

I scanned the far walls. There were a few empty trash bins and some motorbikes chained up beside a stairwell. Some chunks of metal had been etched by enterprising street artists. They weren't supposed to do that, but the people encouraged them, quietly. It was one of the only forms of rebellion the common people ever engaged in.

"Well, we can wait here staring until they *do* come," Cody said, rubbing his face with a leathery finger, "or we can just go. Let's be on with it." He stood up.

One of the large trash bins shimmered.

"Wait!" I said, grabbing Cody and pulling him down, my heart leaping.

"What?" he said, anxious, unslinging his rifle. It was of a very fine make, old but well maintained, with a large scope and a state-of-the-art suppressor on the front. I'd never been able to get my hands on one of those. The cheaper ones worked poorly, and I found it too hard to aim with them.

"There," I said, pointing at the trash bin. "Watch it."

He frowned but did what I asked. My mind raced, sorting through fragments of remembered research. I needed my notes. Shimmering . . . illusionist Epic . . . who was that?

Refractionary, I thought, seizing on a name. *A class C illusionist with personal invisibility capabilities.*

"What am I watching for?" Cody asked. "Did you get spooked by a cat or something—" He cut off as the bin shimmered again. Cody frowned, then crouched down farther. "What is that?"

"An Epic," Megan said, her eyes narrowing. "Some of the lesser Epics with illusion powers have trouble maintaining an exact illusion."

"Her name is Refractionary," I said softly. "She's pretty skilled, capable of creating complex visual manifestations. But she's not terribly powerful, and her illusions always have tells to them. Usually they shimmer as if light is reflecting off them."

Cody aimed his rifle, sighting on the trash bin. "So you're saying that bin isn't really there. It's hiding something else. Enforcement officers, probably?"

"I'd guess so," I said.

"Can she be harmed by bullets, lad?" Cody asked.

"Yes, she's not a High Epic. But Cody, she might not be in there."

"You just said—"

"She's a class C illusionist," I explained. "But her secondary power is class B personal invisibility. Illusions and invisibility often go hand in hand. Anyway, she can make herself invisible, but not anything else—others, she has to create an illusion around. I'd be certain she's hiding an Enforcement squad in that fake trash bin illusion, but if she's smart—and she is—she'll be somewhere else."

I felt an itch in the small of my back. I *hated* illusionist Epics. You never knew where they'd be. Even the weakest of them—class D or E, by my own notation system—could make an illusion big enough for themselves to hide in. If they had personal invisibility, it was even worse.

"There," Megan whispered, pointing toward a large piece of playground equipment—a kind of wooden fort for climbing. "See those boxes on the top of that playground tower? They just shimmered. Someone's hiding in them."

"That's only big enough for one person," I whispered. "From that position, whoever is there could see right into my apartment through the door. Sniper?"

"Most likely," Megan said.

"Refractionary is close, then," I said. "She'll need to be able to see both that playground equipment and the fake garbage bins to keep the illusions going. The range on her powers isn't great."

"How do we draw her out?" Megan asked.

"She likes to be involved, from what I remember," I said. "If we can get the Enforcement soldiers to move, she'll stay close to them, in case she needs to give orders or make illusions to support them."

"Sparks!" Cody whispered. "How do you know all of this, lad?"

"Weren't you listening?" Megan asked softly. "This is what he does. It's what he has built his life around. He studies them."

Cody stroked his chin. He looked as if he'd assumed everything I said before was bravado. "You know her weakness?"

"It's in my notes," I said. "I'm trying to remember. Uh . . . well, illusionists usually can't see if they turn themselves completely invisible. They need light to strike their irises. So you can watch for the eyes. But a really skilled illusionist can make their eyes match the color of their surroundings. But that's not really her weakness, more a limitation of illusions themselves."

What was it? "Smoke!" I exclaimed, then blushed at the sound of it. Megan shot me a glare. "It's her weakness," I whispered. "She always avoids people who are smoking, and stays away from any kind of fire. It's pretty well known, and reasonably substantiated, as far as Epic weaknesses go."

"Guess we're back to starting the place on fire after all," Cody said. He seemed excited by the prospect.

"What? No."

"Prof said—"

"We can still get the information," I said. "They're waiting for me, but they only sent a minor Epic. That means they want me, but they haven't sorted through that the Reckoners were behind the assassination tonight—or maybe they don't know how I was involved. They probably haven't cleaned out my room yet, even if they did break in and scan through what's there."

"Excellent reason to burn the place," Megan said. "I'm sorry, but if they're that close . . ."

"But see, it's essential that we go in now," I said, growing more anxious. "We have to see what has been disturbed, if anything. That'll tell us what they've discovered. We burn the place down now, and we blind ourselves."

The other two hesitated.

"We can stop them," I said. "And we might be able to kill us an Epic in the process. Refractionary has plenty of blood on her hands. Just last month someone cut her off in traffic. She created an illusion of the road turning up ahead and drove the offender off the freeway and into a home. Six dead. Children were in the car."

Epics had a distinct, even incredible, lack of morals or conscience. That bothered some people, on a philosophical level. Theorists, scholars. They wondered at the sheer inhumanity many Epics manifested. Did the Epics kill because Calamity chose—for whatever reason—only terrible people to gain powers? Or did they kill because such amazing power twisted a person, made them irresponsible?

There were no conclusive answers. I didn't care; I wasn't a scholar. Yes, I did research, but so did a sports fan when he followed his team. It didn't matter to me why the Epics did what they did any more than a baseball fan wondered at the physics of a bat hitting a ball.

Only one thing mattered—Epics gave no thought for ordinary human life. A brutal murder was a fitting retribution, in their minds, for the most minor of infractions.

"Prof didn't approve hitting an Epic," Megan said. "This isn't in the procedures."

Cody chuckled. "Killing an Epic is always in the procedures, lass. You just haven't been with us long enough to understand."

"I have a smoke grenade in my room," I said.

"What?" Megan asked. "How?"

"I grew up working at a munitions plant," I said. "We mostly made rifles and handguns, but we worked with other factories. I got to pick up the occasional goody from the QC reject pile."

"A smoke grenade is a goody?" Cody asked.

I frowned. What did he mean? Of course it was. Who wouldn't want a smoke grenade when offered one? Megan actually showed the faintest of smiles. She understood.

I don't get you, girl, I thought. She carried explosives in her shirt and was an excellent shot, but she was worried about procedures when she got a chance to kill an Epic? And as soon as she caught me looking at her, her expression grew cold and aloof once again.

Had I done something to offend her?

"If we can get that grenade, I can use it to negate Refractionary's powers," I said. "She likes to stay near her teams. So if we can draw the soldiers into an enclosed space, she'll probably follow. I can blow the grenade, then shoot her when it makes her appear."

"Good enough," Cody said. "But how are we going to manage all of that *and* get your notes?"

"Easy," I said, reluctantly handing my rifle to Megan. I'd have a better chance of fooling them if I wasn't armed. "We give them the thing they're waiting for. Me."

10

I crossed the street toward my flat, hands in the pockets of my jacket, fingering the roll of industrial tape I usually kept there. The other two hadn't liked my plan, but they hadn't come up with anything better. Hopefully they'd be able to fulfill their parts in it.

I felt completely naked without my rifle. I had a couple of handguns stashed in my room, but a man wasn't really dangerous unless he had a rifle. At least, he wasn't consistently dangerous. Hitting something with a handgun always felt like an accident.

Megan did it, I thought. *She not only hit, but hit a High Epic in the middle of a dodge, firing two guns at once, one from the hip.*

She'd shown emotion during our fight with Fortuity. Passion, anger, annoyance. The second two toward me, but it had been something. And then, for a few moments after he fell . . . there had been a connection. Satisfaction, and appreciation of me that had come out when she'd spoken on my behalf to Prof.

Now that was gone. What did it mean?

I stopped at the edge of the playground. Was I really thinking about a girl *now*? I was only about five paces from where a group of Enforcement officers were hiding, probably with automatic or energy weapons trained on me.

Idiot, I thought, heading up the metal stairway toward my apartment. They'd wait to see if I got out anything incriminating before grabbing me. Hopefully.

Climbing steps like that, with my back to the enemy, was excruciating. I did what I always did when I grew afraid. I thought of my father falling, bleeding beside that pillar in the broken bank lobby while I hid. I hadn't helped.

I would never be that coward again.

I reached the door to my apartment, then fiddled with the keys. I heard a distant scrape but pretended not to notice. That would be the sniper on top of the playground equipment nearby, repositioning to aim at me. Yes, from this angle I saw for certain. That playground piece was just tall enough that the sniper would be able to shoot through the door into my apartment.

I stepped inside my single room. No hallways or anything else, just a hole cut into the steel, like most dwellings in the understreets. It might not have had a bathroom or running water, but I was still living quite well, by understreets standards. A whole room for a single person?

I kept it messy. Some old, disposable noodle bowls sat in a pile beside the door, smelling of spice. Clothing was strewn across the floor. I had a bucket of two-day-old water sitting on the table, and dirty, beat-up silverware sat in a pile beside it.

I didn't use those to eat. They were for show. So was the clothing; I didn't wear any of it. My actual clothing—four sturdy outfits, always clean and washed—was folded in the trunk beside my mattress on the floor. I *kept* my room messy, intentionally. It actually itched at me, as I liked things neat.

I'd found that sloppiness put people off guard. If my landlady came snooping up here, she'd find what she expected. A teenager just into his majority blowing his earnings on an easy life for a year before responsibility hit him. She wouldn't poke or prod for secret compartments.

I hurried to the trunk. I unlocked it and pulled out my backpack—already packed with a change of clothing, spare shoes, some dry rations, and two liters of water. There was a handgun in a pouch on one side, and the smoke grenade was in a pouch on the other side.

I walked to my mattress and unzipped the case. Inside was my life. Dozens of folders, filled with clippings from newspapers or scraps of information. Eight notebooks filled with my thoughts and findings. A larger notebook with my indexes.

Maybe I should have brought all of this with me when going to watch the Fortuity hit. After all, I'd hoped to leave with the Reckoners. I'd debated it but had eventually decided that it wouldn't be reasonable. There was so much of it, for one thing. I could lug it all if I needed to, but it slowed me down.

And it was just too precious. This research was the most valuable thing in my life. Collecting some of it had nearly gotten me killed—spying on Epics, asking questions better left unasked, making payments to shady informants. I was proud of it, not to mention frightened about what might happen to it. I'd thought it safer here.

Boots shook the metal landing of the stairway outside. I looked over my shoulder and saw one of the most feared sights in the understreets: fully geared Enforcement officers. They stood on the landing, automatic rifles in their hands, sleek black helmets on their heads, military-grade armor on their chests, knees, arms. There were three of them.

Their helmets had black visors that came down over their eyes, leaving their mouths and chins exposed. The eye shields gave them night vision and glowed faintly green, with a strange smoky pattern that swirled and undulated across the front. It was transfixing, which was said to be the point.

I didn't need to act to make my eyes go wide, my muscles taut.

"Hands on your head," the lead officer said, rifle up at his shoulder and the barrel trained on me. "Down on your knees, subject."

That was what they called people, *subject*. Steelheart didn't bother with any kind of silly pretense that his empire was a republic or a representative government. He didn't call people *citizens* or *comrades*. They were subjects of his empire. That was that.

I quickly raised my hands. "I didn't do anything!" I whined. "I was just there to watch!"

"HANDS UP, KNEES DOWN!" the officer yelled.

I complied.

They entered the room, leaving the doorway conspicuously open so that their sniper had a view through the door. From what I'd read, these three would be part of a five-person squad known as a Core. Three regular troops, one specialist—in this case a sniper—and one minor Epic. Steelheart had about fifty Cores like this.

Almost all of Enforcement was made of special-operations teams. If there was any large-scale fighting to be done, something *very* dangerous, Steelheart, Nightwielder, Firefight, or maybe Conflux—who was head of Enforcement—would deal with it personally. Enforcement was used for the smaller problems in the city, the ones Steelheart didn't want to bother with himself. In a way he didn't need Enforcement. They were like a homicidal dictator's version of valet parking attendants.

One of the three soldiers kept an eye on me while the other two rifled through the contents of my mattress. *Is she in here?* I wondered. *Invisible somewhere?* My instincts, and my memory of researching her, told me she'd be near.

I just had to hope she was in the room. I couldn't move until

Cody and Megan fulfilled their part of my plan, though, so I waited, tense, for them to do so.

The two soldiers pulled notebooks and folders out from between the two pieces of foam that made up my mattress. One flipped through the notes. "This is information on Epics, sir," he said.

"I thought I'd be able to see Fortuity fight another Epic," I said, staring at the floor. "When I found out something terrible was happening, I tried to get away. I was only there to see what would happen, you know?"

The officer began looking through the notebooks. The soldier watching me seemed uncomfortable about something. He kept glancing at me, then at the others.

I felt my heart thumping, waiting. Megan and Cody would attack soon. I had to be ready.

"You are in serious trouble, subject," the officer said, tossing one of my notebooks to the floor. "An Epic, and an important one, is dead."

"I didn't have anything to do with it!" I said. "I swear. I—"

"Bah." The lead officer pointed toward one of the other soldiers. "Gather this up."

"Sir," said the soldier watching me. "He's probably telling the truth."

I hesitated. That voice . . .

"Roy?" I said, shocked. He'd hit majority the year before me . . . and had joined Enforcement after that.

The officer glanced back at me. "You know this subject?"

"Yes," Roy said, sounding reluctant. He was a tall redhead. I'd always liked him. He'd been an adjunct at the Factory, which was a position Martha gave to senior boys—they were meant to stop the young or weaker workers from being picked on. He'd done his job well.

"You didn't say anything?" the lead officer said, his voice hard.

"I . . . sir, I'm sorry. I should have. He's always had a fascination with Epics. I've seen him cross half the city on foot and wait in the rain just because he heard a new Epic might be passing through town. If he heard something about two of them fighting, he'd have gone to watch, whether it was a good idea or not."

"Sounds exactly like the kind of person who should be off the streets," the officer said. "Gather this. Son, you're going to come tell us *exactly* what you saw. If you do a good job, perhaps you might even live through the night. It—"

A gunshot sounded outside. The officer's face blossomed red, the front of his helmet exploding as a bullet hit him.

I rolled toward my backpack. Cody and Megan had done their job, quietly taking down the sniper and getting into position to support me.

I ripped open the Velcro on the side of my pack and pulled out my handgun, then fired rapidly at Roy's thighs. The bullets hit an open spot in his advanced plastic armor, dropping him, though I almost missed. Sparking pistols.

The other soldier fell to a well-placed shot from Cody, who would be on that playground equipment outside. I didn't stop to make sure the third soldier was dead—Refractionary might be in the room, armed and ready to shoot. I pulled out the smoke grenade and removed the pin.

I dropped the grenade. A burst of grey smoke jetted from the canister, filling the room. I held my breath, handgun up. Refractionary's powers would be negated when the smoke touched her. I waited for her to appear.

Nothing happened. She wasn't in the room.

Smothering a curse, still holding my breath, I glanced at Roy. He was trying to move, holding his leg and trying to point his rifle toward me. I leaped through the smoke and kicked the rifle aside. Then I pulled his sidearm out of its holster and tossed it. Both guns would be useless to me; they'd be keyed to his gloves.

Roy's hand was in his pocket. I put my gun to his temple and yanked his hand out. He'd been trying to dial his mobile. I cocked the gun, and he dropped the mobile.

"It's too late anyway, David," Roy spat, then started coughing at the smoke. "Conflux will know the moment we go offline. Other Cores are on their way here. They'll send spying eyes down to watch. Those are probably already here."

Breath still held, I checked the pockets on his cargo pants. There were no other weapons.

"You're being a fool, David," Roy said, coughing. I ignored him and scanned the room. I had to start breathing, and the smoke was getting overpowering.

Where was Refractionary? On the landing, maybe. I kicked the smoke grenade out, hoping she was there.

Nothing. Either I had her weakness wrong, or she'd decided not to join her team in coming to get me.

What if she was sneaking up on Megan and Cody? They'd never see her coming.

I glanced down. Roy's mobile.

Worth a try.

I snatched the phone and opened the address book. Refractionary was listed under her Epic name. Most Epics preferred to use them.

I dialed.

Almost immediately, a gunshot sounded from the playground outside.

I couldn't hold my breath any longer. I ducked outside, staying low, and kicked the smoke grenade off the landing. I started down the stairwell and took a deep breath.

Then, eyes watering, I scanned the playground. Cody knelt on top of the playground equipment, rifle out. At the base of the tower, Megan stood with her gun out, a body in black and yellow at her feet. Refractionary.

Megan fired again into the body, just to be certain, but the woman was obviously dead.

Another Epic eliminated.

11

MY first move was to go back in and toss Roy's rifle, which he had been crawling toward, out the door. Then I checked on the two other soldiers. One was dead; the other had a weak pulse—but he wasn't going to be waking anytime soon.

Time to move quickly. I pulled the notebooks from my mattress and stuffed them in my backpack. Six thick notebooks and one index caused the backpack to bulge. I thought for a moment, then took my extra pair of shoes out of the pack. I could buy new shoes, but I couldn't replace these notebooks.

The last two fit, and beside them I slid the folders about Steelheart, Nightwielder, and Firefight. After a moment I added the one about Conflux. It was the thinnest. Very little was known about the clandestine High Epic who ran Enforcement.

Roy was still coughing, though the smoke had cleared out. He pulled off his helmet. It was surreal to see that familiar face—one I'd known for years—wearing the uniform of the enemy. We hadn't been friends; I didn't really have those, but I'd looked up to him.

"You're working with the Reckoners," Roy said.

I needed to try to lay down a false trail, get him to think I was working for someone else. "What?" I said, doing my best to look baffled.

"Don't try to hide it, David. It's obvious. Everyone knows the Reckoners hit Fortuity."

I knelt down beside him, pack slung over my shoulder. "Look, Roy, don't let them heal you, okay? I know Enforcement has Epics who can do that. Don't let them, if you can manage it."

"What, why—"

"You want to be laid out sick for this next part, Roy," I said softly, intensely. "Power is going to change hands in Newcago. Limelight is coming for Steelheart."

"Limelight?" Roy said. "Who the hell is that?"

I walked over to the rest of my folders, then reluctantly took a can of lighter fluid from my trunk and poured it on the bed.

"You're working for an Epic?" Roy whispered. "You really think anyone can challenge Steelheart? Sparks, David! How many rivals has he killed?"

"This is different," I said, then got out some matches. "Limelight is different." I lit the match.

I couldn't take the remaining folders. They were source material, facts and articles for the information I'd collected in my notebooks. I wanted to take them, but there was no more room in my bag.

I dropped the match. The bed started aflame.

"One of your friends might still be alive," I said to Roy, nodding to the two Enforcement officers who were down. The leader had been shot in the head, but the other one only in the side. "Get him out. Then stay out of things, Roy. Dangerous days are coming."

I slung the pack over my shoulder and hastened out the door and onto the stairwell. I met Megan on the way down the steps.

"Your plan failed," she said quietly.

"Worked well enough," I said. "An Epic is dead."

"Only because she left her mobile on vibrate," Megan said, hurrying down the steps beside me. "If she hadn't been sloppy . . ."

"We were lucky," I agreed. "But we still won."

Mobiles were just a part of daily life. The people might live in hovels, but they all had a mobile for entertainment.

We met Cody at the base of the playground tower near Refractionary's corpse. He handed back my rifle. "Lad," he said, "that was *awesome*."

I blinked. I'd been expecting another berating, like Megan had given me.

"Prof is going to be jealous he didn't come himself," Cody said, slinging his rifle over his shoulder. "Were you the one who called her?"

"Yeah," I said.

"Awesome," Cody said again, slapping me on the back.

Megan didn't look nearly as pleased. She gave Cody a sharp look, then reached for my pack.

I resisted.

"You need two hands for the rifle," she said, pulling it free and slinging it over her shoulder. "Let's move. Enforcement will . . ." She trailed off as she noticed Roy barely managing to tow the other Enforcement officer out of the burning room and onto the landing.

I felt bad, but only a little. Copters were thumping above; he'd have help soon. We scurried across the park, heading toward the tunnels that led deeper into the understreets.

"You left them alive?" Megan asked as we ran.

"This was more useful," I said. "I laid us a false trail. I told him a lie that I was working for an Epic who wants to challenge Steelheart. Hopefully it will keep them from searching for the Reckoners." I hesitated. "Besides. They're not our enemies."

"Of course they are," she snapped.

"No," Cody said, jogging beside her. "He's right, lass. They aren't. They may work for the enemy, but they're just regular folks. They do what they can to get by."

"We can't think like that," she said as we reached a branching tunnel. She glared at me, eyes cold. "We can't show them mercy. They won't show it to us."

"We can't become them, lass," Cody said, shaking his head. "Listen to Prof talk about it sometime. If we have to do what the Epics do to beat them, then it's not worth it."

"I've heard him talk," she said, still looking at me. "I'm not worried about him. I'm worried about Knees here."

"I'll shoot an Enforcement officer if I have to," I said, meeting her eyes. "But I won't get distracted hunting them down. I have a goal. I'll see Steelheart dead. That is all that matters."

"Bah," she said, turning away from me. "That's not an answer."

"Let's keep moving," Cody said, nodding toward a stairwell down to deeper tunnels.

"He's a scientist, lad," Cody explained as we walked through the narrow corridors of the steel catacombs. "Studied Epics in the early days, created some pretty remarkable devices, based on what we learned from them. That's why he's called Prof, other than that last-name thing."

I nodded thoughtfully. Now that we were deep, Cody had relaxed. Megan was still stiff. She walked ahead, holding her mobile and using it to send Prof a report on the mission. Cody had his set to flashlight, hooked to the upper left of his camo jacket. I'd removed the network card from mine, which he said was a good idea until Abraham or Tia had a chance to tweak it.

It turned out that they didn't trust even the Knighthawk Foundry. The Reckoners usually left their mobiles linked only to one another, and had the transmissions encrypted on both ends, not using the regular network. Until I got the encryption too, I could at least use my mobile as a camera or a glorified flashlight.

Cody walked with a relaxed posture, rifle up on his shoulder, arm looped over it and hand hanging down. I seemed to have earned his approval with Refractionary's death.

"So where did he work?" I asked, hungry for information about Prof. There were so many rumors about the Reckoners, but few real facts.

"Don't know," Cody admitted. "Nobody's sure what Prof's past is, though Tia probably knows something. She doesn't talk about it. Abe and I have bets going 'bout what Prof's specific workplace was. I'm pretty sure he was at some kind of secret government organization."

"Really?" I asked.

"Sure," Cody said. "I wouldn't be surprised if it was the same one that caused Calamity."

That was one of the theories, that the United States government—or sometimes the European Union—had somehow set off Calamity while trying to start a superhuman project. I thought it was pretty far-fetched. I'd always figured it was some kind of comet that got caught in Earth's gravity, but I didn't know if the science of that made any sense. Maybe it was a satellite. That could fit Cody's theory.

He wouldn't be the only one who thought it reeked of conspiracy. There *were* a lot of things about the Epics that didn't add up.

"Oh, you got that look," Cody said, pointing at me.

"That look?"

"Y'all think I'm crazy."

"No. No, of course not."

"You do. Well, it's okay. I know what I know, even if Prof rolls his eyes whenever I say anything about it." Cody smiled. "But that's another story. As for Prof's line of work, I think it *must* have been some kind of weapons facility. He created the tensors, after all."

"The tensors?"

"Prof wouldn't want you talking about that," Megan said, looking over her shoulder. "Nobody gave authorization for *him* to know about it," she added, glancing at me.

"I'm giving it," Cody said, relaxed. "He's going to see anyway, lass. And *don't* quote Prof's rules at me."

She closed her mouth; she looked like she'd been about to do just that.

"The tensors?" I asked again.

"Something Prof invented," Cody said. "Either right before or right after he left the lab. He's got a couple of things like that, inventions that give us our main edge against the Epics. Our jackets are one of those—they can take a lot of punishment—and the tensors are another."

"But what *are* they?"

"Gloves," Cody said. "Well, devices in the form of gloves. They create vibrations that disrupt solid objects. Works best on dense stuff, like stone and metal, some kinds of wood. Turns that kind of material to dust, but won't do anything to a living animal or person."

"You're kidding." In all my years of research I'd never heard of any technology like that.

"Nope," Cody said. "They're difficult to use, though. Abraham and Tia are the most skilled. But you'll see—the tensors, they let us go where we're not supposed to be. Where we're not expected to be."

"That's amazing," I said, my mind racing. The Reckoners *did* have a reputation for being able to get where nobody thought they could. There were stories . . . Epics killed in their own chambers, well guarded and presumed safe. Near-magical escapes by the Reckoners.

A device that could turn stone and metal to powder . . . You could get through locked doors, regardless of the security devices. You could sabotage vehicles. Maybe even knock down buildings. Suddenly, some of the most baffling mysteries surrounding the Reckoners made sense to me. How they'd gotten in to trap Daystorm, how they'd escaped the time when Calling War had nearly cornered them.

They'd have to be clever about how they entered, so as to not leave obvious holes that gave them away. But I could see how it would work. "But why . . . ," I asked, dazed, "why are you telling me this?"

"As I said, lad," Cody explained. "You're going to see them at work soon anyway. Might as well prepare you for it. Besides, you already know so much about us that one more thing won't matter."

"Okay." I said it lightly, then caught the somber tone of his voice. He'd left something unsaid: I already knew so much that I couldn't be allowed to go free.

Prof had given me my chance to leave. I'd insisted they bring me. At this point I either convinced them utterly that I wasn't a threat and joined them, or they left me behind. Dead.

I swallowed uncomfortably, my mouth suddenly dry. *I asked for this,* I told myself sternly. I'd known that once I joined them—if I joined them—I wouldn't ever be leaving. I was in, and that was that.

"So . . ." I tried to force myself not to dwell on the fact that this man—or any of them—might someday decide I needed to be shot in the name of the common good. "So how did he figure these gloves out? The tensors? I've never heard of anything *like* them."

"Epics," Cody said, his voice growing amiable again. "Prof let it drop once. The technology came from studying an Epic who could do something similar. Tia says it happened in the early days—before society collapsed, some Epics were captured and held. Not all of them are so powerful they can escape captivity with ease. Different labs ran tests on them, trying to figure out how their powers worked. The technology for things like the tensors came from those days."

I hadn't heard that, and some things started to click into place for me. We'd made great advances in technology back then, right around the arrival of Calamity. Energy weapons, advanced power sources and batteries, new mobile technology—which was why ours worked underground and at a significant range without using towers.

Of course, we lost much of it when the Epics started to take over. And what we didn't lose, Epics like Steelheart controlled. I tried to imagine those early Epics being tested. Was that why so many were evil? They resented this testing?

"Did any of them go to the testing willingly?" I asked. "How many labs were doing this?"

"I don't know," Cody said. "I reckon it's not very important."

"Why wouldn't it be?"

Cody shrugged, rifle still over his shoulder, the light of his mobile illuminating the tomblike metal corridor. The catacombs smelled of dust and condensation. "Tia is always talking about the scientific foundation of the Epics," he said. "I don't think they can be explained that way. Too much about them breaks what science says should happen. I sometimes wonder if they came along *because* we thought we could explain everything."

It didn't take much longer for us to arrive. I'd noticed that Megan was leading us by way of her mobile, which showed a map on its screen. That was remarkable. A map of the steel catacombs? I didn't think such a thing existed.

"Here," Megan said, waving to a thick patch of wires hanging down like a curtain in front of a wall. Sights like that were common down here, where the Diggers had left things unfinished.

Cody walked up and banged on a plate near the wires. A distant bang came back at him a few moments later.

"In you go, Knees," he said to me, gesturing toward the wires.

I took a breath and stepped forward, pushing them aside with the barrel of my rifle. There was a small tunnel beyond, leading steeply upward. I would have to crawl. I looked back at him.

"It's safe," he promised. I couldn't tell if he was making me go first because of some latent mistrust, or because he liked seeing me squirm. It didn't seem the time to question him or back down. I started crawling.

The tunnel was small enough to make me worry that if I slung my rifle on my back, a good scrape stood a chance of knocking the scope or sights out of alignment. So I kept it in my right hand as I crawled, which made it all the more awkward. The tunnel led toward a distant, soft light, and the crawl took long enough that my knees were aching by the time I reached the light. A strong hand took me by the left arm, helping me out of the tunnel. Abraham. The dark-skinned man had changed into cargo pants and a green tank top, which showed well-muscled arms. I hadn't noticed before, but he was wearing a small silver pendant around his neck, hanging out of his shirt.

The room I stepped into was unexpectedly large. Big enough for the team to have laid out their equipment and several bedrolls without it feeling cramped. There was a large table made of metal that grew right out of the floor, as well as benches at the walls and stools around the table.

They carved it there, I realized, looking at the sculpted walls. *They made this room with the tensors. Carved furniture right into it.*

It was impressive. I gawked as I stepped back and let Abraham help Megan out of the tunnel. The chamber had two doorways into other rooms that looked smaller. It was lit by lanterns, and there were cords on the floor—taped in place and out of the way—leading down another small tunnel.

"You have electricity," I said. "How did you get electricity?"

"Tapped into an old subway line," Cody said, crawling out of the tunnel. "One that was half completed, then forgotten about. The nature of this place is that even Steelheart doesn't know all of its nooks and dead ends."

"Just more proof the Diggers were mad," Abraham said. "They wired things in strange ways. We've found rooms that were sealed completely but had lights left on inside, shining for years by themselves. *Repaire des fantômes.*"

"Megan tells me," Prof said, appearing from one of the other rooms, "that you recovered the information, but that your means were . . . unconventional." The aging but sturdy man still wore his black lab coat.

"Hell yeah!" Cody said, shouldering his rifle.

Prof snorted. "Well, let's see what you recovered before I decide if I should yell at you or not." He reached for the backpack in Megan's hand.

"Actually," I said, stepping toward it, "I can—"

"You'll sit down, son," Prof said, "while I have a look at this. All of it. Then we'll talk."

His voice was calm, but I got the message. I pensively sat down beside the steel table as the others gathered around the pack and began rifling through my life.

12

"**WOW,**" Cody said. "Honestly, lad, I thought you were exaggerating. But y'all really are a full-blown supergeek, aren't you?"

I blushed, still sitting on my stool. They had opened the folders I'd packed and spread out the contents, then moved on to my notebooks, passing them around and studying them. Cody had eventually lost interest and moved over to sit by me, his back to the table and elbows hitched up on it behind him.

"I had a job to do," I said. "I decided to do it well."

"This *is* impressive," Tia said. She sat cross-legged on the floor. She had changed to jeans but was still wearing her blouse and blazer, and her short red hair was still perfectly styled. Tia held up one of my notebooks. "It's rudimentary in organization," she said, "and doesn't use standard classifications. But it is exhaustive."

"There are standard classifications?" I asked.

"Several different systems," she said. "It looks like you've got a few of the terms here that cross between the systems, like High Epic—though I personally prefer the tier system. In other places, what you've come up with is interesting. I do like some of your terminology, like *prime invincibility*."

"Thanks," I said, though I felt a little embarrassed. Of course there were ways of classifying Epics. I hadn't the education—or the resources—to learn such things, so I'd made up my own.

It was surprising how easy it had been. There were outliers, of course—bizarre Epics with powers that didn't fit any of the classifications—but a surprising number of the others showed similarities. There were always individual quirks, like the glimmering of Refractionary's illusions. The core abilities, however, were often very similar.

"Explain this to me," Tia said, holding up a different notebook.

Hesitantly, I slid off my stool and joined her on the floor. She was pointing toward a notation I'd made at the bottom of the entry for a particular Epic named Strongtower.

"It's my Steelheart mark," I said. "Strongtower shows an ability like Steelheart has. I watch Epics like that carefully. If they get killed, or they manifest a limitation to their powers, I want to be aware of them."

Tia nodded. "Why didn't you lump the mental illusionists with the photon-manipulators?"

"I like to make groupings based on limitations," I said, getting out my index and flipping to a specific page for her. Epics with illusion powers fell into two groups. Some created actual changes in the way light behaved, crafting illusions with photons themselves. Others made illusions by affecting the brains of the people around them. They really created hallucinations, not true illusions.

"See," I said, pointing. "The mental illusionists tend to be limited in similar ways to other mentalists—like those with hypnotism powers, or mind-control effects. Illusionists that can alter light work differently. They are far more similar to the electricity-manipulation Epics."

Cody whistled softly. He'd gotten out a canteen and held it in one hand while still leaning back against the table. "Lad, I think we need to have a conversation about how much time you've got on your hands and how we can put it to better use."

"Better use than researching how to kill Epics?" Tia asked with a raised eyebrow.

"Sure," Cody said, taking a swig from his canteen. "Think of what he could do if I got him to organize all of the pubs in town, by brew!"

"Oh please," Tia said drily, turning a page in my notes.

"Abraham," Cody said. "Ask me why it's tragic for the young David to have spent so much time on these notebooks."

"Why is it tragic for the boy to have done such research?" Abraham said, still cleaning his gun.

"That's a very astute question," Cody said. "Thank you very much for asking."

"It is my pleasure."

"Anyway," Cody said, raising his canteen, "why do you want so badly to kill these Epics?"

"Revenge," I said. "Steelheart killed my father. I intend—"

"Yes, yes," Cody said, cutting me off. "Y'all intend to see him bleed again, and all that. Very dedicated and familial of you. But I'm telling you, that ain't enough. You've got passion to kill, but you need to find passion to live. At least that's what I think."

I didn't know how to respond to that. Studying Steelheart, learning about Epics so that I could find a way to kill him, *was* my passion. If there was a place I fit in, wasn't it with the Reckoners? That was their life's work too, wasn't it?

"Cody," Prof said, "why don't you go finish working on the third chamber?"

"Sure thing, Prof," the sniper said, screwing on the lid of his canteen. He sauntered out of the room.

"Don't listen too much to Cody, son," Prof said, setting one of my notebooks on the stack. "He says the same things to the rest of us. He worries we'll focus so hard on killing the Epics that we'll forget to live our lives."

"He might be right," I said. "I . . . I really haven't had much of a life, other than this."

"The work we do," Prof said, "is not about living. Our job is killing. We'll leave the regular people to live their lives, to find joy in them, to enjoy the sunrises and the snowfalls. Our job is to get them there."

I had memories of the world before. It had only been ten years ago, after all. It's just that it was difficult to remember a world of sunshine when darkness was all you saw each day. Remembering that time . . . it was like trying to recall the specifics of my father's face. You forget things like that, gradually.

"Jonathan," Abraham said to Prof, slipping the barrel back onto his gun, "have you considered the things this boy said?"

"I'm not a boy," I said.

They all looked at me. Even Megan, standing beside the doorway.

"I just wanted to note it," I said, suddenly uncomfortable. "I mean, I'm eighteen. I've hit my majority. I'm not a child."

Prof eyed me. Then, surprisingly, he nodded. "Age has nothing to do with it, but you've helped kill two Epics, which is good enough for me. It should be for any of us."

"Very well," Abraham said, voice soft. "But Prof, we have spoken of this before. By killing Epics like Fortuity, are we really achieving anything?"

"We fight back," Megan said. "We're the only ones who do. It's important."

"And yet," Abraham said, snapping another piece onto his gun, "we are afraid to fight the most powerful. And so, the domination of the tyrants continues. So long as they do not fall, the others will not truly fear us. They will fear Steelheart, Obliteration, and Night's

Sorrow. If we will not face creatures such as these, is there any hope that others will someday stand up to them?"

The steel-walled room went quiet, and I held my breath. The words were nearly the same I had used earlier, but coming from Abraham's soft-spoken, lightly accented voice, they seemed to hold more weight.

Prof turned to Tia.

She held up a photograph. "This is really Nightwielder?" she asked me. "You're sure of it?"

The picture was a prize of my possessions, a photograph of Nightwielder beside Steelheart on the Day of Annexation, just before his darkness had come upon the city. As far as I knew, it was one of a kind, sold to me by an urchin whose father had taken it with an old Polaroid camera.

Nightwielder was normally translucent, incorporeal. He could move through solid objects and control darkness itself. He appeared often in the city, but was always in his incorporeal form. In this picture he was solid, wearing a sharp black suit and hat. He had Asian features and black shoulder-length hair. I had other pictures of him in his incorporeal form. The face was the same.

"It's obviously him," I said.

"And the photo wasn't doctored," Tia said.

"I . . ." That I couldn't prove. "I can't promise it wasn't, though its being a Polaroid makes that less likely. Tia, he has to be corporeal *some* of the time. That photo is the best clue, but I have others. People who have smelled phosphorus and spotted someone walking by who matches his description." Phosphorus was one of the signs of him using his powers. "I've found a dozen sources that all match this idea. It's *sunlight* that makes the difference—I suspect it's the ultraviolet part of sunlight that matters. Bathed in it, he turns corporeal."

Tia held the photo before her, contemplating it. Then she began scanning through my other notes on Nightwielder. "I think we need to investigate it, Jon," she said. "If there's a chance we can actually get to Steelheart . . ."

"We can," I said. "I have a plan. It will work."

"This is stupidity," Megan cut in. She stood by the wall with her arms crossed. "Sheer stupidity. We don't even know his weakness."

"We can figure it out," I shot back. "I'm sure of it. We have the clues we need."

"Even if we did figure it out," Megan said, throwing a hand up into the air, "it would be practically useless. The obstacles in even *getting* to Steelheart are insurmountable!"

I locked eyes with her, fighting down my anger. I got the feeling she was arguing with me not because she actually disagreed, but because she found me offensive for some reason.

"I—" I began, but Prof interrupted me.

"Everyone follow me," he said, standing up.

I shared a glare with Megan, and then we all moved, joining him as he walked toward the smaller room to the right of the main chamber. Even Cody made his way in from the third room— unsurprisingly, he'd been listening. He wore a glove on his right hand. It glowed with a soft green light at the palm.

"Is the imager ready?" Prof asked.

"Mostly," Abraham said. "It's one of the first things I set up." He knelt beside a device on the floor connected to the wall by several wires. He turned it on.

Suddenly, all of the metal surfaces in the room turned black. I jumped. It felt like we were floating in darkness.

Prof raised a hand, then tapped on the wall in a pattern. The walls changed to show a view of the city, presenting it as if we were standing atop a six-story building. Lights sparkled in the blackness, shining from the hundreds of steel buildings that made up Newcago. The old buildings were less uniform; the new buildings, spreading out onto what had once been the lake, were more modern. They had been built from other materials, then intentionally transformed to steel. You could do some interesting things with architecture, I'd heard, when you had that option.

"This is one of the most advanced cities in the world," Prof said. "Ruled by arguably the most powerful Epic in North America. If we move against him, we raise the stakes dramatically—and we're already betting up to the limits of what we can pay. Failure could mean the end of the Reckoners completely. It could bring disaster, could end the last bit of resistance against the Epics that mankind has left."

"Just let me tell you the plan," I said. "I think it will persuade you." I had a hunch. Prof *wanted* to go after Steelheart. If I could make my case, he'd side with me.

Prof turned to me, meeting my eyes. "You want us to do this? Fine, I'll give you your shot. But I don't want you to persuade me." He pointed to Megan, who stood beside the doorway, her arms still crossed. "Persuade *her*."

13

PERSUADE her. *Great,* I thought. Megan's eyes could have drilled holes through . . . well, anything, I guess. I mean, eyes can't normally drill holes through things, so the metaphor works regardless, right?

Megan's eyes could have drilled holes through butter. *Persuade her?* I thought. *Impossible.*

But I wasn't going to give up without trying. I stepped up to the wall of glistening metal overlaid with the outline of Newcago.

"The imager can show us anything?" I asked.

"Anything the basic spynet watches or listens to," Abraham explained, standing up from the imaging device.

"The spynet?" I said, suddenly feeling uncomfortable. I walked forward. This device was remarkable; it made me feel as if we really were standing on top of a building outside in the city, rather than in a box of a room. It wasn't a perfect illusion—if I looked around closely I could still see the corners of the room we were standing in, and the 3-D imaging wasn't great for things nearby.

Still, so long as I didn't look too closely—and didn't pay attention to the lack of wind or scents of the city—I really could imagine I was outside. They were constructing this image using the spynet? That was Steelheart's surveillance system for the city, the means by which Enforcement kept tabs on what the people in Newcago were doing.

"I knew he was watching us," I said, "but I hadn't realized that the cameras were so . . . extensive."

"Fortunately," Tia said, "we've found some ways to influence what the network sees and hears. So don't worry about Steelheart spying on us."

I still felt uncomfortable, but it wasn't worth thinking on at the moment. I stepped up to the edge of the roof, looking down at the street below. A few cars passed, and the imager relayed the sounds of their driving. I reached forward and placed my hand on the wall of the room—seemingly touching something invisible in midair. This was going to be very disorienting.

Unlike the tensors, room imagers I'd heard of—people paid good money to visit imager films. My conversation with Cody left me thinking. Had we learned how to do things like this from Epics with illusion powers?

"I—" I began.

"No," Megan said. "If he has to convince me, then I'm driving this conversation." She stepped up beside me.

"But—"

"Go ahead, Megan," Prof said.

I grumbled to myself and stepped back to where I didn't feel I was on the verge of a multistory plummet.

"It's simple," Megan said. "There's one enormous problem in facing Steelheart."

"One?" Cody asked, leaning back against the wall. It made

him look like he was leaning against open air. "Let's see: incredible strength, can shoot deadly blasts of energy from his hands, can transform anything nonliving around him into steel, can command the winds and fly with perfect control . . . oh, and he's utterly impervious to bullets, edged weapons, fire, radiation, blunt trauma, suffocation, and explosions. That's like . . . *three* things, lass." He held up four fingers.

Megan rolled her eyes. "All true," she said, then turned back to me. "But none of that is even the first problem."

"Finding him is the first problem," Prof said softly. He'd set out a folding chair, Tia as well, and the two were sitting in the center of the imaged rooftop. "Steelheart is paranoid. He makes certain nobody knows where he is."

"Exactly," Megan said, raising her hands and using a thumbs-out gesture to control the imager. We zoomed through the city, the buildings a blur beneath us.

I wobbled, my stomach flip-flopping. I reached for the wall, but I wasn't certain where it was, and stumbled to the side until I found it. Abruptly we halted, hanging in midair, looking at Steelheart's palace.

It was a dark fortress of anodized steel that rose from the edge of the city, built upon the portion of the lake that had been transformed to steel. It spread out in either direction, a long line of dark metal with towers, girders, and walkways. Like some mash-up of an old Victorian manor, a medieval castle, and an oil rig. Violent red lights shone from deep within the various recesses, and smoke billowed from chimneys, black against a black sky.

"They say he intentionally built the place to be confusing," Megan said. "There are hundreds of chambers, and he sleeps in a different one each night, eats in a different one for each meal. Supposedly even the staff doesn't know where he'll be." She turned to me, hostile. "You'll never find him. *That's* the first problem."

I swayed, still feeling as if I were standing in midair, though none of the others seemed to be having trouble. "Could we . . . ," I asked nauseously, looking back at Abraham.

He chuckled, making some gestures and pulling us back to the top of a nearby building. There was a small chimney on it, and as we "landed" the chimney squished flat, becoming two-dimensional on the floor. This wasn't a hologram—so far as I knew, nobody had mimicked that level of illusion power with technology. It was just a very advanced use of six screens and some 3-D imaging.

"Right," I said, feeling steadier. "Anyway, that *would be* a problem."

"Except?" Prof asked.

"Except we don't need to find Steelheart," I said. "He'll come to us."

"He rarely comes out in public anymore," Megan said. "And when he does, it's erratic. How in Calamity's fires are you going to—"

"Faultline," I said. The Epic who had made the earth swallow the bank on that terrible day when my father had been killed, and who had later challenged Steelheart.

"David has a point," Abraham said. "Steelheart *did* come out of hiding to fight her when she tried to take Newcago."

"And when Ides Hatred came here to challenge him," I said. "Steelheart met the challenge personally."

"As I recall," Prof said, "they destroyed an entire city block in that conflict."

"Sounds like quite the party," Cody noted.

"Yes," I said. I had pictures of that fight.

"So you're saying we need to convince a powerful Epic to come to Newcago and challenge him," Megan said, her voice flat. "Then we'll know where he's going to be. Sounds easy."

"No, no," I said, turning to face them, my back to the dark, smoldering expanse of Steelheart's palace. "That's the first part of the plan. We make Steelheart *think* a powerful Epic is coming here to challenge him."

"How would we do that?" Cody asked.

"We've already started," I explained. "Now we spread word that Fortuity was killed by agents of a new Epic. We start hitting more Epics, leaving the impression that it's all the work of the same rival. Then we deliver an ultimatum to Steelheart that if he wants to stop the murder of his followers, he'll need to come out and fight.

"And he *will* come. So long as we're convincing enough. You said he's paranoid, Prof. You're right. He is—and he can't stand a challenge to his authority. He always deals with rival Epics in person, just like he did with Deathpoint all those years ago. If there's one thing that the Reckoners are good at, it's killing Epics. If we hunt down enough of them in the city in a short time, it will be a threat to Steelheart. We can draw him out, choose our own battlefield. We can make him come to us and walk right into our trap."

"Won't happen," Megan said. "He'll just send Firefight or Nightwielder."

Firefight and Nightwielder, two immensely powerful High Epics who acted as Steelheart's bodyguards and right-hand men. They were nearly as dangerous as he was.

"I've shown you Nightwielder's weakness," I said. "It's sunlight—ultraviolet radiation. He doesn't know that anyone is aware of it. We can use that to trap him."

"You haven't proven anything," Megan said. "You've shown us he *has* a weakness. But every Epic does. You don't know it's the sunlight."

"I glanced through his sources," Tia said. "It . . . it really does look like David might have something."

Megan clenched her jaw. If this came down to me convincing her to agree to my plan, I was going to fail. She didn't look like she'd agree no matter how good my arguments.

But I wasn't convinced I needed her support, regardless of what Prof said. I'd seen how the other Reckoners looked to him. If he decided this was a good idea, they'd follow. I just had to hope that my reasoning would be good enough for him, even though he'd said I needed to convince Megan.

"Firefight," Megan said. "What about him?"

"Easy," I said, my mood lifting. "Firefight isn't what he seems."

"What does that mean?"

"I'll need my notes to explain," I said. "But he'll be the easiest of the three to take down—I promise you that."

Megan made a face as if she were offended by this, annoyed that I wasn't willing to engage her without my notes. "Whatever," she said, then made a gesture, spinning the room around in a circle and sending me stumbling again, though there was no momentum. She glanced at me, and I saw a hint of a smile on her lips. Well, at least I knew one thing that broke through her coldness: nearly making me lose my lunch.

When the room stopped rotating, our view pointed upward at an angle. Every part of me said I should be sliding backward into the wall, but I knew it was all just done with perspective.

Directly ahead of us a group of three copters moved through the air low, just above the city. They were sleek and black, with two large rotors each. The sword-and-shield emblem of Enforcement painted in white on their sides.

"It probably won't even come to Firefight and Nightwielder," she said. "I should have brought this up first: Enforcement."

"She's right," Abraham said. "Steelheart is always surrounded by Enforcement soldiers."

"So we take them out first," I said. "It's what a rival Epic would probably do anyway—disable Steelheart's army so they could move in on the city. That will only help convince him that we're a rival Epic. The Reckoners would never do something like take on Enforcement."

"We wouldn't do it," Megan said, "because it would be pure idiocy!"

"It does seem a little outside our capabilities, son," Prof said, though I could tell I had him hooked. He watched with interest. He liked the idea of drawing Steelheart out. It was the sort of thing the Reckoners *did* do, playing on an Epic's arrogance.

I raised my hands, imitating the gestures the others had been making, then thrust them forward to try moving the viewing room toward Enforcement headquarters. The room lurched awkwardly, tipping sideways and streaking through the city to slam into the side of a building. It froze there, unable to continue into the structure because the spynet didn't look there. The entire room quivered, as if desperate to fulfill my demand but uncertain where to go.

I toppled sideways into the wall, then plopped down on the ground, dizzy. "Uh . . ."

"Y'all want me to get that for you?" Cody asked, amused, from the doorway.

"Yeah. Thanks. Enforcement headquarters, please."

Cody made the gestures and raised the room up, leveled it out, then spun it about and moved it over the city until we were hovering near a large black box of a building. It looked vaguely like a prison, though it didn't house criminals. Well, just the state-sanctioned kinds of criminals.

I righted myself, determined not to look like a fool in front of the others. Though I wasn't certain if that was possible at this point. "There's one simple way to neuter Enforcement," I said. "We take out Conflux."

For once an idea of mine didn't prompt an outcry from the others. Even Megan looked thoughtful, standing just a short distance from me, her arms crossed. *I'd love to see her smile again,* I thought, then immediately forced my mind away from that. I had to stay focused. This wasn't a time to let my feet get swept out from underneath me. Well . . . in a figurative sense, at least.

"You've considered this," I guessed, looking around the room. "You hit Fortuity, but you talked about trying for Conflux instead."

"It would be a powerful blow," Abraham said softly, leaning against the wall near Cody.

"Abraham suggested it," Prof said. "He fought for it, actually. Using some of the same arguments that you made—that we weren't doing enough, that we weren't targeting Epics who were important enough."

"Conflux is more than just the head of Enforcement," I said, excited. They finally seemed like they were listening. "He's a gifter."

"A what?" Cody asked.

"It's a slang term," Tia said, "for what we call a transference Epic."

"Yes," I said.

"Great," Cody said. "So what's a transference Epic?"

"Don't you *ever* pay attention?" Tia asked. "We've talked about this."

"He was cleaning his guns," Abraham said.

"I'm an artist," Cody said.

Abraham nodded. "He's an artist."

"And cleanliness is next to deadliness," Cody added.

"Oh please," Tia said, turning back to me.

"A gifter," I said, "is an Epic who has the ability to transfer his powers to other people. Conflux has two powers he can give others, and both are incredibly strong. Maybe even stronger than those of Steelheart."

"So why doesn't *he* rule?" Cody asked.

"Who knows?" I shrugged. "Probably because he's fragile. He isn't said to have any immortality powers. So he stays hidden. Nobody even knows what he looks like. He's been with Steelheart for over half a decade, though, quietly managing Enforcement." I looked back at Enforcement headquarters. "He can create enormous stores of energy from his body. He gives this electricity to team leaders of Enforcement Cores; that's how they run their mechanized suits and their energy rifles. No Conflux means no power armor and no energy weapons."

"It means more than that," Prof said. "Taking out Conflux might knock out power to the city."

"What?" I asked.

"Newcago uses more electricity than it generates," Tia explained. "All of those lights, on all the time . . . it's a huge drain, on a level that would have been hard to sustain even back before Calamity. The new Fractured States don't have the infrastructure to provide Steelheart with enough power to run this city, yet he does."

"He's using Conflux to augment his power stores," Prof said. "Somehow."

"So that makes Conflux an even better target!" I said.

"We talked about this months ago," Prof said, leaning forward, fingers laced before him. "We decided he was too dangerous to hit. Even if we succeeded, we'd draw too much attention, be hunted down by Steelheart himself."

"Which is what we want," I said.

The others didn't seem convinced. Take this step, move against Steelheart's empire, and they'd be exposing themselves. No more hiding in the various urban undergrounds, hitting carefully chosen targets. No more quiet rebellion. Kill Conflux, and there would be no backing down until Steelheart was dead or the Reckoners were captured, broken, and executed.

He's going to say no, I thought, looking into Prof's eyes. He looked older than I'd always imagined him being. A man in his middle years, with grey speckling his hair, and with a face that showed he had lived through the death of one era and had worked ten hard years trying to end the next era. Those years had taught him caution.

He opened his mouth to say the words, but was interrupted when Abraham's mobile chirped. Abraham unhooked it from its shoulder mount. "Time for Reinforcement," he said, smiling.

Reinforcement. Steelheart's daily message to his subjects. "Can you show it on the wall here?" I asked.

"Sure," Cody said, turning his mobile toward the projector and tapping a button.

"That won't be ne—" Prof began.

The program had already started. It showed Steelheart this time. Sometimes he appeared personally, sometimes not. He stood atop one of the tall radio towers on his palace. A pitch-black cape spread out behind him, rippling in the wind.

The messages were all prerecorded, but there was no way to tell when; as always there was no sun in the sky, and no trees grew in the city any longer to give an indication of the season either. I'd almost forgotten what it was like to be able to tell the time of day just by looking out the window.

Steelheart was illuminated by red lights from below. He placed one foot on a low railing, then leaned forward and scanned his city. His dominion.

I shivered, staring at him, presented in large scale on the wall in front of me. My father's murderer. The tyrant. He looked so calm, so thoughtful, in this picture. Long jet-black hair that curled softly down to his shoulders. Shirt stretched across an inhumanly strong physique. Black slacks, an upgrade from the loose pants he'd worn on that day ten years ago. This shot of him seemed like it wanted to present him as the thoughtful and concerned dictator, like the early communist leaders I'd learned about back in the Factory school.

He raised a hand, staring intently at the city beneath him, and the hand started to glow with a wicked power. Yellow-white, to contrast the violent red below. The power around his hand wasn't electricity but raw *energy*. He built it up for a time, until it was shining so brightly the camera couldn't distinguish anything but the light and the shadow of Steelheart in front of it.

Then he pointed and launched a bolt of blazing yellow force into the city. The power hit a building, blasting a hole through the side, sending flames and debris exploding out the opposite windows. As the building smoldered, people fled from it. The camera zoomed in, making sure to catch sight of them. Steelheart wanted us to know he was firing on an inhabited structure.

Another bolt followed, causing the building to lurch, the steel of one side melting and caving inward. He fired twice more into a building beside it, starting the innards there aflame as well, walls melting from the enormous power of the energy he threw.

The camera pulled back and turned to Steelheart again, still in the same half-crouched stance. He looked down at the city, face impassive, red light from beneath limning a strong jaw and contemplative eyes. There was no explanation of why he'd destroyed those buildings, though perhaps a later message would explain the sins—real or perceived—that the inhabitants were guilty of.

Or perhaps not. Living in Newcago brought risks; one of them was that Steelheart could decide to execute you and your family without explanation. The flip side was that for those risks, you got to live in a place with electricity, running water, jobs, and food. Those were rare commodities in much of the land now.

I took a step forward, walking right up to the wall to study the creature that loomed there. *He wants us to be terrified,* I thought. *It's what this is all about. He wants us to think no one can challenge him.*

Early scholars had wondered if perhaps Epics were some new stage in human development. An evolutionary breakthrough. I didn't accept that. This thing wasn't human. It never had been. Steelheart turned to look toward the camera, and there was a hint of a smile on his lips.

A chair scraped behind me and I turned. Prof had stood up and was staring at Steelheart. Yes, there was hatred there. Deep hatred. Prof looked down and met my eyes. It happened again, that moment of understanding.

Each of us knew where the other stood.

"You haven't said how you'll kill him," Prof said to me. "You haven't convinced Megan. All you've shown is that you have a fragile half of a plan."

"I've seen him bleed," I said. "The secret is in my head somewhere,

Prof. It's the best chance you or anyone will ever have at killing him. Can you pass that up? Can you *really* walk away when you've got a shot?"

Prof met my eyes. He stared into them for a long moment. Behind me Steelheart's transmission ended, and the wall went black.

Prof was right. My plan, clever though it had once seemed to me, depended on a lot of speculation. Draw Steelheart out with a fake Epic. Take down his bodyguards. Upend Enforcement. Kill him using a secret weakness that might be hidden in my memory somewhere.

A fragile half plan indeed. That was why I had needed to come to the Reckoners. They could make it happen. This man, Jonathan Phaedrus, could make it happen.

"Cody," Prof said, turning, "start training the new kid with a tensor. Tia, let's see if we can start tracking Conflux's movements. Abraham, we're going to need some brainstorming on how to imitate a High Epic, if that's even possible."

I felt my heart jump. "We're going to do it?"

"Yes," Prof said. "God help us, we are."

PART TWO

14

"**NOW,** y'all gotta be *gentle* with her," Cody said. "Like caressing a beautiful woman the night before the big caber toss."

"Caber toss?" I said as I raised my hands toward the chunk of steel on the chair in front of me. I sat cross-legged on the floor of the Reckoner hideout, Cody on the ground beside me, his back to the wall and legs stretched out in front of him. It had been a week since the hit on Fortuity.

"Yeah, caber toss," Cody said. Though his accent was purely Southern—and strongly that—he always talked as if he were from Scotland. I guessed his family was from there or something. "It's this sport we had back in the homeland. Involved throwing trees."

"Little saplings? Like javelins?"

"No, no. The cabers had to be so wide that your fingers couldn't touch on the other side when you reached your arms around them. We'd rip 'em out of the ground, then hurl them as far as we could."

I raised a skeptical eyebrow.

"Bonus points if you could hit a bird out of the air," he added.

"Cody," Tia said, walking by with a sheaf of papers, "do you even know what a caber is?"

"A tree," he said. "We used them to build show houses. It's where the word *cabaret* came from, lass." He said it with such a straight face that I had trouble determining if he was sincere or not.

"You're a buffoon," Tia said, sitting down at the table, which was spread with various detailed maps that I hadn't been able to make sense of. They appeared to be city plans and schematics, dating from before the Annexation.

"Thank you," Cody said, tipping his camo baseball cap toward her.

"It wasn't a compliment."

"Oh, you didn't mean it as one, lass," Cody said. "But the word *buffoon,* it comes from the word *buff,* meaning strong and handsome, which in turn—"

"Aren't you supposed to be helping David learn the tensors?" she interrupted. "And *not* bothering me."

"It's all right," Cody said. "I can do both. I'm a man of many talents."

"None of which involve remaining silent, unfortunately," Tia muttered, leaning down and making a few notations on her map.

I smiled, though even after a week with them I wasn't certain what to make of the Reckoners. I'd imagined each pod of them as an elite special forces group, tightly knit and intensely loyal to one another.

There was some of that in this group; even Tia and Cody's banter was generally good-natured. However, there was also a lot of individuality to them. They each kind of . . . did their own thing. Prof didn't seem so much a leader as a middle manager. Abraham worked on the technology, Tia the research, Megan information gathering, and Cody odd jobs—filling in the spaces with mayonnaise, as he liked to call it. Whatever that meant.

It was bizarre to see them as people. A part of me was actually disappointed. My gods were regular humans who squabbled, laughed, got on one another's nerves, and—in Abraham's case—snored when they slept. Loudly.

"Now, *that's* the right look of concentration," Cody said. "Nice work, lad. Y'all've got to keep a keen mind. Focused. Like Sir William himself. Soul of a warrior." He took a bite of his sandwich.

I hadn't been focused on my tensor, but I didn't let on to that fact. Instead I raised my hand, doing as I'd been instructed. The thin glove I wore had lines of metal along the front of each finger. The lines joined in a pattern at the palm and all glowed softly green.

As I concentrated my hand began to vibrate softly, as if someone were playing music with a lot of bass somewhere nearby. It was hard to focus with that strange pulsation running up my arm.

I raised my hand toward the chunk of metal; it was the remnant of a section of pipe. Now, apparently, I needed to *push* the vibrations away from me. Whatever that meant. The technology hooked right into my nerves using sensors inside the glove, interpreting electrical impulses from my brain. So Abraham had explained.

Cody had said it was magic, and had told me not to ask any questions lest I "anger the wee daemons inside who make the gloves work and our coffee taste good."

I still hadn't managed to make the tensors do anything, though I felt I was getting close. I had to remain focused, keep my hands steady, and *push* the vibrations out. Like blowing a ring of smoke, Abraham had said. Or like using your body warmth in a hug—without the arms. That had been Tia's explanation. Everyone thought of it their own way, I guess.

My hand started to shake more vigorously.

"Steady," Cody said. "Don't lose control, lad."

I stiffened my muscles.

"Whoa. Not too stiff," Cody said. "Secure, strong, but calm. Like you're caressing a beautiful woman, remember?"

That made me think of Megan.

I lost control, and a green wave of smoky energy burst from my hand and flew out in front of me. It missed the pipe completely, but vaporized the metal leg of the chair it sat on. Dust showered down and the chair went lopsided, dumping the pipe to the floor with a *clang*.

"Sparks," Cody said. "Remind me to never let you caress me, lad."

"I thought you told him to think of a beautiful woman," Tia said.

"Yeah," Cody replied. "And if that's how he treats one of them, I don't want to *know* what he'd do to an ugly Scotsman."

"I did it!" I exclaimed, pointing at the powdered metal that was the remains of the chair leg.

"Yeah, but you missed."

"Doesn't matter," I said. "I finally made it work!" I hesitated. "It wasn't like blowing smoke. It was like . . . like singing. From my hand."

"That's a new one," Cody said.

"It's different for everyone," Tia said from her table, head still down. She opened a can of cola as she scribbled notes. Tia was useless without her cola. "Using the tensors isn't natural to your mind, David. You've already built neural pathways, and so you have to kind of hotwire your brain to figure out what mental muscles to flex. I've always wondered if we gave a tensor to a child, if they'd be able to incorporate using it better, more naturally, as just another kind of 'limb' to practice with."

Cody looked at me. Then he whispered, "Wee daemons. Don't let her fool you, lad. I think she works for them. I saw her leaving out pie for them the other night."

Trouble was, he was *just* serious enough to make me question whether he really believed that. The twinkle to his eye indicated he was being silly, but he had such a perfectly straight face. . . .

I took off the tensor and handed it over. Cody slipped it on, then absently raised a hand—palm first—to the side and thrust it outward. The tensor began vibrating as his hand moved, and when it stopped a faint, smoky green wave continued on, hitting the fallen chair and the pipe. Both vaporized to dust, falling to the ground in a puff.

Each time I saw the tensors work, I was amazed. The range was very limited, only a few feet at most, and they couldn't affect flesh. They weren't much good in a fight—sure, you could vaporize someone's gun, but only if they were very close to you. In which case taking the time to concentrate and fight with the tensors would probably be less effective than just punching the guy.

Still, the opportunities they afforded were incredible. Moving through the bowels of Newcago's steel catacombs, getting in and out of rooms. If you managed to keep the tensor hidden, you could escape from any bond, any cell.

"You keep training," Cody said. "You show talent, so Prof will want you to get good with these. We need another member of the team who can use them."

"Not all of you can?" I asked, surprised.

Cody shook his head. "Megan can't make them work, and Tia's rarely in a position to use them—we need her back giving support while on missions. So it usually comes down to Abraham and me using them."

"What about Prof?" I asked. "He invented them. He's got to be pretty good with them, right?"

Cody shook his head. "Don't know. He refuses to use them. Something about a bad experience in the past. He won't talk about it. Probably shouldn't. We don't need to know. Either way, you should practice." Cody shook his head and took off the tensor, tucking it into his pocket. "What I'd have given for one of these before. . . ."

The other pieces of Reckoner technology were awesome too. The jackets, which supposedly worked a little like armor, were one.

Cody, Megan, and Abraham each wore a jacket—different on the outside, but with a complicated network of diodes inside that somehow protected them. The dowser, which told if someone was Epic, was another piece of such technology. The only other piece I'd seen was something they called the harmsway, a device that accelerated a body's healing abilities.

It's so sad, I thought, as Cody fetched a broom to clean up the dust. *All of this technology . . . it could have changed the world. If the Epics hadn't done that first.* A ruined world couldn't enjoy the benefits.

"What was your life like back then?" I asked, holding the dustpan for Cody. "Before all of this happened? What did you do?"

"You wouldn't believe me," Cody said, smiling.

"Let me guess," I said, anticipating one of Cody's stories. "Professional footballer? High-paid assassin and spy?"

"A cop," Cody said, subdued, looking down at the pile of dust. "In Nashville."

"What? Really?" I *was* surprised.

Cody nodded, then waved for me to dump the first pile of dust into the trash bin while he swept up the rest of it. "My father was a cop too in his early years, over in the homeland. Small city. You wouldn't know it. He moved here when he married my mother. I grew up over here; ain't never actually been to the homeland. But I wanted to be just like my pa, so when he died, I went to school and joined the force."

"Huh," I said, stooping down again to collect the rest of the dust. "That's a lot less glamorous than I'd been imagining."

"Well, I did take down an entire drug cartel by myself, you understand."

"Of course."

"And there was the time the president's Secret Service were shuttling him through the city, and they all ate a bad mess of scones and got sick, and we in the department had to protect him from an assassination plot." He called over to Abraham, who was tinkering with one of the team's shotguns. "It was them Frenchies who were behind it, you know."

"I'm not French!" Abraham called back. "I'm Canadian, you slontze."

"Same difference!" Cody said, then grinned and looked back at me. "Anyway, maybe it wasn't glamorous. Not all the time. But I enjoyed it. I like doing good for people. Serve and protect. And then . . ."

"Then?" I asked.

"Nashville got annexed when the country collapsed," Cody explained. "A group of five Epics took charge of most of the South."

"The Coven," I said, nodding. "There's actually six of them. One pair are twins."

"Ah, right. Keep forgetting that y'all are freakishly informed about this stuff. Anyway, they took over, and the police department started serving them. If we didn't agree, we were supposed to turn in our badges and retire. The good ones did that. The bad ones stayed on, and they got worse."

"And you?" I asked.

Cody fingered the thing he kept at his waist, tied to his belt on the right side. It looked like a thin wallet. He reached down and undid the snap, showing a scratched—but still polished—police badge.

"I didn't do either one," he said, subdued. "I took an oath. Serve and protect. I ain't going to stop that because some thugs with magic powers start shoving everybody around. That's that."

His words gave me a chill. I stared at that badge, and my mind flipped over and over like a pancake on a griddle, trying to figure out this man. Trying to reconcile the joking, storytelling blowhard with the image of a police officer still on his beat. Still serving after the city government had fallen, after the precinct had been shut down, after everything had been taken from him.

The others probably have similar stories, I thought, glancing at Tia, who was busy working away, sipping her cola. What had drawn her to fighting what most would call a hopeless battle, living a life of constant running, bringing justice to those the law should have condemned—but could not touch? What had drawn Abraham, Megan, the professor himself?

I looked back at Cody, who was moving to close his badge holder. There was something tucked behind the plastic opposite it in the holder—a picture of a woman, but with a section removed, a bar shape that had contained her eyes and much of her nose.

"Who was that?"

"Somebody special," Cody said.

"Who?"

He didn't answer, snapping the badge holder closed.

"It's better if we don't know, or ask, about each other's families," Tia said from the table. "Usually a stint in the Reckoners ends with death, but occasionally one of us gets captured. Better if we can't reveal anything about the others that will put their loved ones in danger."

"Oh," I said. "Yeah, that makes sense." It just wasn't something I'd have considered. I didn't have any loved ones left.

"How is it going there, lass?" Cody asked, sauntering over to the table. I joined him and saw that Tia had spread out lists of reports and ledgers.

"It's not going at all," Tia said with a grimace. She rubbed her eyes beneath her spectacles. "This is like trying to re-create a complex puzzle after being given only one piece."

"What are you doing?" I asked. I couldn't make sense of the ledgers any more than I'd been able to make sense of the maps.

"Steelheart was wounded that day," Tia said. "If your recollection is correct—"

"It is," I promised.

"People's memories fade," Cody said.

"Not mine," I said. "Not about this. Not about that day. I can tell you what color tie the mortgage man was wearing. I can tell you how many tellers there were. I could probably count the ceiling tiles in the bank for you. It's there, in my head. Burned there."

"All right," Tia said. "Well, if you *are* correct, then Steelheart was impervious for most of the fight and only harmed near the end. Something changed. I'm working through all possibilities—something about your father, the location, or the situation. The most likely seems the possibility you mentioned, that the vault was involved. Perhaps something inside it weakened Steelheart, and once the vault was blown open it could affect him."

"So you're looking for a record of the bank vault's contents."

"Yes," Tia said. "But it's an impossible task. Most of the records would have been destroyed with the bank. Off-site records would have been stored on a server somewhere. First Union was hosted by a company known as Dorry Jones LLC. Most of their servers were located in Texas, but the building was burned down eight years back during the Ardra riots.

"That leaves the off chance that they had physical records or a digital backup at another branch, but that building housed the main offices, so the chances of that are slim. Other than that, I've been looking for patron lists—the rich or notable who were known to frequent the bank and have boxes in the vault. Perhaps they stored something in there that will be part of the public record. A strange rock, a specific symbol that Steelheart might have seen, something."

I looked at Cody. Servers? Hosted? What was she talking about? He shrugged.

The problem was, an Epic weakness could be just about anything. Tia mentioned symbols—there were some Epics who, if they saw a specific pattern, lost their powers for a few moments. Others were weakened by thinking certain thoughts, not eating certain foods, or eating the wrong foods. The weaknesses were more varied than the powers themselves.

"If we don't figure out this puzzle," Tia said, "the rest of the plan is useless. We're starting down a dangerous path, but we don't yet know if we'll be capable of doing what we need to at the end. That bothers me greatly, David. If you think of anything—*anything*—that could give me another lead to work on, speak of it."

"I will," I promised.

"Good," she said. "Otherwise, take Cody and *please* let me concentrate."

"You really should learn to do two things at once, lass," Cody said. "Like me."

"It's easy to both be a buffoon and make messes of things, Cody," she replied. "Putting those messes back together while dealing with said buffoon is a much more difficult prospect. Go find something to shoot, or whatever it is you do."

"I thought I *was* doing whatever it is I do," he said absently. He stabbed a finger at a line on one of the pages, which looked like it listed clients of the bank. It read *Johnson Liberty Agency*.

"What are you—" Tia began, then cut herself off as she read the words.

"What?" I asked, reading the document. "Are those people who stored things at the bank?"

"No," Tia said. "This isn't a list of clients. It's a list of people the bank was paying. That's . . ."

"The name of their insurance company," Cody said, smirking.

"Calamity, Cody," Tia swore. "I hate you."

"I know you do, lass."

Oddly, both of them were smiling as they said it. Tia immediately began shuffling through papers, though she noticed—with a dry look—that Cody had left a smudged bit of mayonnaise from his sandwich on the paper where he'd pointed.

He took me by the shoulder and steered me away from the table.

"What just happened?" I asked.

"Insurance company," Cody said. "The people who First Union Bank paid piles of money to cover the stuff they had in their vault."

"So that insurance company . . ."

"Would have kept a detailed, day-by-day record of just what they were insuring," Cody said with a grin. "Insurance people are a wee bit anal about things like that. Like bankers. Like Tia, actually. If we're lucky, the bank filed an insurance claim following the loss of the building. That would leave an additional paper trail."

"Clever," I said, impressed.

"Oh, I'm just good at finding things that are hovering around under my nose. I have keen eyes. I once caught a leprechaun, you know."

I looked at him skeptically. "Aren't those Irish?"

"Sure. He was over in the homeland on an exchange basis. We sent the Irish three turnips and a sheep's bladder in trade."

"Doesn't seem like much of a trade."

"Oh, I think it was a sparking good one, seeing as to how leprechauns are imaginary and all. Hello, Prof. How's your kilt?"

"As imaginary as your leprechaun, Cody," Prof said, walking into the chamber from one of the side rooms, the one he'd appropriated as his "thinking room," whatever that meant. It was the one with the imager in it, and the other Reckoners stayed away from it. "Can I borrow David?"

"Please, Prof," Cody said, "we're friends. You should know by now that you needn't ask something like that . . . you should be *well* aware of my standard charge for renting one of my minions. Three pounds and a bottle of whiskey."

I wasn't sure if I should be more insulted at being called a minion, or at the low price to rent me.

Prof ignored him, taking me by the arm. "I'm sending Abraham and Megan to Diamond's place today."

"The weapons dealer?" I asked, eager. They'd mentioned that he might have some technology for sale that could help the Reckoners pretend to be an Epic. The "powers" manifested would have to be flashy and destructive, to get Steelheart's attention.

"I want you to tag along," Prof said. "It will be good experience for you. But follow orders—Abraham is in charge—and let me know if anyone you meet seems to recognize you."

"I will."

"Go get your gun, then. They're leaving soon."

15

"**WHAT** about the gun?" Abraham said as we walked. "The bank, the vault contents, those could be a false lead, could they not? What if there was something special about the gun that your father fired at him?"

"That gun was dropped by a random security officer," I said. "Smith and Wesson M&P nine-millimeter, semiauto. There was nothing special about it."

"You remember the *exact gun*?"

I kicked a bit of trash as we walked through the steel-walled underground tunnel. "As I said, I remember that day. Besides, I know guns." I hesitated, then admitted more. "When I was young, I assumed the type of gun must have been special. I saved up, planning to buy one, but nobody would sell to a kid my age. I was planning to sneak into the palace and shoot him."

"Sneak into the palace," Abraham said flatly.

"Uh, yes."

"And shoot *Steelheart*."

"I was ten," I said. "Give me a little credit."

"To a boy with aspirations like that, I would extend my respect—but not credit. Or life insurance." Abraham sounded amused. "You are an interesting man, David Charleston, but you sound like you were an even *more* interesting child."

I smiled. There was something invitingly friendly about this soft-spoken, articulate Canadian, with his light French accent. You almost didn't notice the enormous machine gun—with mounted grenade launcher—resting on his shoulder.

We were still in the steel catacombs, where even such a high level of armament didn't draw particular attention. We passed occasional groups of people huddled around burning fires or heaters plugged into pirated electrical jacks. More than a few of the people we passed carried assault rifles.

Over the last few days I'd ventured out of the hideout a couple times, always in the company of one of the other Reckoners. The babysitting bothered me, but I got it. I couldn't exactly hope for them to trust me yet. Not completely. Besides—though I would never admit it out loud—I didn't want to walk the steel catacombs alone.

I'd avoided these depths for years. At the Factory they told stories about the depraved people—terrible monsters—who lived down here. Gangs that literally fed on the foolish who wandered into forgotten hallways, killing them and feasting on their flesh. Murderers, criminals, addicts. Not the normal sort of criminals and addicts we had up above, either. Specially depraved ones.

Perhaps those were exaggerations. The people we passed did seem dangerous—but more in a hostile way, not in an insane way. They watched with grim expressions and eyes that tracked your every movement until you passed out of their view.

These people wanted to be alone. They were the outcasts of the outcasts.

"Why does he let them live down here?" I asked as we passed another group.

Megan didn't respond—she was walking ahead of us, keeping to herself—but Abraham glanced over his shoulder, looking toward the firelight and the line of people who had stepped up to make sure we left.

"There will always be people like them," Abraham said. "Steelheart knows it. Tia, she thinks he made this place for them so he would know where they were. It is useful to know where your outcasts are gathering. Better the ones you know about than the ones you cannot anticipate."

That made me uncomfortable. I'd thought we were completely outside Steelheart's view down here. Perhaps this place wasn't as safe as I'd assumed.

"You cannot keep all men confined all the time," Abraham said, "not without creating a strong prison. So instead you allow some measure of freedom for those who really, really want it. That way, they do not become rebels. If you do it right."

"He did it wrong with us," I said softly.

"Yes. Yes, indeed he did."

I kept glancing back as we walked. I couldn't shake the worry that some of those in the catacombs would attack us. They never did, though. They—

I started as I realized that at that moment, some of them *were* following us. "Abraham!" I said softly. "They're following."

"Yes," he said calmly. "There are some waiting for us ahead too."

In front of us the tunnel narrowed. Sure enough, a group of shadowed figures were standing there, waiting. They wore the mismatched cast-off clothing common to many catacombers, and they carried old rifles and pistols wrapped in leather—the type of guns that probably only worked one day out of two and had been carried by a dozen different people over the last ten years.

The three of us stopped walking, and the group behind caught up, boxing us in. I couldn't see their faces. None carried mobiles, and it was dark without their glow.

"That's some nice equipment, friend," said one of the figures in the group in front of us. Nobody made any overtly hostile moves. They held their weapons with barrels pointed to the sides.

I carefully started to unsling my gun, my heart racing. Abraham, however, laid a hand on my shoulder. He carried his massive machine gun in his other hand, barrel pointed upward, and wore one of the Reckoner jackets, like Megan, though his was grey and white, with a high collar and several pockets, while hers was standard brown leather.

They always wore their jackets when they left the hideout. I'd never seen one work, and I didn't know how much protection they could realistically offer.

"Be still," Abraham said to me.

"But—"

"I will deal with this," he said, his voice perfectly calm as he took a step forward.

Megan stepped up beside me, hand on the holster of her pistol. She didn't look any calmer than I was, both of us trying to watch the people ahead and behind us at once.

"You like our equipment?" Abraham asked politely.

"You should leave the guns," the thug said. "Continue on."

"This would not make any sense," Abraham said. "If I have weapons that you want, the implication is that my firepower is greater than yours. If we were to fight, you would lose. You see? Your intimidation, it does not work."

"There are more of us than you, friend," the guy said softly. "And we're ready to die. Are you?"

I felt a chill at the back of my neck. No, these *weren't* the murderers I'd been led to believe lived down here. They were something more dangerous. Like a pack of wolves.

I could see it in them now, in the way they moved, in the way groups of them had watched us pass. These were outcasts, but outcasts who had banded together to become one. They no longer lived as individuals, but as a group.

And for this group, guns like the ones Abraham and Megan carried would increase their chances of survival. They'd take them, even if it meant losing some of their numbers. It looked to be about a dozen men and women against just three, and we were surrounded. They were terrible odds. I itched to lower my rifle and start shooting.

"You didn't ambush us," Abraham pointed out. "You hope to be able to end this without death."

The thieves didn't reply.

"It is very kind of you to offer us this chance," Abraham said, nodding to them. There was a strange sincerity to Abraham; from another person, words like those might have sounded condescending or sarcastic, but from him they sounded genuine. "You have let us pass several times, through territory you consider to be your own. For this also, I give you my thanks."

"The guns," the thug said.

"I cannot give them to you," Abraham said. "We need them. Beyond this, if we were to give them to you, it would go poorly for you and yours. Others would see them, and would desire them. Other gangs would seek to take them from you as you have sought to take them from us."

"That isn't for you to decide."

"Perhaps not. However, in respect of the honor you have shown us, I will offer you a deal. A duel, between you and me. Only one man need be shot. If we win, you will leave us be, and allow us to pass freely through this area in the future. If you win, my friends will deliver up their weapons, and you may take from my body that which you wish."

"These are the steel catacombs," the man said. Some of his companions were whispering now, and he glared at them with shadowed eyes, then continued. "This is not a place of deals."

"And yet, you already offered us one," Abraham said calmly. "You did us honor. I trust that you will show it to us again."

It didn't seem to be about honor to me. They hadn't ambushed us because they were afraid of us; they wanted the weapons, but they didn't want a fight. They aimed to intimidate us instead.

The lead thug, however, finally nodded. "Fine," he said. "A deal." Then he quickly raised his rifle and fired. The bullet hit Abraham right in the chest.

I jumped, cursing as I scrambled for my gun.

But Abraham didn't fall. He didn't even twitch. Two more shots cracked in the narrow tunnel, bullets hitting him, one in the leg, one in the shoulder. Ignoring his powerful machine gun, he calmly reached to his side and took his handgun out of its holster, then shot the thug in the thigh.

The man cried out, dropping his battered rifle and collapsing, holding his wounded leg. Most of the others seemed too shocked to respond, though a few lowered their weapons nervously. Abraham casually reholstered his pistol.

I felt sweat trickle down my brow. The jacket seemed to be doing its job, and doing it better than I'd assumed. But I didn't have one of those yet. If the other thugs opened fire . . .

Abraham handed his machine gun to Megan, then walked forward and knelt beside the fallen thug. "Place pressure here, please," he said in a friendly tone, positioning the man's hand on his thigh. "There, very good. Now if you don't mind, I'll bandage the wound. I shot you where the bullet could pass through the muscle, so it wouldn't get lodged inside."

The thug groaned at the pain as Abraham took out a bandage and wrapped the leg.

"You cannot kill us, friend," Abraham continued, speaking more softly. "We are not what you thought us to be. Do you understand?"

The thug nodded vigorously.

"It would be wise to be our allies, do you not think?"

"Yes," the thug said.

"Wonderful," Abraham replied, tying the bandage tight. "Change that twice a day. Use boiled bandages."

"Yes."

"Good." Abraham stood and took his gun back and turned to the rest of the thug's group. "Thank you for letting us pass," he said to the others.

They looked confused but parted, creating a path for us. Abraham walked forward and we followed in a hurry. I looked over my shoulder as the rest of the gang gathered around their fallen leader.

"That was *amazing,*" I said as we got farther away.

"No. It was a group of frightened people, defending what little they can lay claim to—their reputation. I feel bad for them."

"They shot you. Three times."

"I gave them permission."

"Only after they threatened us!"

"And only after we violated their territory," Abraham said. He handed his machine gun to Megan again, then took off his jacket as he walked. I could see that one of the bullets had penetrated it. Blood was seeping out around a hole in his shirt.

"The jacket didn't stop them all?"

"They aren't perfect," Megan said as Abraham took off the shirt. "Mine fails all the time."

We stopped as Abraham cleaned the wound with a handkerchief, then pulled out a little shard of metal. It was all that was left of the bullet, which had apparently disintegrated upon hitting his jacket. Only one little shard had made it through to his skin.

"What if he'd shot you in the face?" I asked.

"The jackets hide an advanced shielding device," Abraham said. "It isn't the jacket itself that protects, really, but the field the jacket extends. It offers some protection for the entire body, an invisible barrier to resist force."

"What? Really? That's amazing."

"Yes." Abraham hesitated, then pulled his shirt back on. "It probably would not have stopped a bullet to the face, however. So I am fortunate they did not choose to shoot me there."

"As I said," Megan interjected, "they are far from perfect." She seemed annoyed with Abraham. "The shield works better with things like falls and crashes—bullets are so small and hit with so much velocity, the shields overload quickly. Any of those shots could have killed you, Abraham."

"But they did not."

"You still could have been hurt." Megan's voice was stern.

"I *was* hurt."

She rolled her eyes. "You could have been hurt worse."

"Or they could have opened fire," he said, "and killed us all. It was a gamble that worked. Besides, I believe they now think we are Epics."

"*I* almost thought you were one," I admitted.

"Normally we keep this technology hidden," Abraham said, putting on his jacket again. "People cannot wonder whether the Reckoners are Epics; it would undermine what we stand for. However, in this case, I believe it will go well for us. Your plan calls for there to be rumors of new Epics in the city, working against Steelheart. These men will hopefully spread that rumor."

"I guess," I said. "It was a good move, Abraham, but *sparks*. For a moment, I thought we were dead."

"People rarely want to kill, David," Abraham said calmly. "It's not basic to the makeup of the healthy human mind. In most situations they will go to great lengths to avoid killing. Remember that, and it will help you."

"I've seen a lot of people kill," I replied.

"Yes, and that will tell you something. Either they felt they had no choice—in which case, if you could give them another choice, they would likely have taken it—or they were not of healthy mind."

"And Epics?"

Abraham reached to his neck and fingered the small silver necklace he wore there. "Epics are not human."

I nodded. With that, I agreed.

"I believe our conversation was interrupted," Abraham said, taking his gun from Megan and casually resting it on his shoulder as we walked onward. "How did Steelheart get wounded? It *could* have been the weapon your father used. You never tried your brave plan of finding an identical gun, then doing . . . what was it you said? Sneaking into Steelheart's palace and shooting him?"

"No, I didn't get to try it," I said, blushing. "I came to my senses. I don't think it was the gun, though. M&P nine-millimeters aren't exactly uncommon. Someone's *got* to have tried shooting him with one. Besides, I've never heard of an Epic whose weakness was being shot by a specific caliber of bullet or make of gun."

"Perhaps," Abraham said, "but many Epic weaknesses do not make sense. It could have something to do with that specific gun manufacturer. Or instead, it could have something to do with the composition of the bullet. Many Epics are weak to specific alloys."

"True," I admitted. "But what would be different about that particular bullet that wasn't the same for all of the others fired at him?"

"I don't know," Abraham said. "But it is worth considering. What do *you* think caused his weakness?"

"Something in the vault, like Tia thinks," I said with only some measure of confidence. "Either that or something about the situation. Maybe my father's specific age let him get through—weird, I know, but there was an Epic in Germany who could only be hurt by someone who was thirty-seven exactly. Or maybe it was the number of people firing on him. Crossmark, an Epic down in Mexico, can only be hurt if five people are trying to kill her at once."

"It doesn't matter," Megan interrupted, turning around in the hallway and stopping in the tunnel to look at us. "You're never going to figure it out. His weakness could be virtually *anything*. Even with David's little story—assuming he didn't just make it up—there's no way of knowing."

Abraham and I stopped in place. Megan's face was red, and she seemed barely in control. After a week of her acting cold and professional, her anger was a big shock.

She spun around and kept walking. I glanced at Abraham, and he shrugged.

We continued on, but our conversation died. Megan quickened her pace when Abraham tried to catch up to her, and so we just left her to it. Both she and Abraham had been given directions to the weapons merchant, so she could guide us just as well as he could. Apparently this "Diamond" fellow was only going to be in town for a short time, and when he came he always set up shop in a different location.

We walked for a good hour through the twisting maze of catacombs before Megan stopped us at an intersection, her mobile illuminating her face as she checked the map Tia had uploaded to it.

Abraham took his mobile off the shoulder of his jacket and did the same. "Almost there," he told me, pointing. "This way. At the end of this tunnel."

"How well do we trust this guy?" I asked.

"Not at all," Megan said. Her face had returned to its normal impassive mask.

Abraham nodded. "Best to never trust a weapons merchant, my friend. They all sell to both sides, and they are the only ones who win if a conflict continues indefinitely."

"Both sides?" I asked. "He sells to Steelheart too?"

"He won't admit it if you ask," Abraham said, "but it is certain that he does. Even Steelheart knows not to harm a good weapons dealer. Kill or torture a man like Diamond, and future merchants won't come here. Steelheart's army will never have good technology compared to the neighbors. That's not saying that Steelheart likes it—Diamond, he could never open his shop up in the overstreets. Down here, however, Steelheart will turn a blind eye, so long as his soldiers continue to get their equipment."

"So . . . whatever we buy from him," I said, "Steelheart will know about it."

"No, no," Abraham said. He seemed amused, as if I were asking questions about something incredibly simple, like the rules to hide-and-seek.

"Weapons merchants don't talk about other clients," Megan said. "As long as those clients live, at least."

"Diamond arrived back in the city just yesterday," Abraham said, leading the way down the tunnel. "He will be open for one week's time. If we are first to get to him, we can see what he has before Steelheart's people do. We can get an advantage this way, eh? Diamond, he often has very . . . interesting wares."

All right, then, I thought. I guess it didn't matter that Diamond was slime. I'd use any tool I could to get to Steelheart. Moral considerations had stopped bothering me years ago. Who had time for morals in a world like this?

We reached the corridor leading to Diamond's shop. I expected guards, perhaps in full powered armor. The only person there, though, was a young girl in a yellow dress. She was lying on a blanket on the floor and drawing pictures on a piece of paper with a silver pen. She looked up at us and began chewing on the end of the pen.

Abraham politely handed the girl a small data chip, which she took and examined for a moment before tapping it on the side of her mobile.

"We are with Phaedrus," Abraham said. "We have an appointment."

"Go on," the girl answered, tossing the chip back to him.

Abraham snatched it from the air, and we continued down the corridor. I glanced over my shoulder at the girl. "That's not very strong security."

"It's always something new with Diamond," Abraham said, smiling. "There is probably something elaborate behind the scenes—some kind of trap the girl can spring. It probably has to do with explosives. Diamond likes explosives."

We turned a corner and stepped into heaven.

"Here we are," Abraham announced.

16

DIAMOND'S shop wasn't set up in a room, but instead in one of the long corridors of the catacombs. I assumed that the other end of the corridor was either a dead end or had guards. The space was lit from above by portable lights that were almost blinding after the general darkness of the catacombs.

Those lights shone on guns—hundreds of them hung on the walls of the hallway. Beautiful polished steel and deep, muted blacks. Assault rifles. Handguns. Massive, electron-compressed beasts like the one Abraham carried, with full gravatonics. Old-style revolvers, grenades in stacks, *rocket launchers*.

I'd only ever owned two guns—my pistol and my rifle. The rifle was a good friend. I'd had her for three years now, and I'd come to rely on her a lot. She worked when I needed her. We had a great relationship—I cared for her, and she cared for me.

At the sight of Diamond's shop, though, I felt like a boy who'd only ever owned a single toy car and had just been offered a showroom full of Ferraris.

Abraham sauntered into the hallway. He didn't give the weapons much of a look. Megan entered and I followed on her heels, staring at the walls and their wares.

"Wow," I said. "It's like . . . a banana farm for guns."

"A banana farm," Megan said flatly.

"Sure. You know, how bananas grow from their trees and hang down and stuff?"

"Knees, you *suck* at metaphors."

I blushed. *An art gallery,* I thought. *I should have said "like an art gallery for guns." No, wait. If I said it that way, it would mean the gallery was intended for guns to come visit. A gallery* of *guns, then?*

"How do you even know what bananas are?" Megan said quietly as Abraham greeted a portly man standing beside a blank portion of wall. This could only be Diamond. "Steelheart doesn't import from Latin America."

"My encyclopedias," I said, distracted. *A gallery of guns for the criminally destructive. I should have said that. That sounds impressive, doesn't it?* "Read them a few times. Some of it stuck."

"Encyclopedias."

"Yeah."

"Which you read 'a few times.' "

I stopped, realizing what I'd said. "Er. No. I mean, I just browsed them. You know, looking for pictures of guns. I—"

"You are such a nerd," she said, walking ahead to join Abraham. She sounded amused.

I sighed, then joined them and tried to get her attention to show off my new metaphor, but Abraham was introducing us.

". . . new kid," he said, gesturing to me. "David."

Diamond nodded to me. He had on a brightly colored floral-pattern shirt, like people supposedly once wore in the tropics.

Maybe that was where I'd gotten the whole banana metaphor. He had a white beard and long white hair, though he was balding at the front, and wore a huge smile that sparkled in his eyes.

"I assume," he said to Abraham, "you want to see what's new. What's exciting. You know, my—*ahem*—other clients haven't even been through here yet! You're the first. First picks!"

"And highest prices," Abraham said, turning to look at the wall of guns. "Death comes at such a premium these days."

"Says the man carrying an electron-compressed Manchester 451," Diamond said. "With gravatonics and a full grenade dock. Nice explosions on those. Little on the small side, but you can bounce them in really fun ways."

"Show us what you have," Abraham said politely, though his voice seemed strained. I could swear he had sounded more calm talking to the thugs who had shot him. Curious.

"I'm getting some things ready to show you," Diamond said. He had a smile like a parrot fish, which I've always assumed look like parrots, though I've never actually seen either. "Why don't you just have a look around? Browse a bit. Tell me what suits your fancy."

"Very well," Abraham said. "Thank you." He nodded to us—we knew what we were supposed to do. Look for anything out of the ordinary. A weapon that could cause a lot of destruction—destruction that could seem like the work of an Epic. If we were going to imitate one, we'd need something impressive.

Megan stepped up beside me, studying a machine gun that fired incendiary rounds.

"I'm *not* a nerd," I hissed at her softly.

"Why does it matter?" she asked, her tone neutral. "There's nothing wrong with being smart. In fact, if you *are* intelligent, you'll be a stronger asset to the team."

"I just . . . I . . . I just don't like being called that. Besides, who ever heard of a nerd jumping from a moving jet and shooting an Epic in midair while plummeting toward the ground?"

"I've never heard of *anyone* doing that."

"Phaedrus did it," I said. "Execution of Redleaf, three years ago up in Canada."

"That story was exaggerated," Abraham said softly, walking by. "It was a helicopter. And it was all part of the plan—we were very careful. Now please, keep focused on our current task."

I shut my mouth and began studying the weapons. Incendiary rounds were impressive, but not particularly original. That wasn't flashy enough for us. In fact, any type of basic gun wouldn't work— whether it shot bullets, rockets, or grenades, it wouldn't be convincing. We needed something more like the energy weapons Enforcement had. A way to mimic an Epic's innate firepower.

I moved down the hallway, and the weapons seemed to grow more unusual the farther I walked. I stopped beside a curious group of objects. They appeared to be innocent enough—a water bottle, a mobile phone, a pen. They were attached to the wall like the weapons.

"Ah . . . you are a discerning man, are you, David?"

I jumped, turning to see Diamond grinning behind me. How could a fat man move so quietly?

"What are they?" I asked.

"Advanced stealth explosives," Diamond answered proudly. He reached up and tapped a section of the wall, and an image appeared on it. He had an imager hooked up here, apparently. It showed a water bottle sitting on a table. A businessman strolled past, looking at some papers in his hand. He set them on the table, then twisted the cap off the water.

And exploded.

I jumped back.

"Ah," Diamond said. "I hope you appreciate the value of this footage—it's rare that I get good shots of a stealth explosive being deployed in the field. This one is quite remarkable. Notice how the explosion flung the body back but didn't damage too much nearby?

That's important in a stealth explosive, particularly if the person to be assassinated might have valuable documents on them."

"That's disgusting," I said, turning away.

"We are in the business of death, young man."

"The video, I mean."

"He wasn't a very nice person, if it helps." I doubted that mattered to Diamond. He seemed affable as he tapped the wall. "Good explosion. I'll be honest—I half keep these to sell just because I like showing off that video. It's one of a kind."

"Do they all explode?" I asked, examining the innocent-looking devices.

"The pen is a detonator," Diamond said. "Click the back and you set off one of those little eraser devices next to it. They're universal blasting caps. Stick them close to something explosive, trigger them, and they can usually set it off. Depends on the substance, but they're programmed with some pretty advanced detection algorithms. They work on most explosive substances. Stick one of those to some guy's grenade, walk away, then click the pen."

"If you could clip one of those to his grenade," Megan said, approaching, "you could have just pulled the pin. Or better yet, shot him."

"It's not for every situation," Diamond said defensively. "But they can be *very* fun. What's better than detonating your enemy's own explosives when he's not expecting it?"

"Diamond," Abraham called from down the corridor. "Come tell me about this."

"Ah! Excellent choice. *Wonderful* explosions from that one . . ." He scuttled off.

I looked at the panel full of innocent yet deadly objects. Something about them felt very wrong to me. I'd killed men before, but I'd done it honestly. With a gun in my hands, and only because I'd been forced to. I didn't have many philosophies about life, but one of them was something my father had taught me: never throw the first punch. If you have to throw the second, try to make sure they don't get up for a third.

"These *could* be useful," Megan said, arms still crossed. "Though I doubt that blowhard really understands what for."

"I know," I said, trying to redeem myself. "I mean, recording some poor guy's death like that? It was totally unprofessional."

"Actually, he sells explosives," she said, "so having a recording like that *is* professional of him. I suspect he has recordings of each of these weapons being fired, as we can't test them hands-on down here."

"Megan, that was a recording of some guy *blowing up*." I shook my head, revolted. "It was awful. You shouldn't show off stuff like that."

She hesitated, looking troubled about something. "Yes. Of course." She looked at me. "You never did explain why you were so bothered by being called a nerd."

"I told you. I don't like it because, you know, I want to do awesome stuff. And nerds don't—"

"That's not it," she said, staring at me coolly. *Sparks,* but her eyes were beautiful. "There's something deeper about it that bothers you, and you need to get over it. It's a weakness." She glanced at the water bottle, then turned and walked over to the thing Abraham was inspecting. It was some kind of bazooka.

I secured my rifle over my shoulder and stuck my hands in my pockets. It seemed that I was spending a lot of time lately getting lectured. I'd thought that leaving the Factory would end all of that, but I guess I should have known better.

I turned from Megan and Abraham and looked across at the wall nearest me. I was having trouble focusing on the guns, which was a first for me. My mind was working over what she'd asked. Why did being called a nerd bother me?

I walked over to her side.

"... don't know if it's what we want," Abraham was saying.

"But the explosions are *so big*," Diamond replied.

"It's because they took the smart ones away," I said softly to Megan.

I could feel her eyes on me, but I continued staring at the wall.

"A lot of kids at the Factory tried so hard to prove how smart they were," I said quietly. "We had school, you know. You went to school half the day, worked the other half, unless you got expelled. If you did poorly the teacher just expelled you, and after that you worked full days. School was easier than the Factory, so most of the kids tried really hard.

"The smart ones, though ... the really smart ones ... the nerds ... they left. Got taken to the city above. If you showed some skill with computers, or math, or writing, off you went. They got good jobs, I hear. In Steelheart's propaganda corps or his accounting offices or something like that. When I was young I'd have laughed about Steelheart having accountants. He's got a lot of them, you know. You need people like them in an empire."

Megan looked at me, curious. "So you ..."

"Learned to be dumb," I said. "Rather, to be mediocre. The dumb ones got kicked out of school, and I wanted to learn—knew I *needed* to learn—so I had to stay. I also knew that if I went up above, I'd lose my freedom. He keeps a lot better watch over his accountants than he does his factory workers.

"There were other boys like me. A lot of the girls moved on fast, the smart ones. Some of the boys I knew, though, they started to see it as a mark of pride that they weren't taken above. You didn't want to be one of the smart ones. I had to be extra careful, since I asked so many questions about the Epics. I had to hide my notebooks, find ways to throw off those who thought I was smart."

"But you're not there anymore. You're with the Reckoners. So it doesn't matter."

"It does," I said. "Because it's not who I am. I'm not smart, I'm just persistent. My friends who were smart, they didn't have to study at all. I had to study like a horse for every test I took."

"Like a horse?"

"You know. Because horses work hard? Pulling carts and plows and things?"

"Yeah, I'll just ignore that one."

"I'm *not* smart," I said.

I didn't mention that part of the reason I had to study so hard was because I needed to know the answer to each and every question perfectly. Only then could I ensure that I would get the *exact* number of questions wrong to remain in the middle of the pack. Smart enough to stay in school, but not worthy of notice or attention.

"Besides," I continued. "The people I knew who were really smart, they learned because they loved it. I didn't. I hated studying."

"You read the encyclopedia. *A few times.*"

"Looking for things that could be Epic weaknesses," I said. "I needed to know different types of metal, chemical compounds, elements, and symbols. Practically anything could be a weakness. I hoped something would spark in my head. Something about him."

"So it's all about him."

"Everything in my life is about him, Megan," I said, looking at her. "Everything."

We fell silent, though Diamond continued blabbing on. Abraham had turned to look at me. He seemed thoughtful.

Great, I realized. *He heard. Just great.*

"That will be enough, please, Diamond," Abraham said. "That weapon really won't work."

The weapons merchant sighed. "Very well. But perhaps you can give me a clue as to what *might* work."

"Something distinctive," Abraham said. "Something nobody has seen before, but also something destructive."

"Well, I don't have much that *isn't* destructive," Diamond said. "But distinctive . . . Let me see. . . ."

Abraham waved for us to keep searching. As Megan moved off, however, he took me by the arm. He had quite a strong grip. "Steelheart takes the smart ones," Abraham said softly, "because he fears them. He knows, David. All of these guns, they do not frighten him. They won't be what overthrows him. It will be the person clever enough, *smart* enough, to figure out the chink in his armor. He knows he can't kill them all, so he employs them. When he dies it will be because of someone like you. Remember that."

He released my arm and walked after Diamond.

I watched him go, then walked over to another group of weapons. His words didn't really change anything, but oddly, I did feel myself standing a little taller as I looked at a line of guns and was able to identify each of the manufacturers.

I'm totally not a nerd though. I still know the truth at least.

I looked over the guns for a few minutes, proud of how many I could identify. Unfortunately none of them seemed distinctive enough. Actually, the fact that I could identify them guaranteed that they weren't distinctive enough. We needed something nobody had seen before.

Maybe he won't have anything, I thought. *If he has a rotating stock, then we may have picked the wrong time to visit. Sometimes a grab bag doesn't give anything worthwhile. It—*

I stopped as I noticed something different. Motorcycles.

There were three of them in a row near the far side of the hallway. I hadn't seen them at first, as I'd been focused on the guns. They were sleek, their bodies a deep green with black patterns running up their sides. They made me want to hunch over and crouch down to make myself have less wind resistance. I could imagine shooting through the streets on one of these. They looked so dangerous, like alligators. Really fast alligators wearing black. Ninja alligators.

I decided not to use that one on Megan.

They didn't have any weapons on them that I could see, though there were some odd devices on the sides. Maybe energy weapons? They didn't seem to fit with much of what Diamond had here, but then again, what he had was pretty eclectic.

Megan walked past me and I raised a finger to point at the motorcycles.

"No," she said, not even looking.

"But—"

"No."

"But they're awesome!" I said, holding up my hands, as if that should have been enough of an argument. And, sparks, it should have been. They were *awesome*!

"You could barely drive some lady's sedan, Knees," Megan said. "I don't want to see you on the back of something with gravatonics."

"Gravatonics!" That was even *more* awesome.

"No," Megan said firmly.

I looked toward Abraham, who was inspecting something nearby. He glanced at me, then over at the bikes, and smiled. "No."

I sighed. Wasn't shopping for weapons supposed to be more fun than this?

"Diamond," Abraham called to the dealer. "What is this?"

The weapons merchant began waddling over. "Oh, it's wonderful. Great explosions. It . . ." His face fell as he neared and saw what Abraham was actually looking at. "Oh. That. Um, it is *quite* wonderful, though I don't know if it would suit your needs. . . ."

The item in question was a large rifle with a very long barrel and a scope on top. It looked a little bit like an AWM—one of the sniper rifles the Factory had used as a model in building their products. The barrel was larger, however, and there were some odd coils around the forestock. It was painted a dark black-green and had a big hole where the magazine should have fit.

Diamond sighed. "This weapon is wonderful, but you are a good customer. I should warn you that I don't have the resources to make it work."

"What?" Megan asked. "You're selling a broken gun?"

"It's not that," Diamond said, tapping the section of wall beside the gun. An image displayed of a man set up on the ground, holding the rifle and looking through the scope at some run-down buildings. "This is called a gauss gun, developed using research on some Epic or another who throws bullets at people."

"Rick O'Shea," I said, nodding. "An Irish Epic."

"That's really his name?" Abraham asked softly.

"Yeah."

"That's horrible." He shivered. "Taking a beautiful French word and turning it into . . . into something Cody would say. *Câlice!*"

"Anyway," I said. "He can make objects unstable by touching them; then they explode when subjected to any significant impact. Basically he charges rocks with energy, throws them at people, and they explode. Standard kinetic energy Epic."

I was more interested in the idea that the technology had been developed based on his powers. Ricky was a newer Epic. He wouldn't have been around back in the old days when, as the Reckoners had explained, Epics had been imprisoned and experimented on. Did this mean that kind of research was still going on? There was a place where Epics were being held captive? I'd never heard of such a thing.

"The gun?" Abraham asked Diamond.

"Well, like I said." Diamond tapped the wall and the video started playing. "It's a type of gauss gun, only it uses a projectile that has been charged with energy first. The bullet, once turned explosive, is propelled to extreme speeds using tiny magnets."

The man holding the gun in the video flipped a switch and the coils lit up green. He pulled the trigger and there was a *burst* of energy, though the thing seemed to have almost no recoil. A splash of green light spat from the front of the gun's barrel, leaving a line in the air. One of the distant buildings exploded, giving off a strange shower of green that seemed to warp the air.

"We're . . . not sure why it does that," Diamond admitted. "Or even how. The technology changes the bullet into a charged explosive."

I felt a shiver, thinking about the tensors, the jackets—the technology used by the Reckoners. Actually, a lot of the technology we now used had come with the advent of the Epics. How much of it did we really understand?

We were relying on half-understood technology built from studying mystifying creatures who didn't even know how they did what they did themselves. We were like deaf people trying to dance to a beat we couldn't hear, long after the music actually stopped. Or . . . wait. I don't know what that actually was supposed to mean.

Anyway, the lights given off by that gun's explosion were very distinctive. Beautiful, even. There didn't seem to be much debris, just some green smoke that still floated in the air. Almost as if the building had been transformed directly to energy.

Then it hit me. "Aurora borealis," I said, pointing. "It looks like the pictures I've seen of it."

"Destructive capability looks good," Megan said. "That building was almost completely knocked down by one shot."

Abraham nodded. "It might be what we need. However, Diamond, might I inquire about what you mentioned earlier? You said it didn't work."

"It works just fine," the merchant said quickly. "But it requires an energy pack to fire. A powerful one."

"How powerful?"

"Fifty-six KC," Diamond said, then hesitated. "Per shot."

Abraham whistled.

"Is that a lot?" Megan asked.

"Yeah," I said, in awe. "Like, several thousand standard fuel cells' worth."

"Usually," Diamond said, "you need to hook it up by cord to its own power unit. You can't just plug this bad boy into a wall socket. The shots on this demo were fired using several six-inch cords running back to a dedicated generator." He looked up at the weapon. "I bought it hoping I could trade *a certain client* for some of his high-energy fuel cells, then be able to actually sell the weapon in working condition."

"Who knows about this weapon?" Abraham asked.

"Nobody," Diamond said. "I bought it directly from the lab that created it, and the man who made this video was in my employ. It's never been on the market. In fact, the researchers who developed it died a few months later—blew themselves up, poor fools. I guess that's what you get when you routinely build devices that supercharge matter."

"We'll take it," Abraham said.

"You will?" Diamond looked surprised, and then a smile crossed his face. "Well . . . what an excellent choice! I'm certain you'll be happy. But again, to clarify, this will *not* fire unless you find your own energy source. A very powerful one, likely one you won't be able to transport. Do you understand?"

"We will find one," Abraham said. "How much?"

"Twelve," Diamond said without missing a beat.

"You can't sell it to anyone else," Abraham said, "and you can't make it work. You'll be getting four. Thank you." Abraham got out a small box. He tapped it, and handed it over.

"And we want one of those pen exploder things thrown in," I said on a whim as I held my mobile up to the wall and downloaded the video of the gauss gun in action. I almost asked for one of the motorcycles, but figured that would *really* be pushing things.

"Very well," Diamond said, holding up the box Abraham had given him. What *was* that, anyway? "Is Fortuity in here?" he asked.

"Alas," Abraham said, "our encounter with him did not leave time for proper harvesting. But four others, including Absence."

Harvesting? What did *that* mean? Absence was an Epic the Reckoners had killed last year.

Diamond grunted. I found myself *very* curious as to what was in that box.

"Also, here." Abraham handed over a data chip.

Diamond smiled, taking it. "You know how to sweeten a deal, Abraham. Yes you do."

"Nobody finds out that we have this," Abraham said, nodding toward the gun. "Do not even tell another person that it exists."

"Of course not," Diamond said, sounding offended. He walked over to pull a standard rifle bag out from under his desk, then began to get the gauss gun down.

"What did we pay him with?" I asked Megan, speaking very softly.

"When Epics die, something happens to their bodies," she replied.

"Mitochondrial mutation." I nodded. "Yeah."

"Well, when we kill an Epic, we harvest some of their mitochondria," she said. "It's needed by the scientists who build all this kind of stuff. Diamond can trade it to secret research labs."

I whistled softly. "Wow."

"Yeah," she said, looking troubled. "The cells expire after just a few minutes if you don't freeze them, so that makes it hard to harvest. There are some groups out there who make a living harvesting cells—they don't kill the Epics, they just sneak a blood sample and freeze it. This sort of thing has become a secret, high-level currency."

So *that* was how it was happening. The Epics didn't even need to know about it. It worried me more deeply, however, to learn about this. How much of the process did we understand? What would the Epics think of their genetic material being sold at market?

I'd never heard of any of this, despite my research into Epics. It served as a reminder. I might have figured a few things out, but there was an entire world out there beyond my experience.

"What about the data chip Abraham gave him?" I asked. "The thing Diamond called a deal sweetener?"

"That has explosions on it," she said.

"Ah. Of course."

"Why do you want that detonator?"

"I don't know," I said. "It just sounded fun. And since it looks like a while till I'll get one of those bikes—"

"You'll *never* get one of those bikes."

"—I thought I'd ask for something."

She didn't reply, though it seemed as if I'd unintentionally annoyed her. Again. I was having a tough time deciding what was bothering her—she seemed to have her own special rules for what constituted being "professional" and what didn't.

Diamond packed up the gun and, to my delight, tossed in the pen detonator and a small pack of the "erasers" that worked with it. I was feeling pretty good about getting something extra. Then I smelled garlic.

I frowned. It wasn't *quite* garlic, but it was close. What was . . .

Garlic.

Phosphorus smelled like garlic.

"We're in trouble," I said immediately. "Nightwielder is here."

17

"THAT'S impossible!" Diamond said, checking his mobile. "They're not supposed to be here for another hour or two." He paused, then held his ear—he wore a small earpiece—his mobile twinkling in his hand.

He grew pale, likely getting news of an early arrival from the girl outside. "Oh dear."

"Sparks," Megan said, slinging the gauss gun's bag over her shoulder.

"You had an appointment with Steelheart *today*?" Abraham said.

"It won't be him," Diamond said. "Assuming he were a client of mine, he would never come himself."

"He just sends Nightwielder," I said, sniffing the air. "Yeah, he's here. Can you smell that?"

"Why didn't you warn us?" Megan said to Diamond.

"I don't speak of other clients to—"

"Never mind," Abraham said. "We leave." He pointed down the hallway, opposite the way we'd come in. "Where does it lead?"

"Dead end," Diamond said.

"You left yourself without a way out?" I asked, incredulous.

"Nobody would attack me!" Diamond said. "Not with the hardware I've got in here. Calamity! This is *not* supposed to happen. My clients know not to arrive early."

"Stop him outside," Abraham said.

"Stop Nightwielder?" Diamond asked, incredulous. "He's incorporeal. He can walk through walls for Calamity's sake."

"Then keep him from walking all the way down the hallway," Abraham said calmly. "There are some shadows back there. We'll hide."

"I don't—" Diamond started.

"There isn't time to argue, my friend," Abraham said. "Everyone pretends to not care that you sell to all sides, but I doubt Nightwielder will treat you well if he discovers us here. He'll recognize me; he's seen me before. If he finds me here, we all die. Do you understand?"

Diamond, still pale, nodded again.

"Come on," Abraham said, shouldering his gun and jogging down the hallway past the rear of the store. Megan and I joined him. My heart was thumping. Nightwielder would recognize Abraham? What history did they have together?

There were piles of crates and boxes at the other end of the hallway. It was indeed a dead end, but there were no lights. Abraham waved for us to take cover behind the boxes. We could still see the walls full of weapons back where we'd been. Diamond stood there, wringing his hands.

"Here," Abraham said, setting his large gun down on a box and aiming it directly at Diamond. "Man this, David. Don't fire unless you *must*."

"Won't work against Nightwielder anyway," I said. "He has

prime invincibility—bullets, energy weapons, explosions all pass through him." Unless we could get him into the sunlight, assuming I was right. I put up a good front for the others, but the truth was, all I had was hearsay.

Abraham dug in the pocket of his cargo pants and pulled something out. One of the tensors.

I immediately felt a surge of relief. He was going to cut us a path to freedom. "So we're not going to wait it out?"

"Of course not," he said calmly. "I feel like a rat in a trap. Megan, contact Tia. We need to know the tunnel nearest to this one. I'll dig us a route to it."

Megan nodded, kneeling down and cupping her mouth as she whispered into her mobile. Abraham warmed up the tensor, and I folded out the scope on his machine gun, flipping the switch to burst mode. He nodded appreciatively at the move.

I sighted through the scope. It was a nice one, far nicer than my own, with distance readouts, wind speed monitors, and optional low-light compensators. I had a pretty good view of Diamond as he welcomed his new customers with hands open and a wide smile on his face.

I grew tense. There were eight of them—two men and a woman in suits alongside four Enforcement soldiers. And Nightwielder. He was a tall Asian man who was only half there. Faint, incorporeal. He wore a fine suit, but the long jacket had an Eastern flair to it. His hair was short, and he walked with hands clasped behind his back.

My finger twitched toward the trigger. This creature was Steelheart's right-hand Epic, the source of the darkness that cut Newcago off from the sun and stars. Similar darkness stirred on the ground around him, sliding toward shadows and pooling there. He could kill with that, could make tendrils of that dark mist turn solid and spear a man.

Those—the incorporeity and the manipulation of that mist— were his only two known powers, but they were doozies. He could move through solid matter, and like all incorporeals, he could fly at a steady speed. He could make a room completely black, then spear you with that darkness. And he could hold an entire city in perpetual night. Many assumed that he dedicated most of his energies to this.

That had always worried me. If he weren't so busy keeping the city in darkness, he might have been as powerful as Steelheart himself. Either way, he'd be more than enough to handle the three of us, unprepared as we were.

He and two of his minions were in conversation with Diamond. I wished I could hear what they were saying. I hesitated, then pulled back from the scope. A lot of advanced guns had . . .

Yes. I flipped the switch on the side, activating the scope's directional sound amplifier. I pulled the earphone out of my mobile and waved it past the chip on the scope to pair it, then stuck it in my ear. I leaned in and aimed the scope right at the group. The receiver picked up what was being said.

". . . is interested in specific kinds of weapons, this time," one of Nightwielder's minions was saying. She wore a pantsuit and had her black hair cut short up over her ears. "Our emperor is worried that our forces rely too much on the armor units for heavy support. What do you have for more mobile troops?"

"Er, plenty," Diamond said.

Sparks, but he looks nervous. He didn't glance at us, but he fidgeted and looked as if he might be sweating. For a man who dealt in the underground weapons trade, he certainly seemed bad at handling stress.

Diamond glanced from the woman toward Nightwielder, whose hands were clasped behind his back. According to my notes, he rarely spoke directly during business interactions. He preferred to use minions. It was some kind of Japanese culture thing.

The conversation continued, and Nightwielder continued to stand straight-backed and silent. They didn't go look at the guns on the walls, even when Diamond hinted that they could. They made him bring the weapons to them, and one of the assistants always handled the inspection and the questions.

That's pretty handy, I thought, a bead of nervous sweat dripping down my temple. *He can focus on Diamond—study and think, without bothering to make conversation.*

"Got it," Megan whispered. I glanced back to see her twisting her mobile around, her hand shading its light, to show Abraham the map Tia had sent. Abraham had to lean in close to make anything out; she had the mobile's screen dimmed almost to black.

He grunted softly. "Seven feet straight back, a few degrees down. That's going to take a few minutes."

"You should get at it, then," Megan said.

"I'll need your help to pile out the dust."

Megan shuffled to the side and Abraham placed his hands against the back wall, near the ground, and engaged the tensor. A large disk of steel began to disintegrate beneath his touch, creating a tunnel we could crawl through. Megan began scooping up and moving the steel dust as Abraham concentrated.

I turned back to watching, trying to breathe as quietly as possible. The tensors didn't make much noise, just a soft buzzing. Hopefully nobody would notice.

". . . master thinks that this weapon is of poor quality," the servant said, handing back a machine gun. "We are growing disappointed in your selection, merchant."

"Well, you want heavy gear, but no launchers. That's a difficult prospect to match. I—"

"What was in this place on the wall?" a soft, eerie voice asked. It sounded something like a loud whisper, faintly accented, yet piercing. It made me shiver.

Diamond stiffened. I shifted the view on the scope slightly. Nightwielder stood beside the wall of weapons. He was pointing toward an open space where hooks jutted from the wall—where the gauss gun had been.

"There was something here, was there not?" Nightwielder asked. He almost never spoke to someone directly like this. It didn't seem to be a good sign. "You only opened today. You have already had business?"

"I . . . don't discuss other clients," Diamond said. "You know this."

Nightwielder looked back at the wall. At that moment, Megan bumped a box as she was moving steel dust. It didn't make a loud noise—in fact, she didn't even seem to notice she'd done it. But Nightwielder swiveled his head in our direction. Diamond followed his gaze; the weapons merchant looked so nervous you could have turned milk into butter by sticking his hand in it.

"He's noticed us," I said softly.

"What?" Abraham said, still concentrating.

"Just . . . keep at it," I said, standing. "And stay quiet."

It was time for a little more improvising.

18

I shouldered Abraham's gun, ignoring Megan's soft curse. I trotted out from behind the boxes before she could restrain me, and at the last moment I remembered to pop the earpiece out of my ear and stow it.

As I left the shadows, Nightwielder's soldiers trained guns on me with quick motions. I felt a spike of anxiety, the prickling sensation of defenselessness. I hate it when people point guns at me . . . though I guess that makes me like pretty much everyone else.

I continued on. "Boss," I called, patting the weapon. "I got it working. Magazine comes out easily now."

Nightwielder's soldiers glanced toward him, as if looking for permission to shoot. The Epic clasped his hands behind his back, studying me with ethereal eyes. He didn't seem to notice, but his elbow brushed the wall and passed right through the solid steel.

He studied me but remained motionless. The goons didn't shoot. Good sign.

Come on, Diamond, I thought, trying to contain my nervousness. *Don't be an idiot. Say someth—*

"Was it the release pin?" Diamond asked.

"No, sir," I said. "The magazine was bent slightly on one side." I gave a respectful nod to Nightwielder and his flunkies, then moved over to set the gun in the spot on the wall. It fit, fortunately. I'd guessed it would, considering it was close to the same size as the gauss gun.

"Well, Diamond," Nightwielder's female attendant said. "Perhaps you can tell us of this new addition. It looks like it—"

"No," Nightwielder said softly. "I will hear it from the boy."

I froze, then turned around, nervous. "Sir?"

"Tell me about this gun," Nightwielder said.

"The boy's a new hire," Diamond said. "He doesn't—"

"It's all right, boss," I said. "That's a Manchester 451. The weapon is a powerhouse—fifty caliber, with electron-compressed magazines. Each holds eight hundred rounds. The select-fire system supports single shot, burst, and full auto capabilities. It has gravatonic recoil reduction for shoulder firing, with optional advanced magnitude scope including audio receiving, range finding, and a remote firing mechanism. It also includes the optional grenade launcher. Equipped rounds are armor-piercing incendiary, sir. You couldn't ask for a better gun."

Nightwielder nodded. "And this?" he said, pointing to the gun next to it.

My palms were sweating. I shoved them in my pockets. That was . . . it was a . . . Yes, I knew. "Browning M3919, sir. An inferior gun, but very good for the price. Also fifty caliber, but without the recoil suppression, the gravatonics, or the electron compression. It is excellent as a mounted weapon—with the advanced heat sinks on the barrel, it can fire around eight hundred rounds a minute. Over a mile effective range with remarkable accuracy."

The corridor fell still. Nightwielder regarded the gun, then turned to his minions and made a curt gesture. That nearly made me jump with alarm, but the others seemed to relax. I'd passed Nightwielder's test, apparently.

"We will want to see the Manchester," the woman said. "This is exactly what we are looking for; you should have mentioned it earlier."

"I . . . was embarrassed about the magazine sticking," Diamond said. "It's a known problem with Manchesters, I'm afraid. Every gun has its quirks. I've heard that if you file down one of the top edges of the magazine, it slides much more easily. Here, let me get that back down for you. . . ."

The conversation continued, but I was forgotten. I was able to step back to where I wouldn't be in the way. *Should I try to slip away?* I wondered. It would seem suspicious if I went to the back of the hallway again, wouldn't it? Sparks. It looked like they were going to buy Abraham's gun. I hoped he'd forgive me for that.

If Abraham and Megan got out through the hole, I could just wait here until Nightwielder left, then meet up with them. Staying put seemed like the best move for the moment.

I found myself staring at Nightwielder's back as his minions continued negotiations. I was . . . what, three steps away from him? One of Steelheart's three most trusted, one of the most powerful living Epics. He was right there. And I couldn't touch him. Well, I couldn't touch him literally, since he was incorporeal—but I meant figuratively too.

That was the way it had always been, ever since Calamity appeared. So few dared resist the Epics. I'd watched children be murdered in front of their parents, with nobody brave enough to lift a hand to try to stop it. Why would they try? They'd just be killed.

He did it to me too, to an extent. I was here with him, but all I wanted to do was escape. *You make us all selfish,* I thought at Nightwielder. *That's why I hate you. All of you.* But Steelheart most of all.

". . . could use some better forensic tools," Nightwielder's female minion said. "I realize it's not your specialty."

"I always bring some along to Newcago," Diamond replied. "Just for you. Here, let me show you what I have."

I blinked. They were done with the conversation about the Manchester, and apparently they'd bought it—and ordered a shipment of three hundred more from Diamond, who'd happily made the sale even though this one wasn't his to sell.

Forensics . . . , I thought. Something about that itched at my memory.

Diamond waddled over to rummage under his desk for a few boxes. He noticed me and waved me away. "You can go back to the stockpile and continue your inventory, kid. I don't need you here any longer."

I should probably have done as he said, but I did something stupid instead. "I'm almost finished with that, boss," I said. "I'd like to stay, if I can. I still don't know a lot about the forensic equipment."

He stopped, studying me, and I tried my best to look innocent, hands stuffed in the pockets of my jacket. A little voice in my head was muttering, *You are so stupid, you are so stupid, you are so stupid.* But when was I going to get a chance like this again?

Forensic equipment would include the kinds of things one used for studying a crime scene. And I knew a little more about that sort of thing than I'd just implied to Diamond. I'd read about it, at least.

And I remembered that you could find DNA and fingerprints by shining UV light on them. UV light . . . the very thing my notes claimed was Nightwielder's weakness.

"Fine." Diamond went back to rummaging. "Just stay out of the Great One's way."

I took a few steps back and kept my eyes down. Nightwielder paid me no heed, and his minions stood with arms crossed as Diamond got out an array of boxes. He began asking what they needed, and I could soon tell from their responses that someone in the

Newcago government—Nightwielder, maybe Steelheart himself—was troubled by Fortuity's assassination.

They wanted equipment to detect Epics. Diamond didn't have such a thing; he said he'd heard of some for sale in Denver, but it had turned out to be only a rumor. It appeared that dowsers like the Reckoners had weren't easy to come by even for someone like Diamond.

They also wanted equipment to better determine the origins of bullet shells and explosives. This request he could accommodate, particularly tracking down explosives. He unpacked several devices from their Styrofoam and cardboard, then showed a scanner that identified the chemicals in an explosive by analyzing the ash produced.

I waited, tense, as one of the minions picked up something that looked like a metal briefcase with locks on the sides. She flipped it open, revealing a bunch of smaller devices situated in foam holes. That looked just like the forensic kits I'd read about.

A small data chip was attached to the top, glowing faintly now that the case was open. That would be the manual. The minion waved her mobile in front of it absently, downloading the instructions. I stepped over and did likewise, and though she glanced at me, she soon dismissed me and turned back to her inspection.

My heart beating more quickly, I scanned through the manual's contents until I found it. UV fingerprint scanner with attached video camera. I skimmed the instructions. Now, if I could just get it out of the case. . . .

The woman took out a device and inspected it. It wasn't the fingerprint scanner, so I didn't pay attention. I snatched that scanner the second she looked away, and then I pretended to just be fiddling with it, trying my best to look idly curious.

In the process I got it turned on. It glowed blue at the front and had a screen on the back—it worked like a digital camcorder, but with a UV light on the front. You shined the light over objects and recorded images of what that revealed. That would be handy if doing a sweep of a room for DNA—it would give you a record of what you'd seen.

I turned on the record function. What I was about to do could easily get me killed. I'd seen men murdered for far less. But I knew Tia wanted stronger proof. It was time to get her some.

I turned the UV light and shined it on Nightwielder.

19

NIGHTWIELDER spun on me immediately.

I turned the UV light to the side, my head down as if I were studying the device and trying to figure out how it worked. I wanted it to seem like I'd shined the light on him by happenstance while fiddling with it.

I didn't look at Nightwielder. I *couldn't* look at Nightwielder. I didn't know if the light had worked on him, but if it had and he so much as suspected that I'd seen, I'd die.

I might die anyway.

It was painful not to know what effect the light had produced, but the device *was* recording. I turned away from Nightwielder, and with one hand I tapped some buttons on the device as if trying to make it work. With the other—fingers trembling nervously—I slid out the data chip and hid it in the palm of my hand.

Nightwielder was still watching me. I could feel his eyes, as if they were drilling holes into my back. The room seemed to grow darker, shadows lengthening. To the side, Diamond continued chatting about the features of the device he was demonstrating. Nobody seemed to have noticed that I'd drawn Nightwielder's attention.

I pretended not to notice either, though my heart was pounding even harder in my chest. I fiddled with the machine some more, then held it up as if I'd finally figured out how it worked. I stepped forward and pressed my thumb on the wall, then stepped back to try to see the thumbprint show up in the UV light.

Nightwielder hadn't moved. He was considering what to do. Killing me would protect him if I'd noticed what the UV light did. He could do it. He could claim that I'd impinged on his personal space, or looked at him wrong. Sparks, he didn't even need to give an excuse. He could do what he wanted.

However, that could be dangerous for him. When an Epic killed erratically or unexpectedly, people always wondered if it was an attempt to hide their weakness. His minions had seen me holding a UV scanner. They might make a connection. And so, to be safe, he'd probably have to kill Diamond and the Enforcement soldiers as well. Probably his own assistants too.

I was sweating now. It felt awful to stand there, to not even be facing him as he considered murdering me. I wanted to spin, look him in the eyes, and spit at him as he killed me.

Steady, I told myself. Keeping the defiance from my face, I looked over and pretended to notice—for the first time—that Nightwielder was staring at me. He stood as he had earlier, hands behind his back, black suit and thin black necktie making him look all lines. Motionless gaze, translucent skin. There was no sign of what had happened, if indeed anything *had* happened.

Upon seeing him I jumped in shock. I didn't have to feign fear; I felt my skin grow pale, the color drain from my face. I dropped the fingerprint scanner and yelped softly. The scanner cracked as it hit the ground. I immediately cursed, crouching down beside the broken device.

"What are you doing, you fool!" Diamond bustled over to me. He didn't seem very worried about the scanner, more about my offending Nightwielder somehow. "I'm so sorry, Great One. He is a bumbling idiot, but he's the best I've been able to find. It—"

Diamond hushed as the shadows nearby lengthened, then swirled upon themselves, becoming thick black cords. He stumbled away and I jumped to my feet. The darkness didn't strike at me, however, but scooped up the fallen fingerprint scanner.

The blackness seemed to pool on the floor, writhing and twisting about itself. Tendrils of it raised the scanner up into the air in front of Nightwielder, and he studied it with an indifferent gaze. He looked to us, and then more of the blackness rose up and surrounded the scanner. There was a sudden *crunch,* like a hundred walnuts being cracked at once.

The intended message was clear. Annoy me, and you will meet the same fate. Nightwielder neatly obscured his fear of the scanner, and his desire to destroy it, behind the guise of a simple threat.

"I . . ." I said softly. "Boss, why don't I just go to the back and keep working on that inventory, like you said?"

"What you should have done from the first," Diamond said. "Off with you."

I turned and scrambled away, hand held to my side, clutching the data chip from the UV scanner. I hurried my pace, not minding how I looked, until I was running. I reached the boxes and the relative safety of their shadows. There, close to the floor, I found a completed tunnel burrowed through the back wall.

I lurched to a stop. I took a breath, got on my hands and knees, and scrambled into the opening. I slid through the seven feet of steel and came out the other side.

Something grabbed my arm and I pulled back by instinct. I looked up, logic fleeing as I thought of how Nightwielder had made the shadows themselves come alive, but was relieved to see a familiar face.

"Hush!" Abraham said, holding my arm. "Are they chasing?"

"I don't think so," I said softly.

"Where's my gun?"

"Um . . . I kind of sold it to Nightwielder."

Abraham raised an eyebrow at me, then towed me to the side, where Megan covered us with my rifle. She was the definition of professional—lips a terse line, eyes searching the tunnels nearby for danger. The only light came from the mobiles she and Abraham wore strapped to their shoulders.

Abraham nodded to her, and there was no further conversation as the three of us made our escape down the corridor. At the next intersection of the catacombs, Megan tossed my rifle to Abraham— ignoring that I'd put my hand out for it—and unholstered one of her handguns. She nodded to him, then took point, hurrying ahead down the steel tunnel.

We continued that way, no talk, for a time. I'd been hopelessly lost before, but now I was turned around so much I barely knew which direction was up.

"Okay," Abraham finally said, holding up a hand to wave Megan back. "Let's take a breather and see if anyone is following." He settled down in a small alcove in the hallway where he could watch the stretch behind us and see if anyone had followed. He seemed to be favoring the arm opposite the shoulder that had been shot.

I crouched beside him and Megan joined us.

"That was an unexpected move you made up there, David," Abraham said softly, calmly.

"I didn't have time to think about it," I said. "They heard us working."

"True, true. And then Diamond suggested you go back, but you said you wanted to stay?"

"So . . . you heard that?"

"I could not have just mentioned it if I hadn't." He continued looking down the hallway.

I glanced at Megan, who gave me a frosty stare. "Unprofessional," she muttered.

I fished in my pocket and brought out the data chip. Abraham glanced at it, then frowned. He obviously hadn't stayed long enough to see what I was doing with Nightwielder. I tapped the chip to my mobile, downloading the information. Three taps later, it started displaying the video from the UV scanner. Abraham glanced over, and even Megan craned her neck to see what it was showing.

I held my breath. I still didn't know for certain if I was right about Nightwielder—and even if I was, there was no telling whether my hasty spin of the scanner had captured any useable images.

The video image showed the ground, with me waving my hand in front of the lens. Then it turned on Nightwielder and my heart leaped. I tapped the screen, freezing the image.

"You clever little slontze," Abraham murmured. There, on the screen, Nightwielder stood with half his body fully corporeal. It was difficult to make out, but it was there. Where the UV light shone, he wasn't translucent, and his body seemed to have *settled* more.

I tapped the screen again and the UV light panned past, letting Nightwielder become incorporeal again. The video was only a second or two, but it was enough. "UV forensics scanner," I explained. "I figured this was the best chance we'd get to know for certain. . . ."

"I can't believe you took that chance," Megan said. "Without asking anyone. You could have gotten *all three* of us killed."

"But he didn't," Abraham said, plucking the data chip from my hand. He studied it, seeming oddly reverent. Then he looked up, as if remembering he'd been planning to watch the hallway for signs of people following. "We need to get this chip to Prof. Now." He hesitated. "Nice work."

He stood up to go, and I found myself beaming. Then I turned to Megan, who gave me an even colder, more hostile look than she had earlier. She rose and followed Abraham.

Sparks, I thought. What would it take to impress that girl? I shook my head and jogged after them.

20

WHEN we returned, Cody was off on a mission to do some scouting for Tia. She waved toward some rations on the back table of the main room, awaiting devourment. Devouration. Whatever that word is.

"Go tell Prof what you found," Abraham said softly, walking toward the storage room. Megan made her way to the rations.

"Where are you going?" I asked Abraham.

"I need a new gun, it seems," he said with a smile, ducking through the doorway. He hadn't chided me for what I'd done with his gun—he saw that I'd saved the team. At least I hoped that was how he viewed it. Still, there was a distinct sense of loss in his voice. He'd liked that gun. And it was easy to see why—I'd *never* owned a weapon as nice as that one.

Prof wasn't in the main room, and Tia glanced at me, raising an eyebrow. "What are you telling Prof?"

"I'll explain," Megan said, sitting down beside her. As usual, Tia had her table covered with papers and cans of cola. It looked like she'd gotten the insurance records Cody mentioned, and she had them up on the screen in front of her.

If Prof wasn't in here, I figured he was probably in his thinking room with the imager. I walked over and knocked softly on the wall; the doorway was only draped with a cloth.

"Come in, David," Prof's voice called from inside.

I hesitated. I hadn't been in the room since I had told the team my plan. The others rarely entered. This was Prof's sanctum, and he usually came out—rather than inviting people in—when they needed to speak to him. I glanced at Tia and Megan, both of whom looked surprised, though neither said anything.

I pushed past the cloth and stepped into the room. I'd imagined what Prof was doing with the wall imagers—maybe exploiting the team's hack of the spy network, moving through the city and studying Steelheart and his minions. It wasn't anything so dramatic.

"Chalkboards?" I asked.

Prof turned from the far wall, where he'd been standing and writing with a piece of chalk. All four walls, along with ceiling and floor, had been turned slate-black, and they were covered in white scribbled writing.

"I know," Prof said, waving me in. "It's not very modern, is it? I have technology capable of representing just about anything I want, in any form I want. And I choose chalkboards." He shook his head, as if in amusement at his own eccentricity. "I think best this way. Old habits, I guess."

I stepped up to him. I could see now that he wasn't actually writing on the walls. The thing in Prof's hand was just a little stylus shaped like a piece of chalk. The machine was interpreting his writings, making the words appear on the wall as he scribbled them.

The drape had fallen back into place, masking the light from the other rooms. I could barely make Prof out; the only light came from the soft glow of the white script on all six walls. I felt as if I were floating in space, the words *stars* and *galaxies* shining at me from distant abodes.

"What *is* this?" I asked, looking upward, reading the script that covered the ceiling. Prof had certain bits of it boxed away from others, and had arrows and lines pointing to different sections. I couldn't make much sense of what it said. It was written in English, kind of. But many of the words were very small and seemed to be in some kind of shorthand.

"The plan," Prof said absently. He didn't wear his goggles or coat—both sat in a pile beside the door—and the sleeves of his black button-up shirt were rolled to the elbows.

"My plan?" I asked.

Prof's smile was lit by the pale glowing chalk lines. "Not any longer. There are some seeds of it here, though."

I felt a sharp sinking feeling. "But, I mean . . ."

Prof glanced at me, then laid a hand on my shoulder. "You did a great job, son. All things considered."

"What was wrong with it?" I asked. I'd spent years . . . really, my *entire life* on that plan, and I was pretty confident in what I'd come up with.

"Nothing, nothing," Prof said. "The ideas are sound. Remarkably so. Convince Steelheart that there's a rival in town, lure him out, hit him. Though there is the glaring fact that you don't know what his weakness is."

"Well, there is that," I admitted.

"Tia is working hard on it. If anyone can tease out the truth, it will be her," Prof said, then paused for a moment before he continued. "Actually, no—I shouldn't have said that this isn't your plan.

It is, and there are more than just seeds of it here. I looked through your notebooks. You thought through things very well."

"Thank you."

"But your vision was too narrow, son." Prof removed his hand from my shoulder and walked up to the wall. He tapped it with his imitation chalk stylus, and the room's text rotated. He didn't appear to even notice, but I grew dizzy as the walls seemed to tumble about me, spinning until a new wall of text popped up in front of Prof.

"Let me start with this," he said. "Other than not specifically knowing Steelheart's weakness, what's the biggest flaw in your plan?"

"I . . ." I frowned. "Taking out Nightwielder, maybe? But Prof, we just—"

"Actually," Prof said, "that's not it."

My frown deepened. I hadn't thought there *was* a flaw in my plan. I'd worked all those out, smoothing them away like cleanser removing the pimples from a teenager's chin.

"Let's break it down," Prof said, raising his arm and sweeping an opening on the wall, like he was wiping mud from a window. The words scrunched to the side, not vanishing but bunching up like he'd pulled a new section of paper from a spool. He raised his chalk to the open space and started to write. "Step one, imitate a powerful Epic. Step two, start killing Steelheart's important Epics to make him worried. Step three, draw him out. Step four, kill him. By doing this you restore hope to the world and encourage people to fight back."

I nodded.

"Except there's a problem," Prof said, still scribbling on the wall. "If we *actually* manage to kill Steelheart, we'll have done it by imitating a powerful Epic. Everyone's going to assume, then, that an *Epic* was behind the defeat. And so, what do we gain?"

"We could announce it was the Reckoners after the fact."

Prof shook his head. "Wouldn't work. Nobody would believe us, not after all the trouble we'll need to go through to make Steelheart believe."

"Well, does it matter?" I asked. "He'll be dead." Then, more softly, I added, "And I get revenge."

Prof hesitated, chalk pausing on the wall. "Yes," he said. "I guess you'd still have that."

"You want him dead too," I said, stepping up beside him. "I know it. I can see it."

"I want all Epics dead."

"It's more than that," I said. "I've seen it in you."

He glanced at me, and his gaze grew stern. "That doesn't matter. It is *vital* that people know we were behind this. You've said it yourself—we can't kill every Epic out there. The Reckoners are spinning in circles. The only hope we have, the only hope that humankind has, is to convince people that we *can* fight back. For that to happen, Steelheart has to fall by human hands."

"But for him to come out, he has to believe an Epic is threatening him," I said.

"You see the problem?"

"I . . ." I was starting to. "So we're not going to imitate an Epic?"

"We are," Prof said. "I like the idea, the spark of that. I'm just pointing out problems we have to work through. If this . . . Limelight is going to kill Steelheart, we need a way to make certain that after the fact, we can convince people it was really us. Not impossible, but it is why I had to work more on the plan, expand it."

"Okay," I said, relaxing. So we were still on track. A false Epic . . . the soul of my plan was there.

"There's a bigger problem, unfortunately," Prof said, tapping his chalk against the wall. "Your plan calls for us to kill Epics in Steelheart's administration to threaten him and draw him out. You indicate that we should do this to prove that a new Epic has come to town. Only, that's not going to work."

"What? Why?"

"Because it's what the Reckoners would do," Prof said. "Killing Epics quietly, never coming out into the open? It'll make him suspicious. We need to think like a *real* rival would. Anyone who wants Newcago would think bigger than that. Any Epic out there can have a city of his own; it's not that hard. To want Newcago, you'd have to be ambitious. You'd have to want to be a *king*. You'd have to want Epics at your beck and call. And so, killing them off one by one wouldn't make sense. You see?"

"You'd want them alive so they'd follow you," I said, slowly understanding. "Every Epic you kill would lessen your power once you actually took Newcago."

"Exactly," Prof said. "Nightwielder, Firefight, maybe Conflux . . . they'll have to go. But you'd be very careful who to kill and who to try to bribe away."

"Only we *can't* bribe them away," I said. "We wouldn't be able to convince them that we're an Epic, not long term."

"So you see another problem," Prof said.

He was right. I wilted, like soda going flat in a cup left out overnight. How had I not seen this hole in my plan?

"I've been working on these two problems," Prof said. "If we're going to imitate an Epic—and I think we still should—we need to be able to prove that we were behind it all along. That way the truth can flood Newcago and spread across the Fractured States from there. We can't just kill him; we have to film ourselves doing so. And we need to, at the last minute, send information about our plan to the right people around the city—so that they know and can vouch for us. People like Diamond, non-Epic crime magnates, people with influence but no direct connection to his government."

"Okay. But what about the second problem?"

"We need to hit Steelheart where it hurts," Prof said, "but we can't spread it out over too much time, and we can't focus on Epics. We need one or two massive hits that make him bleed, make him see us as a threat, and we need to do it as a rival seeking to take his place."

"So . . ."

Prof tapped the wall, rotating the text from the floor up in front of him. He tapped a section and some of the text started glowing green.

"Green?" I said, amused. "What was that about liking things old-fashioned?"

"You can use colored chalk on a chalkboard," he said gruffly as he circled a pair of words: *sewage system*.

"Sewage system?" I said. I'd been expecting something a little more grand, and a little less . . . crappy.

Prof nodded. "The Reckoners never attack facilities; we focus only on Epics. If we hit one of the city's main points of infrastructure, it will make Steelheart believe it's not the Reckoners working against him, but some other force. Someone specifically trying to take down Steelheart's rule—either rebels in the city, or another Epic moving on his territory.

"Newcago works on two principles: fear and stability. The city has the basic infrastructure that many others don't, and that draws people here. The fear of Steelheart keeps them in line." He rolled the words on the walls again, bringing over a network of drawings he'd done in "chalk" on the far wall. It looked like a crude blueprint. "If we start attacking his infrastructure he'll move on us faster than if we'd attacked his Epics. Steelheart is smart. He knows why people come to Newcago. If he loses the basic things—sewage, power, communications—he'll lose the city."

I nodded slowly. "I wonder why."

"Why? I just explained. . . ." Prof trailed off, looking at me. He frowned. "That's not what you mean."

"I wonder why he cares. Why does he go to so much trouble to create a city where people want to live? Why does he care if they have food, or water, or electricity? He kills them so callously, yet he also sees that they're provided for."

Prof fell silent. Eventually he shook his head. "What is it to be a king if you have nobody to follow you?"

I thought back to that day, the day when my father died. *These people are mine. . . .* As I considered it I realized something about the Epics. Something that, despite all my years of study, I'd never quite understood before.

"It isn't enough," Prof whispered. "It isn't *enough* to have godly powers, to be functionally immortal, to be able to bend the elements to your will and soar through the skies. It isn't enough unless you can use it to make others follow you. In a way, the Epics would be nothing without the regular people. They need someone to dominate; they need some way to show off their powers."

"I hate him," I hissed, though I hadn't meant to say it out loud. I hadn't even realized I'd been thinking it.

Prof looked at me.

"What?" I asked. "Are you going to tell me that my anger doesn't do any good?" People had tried to tell me that in the past, Martha foremost among them. She claimed the thirst for vengeance would eat me alive.

"Your emotions are your own business, son," Prof said, turning away. "I don't care *why* you fight, so long as you do fight. Maybe your anger will burn you away, but better to burn yourself away than to shrivel up beneath Steelheart's thumb." He paused. "Besides, telling you to stop would be a little like a hearth telling the oven to cool down."

I nodded. He understood. He felt it too.

"Regardless, the plan is now realigned," Prof said. "We'll strike at the wastewater treatment plant, as it's the least well guarded. The trick will be making sure Steelheart connects the attack to a rival Epic, rather than just rebels."

"Would it be so bad if people thought there was a rebellion?"

"It wouldn't draw Steelheart out, for one," Prof said. "And if he thought the people were rebelling, he'd make them pay. I won't have innocents dying in retaliation for things we've done."

"But, I mean, isn't that the point? To show the others that we can fight back? Actually, as I think about it, maybe we could set up here in Newcago for good. If we win, maybe we could lead the place once—"

"Stop."

I frowned.

"We kill Epics, son," Prof said, his voice suddenly quiet, intense. "And we're good at it. But don't get it into your mind that we're revolutionaries, that we're going to tear down what's out there and put ourselves in its place. The *moment* we start to think like that, we derail.

"We want to make others fight back. We want to inspire them. But we dare not take that power for ourselves. That's the end of it. We're killers. We'll rip Steelheart from his place and find a way to pull his heart from his chest. After that, let someone else decide what to do with the city. I want no part of it."

The ferocity of those words, soft though they were, quieted me. I didn't know how to respond. Maybe Prof did have a point, though. This was about killing Steelheart. We had to stay focused.

It still felt odd that he hadn't challenged me on my passion for vengeance. He was pretty much the first person who hadn't served me some platitude on revenge.

"Fine," I said. "But I think the sewage station is the wrong place to hit."

"Where would you go?"

"The power station."

"Too well guarded." Prof examined his notes, and I could see that he had a schematic of the power station as well, with notations around the perimeter. He'd considered it.

I got a thrill from the idea that the two of us thought along the same lines.

"If it's well guarded," I said, "then blowing it up will look that much more impressive. And we could steal one of Steelheart's power cells while we're there. We brought back a gun from Diamond, but it's dry. It needs a powerful energy source to run." I raised my mobile to the wall and uploaded the video of the gauss gun firing. The video appeared on the wall, shoving aside some of Prof's chalk writings, and played.

He watched in silence, and when it was done he nodded. "So our fake Epic will have energy powers."

"And that's why he'd destroy the power station," I said. "It's in theme." Epics liked themes and motifs.

"It's too bad that removing the power station wouldn't stop Enforcement," Prof said. "Conflux powers them directly. He powers some of the city directly too, but our intel says he does it by charging power cells that are stored here." He pulled up his schematics of the power station. "One of those cells could power this gun—they're extremely compact, and they each have more juice packed into them than should be physically possible. If we blow the station, and the rest of those cells, it will cause serious damage to the city." He nodded. "I like it. Dangerous, but I like it."

"We'll still have to hit Conflux," I said. "It would make sense, even for a rival Epic. First remove the power station, then take out the police force. Chaos. It will work particularly well if we can kill Conflux using that gun, giving off a big light show."

Prof nodded. "I'll need to do more planning," he said, raising a hand and wiping away the video. It came off like it had been drawn in chalk. He pushed aside another pile of writing and raised his stylus to start working. He stopped, however, then looked at me.

"What?" I asked.

He walked over to his Reckoner jacket, which sat on a table, and took something out from under it. He walked back and handed it to me. A glove. One of the tensors. "You've been practicing?" he asked me.

"I'm not very good yet."

"Get better. Fast. I won't have the team underpowered, and Megan can't seem to make the tensors work."

I took the glove, saying nothing, though I wanted to ask the question. *Why not you, Prof? Why do you refuse to use your own invention?* Tia's warning not to pry too much made me hold my tongue.

"I confronted Nightwielder," I blurted out, only now remembering the reason I'd come to talk with Prof.

"What?"

"He was there, at Diamond's place. I went out and pretended to be one of Diamond's helpers. I . . . used a UV fingerprint scanner he had to confirm Nightwielder's weakness."

Prof studied me, his face betraying no emotions. "You've had a busy afternoon. I assume you did this at great risk to the entire team?"

"I . . . Yes." Better he heard it from me, rather than Megan, who would undoubtedly report—in great detail—of how I'd deviated from the plan.

"You show promise," Prof said. "You take risks; you get results. You have proof of what you said about Nightwielder?"

"I got a recording."

"Impressive."

"Megan wasn't very happy with it."

"Megan liked the way things were before," Prof said. "Adding a new team member always upends the dynamic. Besides, I think she's worried you're showing her up. She's still smarting from being unable to make the tensors work."

Megan? Worried that *I* was showing *her* up? Prof must not know her very well.

"Out with you, then," Prof said. "I want you up to speed with the tensor by the time we hit the power plant. And don't worry too much about Megan . . ."

"I won't. Thank you."

". . . worry about me."

I froze.

Prof started writing on the board and didn't turn back when he spoke, but his words were sharp. "You got results by risking the lives of my people. I assume nobody was hurt, otherwise you'd have mentioned it by now. You show promise, as I said. But if you brashly get one of my people killed, David Charleston, Megan will not be your problem. I won't leave enough of you for her to bother with."

I swallowed. My mouth had suddenly gone dry.

"I trust you with their lives," Prof said, still writing, "and them with yours. Don't betray that trust, son. Keep your impulses in check. Don't just act because you can; act because it's the right thing to do. If you keep that in mind, you'll be all right."

"Yes sir," I said, leaving with a quick step out the cloth-covered doorway.

21

"HOW'S the signal?" Prof asked through the earpiece.

I raised my hand to my ear. "Good," I said. I wore my mobile—newly tuned to the Reckoner mobiles and made completely secure from Steelheart's prying—on my wrist mount. I'd also been given one of the jackets. It looked like a thin black and red sports-style jacket—though it had wiring all around the inside lining and a little power pack sewn into the back. That was the part that would extend a concussion field around me if I was hit hard.

Prof had built it for me himself. He said it would protect me from a short fall or a small explosion, but I shouldn't try jumping off any cliffs or getting shot in the face. Not like I was intending to do either.

I wore it proudly. I'd never been officially told I was a member of the team, but these two changes seemed essentially the same thing. Of course, going on this mission was probably a good indication too.

I glanced at my mobile; it showed that I was only on the line with Prof. Tapping the screen could move me to a line to everyone in the team, cycle me to a single member, or let me pick a few of them to talk to.

"You in position?" Prof asked.

"We are." I stood in a dark tunnel of pure steel, the only light that of my mobile and Megan's up ahead. She wore a pair of dark jeans and her brown leather jacket, open at the front, over a tight T-shirt. She was inspecting the ceiling.

"Prof," I said softly, turning away, "you sure I can't pair up with Cody for this mission?"

"Cody and Tia are interference," Prof said. "We've been over this, son."

"Maybe I could go with Abraham, then. Or you." I glanced over my shoulder, then spoke even more softly. "She doesn't really like me much."

"I won't have two members of my crew not getting along," Prof said sternly. "You will learn to work together. Megan is a professional. It'll be fine."

Yes, she's professional, I thought. *Too professional.* But Prof wasn't hearing any of it.

I took a deep breath. Part of my nervousness, I knew, was because of the job. One week had passed since my conversation with Prof, and the rest of the Reckoners had agreed that hitting the power station—and imitating a rival Epic while doing so—was the best plan.

Today was the day. We'd sneak in and destroy Newcago's power plant. This would be my first real Reckoner operation. I was finally a member of the team. I didn't want to be the weak one.

"You good, son?" Prof asked.

"Yeah."

"We're moving. Set your timer."

I set my mobile for a ten-minute countdown. Prof and Abraham were going to break in first on the other side of the station, where all the huge equipment was. They'd work their way upward, setting charges. At the ten-minute mark, Megan and I would go in and steal a power cell to use with the gauss gun. Tia and Cody would come in last, entering through the hole Prof and Abraham had made. They were a support team; ready to move and help us extract if we needed to, but otherwise hanging back and giving us information and guidance.

I took another deep breath. On the hand opposite my mobile, I wore the black leather tensor, with glowing green strips from the fingertips to the palm. Megan eyed me as I strode up to the end of the tunnel that Abraham had dug the day before during a scouting mission.

I showed her the countdown.

"You're sure you can do this?" she asked me. There was a hint of skepticism in her voice, though her face was impassive.

"I've gotten a lot better with the tensors," I said.

"You forget that I've watched most of your practice sessions."

"Cody didn't need those shoes," I said.

She raised an eyebrow at me.

"I can do it," I said, stepping up to the end of the tunnel, where Abraham had left a pillar of steel jutting from the ground. It was short enough that I could step up on it to reach the low ceiling. The clock ticked down. We didn't speak. I mentally sounded out a few ways to start conversation, but each one died on my lips as I opened my mouth. Each time I was confronted by Megan's glassy stare. She didn't want to chat. She wanted to do the job.

Why do I even care? I thought, looking up at the ceiling. *Other than that first day, she's never shown me anything other than coldness and the occasional bit of disdain.*

Yet . . . there was something about her. More than the fact that she was beautiful, more than the fact that she carried tiny grenades in her top—which I still thought was awesome, by the way.

There had been girls at the Factory. But, like everyone else, they were complacent. They'd just call it living their lives, but they were afraid. Afraid of Enforcement, afraid that an Epic would kill them.

Megan didn't seem afraid of anything, ever. She didn't play games with men, fluttering her eyes, saying things she didn't mean. She did what needed to be done, and she was very good at it. I found that *incredibly* attractive. I wished I could explain that to her. But getting the words out of my mouth felt like trying to push marbles through a keyhole.

"I—" I began.

My mobile beeped.

"Go," she said, looking upward.

Trying to tell myself I wasn't relieved by the interruption, I raised my hands up to the ceiling and closed my eyes. I *was* getting better with the tensor. I still wasn't as good as Abraham, but I wasn't an embarrassment any longer. At least not most of the time. I pressed my hand flat against the metal ceiling of the tunnel and pushed, holding my hand in place as the vibrations began.

The buzzing was like the eager purr of a muscle car that had just been started, but left in neutral. That was another of Cody's metaphors for it; I'd said the sensation felt like an unbalanced washing machine filled with a hundred epileptic chimpanzees. Pretty proud of that one.

I pushed and kept my hand steady, humming softly to myself in the same tone as the tensor. That helped me focus. The others didn't do it, and they didn't always have to keep their hand pressed against a wall either. I eventually wanted to learn to do it like they did, but this would work for now.

The vibrations built, but I contained them, held them in my hand. Kept hold of them until it felt like my fingernails were going to rattle free. Then I pulled my hand back and *pushed* somehow.

Imagine holding a swarm of bees in your mouth, then spitting them out and trying to keep them pointed in a single direction by the sheer force of your breath and will. It's kind of like that. My hand flew back and I launched the half-musical vibrations away, into the ceiling, which rattled and shook with a quiet hum. Steel dust fell down around my arm, showering to the ground below like someone had taken a cheese grater to a refrigerator.

Megan crossed her arms and watched, a single eyebrow raised. I prepared myself for some cold, indifferent comment. She nodded and said, "Nice work."

"Yeah, well, you know, I've been practicing a lot. Hitting the old wall-vaporizing gym."

"The what?" She frowned as she pulled over the ladder we'd brought with us.

"Never mind," I said, climbing up the ladder and peeking my head into the basement of Station Seven, the power station. I'd never been inside any of the city stations, of course. They were like bunkers, with high steel walls and fences surrounding them. Steelheart liked to keep things under a watchful eye; a place like this wouldn't just be a power station but would have government offices on the upper floors as well. All carefully fenced, guarded, and observed.

The basement, fortunately, had no cameras watching it. Most of those were in the hallways.

Megan handed me my rifle, and I climbed out into the room above. We were in a storage chamber, dark save for a few of those glowing "always on" lights that places tend to . . . well, always leave on. I moved to the wall and tapped my mobile. "We're in," I said softly.

"Good," Cody's voice came back.

I blushed. "Sorry. I meant to send that to Prof."

"You did. He told me to watch over y'all. Turn on the video feed from your earpiece."

The earpiece was one of those wraparound kinds and had a little camera sticking out over my ear. I tapped a few times on my mobile screen, activating it.

"Nice," Cody said. "Tia and I have set up here at Prof's entrance point." Prof liked contingencies, and that usually meant leaving a person or two back to create diversions or enact plans if the main teams got pinned down.

"I don't have much to do here," Cody continued, his Southern drawl as thick as ever, "so I'm going to bother you."

"Thanks," I said, glancing back at Megan as she climbed up out of the hole.

"Don't mention it, lad. And stop looking down Megan's shirt."

"I'm not—"

"Just teasing. I hope you keep doing it. It'll be fun to watch her shoot you in the foot when she catches you."

I looked away pointedly. Fortunately it didn't appear that Cody had included Megan in that particular conversation. I actually found myself breathing a little easier, knowing that Cody was watching over us. Megan and I were the two newest members of the team; if anyone could use coaching it would be us.

Megan carried our pack on her back, filled with the things we'd need for the infiltration. She had out a handgun, which honestly would be more useful in close quarters than my rifle. "Ready?" she asked.

I nodded.

"How much 'improvising' do I have to be ready for from you today?" she asked.

"Only as much as needed," I grumbled, raising my hand to the wall. "If I knew when it would be needed, it wouldn't be improvising, would it? It would be planning."

She chuckled. "A foreign concept to you."

"Foreign? Did you not see all the notebooks of plans I brought to the team? You know, the ones we all almost died retrieving?"

She turned away, not looking at me, and her posture grew stiff.

Sparking woman, I thought. *Try making some sense for once.* I shook my head, placing my hand against the wall.

One of the reasons that the city stations were considered

impregnable was because of the security. Cameras in all of the hallways and stairwells; I had thought we'd hack into security and change the camera feeds. Prof said we'd certainly hack the feeds to watch them, but changing those feeds to cover sneaking rarely worked as well as it did in the old movies. Steelheart didn't hire stupid security officers, and they'd notice if their video looped. Besides, soldiers patrolled the hallways.

However, there was a much simpler way to make sure we weren't seen. We just had to stay out of the hallways. There weren't cameras in most of the rooms, as the research and experiments done there were kept secret, even from the security watching the building. Besides, logically, if you kept really close watch on all the hallways, you could catch intruders. How else would people move from room to room?

I raised my hand and, with some concentration, vaporized a four-foot-wide hole in the wall. I glanced through it, shining my mobile. I'd ruined some computer equipment on the wall, and I had to shove a desk out of the way to get in, but there was nobody inside. At this hour of the night much of the station was unoccupied, and Tia had drawn up our path very carefully, with the goal of minimizing the chances that we'd run into anyone.

After we crawled through, Megan took something from the pack and placed it on the wall beside the hole I'd made. It had a small red light that blinked ominously. We were to place explosive charges beside each hole we created so that when we detonated the building, it would be impossible to find out about the tensors from the wreckage.

"Keep moving," Cody said. "Every minute y'all are in there is a minute longer that someone might wander into a room and wonder where all those bloody holes came from."

"I'm on it," I said, sliding my finger across my mobile's screen and bringing up Tia's map. If we continued straight ahead through three rooms, we'd reach an emergency stairwell with fewer security cameras. We could avoid those, hopefully, by looping through some walls and moving up two floors. Then we needed to make our way into the main storage chamber for energy cells. We'd set the rest of our charges, steal a power cell or two, and bolt.

"Are you talking to yourself?" Megan asked, watching the door, her gun at chest level and arm straight and ready.

"Tell her you're listening to ear demons," Cody suggested. "Always works for me."

"Cody is on the line," I said, working on the next wall. "Giving me a delightful running commentary. And telling me about ear demons."

That almost provoked a smile from her. I swore I saw one, for a moment at least.

"Ear demons are totally real," Cody said. "They're what make microphones like these ones work. They're also what tell you to eat the last slice of pie when you know Tia wanted it. Hold for a second. I'm patched into the security system, and there's someone coming down the hall. Hold."

I froze, then hastily quieted the tensor.

"Yeah, they're entering that room next to you," Cody said. "Lights were already on. Might be someone else in it too—can't tell from the security feed. Y'all might have just dodged a bullet. Or rather, dodged having to dodge quite a few of them."

"What do we do?" I asked tensely.

"About Cody?" Megan asked, frowning.

"Cody, could you just patch her in too?" I asked, exasperated.

"You really want to talk about her cleavage when she's on the line?" Cody asked innocently.

"No! I mean. Don't talk about that at all."

"Fine. Megan, there's someone in the next room."

"Options?" she asked, calm.

"We can wait, but the lights were already on. My guess is some late-night scientists still working."

Megan raised her gun.

"Uh . . . ," I said.

"No, lass," Cody said. "You know how Prof feels about that. Shoot guards if you have to. Nobody else." The plan included pulling an alarm and evacuating the building before we detonated our charges.

"I wouldn't have to shoot the people next door," Megan said calmly.

"And what else would you do, lass?" Cody asked. "Knock them out, then leave them for when we blow up the building?"

Megan hesitated.

"Okay," Cody said. "Tia says there's another way. You're going to have to go up an elevator shaft, though."

"Lovely," Megan said.

We hurried back to the first room we'd come through. Tia uploaded a new map for me, with tensor points, and I got to work. I was a little more nervous this time. Were we going to find random scientists and workers just hanging around all over? What *would* we do if someone surprised us? What if it was some innocent custodian?

For the first time in my life, I found myself nearly as worried about what I might end up doing as I was about what someone might do to me. It was an uncomfortable situation. What we were doing was, basically, terrorism.

But we're the good guys, I told myself, breaking open the wall and letting Megan slide through first. Of course, what terrorist *didn't* think he or she was the good guy? We were doing something important, but what would that matter to the family of the cleaning woman we accidentally killed? As I hastened through the next darkened room—this one was a lab chamber, with some beakers and other glasswork set up—I had trouble shaking off these questions.

And so, I focused on Steelheart. That awful, hateful sneer. Standing there with the gun he'd taken from my father, barrel pointed down at the inferior human.

That image worked. I could forget everything else when I thought of it. I didn't have all the answers, but at least I had a goal. Revenge. Who cared if it would eat me up inside and leave me hollow? So long as it drove me to make life better for everyone else. Prof understood that. I understood it too.

We reached the elevator shaft without incident, entering it through a storage room that bordered it. I vaporized a large hole in the wall, and then Megan poked her head in and looked up the tall, dark shaft. "So, Cody, there's supposed to be a way up?"

"Sure. Handholds on the sides. They put them in all elevator shafts."

"Looks like someone forgot to inform Steelheart of that," I said, looking in beside Megan. "These walls are completely slick. No ladder or anything like that. No ropes or cords either."

Cody cursed.

"So we're back to going the other way?" Megan asked.

I scanned the walls again. The blackness seemed to extend forever above and below us. "We could wait for the elevator to come."

"The elevators have cameras," Cody said.

"So we ride on top of it," I said.

"And alert the people inside when we drop onto it?" Megan asked.

"We just wait for one that doesn't have anyone in it," I said. "Elevators are empty about half the time, right? They're responding to calls people make."

"All right," Cody said. "Prof and Abraham have hit a small snag—waiting for a room to clear out so they can move through. Prof says you have five minutes to wait. If nothing happens by then, we're scrapping the job."

"Okay," I said, feeling a stab of disappointment.

"I'm going to run some visuals for them," Cody said. "I'll be off-line from you for a bit; call me if you need me. I'll watch the elevator. If it moves, I'll let you know." The line clicked as Cody switched frequencies, and we started waiting.

We both sat quietly, straining to hear any sounds of the elevator moving, though we'd never spot it before Cody did with his video feeds.

"So . . . how often is it like this?" I asked after a few minutes of kneeling beside Megan, stuck in the room beside the hole I'd burrowed into the side of the elevator shaft.

"Like what?" she asked.

"The waiting."

"More than you'd think," she said. "The jobs we do, they're often all about timing. Good timing requires a lot of waiting around." She glanced at my hand, and I found that I'd been nervously tapping the side of the wall.

I forced myself to stop.

"You sit," she said, voice growing softer, "and you wait. You go over and over the plan, picture it in your mind. Then it usually goes wrong anyway."

I eyed her suspiciously.

"What?" she asked.

"The thing you just said. It's exactly what I think too."

"So?"

"So if something usually goes wrong, why are you always on my back about improvising?"

She grew thin-lipped.

"No," I said. "It's time you leveled with me, Megan. Not just about this mission, but about everything. What is with you? Why do you treat me like you hate me? *You* were the one who originally spoke up for me when I wanted to join! You sounded impressed with me at first—Prof might never have listened to my plan at all if you hadn't said what you did. But since then you've acted like I was a gorilla at your buffet."

"A . . . *what*?"

"Gorilla at your buffet. You know . . . eating all your food? Making you annoyed? That kind of thing?"

"You're a very special person, David."

"Yeah, I take a specialness pill each morning. Look, Megan, I'm *not* letting go of this. The whole time I've been with the Reckoners, it seems like I've been doing something that bothers you. Well, what is it? What made you turn on me like that?"

She looked away.

"Is it my face?" I asked. "Because that's the only thing I can think of. I mean, you were all for me after the Fortuity hit. Maybe it's my face. I don't think it's too bad a face, as far as faces go, but it does look kind of stupid sometimes when I—"

"It's not your face," she interrupted.

"I didn't think it was, but I need you to talk to me. Say something." *Because I think you're hotter than hell and I can't understand what went wrong.* Fortunately I stopped myself from saying that part out loud. I also kept my eyes straight at her head, just in case Cody was watching in.

She said nothing.

"Well?" I prompted.

"Five minutes is up," she said, checking her mobile.

"I'm not going to let this go so easily, this—"

"Five minutes is up," Cody suddenly said, cutting in. "Sorry, kids. This mission is a bust. Nobody is moving the elevators."

"Can't you send one for us?" I asked.

Cody chuckled. "We're tapped into the security feed, lad, but that's a far cry from being able to control things in the building. If Tia could hack us in that far, we could blow the building from the inside by overpowering the plants or something."

"Oh." I looked up the cavernous shaft. It resembled an enormous throat, stretching upward . . . one we needed to get up . . . which made us . . .

Bad analogy. Very bad. Regardless, there was a twisting feeling in my gut. I hated the idea of backing down. Above lay the path to destroying Steelheart. Behind lay more waiting, more planning. I'd been planning for years.

"Oh no," Megan said.

"What?" I asked absently.

"You're going to improvise, aren't you?"

I reached out into the shaft with the hand that wore the tensor, pressed it flat against the wall, and began a small vibrative burst. Abraham had taught me to make bursts of different sizes; he said that a master with the tensors could control the vibrations, leaving patterns or even shapes in your target.

I pushed my hand hard, flat, feeling the glove shake. It wasn't just the glove, though. It was my whole hand. That had confused me at first. It seemed like *I* was creating the power, not the glove—the glove just helped shape the blast somehow.

I couldn't fail at this. If I did the operation was over. I should have felt stress at that, but I didn't. For some reason, I was realizing, when things got really, really tense I found it easier to relax.

Steelheart looming above my father. A gunshot. I *would not back down*.

The glove vibrated; dust fell away from the wall in a little patch around my hand. I slipped my fingers forward and felt what I'd done.

"A handhold," Megan said softly, shining the light of her mobile.

"What, really?" Cody asked. "Turn on your camera, lass." A moment later he whistled. "You've been holding back on me, David. I didn't think you were nearly practiced enough to do something like that. I might have suggested it myself if I'd thought you could."

I moved my hand to the side and made another handhold, placing it beside the other in the shaft just next to the hole in the wall. I made two more for my feet, then swung out of the hole in the wall and into the elevator shaft, placing my hands and feet in the handholds.

I stretched up and made another set of holds above. I climbed up, rifle slung over my shoulder. I did *not* look down but made another set of holds and continued. Climbing and carving with the tensor wasn't by any means easy, but I was able to shape the tensor blasts to leave a ridge at the front of each handhold, making them easy to grip.

"Can Prof and Abraham stall for a little longer?" Megan asked from below. "David seems to be working at a good clip, but it might take us about fifteen minutes to get up."

"Tia's calculating," Cody said.

"Well, I'm going after David," Megan said. She sounded muffled. I glanced over my shoulder; she'd wrapped a scarf around her face.

The dust from the handholds; she doesn't want to breathe it in. Smart. I was having trouble avoiding it, and steel dust did *not* seem like a smart thing to inhale. Abraham said tensor dust wasn't as dangerous as it seemed, but I still didn't think it would be a good idea, so I ducked my head and held my breath each time I made a new hole.

"I'm impressed," a voice said in my ear. Prof's voice. It nearly made me leap in shock, which would have been a very bad thing. He must have patched into my visual feed with his mobile, and could see the images made by the camera on my earpiece.

"Those holes are crisp and well formed," Prof continued. "Keep at it and you'll soon be as good as Abraham. You might already have passed up Cody."

"You sound worried about something," I said between making handholds.

"Not troubled. Just surprised."

"It needed to be done," I said, grunting as I pulled myself up past another floor.

Prof was silent for a few moments. "That it did. Look, we can't have you extract down this same route. It will take too long, so you'll have to go out another way. Tia will let you know where. Wait for the first explosion."

"Affirmative," I said.

"And, David," Prof added.

"Yeah?"

"Good work."

I smiled, pulling myself up again.

We continued at it, climbing up the elevator shaft. I worried that the elevator would come down at some point, though if it did it should miss us by a few inches. We were on the side of the shaft where there *should* have been a ladder. They just hadn't installed one.

Perhaps Steelheart has watched the same movies that we have, I thought with a grimace as we finally passed the second floor. One more to go.

My mobile clicked in my ear. I glanced at it on my wrist— someone had muted our channel.

"I don't like what you've done to the team," Megan called up, her voice muffled.

I glanced over my shoulder at her. She wore the backpack with our equipment in it, and her nose and mouth were covered with the scarf. Those eyes of hers glared at me, softly lit by the glow of the mobile strapped to her forearm. Beautiful eyes, peeking out above the shroud of a scarf.

With a huge, black pit stretching behind her. Whoa. I lurched woozily.

"Slontze," she called. "Stay focused."

"You're the one who said something!" I whispered, turning back around. "What do you mean you don't like what I did to the team?"

"Before you showed up we were going to move out of Newcago," Megan said from below. "Hit Fortuity, then leave. You made us stay."

I continued climbing. "But—"

"Oh, just shut up and let me talk for once."

I shut up.

"I joined the Reckoners to kill Epics who deserved it," Megan continued. "Newcago is one of the safest, most stable places in the entire Fractured States. I don't think we should be killing Steelheart, and I don't like how you've hijacked the team to fight your own personal war against him. He's brutal, yes, but he's doing a better job than most Epics. He doesn't deserve to die."

The words stunned me. She didn't think we should kill Steelheart? He didn't *deserve* to die? It was insanity. I resisted the urge to look down again. "Can I talk now?" I asked, making another pair of handholds.

"Okay, fine."

"Are you *crazy*? Steelheart is a monster."

"Yes. I'll admit that. But he's an *effective* monster. Look, what are we doing today?"

"Destroying a power plant."

"And how many cities out there still have power plants?" she asked. "Do you even know?"

I kept climbing.

"I grew up in Portland," she said. "Do you know what happened there?"

I did, though I didn't say. It hadn't been good.

"The turf wars between Epics left the city in ruins," Megan continued, her voice softer now. "There is nothing left, David. *Nothing.* All of Oregon is a wasteland; even the trees are gone. There aren't any power plants, sewage treatment plants, or grocery stores. That was what Newcago would have become, if Steelheart hadn't stepped in."

I continued climbing, sweat tickling the back of my neck. I thought about the change in Megan—she'd grown cold toward me right after I'd first talked about taking down Steelheart. The times when she'd treated me the worst had been when we'd been making breakthroughs. When we'd gone to fetch my plans and when I'd found out how to kill Nightwielder.

It hadn't been my "improvising" that had set her against me. It had been my intentions. My successes in getting the team to target Steelheart.

"I don't want to be the cause of something like Portland

happening again," Megan continued. "Yes, Steelheart is terrible. But he's a kind of terrible that people can live with."

"So why haven't you quit?" I asked. "Why are you here?"

"Because I'm a Reckoner," she said. "And it's not my job to contradict Prof. I'll do my job, Knees. I'll do it well. But this time, I think we're making a mistake."

She was using that nickname of hers for me again. It actually seemed like a good sign, as she only seemed to use it when she was less annoyed at me. It was kind of affectionate, wasn't it? I just wished the nickname hadn't been a reference to something so embarrassing. Why not . . . Super-Great-Shot? That kind of rolled off the tongue, didn't it?

We climbed the rest of the way in silence. Megan turned our audio feed to the rest of the team back on, which seemed an indication that she thought the conversation was over. Maybe it was—I certainly didn't know what else to say. How could she possibly think that living under Steelheart was a *good* thing?

I thought of the other kids at the Factory, of the people in the understreets. I guessed that many of them thought the same way— they'd come here knowing that Steelheart was a monster, but they still thought life was better in Newcago than in other places.

Only they were complacent—Megan was anything but that. She was active, incredible, capable. How could *she* think like they did? It shook what I knew of the world—at least, what I thought I knew. The Reckoners were supposed to be different.

What if she was right?

"Oh *sparks*!" Cody suddenly said in my ear.

"What?"

"Y'all've got trouble, lad. It's—"

At that moment the doors to the elevator shaft just above—the ones on the third floor—slid open. Two uniformed guards stepped up to the ledge and peered down into the darkness.

22

"I'M telling you, I heard something," one of the guards said, squinting downward. He seemed to be looking right at me. But it was dark in the elevator shaft—darker than I'd thought it would be, with the doors open.

"I don't see anything," the other said. His voice echoed softly.

The first pulled his flashlight off his belt.

My heart lurched. *Uh-oh.*

I pressed my hand against the wall; it was the only thing I could think to do. The tensor started vibrating, and I tried to concentrate, but it was *hard* with them up there. The flashlight clicked.

"See? Hear that?"

"Sounds like the furnace," the second guard said drily.

My hand rattling against the side of the wall did have a kind of mechanical sound to it. I grimaced but kept on. The light of the flashlight shone in the shaft. I nearly lost control of the vibration.

There was no way they could have missed seeing me with that light. They were too close.

"Nothing there," the guard said with a grunt.

What? I looked up. Somehow, despite being only a short distance away, it seemed they hadn't seen me. I frowned, confused.

"Huh," the other guard said. "I do hear a sound, though."

"It's coming from . . . you know," the first guard said.

"Oh," the other said. "Right."

The first guard stuffed the flashlight back into place on his belt. How could he have missed seeing me? He'd shined it right in my direction.

The two backed away from the opening and let the doors slide shut.

What in Calamity's fires? I thought. Could they have actually missed us in the darkness?

My tensor went off.

I'd been preparing to vaporize a pocket into the wall to hide in— get us out of their line of fire if it came to that. But because I wasn't focusing the blast, I took a large chunk out of the wall in front of me, and in an instant my handhold disappeared. I grabbed at the side of the hole I'd made, barely finding a grip.

A burst of dust fell back over me and cascaded over Megan in an enormous shower. Holding tight to the side of the hole, I glanced down to find her glaring up at me, blinking dust from her eyes. Her hand actually seemed to be inching toward her gun.

Calamity! I thought with a start. Her scarf and skin were dusted silver, and her eyes were *angry*. I don't think I'd ever seen an expression like that in a person's eyes before—not directed at me at least. It was like I could feel the hate coming off her.

Her hand kept inching toward the handgun at her side.

"M-Megan?" I asked.

Her hand stopped. I didn't know what I'd seen, but it was gone in a moment. She blinked, and her expression softened. "You need to watch what you're destroying, Knees," she snapped, reaching up to wipe some of the dust off her face.

"Yeah," I said, then looked back up into the hole I was hanging onto. "Hey, there's a room here." I raised my mobile, shining light into it to get a better look.

It was a small room—a few orderly desks outfitted with computer terminals lined one wall and filing cabinets ran along the other. There were two doors, one a reinforced metal security door with a keypad.

"Megan, there's definitely a room here. And it doesn't look like there's anyone in it. Come on." I pulled myself up and crawled through.

As soon as I was in I helped Megan up and out of the shaft. She hesitated before taking my hand, then once she was out she walked past me without a word. She seemed to have gone back to being cold toward me, maybe even a little mean.

I knelt beside the hole back into the elevator shaft. I couldn't shake the feeling that something very strange had just happened. First the guard hadn't seen us, then Megan went from opening up to me to totally closing off in seconds flat. Was she having second thoughts about what she'd shared with me? Was she worried I'd tell Prof that she didn't support killing Steelheart?

"What *is* this place?" Megan said from the center of the small room. The ceiling was low enough that she almost had to stoop—I would definitely have to. She unwrapped her scarf, releasing a puff of metal dust, grimaced, and then began shaking out her clothing.

"No idea," I said, checking my mobile and the map Tia had uploaded. "The room's not on the map."

"Low ceilings," Megan said. "Security door with a code. Interesting." She tossed her pack to me. "Put an explosive on the hole you made. I'll check things out here."

I fished in the pack for an explosive as she cracked open the door that didn't have the security pad and then stepped through.

I attached the small device to the hole I'd made, then noticed some exposed wires in the lower part of the wall.

I followed them down and was prying up a section of the floor when Megan came back.

"There are two other rooms like this," she said. "No people in them, small and built up against the elevator shaft. Best I can figure, this is where furnace equipment and elevator maintenance is supposed to be, but they hid some rooms here instead and took them off the building schematics. I wonder if there's space between other floors—if there are rooms hidden there too."

"Look at this," I said, pointing at what I'd discovered.

She knelt beside me and eyed the wall and the wiring.

"Explosives," she said.

"The room's *already* set to blow," I said. "Creepy, eh?"

"Whatever is in here," Megan said, "it must be important. Important enough that it's worth destroying the entire power plant to keep it from being discovered."

We both looked up at the computers.

"What are you two doing?" Cody's voice came back onto our feed.

"We found this room," I said, "and—"

"Keep moving," Cody said, cutting me off. "Prof and Abraham just ran into some guards and were forced to shoot them. The guards are down, bodies hidden, but they'll be missed soon. If we're lucky we'll have a few minutes before someone realizes they're not on their patrol anymore."

I cursed, fishing in my pocket.

"What's that?" Megan asked.

"One of the universal blasting caps I got from Diamond," I said. "I want to see if they work." I nervously used my electrical tape to stick the little round nub on the explosives we'd found under the floor. In my pocket I carried its detonator—the one that looked like a pen.

"By the map Tia gave us," Megan said, "we're only two rooms

over from the storage area with the energy cells, but we're a little below it."

We shared a glance, then split up to scour the hidden room. We might not have much time, but we needed to at least *try* to find out what information this place contained. She pulled open a filing cabinet and grabbed a handful of folders. In an instant I was up and opening desk drawers. One had a couple of data chips. I grabbed them, waved them at Megan, then tossed them in her bag. She threw the folders in, then searched another desk while I raised a hand to the right wall and made us a hole.

Since the hidden room was halfway between two floors, I wasn't certain how that related to the rest of the building. I made a hole in the wall in the direction we wanted to go, but I made it near the ceiling.

That opened up into a room on the third floor, but near the floor. So there was some overlap between our hidden room and the third floor. With a glance at the map, I could see how they'd hidden the room. On the schematics the elevator shaft was shown as slightly bigger than it actually was. It also included a maintenance shaft that wasn't actually there—and that explained the lack of handholds in the elevator. The builders assumed the maintenance shaft would provide a way to service the elevator, not knowing that the hidden room would actually go in that space.

Megan and I climbed through the hole and onto the third floor. We crossed that room—a conference room of some sort—and passed through another, which was a monitoring station. I vaporized the wall and opened a hole into a long, low-ceilinged storage area. This was our target: the room where the power cells were kept.

"We're in," Megan said to Cody as we slipped inside. The room was filled with shelves, and on them were various pieces of electrical equipment, none of which we wanted.

We went in different directions, searching hastily.

"Awesome," Cody said. "The power cells should be in there

somewhere. Look for cylinders about a handspan wide and about as tall as a boot."

I spied some large storage lockers on the far wall, with locks on the doors. "Might be in here," I said to Megan, moving toward them. I made quick work of the locks with the tensor and pulled the doors open as she joined me. Inside one was a tall column of green cylinders stacked on top of one another on their sides. Each cylinder looked vaguely like a cross between a very small beer keg and a car battery.

"Those are the power cells," Cody said, sounding relieved. "I was half worried there wouldn't be any. Good thing I brought my four-leaf clover on this operation."

"Four-leaf clover?" Megan said with a snort as she fished something out of her pack.

"Sure. From the homeland."

"That's the Irish, Cody, not the Scottish."

"I know," Cody said without missing a beat. "I had to kill an Irish dude to get mine."

I pulled out one of the power cells. "They aren't as heavy as I thought they'd be," I said. "Are we sure these will have enough juice to power the gauss gun? That thing needs a *lot* of energy."

"Those cells were charged by Conflux," Cody said in my ear. "They're more powerful by magnitudes than anything we could make or buy. If they won't work, nothing will. Grab as many as you can carry."

They might not have been as heavy as I'd thought, but they were still kind of bulky. We took the rest of the equipment out of Megan's pack, then retrieved the smaller sack we had stuffed in the bottom. I managed to stuff four of the cells in the pack while Megan transferred the rest of our equipment—a few explosive charges, some rope, and some ammunition—to her smaller sack. There were also some lab coats for disguises. I left these out—I suspected we'd need them to escape.

"How are Prof and Abraham?" I asked.

"On their way out," Cody said.

"And our extraction?" I asked. "Prof said we shouldn't go back down the elevator shaft."

"You have your lab coats?" Cody asked.

"Sure," Megan said. "But if we go in the hallways, they might record our faces."

"That's a risk we'll have to take," Cody said. "First explosion is a go in two minutes."

We threw on the lab coats, and I squatted down and let Megan help me put on the backpack with the power cells. It was heavy, but I could still move reasonably well. Megan threw on her lab coat. It looked good on her, but pretty much anything would. She swung her own lighter pack over her shoulder, then eyed my rifle.

"It can be disassembled," I explained as I pulled the stock from the rifle, then popped out the magazine and removed the cartridge from the chamber. I slid on the safety just in case, then stuffed the pieces in her sack.

The coats were embroidered with Station Seven's logo, and we both had fake security badges to go with them. The disguises would never have worked getting us in—security was far too tight—but in a moment of chaos, they should get us out.

The building shook with an ominous rumble—explosion number one. That was mostly to prompt an evacuation rather than to inflict any real damage.

"Go!" Cody yelled in our ears.

I vaporized the lock on the door to the room and the two of us burst out into the hallway. People were peeking out of doors—it seemed to be a busy floor, even at night. Some of the people were cleaning staff in blue overalls, but others were technicians in lab coats.

"Explosion!" I did my best to seem panicked. "Someone's attacking the building!"

The chaos started immediately, and we were soon swept up into the crowd fleeing from the building. About thirty seconds later, Cody triggered the second explosion, on an upper floor. The ground trembled and people in the hallway around us screamed, glancing at the ceiling. Some of the dozen or so people clutched small computers or briefcases.

There wasn't actually anything to be frightened of. These initial explosions had been set in unpopulated locations that wouldn't bring down the building. There would be four of those early blasts, and they'd been placed to shepherd all the civilians out of the structure. Then the real explosions could begin.

We made a hasty flight through hallways and down stairwells, being careful to keep our heads down. Something felt odd about the place, and as we ran I realized what it was. The building was clean. The floors, the walls, the rooms . . . too clean. It had been too dark for me to notice it when we were making our way in, but in the light, it seemed stark to me. The understreets weren't ever this clean. It didn't feel right for everything to be so scrubbed, so neat.

As we ran it became clear that the place was big enough that any one employee wouldn't know everyone else who worked there, and though our intelligence said that the security officers had the faces of all employees in portfolios that they checked against security feeds, no one challenged us.

Most of the security officers were running with the growing crowd, just as worried about the explosions as everyone else, and that dampened my fears even more.

As a group we flooded down the last flight of stairs and burst out into the lobby. "What's going on?" a security officer yelled. He was standing by the exit with his gun out and aimed. "Did anyone see anything?"

"An Epic!" Megan said breathlessly. "Wearing green. I saw him walking through the building throwing out blasts of energy!"

The third explosion went off, shaking the building. It was followed by a series of smaller explosions. Other groups of people flooded out of adjacent stairwells and from the ground-floor hallways.

The guard cursed, then did the smart thing. He ran too. He wouldn't be expected to face an Epic—indeed, he could get in trouble for doing it, even if that Epic was working against Steelheart. Ordinary men left Epics alone, end of story. In the Fractured States that was a law greater than any other.

We burst out of the building and onto the grounds. I glanced back to see trails of smoke rising from the enormous structure. Even as I watched, another series of small explosions went off in an upper row of windows, each one flashing green. Prof and Abraham hadn't just planted bombs, they'd planted a light show.

"It *is* an Epic," a woman near me breathed. "Who would be so foolish . . ."

I flashed a smile at Megan, and we joined the flood of people running to the gates in the wall surrounding the grounds. The guards there tried to hold people in, but when the next explosion went off they gave up and opened the gates. Megan and I followed the others out into the dark streets of the city, leaving the smoldering building behind.

"Security cameras are still up," Cody reported on the open channel to everyone. "Building is still evacuating."

"Hold the last explosions," Prof said calmly. "But blow the leaflets."

There was a soft pop from behind, and I knew that the leaflets proclaiming that a new Epic had come to town had been blasted from the upper floors and were floating down to the city. Limelight, we were calling him—the name I'd chosen. The flyer was filled with propaganda calling Steelheart out, claiming that Limelight was the new master of Newcago.

Megan and I were to our car before Cody gave the all clear. I climbed in the driver's side, and Megan followed through the same door, shoving me over into the passenger seat.

"I can drive," I said.

"You destroyed the last car going around one block, Knees," she said, starting the vehicle. "Knocked down two signs, I believe. And I think I saw the remains of some trash cans as we fled." There was a faint smile on her lips.

"Wasn't my fault," I said, thrilled by our success as I looked back at Station Seven rising into the dark sky. "Those trash cans were totally asking for it. Cheeky slontzes."

"I'm triggering the big one," Cody said in my ear.

A line of blasts sounded in the building, including the explosives Megan and I had placed, I guessed. The building shook, fires burning out the windows.

"Huh," Cody said, confused. "Didn't bring it down."

"Good enough," Prof answered. "Evidence of our incursion is gone, and the station won't be operating anytime soon."

"Yeah," Cody said. I could hear the disappointment in his voice. "I just wish it had been a little more dramatic."

I pulled the pen detonator from my pocket. It probably wouldn't do anything—the explosives we'd placed on the walls had probably already set off the ones in the floor. I clicked the top of the pen anyway.

The following explosion was about ten times as strong as the previous one. Our car shook and debris sprayed out over the city, dust and bits of rock raining down. Megan and I both spun around in our seats in time to catch the building collapse in an awful-sounding crunch.

"Wow," Cody said. "Look at that. I guess some of the power cells went up."

Megan glanced at me, then at the pen, then rolled her eyes. In seconds we were racing down the street in the opposite direction of fire trucks and emergency responders, heading for the rendezvous point with the other Reckoners.

PART THREE

23

I grunted, hauling the rope hand over hand. A plaintive squeak came from the pulley system with each draw, as if I had strapped some unfortunate mouse to a torture device and was twisting with glee.

The construction had been set up around the tunnel into the Reckoner burrow, which was the only way in or out. It had been five days since our attack on the power station, and we'd been lying low during most of that, planning our next move—the hit on Conflux to undermine Enforcement.

Abraham had just gotten back from a supply run. Which meant that I'd stopped being one of the team's tensor specialists and started being their source of free teenage labor.

I continued pulling, sweat dripping from my brow and beginning to soak through my T-shirt. Eventually the crate appeared from the depths of the hole, and Megan pulled it off its rollers and heaved it into the room. I let go of the rope, sending the roller board and rope back down the tunnel so Abraham could tie on another crate of supplies.

"You want to do the next one?" I asked Megan, wiping my brow with a towel.

"No," she said lightly. She heaved the crate onto a dolly and wheeled it over to stack it with the others.

"You sure?" I asked, arms aching.

"You're doing such a fine job," she said. "And it's good exercise." She settled the crate, then sat down on a chair, putting her feet up on the desk and sipping a lemonade while reading a book on her mobile.

I shook my head. She was unbelievable.

"Think of it as being chivalrous," Megan said absently, tapping the screen to scroll down more text. "Protecting a defenseless girl from pain and all that."

"Defenseless?" I asked as Abraham called up. I sighed, then started pulling the rope again.

She nodded. "In an abstract way."

"How can someone be *abstractly* defenseless?"

"Takes a lot of work," she said, then sipped her drink. "It only *looks* easy. Just like abstract art."

I grunted. "Abstract art?" I asked, heaving on the rope.

"Sure. You know, guy paints a black line on a canvas, calls it a metaphor, sells it for millions."

"That never happened."

She looked up at me, amused. "Sure it did. You never learned about abstract art in school?"

"I was schooled at the Factory," I said. "Basic math, reading, geography, history. Wasn't time for anything else."

"But before that. Before Calamity."

"I was eight," I said. "And I lived in inner-city Chicago, Megan.

My education mostly involved learning to avoid gangs and how to keep my head down at school."

"That's what you learned when you were *eight*? In grade school?"

I shrugged and kept pulling. She seemed troubled by what I'd said, though I'll admit, I was troubled by what she'd said. People hadn't really paid that much money for such simple things, had they? It baffled me. Pre-Calamity people had been a strange lot.

I hauled the next crate up, and Megan hopped down from her chair again to move it. I couldn't imagine that she was getting much reading done, but she didn't seem bothered by the interruptions. I watched her, taking a long gulp from my cup of water.

Things had been . . . different between us since her confession in the elevator shaft. In a lot of ways she was more relaxed around me, which didn't make that much sense. Shouldn't things have been more awkward? I knew she didn't support our mission. That felt like a pretty big deal to me.

She really *was* a professional, though. She didn't agree that Steelheart should be killed, but she didn't abandon the Reckoners, or even ask for a transfer to another Reckoner cell. I didn't know how many of those there were—apparently only Tia and Prof knew—but there was at least one other.

Either way, Megan stayed on board and didn't let her feelings distract her from her job. She might not agree that Steelheart needed to die, but from what I'd pried from her, she believed in fighting the Epics. She was like a soldier who believed a certain battle wasn't tactically sound, yet supported the generals enough to fight it anyway.

I respected her for that. Sparks, I was liking her more and more. And though she hadn't been particularly affectionate toward me lately, she wasn't openly hostile and cold any longer. That left me room to work some seductive magic. I wished I knew some.

She got the crate in place, and I waited for Abraham to call up that I should start pulling again. Instead he appeared at the mouth of the tunnel and started to unhook the pulley system. His shoulder had been healed from the gunshot using the harmsway, the Reckoner device that helped flesh heal extraordinarily fast.

I didn't know much about it, though I'd spoken to Cody—he'd called it the "last of the three." Three bits of incredible technology brought to the Reckoners from Prof's days as a scientist. The tensors, the jackets, the harmsway. From what Abraham told me, Prof had developed each technology and then stolen them from the lab he'd worked in, intent on starting his own war against the Epics.

Abraham got the last parts of the pulley down.

"Are we done?" I asked.

"Indeed."

"I counted more crates than that."

"The others are too big to fit through the tunnel," Abraham said. "Cody's going to drive them over to the hangar."

That was what they called the place where they kept their vehicles. I'd been there; it was a large chamber with a few cars and a van inside. It wasn't nearly as secure as this hideout was—the hangar had to have access to the upper city and couldn't be part of the understreets.

Abraham walked over to the stack of a dozen crates we'd heaved into the hideout. He rubbed his chin, inspecting them. "We might as well unload these," he said. "I've got another hour to spare."

"Before what?" I asked, joining him at the crates.

He didn't reply.

"You've been gone a lot these last few days," I noted.

Again, he didn't reply.

"He's not going to tell you where he's been, Knees," Megan said from her lounging position at the desk. "And get used to it. Prof sends him out on secret errands a lot."

"But . . . ," I said, feeling hurt. I'd thought I'd earned my place on the team.

"Do not be saddened, David," Abraham said, grabbing a crowbar to crack open one of the crates. "It is not a matter of trust. We must keep some things secret, even within the team, should one of us be taken captive. Steelheart has his way of getting to what one hides—nobody except Prof should know everything we are doing."

It was a good rationale, and it was probably why I couldn't know about other Reckoner cells either, but it was still annoying. As Abraham cracked open another crate, I reached to the pouch at my side and slipped out my tensor. With that, I vaporized the wooden lids off a few crates.

Abraham raised an eyebrow at me.

"What?" I said. "Cody told me to keep practicing."

"You are growing quite good," Abraham said. Then he reached into one of the crates I'd opened and fished out an apple, which was now covered in sawdust. It made something of a mess getting it out. "Quite good," he continued. "But sometimes, the crowbar is more effective, eh? Besides, we may wish to reuse these crates."

I sighed, but nodded. It was just . . . well, hard. The sense of strength I'd felt during the power station infiltration was difficult to forget. Opening the holes in the walls and creating those handholds, I'd been able to bend matter to my will. The more I used the tensor, the more excited I grew about the possibilities it offered.

"It is also important," Abraham said, "to avoid leaving traces of what we can do. Imagine if everyone knew about these things, eh? It would be a different world, more difficult for us."

I nodded, reluctantly putting the tensor away. "Too bad we had to leave that hole for Diamond to see."

Abraham hesitated, just briefly. "Yes," he said. "Too bad."

I helped him unload the supplies, and Megan joined us, working with characteristic efficiency. She ended up doing a lot of supervising, telling us where to stow the various foodstuffs. Abraham accepted her direction without complaint, even though she was the junior member of the team.

About halfway through the unloading, Prof came out of his planning room. He walked over to us while scanning through some papers in a folder.

"Did you learn anything, Prof?" Abraham asked.

"Rumors are going our way, for once," Prof said, tossing the folder onto Tia's desk. "The city's buzzing with the news of a new Epic come to challenge Steelheart. Half the city is talking about it, while the other half is bunkering down in their basements, waiting for the fighting to blow over."

"That's great!" I said.

"Yes." Prof seemed troubled.

"What's wrong, then?" I asked.

He tapped the folder. "Did Tia tell you what was on those data chips you brought back from the power plant?"

I shook my head, trying to hide my curiosity. Was he going to tell me? Perhaps it would give me a clue to what Abraham had been up to the last few days.

"It's propaganda," Prof said. "We think you found a hidden public manipulation wing of Steelheart's government. The files you brought back included press releases, outlines of rumors planned to be started, and stories of things Steelheart has done. Most of those stories and rumors are false, so far as Tia can determine."

"He wouldn't be the first ruler to fabricate a grand history for himself," Abraham noted, stowing some canned chicken on one of the shelves that had been carved to fill the entire wall of the back room.

"But why would Steelheart need to do that?" I asked, wiping my brow. "I mean . . . he's practically immortal. It's not like he needs to look more powerful than he is."

"He's arrogant," Abraham said. "Everybody knows this. You can see it in his eyes, in how he speaks, in what he does."

"Yes," Prof said. "Which is why these rumors are so confusing. The stories aren't meant to bolster him—or if they are, he has an odd way of going about it. Most of the stories are about atrocities he's committed. People he's murdered, buildings—even small towns—he has supposedly wiped out. But none of it has actually happened."

"He's spreading rumors about having slaughtered towns full of people?" Megan asked, sounding troubled.

"So far as we can tell," Prof said. He joined in, helping unload the crates. Megan had stopped giving orders, I noticed, now that he was around. "Someone, at least, wants Steelheart to sound more terrible than he really is."

"Maybe we found some kind of revolutionary group," I said, eager.

"Doubtful," Prof said. "Inside one of the major government buildings? With that kind of security? Besides, what you told me seems to imply the guards knew of the place. Anyway, many of these stories are accompanied by documentation claiming they were devised by Steelheart himself. It even notes their falsehood, and the need to substantiate them with made-up facts."

"He's been bragging," Abraham said, "and making things up—only now, his ministry has to make all of his claims sound true. Otherwise he'll look foolish."

Prof nodded, and my heart sank. I'd assumed that we'd found something important. Instead all I'd discovered was a department dedicated to making Steelheart look good. And more evil. Or something.

"So Steelheart is not as terrible as he would like us to think," Abraham said.

"Oh, he's pretty terrible," Prof said. "Wouldn't you say, David?"

"Over seventeen thousand confirmed deaths to his name," I said absently. "It's in my notes. Many were innocents. They can't all be fabrications."

"And they're not," Prof said. "He's a terrible, awful individual. He just wants to make sure that we all know it."

"How strange," Abraham said.

I dug into a crate of cheeses, getting out the paper-wrapped blocks and loading them in the cold-storage pit on the far side of the room. So many of the foods the Reckoners ate were things I'd never been able to afford. Cheese, fresh fruit. Most food in Newcago had to be shipped in because of the darkness. It was impossible to grow fruit and vegetables outside, and Steelheart was careful to keep a firm hold on the farmlands surrounding the city.

Expensive foods. I was already getting used to eating them. Odd, how quickly that could happen.

"Prof," I said, placing a cheese wheel in the pit, "do you ever wonder if maybe Newcago will be worse without Steelheart than it is with him?"

At the other side of the room, Megan turned sharply to look at me, but I didn't look at her. *I won't tell him what you said, so stop glaring at me. I just want to know.*

"It probably will be," Prof said. "For a while at least. The infrastructure of the city will probably collapse. Food will get scarce. Unless someone powerful takes Steelheart's place and secures Enforcement, there will be looting."

"But—"

"You want your revenge, son? Well, that's the cost. I won't sugarcoat it. We try to keep from hurting innocents, but when we kill Steelheart, we'll cause suffering."

I sat down beside the cold-storage hole.

"Did you never think of this?" Abraham asked. He'd gotten that necklace out from underneath his shirt and was rubbing his finger on it. "In all those years of planning, preparing to kill the one you hated, did you never consider what would happen to Newcago?"

I blushed, but then I shook my head. I hadn't. "So . . . what do we do?"

"Continue as we have," Prof said. "Our job is to cut out the infected flesh. Only then can the body start to heal—but it's going to hurt a lot first."

"But . . ."

Prof turned to me, and I saw something in his expression. A deep exhaustion, the tiredness of one who had been fighting a war for a long, long time. "It's good for you to think of this, son. Ponder. Worry. Stay up nights, frightened for the casualties of your ideology. It will do you good to realize the price of fighting.

"I need to warn you of something, however. There aren't any answers to be found. There are no good choices. Submissiveness to a tyrant or chaos and suffering. In the end I chose the second, though it flays my soul to do so. If we don't fight, humankind is finished. We slowly become sheep to the Epics, slaves and servants—stagnant.

"This isn't just about revenge or payback. It's about the survival of our race. It's about men being the masters of their own destiny. I choose suffering and uncertainty over becoming a lapdog."

"That's all well and good," Megan said, "to choose for yourself. But Prof, you're *not* just choosing for yourself. You're choosing for everyone in the city."

"So I am." He slid some cans onto the shelf.

"In the end," Megan said, "they *don't* get to be masters of their own destinies. They get to be dominated by Steelheart or left to fend for themselves—at least until another Epic comes along to dominate them again."

"Then we'll kill him too," Prof said softly.

"How many can you kill?" Megan said. "You can't stop all of the Epics, Prof. Eventually another one will set up here. You think he'll be *better* than Steelheart?"

"Enough, Megan," Prof said. "We've spoken of this already, and I made my decision."

"Newcago is one of the best places in the Fractured States to live," Megan continued, ignoring Prof's comment. "We should be focusing on Epics who *aren't* good administrators, places where life is worse."

"No," Prof said, his voice sounding gruffer.

"Why not?"

"Because that's the problem!" he snapped. "Everyone talks about how great Newcago is. But it's *not* great, Megan. It's good by comparison only! Yes, there are worse places, but so long as this hellhole is considered the ideal, we'll never get anywhere. *We cannot let them convince us this is normal!*"

The room fell still, Megan looking taken aback by Prof's outburst. I sat down, my shoulders slumping.

This wasn't anything like I'd imagined. The glorious Reckoners, bringing justice to the Epics. I hadn't once thought of the guilt they'd bear, the arguments, the uncertainty. I could see it in them, the same fear I'd had in the power plant. The worry that we might be making things worse, that we might end up as bad as the Epics.

Prof stalked away, waving a hand in frustration. I heard the curtain rustle as he retreated back to his thinking room. Megan watched him go, red-faced with anger.

"It is not so bad, Megan," Abraham said quietly. He still seemed calm. "It will be all right."

"How can you say that?" she asked.

"We don't need to defeat all of the Epics, you see," Abraham said. He was holding a chain in his dark-skinned hand, with a small pendant dangling from it. "We just need to hold out long enough."

"I'm not going to listen to your foolishness, Abraham," she said. "Not right now." With that she turned and left the storage room. She crawled into the tunnel that led down to the steel catacombs and vanished.

Abraham sighed, then turned to me. "You look unwell, David."

"I feel sick," I said honestly. "I thought . . . well, if anyone had the answers, I thought it would be the Reckoners."

"You mistake us," Abraham said, walking over to me. "You mistake Prof. Do not look to the executioner for the reason his blade falls. And Prof *is* society's executioner, the warrior for mankind. Others will come to rebuild."

"But doesn't it bother you?" I asked.

"Not unduly," Abraham answered simply, putting his necklace back on. "But then, I have a hope the others do not."

I could now see the pendant he wore. It was small and silver, with a stylized *S* symbol on it. I thought I recognized that symbol from somewhere. It reminded me of my father.

"You're one of the Faithful," I guessed. I'd heard of them, though I'd never met one. The Factory raised realists, not dreamers, and to be one of the Faithful you had to be a dreamer.

Abraham nodded.

"How can you still believe that good Epics will come?" I asked. "I mean, it's been over ten years."

"Ten years is not so long," Abraham said. "Not in the big picture of things. Why, humankind is not so old a species, compared to the big picture! The heroes *will* come. Someday we will have Epics that do not kill, do not hate, do not dominate. We will be protected."

Idiot, I thought. It was a gut reaction, though I immediately felt bad about it. Abraham wasn't an idiot. He was a wise man, or had seemed so until this moment. But . . . how could he really still think there would be *good* Epics? It was the same reasoning that had gotten my father killed.

Though at least he has something to look forward to, I thought. Would it be so bad, to wish for some mythical group of heroic Epics—to wait for them to come and provide salvation?

Abraham squeezed my shoulder and gave me a smile, then walked away. I stood and caught sight of him following Prof into the thinking room, something I'd never seen any of the others do. I soon heard soft conversation.

I shook my head. I considered continuing with the unloading, but found I didn't have a heart for it. I glanced at the tunnel down to the catacombs. On a whim I climbed in and went to see if I could find Megan.

24

MEGAN hadn't gone far. I found her at the bottom of the tunnel, sitting on a pile of old crates just outside the hideout. I walked up, hesitantly, and she shot me a suspicious glance. Her expression softened after a moment, and she turned back to studying the darkness in front of her. She had her mobile turned all the way up to give light.

I climbed up on the crates beside her and sat, but didn't speak. I wanted to have the perfect thing to say, and—as usual—I couldn't figure out what that would be. Trouble was, I basically agreed with Prof, even though it made me feel guilty that I did. I didn't have the schooling to predict what would happen to Newcago if its leader were killed. But I *did* know Steelheart was evil. No court would convict him, but I had a right to seek justice for the things he had done to me and mine.

So I just sat there, trying to formulate something to say that wouldn't offend her but that also wouldn't sound lame. It's harder than it seems—which is probably why I just say what comes to me most of the time. When I stop to think, I can never come up with anything.

"He really is a monster," Megan eventually said. "I know that he is. I hate sounding like I'm defending him. I just don't know if killing him is going to be good for the very people we're trying to protect."

I nodded. I got it, I really did. We fell silent again. As we sat I could hear distant sounds in the corridors, distorted by the bizarre composition and acoustics of the steel catacombs. Sometimes you could hear water rushing, as the city sewage pipes ran nearby. Other times I swore I could hear rats, though it baffled me what they could be living on down here. Other times the land seemed to be groaning softly.

"What *are* they, Megan?" I asked. "Have you ever wondered that?"

"You mean the Epics?" she asked. "Lots of people have theories."

"I know. But what do you think?"

She didn't reply immediately. Lots of people did have theories, and most would be happy to tell you about them. The Epics were the next stage in human evolution, or they were a punishment sent by this god or that, or they were really aliens. Or they were the result of a secret government project. Or it was all fake and they were using technology to pretend they had powers.

Most of the theories fell apart when confronted by facts. Normal people had gained powers and become Epics; they weren't aliens or anything like that. There were enough direct stories of a family member manifesting abilities. Scientists claimed to be baffled by the genetics of Epics, but I didn't know much about that kind of thing. Besides, most of the scientists were either gone now or worked for one of the more powerful Epics.

Anyway, a lot of the rumors were silly, but that had never stopped them from spreading, and probably never would.

"I think they're a test of some kind," Megan said.

I frowned. "You mean, like religiously?"

"No, not a test of faith or anything like that," Megan said. "I mean a test of what we'll do, if we have power. Enormous power. What would it do to us? How would we deal with it?"

I sniffed. "If the Epics are an example of what we'd do with power, then it's better if we never get any."

She fell silent. A few moments later I heard another odd sound. Whistling.

I turned and was surprised to see Cody walking down the corridor. He was alone, and on foot, which meant he'd left the industrial scooter—which had pulled the crates of supplies—in the hangar. He had his gun over his shoulder and wore his baseball cap embroidered with the supposed coat of arms of his Scottish clan. He tipped the cap to us.

"So . . . we having a party?" he asked. He checked his mobile. "Is it time for tea?"

"Tea?" I asked. "I've never seen you drink tea."

"I usually have some fish sticks and a bag of potato chips," Cody said. "It's a British thing. Y'all are Yanks and wouldn't understand."

Something seemed off about that statement, but I didn't know enough to call him on it.

"So why the dour expressions?" Cody asked, hopping up beside us on the crates. "You two look like a pair of coon hunters on a rainy day."

Wow, I thought. *Why can't I come up with metaphors like that?*

"Prof and I got into an argument," Megan said with a sigh.

"Again? I thought you two were past that. What was it about this time?"

"Nothing I want to talk about."

"Fair enough, fair enough." Cody got out his long hunter's knife and began trimming his fingernails. "Nightwielder's been out in the city. People are reporting him all over, passing through walls, looking in on dens of miscreants and lesser Epics. It has everyone on edge."

"That's good," I said. "It means Steelheart is taking the threat seriously."

"Maybe," Cody said. "Maybe. He ain't said anything about the challenge we left him yet, and Nightwielder is checking in on a lot of regular folks. Steelheart might suspect that someone's trying to blow smoke up his kilt."

"Maybe we should hit Nightwielder," I said. "We know his weakness now."

"Might be a good idea," Cody said, fishing a long, slender device out of his hip pack. He tossed it to me.

"What's this?"

"UV flashlight," he said. "I managed to find a place that sold them—or, well, bulbs anyway, which I put in the flashlights and fixed us up a few. Best to be ready in case Nightwielder surprises us."

"Do you think he'll come here?" I asked.

"He'll start in on the steel catacombs eventually," Cody said. "Maybe he's started already. Having a defensible base means nothing if Nightwielder just decides to phase through the walls and strangle us in our sleep."

Cheery thoughts. I shivered.

"At least we can fight him now," Cody said, fishing out another flashlight for Megan. "But I think we're poorly prepared. We still don't know what Steelheart's weakness is. What if he *does* challenge Limelight?"

"Tia will find the answer," I said. "She has a lot of leads in discovering what was in that bank vault."

"And Firefight?" Cody said. "We haven't even *started* planning how to deal with him."

Firefight, the other of Steelheart's High Epic bodyguards. Megan looked at me, obviously curious as to what I'd say next.

"Firefight won't be a problem," I said.

"So you said before, when you pitched this whole thing to us. But you ain't said why yet."

"I've talked it over with Tia," I said. "Firefight's not what you think he is." I was reasonably confident about that. "Come on, I'll show you."

Cody raised an eyebrow but followed as I crawled back up the tunnel. Prof already knew what my notes said, though I wasn't certain he believed. I knew he was planning a meeting to talk about Firefight and Nightwielder, but I *also* knew that he was waiting on Tia before moving too far ahead in the plan. If she didn't come up with the answer to how to kill Steelheart, nothing else would matter.

I didn't want to think about that. Giving up now because we didn't know his weakness . . . it would be like finding out that you'd drawn lots for dessert at the Factory and been only one number off. Only it didn't matter, because Pete already snuck in to steal the dessert, so nobody was going to get any anyway—not even Pete, because it turns out that there had never been any dessert in the first place. Well, something like that. That metaphor's a work in progress.

At the top of the tunnel I led Cody to the box where we kept my notes. I flipped through them for a few minutes, noting that Megan had followed us up. She had an unreadable expression on her face.

I grabbed the folder on Firefight and brought it over to the desk, spreading out some pictures. "What do you know about Firefight?"

"Fire Epic," Cody said, pointing at a photo. It showed a person made of flames, the heat so intense the air around him warped. No photo could capture the details of Firefight's features, as they were composed of solid flames. In fact, each photo I pulled out showed him glowing so brightly that it distorted the picture.

"He's got standard fire Epic powers," Megan said. "He can turn to flame—in fact, he pretty much always remains in fire form. He can fly, throw fire from his hands, and manipulate existing flames. He creates an intense heat field around him, capable of melting bullets—though they likely couldn't hurt him even if they didn't melt. It's a basic fire Epic portfolio."

"Too basic," I said. "Every Epic has quirks. Nobody has *exactly* the same portfolio of powers. That was what first tipped me off. Here's the other clue." I tapped the series of photographs—each was a shot of Firefight taken on a different day, usually with Steelheart and his retinue. Though Nightwielder often went out on missions, Firefight usually remained near Steelheart to act as first-line bodyguard.

"Do you see it?" I asked.

"See what?" Cody asked.

"Here," I said, pointing to a man standing with Steelheart's guards in one of the pictures. He was slender and clean-shaven and wore a stiff suit, a pair of dark shades, and a wide-brimmed hat that obscured his face.

I pointed to the next photo. The same person was there. And the next photo. And the next. His face was hard to make out in the other pictures too—none of them were focused on him specifically, and the hat and shades always masked his features.

"This person is always there when Firefight appears," I said. "It's suspicious. Who is it, and what is he doing there?"

Megan frowned. "What are you implying?"

"Here," I said, "take a look at these." I got out a sequence of five photos, a rapid-fire series of shots capturing a few moments. The scene was Steelheart flying through the city with a procession of his minions. He did that sometimes. Though he always looked like he was going somewhere important, I suspected these were really just his version of a parade.

Nightwielder and Firefight were with him, flying about ten feet above the ground. A cavalcade of cars drove beneath, like a military convoy. I couldn't make out any faces, though I suspected the suspicious person was among them.

Five pictures. Four of them showed the trio of Epics flying side by side. And in one of them—right in the middle of the sequence—Firefight's shape had fuzzed and gone translucent.

"Firefight can go incorporeal, like Nightwielder?" Cody guessed.

"No," I said. "Firefight's not real."

Cody blinked. "What?"

"He's not real. At least, not in the way we think. Firefight is an incredibly intricate—and incredibly clever—illusion. I suspect that the person we're seeing in those photos, the one wearing the suit and hat, is the true Epic. He's an illusionist, capable of manipulating light to create images, a lot like Refractionary—only on a much more powerful level. Together the real Firefight and Steelheart concocted the idea of a fake Epic much the same way we're concocting Limelight. In these photos we're catching a moment of distraction, when the real Epic wasn't concentrating on his illusion and it wobbled and nearly vanished."

"A fake Epic?" Megan said, dismissive. "What would be the point? Steelheart wouldn't need to do that."

"Steelheart has a strange psychology," I said. "Trust me. I'll bet I know him better than anyone other than his closest allies. He's arrogant, like Abraham said, but he's *also* paranoid. Much of what he does is about holding on to power, about forcing people into line. He moves the location of his sleeping quarters. Why would he need to do that? He's immune to harm, right? He's paranoid, scared that someone will discover his weakness. He destroyed the entire bank because we might have had a *hint* at how he was hurt."

"Lots of Epics would do that," Cody noted.

"That's because most Epics are equally paranoid. Look, what better way to surprise would-be assassins than to make them prepare for an Epic that isn't there? If they spend all their time planning how to kill Firefight, then go up against an illusionist instead, they'll be caught totally off guard."

"So will we, if you're right," Cody said. "Fighting illusionists is tough. I hate not being able to trust my eyes."

"Look, an illusionist Epic can't explain everything," Megan said. "There are recorded events of Firefight melting bullets."

"Firefight made the bullets vanish when they reached the illusion, then made illusory melted bullets drop to the ground. Later some of Steelheart's minions went and spread some actual melted bullets down as proof." I took out another pair of pictures. "I've got evidence of them doing just that. I have mountains of documentation on this, Megan. You're welcome to read through it. Tia agrees with me."

I picked up a few more pictures from the stack. "Take this. Here, we've got photos of a time that Firefight 'burned' down a building. I took these pictures myself; see how he's throwing fire? If you look at the scorch marks on the walls the following day in this next set, they're different from the blasts Firefight created. The real scorch marks were added by a team of workers in the night. They cleared everyone from the scene, so I couldn't get pictures of them, but the next day's evidence is clear."

Megan looked deeply troubled.

"What?" Cody said.

"It's what you said," she replied. "Illusionists. They're annoying. I'm just hoping we don't have to face one."

"I don't think we'll have to," I said. "I've thought it through and, despite Firefight's reputation, he doesn't seem terribly dangerous. I can't squarely attribute any deaths to him, and he rarely fights. It has to be because he wants to be careful not to reveal what he really is. I've got the facts in these folders. As soon as Firefight appears, all we have to do is shoot the one creating the illusion—this man in the photos—and all of his illusions will go down. It shouldn't be too hard."

"Y'all might be right about the illusions," Cody said, looking through another group of photos. "But I'm not sure about this person you think is making them. If Firefight were smart, he'd create the illusion, then turn himself invisible."

"It's possible he can't," I said. "Not all illusionists are capable of that, even powerful ones." I hesitated. "But you're right. We can't know for certain who's making the fake Firefight, but I still think Firefight won't be a problem. All we need to do is spook him—set up a trap that will expose his illusion as fake. When he's threatened with being revealed, I'll bet he bolts. From what I've been able to determine about him, he seems like something of a coward."

Cody nodded thoughtfully.

Megan shook her head. "I think you're taking this too lightly." She sounded angry. "If Steelheart really has been fooling everyone all this time, then it's likely that Firefight is even more dangerous than we thought. Something about this bothers me; I don't think we're prepared for it."

"You're looking for a reason to call off this mission anyway," I said, annoyed at her.

"I never said that."

"You didn't need to. It—"

I was interrupted by motion at the tunnel into the hideout and I turned in time to see Tia climbing through, wearing old jeans and her Reckoner jacket. Her knees were dusty. She stood up, smiling. "We've found it."

My heart leaped in my chest and sent what felt like electricity jolting through my body. "Steelheart's weakness? You found out what it is?"

"No," she said, her eyes seeming to glow with excitement. "But this should lead to the answers. I found *it*."

"What, Tia?" Cody asked.

"The bank vault."

25

"I first started considering this possibility when you told your story, David," Tia explained. The entire team of Reckoners was following her down a tunnel in the steel catacombs. "And the more I investigated the bank, the more curious I became. There are oddities."

"Oddities?" I asked. The group moved in a tense huddle, Cody taking point, Abraham watching our tail. He had replaced his very nice machine gun with a similar one, only without quite as many bells and whistles.

I felt pretty comfortable with him at our back. These narrow confines would make a heavy machine gun especially deadly to anyone trying to approach us; the walls would work like bumpers on the sides of a bowling lane, and Abraham wouldn't have any trouble at all getting strikes.

"The Diggers," Prof said. He was at my side. "They weren't allowed to excavate the area beneath where the bank had stood."

"Yes," Tia said, speaking eagerly. "It was very irregular. Steelheart barely gave them any direction. The chaos of these lower catacombs proves that; their madness made them hard to control. But one order he was firm on: the area beneath the bank was to be left alone. I wouldn't have thought twice about that if it hadn't been for what you described, that Steelheart had most of the main room of the bank turned to steel by the time Faultline came that afternoon. Her powers had two parts, it—"

"Yes," I said, too excited not to interrupt. Faultline—the woman Steelheart had brought to bury the bank after I'd escaped. "I know. Power duality—melding two second-tier abilities creates a first-tier one."

Tia smiled. "You've been reading my classification system notes."

"I figure we might as well use the same terminology." I shrugged. "I have no trouble switching over."

Megan glanced at me, the hint of a smile on the corners of her lips.

"What?" I asked.

"Nerd."

"I am not—"

"Stay focused, son," Prof said, shooting a hard look at Megan, whose eyes shone with amusement. "I happen to have a fondness for nerds."

"I never said that I didn't," Megan replied lightly. "I'm just interested whenever someone pretends to be something they're not."

Whatever, I thought. Faultline was a tier-one Epic, by Tia's classification, without an immortality benefit. That made her powerful, but fragile. She should have realized that; when she'd tried to seize Newcago a few years back, she'd never had a chance.

Anyway, she was an Epic who had several smaller powers that worked together to create what seemed to be a single, more impressive power. In her case, she could move earth—but only if it wasn't too rigid. However, she *also* had the ability to turn ordinary stone and earth into a kind of sandy dust.

What had looked like her creating an earthquake had actually been her softening the ground, then pulling back the earth. There were true earthquake-creating Epics, but they were ironically less powerful—or at least less useful. The stronger ones could destroy a city with their powers but couldn't bury a single building or group of people at will. Plate tectonics just worked on too massive a scale to allow for precision.

"Don't you see?" Tia asked. "Steelheart turned the bank's main room—walls, much of the ceiling, floor—to steel. Then Faultline softened the ground beneath it and let it sink. I began thinking, there might be a chance that—"

"—that it would still be there," I said softly. We turned a corner in the catacombs, and then Tia stepped forward, moving some pieces of junk to reveal a tunnel. I had enough practice by now to tell it was probably tensor-made. The tensors, unless controlled precisely, always created circular tunnels, while the Diggers had created square or rectangular corridors.

This tunnel burrowed through the steel at a slight decline. Cody walked up, shining his light in. "Well, I guess now we know what you and Abraham have been working on for the last few weeks, Tia."

"We had to try several different avenues of approach," Tia explained. "I wasn't certain how deep the bank room ended up sinking, or even if it retained structural integrity."

"But it did?" I asked, suddenly feeling a strange numbness.

"It did!" Tia said. "It's amazing. Come see." She led the way down the tunnel, which was tall enough to walk through, though Abraham would have to stoop.

I hesitated. The others waited for me to follow, so I forced myself forward, joining Tia. The rest of them came along behind, our mobiles providing the only light.

No, wait. There was light up ahead; I could barely make it out, around the shadows of Tia's slender figure. We eventually reached the end of the tunnel, and I stepped into a memory.

Tia had set up a few lights in corners and on tables, but they did little more than give a ghostly cast to the large, dark chamber. The room had settled at an angle, with the floor sloping downward. The skewed perspective only enhanced the surreal sensation of this place.

I froze in the mouth of the tunnel. The room was as I remembered it, shockingly well preserved. Towering pillars—now made of steel—and scattered desks, counters, rubble. I could still make out the tile mosaic on the floor, though only its shape. Instead of marble and stone it was now all a uniform shade of silver broken by ridges and bumps.

There was almost no dust, though some motes dodged lazily in the air, creating little halos around the white lanterns Tia had set up.

Realizing that I was still standing in the mouth of the tunnel, I stepped down into the room. *Oh sparks . . .* , I thought, my chest constricting. I found my hands gripping my rifle, though I knew I was in no danger. The memories were coming back in a flood.

"In retrospect," Tia was explaining—I listened with only half an ear—"I shouldn't have been surprised to find it so well preserved. Faultline's powers created a kind of cushion of earth as the room sank, and Steelheart turned almost all of that earth to metal. The other rooms in the building were destroyed in his assault on the bank, and they broke off as the structure sank. But this one, and the attached vault, were ironically preserved by Steelheart's own powers."

By coincidence we'd entered through the front of the bank. There had been wide, beautiful glass doors here; those had been destroyed in the gunfire and energy blasts. Steel rubble and some steel bones from Deathpoint's victims littered the ground to both sides. As I stepped forward I followed the path Steelheart had taken into the building.

Those are the counters, I thought, looking directly ahead. *The ones where the tellers worked.* One section had been destroyed; as a child I'd crawled through that gap before making my way to the vault. The ceiling nearby was broken and misshapen, but the vault itself had been steel before Steelheart's intervention. Now that I thought about it, that might have helped preserve its contents, because of how his transfersion abilities worked.

"Most of the rubble is from where the ceiling fell in," Tia said from behind, her voice echoing in the vast chamber. "Abraham and I cleaned as much out as we could. A large amount of dirt had tumbled through the broken wall and ceiling, filling one part of the chamber over by the vault. We used the tensors on that pile, then made a hole in the corner of the floor—it opens into a pocket of space underneath the building—and shoved the dust in there."

I moved down three steps to the lower section of the floor. Here, in the center of the room, was where Steelheart had faced Deathpoint. *These people are mine. . . .* By instinct, I turned to the left. Huddling beside the pillar I found the body of the woman whose child had been killed in her arms. I shivered. She was now a statue made of steel. When had she died? How? I didn't remember. A stray bullet, maybe? She wouldn't have been turned to steel unless she'd already been dead.

"What *really* saved this place," Tia continued, "was the Great Transfersion, when Steelheart turned everything in the city to steel. If he hadn't done that, dirt would have filled this room completely. Beyond that, the settling of the ground probably would have caved in the ceiling. However, the transfersion turned the remaining things in the room to steel, as well as the earth around it. In effect he locked the room into place, preserving it, like a bubble in the middle of a frozen pond."

I continued forward until I could see the sterile little mortgage cubicle I'd hidden in. Its windows were now opaque, but I could see in through the open front. I walked in and ran my fingers along the desk. The cubicle felt smaller than I remembered.

"The insurance records were inconclusive," Tia continued. "But there *was* a claim submitted on the building itself, an earthquake claim. I wonder if the bank owners really thought the insurance company would pay out on that. Seems ridiculous—but of course, there was still a lot of uncertainty surrounding Epics in those days. Anyway, that made me investigate records surrounding the bank's destruction."

"And that led you here?" Cody asked, his voice coming from the darkness as he poked around the perimeter of the room.

"No, actually. It led me to find something curious. A cover-up. The reason I couldn't find anything in the insurance reports, and why I couldn't find any lists of what was in the vault, was because some of Steelheart's people had already gathered and hidden the information. I realized that since he had made a dedicated attempt to cover this up, I would never discover anything of use in the records. Our only chance would be to come to the bank, which Steelheart had assumed was buried beyond reach."

"It's a good assumption," Cody said, sounding thoughtful. "Without the tensors—or some kind of Epic power like the Diggers had—getting here would have been near impossible. Burrowing through fifty feet of solid steel?" The Diggers had started out as normal humans and had been granted their strange powers by an Epic known as Digzone, who was a gifter like Conflux. It . . . hadn't gone well for them. Not all Epic powers were meant to be used by mortal hands, it appeared.

I was still standing in the cubicle. The mortgage man's bones were there, scattered on the floor around the desk, peeking out from some rubble. All of it was metal now.

I didn't want to look, but I had to. I *had to.*

I turned around. For a moment I couldn't tell the past from the present. My father stood there, determined, gun raised to defend a monster. Explosions, shouts, dust, screams, fire.

Fear.

I blinked, trembling, hand to the cold steel of the cubicle wall. The room smelled of dust and age, but I thought I could smell blood. I thought I could smell terror.

I stepped out of the cubicle and walked to where Steelheart had stood, holding a simple pistol, arm extended toward my father. Bang. One shot. I could remember hearing it, though I didn't know if my mind had constructed that. I'd been deafened by the explosions by then.

I knelt beside the pillar. A mound of silvery rubble covered everything in front of me, but I had my tensor. The others continued talking, but I stopped paying attention, and their words became nothing more than a low hum in the background. I put on my tensor, then reached forward and—very carefully—began vaporizing bits of rubble.

It didn't take long; the bulk of it was made of one large piece of ceiling panel. I destroyed it, then froze.

There he was.

My father lay slumped against the pillar, head to the side. The bullet wound was frozen in the steel folds of his shirt. His eyes were still open. He looked like a statue, cast with incredible detail—even the pores of the skin were clear.

I stared, unable to move, unable to even lower my arm. After ten years, the familiar face was almost crushing to me. I didn't have any pictures of him or my mother; I hadn't dared go home after surviving, though Steelheart couldn't have known who I was. I'd been paranoid and traumatized.

Seeing his face brought that all back to me. He looked so . . . normal. Normal in a way that hadn't existed for years; normal in a way that the world didn't deserve any longer.

I wrapped my arms around myself, but I kept looking at my father's face. I couldn't turn away.

"David?" Prof's voice. He knelt down beside me.

"My father . . . ," I whispered. "He died fighting back, but he also died protecting Steelheart. And now here I am, trying to kill the thing he rescued. It's funny, eh?"

Prof didn't respond.

"In a way," I said, "this is all his fault. Deathpoint was going to kill Steelheart from behind."

"It wouldn't have worked," Prof said. "Deathpoint didn't know how powerful Steelheart was. Nobody knew back then."

"I guess that's true. But my father was a fool. He couldn't believe that Steelheart was evil."

"Your father believed the best about people," Prof said. "You could call that foolish, but I'd never call it a fault. He was a hero, son. He stood up to, and killed, Deathpoint—an Epic who had been slaughtering wantonly. If, in doing so, he let Steelheart live . . . well, Steelheart hadn't done terrible things at that point. Your father couldn't know the future. You can't be so frightened of what *might* happen that you are unwilling to act."

I stared into my father's dead eyes, and I found myself nodding. "That's the answer," I whispered. "It's the answer to what you and Megan were arguing about."

"It isn't her answer," Prof said. "But it's mine. And maybe yours too." He gave my shoulder a squeeze, then went to join the rest of the Reckoners, who were standing near the vault.

I'd never expected to see my father's face again; I'd left that day feeling like a coward, seeing him mouth the plea for me to run and escape. I'd lived ten years with a single dominating emotion: the need for vengeance. The need to prove I was not a coward.

Now, here he was. Looking into those steel eyes, I knew my father wouldn't care about vengeance. But he'd kill Steelheart all the same if he had the chance, to stop the murders. Because sometimes, you need to help the heroes along.

I stood up. Somehow I knew, in that moment, that the bank vault and its contents were a false lead. That hadn't been the source of Steelheart's weakness. It had been my father, or something about him.

I left the corpse for the moment, joining the others. ". . . very careful as we open the vault boxes," Tia was saying. "We don't want to destroy what might be inside."

"I don't think it will work," I said, drawing all of their eyes. "I don't think the vault contents are to blame."

"You said Steelheart looked at the vault after the rocket blew it open," Tia said. "And his agents worked very hard to obtain and hide any lists of what was in here."

"I don't think he knew how he got hurt," I said. "A lot of Epics don't know their weaknesses at first. He quietly had his people gather those records and analyze them so he could try to figure it out."

"So maybe he found the answer there," Cody said with a shrug.

I raised an eyebrow. "If he'd found out this vault contained something that made him vulnerable, do you think this place would still be here?"

The others grew silent. No, it wouldn't still be there. If that had been the case, Steelheart would have burrowed down and destroyed the place, no matter the difficulty in doing so. I was increasingly certain that it wasn't an object that had made him weak; it was something about the situation.

Tia's face looked dark; she probably wished I'd mentioned this before she spent days excavating. I couldn't help it, though, since nobody had told me what she was doing.

"Well," Prof said. "We're going to search this vault. David's theory has merit, but so does the theory that something in here weakened him."

"Will we even be able to find anything?" Cody asked. "Everything's been turned to steel. I don't know that I'll be able to recognize much if it's all fused together."

"Some things might have survived in their original form," Megan said. "In fact, it's likely that they did. Steelheart's transfersion powers are insulated by metal."

"They're what?" Cody asked.

"Insulated by metal," I repeated. "He exerts a kind of . . . ripple of transfersion that travels through and changes nonmetal substances like sound travels through air or waves move through a pool of water. If the wave hits metal—particularly iron or steel—it stops. He can affect other kinds of metal, but the wave moves more slowly. Steel stops it entirely."

"So these safe-deposit boxes . . . ," Cody said, stepping into the vault.

"Might have insulated their contents," Megan finished, following him in. "Some of it will have been transformed—the wave that created the transfersion was enormously powerful. I think we might find something, though, particularly since the vault itself was metal and would work as a primary insulator." She glanced over her shoulder and caught me looking at her. "What?" she demanded.

"Nerd," I said.

Uncharacteristically, she blushed furiously. "I pay attention to Steelheart. I wanted to be familiar with his powers, since we were coming into the city."

"I didn't say it was a bad thing," I said lightly, stepping into the vault and raising my tensor. "I just pointed it out."

Never has getting glared at felt so good.

Prof chuckled. "All right," he said. "Cody, Abraham, David, vaporize the fronts of the safe-deposit boxes but *don't* destroy the contents. Tia, Megan, and I will start pulling them out and going through them for anything that looks interesting. Let's get to work; this is going to take a while. . . ."

26

"WELL," Cody said, looking over the heap of gemstones and jewelry, "if this achieved nothing else, it at least made me rich. That's a failure I can live with."

Tia snorted, picking through the jewelry. We four, including Prof, sat around a large desk in one of the cubicles. Megan and Abraham were on guard duty, watching the tunnel into the bank chamber.

There was a hallowed feeling to the room—like I somehow had to show respect—and I think the others must have sensed it too. They spoke in low, muted voices. All except Cody. He tried to lean back on his chair as he held up a large ruby, but—of course—the steel chair legs were fused to the steel floor.

"That once might have made you rich, Cody," Tia said, "but you'd have some trouble selling it now."

That was true. Jewelry was practically worthless these days. There were a couple Epics who could create gemstones.

"Maybe," Cody said, "but gold remains a standard." He scratched his head. "Not sure why, though. You can't eat it, which is all most people are interested in."

"It's familiar," Prof said. "It doesn't rust, it's easy to shape, and it's hard to fake. There aren't any Epics who can make it. Yet. People need to have a way to trade, particularly across kingdom or city boundaries." He fingered a gold chain. "Cody's actually right."

"I am?" Cody looked surprised.

Prof nodded. "Whether or not we take on Steelheart, the gold we've recovered here can fund the Reckoners for a few years on its own."

Tia set her notebook on the desk, tapping it absently with her pen. On the other mortgage cubicle desks we'd arranged what we'd found in the vault. About three-quarters of the boxes' contents had been recoverable.

"Mostly we have a lot of wills," Tia said, opening a can of cola, "stock certificates, passports, copies of driver's licenses . . ."

"We could fill a whole city with fake people if we wanted," Cody said. "Imagine the fun."

"The second-largest grouping," Tia continued, "is the aforementioned pile of jewelry, both valuable and worthless. If something in there affected Steelheart, then by pure volume this is the most likely group."

"But it's not," I said.

Prof sighed. "David, I know what you—"

"What I mean," I interrupted, "is that jewelry doesn't make sense. Steelheart didn't attack other banks, and he hasn't done anything— either directly or indirectly—to forbid people from wearing jewelry in his presence. Jewelry is common enough among Epics that he'd have to take measures."

"I agree," Tia said, "though only in part. It's possible we've missed something. Steelheart has proven subtle in the past; perhaps he has a secret embargo on a certain type of gemstone. I'll look into it, but I think David's right. If something *did* affect Steelheart, then it's likely one of the oddities."

"How many of those are there?" Prof asked.

"Over three hundred," Tia said with a grimace. "Mostly mementos or keepsakes of no intrinsic value. Anything among them could be our culprit, theoretically. But then there's a chance it was something one of the people in the room was carrying on them. Or it could be, as David seems to think, something about the situation."

"It's very rare for an Epic's weakness to be influenced just by proximity to something mundane," I said, shrugging. "Unless an object in the vault emitted a kind of radiation or a light or a sound—something that actually reached Steelheart—the chances are slim it was the culprit."

"Look through the items anyway, Tia," Prof said. "Maybe we can find a correlation to something Steelheart has done in the city."

"What about the darkness?" Cody asked.

"Nightwielder's darkness?"

"Sure," Cody said. "I've always thought it was strange that he kept it so dark here."

"That's probably because of Nightwielder himself," I said. "He doesn't want sunlight shining on him and making him corporeal. I wouldn't be surprised if that was part of the deal between them, one of the reasons Nightwielder serves beneath Steelheart. Steelheart's government provides infrastructure—food, electricity, crime prevention—to compensate for it always being dark."

"I suppose that makes sense," Cody said. "Nightwielder needs darkness, but can't have it unless he's got a good city to work from. Kind of like a piper needs a good city to support him, so he can stand on the cliff tops and play."

"A . . . piper?" I asked.

"Oh please, don't get him started," Tia said, raising a hand to her head.

"Bagpiper," Cody said.

I looked at him blankly.

"You've never heard of *bagpipes*?" Cody asked, sounding aghast. "They're as Scottish as kilts and red armpit hair!"

"Um . . . yuck?" I said.

"That's it," Cody said. "Steelheart has to fall so we can get back to educating children properly. This is an offense against the dignity of my motherland."

"Great," Prof said, "I'm glad we now have proper motivation." He tapped the desk idly.

"You're worried," Tia said. She seemed to be able to read Prof pretty well.

"We're getting closer and closer to a confrontation. If we continue on this course we'll draw Steelheart out but will be unable to fight him."

The people at the desk grew still. I looked up, gazing at the high ceiling; the sterile white lights around the room provided insufficient glow to reach the room's farthest corners. It was cold in this room, and quiet. "When's the last moment we could pull out?"

"Well," Prof said, "we could draw him to a confrontation with Limelight, then not show."

"That might be kind of fun on its own merits," Cody noted. "I doubt Steelheart gets stood up very often."

"He'd react poorly to the embarrassment," Prof said. "Right now the Reckoners are a thorn—an annoyance. We've only done three hits in his city and have never killed anyone vital to his organization. If we run, what we've been doing will get out. Abraham and I set in place evidence that will prove we're behind this—that is the only way to make sure our victory, if we obtain one, isn't attributed to an Epic instead of ordinary men."

"So if we run . . . ," Cody said.

"Steelheart will know that Limelight was a fake and that the Reckoners were working on a way to assassinate him," Tia said.

"Well," Cody said, "most Epics already want to kill the lot of us. So maybe nothing will change."

"This will be worse," I said, still looking up at the ceiling. "He killed the *rescue workers,* Cody. He's paranoid. He'll hunt us actively if he finds out what we've been up to. The thought that we tried to get to him . . . that we were researching his weakness . . . he won't take that sitting down."

The shadows flickered, and I looked down to see Abraham walking up to our cubicle. "Prof, you asked me to warn you when we reached the hour."

Prof checked his mobile, then nodded. "We should be getting back to the hideout. Everyone grab a sack and fill it with the things we found. We'll sort through them further in a more controlled environment."

We got up from our seats, Cody patting the head of the dead— and steel-frozen—bank patron who slumped beside the wall of this particular cubicle. As they left, Abraham set something down on the desk. "For you."

It was a handgun. "I'm no good with . . ." I trailed off. It looked familiar. *The gun . . . the one my father picked up.*

"I found it in the rubble beside your father," Abraham said. "The transfersion turned the grip and frame to metal, but most of the parts were already good steel. I removed the magazine and cleared the chamber, and the slide and trigger still function as expected. I wouldn't completely trust it until I give it a thorough once-over back at base, but there's a good chance it will fire reliably."

I picked up the gun. This was the weapon that had killed my father. Holding it felt wrong.

But it was also, so far as I knew, the only weapon ever to have wounded Steelheart.

"We can't know if it was something about the gun that allowed Steelheart to be hurt," Abraham said. "I felt it would be worth digging out. I'll take it apart and clean it for you, check over the cartridges. They should still be good, though I might need to change the powder, if the casings didn't insulate against the transfersion. If it all checks out, you can carry it. If the opportunity presents itself, you can try shooting him with it."

I nodded in thanks, then ran to get a sack and haul out my part of what we'd found.

"Piping is the most sublime sound y'all have ever heard," Cody explained, gesturing widely as we walked down the corridor toward the hideout. "A sonorous mix of power, frailty, and wonder."

"It sounds like dying cats being stuffed into a blender," Tia said to me.

Cody looked wistful. "Aye, and a beauteous melody that is, lass."

"So, wait," I said, holding up a finger. "These bagpipes. To make them, you . . . what was it you said? 'Y'all need to kill yourself a wee dragon, which are totally real and not at all mythological—they live in the Scottish Highlands to this day.'"

"Aye," Cody said. "It's important y'all pick a *wee* one. The big ones are too dangerous, you see, and their bladders don't make good pipes. But you have to kill it yourself, you see. A piper needs to have slain his own dragon. It's part of the code."

"After that," I said, "you need to cut out the bladder, and attach . . . what was it?"

"Carved unicorn horns to make the pipes," Cody said. "I mean, you *could* use something less rare, like ivory. But if you're going to be a purist, it has to be unicorn horns."

"Delightful," Tia said.

"A grand word to choose," Cody said. "It, of course, is originally a Scottish term. *Del* coming from Dál Riata, the ancient and great Scottish kingdom of myth. Why, I think one of the great piping songs is from that era. *'Abharsair e d' a chois e na Dùn Èideann.'"*

"Ab . . . ha . . . what?" I asked.

"Abharsair e d' a chois e na Dùn Èideann," Cody said. "It is a sweetly poetic name that doesn't really translate to English—"

"It means 'The Devil Went Down to Edinburgh' in Scottish Gaelic," Tia said, leaning in toward me but speaking loudly enough that Cody could hear.

Cody, for once, missed a step. "You speak Scottish Gaelic, lass?"

"No," Tia said. "But I looked that up *last* time you told this story."

"Er . . . you did, eh?"

"Yes. Though your translation is questionable."

"Well, now. I always did say you were a smart one, lass. Yes indeed." He coughed into his hand. "Ah, look. We're at the base. I'll continue the story later." The others had arrived at the hideout just ahead and Cody scurried up to meet them, then followed Megan up the tunnel.

Tia shook her head, then walked with me to the tunnel. I went last, making sure the cords and cables that hid the entrance were in place. I turned on the hidden motion sensors that would alert us if someone came in, then crawled up myself.

". . . just don't know, Prof," Abraham was saying in his soft voice. "I just don't know." The two of them had spent the trip back walking ahead, speaking softly. I'd tried to edge up to hear them, but Tia had pointedly placed a hand on my shoulder and drawn me back.

"So?" Megan asked, crossing her arms as we all gathered around the main table. "What's going on?"

"Abraham doesn't like the way the rumors are going," Prof said.

"The general public does seem to accept our tale of Limelight," Abraham said. "They are scared, and our hit on the power station has had an effect—there are rolling blackouts all over the city. However, I see no proof that Steelheart believes. Enforcement is sweeping the understreets. Nightwielder is scouring the city. Everything I hear from informants is that Steelheart is searching for a group of rebels, not a rival Epic."

"So we hit back with a fury," Cody said, crossing his arms and leaning back against the wall beside the tunnel. "Kill a few more Epics."

"No," I said, remembering my conversation with Prof. "We need to be more focused. We can't just take out random Epics; we have to think like someone trying to capture the city."

Prof nodded. "Each and every hit we make without having Limelight appear in the open will make Steelheart more suspicious."

"We're giving up?" Megan said, a hint of eagerness in her voice, though she obviously tried to cover it.

"Not by a mile," Prof said. "Perhaps I will still decide we need to pull out—if we aren't confident enough about Steelheart's weakness, I might do just that. We aren't there yet. We're going to keep on with this plan, but we need to do something big, preferably with an appearance by Limelight. We need to squeeze Steelheart as hard as we can and drive that temper of his. *Force* him out."

"And we do that how?" Tia asked.

"It's time to kill Conflux," Prof said. "And bring down Enforcement."

27

CONFLUX.

In many ways he was the backbone of Steelheart's rule. A mysterious figure, even when compared to the likes of Firefight and Nightwielder.

I had no good photos of Conflux. The few I'd paid dearly to get were blurry and unspecific. I couldn't even know if he was real.

The van thumped as it moved through the dark streets of Newcago; it was stuffy inside. I sat in the passenger seat, with Megan driving. Cody and Abraham were in the back. Prof was running point in a different vehicle, and Tia was running support back at our base, watching the spy videos of the city streets. It was a frigid day and the heater in our van didn't work—Abraham hadn't gotten around to fixing it.

Prof's words ran through my mind. *We've considered hitting*

Conflux before, but discarded the idea because we thought it would be too dangerous. We still have the plans we made. It's no less dangerous now, but we're in deep. No reason not to move forward.

Was Conflux real? My gut said he was. Much as the clues pointed to Firefight being a fabrication, the clues surrounding Conflux added up to *something* being there. A powerful but fragile Epic.

Steelheart moves Conflux around, Prof had said, *never letting him stay long in the same place. But there's a pattern to how he's moved. He often uses an armored limo with six guards and a two-motorcycle escort. If we watch for that, wait until he uses that convoy to move, we can hit him on the streets in transit.*

The clues. Even with power plants Steelheart didn't have enough electricity to run the city, and yet he somehow produced those fuel cells. The mechanized armor units didn't pack power sources, and neither did many of the copters. The fact that they were powered directly by high-ranking members of Enforcement wasn't much of a secret. Everyone knew it.

He was out there. A gifter who could make energy in a form that could power vehicles, fill fuel cells, even light a large chunk of the city. That level of power was awesome, but no more so than what Nightwielder or Steelheart held. The most powerful Epics set their own scale of strength.

The van bumped, and I gripped my rifle—held low, safety on, barrel pointed down and toward the door. Out of sight, but handy. Just in case.

Tia had spotted the right kind of limo convoy today, and we'd scrambled. Megan drove us toward a point where our road would intersect with Conflux's limo. Her eyes were characteristically intense, though there was a particular edge to her today. Not fear. Just . . . worry, maybe?

"You don't think we should be doing this, do you?" I asked.

"I think I made that clear," Megan said, her voice even, eyes ahead. "Steelheart doesn't need to fall."

"I'm talking about Conflux specifically," I said. "You're nervous. You're normally not nervous."

"I just don't think we know enough about him," she said. "We shouldn't be hitting an Epic we don't even have photographs of."

"But you *are* nervous."

She drove, eyes forward and hands tight on the wheel.

"It's okay," I said. "I feel like a brick made of porridge."

She looked at me, brow scrunching up. The van's cab fell silent. Then Megan started to laugh.

"No, no," I said. "It makes sense! Listen. A brick is supposed to be strong, right? But if one were secretly made of porridge, and all of the other bricks didn't know, he'd sit around worrying that he'd be weak when the rest of them were strong. He'd get smooshed when he was placed in the wall, you see, maybe get some of his porridge mixed with that stuff they stick between bricks."

Megan was laughing even harder now, so hard she was actually gasping for breath. I tried to keep explaining but found myself smiling. I don't think I'd ever heard her laugh, *really* laugh. Not chuckle, not part her lips in wry mockery, but truly laugh. She was almost in tears by the time she got control of herself. I think we were fortunate she didn't crash into a post or something.

"David," she said between gasps, "I think that is the most ridiculous thing I've ever heard anyone say. The most outlandishly, audaciously ridiculous."

"Um . . ."

"Sparks," she said, exhaling. "I needed that."

"You did?"

She nodded.

"Can we . . . pretend that's why I said it, then?"

She looked at me, smiling, eyes sparkling. The tension was still there, but it had retreated somewhat. "Sure," she said. "I mean, bad puns are something of an art, right? So why not bad metaphors?"

"Exactly."

"And if they're an art, you are a master painter."

"Well, actually," I said, "that won't work, you see, because the metaphor makes too much sense. I'd have to be, like, the ace pilot or something." I cocked my head. "Actually, that makes a little bit of sense too." Sparks, doing it badly intentionally was hard too. I found that decidedly unfair.

"Y'all okay up there?" Cody said in our ears. The back of the van was separated from the cab by a metal partition, like a service van. There was a little window in it, but Cody preferred to use the mobiles to communicate.

"We're fine," Megan said. "Just having an abstract conversation about linguistic parallelism."

"You wouldn't be interested," I said. "It doesn't involve Scotsmen."

"Well, actually," Cody said, "the original tongue of my motherland . . ."

Megan and I looked at each other, then both pointedly reached to our mobiles and muted him.

"Let me know when he's done, Abraham," I said into mine.

Abraham sighed on the other end of the line. "Want to trade places? I'd sure like to be able to mute Cody myself right about now. It is regrettably difficult when he's sitting beside you."

I chuckled, then glanced at Megan. She was still grinning. Seeing her smile made me feel like I'd done something grand.

"Megan," Tia said in our ears, "keep on straight as you are. The convoy is progressing along the road, without deviations. You should meet up in another fifteen minutes or so."

"Affirmative."

Outside the streetlights flickered, as did the lights inside an apartment complex we were passing. Another brownout.

So far there hadn't been any looting. Enforcement walked the streets, and people were too frightened. Even as we drove past an intersection, I saw a large, mechanized armor unit lumbering down a side street. Twelve feet tall with arms that were little more than machine-gun barrels, the mechanized armor was accompanied by a five-man Enforcement Core. One soldier bore a distinctive energy weapon, painted bright red in warning. A few blasts from that could level a building.

"I've always wanted to pilot one of those armor units," I noted as we drove on.

"It's not much fun," Megan said.

"You've done it?" I asked, shocked.

"Yeah. They're stuffy inside, and they respond very sluggishly." She hesitated. "I'll admit that firing both rotary guns with wild abandon can be rather fulfilling, in a primal sort of way."

"We'll convert you away from those handguns yet."

"Not a chance," she said, reaching over and patting her underarm holster. "What if I got stuck in close confines?"

"Then you hit 'em with the stock of the gun," I said. "If they're too far away for that, it's always better to have a gun you can actually *hit* with."

She gave me a flat stare as she drove. "Rifles take too much time. They're not . . . spontaneous enough."

"This from the woman who complains when people improvise."

"I complain when *you* improvise," she said. "That's different from improvising myself. Besides, not all handguns are inaccurate. Have you ever fired an MT 318?"

"Nice gun, that," I admitted. "If I *had* to carry a handgun, I'd consider an MT. Problem is, the thing is so weak, you might as well just be throwing the bullets at someone. Likely to hurt them about as much."

"If you're a good shot, it doesn't matter how much stopping power a gun has."

"If you're a good shot," I said solemnly, raising a hand to my breast, "you're probably already using a rifle."

She snorted. "And what handgun *would* you pick, given the choice?"

"Jennings .44."

"A Spitfire?" she asked, incredulous. "Those things shoot about as accurately as tossing a handful of bullets into a fire."

"Sure. But if I'm using a handgun, that means someone is in my face. I might not have a chance for a second shot, so I want to down them fast. At that point accuracy doesn't matter, since they're so close anyway."

Megan just rolled her eyes and shook her head. "You're hopeless. You're buying into assumptions. You can be just as accurate with a handgun as you can with a rifle, and you can use it at more immediate ranges. In a way, because it's harder, *truly* skilled people use the handgun. Any slontze can hit with a rifle."

"You did *not* just say that."

"I did, and I'm driving, so I get to decide when the argument is over."

"But . . . but that makes no sense!"

"It doesn't need to," she said. "It's a brick made out of porridge."

"You know," Tia said in our ears, "you two *could* just each carry both a rifle *and* a handgun."

"That's not the point," I said at exactly the same time that Megan said, "You don't understand."

"Whatever," Tia answered. I could hear her sipping cola. "Ten minutes." Her tone said she was bored with our arguing. She, however, couldn't see that both of us were grinning.

Sparks, I like this girl, I thought, eyeing Megan. Who seemed to think she'd won the argument.

I tapped the mute-all button on my mobile. "I'm sorry," I found myself saying.

Megan raised an eyebrow at me.

"For doing what I did to the Reckoners," I said. "For making everything go a different way than you wanted it to. For dragging you into this."

She shrugged, then tapped her own mute button. "I'm past it."

"What changed?"

"Turns out I like you too much to hate you, Knees." She eyed me. "Don't let it go to your head."

I wasn't worried about my head. My heart, on the other hand, was another matter. A wave of shock ran through me. Had she really just said that?

Before I could melt too far, however, my mobile flashed. Prof was trying to contact us. I tapped it with a quick snap.

"Stay sharp, you two," he told us. He sounded a little suspicious. "Keep the lines up."

"Yes sir," I said immediately.

"Eight minutes," Tia said. "The convoy has taken a left on Frewanton. Turn right at the next intersection to continue on an intercept course."

Megan focused on her driving, and so—to keep *me* from focusing too much on *her*—I went over the plan a few times in my head.

We're going to do this one simply, Prof had said. *Nothing fancy at all. Conflux is fragile. He's a schemer, an organizer, a string puller, but he has no powers that will protect him.*

We pull up close to the motorcade, and Abraham uses the dowser to determine if a powerful Epic is really in the car. The van pulls forward in front of the convoy; we throw open the back doors, where Cody stands in costume.

Cody raises his hands; Abraham fires the gauss gun from behind. In the confusion, we'll hope it looks like he launched the bolt from his hand. We hit the entire limo, leave nothing but slag, and then flee. The surviving motorcycle guards can spread the story.

It *would* work. Hopefully. And without Conflux gifting his abilities to high-level Enforcement soldiers, the mechanized armor, the energy weapons, and the copters would all stop working. Fuel cells would run dry, and the city would run out of power.

"We're getting close," Tia said softly in our ears. "The limo is turning right on Beagle. Prof, use the beta formation; I'm pretty sure they're heading uptown, and that means they'll turn onto Finger Street. Megan, you're still on target."

"Got it," Prof said. "I was heading that way."

We passed an abandoned park from the old days. You could tell because of the frozen weeds and fallen branches transformed to steel. Only the dead ones had been changed—Steelheart couldn't affect living matter. In fact, his pulses had trouble with anything too close to a living body. A person's clothing often wouldn't be transformed, but the ground around them would change.

That kind of oddity was common in Epic powers; it was one of the things that didn't make scientific sense. A dead body and a living one could be very similar, scientifically. But one could be affected by many of the odder Epic powers while the other could not.

My breath fogged the window as we passed the playground, which was no longer safe for play. The weeds were now jagged bits of metal. Steelheart's steel didn't rust, but it could break, leaving sharp edges.

"Okay," Prof said a few minutes later. "I'm here. Climbing up the outside of the building. Megan, I want you to repeat back to me our contingencies."

"Nothing is going to go wrong," Megan said, her voice sounding both beside me and in my ear comm.

"Something always goes wrong," Prof said. I could hear him puffing as he climbed, though he had a gravatonic belt to help him. "Contingencies."

"If you or Tia give the word," Megan said, "we'll pull out and split up. You'll create a distraction. The four of us in the van will break into two squads and go opposite directions, heading for rally point gamma."

"That's what I don't get," I said. "How exactly are we going to go separate directions? We've only got one van."

"Oh, we've got a little surprise back here, lad," Cody said; I'd unmuted him when I'd unmuted Prof and the rest. "I'm actually hoping something goes wrong. I kinda want to use it."

"Never hope for something to go wrong," Tia said.

"But always expect it to," Prof added.

"You're paranoid, old man," Tia said.

"Damn right," Prof said, voice muffled, probably because he was hunkering down with his rocket launcher. I had assumed they'd put Cody in that position with a sniper rifle, but Prof said that he'd rather have something heavier when Enforcement might be involved. Diamond would have been proud.

"You're getting close, Megan," Tia said. "You should be on them in another few minutes. Maintain your speed; the limo is driving faster than it usually does."

"Do they suspect something?" Cody asked.

"They'd be fools not to," Abraham said softly. "Conflux will take extra care these days, I should think."

"It's worth the risk," Prof said. "Just be careful."

I nodded. With widespread power outages in the city, disabling Enforcement would leave the city in disorder. It would force Steelheart to step forward and take a firm hand to prevent looting or riots. That would mean revealing himself one way or another.

"He's never afraid to fight other Epics," I said.

"What are you talking about?" Prof asked.

"Steelheart. He'll face other Epics, no problem. But he doesn't like putting down riots by himself. He always uses Enforcement. We assumed it's because he doesn't want to bother, but what if it's something more? What if he's afraid of crossfire?"

"Who's that?" Abraham asked.

"No, not an Epic. It just occurred to me—what if Steelheart is afraid of getting hit accidentally? What if that's his weakness? He got hurt by my father, but my father wasn't aiming for him. What if he can only be hurt if the bullet was meant for someone else?"

"Possible," Tia said.

"We need to stay focused," Prof answered. "David, shelve that idea for the moment. We'll come back to it."

He was right. I was letting myself get distracted, like a rabbit doing math problems instead of looking for foxes.

Still . . . *If I'm right, he wouldn't ever be in danger in a one-on-one fight. He's faced other Epics with impunity. What he seems to be afraid of is a big battle, where bullets are flying around.* There was a sense to it. It was a simple thing, but most Epic weaknesses *were* simple.

"Slow down just a tad," Tia said softly.

Megan complied.

"Here it comes. . . ."

A sleek black car pulled out onto the dark street in front of us, going the same direction we were. It was flanked by a couple of motorcycles—good security, but not great. We knew from the Reckoners' original plan to hit Conflux that this convoy was probably his. We'd use the dowser to make sure, though.

We continued along behind the limo. I was impressed; even though they didn't know where the limo was going, Tia and Megan had timed it so that the limo came onto *our* street, not the other way around. We'd look far less suspicious this way.

My job was to keep my eyes open and, if things went wrong, to return fire so Megan could drive. I slipped a small pair of binoculars out of my pocket and hunkered down, sighting through them and inspecting the limo ahead.

"Well?" Prof asked in my ear.

"Looks good," I said.

"I'm going to pull up beside them at the next light," Megan said. "It will feel natural. Be ready, Abraham."

I slipped the binoculars into my pocket and tried to look nonchalant. The next light was green when we hit it, so Megan kept trailing the limo at a safe distance. The light after that, however, turned red before the limo reached it.

We pulled up slowly beside the limo, on the left side.

"There's an Epic near us for sure," Abraham said from the back of our van. He whistled softly. "A powerful one. *Very* powerful. The dowser is focusing in. I'll have more in a second."

One of the motorcycle drivers looked us over. He wore an Enforcement helmet and had an SMG strapped to his back. I tried to peer through the windows of the limo and catch a glimpse of Conflux. I'd always wondered what he looked like.

I couldn't see through the tinted rear glass. But as we pulled forward, I caught sight of someone sitting in the passenger seat. A woman who was vaguely familiar. She met my eyes but then looked away.

Business suit, black hair cut short over her ears. She was Nightwielder's assistant, the one who had been with him at Diamond's. She was probably a liaison to Enforcement; it made sense for her to be in the limo.

Something still made me suspicious. She'd met my eyes; she should have recognized me. Maybe . . . she *had* recognized me, but hadn't been surprised to see me.

We pulled forward, the light green, and I felt a spike of alarm. "Prof, I think it's a trap."

At that moment Nightwielder himself flew through the top of the limo, his arms spread wide, lines of darkness stretching from his fingers out into the night.

28

MOST people have never seen a High Epic in their glory. That's what we call it when they summon their powers in earnest—when they rise up in their might, their emotions kindled to wrath and fury.

There is a *glow* about them. The air grows sharp, like it's become full of electricity. Heartbeats still. The wind holds its breath. Nightwielder's rising made this the third time I'd seen something like it.

He was clothed in night, and blackness writhed and twisted about him. His face was pale, translucent, but his eyes were alight, his lips drawn in a sneer of hatred. It was the sneer of a god, barely tolerant of even his allies. He had come to destroy.

Looking upon him, I found myself terrified.

"Calamity!" Megan cursed, slamming her foot down on the gas and swerving the van to the side as shadows leaped from around Nightwielder toward us. They moved like ghostly fingers.

"Abort!" Tia called. "Get out of there!"

There was no time. Nightwielder moved in the air, ignoring things like wind and gravity. He flew like a specter out in front of his car and toward us. He wasn't the true danger, though—the true danger was those tendrils of blackness. The van could not avoid them; there were dozens.

Shoving aside my fear, I raised my rifle. The van rattled and jolted around me. Wisps of darkness moved up, wrapping around the vehicle.

Idiot, I thought. I dropped my rifle and shoved my hand into my coat pocket. The flashlight! Panicked, I flipped it on and shined it right in Nightwielder's face as he floated up beside my window. He was flying face-first, like he was swimming in the air.

The reaction was immediate. Though the flashlight gave off little light that I could see, Nightwielder's face immediately lost its incorporeity. His eyes stopped glowing, and the shadows vanished from around his head. The beam of invisible light pierced the dark tendrils like a laser through a pile of sheep.

In that UV light, Nightwielder's face didn't look divine. It looked frail, human, and very, very surprised. I struggled to get my gun up to fire at him, but the rifle was too unwieldy and my father's handgun was strapped under my arm where I couldn't get at it while holding the flashlight.

Nightwielder looked at me for the space of a single heartbeat, his eyes wide with terror. Then he fled in a blink, streaking sideways away from the van. I wasn't sure, but it seemed like he'd been losing altitude as I shined the light on him, as if all his powers were weakening.

He vanished down a side street, and the shadows that had been moving around the van retreated with him. I had a feeling he wasn't going to be back anytime soon, not after the scare I'd just given him.

Submachine-gun fire erupted around us, bullets pelting the side of the van with metallic *ping*s. I cursed, ducking down as my window shattered. The motorcyclists had opened fire. Though I was crouched low, I could still see a terrible sight: a sleek black Enforcement copter was rising from behind the commercial buildings in front of us.

"Calamity, Tia!" Megan screamed, twisting the wheel. "How did you miss *that*?"

"I don't know," Tia said. "I—"

A ball of light propelled by a long smoke trail snaked through the sky, exploding into the side of the copter. It tipped in the air, flames chewing its side, bits of debris fluttering through the sky.

Rotors slowing, it began to fall.

Rocket launcher, I realized. *Prof.*

"Don't panic." Prof's voice was steady. "We can survive this. Cody, Abraham, prep for the split."

"Prof!" Abraham said. "I think you—"

"Four more copters coming!" Tia cut in. "It looks like they had them hidden in warehouses all along the limo's route. They didn't know where we'd hit them; that one was just the closest. I . . . Megan, what are you *doing*?"

The copter was out of control. Smoke billowing from one side, it was spinning in a crooked circle and coming down toward the roadway right in front of us. Megan wasn't turning; she'd punched up the speed, leaning over the wheel and driving the van forward in a frenzied, insane rush right toward where the copter would hit.

I tensed, pushing myself back in my seat and grabbing the side of my door in a panic. She'd lost her mind!

There was no time to object. Bullets pelting us, streets outside a blur, Megan drove the van right under the copter as it crashed to the street with force enough to make the earth beneath us tremble.

Something clipped the top of the van with a ghastly screech of metal on metal, and we spun out to the side, hitting the wall of a brick building and grinding my side of the van along it. Noise, chaos, sparks. My door ripped free. Bricks ground against steel mere inches from me. It seemed to last forever.

Then, a second later, the van lurched to a halt. Trembling, I took a deep breath. I was covered in pebbles of safety glass; the windshield had shattered.

Megan sat breathing hard in the driver's seat—a mad grin on her face, eyes wide. She looked at me.

"Calamity!" I said, looking in Megan's side mirror back at the burning copter. It had hit the roadway right after we passed under it, blocking off the bikers and the pursuit. "Calamity, Megan! *That was awesome!*"

Megan's grin broadened. "You two okay back there?" she called, looking through the little window into the back of the van.

"I feel like I've been in a centrifuge," Cody complained, groaning. "I think the Scotsman drained to my feet and the American floated up to my ears."

"Prof," Abraham said. "I still had the dowser on as Nightwielder fled, and it was focusing on Epic locations. I got confusing readings, but there is *another Epic* in that limo. Maybe a third. That doesn't make sense. . . ."

"No, it does," Megan said, hurriedly pushing open her door and hopping out onto the street. "They really *were* transporting Conflux; they didn't know if we'd strike. They just wanted to be ready if we did. He was in that car. That's what you're sensing, Abraham. Probably a third, lesser Epic as another safety measure."

I hastily reached to undo my seat belt, then realized the right half had been ripped free as we skidded against the wall. I shivered, then scrambled out of the van through Megan's side.

"Hurry up, you four," Prof said. I heard an engine revving on his side of the link. "Those other copters are almost upon you, and those cycles will circle around."

"I'm watching them," Tia said. "You've got maybe a minute."

"Where's Nightwielder?" Prof asked.

"David scared him off with a flashlight," Megan said, reaching the back of the van and pulling the doors open.

"Nice work," Prof said.

I grinned in satisfaction as I reached the back of the van. I was just in time to see Cody and Abraham push the back off a huge crate inside. I hadn't seen them load up the van—that had happened in the hangar.

Cody was wearing a dark green jacket and glasses, the uniform we'd devised for Limelight. My eyes were drawn to the items in the crate: three shiny green motorcycles.

"The cycles from Diamond's shop!" I exclaimed, pointing. "You *did* buy them!"

"Sure did," Abraham said, running his hand along the sleek, dark green finish on one of the cycles. "Wasn't about to let machines like *this* pass us by."

"But . . . you told me no!"

Abraham laughed. "I've heard how you drive, David." He pushed a ramp out from the back of the van and rolled one of the bikes down to Megan. She climbed on, starting it up. Small ovals mounted to the sides of the cycles glowed a bright green. I'd noticed those at Diamond's.

Gravatonics, I thought. *To make the cycles lighter, maybe?* Gravatonics couldn't make things fly; they were just used to reduce recoil or to make heavy items easier to move.

Abraham rolled the next vehicle down.

"You *were* going to get to drive one, David," Cody said, quickly gathering things out of the back of the van, including the dowser. "But somebody wrecked the van."

"It would never stay ahead of the copters anyway," Megan said. "Two of us will have to ride tandem."

"I'll take David on mine," Cody said. "Grab that pack, lad. Where are the helmets?"

"Hurry!" Tia exclaimed, her voice urgent.

I jumped to grab the pack Cody pointed out. It was heavy. "I can drive!" I said.

Megan glanced at me as she pulled on her helmet. "You took out two signs trying to drive around *one* corner."

"Small ones!" I said, slinging on the pack and dashing toward Cody's cycle. "And I was under a lot of pressure!"

"Really?" Megan said. "Kind of like we are now?"

I hesitated. *Wow. I walked into that one, didn't I?*

Cody and Abraham started up their cycles. There were only three helmets. I didn't ask for one—hopefully my Reckoner jacket would be enough.

Before I could reach Cody, I heard the thumping sounds of a copter overhead. An Enforcement armored van appeared out of a side street, a man in the machine-gun turret on the top. He opened fire.

"Calamity!" Cody said, kicking his cycle forward with a burst of speed as the bullets hit the ground near him. I fell back beside the wreckage of our van.

"Get on," Megan yelled to me; she was closest. "Now!"

I ducked down and ran to her cycle, throwing myself up behind her and grabbing her waist as she revved the engine. We lurched away, zipping down an alleyway as Enforcement cycles came roaring out of another side street.

We lost Cody and Abraham in a flash. I held tight to Megan— something I'll admit I wished I could have done under less insane circumstances. Cody's bag thumped against my back.

I left my rifle in the van, I realized with a sinking feeling. I hadn't noticed in the panic to grab Cody's bag and get to a cycle.

I felt terrible, like I'd abandoned a friend.

We burst out of the alleyway and Megan turned onto a dark city street, increasing our speed to what I felt was a pretty ridiculous level. The wind blew against my face so powerfully, I had to squeeze in close and low against her back.

"Where are we going?" I yelled.

Fortunately we still had our mobiles and our earpieces. Though I couldn't hear her naturally, her voice spoke in my ear. "There's a plan! We all go different ways and meet up!"

"Except you're going the wrong way," Tia said, sounding exasperated. "And so is Abraham!"

"Where is the limo?" Abraham asked; even with his voice in my ear, it was hard to hear him over the wind.

"Forget the limo," Prof ordered.

"I can still get to Conflux," Abraham said.

"It doesn't matter," Prof said.

"But—"

"It's over," Prof said, voice harsh. "We ran."

We ran.

Megan hit a bump and I jolted, but hung on tight. My mind reeled as I realized what Prof meant. An Epic who truly sought to defeat Steelheart wouldn't have run from Enforcement; he'd have been able to handle a few squads of them on his own.

By fleeing, we proved what we really were. Steelheart would never face us in person now.

"Then I want to do something," Abraham said, "make him hurt before we abandon the city. Half of Enforcement is going to be out chasing us. That limo is unguarded, and I've got some grenades."

"Jon, let him try," Tia said. "This is already a disaster. At least we can make it cost Steelheart."

Streetlights were a blur. I could hear cycles behind us, and I risked glancing over my shoulder. *Calamity!* I thought. They were close, their headlights illuminating the street.

"You'll never make it," Prof said to Abraham. "Enforcement is on you."

"We'll draw them off him," I said.

"Wait," Megan said. "We'll *what?*"

"Thanks," Abraham said. "Meet up with me at Fourth and Nodell; see if you can take the pressure away from me."

Megan tried to twist around and glare at me through her helmet's visor.

"Keep driving!" I said urgently.

"Slontze," she said, then took the next turn. *Without slowing down.*

I screamed, certain we were dead. The bike went almost parallel to the ground, skidding against the street, but the gravatonics on the side glowed brightly, keeping us from toppling. We half skidded, half drove around the corner, almost like we were tethered to it.

We came upright, my scream dying off.

There was an explosion from behind us and the steel street trembled. I looked over my shoulder, hair whipping in the wind. One of the black Enforcement cycles had just failed to take the corner at speed, and was now a smoking wreck pasted to the side of a steel building. Their gravatonics didn't seem as good as ours, if they even had any.

"How many are there?" Megan asked.

"Three now. No, wait, there are two more. *Five.* Sparks!"

"Great," Megan muttered. "How exactly do you expect us to take heat off Abraham?"

"I don't know. Improvise!"

"They're setting up roadblocks on nearby streets," Tia warned in our ears. "Jon, copter on Seventeenth."

"On my way."

"What are you doing?" I asked.

"Trying to keep you kids alive," Prof said.

"Sparks," Cody cursed. "Roadblock on Eighth. Taking an alleyway over to Marston."

"No," Tia said. "They're trying to get you to go that way. Circle back around. You can escape into the understreets on Moulton."

"Right," Cody said.

Megan and I burst out onto a large roadway, and a second later Abraham's cycle came skidding out of a side street in front of us, almost level to the ground, the gravatonics keeping it from tipping over completely. It was impressive; the bike turned almost on its side, wheels spinning, sparks spraying out from underneath it. The gravatonic mechanisms cushioned the momentum so the wheels could grip the road and the cycle could turn, but only after an extended skid.

I'll bet I could drive one of these things, I told myself. *It doesn't look too hard.* Like slipping on a banana peel around a corner at eighty miles an hour. Piece of cake.

I glanced over my shoulder. There were at least a dozen black cycles behind us now, though we were going too fast for them to dare shooting at us. Everyone needed to concentrate on their driving. That was probably the idea behind going so fast in the first place.

"Armored unit!" Tia exclaimed. "Just ahead!"

We barely had time to react as a juggernaut of an armor unit, on two legs and standing fifteen feet high, lumbered out onto the street and opened fire with both rotary guns. Bullets hit the steel building wall beside us, creating a spray of sparks. I kept my head down and my jaw clenched as Megan kicked a lever on the cycle and sent us down in a long gravatonic skid, almost parallel to the ground, to pass under the bullets.

Wind ripped at my jacket, sparks blinded my vision. I could barely make out two enormous feet of steel on either side as we slid between the armor's legs. Megan brought the cycle up in a wide spin as we turned a corner. Abraham got around the armor to one side, but his cycle was trailing smoke.

"I'm hit," Abraham said.

"Are you all right?" Tia asked, alarmed.

"Jacket kept me in one piece," Abraham said with a grunt.

"Megan," I said softly. "He doesn't look good." Abraham was slowing, one hand holding his side.

She glanced at him, then turned quickly back to the road. "Abraham, as we take the next curve, I want you to break right into the first alleyway. They're far enough behind that they might not see. I'll keep straight and draw them after."

"They'll wonder where I went," Abraham said. "It—"

"Do it!" Megan said sharply.

He didn't object further. We took the next corner but had to slow down to keep from outpacing Abraham. I could see he was trailing blood, his cycle riddled with bullet holes. It was a wonder it was still moving.

As we came around, Abraham turned and darted right. Megan punched her cycle and the wind rose to a howl as we raced down a dark street. I risked a glance behind me and almost lost Cody's pack as it slipped down my shoulder. I had to release Megan for a moment with one hand and hold it, which threw me off balance and nearly sent me tumbling to the ground.

"Be careful," Megan said with a curse.

"Right," I said, confused. In that jumbled moment, I *thought* I'd seen another green cycle like our own, following us close behind.

I looked again. The Enforcement cycles seemed to have taken the bait and were following us and not Abraham. Their headlights were a wave of light on the street, helmets reflecting streetlights. Of the phantom cycle I'd thought I'd seen, there was no sign.

"Sparks," Tia said. "Megan, they've got blockades going up all around you, particularly in places that lead to the understreets. They seem to have guessed that's where we're trying to run."

In the distance I saw the flash of an explosion in the sky, and another copter began trailing smoke. There was yet another heading our way, however—a black form with blinking lights against the dark sky.

Megan sped up.

"Megan?" Tia said, her voice laced with urgency. *"You're heading straight for a blockade."*

Megan gave no response. I could feel her body growing more

and more rigid in my grip. She leaned forward, and intensity seemed to *stream* off her.

"Megan!" I said, noticing the lights flashing ahead as Enforcement set up their blockade. Cars, vans, trucks. A dozen or more soldiers, a mechanized unit.

"MEGAN!" I screamed.

She seemed to shake for a moment, then cursed and punched us to the side as gunfire pelted the street around us. We tore down an alleyway, the wall an inch from my elbow, then hit the next street and went down in a long turn, throwing sparks as we took the corner.

"I'm out," Abraham said softly, grunting. "Abandoning the cycle. I can make it to one of the bolt-holes. They didn't spot me, but some soldiers came down and started setting up in the stairway after I passed."

"Sparks," Cody murmured. "Are you monitoring the Enforcement audio lines, Tia?"

"Yeah," Tia said. "They're confused. They think this is a full-out assault on the city. Prof keeps blasting copters out of the air, and we all went different directions. Enforcement seems to think they're fighting dozens, maybe hundreds of insurgents."

"Good," Prof said. "Cody, are you clear?"

"I'm still dodging a few cycles," he said. "I've ended up looping around." He hesitated. "Tia, where's the limo? Is it still out?"

"It's breaking for Steelheart's palace," she said.

"I'm heading along that way too," Cody said. "What street?"

"Cody . . . ," Prof said.

Gunfire from behind distracted me from the rest of the conversation. I caught a glimpse of cycles, their drivers holding out SMGs and firing. We were going more slowly now; Megan had driven us into a slum neighborhood where the streets were smaller, and she was weaving us through lots of twists and turns.

"Megan, that's dangerous," Tia said. "There are a lot of dead ends in there."

"The other way is all dead ends," Megan answered. She seemed to have recovered from whatever lapse had almost led her to drive us right into a blockade.

"I'm going to have trouble leading you," Tia said. "Try to take the next right."

Megan started to break that direction, but an approaching cycle moved to cut us off, the soldier firing an SMG one-handed toward us in a spray. Megan cursed and slowed, sending the soldier on ahead, then she broke left down an alleyway. We nearly slammed into a large garbage bin, but she managed to weave around it. I guessed that we were barely going twenty.

Barely going twenty, I thought. Twenty mph down narrow alleys while being shot at. It was still insane, just a different kind of insane.

I could hold on pretty well with one arm at these speeds, Cody's pack thumping against my back. I probably should have dropped that by now. I didn't even know what was . . .

I felt at the pack, realizing something. I carefully slung it down in front of me, between Megan and myself. I gripped the cycle between my knees, let go of Megan, and unzipped the pack.

The gauss gun lay inside. Shaped like a regular assault rifle, perhaps a little longer, it had one of the power cells we'd recovered hooked up at the side. I pulled it out. With the power cell it was heavy, but I could still maneuver it.

"Megan!" Tia said. "Blockade ahead."

We turned into another alley, and I nearly lost the gun as I grabbed onto Megan with one arm.

"No!" Tia said. "Not right. That's—"

A motorcycle followed us into the alleyway. Bullets hit the wall just above my head. And right in front of us the alley ended in a wall. Megan tried to brake.

I didn't think. I grabbed the gun with both hands, leaned back, and raised the barrel right over Megan's shoulder.

Then I fired at the wall.

29

THE wall before us went up in a flash of green energy. Megan tried to turn the cycle and stop. We skidded through the churning green smoke, pebbles scattering under our tires, and slid out onto the street on the other side, where we came to a halt. Megan's body was braced for impact. She seemed stunned.

The Enforcement cyclist burst from the smoke. I swung the gauss gun and blasted his cycle out from underneath him. The shot turned the whole motorcycle into a flash of green energy, vaporizing it and part of the officer on it. His body went rolling.

The gun was amazing—there was no recoil, and the shots *vaporized* instead of really *exploding*. That left little debris, but gave a great light show and a lot of smoke.

Megan turned toward me, a grin splitting her lips. "About time you started doing something useful back there."

"Go," I said. The sound of more cycles was coming from the alleyway.

Megan revved our motorcycle, then led us in a darting, stomach-churning pattern through the narrow streets of the slum. I couldn't turn to fire the gun behind us as we drove, so instead I clung to her waist with one hand and settled the gun on her shoulder to steady it, using the iron sights, scope folded down to the side.

We roared out of an alleyway and skidded toward a blockade. I blasted a hole through a truck for us, then for good measure hit the armored unit with a shot to the leg. Soldiers scattered, yelling, some trying to fire as we sped through the opening I'd made. The armor unit collapsed and Megan dodged to the side, down a dark alley. Shouts and curses sounded behind as some of the cycles chasing us got caught up in the confusion.

"Nice work," Tia said in our ears, her voice calm again. "I think I can get you to the understreets. There's an old tunnel up ahead at the bottom of a flood gulley. You might have to blast your way through some walls, though."

"I think I can hit a wall or two," I said. "So long as they aren't good at dodging."

"Be careful," Prof said. "That gun drinks energy like Tia with a six-pack of cola. That power cell could run a small city, but it will give you only a dozen shots at best. Abraham, you still with us?"

"I'm here."

"You in the bolt-hole?"

"Yes. Bandaging my wound. It's not too bad."

"I'll be the judge of that. I'm almost to you. Cody, status?"

"I can see the limo," Cody said in my ear as Megan took another corner. "I've mostly shaken pursuit. I've got a tensor; I'll hit the limo with a grenade, then use the tensor to drill myself down to the understreets."

"Not an option," Prof said. "It'll take you too long to drill down that far."

"Wall!" Tia said.

"Got it," I said, blasting a hole through a wall at the end of an alleyway. We roared out into a backyard, and I blasted a hole in another wall, letting us cut into the next yard. Megan turned us to the right, then drove us through a very narrow slot between two houses.

"Go left," Tia said as we reached the street.

"Prof," Cody said. "I can *see* the limo. I can hit it."

"Cody, I don't—"

"I'm taking the shot, Prof," Cody said. "Abraham's right. Steelheart's going to come for us after this. We need to hurt him as much as we can, while we can."

"All right."

"Turn right," Tia said.

We turned.

"I'm sending you through a large building," Tia said. "Can you handle that?"

Gunfire sprayed against the wall beside us, and Megan cursed, hunkering down farther. I held the gauss gun in a sweaty grip, feeling terribly exposed with my back to the enemy. I could hear the cycles back there.

"They *really* seem to want you two," Tia said softly. "They're pulling a lot of resources toward you, and . . . Calamity!"

"What?" I said.

"My video feed just went out," Tia said. "Something's wrong. Cody?"

"Little busy," he grunted.

More gunfire sounded from behind. Something hit the cycle, jarring us, and Megan cursed.

"The building, Tia!" I said. "How do we find that building? We'll lose them inside."

"Second right," Tia told us. "Then straight to the end of the road. It's an old mall, and the gulley is just behind it. I was looking for other routes, but—"

"This will work," Megan said curtly. "David, be ready to open the place up for us."

"Got it," I said, steadying the gun, though it was harder now that she'd picked up speed. We took a corner, then turned toward a large, flat structure at the end of the road. I vaguely remembered malls from the days before Calamity. They'd been marketplaces, all enclosed.

Megan was driving fast and heading right at it. I took aim carefully and blasted through a set of steel doors in the front. We shot through the smoke, entering the heavy blackness of an abandoned building. The headlight of the cycle showed shops on either side of us.

The place had been looted long ago, though a lot of wares remained in the shops. Clothing that had been turned to steel wasn't particularly useful.

Megan wove easily through the mall's open corridors, taking us up a frozen escalator onto the second floor. Engines echoed throughout the building as Enforcement cycles followed us in.

Tia couldn't guide us any longer, it appeared, but Megan seemed to have an idea of what she was doing. From the balcony above, I got a shot at the cycles following us. I hit the ground in front of them, taking a chunk out of the floor and causing several to skid out, the others scattering for cover. None seemed to have drivers as skilled as Megan.

"Wall up ahead," Megan said.

I blasted it, then glanced at the energy meter on the side of the gauss gun. Prof was right; I'd drained it pretty quickly. We had maybe a couple of shots left.

We roared out into open air and the gravatonics on the cycle engaged, softening our landing as we fell one story to the street below. We still hit hard; the cycle wasn't intended to take jumps that high. I grunted, my backside and legs hammered from the impact. Megan immediately punched the vehicle forward down a narrow alleyway behind the mall.

I could see the ground fall away up ahead. The gulley. We only had to—

A sleek black copter rose out of the gulley in front of us, and the rotary guns on its sides began to spin up.

Not a chance, I thought, raising the gauss gun with both hands, sighting. Megan ducked lower and the cycle hit the edge of the gulley. The copter started firing. I could see the pilot's helmet through the glass of the cockpit.

I took the shot.

I'd often dreamed of doing incredible things. I'd imagined what it would be like to work with the Reckoners, to fight the Epics, to actually *do* things instead of sitting around thinking about them. With that shot, I finally got my chance.

I hung in the air, staring down a hundred-ton death machine, and squeezed the trigger. I popped the copter's canopy dead on, vaporizing it and the pilot inside. For a moment I felt like the Epics must. Like a god.

And then I fell out of the seat.

I should have expected it—going into free fall in a twenty-foot ravine with two hands on my gun and none on my ride made it kind of inevitable. I won't say I was happy to find myself plummeting toward broken legs and probably worse.

But that shot . . . That shot had been worth it.

I didn't feel much of the fall. It happened so fast. I hit mere moments after realizing I'd lost my seat, and I heard a crunch. That was followed by a *boom* that deafened me, and that was followed by a wave of heat.

I lay there, stunned, as my vision swam. I found myself facing the wreckage of the copter, which burned nearby. I felt numb.

Suddenly Megan was shaking me. I coughed, rolling over, and looked up at her. She'd pulled off her helmet, so I could see her face. Her beautiful face. She actually seemed concerned about me. That made me smile.

She was saying something. My ears rang, and I squinted, trying to read her lips. I could barely hear the words. ". . . up, you slontze! Get up!"

"You aren't supposed to shake someone who's suffered a fall," I mumbled. "Might have a broken back."

"You'll have a broken head if you don't *start moving*."

"But—"

"Idiot. Your jacket absorbed the blow. Remember? The one you wear to keep you from getting killed? They're supposed to make up for you doing stupid things like letting go of me in midair."

"It's not my intention to let go of you," I mumbled. "Not ever."

She froze.

Wait. Had I just said that out loud?

Jacket, I thought, wiggling my toes, then raising both arms. *The jacket's shielding device protected me. And . . . and we're still being chased.*

Calamity! I *was* a slontze. I rolled onto my knees and let Megan help me to my feet. I coughed a few times but felt more stable by the moment. I let go of her and was pretty steady by the time we reached the cycle, which she'd landed without crashing.

"Wait," I said, looking around. "Where is . . ."

The gauss gun lay in several pieces where it had fallen and hit a steel rock. I felt a sinking feeling, though I knew the gun wasn't nearly as useful to us now. We couldn't use it to pretend to be an Epic any longer, not now that Enforcement had seen me shooting it.

Still, it was a pity to lose such a nice weapon. Particularly after leaving my own rifle in the van. I was making a real habit of that sort of thing.

I climbed onto the cycle behind Megan, who pulled on her helmet again. The poor machine was looking pretty ragged, scratched and dented, the windshield cracked. One of the gravatonics—a palm-size oval on the right side—didn't light up like the others anymore. But the cycle still started, and the engine roared as Megan drove us down the ravine toward a large tunnel up ahead. It looked like it led into the sewage system, but a lot of things like that were misleading in Newcago, what with the Great Transfersion and the creation of the understreets.

"Hey, all y'all?" Cody said softly in our ears. By some miracle I'd kept my mobile and earpiece through the fall. "Something strange is going on. Something very, very strange is going on."

"Cody," Tia said. "Where are you?"

"Limo's down," he said. "I shot out one of the tires and it drove itself into a wall. I had to eliminate six soldiers before I could approach."

Megan and I passed into the tunnel, the darkness deepening. The ground sloped downward. I was vaguely familiar with the area, and I figured this would lead us into the understreets near Gibbons Street, a relatively unpopulated area.

"What about Conflux?" Prof asked Cody.

"He wasn't inside the limo."

"Maybe one of the Enforcement officers you shot was actually Conflux," Tia said.

"Nah," Cody said. "I found him. In the trunk."

The line was quiet for a moment.

"You're sure it's him?" Prof asked.

"Well, no," Cody said. "Maybe they had some *other* Epic tied up in their trunk. Either way, the dowser says this lad's *very* powerful. But he's unconscious."

"Shoot him," Prof said.

"No," Megan said. "Bring him."

"I think she's right, Prof," Cody said. "If he's tied up, he can't be that strong. Either that, or they've used his weakness to make him impotent."

"We don't know his weakness, though," Prof said. "Put him out of his misery."

"I'm not shooting an unconscious fellow, Prof," Cody said. "Not even an Epic."

"Then leave him."

I was torn. Epics deserved to die. All of them. But why was he unconscious—what were they doing with him? Was it even Conflux?

"Jon," Tia said. "We might need this. If it *is* Conflux, he could tell us things. We might even be able to use him against Steelheart, or bargain for our escape."

"He's not supposed to be very dangerous," I admitted, speaking into the line. My lip was bleeding. I'd bit it when I'd fallen, and now that I was a little more aware of things I realized my leg was aching and my side was *throbbing*. The jackets helped, but they were far from perfect.

"Fine," Prof said. "Bolt-hole seven, Cody. Don't take him to the base. Leave him tied up, blindfolded, and gagged. Do *not* talk to him. We need to deal with him together."

"Right," Cody said. "I'm on it."

"Megan and David," Prof said, "I want you to—"

I lost the rest as gunfire erupted around us. The cycle—battered as it was—spun out and went down.

Right onto the side where the gravatonics were broken.

30

WITHOUT the gravatonics, the cycle reacted like any normal motor-cycle would when falling onto its side at very high speed.

Which isn't a good thing.

I was immediately ripped free, the cycle skidding out from underneath me as my leg hit the ground and the friction pulled me backward. Megan wasn't so lucky. She got pinned under the cycle, its weight grinding her against the ground. It collided with the wall of the tubular steel corridor.

The tunnel wavered, and my leg burned with pain. As I rolled to a halt and things stopped shaking, I realized that I was still alive. I actually found that surprising.

Behind us, from an alcove we had driven past, two men in full Enforcement armor stepped out of the shadows. There were some small, faint lights ringing the edge of the alcove. By that light I could see that the soldiers looked relaxed. I swore I could hear one chuckling inside his helmet as he said something over the comm unit to his companion. They assumed Megan and I would both be dead—or at least knocked out of fighting shape—by such a crash.

To Calamity with that, I thought, cheeks hot with anger. Before I'd had time to think, I'd unholstered the pistol under my arm—the pistol that had killed my father—and unloaded four shots at nearly point-blank range into the men. I didn't aim for their chests, not with their armor. The sweet spot was the neck.

Both men fell. I breathed in a deep, ragged breath, my hand and gun shaking in front of me. I blinked a few times, shocked that I'd managed to hit them. Maybe Megan was right about handguns.

I groaned, then managed to sit up. My Reckoner jacket was in tatters; many of the diodes along its inside—the ones that generated the protective field—were smoking or entirely ripped free. My leg was scraped badly along one side. Though it hurt fiercely, the lacerations weren't too deep. I was able to stumble to my feet and walk. Kind of.

The pain was . . . rather unpleasant.

Megan! The thought came through the daze, and—stupid though it was—I didn't check to see if the two soldiers were actually dead. I limped over to where the fallen cycle had skidded up against the wall. The only light here was from my mobile. I pushed aside the wreckage and found Megan sprawled beneath, her jacket in even worse shape than mine.

She didn't look good. She wasn't moving, her eyes were closed, and her helmet was cracked, only halfway on. Blood trailed down her cheek. It was the color of her lips. Her arm was twisted at an awkward angle, and her entire side—leg up to torso—was bloodied. I knelt, aghast, the cool, calm light of my mobile revealing horrible wounds everywhere I turned it.

"David?" Tia's voice came softly from my mobile, which hung in its place from my jacket. It was a miracle it still functioned, though I'd lost my earpiece. "David? I can't reach Megan. What's going on?"

"Megan's down," I said numbly. "Her mobile is gone. Shattered, probably." It had been attached to her jacket, which was mostly gone also.

Breathing. I have to see if she's breathing. I leaned down, trying to use my mobile screen to catch her breath. Then I thought to check for a pulse. *I'm in shock. I'm not thinking right.* Could you think that, when you weren't thinking right?

I pressed my fingers against Megan's neck. The skin felt clammy.

"David!" Tia said urgently. "David, there's chatter on the Enforcement channels. They know where you are. There are multiple units converging on you. Infantry and armor. Go!"

I felt a pulse. Shallow, light, but there.

"She's alive," I said. "Tia, she's alive!"

"You *have* to get out of there, David!"

Moving Megan could make things worse for her, but leaving her would definitely make things worse. If they took her she'd be tortured and executed. I pulled off my tattered jacket and used it to wrap my leg. As I worked I felt something in the pocket. I pulled it out. The pen detonator and blasting caps.

In a moment of lucidity I stuck one of the blasting caps on the cycle's fuel cell. I'd heard you could destabilize and blow those, if you knew what you were doing—which I didn't. It seemed like a good idea, though. My *only* idea. I took my mobile and attached it to my wrist mount. Then, sucking in a deep breath, I shoved aside the broken motorcycle—the front wheel had been ripped clean off—and lifted Megan.

Her broken helmet slipped free, falling off and cracking against the ground. That made her hair cascade down over my shoulder. She was heavier than she looked. People always are. Though she was small, she was compact, *dense*. I decided she'd probably not like hearing me describe her that way.

I got her up over my shoulders, then began an unsteady hike down the tunnel. Tiny yellow lights hung from the ceiling periodically, giving barely enough light to see by, even for an understreeter like me.

Soon my shoulders and back were complaining. I kept on going, one foot after another. I wasn't moving very quickly. I wasn't thinking very well either.

"David." Prof's voice. Quiet, intense.

"I'm *not* leaving her," I said through clenched teeth.

"I wouldn't have you do something like that," Prof said. "I'd much sooner have you stand your ground and make Enforcement gun you both down."

Not very comforting.

"It's not going to come to that, son," Prof said. "Help is on its way."

"I think I can hear them," I said. I'd finally reached the end of the tunnel; it opened onto a narrow crossroads in the understreets. There were no buildings here, just steel corridors. I didn't know this part of town well.

The ceiling was solid, with no gaps up to the air above like there were in the area where I'd grown up. Those were definitely shouts I heard echoing from the right. I heard *clank*s from behind, steel feet pounding against the steel ground. More shouts. They'd found the cycle.

I leaned up against the wall, shifting Megan's weight, then pressed the button on my pen detonator. I was relieved to hear a *pop* from behind as the cycle's fuel cell blew. The shouts rose. Maybe I'd caught a few of them in the blast; if I was really lucky they'd assume I was hiding somewhere near the wreckage and had tossed a grenade or something.

I hefted Megan, then took the left turn at the crossroads. Her blood had soaked my clothing. She was probably dead by—

No. I wouldn't think about that. One foot in front of the other. Help was coming. Prof *promised* help was coming. It would come. Prof didn't lie. Jonathan Phaedrus, founder of the Reckoners, a man I somehow understood. If there was anything in this world I felt I could trust, it was him.

I walked a good five minutes before I was forced to pull up short. The tunnel in front of me ended in a flat wall of steel. Dead end. I glanced over my shoulder to see flashlights and shadows moving. No escape that way.

The corridor around me was wide, maybe twenty paces across, and tall. There was some old construction equipment on the ground, though most of it looked to have been picked over by opportunists. There were a few heaps of broken bricks and cinder blocks. Some-one had been building more rooms down here recently. Well, those might provide some cover.

I stumbled over and laid Megan down behind the largest of the piles, then I flipped my mobile to manual response. Prof and the others wouldn't be able to hear me unless I touched the screen to broadcast, but it also meant they wouldn't give away my position by trying to contact me.

I crouched down behind the bricks. The pile didn't give me com-plete cover, but it was better than nothing. Cornered, outgunned, with no way to . . .

Suddenly I felt like an idiot. I dug in the zip pocket on my trou-ser leg, fishing for my tensor. I pulled it out triumphantly. Maybe I could dig down to the steel catacombs, or even just dig out to the side and find a safer path.

I pulled on the glove, and only then did I realize that the tensor had been shredded. I stared at it with a sinking despair. It had been in the pocket on the leg I'd landed on when falling, and the pouch had been ripped at the bottom. The tensor was missing two fingers, and the electronics had been shattered, pieces hanging off like eyes drooping out of a zombie's sockets in an old horror movie.

I almost laughed as I settled back down. The Enforcement soldiers were searching the corridors. Shouts. Footsteps. Flashlights. Getting closer.

My mobile blinked softly. I turned the volume way down, then pressed the screen and leaned in. "David?" Tia asked in a very quiet voice. "David, where are you?"

"I reached the bottom of the tunnel," I whispered back, holding the mobile up to my mouth. "I turned left."

"Left? That's a dead end. You need to—"

"I know," I said. "There were soldiers the other directions." I glanced at Megan, lying slumped on the floor. I tested her neck again.

Still a pulse. I closed my eyes in relief. *Not that it matters now.*

"Calamity," Tia swore. I heard gunfire and jumped, thinking it was from my position. But it wasn't. It was from the line.

"Tia?" I hissed.

"They're here," she said. "Don't worry about me. I can hold this place. David, you have to—"

"Hey, you!" a voice called from the intersection.

I ducked down, but the mound of bricks wasn't large enough to hide me completely unless I was practically lying flat.

"There's someone over there!" the voice shouted. Powerful, Enforcement-issue flashlights pointed my direction. Most of those would be on the ends of assault rifles.

My mobile flashed. I tapped it. "David." Prof's voice. He sounded winded. "Use the tensor."

"Broken," I whispered. "I ruined it in the crash."

Silence.

"Try it anyway," Prof urged.

"Prof, it's dead." I peeked over the bricks. A large crowd of soldiers was gathering at the other end of the hall. Several were kneeling with guns pointed in my direction, eyes to scopes. I kept low.

"Just do it," Prof ordered.

I sighed, then pressed my hand against the ground. I closed my eyes, but it wasn't easy to concentrate.

"Hold up your arms and walk forward slowly!" a voice shouted down the hall toward me. "If you do not show yourself, we will be forced to open fire."

I tried as best I could to ignore them. I focused on the tensor, on the vibrations. For a moment I thought I felt something, a low hum—deep, powerful.

It was gone. This was stupid. Like trying to saw a hole in a wall using only a bottle of soda.

"Sorry, Prof," I said. "It's busted up good." I checked the magazine on my father's gun. Five rounds left. Five precious rounds that might be able to hurt Steelheart. I'd never have the chance to find out.

"You are running out of time, friend!" the soldier called toward me.

"You have to hold out," Prof said urgently. His voice sounded frail with the volume down so low.

"You should go to Tia," I said, preparing myself.

"She'll be fine," Prof said. "Abraham is on his way to help her, and the hideout was designed with an attack in mind. She can seal the entrance and wait them out. David, you *must* hang on long enough for me to arrive."

"I'll see that they don't take us alive, Prof," I promised. "The safety of the Reckoners is more important than I am." I fished at Megan's side, getting out her handgun and then flipping off its safety. SIG Sauer P226, .40 caliber. A nice gun.

"I'm coming, son," Prof said softly. *"Hold out."*

I peeked up. The officers were advancing, guns raised. They probably wanted to take me alive. Well, maybe that would let me take a few of them out before I fell.

I lifted Megan's gun and let loose a burst of rapid-fire shots. They had the intended effect; the officers scattered, seeking cover.

Some fired back, and chips sprayed across me as bricks exploded to automatic-weapon fire.

Well, so much for hoping they wanted me alive.

I was sweating. "Hell of a way to go, eh?" I found myself saying to Megan as I ducked around and fired on an officer who'd gotten too close. I think one of the bullets actually got through his armor—he was limping as he jumped behind a few rusty barrels.

I hunkered down again, assault-rifle fire sounding like firecrackers in a tin can. Which was, as I thought about it, kind of what this was. *I'm getting better.* I smiled wryly as I dumped the magazine from Megan's gun and locked a new one in.

"I'm sorry to let you down," I said to her immobile form. Her breathing had grown more shallow. "You deserved to live through this, even if I didn't."

I tried to fire off more rounds, but gunfire drove me back to cover before I could get off a single shot. I breathed hard, wiping some blood from my cheek. Some of the exploding rubble had hit hard enough to cut me.

"You know," I said, "I think I fell for you that first day. Stupid, huh? Love at first sight. What a cliché." I got off three shots, but the soldiers were acting less scared now. They had figured out there was only one of me, and that my gun was only a handgun. I was probably only alive because I'd blown the cycle, which made them worry about explosives.

"I don't even know if I can call it love," I whispered, reloading. "Am I in love? Is it just infatuation? We've known each other for less than a month, and you've treated me like dirt about half that time. But that day fighting Fortuity and that day in the power plant, it seems like we had something. A . . . I don't know. Something together. Something I wanted."

I glanced at her pale, motionless figure.

"I think," I said, "that a month ago, I would have left you by the cycle. Because I wanted so badly to get my vengeance on *him*."

Bam, bam, bam!

The pile of bricks shook, as if the officers were trying to cut through them to get to me.

"That scares me about myself," I said softly, not looking at Megan. "For what it's worth, thank you for making me care about something other than Steelheart. I don't know if I love you. But whatever the emotion is, it's the strongest one I've felt in years. Thank you." I fired widely but fell back as a bullet grazed my arm.

The magazine was empty. I sighed, dropping Megan's gun and raising my father's. Then I pointed it at her.

My finger hesitated on the trigger. It would be a mercy. Better a quick death than to suffer torture and execution. I tried to force myself to pull the trigger.

Sparks, she looks beautiful, I thought. Her unbloodied side was toward me, her golden hair fanning out, her skin pale and eyes closed as if asleep.

Could I really do this?

The gunshots had paused. I risked glancing over my crumbling pile of bricks. Two enormous forms were mechanically clomping down the hallway. So they *had* brought in armor units. A piece of me felt proud that I was such a problem for them. The chaos the Reckoners had caused this day, the destruction we'd brought to Steelheart's minions, had driven them to overkill. A squad of twenty men and two mechanized armors had been sent to take down one guy with a pistol.

"Time to die," I whispered. "I think I'll do it while firing a handgun at a fifteen-foot-tall suit of powered armor. At least it will be dramatic."

I took a deep breath, nearly surrounded by Enforcement forms creeping forward in the dark corridor. I began to stand, my gun leveled at Megan more firmly this time. I'd shoot her, then force the soldiers to gun me down.

I noticed that my mobile was blinking.

"Fire!" a soldier yelled.

The ceiling melted.

I saw it distinctly. I was looking down the tunnel, not wanting to watch Megan as I shot her. I had a clear view of a circle in the ceiling becoming a column of black dust, cascading in a shower of disintegrated steel. Like sand from an enormous spigot, the particles hit the floor and billowed outward in a cloud.

The haze cleared. My finger twitched, but I had not pulled the trigger. A figure stood from a crouch amid the dust; he had fallen from above. He wore a black coat—thin, like a lab coat—dark trousers, black boots, and a small pair of goggles over his eyes.

Prof had come, and he wore a tensor on each hand, the green light glowing with a phantom cast.

The officers opened fire, releasing a storm of bullets down the hallway. Prof raised his hand and thrust forward the glowing tensor. I could almost *feel* the device hum.

Bullets burst in midair, crumbling. They hit Prof as little shavings of fluttering steel, no more dangerous than pinches of dirt. Hundreds of them pelted him and the ground around him; the ones that missed flew apart in the air, catching the light. Suddenly I understood why he wore the goggles.

I stood up, slack jawed, gun forgotten in my fingers. I'd assumed *I* was getting good with my tensor, but destroying those bullets . . . that was beyond anything I'd been able to comprehend.

Prof didn't give the baffled soldiers time to recover. He carried no weapon that I could see, but he leaped free of the dust and dashed right toward them. The mechanized units started firing, but they used their rotary guns—as if they couldn't believe what they'd seen and figured a higher caliber was the answer.

More bullets popped in the air, shattered by Prof's tensors. His feet skidded across the ground on the dust, and then he reached the Enforcement troops.

He attacked fully armored men with his fists.

My eyes widened as I saw him drop a soldier with a fist to the face, the man's helmet melting to powder before his attack. *He's vaporizing the armor as he attacks.* Prof spun between two soldiers, moving gracefully, slamming a fist into the gut of one, then spinning and slamming an arm into the leg of the other. Dust sprayed out as their armor failed them, disintegrating just before Prof hit.

As he came up from the spin he pounded a hand against the side of the steel chamber. The pulverized metal poured away, and something long and thin fell from the wall into his hand. A sword, carved from the steel by an incredibly precise tensor blast.

Steel flashed as Prof struck at the disordered officers. Some tried to keep firing, and others were going in with batons—which Prof destroyed just as easily as he had the bullets. He wielded the sword in one hand, and his other hand sent out near-invisible blasts that reduced metal and kevlar to nothing. Dust streamed off soldiers who got too close to him, making them slip and stumble, suddenly unbalanced as helmets melted around their heads and body armor fell away.

Blood flew in front of high-powered flashlights, and men collapsed. It had been mere heartbeats since Prof had dropped into the room, but a good dozen of the soldiers were down.

The armored units had drawn their shoulder-mounted energy cannons, but Prof had gotten too close. He hit a patch of steel dust at a sprint, then slid in a crouch forward, moving on the dust with obvious familiarity. He twisted to the side and swung his forearm, *smashing* through the armored unit's leg. Powder sprayed out the back as Prof's arm passed completely through it.

He slid to a stop, still on one knee. The armor collapsed with a resounding *thud* as Prof leaped forward and drilled his fist through the second armor's leg. He pulled his hand out and the leg bent, then snapped, the unit collapsing sideways. It fired a yellow-blue blast into the ground as it fell, melting a portion of the floor.

One foolhardy member of Enforcement tried to charge Prof, who stood over the fallen armors. Prof didn't bother with the sword. He dodged to the side, then slammed his fist forward. I could see the fist approach the soldier's face, could see the helmet's visor vaporizing just in front of Prof's punch.

The soldier dropped. The hallway grew silent. Sparkling steel flakes floated in beams of light like snow at midnight.

"I," Prof said in a powerful, self-assured voice, "am known as Limelight. Let your master know that I am *more* than aggravated by being forced to bother myself with you worms. Unfortunately, my minions are fools, and are incapable of following the simplest of orders.

"Tell your master that the time for dancing and playing is through. If he does not come to face me himself, I will dismantle this city piece by piece until I find him." Prof strode past the remaining soldiers without sparing them a glance.

He walked toward me, his back to the soldiers. I grew tense, waiting for them to try something. But they didn't. They cowered. Men did not fight Epics. They had been taught this, had it drilled into them.

Prof reached me, face shrouded in shadows, light shining from behind.

"That was *genius,*" I said softly.

"Get the girl."

"I can't believe that you—"

Prof looked at me, and I finally caught sight of his features. Jaw clenched, eyes seeming to blaze with intensity. There was *contempt* in those eyes, and the sight of it caused me to stumble back in shock.

Prof seemed to be shaking, his hands forming fists, as if he were holding back something terrible. "Get. The. Girl."

I nodded dumbly, stuffing my gun back in my pocket and picking up Megan.

"Jon?" Tia's voice came from his mobile; mine was still on silent. "Jon, the soldiers have pulled out from my position. What's going on?"

Prof didn't reply. He waved a tensored hand and the ground before us melted away. The dust drained, like sand in an hourglass, revealing an improvised tunnel to the lower levels below.

I followed him through the tunnel, and we made our escape.

PART FOUR

31

"**ABRAHAM,** more blood," Tia said, working with a frantic urgency. Abraham—his arm in a sling, which was stained red with his own blood—hastened to the cooler.

Megan lay on the steel conference table in the main room of our hideout. Stacks of paper and some of Abraham's tools lay on the floor where I'd swept them. Now I sat to the side, feeling helpless, exhausted, and terrified. Prof had burrowed us a path into the hideout from the back; the front entrance had been sealed by Tia using some metal plugs and a special type of incendiary grenade.

I didn't understand much of what Tia was doing as she worked on Megan. It involved bandages and attempts to stitch wounds. Apparently Megan had internal injuries. Tia found those even more distressing than the huge amounts of blood Megan had lost.

I could see Megan's face. It was turned toward me, angel's eyes closed softly. Tia had cut free most of Megan's clothing, revealing the extent of her wounds. Horrible wounds.

It seemed strange that her face was so serene. But I felt like I understood. I felt numb myself.

One step after another . . . I'd carried her back to the hideout. That time was a blur, a blur of pain and fright, of aching and dizziness.

Prof hadn't offered to help a single time. He'd almost left me behind at several points.

"Here," Abraham said to Tia, arriving with another pouch of blood.

"Hook it up," Tia said distractedly, working on Megan's side opposite me. I could see her bloodied surgical gloves reflecting the light. She hadn't had time to change, and her regular clothing—a cardigan over a blouse and jeans—was now stained with streaks of red. She worked with intense concentration, but her voice betrayed panic.

Tia's mobile beeped a soft rhythm; it had a medical package, and she had set it on Megan's chest to detect her heartbeat. Tia occasionally picked it up to take quick ultrasounds of Megan's abdomen. With the part of my brain that could still think, I was impressed by the Reckoners' preparations. I hadn't even known that Tia had medical training, let alone that we had blood and surgical equipment in storage.

She shouldn't look that way, I thought, blinking out tears I hadn't realized were forming. *So vulnerable. Naked on the table. Megan is stronger than that. Shouldn't they cover her a little with a sheet or something as they work?*

I caught myself rising to fetch something to cover her, something to give a semblance of modesty, but then realized how stupid I was being. Each moment was crucial here, and I couldn't go blundering in and distract Tia.

I sat down. I was covered in Megan's blood. I couldn't smell it anymore; I guess my nose had gotten used to it.

She has to be okay, I thought, dazed. *I saved her. I brought her back. She has to be all right, now. That's the way it works.*

"This shouldn't be happening," Abraham said softly. "The harmsway . . ."

"It doesn't work on everyone," Tia said. "I don't know why. I *wish* I knew why, dammit. But it has never worked well on Megan, just like she always had trouble working the tensors."

Stop talking about her weaknesses! I screamed at them in my head.

Megan's heartbeat was getting even weaker. I could hear it, amplified by Tia's phone—*beep, beep, beep.* Before I knew it, I was standing up. I turned toward Prof's thinking room. Cody hadn't returned to the hideout; he was still watching the captured Epic in a separate location, as he'd been ordered. But Prof was here, in the other room. He'd walked straight there after arriving, not once looking at Megan or me.

"David!" Tia said sharply. "What are you doing?"

"I . . . I . . . ," I stammered, trying to get out the words. "I'm going to get Prof. He'll do something. He'll save her. He knows what to do."

"Jon can't do anything here," Tia said. "Sit back down."

The sharp order cut through my dazed confusion. I sat and watched Megan's closed eyes as Tia worked, swearing softly to herself. The curses almost matched the beat of Megan's heart. Abraham stood to the side, looking helpless.

I watched her eyes. Watched her serene, calm face as the beeps slowed. Then stopped. There was no flatline sound from the mobile. Just silence that carried a weight of meaning. Nothingness laden with data.

"This . . . ," I said, blinking tears. "I mean, I carried her all the way here, Tia. . . ."

"I'm sorry," Tia said. She raised a hand to her face, leaving a bloody mark on her forehead. Then she sighed and leaned back against the wall, looking exhausted.

"Do something," I said. Not an order. A plea.

"I've done what I can," Tia said. "She's gone, David."

Silence.

"Those wounds were bad," Tia continued. "You did everything you could. It's not your fault. To be honest, even if you'd been able to get her here immediately, I don't know if she'd have made it."

"I . . ." I couldn't think.

Cloth rustled. I glanced to the side. Prof stood in the doorway to his room. He'd dusted off his clothing, and he looked clean and dignified, a sharp contrast to the rest of us. His eyes flickered to Megan. "She's gone?" he asked. His voice had softened a little from before, though he still didn't sound like I felt he should.

Tia nodded.

"Gather what you can," Prof said, slinging a pack over his shoulder. "We're abandoning this position. It's been compromised."

Tia and Abraham nodded, as if they'd been expecting this order. Abraham did pause to lay a hand on Megan's shoulder and bow his head, and then he moved his hand to the pendant at his neck. He hurried off to gather his tools.

I took a blanket from Megan's bedroll—it didn't have sheets—and brought it back to lay over her. Prof looked at me, and he seemed about to object to the frivolous action, but he held his tongue. I tucked the blanket around Megan's shoulders but left her head exposed. I don't know why people cover the face after someone dies. The face is the only thing left that is still right. I brushed it with my fingers. The skin was still warm.

This isn't happening, I thought numbly. *The Reckoners don't fail like this.*

Unfortunately, facts—my own facts—flooded my mind. The

Reckoners *did* fail; members of the Reckoners *did* die. I'd researched this. I'd studied this. It happened.

It just shouldn't have happened to Megan.

I need to see her body cared for, I thought, bending down to pick her up.

"Leave the corpse," Prof said.

I ignored him, then felt him gripping my shoulder. I looked up through bleary eyes and found his expression harsh, eyes wide and angry. They softened as I looked at him.

"What's done is done," Prof said. "We'll burn out this hole, and that will be a fitting burial for her. Regardless, trying to bring the body would just slow us down, maybe get us killed. The soldiers are probably still watching the front position. We can't know how long it will take them to find the new hole I cut in here." He hesitated. "She's gone, son."

"I should have run faster," I whispered, in direct contrast to what Tia had said. "I should have been able to save her."

"Are you angry?" Prof asked.

"I . . ."

"Abandon the guilt," Prof said. "Abandon the denial. Steelheart did this to her. He's our goal. That has to be your focus. We don't have time for grief; we only have time for vengeance."

I found myself nodding. Many would have called those the wrong words, but they worked for me. Prof was right. If I moped and grieved, I'd die. I needed something to replace those emotions, something strong.

Anger at Steelheart. That would do it. He'd taken my father from me, and now he'd taken Megan too. I had a lurking understanding that so long as he lived, he'd take everything I loved from me.

Hate Steelheart. Use that to keep me going. Yes . . . I could do that. I nodded.

"Gather your notes," Prof said, "and then pack up the imager.

We're leaving in ten minutes, and we'll destroy anything we leave behind."

I looked back down the new tunnel Prof had cut into the hideout. Harsh red light glowed at its end, a funeral pyre for Megan. The blast Abraham had rigged was hot enough to melt steel; I could feel the heat from here, far away.

If Enforcement managed to cut into the hideout, all they'd find would be slag and dust. We had carried out what we could, and Tia had stashed a little more in a hidden pocket she'd had Abraham cut into a nearby corridor. For the second time in a month, I watched a home I'd known burn.

This one took something very dear with it. I wanted to say good-bye, to whisper it or at least think it. I couldn't get the word to form. I just . . . I guess I just wasn't ready.

I turned and followed the others, hiking away into the darkness.

An hour later I was still walking through the dark corridor, head down, pack slung on my back. I was so tired I could barely think.

It was odd, though—as strong as my hatred had been for a short time, now it was just lukewarm. Replacing Megan with hatred seemed a poor trade.

There was motion ahead and Tia fell back. She'd changed quickly from her bloodstained clothing. She'd also forced me to do so before abandoning the hideout. I'd washed my hands too, but there was still blood crusted under my fingernails.

"Hey," Tia said. "You're looking pretty tired."

I shrugged.

"Do you want to talk?"

"Not about her. Just . . . not right now."

"Okay. Then something else, maybe?" Something to distract you, her tone implied.

Well, maybe that would be nice. Except the only other thing I wanted to talk about was nearly as distressing. "Why is Prof so mad at me?" I asked softly. "He looked . . . He looked *indignant* that he had to come rescue me."

That made me sick. When he'd spoken to me via mobile, he'd seemed encouraging, determined to help. And then after . . . he felt like another person. It lingered with him still, as he walked alone at the front of the group.

Tia followed my gaze. "Prof has some . . . bad memories attached to the tensors, David. He hates using them."

"But—"

"He's not mad at you," Tia said, "and he's *not* bothered by having to rescue you, regardless of how it might have seemed. He's mad at himself. He just needs some time alone."

"But he was so *good* with them, Tia."

"I know," she said softly. "I've seen it. There are troubles there you can't understand, David. Sometimes doing things we used to do reminds us of who we used to be, and not always in good ways."

That didn't make much sense to me. But then, my mind wasn't exactly the most crisp it had ever been.

We eventually reached the new bolt-hole, which was much smaller than the hideout—only two small rooms. Cody met us but spoke with a subdued tone. He'd been briefed, obviously, about what had happened. He helped us carry our equipment up into the main chamber of the new hideout.

Conflux, the head of Enforcement, was captive in there somewhere. Were we foolhardy to think we could hold him? Was this all part of another trap? I had to assume that Prof and Tia knew what they were doing.

As he worked, Abraham flexed his arm—the one that had taken a bullet. The little diodes of the harmsway flashed on his biceps, and the bullet holes had scabbed over already. A night sleeping with those diodes on and he'd be able to use the arm without trouble in the morning. A few days and the wound would only be a scar.

And yet, I thought, handing my pack to Cody and crawling through the tunnel to the upper chamber, *it didn't help Megan. Nothing we did helped Megan.*

I had lost a lot of people in the last ten years. Life in Newcago wasn't easy, particularly for orphans. But none of those losses had affected me this profoundly since my father's death. I guess it was a good thing—it meant I was learning to care again. Still, it felt pretty crappy at the moment.

When I came out of the entry tunnel and into the new hideout, Prof was telling everyone to bed down for the night. He wanted us to have some sleep in us before we dealt with the captive Epic. As I arranged my bedroll, I heard him speaking with Cody and Tia. Something about injecting the captive Epic with a sedative so that he remained unconscious.

"David?" Tia asked. "You're wounded. I should hook up the harmsway to you and . . ."

"I'll live," I said. They could heal me tomorrow. I didn't care at the moment. Instead I lay down on my bedroll and turned over to face the wall. Then I finally let the tears come in force.

32

ABOUT sixteen hours later I sat on the floor of the new hideout, eating a bowl of oatmeal sprinkled with raisins, harmsway diodes flashing on my leg and side. We'd had to leave most of our good food behind and were relying on storage that had been packed in the bolt-hole.

The other Reckoners gave me space. I found that odd, since they'd all known Megan longer than I had. It wasn't like she and I had actually shared anything special, even if she *had* begun warming up to me.

In fact, as I looked back on it, my reaction to her death seemed silly. I was just a boy with a crush. It still hurt, though. Badly.

"Hey, Prof," Cody said, sitting in front of a laptop. "You should see this, mate."

"Mate?" Prof asked.

"I've got a little bit of Australian in me," Cody said. "My father's grandfather was one-quarter Aussie. Been meaning to try it out for a spin."

"You're a bizarre little man, Cody," Prof said. He was back to his normal self, for the most part—maybe a little more solemn today. So were the rest of them, even Cody. Losing a teammate wasn't a pleasant experience, though I got the sense that they'd been through all of this before.

Prof studied the screen for a moment, then raised an eyebrow. Cody tapped, then tapped again.

"What is it?" Tia asked.

Cody turned the laptop around. None of us had chairs; we were all just sitting on our bedrolls. Even though this hideout was smaller than the other, it felt empty to me. There weren't enough of us.

The screen was blue, with simple block letters in black. PICK A TIME AND LOCATION. I WILL COME.

"This," Cody said, "is all people can see on any of the one hundred entertainment channels in Steelheart's network. It's displayed on every mobile that logs on, and on every information screen in the city. Something makes me think we got through to him."

Prof smiled. "This is good. He's letting us pick the place for the fight."

"He usually does that," I said, staring into my oatmeal. "He let Faultline choose. He thinks it sends a message—this city is his, and he doesn't care if you try to find a place that gives you the better ground. He'll kill you anyway."

"I just wish I didn't feel blind," Tia said. She was sitting in the far corner with her datapad. It had her mobile stuck to the back so its display expanded what was on the mobile's screen. "It's baffling. How did they find out that I'd hacked their camera system? I'm locked out on all sides, every hole plugged. I can't see a thing of what's going on in the city."

"We'll pick a place where we can set up our own cameras," Prof said. "You won't be blind when we face him, Tia. It—"

Abraham's mobile beeped. He raised it up. "Proximity alarms say that our prisoner is stirring, Prof."

"Good," Prof said, standing up and looking toward the entrance to the smaller room that held our captive. "That mystery has been itching at me all day." As he turned, his eyes fell on me, and I caught a flash of guilt from him.

He moved past me quickly and began giving orders. We'd interrogate the prisoner with a light shining directly on him, Cody standing behind him with a gun to the Epic's head. Everyone was to wear their jackets. They'd replaced mine with a spare. It was black leather, too large for me by a size or two.

The Reckoners began moving to set things up. Cody and Tia entered the prisoner's room, eventually followed by Prof. I shoved a spoonful of oatmeal in my mouth, then noticed Abraham, who was lingering in the main room.

He walked over to me and knelt on one knee. "Live, David," he said softly. "Live your life."

"I'm doing that," I grumbled.

"No. You are letting Steelheart live your life for you. He controls it, each step of the way. Live your own life." He patted my shoulder, as if that made everything all right, then waved for me to come with him into the next room.

I sighed, climbed to my feet, and followed.

The captive was a spindly older man—perhaps in his sixties— balding and dark skinned. He was turning his head about, trying to figure out where he was, though he was still blindfolded and gagged. He certainly didn't look threatening, strapped into his chair as he was. Of course many an "unthreatening" Epic could kill with little more than a thought.

Conflux wasn't supposed to have powers like that. But then,

Fortuity wasn't supposed to have had heightened dexterity. Besides, we didn't even know if this *was* Conflux. I found myself pondering the situation, which was good. At least it kept me from thinking about her.

Abraham aimed a large floodlight right at the captive's face. Many Epics needed line of sight to use their powers on someone, so keeping the man disoriented had a very real and useful purpose. Prof nodded to Cody, who cut off the prisoner's blindfold and gag, then stepped back and leveled a wicked .357 at the man's head.

The prisoner blinked against the light, then looked about. He cringed in his chair.

"Who are you?" Prof asked, standing by the light where the prisoner wouldn't be able to make out his features.

"Edmund Sense," the prisoner said. He paused. "And you?"

"That is not important to you."

"Well, seeing as to how you have me captive, I suspect it's of *utmost* importance to me." Edmund had a pleasant voice, with a faint Indian accent. He seemed nervous—his eyes kept darting from side to side.

"You're an Epic," Prof said.

"Yes," Edmund answered. "They call me Conflux."

"Head of Steelheart's Enforcement troops," Prof said. The rest of us remained quiet, as instructed, to not give the man an indication of how many were in the room.

Edmund chuckled. "Head? Yes, I suppose you could call me that." He leaned back, closing his eyes. "Though, more appropriately, I might be the heart. Or maybe just the battery."

"Why were you in the trunk of that car?" Prof asked.

"Because I was being transported."

"And you suspected your limo might be attacked, so you hid yourself in the trunk?"

"Young man," Edmund said pleasantly, "if I had wanted to hide, would I have had myself tied up, gagged, and blindfolded?"

Prof was silent.

"You wish for proof that I am who I say," Edmund said with a sigh. "Well, I'd rather not force you to beat it out of me. Do you have a mechanical device that has been drained of energy? No battery power at all?"

Prof looked to the side. Tia fished in her pocket and handed over a penlight. Prof tried it and no light came out. Then he hesitated. Finally he waved us out of the room. Cody remained, gun on Edmund, but the rest of us—Prof included—gathered in the main chamber.

"He might be able to overload it and make it explode," Prof said softly.

"We *will* need proof of who he is, though," Tia said. "If he can power that by touching it, then he's either Conflux or a different Epic with a *very* similar power."

"Or someone who Conflux gifted his abilities to," I said.

"He registers as a powerful Epic on the dowser," Abraham said. "We've tried it on Enforcement officers before who had powers given to them by Conflux, and it didn't register them."

"What if he's a different Epic?" Tia asked. "With some powers gifted by Conflux to show he can give energy to things and make us think he's Conflux? He could act harmless, then when we aren't expecting, turn his full powers on us."

Prof slowly shook his head. "I don't think so. That's just too convoluted, and too dangerous. Why would they think we would decide to kidnap Conflux? We could just as easily have killed him right there when we found him. I think this man is who he says he is."

"Why was he in the trunk, though?" Abraham asked.

"He'll probably answer if we ask him," I said. "I mean, he hasn't exactly been difficult so far."

"That's what worries me," Tia said. "It's too easy."

"Easy?" I asked. "Megan died so we could capture that guy. I want to hear what he has to say."

Prof glanced at me, tapping the penlight against his palm. He nodded, and Abraham fetched a long wooden rod, which we tied the light to. We returned to the room, and Prof used the rod to touch the light to Edmund's cheek.

Immediately the flashlight's bulb started glowing. Edmund yawned, then tried to settle himself in his bonds.

Prof pulled the flashlight back; it continued to shine.

"I recharged the battery for you," Edmund said. "Might that be enough to persuade you to get me a drink . . . ?"

"Two years ago," I said, stepping forward despite Prof's orders, "in July, you were involved in a large-scale project on Steelheart's behalf. What was it?"

"I don't really have a good sense of time . . . ," the man said.

"It shouldn't be hard to remember," I said. "The people of the city don't know about it, but something odd happened to Conflux."

"Summer? Hmm . . . was that when I was taken out of the city?" Edmund smiled. "Yes, I remember the sunlight. He needed me to power some of his war tanks for some reason."

It had been an offensive against Dialas, an Epic in Detroit who had angered Steelheart by cutting off some of his food supplies. Conflux's part had been handled very covertly. Few knew of it.

Prof was looking at me, lips drawn to a tight line. I ignored him. "Edmund," I said, "you came to the city on what date?"

"Spring of 04 AC," he said.

Four years after Calamity. That clinched it for me—most people assumed that Conflux had joined Steelheart in 05 AC, when Enforcement had first gained mechanized units and the power outages of 04 AC had finally begun to stabilize. But inside sources that I'd carefully gathered claimed Steelheart hadn't trusted Conflux at first, and hadn't used him for important projects for nearly a year.

As I looked at this man, a lot of things from my notes about Conflux were starting to make sense. Why was Conflux never seen? Why was he transported as he was? Why the shroud, the mystery? It wasn't just because of Conflux's frailty.

"You're a prisoner," I said.

"Of course he is," Prof said, but Conflux nodded.

"No," I said to Prof. "He's always been a prisoner. Steelheart isn't using him as a lieutenant, but as a power source. Conflux isn't in charge of Enforcement, he's just . . ."

"A battery," Edmund said. "A slave. It's all right, you can say it. I'm quite accustomed to it. I'm a valuable slave, which is actually an enviable position. I suspect it won't be too long before he finds us and kills you all for taking me." He grimaced. "I *am* sorry about that. I hate it terribly when people fight over me."

"All this time . . . ," I said. "Sparks!"

Steelheart *couldn't* let it be known what he was doing to Conflux. In Newcago Epics were all but sacred. The more powerful they were, the more rights they had. It was the foundation of the government. The Epics lived by the pecking order because they knew, even if they were at the bottom, they were still far more important than the ordinary people.

But here was an Epic who was a slave . . . nothing more than a power plant. This had huge ramifications for everyone in Newcago. Steelheart was a liar.

I guess I shouldn't be too surprised, I thought. *I mean, after everything else he's done, this is a minor issue.* Still, it seemed important. Or maybe I was just latching on to the first thing that drew my attention away from Megan.

"Shut it down," Prof said.

"Excuse me?" Edmund said. "Shut down what?"

"You're a gifter," Prof said. "A transference Epic. Draw your power back from the people you've given it to. Remove it from the mechanized armors, the copters, the power stations. I want you to cut off every person you've granted your power."

"If I do that," Edmund said hesitantly, "Steelheart will *not* be pleased with me when he recovers me."

"You can tell him the truth," Prof said, raising a handgun in one hand so that it pointed out in front of the spotlight. "If I kill you, the power will go away. I'm not afraid to take that step. Recover your power, Edmund. Then we'll talk further."

"Very well," Edmund said.

And just like that, he all but shut down Newcago.

33

"I don't really think of myself as an Epic," Edmund said, leaning forward across the makeshift table. We'd made it out of a box and a plank, and we sat on the floor to eat at it. "I was captured and used for power only a month after my transformation. Bastion was my first owner's name. I'll tell you, was *he* unpleasant after we discovered I couldn't transfer my power to him."

"Why do you suppose that is?" I asked, chewing on some jerky.

"I don't know," Edmund said, raising his hands in front of himself. He liked to gesture a lot when he talked; you had to watch yourself, lest you get an accidental ninja punch to the shoulder during a particularly emphatic exclamation about the taste of a good curry.

That was about as dangerous as he got. Though Cody stayed near, his rifle never too far from him, Edmund hadn't been the least bit provocative. He actually seemed pleasant, at least when he wasn't mentioning our inevitable gruesome deaths at Steelheart's hands.

"That's the way it has always worked for me," Edmund continued, pointing at me with his spoon. "I can only gift them to ordinary humans, and I have to touch them to do it. I've never been able to give my powers to an Epic. I've tried."

Nearby, Prof—who had been carrying some supplies past—stopped in place. He turned to Edmund. "What was that you said?"

"I can't gift to other Epics," Edmund said, shrugging. "It's just the way the powers work."

"Is it that way for other gifters?" Prof asked.

"I've never met any," Edmund said. "Gifters are rare. If there are others in the city, Steelheart never let me meet them. He wasn't bothered by not being able to get my powers for himself; he was plenty happy using me as a battery."

Prof looked troubled. He continued on his way, and Edmund looked to me, his eyebrows raised. "What was that about?"

"I don't know," I said, equally confused.

"Well, anyway, continuing my story. Bastion didn't like that I couldn't gift him, so he sold me to a fellow named Insulation. I always thought that was a stupid Epic name."

"Not as bad as the El Brass Bullish Dude," I said.

"You're kidding. There's really an Epic named that?"

I nodded. "From inner LA. He's dead now, but you'd be surprised at the stupid names a lot of them come up with. Incredible cosmic powers do not equate with high IQ . . . or even a sense of what is dramatically appropriate. Remind me to tell you about the Pink Pinkness sometime."

"That name doesn't sound so bad," Edmund said, grinning. "It's actually a little self-aware. Has a smile to it. I'd like to meet an Epic who likes to smile."

I'm talking to one, I thought. I still hadn't quite accepted that.

"Well," I said, "she didn't smile for long. She thought the name was clever, and then . . ."

"What?"

"Try saying it a few times really quickly," I suggested.

He moved his mouth, then a huge grin split his mouth. "Well, well, well . . ."

I shook my head in wonder as I continued eating my jerky. What to make of Edmund? He wasn't the hero people like Abraham and my father were looking for, not by a long shot. Edmund paled when we talked of fighting Steelheart; he was so timid, he often asked for permission to speak before voicing an opinion.

No, he wasn't some heroic Epic born to fight for the rights of men, but he was nearly as important. I'd *never* met, read of, or even caught a story of an Epic who so blatantly broke the stereotype. Edmund had no arrogance, no hatred, no dismissiveness.

It was baffling. Part of me kept thinking, *This is what we get? I finally find an Epic who doesn't want to kill or enslave me, and it's an old, soft-spoken Indian man who likes to put sugar in his milk?*

"You lost someone, didn't you?" Edmund asked.

I looked up sharply. "What makes you ask?"

"Reactions like that one, actually. And the fact that everyone in your team seems to be walking on crumpled tinfoil and trying not to make any sound."

Sparks. Good metaphor. Walking on crumpled tinfoil. I'd have to remember that one.

"Who was she?" Edmund asked.

"Who said it was a she?"

"The look on your face, son," Edmund said, then smiled.

I didn't respond, though that was in part because I was trying to banish the flood of memories washing through my mind. Megan, glaring at me. Megan, smiling. Megan, laughing just a few hours before she died. *Idiot. You only knew her for a couple of weeks.*

"I killed my wife," Edmund said absently, leaning back, staring at the ceiling. "It was an accident. Electrified the counter while trying to power the microwave. Stupid thing, eh? I wanted a frozen burrito. Sara died for that." He tapped the table. "I hope yours died for something greater."

That will depend, I thought, *on what we do next.*

I left Edmund at the table and nodded to Cody, who was standing by the wall and doing a very good job of pretending he wasn't playing guard. I wandered into the other room, where Prof, Tia, and Abraham were sitting around Tia's datapad.

I almost went looking for Megan, my instincts saying she'd be standing guard outside the hideout, since all of the others were in here. Idiot. I joined the team, looking over Tia's shoulder at the screen of the enlarged mobile datapad. She was running it from one of the fuel cells we'd stolen from the power station. Once Edmund had withdrawn his abilities, the city power had gone out, including those wires that sometimes ran through the steel catacombs.

Her pad showed an old steel apartment complex. "No good," Prof said, pointing to some numbers at the side of the screen. "The building next to it is still populated. I'm not going to have a showdown with a High Epic when there are bystanders so close."

"What about in front of his palace?" Abraham asked. "He won't expect that."

"I doubt he's expecting anything in particular," Tia said. "Besides, Cody's done some scouting. The looting has started, so Steelheart has pulled Enforcement in close to his palace. He's really only got infantry left, but that's enough. We'll never get in to make any preparations. And we're going to *need* to prepare the area if we're going to face him."

"Soldier Field," I said softly.

They turned to me.

"Look," I said, reaching over and scrolling along Tia's map of the city. It felt downright primitive compared to the real-time camera views we'd been using.

I got the screen to an old portion of the city that was mostly abandoned. "The old football stadium," I said. "Nobody lives nearby, and there's nothing in the area to loot, so nobody will be around. We can use the tensors to tunnel in from a nearby point in the understreets. That will let us make preparations quietly, without worry that we're being spied on."

"It's so open," Prof said, rubbing his chin. "I'd rather face him in an old building, where we can confuse him and hit him from a lot of sides."

"That will still work here," I said. "He'll almost certainly fly down into the middle of the field. We could put a sniper in the upper seats, and could carve ourselves a few unexpected tunnels— with rope lines—down through the seats into the stadium's innards. We could baffle Steelheart and his minions by putting tunnels where they aren't expected, and the terrain will be unfamiliar to his people—far more so than a simple apartment complex."

Prof nodded slowly.

"We still haven't addressed the real question," Tia said. "We're all thinking it. We might as well talk about it."

"Steelheart's weakness," Abraham said softly.

"We're too effective for our own good," Tia said. "We've got him positioned, and we can bring him out to fight us. We can ambush him perfectly. But will that even matter?"

"So it comes to this," Prof said. "Listen well, people. These are the stakes. We *could* pull out now. It would be a disaster—everyone would find out we'd tried to kill him and failed. That could do as much harm as killing him would do good. People would think that the Epics really are invincible, that even we can't face someone like Steelheart.

"Beyond that, Steelheart would take it upon himself to personally hunt us down. He is not the type to give up easily. Wherever we go, we'd always have to watch and worry about him. But we could go. We don't know his weakness, not for certain. It might be best to pull out while we can."

"And if we don't?" Cody asked.

"We continue with the plan," Prof said. "We do everything we can to kill him, try out every possible clue from David's memory. We set up a trap in this stadium that combines all of those possibilities, and we take a chance. It will be the most uncertain hit I've ever been part of. One of those things could work, but more likely none of them will, and we will have entered into a fight with one of the most powerful Epics in the world. He'll probably kill us."

Everyone sat in silence. No. It couldn't end here, could it?

"I want to try," Cody said. "David's right. He's been right all along. Sneaking about, killing little Epics . . . that's not changing the world. We've got a chance at Steelheart. We have to at least *try*."

I felt a flood of relief.

Abraham nodded. "Better to die here, with a chance at defeating this creature, than to run."

Tia and Prof shared a look.

"You want to do it too, don't you, Jon?" Tia asked.

"Either we fight him here, or the Reckoners are finished," Prof said. "We'd spend the rest of our lives running. Besides, I doubt I could live with myself if I ran, after all we've been through."

I nodded. "We do have to at least try. For Megan's sake."

"I'll bet she would find that ironic," Abraham noted. We looked at him, and he shrugged. "She was the one who didn't want to do this job. I don't know what she'd think of us dedicating the end of it to her memory."

"You can be a downer, Abe," Prof said.

"The truth is not a downer," Abraham said in his lightly accented voice. "The lies that you pretend to accept are the true downer."

"Says the man who still believes the Epics will save us," Prof said.

"Gentlemen," Tia cut in. "Enough. I think we're all in agreement. We're going to try this, ridiculous though it is. We'll try to kill Steelheart without any real idea what his weakness is."

One by one, we all nodded. We had to try.

"I'm not doing this for Megan," I finally said. "But I'm doing it, in part, *because* of her. If we have to stand up and die so that people will know that someone still fights, so be it. Prof, you said that you worry our failure will depress people. I don't see that. They'll hear our story and realize that there's an option other than doing what the Epics command. We may not be the ones to kill Steelheart. But even if we fail, we might be the cause of his death. Someday."

"Don't be so sure we'll fail," Prof said. "If I thought this was suicide for certain, I wouldn't let us continue. As I said, I don't intend to pin our hopes of killing him on a single guess. We'll try everything. Tia, what do your instincts say will work?"

"Something from the bank vault," she said. "One of those items is special. I just wish I knew which one."

"Did you bring them with you when we abandoned the old hideout?"

"I brought the most unusual ones," she said. "I stowed the rest in the pocket we made outside. We can fetch them. So far as I know, Enforcement hasn't found them."

"We take everything and spread it all out here," Prof said, pointing at the steel floor of the stadium, which had once been soil. "David's right; that's where Steelheart will probably land. We don't have to know specifically what weakened him—we can just haul it all over and use it."

Abraham nodded. "A good plan."

"What do you think it is?" Prof asked him.

"If I had to guess? I would say it was David's father's gun or the bullets it shot. Every gun is slightly distinctive in its own way. Perhaps it was the precise composition of the metal."

"That's easy enough to test," I said. "I'll bring the gun, and when I get a chance I'll shoot him. I don't think it will work, but I'm willing to try."

"Good," Prof said.

"And you, Prof?" Tia asked.

"I think it was because David's father was one of the Faithful," Prof said softly. He didn't look at Abraham. "Fools though they are, they're earnest fools. People like Abraham see the world differently than the rest of us do. So maybe it was the way David's father viewed the Epics that let him hurt Steelheart."

I sat back, thinking it over.

"Well, it shouldn't be too hard for me to shoot him too," Abraham said. "In fact, we should probably all try it. And anything else we can think of."

They looked at me.

"I still think it's crossfire," I said. "I think Steelheart can only be harmed by someone who isn't intending to hurt him."

"That's tougher to arrange," Tia said. "If you're right, it probably won't activate if any of us hit him, since we actually want him dead."

"Agreed," Prof said. "But it's a good theory. We'd need to find a way to get his own soldiers to hit him by accident."

"He'd have to *bring* the soldiers first," Tia said. "Now that he's convinced there's a rival Epic in town, he might just bring Nightwielder and Firefight."

"No," I said. "He'll come with soldiers. Limelight has been using minions, and Steelheart will want to be ready—he'll want to have his own soldiers to deal with distractions like that. Besides, while he'll want to face Limelight himself, he'll also want witnesses."

"I agree," Prof said. "His soldiers will probably have orders not to engage unless fired upon. We can make certain they feel they need to start fighting back."

"Then we'll need to be able to stall Steelheart long enough to set up a good crossfire," Abraham said. He paused. "Actually, we'll need to stall him *during* the crossfire. If he assumes this is just an ambush of soldiers, he'll fly off and let Enforcement deal with it." Abraham looked at Prof. "Limelight will have to make an appearance."

Prof nodded. "I know."

"Jon . . . ," Tia said, touching his arm.

"It's what must be done," he said. "We'll need a way to deal with Nightwielder and Firefight too."

"I'm telling you," I said, "Firefight won't be an issue. He's—"

"I know he's not what he seems, son," Prof said. "I accept that. But have you ever fought an illusionist?"

"Sure," I said. "With Cody and Megan."

"That was a weak one," Prof said. "But I suppose it gives you an idea what to expect. Firefight will be stronger. *Much* stronger. I almost wish he was just another fire Epic."

Tia nodded. "He should be a priority. We'll need code phrases, in case he sends in illusory versions of the other members of the team to confuse us. And we'll have to watch for false walls, fake members of Enforcement intended to confuse, things like that."

"Do you think Nightwielder will even show?" Abraham asked. "From what I heard, David's little flashlight show sent him running like a rabbit before the hawk."

Prof looked to me and Tia.

I shrugged. "He might not," I said.

Tia nodded. "Nightwielder's a hard one to read."

"We should be ready for him anyway," I said. "But I'll be perfectly fine if he stays away."

"Abraham," Prof said, "you think you can rig up a UV floodlight or two using the extra power cells? We should arm everyone with some of those flashlights as well."

We fell silent, and I had a feeling we were all thinking the same thing. The Reckoners liked extremely well-planned operations, executed only after weeks or months of preparation. Yet here we were going to try to take down one of the strongest Epics in the world with little more than some trinkets and flashlights.

It was what we had to do.

"I think," Tia said, "we should come up with a good plan for extraction in case none of these things work."

Prof didn't look like he agreed. His expression had grown grim; he knew that if none of these ideas let us kill Steelheart, our chances of survival were slim.

"A copter will work best," Abraham said. "Without Conflux, Enforcement is grounded. If we can use a power cell, or even make him power a copter for us . . ."

"That will be good," Tia said. "But we'll still have to disengage."

"Well, we've still got Diamond in custody," Abraham said. "We could grab some of his explosives—"

"Wait," I said, confused. "In *custody*?"

"I had Abraham and Cody grab him the evening of your little encounter," Prof said absently. "Couldn't risk letting him say what he knew."

"But . . . you said he'd never . . ."

"He saw a hole made by the tensors," Prof said, "and you were linked to him in Nightwielder's mind. The moment they saw you at one of our operations, they'd grab Diamond. It was for his safety as much as our own."

"So . . . what are you doing with him?"

"Feeding him a lot," Prof said, "and bribing him to lie low. He was pretty unsettled by that run-in, and I think he was happy we took him." Prof hesitated. "I promised him a look at how the tensors work in exchange for him remaining in one of our bolt-holes until this all blows over."

I sat back against the wall of the room, disturbed. Prof hadn't said it, but I could read the truth from his tone. The emergence of knowledge of the tensors would change the way the Reckoners worked.

Even if we beat Steelheart, they had lost something great—no longer would they be able to sneak into places unexpectedly. Their enemies would be able to plan, watch, prepare.

I'd brought about the end of an era. They didn't seem to blame me, but I couldn't help feeling some guilt. I was like the guy who had brought the spoiled shrimp cocktail to the party, causing everyone to throw up for a week straight.

"Anyway," Abraham said, tapping the screen of Tia's datapad, "we could dig out a section under the field here with the tensors, leave an inch or so of steel, then pack the hole with explosives. If we have to punch out, we blow the thing, maybe take out some soldiers and use the confusion and smoke to cover our escape."

"Assuming Steelheart doesn't just chase us down and shoot the copter out of the sky," Prof said.

We fell silent.

"I believe you said *I* was a downer?" Abraham asked.

"Sorry," Prof replied. "Just pretend I said something self-righteous about truth instead."

Abraham smiled.

"It's a workable plan," Prof said. "Though we might want to try to set up some kind of decoy explosion, maybe back at his palace, to draw him off. Abraham, I'll let you handle that. Tia, can you send a message to Steelheart through these networks without being traced?"

"I should be able to," she replied.

"Well, give him a response from Limelight. Tell him: 'Be ready on the night of the third day. You'll know the place when the time comes.'"

She nodded.

"Three days?" Abraham said. "Not much time."

"We really don't have much we need to prepare," Prof said. "Besides, anything longer would be too suspicious; he probably expects us to face him tonight. This will have to do, though."

The Reckoners nodded, and the preparations for our last fight began. I sat back, my anxiety rising. I was *finally* going to have my chance to face him. Killing him with this plan seemed almost as much a longshot as ever.

But I would finally get my chance.

34

THE vibrations shook me to the soul. It seemed that my soul vibrated back. I breathed in, shaping the sound with a thought, then thrust my hand forward and sent the music outward. Music only I could hear, music only I could control.

I opened my eyes. A portion of the tunnel in front of me collapsed into fine, powdery dust. I wore a mask, though Prof continued to assure me the stuff wasn't as bad to breathe as I thought.

I wore my mobile strapped to my forehead, shining brightly. The small tunnel through the steel was cramped, but I was alone, so I was able to move as much as I needed to.

As always, using the tensor reminded me of Megan and that day when we'd infiltrated the power station. It reminded me of the elevator shaft, where she'd shared with me things it seemed she hadn't shared with many. I'd asked Abraham if he'd known she was from

Portland, and he'd seemed surprised. He said she never spoke about her past.

I scooped the steel dust into a bucket, then hauled it down the tunnel and dumped it. I did that a few more times, then got back to digging with the tensor. The others were hauling the dust the rest of the way out.

I added a few feet to the tunnel, then checked my mobile to see how I was doing. Abraham had set up three others above to create a kind of triangulation system that let me cut this tunnel with precision. I needed to go a bit more to the right, then I needed to angle upward.

Next time I pick a location to ambush a High Epic, I thought, *I'm going to choose one that's closer to established understreet tunnels.*

The rest of the team agreed with Abraham that they should wire the field with explosives from below, and they also wanted a few hidden tunnels leading up to the perimeter. I was pretty sure we'd be happy to have those when we faced Steelheart, but building all of it was getting *very* tiring.

I almost regretted that I'd shown so much talent with the tensor. Almost. It was still pretty awesome to be able to dig through solid steel with just my hands. I couldn't hack like Tia, scout as well as Cody, or fix machinery like Abraham. This way, at least, I had a place in the team.

Of course, I thought as I vaporized another section of the wall, *Prof's ability makes mine look like a piece of rice. And not even a cooked one.* I was basically only useful in this role because he refused to take it. That dampened my satisfaction.

A thought occurred to me. I raised my hand, summoning the tensor's vibrations. How had Prof done it to make that sword? He'd pounded the wall, hadn't he? I tried to mimic the motion, pounding my fist against the side of the tunnel and directing the burst of energy in my mind from the tensor.

I didn't get a sword. I caused several handfuls of dust to stream out of a pocket in the wall, followed by a long lump of steel that looked vaguely like a bulbous carrot.

Well, it's a start. I guess.

I reached down to pick up the carrot, but caught sight of a light moving up the small tunnel. I quickly kicked the carrot into the pile of dust, then got back to work.

Prof soon moved up behind me. "How's it going?"

"Another couple of feet," I said. "Then I can carve out the pocket for the explosives."

"Good," Prof said. "Try to make it long and thin. We want to channel the explosion upward, not back down the tunnel here."

I nodded. The plan was to weaken the "roof" of the pocket, which would lie just below the center of Soldier Field. Then we'd seal the explosives in with some careful welding by Cody, directing the blast the direction we wanted it to go.

"You keep at it," Prof said. "For now I'll take care of carting off the dust for you."

I nodded, grateful for the chance to just spend more time with the tensor. It was Cody's. He'd given it up for me, as mine was still a ripped, zombie-droopy-eyed mess. I hadn't asked Prof about the two he carried. It didn't seem prudent.

We worked in silence for a time, me carving out chunks of steel, Prof carting off the dust. He found my carrot sword and gave me an odd look. I hoped he didn't see me blush in the faint light.

Eventually my mobile beeped, telling me I was nearing the right depth. I carefully crafted a long hole at shoulder level. Then I reached in and began creating a small "room" to stuff the explosives into.

Prof walked back, carrying his bucket, and saw what I'd done. He checked his mobile, looking up at the ceiling, then rapped softly at the metal with a small hammer. He nodded to himself, though I couldn't tell any difference in the way it sounded.

"You know," I said, "I'm pretty sure these tensors defy the laws of physics."

"What? You mean destroying solid metal with your fingers isn't normal?"

"More than that," I said. "I think we get less dust than we should. It always seems to settle down and take up less space than the steel did—but it couldn't do that unless it was denser than the steel, which it can't possibly be."

Prof grunted, filling another bucket.

"Nothing about the Epics makes sense," I said, pulling a few armfuls of dust out of the hole I was making. "Not even their powers." I hesitated. "Particularly not their powers."

"True enough," Prof said. He continued filling his buckets. "I owe you an apology, son. For how I acted."

"Tia explained it," I said quickly. "She said you've got some things in your past. Some history with the tensors. It makes sense. It's okay."

"No, it's not. But it *is* what happens when I use the tensors. I . . . well, it's like Tia said. Things in my past. I'm sorry for how I acted. There was no justification for it, especially considering what you'd just been through."

"It wasn't so bad," I said. "What you did, I mean." *The rest was horrible.* I tried not to think about that long march with a dying girl in my arms. A dying girl I didn't save. I pushed forward. "You were amazing, Prof. You shouldn't just use the tensors when we face Steelheart. You should use them all the time. Think of what—"

"STOP."

I froze. The tone of his voice sent a spike of shock down my spine.

Prof breathed in and out deeply, his hands buried in steel dust. He closed his eyes. "Don't speak like that, son. It doesn't do me any good. Please."

"All right," I said carefully.

"Just . . . accept my apology, if you are willing."

"Of course."

Prof nodded, turning back to his work.

"Can I ask you something?" I said. "I won't mention . . . you know. Not directly, at least."

"Go ahead, then."

"Well, you invented these things. Amazing things. The harmsway, the jackets. From what Abraham tells me, you had these devices when you founded the Reckoners."

"I did."

"So . . . why not make us something else? Another kind of weapon, based off the Epics? I mean, you sell knowledge to people like Diamond, and he sells it to scientists who are working to create technology like this. I figure you've got to be as good at it as any of them are. Why sell the knowledge and not use it yourself?"

Prof worked in silence for a few minutes, then walked over to help me pull dust out of the hole I was making. "That's a good question. Have you asked Abraham or Cody?"

I grimaced. "Cody talks about daemons or fairies—which he claims the Irish totally stole from his ancestors. I can't tell if he's serious."

"He's not," Prof said. "He just likes to see how people react when he says things like that."

"Abraham thinks it's because you don't have a lab now, like you used to. Without the right equipment, you can't design new technology."

"Abraham is a very thoughtful man. What do *you* think?"

"I think that if you can find the resources to buy or steal explosives, cycles, and even copters when you need them, you could get yourself a lab. There's got to be another reason."

Prof dusted off his hands and turned to look at me. "All right. I can see where this is going. You may ask one question about my past." He said it as if it were a gift, a kind of . . . penance. He had treated me poorly, in part because of something in his past. The recompense he gave was a piece of that past.

I found myself completely unprepared. What did I want to know? Did I ask how he'd come up with the tensors? Did I ask what it was that made him not want to use them? He seemed to be bracing himself.

I don't want to drag him through that, I thought. *Not if it affects him so profoundly.* I wouldn't want to do that any more than I would have wanted someone to drag me through memories of what had happened to Megan.

I decided to pick something more benign. "What *were* you?" I asked. "Before Calamity. What was your job?"

Prof seemed taken aback. "That's your question?"

"Yes."

"You're sure you want to know?"

I nodded.

"I was a fifth-grade science teacher," Prof said.

I opened my mouth to laugh at the joke, but the tone of his voice made me hesitate.

"Really?" I finally asked.

"Really. An Epic destroyed the school. It . . . it was still in session." He stared at the wall, emotion bleeding from his face. He was putting a mask up.

And here I thought it had been an innocent question. "But the tensors," I said. "The harmsway. You worked at a lab at some point, right?"

"No," he said. "The tensors and the harmsway don't belong to me. The others just assume I invented them. I didn't."

That revelation stunned me.

Prof turned away to gather up his buckets. "The kids at the school called me Prof too. It always sticks, though I'm not a professor—I didn't even go to graduate school. I only ended up teaching science by accident. It was the teaching itself that I loved. At least, I loved it back when I thought it would be enough to change things."

He walked off down the tunnel, leaving me to wonder.

"That's it. Y'all can turn around now."

I turned, adjusting the pack I was toting on my back. Cody, balanced on a ladder above me, lifted the welding mask from his face and wiped his brow with the hand not holding the torch. It was a few hours after I had carved out the pocket under the field. Cody and I had spent those hours carving smaller tunnels and holes throughout the stadium, with Cody spot welding where support was needed.

Our most recent project was making the sniper's nest that would be my post at the beginning of the battle. It was at the front of the third level of seats on the west side of the stadium, at about the fifty-yard line, overhanging the top of the first deck. We didn't want it to be visible from above, so I'd used the tensor to carve away a space under the floor, leaving only an inch of metal on top, except for two feet right near the front for my head and shoulders to poke out so I could aim a rifle through a hole in the low wall at the front of the deck.

Cody reached up from his perch on the ladder and jiggled the metal framework he had just welded to the bottom of the area I had hollowed out. He nodded, apparently satisfied it would support me when I lay in wait there in the sniper's nest. The floor of that section of seating was too thin to hollow out a hole deep enough to hide in; the framework was our solution to that problem.

"Where to next?" I asked as Cody climbed down the ladder. "How about we do that escape hole farther up in the third deck?"

Cody slung his welding gear over his shoulder and cracked some kinks out of his back. "Abraham called to say he's going to take care of the UV floodlights now," he said. "He finished packing the explosives under the field a while ago, so it's time for me to go weld down there. Y'all can handle the next hole on your own—but I'll help you carry the ladder there. Good job on these holes so far, lad."

"So you're back to *lad*?" I asked. "What happened to *mate*?"

"I realized something," Cody said, collapsing the ladder and tilting the top to one side. "My Australian ancestors?"

"Yeah?" I lifted the lower end of the ladder and followed him as he walked from the first deck of seats into the stadium innards.

"They came from Scotland originally. So if I want to be *really* authentic, I need to be able to speak Australian with a Scottish accent."

We kept walking through the pitch-black space beneath the stands that was kind of like a large, curved hallway—I think it was called a concourse. The planned lower end for the next escape hole was in one of the restrooms down the hall. "An Australian-Scottish-Tennessean accent, eh?" I said. "You practicing it?"

"Hell no," Cody said. "I'm not crazy, lad. Just a little eccentric."

I smiled, then turned my head to look in the direction of the field. "We're really going to try this, aren't we?"

"We'd better. I bet Abraham twenty bucks that we'd win."

"I just . . . It's hard to believe. I've spent ten years planning for this day, Cody. Over half my life. Now it's here. It's nothing like what I'd pictured, but it's here."

"You should feel proud," Cody said. "The Reckoners have been doing what they've been doing for over half a decade. No changes, no real surprises, no big risks." He reached up to scratch his left ear. "I often wondered if we were getting stagnant. Never could gather the arguments to suggest a change. It took someone coming in from the outside to shake us up a wee bit."

"Attacking Steelheart is just a 'wee bit' of a shakeup?"

"Well, it's not like you've gotten us to do something *really* crazy, like trying to steal Tia's cola."

Outside the restroom, we set the ladder down and Cody wandered over to check on some explosives on the opposite wall. We intended to use them as distractions; Abraham was going to blow them when needed. I paused, then pulled out one of my eraser-like blasting caps. "Maybe I should put one of these on them," I said. "In case we need a secondary person to blow the explosives."

Cody eyed it, rubbing his chin. He knew what I meant. We'd only need a secondary person to blow the explosives if Abraham fell. I didn't like thinking about it, but after Megan . . . Well, we all seemed a whole lot more frail to me now than we once had.

"You know," Cody said, taking the blasting cap from me, "where I'd *really* like to have a backup is on the explosives under the field there. Those are the most important ones to detonate; they're going to cover our escape."

"I suppose," I said.

"Do you mind if I take this and stick it down there before I weld it closed?" Cody asked.

"No, assuming Prof agrees."

"He likes redundancy," Cody said, slipping the blasting cap into his pocket. "Just keep that pen-dealy of yours handy. And *don't* push it by accident."

He sauntered back toward the tunnel under the field, and I took the ladder into the restroom to get to work.

I punched my fist out into open air, then ducked as the steel dust fell around me. *So that's how he did it,* I thought, flexing my fingers. I hadn't figured out the sword trick, but I was getting good at punching and vaporizing things in front of my fist. It had to do with crafting the tensor's sound waves so that they followed my hand in motion, creating kind of an . . . envelope around it.

Done right, the wave would course along with my fist. Kind of like smoke might follow your hand if you punch through it. I smiled, shaking my hand. I'd finally figured it out. Good thing too. My knuckles were feeling pretty sore.

I finished off the hole with a more mundane tensor blast, reaching up from the top of my ladder to sculpt the hole. Through it I could see a pure black sky. *Someday I'd like to see the sun again,* I thought. The only thing up there was blackness. Blackness and Calamity, burning in the distance directly above, like a terrible red eye.

I climbed up off the ladder and out into the upper third deck. I had a sudden, surreal flash of memory. This was near where I'd sat the one time I'd come to this stadium. My father had scrimped and saved to buy us the tickets. I couldn't remember which team we'd played, but I could remember the taste of the hot dog my father bought. And his cheering, his excitement.

I crouched down among the seats, keeping low just in case. Steelheart's spy drones were probably out of commission now that the city was without power, but he might have people scouting the city and looking for Limelight. It would be wise to remain out of sight as much as possible.

Fishing a rope out of my pack, I tied it around the leg of one of the steel seats, then sneaked back to the hole and down the ladder, returning to the bathroom below the second deck. Leaving the rope hanging for a quicker escape than the ladder would allow, I stowed the ladder and my empty pack in one of the stalls and walked out toward the seats.

Abraham was waiting there for me, leaning against the entryway to the lower seating with his muscled arms crossed, his expression thoughtful.

"So, I take it the UV lights are hooked up?" I asked.

Abraham nodded. "It would have been beautiful to use the stadium's own floodlights."

I laughed. "I'd have liked to see that, making a bunch of lights work that had their bulbs turned to steel and fused to their sockets."

The two of us stood there for a time, looking out at our battlefield. I checked my mobile. It was early morning; we planned to summon Steelheart at 5:00 a.m. Hopefully his soldiers would be exhausted from preventing lootings all night without any vehicles or power armor. The Reckoners usually worked on a night schedule anyway.

"Fifteen minutes until projected go time," I noted. "Did Cody finish the welding? Prof and Tia back yet?"

"Cody completed the weld and is moving to his position," Abraham said. "Prof will arrive momentarily. They were able to procure a copter, and Edmund has gifted Tia the ability to power it. She flew it outside of town to park it, so as to not give away our location."

If things went sour, she'd time her flight back in so that she could sweep down and pick us up as the explosives went off. We'd also blast a smokescreen from the stands to cover our escape.

I agreed with Prof, though. You couldn't outfly or outgun Steelheart in a copter. This was the showdown. We defeated him here or we died.

My mobile flashed, and a voice spoke into my ear. "I'm back," Prof said. "Tia's set too." He hesitated a moment. "Let's do this."

35

SINCE my post was right up against the front of the third deck, if I'd been standing I could have looked down over the edge toward the lowest level of seats. Huddled in my improvised hole, however, I couldn't see those—though I had a good view of the field.

This put me high enough to watch what was going on around the stadium, but I also had a route to ground if I needed to try firing my father's gun at Steelheart. The tunnel and rope farther up the deck would get me there quickly.

I'd drop down, then try to sneak up on him, if it came to that. It would be like trying to sneak up on a lion while armed only with a squirt gun.

I huddled in my spot, waiting. I wore my tensor on my left hand, my right hand holding the grip of the pistol. Cody had given me a replacement rifle, but for now it lay beside me.

Overhead, fireworks flared in the air. Four posts around the top of the stadium released enormous jets of sparks. I don't know where Abraham had found fireworks that were pure green, but the signal would undoubtedly be seen and recognized.

This was the moment. Would he really come?

The fireworks began to die down. "I've got something," Abraham said in our ears, his light French accent subtly emphasizing the wrong syllables. He had the high-point sniping position and Cody had the low-point sniping position. Cody was the better shot, but Abraham needed to be farther away, where he could be outside the fight. His job was to remotely turn on the floodlights or blow strategic explosives. "Yes, they're coming indeed. A convoy of Enforcement trucks. No sign of Steelheart yet."

I holstered my father's gun, then reached to the side to pick up the rifle. It felt too new to me. A rifle should be a well-used, well-loved thing. Familiar. Only then can you know that it's trustworthy. You know how it shoots, when it might jam, how accurate the sights are. Guns, like shoes, are worst when they're brand-new.

Still, I couldn't rely on the pistol. I had trouble hitting anything smaller than a freight train with one of those. I'd need to get close to Steelheart if I wanted to try it. It had been decided that we'd let Abraham and Cody test out the other theories first before risking sending me in close.

"They're pulling up to the stadium," Abraham said in my ear. "I've lost them."

"I can see them, Abraham," Tia said. "Camera six." Though she was outside of the city in the copter, with Edmund's gifted abilities to power it, she was monitoring a rig of cameras we'd set up for spying and for recording the battle.

"Got it," Abraham said. "Yes, they're fanning out. I thought they'd come straight in, but they're not."

"Good," Cody said. "That'll make it easier to get a crossfire going."

If Steelheart even comes, I thought. That was both my fear and my hope. If he didn't come, it would mean he didn't believe that Limelight was a threat—which would make it far easier for the Reckoners to escape the city. The operation would be a bust, but not for any lack of trying. I almost wanted that to be the case.

If Steelheart came and killed us all, the Reckoners' blood would be on my hands for leading them on this path. Once that wouldn't have bothered me, but now it itched at my insides. I peered toward the football field but couldn't see anything. I glanced back behind me, toward the upper stands.

I caught a hint of motion in the darkness—what looked like a flash of gold.

"Guys," I whispered. "I think I just saw someone up here."

"Impossible," Tia said. "I've been watching all the entrances."

"I'm telling you, I *saw* something."

"Camera fourteen . . . fifteen . . . David, there's nobody up there."

"Stay calm, son," Prof said. He was hiding in the tunnel we'd made beneath the field, and would come out only when Steelheart appeared. It had been decided that we wouldn't try blowing the explosives down there until after we'd tried all the other ways to kill Steelheart.

Prof wore the tensors. I could tell he hoped he wouldn't have to use them.

We waited. Tia and Abraham gave a quiet running explanation of Enforcement's movements. The ground troops surrounded the stadium, secured all the exits they knew about, then slowly started to infiltrate. They set up gunnery positions at several points in the stands, but they didn't find any of us. The stadium was too large, and we were hidden too well. You could build a lot of interesting hiding places when you could tunnel through what everyone else assumed was un-tunnel-through-able.

"Tap me into the speakers," Prof said softly.

"Done," Abraham replied.

"I am not here to fight worms!" Prof bellowed, his voice echoing through the stadium, blasted from speakers we'd set up. "This is the bravery of the mighty Steelheart? To send little men with popguns to annoy me? Where are you, Emperor of Newcago? Do you fear me so?"

The stadium fell silent.

"You see that pattern the soldiers set up in the stands?" Abraham asked over our line. "They're being very deliberate. It's intended to ensure they don't hit one another with friendly fire. We're going to have trouble catching Steelheart in a crossfire."

I kept glancing over my shoulder. I saw no other movement in the seats behind me.

"Ah," Abraham said softly. "It worked. He's coming. I can see him in the sky."

Tia whistled softly. "This is it, kids. Time for the real party."

I waited, raising my rifle and using the scope to scan the sky. I eventually spotted a point of light in the darkness, getting closer. Gradually it resolved into three figures flying down toward the center of the stadium. Nightwielder floated amorphously. Firefight landed beside him, a burning humanoid form that was so bright he left afterimages in my eyes.

Steelheart landed between them. My breath caught in my throat, and I fell utterly still.

He'd changed little in the decade since he destroyed the bank. He had that same arrogant expression, that same perfectly styled hair. That inhumanly toned and muscled body, shrouded in a black and silver cape. His fists glowed a soft yellow, wisps of smoke rising from them, and there was a hint of silver in his hair. Epics aged far more slowly than regular people, but they did age. ·

Wind swirled about Steelheart, blowing up dust that had collected on the silvery ground. I found I couldn't look away. My father's murderer. He was here, *finally*. He didn't seem to notice the junk from the bank vault. We'd strewn it around the center of the field and mixed it with garbage we'd brought in to mask what we'd done.

The items were easily as close to him now as they had been when he'd been in the bank. My finger twitched on the trigger of my rifle—I hadn't even realized it had moved to the trigger. I carefully removed it. I would see Steelheart dead, but it didn't *have* to be by my hand. I needed to remain hidden; my duty was to hit him with the pistol, and he was too far away for that at the moment. If I shot now, and the shot failed, I'd be revealing myself.

"Guess I get to start this party," Cody said softly. He was going to fire first to test the theory about the vault contents, as his position was the easiest to retreat from.

"Affirmative," Prof said. "Take the shot, Cody."

"All right, you slontze," Cody said softly to Steelheart. "Let's see if that junk was worth the trouble of hauling up here. . . ."

A shot rang in the air.

∃6

I was zoomed in on Steelheart's face in the rifle scope. I could swear that I saw, quite distinctly, the bullet hit the side of his head, disturbing his hair. Cody was right on target, but the bullet didn't even break the skin.

Steelheart didn't flinch.

Enforcement reacted immediately, men shouting, trying to determine the source of the shot. I ignored them, staying focused on Steelheart. He was all that mattered.

More shots fired; Cody was making certain he had hit his mark. "Sparks!" Cody said. "I didn't catch sight of any of the shots. One of those has to have landed, though."

"Can anyone confirm?" Prof asked urgently.

"Hit confirmed," I said, eye still to my scope. "It didn't work."

I heard muttered cursing from Tia.

"Cody, move," Abraham said. "They've caught your location."

"Phase two," Prof said, voice firm—anxious, but in control.

Steelheart turned about with a leisurely air—hands glowing—and regarded the stadium. He was a king inspecting his domain. Phase two was for Abraham to blow some distractions and try to get a crossfire going. My role was to sneak forward with the pistol and get in position. We wanted to keep Abraham's position secret as long as possible, so he could use explosions to try to move the Enforcement officers around.

"Abraham," Prof said. "Get those—"

"Nightwielder's moving!" Tia interrupted. "Firefight too!"

I forced myself to pull back from my scope. Firefight had become a streak of burning light heading toward one of the entrances to the concourse beneath the stands. Nightwielder was moving up into the air.

He was flying right toward where I was hiding.

Impossible, I thought. *He can't—*

Enforcement started firing from the positions they had set up, but they weren't shooting toward Cody. They were shooting toward other areas in the stands. I was confused for a moment until the first hidden UV floodlight exploded.

"They're on to us," I cried, pulling back. "They're shooting out the floodlights!"

"Sparks!" Tia said as each of the other floodlights exploded in a row, shot out by various members of Enforcement. "There's no way they spotted all of those!"

"Something's wrong here," Abraham said. "I'm blowing the first distraction." The stadium shook as I slung my rifle over my shoulder and climbed out of my hole. I raced up a flight of steps in the stands.

The gunfire below sounded soft compared to what I'd experienced a few days ago in the corridors.

"Nightwielder is on to you, David!" Tia said. "He *knew* where you were hiding. They must have been watching this place."

"That doesn't make sense," Prof said. "They'd have stopped us earlier, wouldn't they?"

"What's Steelheart doing?" Cody asked, breathing hard as he ran.

I was barely listening. I dashed for the escape hole in the ground up ahead, not looking over my shoulder. The shadows from the seats around me began to lengthen. Tendrils grew like elongating fingers. In the middle of that, something splashed sparks along the steps in front of me.

"Enforcement sharpshooter!" Tia said. "Targeting you, David."

"Got him," Abraham said. I couldn't pick Abraham's sniper shot out of the gunfire, but no further shots came after me. Abraham might have just revealed himself, though.

Sparks! I thought. This was all going to Calamity really quickly. I hit the rope and fumbled with my flashlight. Those shadows were alive, and they were getting close. I got the flashlight on, shining it to destroy the shadows around the hole, then grabbed the rope with one hand and slid down. Fortunately the UV light affected Nightwielder's shadows as well as it did him personally.

"He's still after you," Tia said. "He . . ."

"What?" I asked urgently, holding the rope with the tensor glove, feet wrapped around it to slow my fall. I passed through open air beneath the third deck of seats, above the second deck. My hand grew hot with the friction, but Prof claimed the tensor could handle that without ripping.

I dropped through the hole in the second deck and through the ceiling of the restroom, emerging into the complete darkness of the concourse. This was where things like the concession stands were. At one time the outside of the place had all been glass—but that was now steel, of course, and so the stadium felt enclosed. Like a warehouse.

I could still hear gunshots, faint, echoing slightly in the hollow confines of the stadium. My flashlight shone mostly UV light through its filter, but it did glow a faint, quiet blue.

"Nightwielder sank into the stands," Tia whispered to me. "I lost track of him. I think he did it to hide from cameras."

So we're not the only ones with that trick, I thought, heart thumping in my chest. He'd come for me. He had a vendetta—he knew I'd been the one to figure out his weakness.

I shined the flashlight about anxiously. Nightwielder would be on me in a second, but he would know that I was armed with UV light. Hopefully that would keep him wary. I unholstered my father's pistol, wielding the flashlight in one hand and the gun in the other, my new rifle slung over my shoulder.

I have to keep moving, I thought. *If I can stay ahead of him, I can lose him.* We had tunnels in and out of places like the restrooms, the offices, the locker rooms, and the concession stands.

The UV flashlight gave off very little visible illumination, but I was an understreeter. It was enough. It did have the odd effect of making things that were white glow with a phantom light, and I worried that would give me away. Should I turn off the flashlight and go by touch?

No. It was also my only weapon against Nightwielder. I wasn't about to go around blind when facing an Epic who could strangle me with shadows. I crept down the tomblike hallway. I needed to—

I froze. What had that been in the shadows ahead? I turned my flashlight back toward it. The light shone across discarded bits of trash that had fused to the ground in the Great Transfersion, some formerly retractable stanchions for line control, a few posters frozen on the wall. Some more recent trash, glowing white and ghostly. What had I . . .

My light fell on a woman standing quietly in front of me. Beautiful hair I knew would be golden if I were seeing it under normal light. A face that seemed too perfect, tinged blue in the UV beam, as if sculpted from ice by a master artist. Curves and full lips, large eyes. Eyes I knew.

Megan.

37

BEFORE I had a chance to do more than gape, the shadows around me started to writhe. I dodged to the side as several of them speared through the air where I'd been standing. Though it seemed as if Nightwielder could animate shadows, really he exuded a black mist that pooled in darkness. That was what he could manipulate.

He could have very fine control over a few tendrils of it, but usually he opted for large numbers of them, probably because it was more intimidating. Controlling so many was more difficult, and he could basically just grab, constrict, or stab. Every patch of darkness around me started forming spears that sought my blood.

I dodged between them, eventually having to roll to the ground to get under a group of attacks. Doing a dodging roll on a steel floor is *not* a comfortable experience. When I came up, my hip was smarting.

I leaped over several of the steel crowd control stanchions, sweating and shining my flashlight at any suspicious shadows. I couldn't turn it all directions at once, though, and I had to keep spinning to avoid the ones at my back. I paid vague attention to the chatter from the other Reckoners in my ear, though I was too busy trying to not be killed to digest much of it. It seemed that things were in chaos. Prof had revealed himself to hold Steelheart's attention; Abraham had been located because of his shot to save me. Both he and Cody were on the run, fighting Enforcement soldiers.

A blast rocked the stadium, the sound traveling down the hallway and washing over me like stale cola through a straw. I threw myself over the last of the steel stanchions and found myself shining the light frantically about me to stop spear after spear of blackness.

Megan was no longer where she'd been standing. I could almost believe she'd been a trick of my mind. Almost.

I can't keep this up, I thought as a black spear struck my jacket and was rebuffed by the shielding. I could feel the hit through my sleeve, and the diodes on the jacket were beginning to flash. This jacket seemed a *lot* weaker than the one I'd worn before. Maybe it was a prototype.

Sure enough, the next spear that caught me ripped through the jacket and sliced my skin. I cursed, shining the light on another patch of inky, oily blackness. Nightwielder was going to have me soon if I didn't change tactics.

I had to fight smarter. *Nightwielder has to be able to see me to use his spears on me,* I thought. So he was nearby—yet the hallway seemed empty.

I stumbled, which saved me from a spear that nearly took off my head. *Idiot,* I thought. He could move through walls. He wouldn't just stand in the open; he'd barely be peeking out. All I needed to do was . . .

There! I thought, catching a glimpse of a forehead and eyes peering out from the far wall. He looked pretty stupid, actually, like a kid in the deep end of a pool thinking he was invisible because he was mostly submerged.

I shined the light on him and tried to get a shot off at the same time. Unfortunately I'd switched hands so I could have the flashlight in my right hand—which meant I was firing with my left. Have I mentioned my thoughts on pistols and their accuracy?

The shot went wild. Like, *way* wild. Like I came closer to hitting a bird flying above the stadium outside than I did Nightwielder. But the flashlight worked. I wasn't sure what would happen if his powers vanished while he was phasing through an object. Unfortunately it looked like it didn't kill him—his face was jerked back through the wall as he became corporeal again.

I didn't know what was on the other side of that wall. It was opposite the field. Was he outside, then? I couldn't stop to look up the map on my phone. Instead I ran for a nearby concession stand. We'd dug a tunnel through there, wrapping down through the floor. Hopefully, if I could keep moving while Nightwielder was outside, he'd have trouble tracking me down once he peeked in again.

I got into the concession stand and crawled inside the tunnel. "Guys," I whispered into my mobile as I moved, "I saw Megan."

"You *what*?" Tia asked.

"I saw *Megan*. She's alive."

"David," Abraham said. "She's dead. We all know this."

"I'm telling you I saw her."

"Firefight," Tia said. "He's trying to get to you."

As I crawled I felt a sharp sinking feeling. Of course—an illusion. But . . . something felt wrong about that.

"I don't know," I said. "The eyes were *right*. I don't think an illusion could be that detailed—that lifelike."

"Illusionists wouldn't be worth much if they weren't able to create realistic puppets," Tia said. "They need to— Abraham, not left! The other way. In fact, throw a grenade down there if you can."

"Thanks," he said, puffing slightly. I could hear an explosion twice—once through his microphone. A distant portion of the stadium shook. "Phase three is a failure, by the way. I got a shot off on Steelheart right after I revealed myself. It didn't do anything."

Phase three was Prof's theory—that one of the Faithful could hurt Steelheart. If Abraham's bullets had bounced off, then it wasn't viable. We only had two other ideas. The first was my theory of crossfire; the other was the theory that my father's gun or bullets were in some way special.

"How's Prof holding up?" Abraham asked.

"He's holding up," Tia said.

"He's *fighting* Steelheart," Cody said. "I've only been able to see a little, but— Sparks! I'm going offline for a moment. They're almost on me."

I crouched in the narrow tunnel, trying to sort through what was happening. I could still hear a lot of gunfire and the occasional blast.

"Prof's keeping Steelheart distracted," Tia said. "We still don't have any confirmed crossfire hits, though."

"We're trying," Abraham said. "I'll get this next group of soldiers to follow me around the corridor, and then let Cody goad them into firing across the field at him. That might work. David, where are you? I might need to set off a distraction blast or two to flush out the soldiers behind cover on your side."

"I'm taking the second concessions tunnel," I said. "I'll be coming out on the ground floor, near the bear. I'll head westward after that." *The bear* meant a giant stuffed bear that had been part of some promotion during the football season, but which was now frozen in place like everything else.

"Got it," Abraham said.

"David," Tia said. "If you saw an illusion, it means you've got both Firefight and Nightwielder on you. On one hand that's good—we were wondering where Firefight ran off to. It's bad for you, though—you've got two powerful Epics to deal with."

"I'm telling you, that wasn't an illusion," I said, cursing as I tried to juggle the gun and the flashlight. I searched in my cargo pocket, fishing out my industrial tape. My father had told me to always keep that industrial tape handy; I'd been surprised, as I grew older, how good that advice had been. "She was real, Tia."

"David, think about that for a moment. How would Megan have gotten here?"

"I don't know," I said. "Maybe they . . . did something to revive her. . . ."

"We flash-burned everything in the hideout. She'd have been cremated."

"There would have been DNA, maybe," I said. "Maybe they have an Epic who can bring someone back or something like that."

"Durkon's Paradox, David. You're searching too hard."

I finished taping the flashlight to the side of the barrel of my rifle—not on the top, as I wanted to be able to use the sights. That left the weapon off balance and clunky, but I felt I'd still be better with it than the handgun. I stuffed that into its holster under my arm.

Durkon's Paradox referred to a scientist who had studied and pondered the Epics during the early days. He'd pointed out that, with Epics breaking known laws of physics, literally anything was possible—but he warned against the practice of theorizing that every little irregularity was caused by an Epic's powers. Often that kind of thinking led to no actual answers.

"Have you *ever* heard of an Epic who could restore another person to life?" Tia said.

"No," I admitted. Some could heal, but none could reanimate someone else.

"And weren't you the one who said we were probably facing an illusionist?"

"Yes. But how would they know what Megan looked like? Why wouldn't they use Cody or Abraham to distract me, someone they know is here?"

"They would have her on video from the Conflux hit," Tia said. "They're using her to confuse you, unhinge you."

Nightwielder *had* nearly killed me while I was staring at the phantom Megan.

"You were right about Firefight," Tia continued. "As soon as that fire Epic was out of sight of the Enforcement officers, it vanished from my video feeds. That was just an illusion, meant to distract. The real Firefight is someone else. David, they're trying to play you so that Nightwielder can kill you. You *have* to accept this. You're letting your hopes cloud your judgment."

She was right. Sparks, but she was right. I halted in the tunnel, breathing in and out deliberately, forcing myself to confront it. Megan was dead. Now Steelheart's minions were playing with me. It made me angry. No, it made me *furious*.

It also brought up another problem. Why would they risk revealing Firefight like that? Letting him vanish after getting out of sight when it was likely we had the place under surveillance? Using an illusion of Megan? These things exposed Firefight for what he was.

That gave me a chill. They knew. They *knew* we were on to them, so they didn't need to pretend. *They also knew where we'd placed the UV floodlights,* I thought, *and where some of us were hiding.*

Something strange was going on. "Tia, I think——"

"Will you fools stop blathering," Prof said, his voice rough, harsh. "I need to concentrate."

"It's all right, Jon," Tia said comfortingly. "You're doing all right."

"Bah! Idiots. All of you."

He's using the tensors, I thought. *It's almost like they turn him into another person.*

There wasn't time to think about that. I simply hoped we all lived long enough for Prof to apologize. I climbed out of the tunnel behind some tall steel equipment cases and panned my rifle with mounted flashlight around the corridor.

I was saved from the strike by a fluke. I thought I saw something in the distance, and I lunged toward it, trying to get more light on it. As I did, three spears of darkness struck at me. One sliced clean through the back of my jacket and cut a line through my flesh. Just another fraction of an inch and it would have severed my spine.

I gasped, spinning around. Nightwielder stood nearby in the cavernous room. I fired a shot at him, but nothing happened. I cursed, getting closer, rifle to my shoulder and the UV light streaming before me.

Nightwielder smiled a devilish grin as I put a bullet through his face. Nothing. The UV wasn't working. I froze in place, panicked. Was I wrong about his weakness? But it had worked before. Why—

I spun about, barely stopping a group of spears. The light dispersed them as soon as it touched them, so it was still working. So what was happening?

Illusion, I thought, feeling stupid. *Slontze. How many times am I going to fall for that?* I scanned the walls. Sure enough, I caught a glimpse of Nightwielder staring out from one of them toward me. He pulled back before I could fire, and the darkness fell motionless again.

I waited, sweating, focused on that point. Maybe he'd peer out again. The fake Nightwielder was just to my right, looking impassive. Firefight was in the room somewhere. Invisible. He could gun me down. Why didn't he?

Nightwielder peeked out again, and I fired, but he was gone in an eyeblink and the shot ricocheted off the wall. He'd probably come at me from another direction, I decided, so I took off running. As I ran I swiped the butt of my gun through the fake Nightwielder. As I expected, it passed right through, the apparition wavering faintly like a projected image.

Explosions sounded. Abraham cursed in my ear.

"What?" Tia asked.

"Crossfire doesn't work," Cody said. "We got a big group of soldiers to fire on each other through the smoke, without their realizing that Steelheart was in the middle."

"At *least* a dozen shots hit him," Abraham said. "That theory is dead. I repeat, accidental fire does *not* hurt him."

Calamity! I thought. And I'd been so sure about that theory. I ground my teeth, still running. *We're not going to be able to kill him,* I thought. *This is all going to be meaningless.*

"I'm afraid that I can confirm," Cody said. "I saw the bullets hit too, and he didn't even notice." He paused. "Prof, you're a machine. Just thought I'd say that."

Prof's only response was a grunt.

"David, how are you handling Nightwielder?" Tia asked. "We need you to activate phase four. Shoot Steelheart with your father's gun. It's all we have left."

"How am I handling Nightwielder?" I asked. "*Poorly.* I'll get out there when I can." I continued jogging down the large, open concourse beneath the seating. Maybe if I could get outside I'd have a better time of it. There were too many hiding places in here.

He was waiting for me when I came out of that tunnel, I thought. *They've got to be listening in on our conversations. That's how they knew so much about our initial setup.*

That, of course, was impossible. Mobile signals were unhackable. The Knighthawk Foundry made sure of that. And beyond that, the Reckoners were on their own network.

Except . . .

Megan's mobile. It was still connected to our network. Had I ever mentioned to Prof and the others that she'd lost it in the fall? I'd assumed it was broken, but if it hadn't been . . .

They listened in on our preparations, I thought. *Did we mention over the lines that Limelight wasn't real?* I thought hard, trying to remember our conversations over the last three days. I came up blank.

Maybe we'd talked about it, but maybe not. The Reckoners tended to be circumspect about their conversations over the network, just to be extra careful.

Further speculation was cut off as I spotted a figure in the hallway in front of me. I slowed, rifle to shoulder, drawing a bead on it. What would Firefight try this time?

Another image of Megan, just standing there. She wore jeans and a tight red button-up shirt—but no Reckoner jacket—her golden hair pulled back in a shoulder-length ponytail. Wary, in case Nightwielder attacked me from behind, I moved past the illusion. It watched me with a blank expression but didn't move otherwise.

How could I find Firefight? He'd be invisible, probably. I wasn't certain he had that power, but it made sense.

Ways of revealing an invisible Epic ran through my mind. Either I had to listen for him or I had to fog the air with something. Flour, dirt, dust . . . maybe I could use the tensor somehow? Sweat trickled down my brow. I *hated* knowing that someone was watching me, someone I couldn't see.

What to do? My initial plan to deal with Firefight had been to reveal I knew his secret, to scare him off as I had Nightwielder during the Conflux hit. That wouldn't work now. He knew we were on to him. He needed to see the Reckoners dead to hide his secret. *Calamity, Calamity, Calamity!*

The illusion of Megan turned its head, following me as I tried to watch all corners of the room and listen for movement.

The illusion frowned. "I know you," she said.

It was her voice. I shivered. *A powerful Epic illusionist would be able to create sounds with their images,* I told myself. *I know that's true. No need to be surprised.*

But it was her voice. How did Firefight know her voice?

"Yes . . . ," she said, walking toward me. "I do know you. Something about . . . about knees." Her eyes narrowed at me. "I should kill you now."

Knees. Firefight couldn't know about that, could he? Had Megan called me that name over the mobile? They couldn't have been listening back then, could they?

I wavered, my gun's sights on her. The illusion. Or was it Megan? Nightwielder would be coming. I couldn't just stand there, but I couldn't run either.

She was walking toward me. Her arrogant expression made her look like she owned the world. Megan had acted like that before, but there was something more here. Her bearing was more confident, even though she had pursed her lips, perplexed.

I had to know. I *had* to.

I lowered the gun and leaped forward. She reacted, but too slowly, and I grabbed her arm.

It was real.

A second later, the hallway exploded.

38

I coughed, rolling over. I was on the ground, my ears ringing. Bits of trash burned nearby. I blinked away the afterimages in my eyes, shaking my head.

"What was that?" I croaked.

"David?" Abraham said in my ear.

"An explosion," I said, groaning and pulling myself up to my feet. I looked around the hallway. Megan. Where was she? I couldn't see her anywhere.

She'd been real. I had felt her. That meant it wasn't an illusion, right? Was I losing my mind?

"Calamity!" Abraham said. "I thought you were down the other end of the concourse. You said you'd go westward!"

"I ran to get away from Nightwielder," I said. "I ran the wrong way. I'm a slontze, Abraham. Sorry."

My rifle. I saw the stock sticking out of a nearby pile of trash. I pulled it out. The rest of the gun wasn't attached. *Sparks!* I thought. *I'm having a devil of a time holding on to these lately.*

I found the rest of the gun nearby. It *might* still work, but without a stock I'd be firing from the hip. The flashlight was still strapped to it, however, and still shining, so I snatched the whole thing up.

"What's your condition?" Tia asked, voice tense.

"A little stunned," I said, "but all right. It wasn't close enough to hit me with anything more than the concussion."

"Those will be amplified in these hallways," Abraham said. "Calamity, Tia. We're losing control of this situation."

"Damn you all," Prof's voice said, sounding feral. "I want David *out here now*. Bring me that gun!"

"I'm coming to help you, lad," Cody said. "Stay put."

A sudden thought struck me. If Steelheart and his people really were listening in on our private line, I could use that.

The idea warred with my desire to hunt for Megan. What if she was hurt? She had to be around here somewhere, and there seemed to be a lot more rubble in the hallway now. I needed to see if . . .

No. I *couldn't* afford to be tricked. Maybe that had been Firefight, wearing Megan's face to distract me.

"Okay," I said to Cody. "You know the restrooms near the fourth bomb position? I'm going to hide in there until you arrive."

"*Got it,*" Cody said.

I dashed away, hoping that Nightwielder, wherever he was, had been disoriented by the blast. I neared the restrooms I'd mentioned to Cody, but I didn't go into them as I'd said. Instead I found a spot nearby and used my tensor to blast a hole into the ground. This was a place where I'd be relatively well hidden but would also have a good view of the rest of the corridor—restrooms included.

I dug the hole deep, then burrowed down in it as Prof had taught me, using the dust to cover up. Soon I was like a soldier in a foxhole, carefully hidden. I turned my mobile to silent and buried my half rifle just under the surface of the dust, so the light from the flashlight was concealed.

Then I watched the door to that restroom. The corridor fell silent. Lit only by burning scraps.

"Is anyone there?" a voice called into the hallway. "I . . . I'm hurt."

I tensed. That was Megan.

It's a trick. It has to be.

I scanned the dim room. There, on the other side of the hallway, I saw an arm wedged in a mountain of rubble from the blast. Chunks of steel, some fallen girders from above. The arm twitched, and blood ran down the wrist. As I looked closer, I could see her face and torso in the shadows. She looked like she was only now beginning to stir, as if she'd been briefly knocked unconscious by the blast.

She was pinned. She was hurt. I had to move, to go help her! I stirred but then forced myself down.

"Please," she said. "Please, someone. Help me."

I didn't move.

"Oh Calamity. Is that my blood?" She struggled. "I can't move my legs."

I squeezed my eyes shut. How were they doing this? I didn't know what to trust.

Firefight is doing it somehow, I told myself. *She's not real.*

I opened my eyes. Nightwielder was emerging from the floor in front of the bathroom. He looked confused, as if he'd been inside looking for me. He shook his head and walked through the corridor, searching about him.

Was that really him, or was it an illusion? Was any of this real? The stadium shook with another blast, but the gunfire outside was dying down. I needed to do something, quickly, or Cody would stumble into Nightwielder.

Nightwielder stopped in the center of the hallway and crossed his arms. His normal calm had been shattered and he looked annoyed. Finally he spoke. "You're in here somewhere, aren't you?"

Dared I take the shot? What if he was the illusion? I could get myself killed by the real Nightwielder if I exposed myself. I turned carefully, examining the walls and floor. I saw nothing other than some darkness creeping from the shadows nearby, tendrils moving like hesitant animals seeking food. Testing the air.

If Firefight was really pretending to be Megan, then shooting her would stop the illusions. I'd be left only with the real Nightwielder, wherever he was. But there was a good chance that the fallen Megan was a full illusion. Sparks, the *girders* could be an illusion. Would a distant blast have really knocked those down?

What if that was Firefight, though, wearing Megan's face so that if I touched her I'd feel something real? I raised my father's gun and sighted on her bloodied face. I hesitated, heart pounding in my ears. Surely Nightwielder could hear that pounding. It was all that I could hear. What would I do to get to Steelheart? Shoot Megan?

She's not real. She can't be real.

But what if she is?

Heartbeats, like thunder.

My breath, held.

Sweat on my brow.

I made my decision and leaped from the foxhole, bringing up the rifle in my left hand—light shining forward—and the handgun in my right. I let loose with both.

On Nightwielder, not Megan.

He spun toward me as the light hit him, eyes wide, and the bullets ripped through him. He opened his mouth in horror and blood sprayed out his back. His *solid* back. He dropped, turning translucent again the moment he got out of the direct line of my flashlight. He hit the ground and began to sink into it.

He only sank halfway. He froze there, mouth open, chest bleeding. He solidified slowly—it was almost like the view from a camera coming into focus—half sunken in the steel floor.

I heard a click and turned. Megan stood there, a gun in her hand. A handgun, a P226 just like she preferred to carry. The other version of her, the one trapped by rubble, vanished in a heartbeat. So did the girders.

"I never did like him," Megan said indifferently, glancing toward Nightwielder's corpse. "You just did me a favor. Plausible deniability and all of that."

I looked into her eyes. I knew those eyes. I *did*. I didn't understand how it was happening, but it was her.

Never did like him . . .

"Calamity," I whispered. "*You're* Firefight, aren't you? You always were."

She said nothing, though her eyes flickered down toward my weapons—the rifle still held at my hip, the handgun in my other hand. Her eye twitched.

"Firefight wasn't male," I said. "He . . . she was a woman." I felt my eyes go wide. "That day in the elevator shaft, when the guards almost caught us . . . they didn't see anything in the shaft. You made an illusion."

She was still staring at my guns.

"And then, when we were on the cycles," I said. "You created an illusion of Abraham riding with us to distract the people following, to keep them from seeing the real him flee to safety. That's what I saw behind us after he split off."

Why was she looking at my guns?

"But the dowser," I said. "It tested you, and it said you weren't an Epic. No . . . wait. Illusions. You could just make it display anything you wanted. Steelheart must have known the Reckoners were coming to town. He sent you to infiltrate. You were the newest of the Reckoners, before me. You never wanted to attack Steelheart. You said you believed in his rule."

She licked her lips, then whispered something. She didn't seem to have been listening to anything I said. "Sparks," she murmured. "I can't believe that actually worked. . . ."

What?

"You checkmated him . . . ," she whispered. "That was amazing. . . ."

Checkmated him? Nightwielder? Was that what she talking about? She looked up at me, and I remembered. She was repeating one of our first conversations, following her shooting Fortuity. She'd held a rifle at her hip and a handgun out forward. Just like I had done to gun down Nightwielder. The sight seemed to have triggered something in her.

"*David,*" she said. "*That's* your name. And I think you're very aggravating." She seemed to only just be recalling who I was. What had happened to her memory?

"Thank you?" I said.

A blast rocked the stadium and she looked over her shoulder. She still had the gun pointed at me.

"Whose side are you on, Megan?" I asked.

"My own," she said immediately, but then she held her other hand to her head, seeming uncertain.

"Someone betrayed us to Steelheart," I said. "Someone warned him we were going to hit Conflux, and someone told him we were hacking the city cameras. Today someone's been listening in on us, reporting to him what we've been doing. It was you."

She looked back at me, and didn't deny it.

"But you also used your illusions to save Abraham," I said. "And you killed Fortuity. I can buy that Steelheart wanted us to trust you, so he let you kill off one of his lesser Epics. Fortuity was out of favor anyway. But why would you betray us, *then* help Abraham escape?"

"I don't know," she whispered. "I . . ."

"Are you going to shoot me?" I asked, looking down the barrel of her gun.

She hesitated. "Idiot. You really don't know how to talk to women, do you, Knees?" She cocked her head as if surprised the words had come out.

She lowered the gun, then turned and ran off.

I've got to follow her, I thought, taking a step forward. Another explosion sounded outside.

No. I ripped my eyes away from her fleeing form. *I've got to get outside and help.*

I dashed past Nightwielder's corpse—still half submerged in steel, frozen, blood seeping down his chest—and headed for the nearest exit out onto the playing field.

Or in this case, the battlefield.

39

"... find that idiot boy and shoot him for me, Cody!" Prof screamed into my ear as I unmuted my mobile.

"We're pulling out, Jon," Tia said, talking over him. "I'm on my way in the copter. Three minutes until I arrive. Abraham will blow the cover explosion."

"Abraham can go to hell," Prof spat. "I'm seeing this to the end."

"You *can't* fight a High Epic, Jon," Tia said.

"I'll do whatever I want! I'm—" His voice cut out.

"I've removed him from the feed," Tia said to the rest of us. "This is bad. I've never heard him go this far. We need to pull him out somehow or we'll lose him."

"Lose him?" Cody asked, sounding confused. I could hear gunfire through the line near him, and could hear the same gunfire up ahead echoing in the wide corridor. I kept running.

"I'll explain later," Tia said in the type of voice that really meant "I'll find a better way to dodge that question later."

There, I thought, catching a bit of light up ahead. It was dark outside, but not as pitch-black as it was in the tunnellike confines of the stadium's innards. The gunfire was louder.

"I'm pulling us out," Tia continued. "Abraham, I need you to blow that explosion in the ground when I say. Cody . . . have you found David yet? Be warned, Nightwielder might be on your back."

She thinks I'm dead, I thought, *because I haven't been answering.* "I'm here," I said.

"David," Tia said, sounding relieved. "What is your status?"

"Nightwielder is down," I said, reaching the tunnel out onto the field, one of the ones that the teams had used when running out to play. "The UV worked. I think Firefight is gone too. I . . . drove him off."

"What? How?"

"Um . . . I'll explain later."

"Fair enough," Tia said. "We have about two minutes until I extract. Get to Cody."

I didn't reply—I was taking in the field. *Battlefield is right,* I thought, stunned. The bodies of Enforcement soldiers lay scattered like discarded trash. Fires burned in several locations, sending smoke twisting up into the dark sky. Red flares blazed across the field, thrown by soldiers to get better light. Chunks had been blown out of the seating and the ground, and blackened scars marred the once-silver steel.

"You guys have been fighting a war," I whispered. Then I caught sight of Steelheart.

He strode across the field, lips parted and teeth clenched in a sneer. His glowing hand was forward, and he blasted shot after shot toward something in front of him. Prof, running behind one of the team benches. Blast after blast nearly hit him, but he ducked and dodged between them, incredibly nimble. He pushed through a wall in the side of the stadium, his tensors vaporizing an opening for him.

Steelheart bellowed in aggravation, firing blasts into the hole. Prof appeared a moment later, breaking out of another wall, steel dust pouring down around him. He whipped his hand forward, throwing a series of crude daggers toward Steelheart; they had likely been cut from the steel itself. They just bounced off the High Epic.

Prof looked frustrated, as if he were annoyed he couldn't hurt Steelheart. For my part, I was amazed. "Has he been doing this the whole time?" I asked.

"Yeah," Cody said. "Like I said, man's a machine."

I scanned the field to my right and picked out Cody behind some rubble. He was leaning forward on his rifle and tracking a group of Enforcement soldiers in the first-level seats. They had set up a large machine gun behind some blast shields, and Cody looked pinned down, which explained why he hadn't been able to come find me. I stuffed my handgun into its holster and unwrapped the flashlight from the stock of my rifle.

"I'm almost there, gentlemen," Tia said. "No more attempts to kill Steelheart. All phases aborted. We need to take this chance and leave while we can."

"I don't think Prof is going to go," Abraham said.

"I'll deal with Prof," Tia said.

"Fine," Abraham answered. "Where are you going to—"

"Guys," I cut in. "Be careful what you say in the general link. I think our lines may be hacked."

"Impossible," Tia said. "Mobile networks are secure."

"Not if you have access to an authorized mobile," I answered. "And Steelheart might have recovered Megan's."

There was silence on the line. "Sparks," Tia said. "I'm an idiot."

"Ah, finally something makes sense," Cody said, firing a shot at the soldiers. "That mobile—"

Something moved in the opening to the building behind Cody. I cursed, raising my rifle—but without the stock it was *very* hard to aim properly. I pulled the trigger as an armed Enforcement soldier leaped out. I missed. He fired a staccato burst.

There was no sound from Cody, but I could see the blood spray. *No, no, NO!* I thought, taking off at a run. I fired again, this time clipping the soldier on the shoulder. It didn't get past his armor, but he turned from Cody, sighting on me.

He fired. I raised my left hand, the one with the tensor. I did it almost by instinct. It was tougher to make the song this time, and I didn't know why.

But I made it work. I let the song out.

I felt something thump against my palm, and a puff of steel dust sprayed off my hand. It smarted something incredible, and the tensor started sparking. A moment later a series of gunshots sounded, and the soldier dropped. Abraham came around the corner behind the man.

Gunfire from above. I dashed and skidded against the ground, sliding behind Cody's cover. He was there, gasping, eyes wide. He'd been hit several times, three in the leg, one in the gut.

"Cover us," Abraham said in his calm voice, whipping out a bandage. He tied it around Cody's leg. "Tia, Cody is hit badly."

"I'm here," Tia said. In the chaos I hadn't noticed the sounds of the copter. "I've created new mobile channels using a direct feed to each of you; that's what we should have done the moment Megan lost her mobile. Abraham, we *need* to extract. Now."

I peeked up over the rubble. Soldiers were climbing down from the stands to move on us. Abraham casually pulled a grenade off his belt and tossed it into the hallway behind us in case someone was trying to sneak up again. It exploded, and I heard shouts.

I swapped my rifle for Cody's, then opened fire on those advancing soldiers. Some went for cover, but others continued moving, bold. They knew we were at the end of our resources. I kept firing but was rewarded with a series of clicks. Cody had been almost out of ammo.

"Here," Abraham said, dropping his large assault rifle beside me. "Tia, where are you?"

"Near your position," she said. "Just outside the stadium. Head straight back and out."

"I'm bringing Cody," Abraham said.

Cody was still conscious, though he was mostly just cursing at the moment, with his eyes squeezed shut. I nodded to Abraham. I'd cover their retreat. I took up Abraham's assault rifle. To be honest, I'd always wanted to fire the thing.

It was a very satisfying weapon to use. The recoil was soft, and the weapon felt lighter than it should have. I set it on the small front tripod and let loose on fully automatic, dozens of rounds ripping through the soldiers trying to get to us. Abraham carried Cody out the back way.

Prof and Steelheart were still fighting. I downed another soldier, Abraham's high-caliber rounds ignoring most of the soldier's armor. As I fired I could feel the handgun under my arm pressing against my side.

We'd never tried firing that, the last of our guesses at how to beat Steelheart. There was no way I could hit Steelheart at this range, though. And Tia had decided to pull us out before we tried it, calling the operation.

I gunned down another soldier. The stadium trembled as Steelheart fired a series of blasts at Prof. *I can't extract now,* I thought, *despite what Tia said—I've got to try the gun.*

"We're in the copter," Abraham said in my ear. "David, time to move."

"I still haven't tried phase four," I said, climbing up to a kneeling position and firing on the soldiers again. One tossed a grenade my direction, but I was already pulling back into the corridor. "And Prof is still out there."

"We're aborting," Tia said. "Retreat. Prof will escape using the tensors."

"He'll never stay ahead of Steelheart," I said. "Besides, do you really want to run without trying this?" I ran my finger along the gun in its holster.

Tia was silent.

"I'm going for it," I said. "If you take heat, pull out." I ran off the field and back into the hallways beneath the stands, holding Abraham's assault rifle and listening to soldiers shout behind me. *Steelheart and Prof were moving this direction,* I thought. *I just need to wrap around and get close enough to fire on him. I can do it from behind.*

It would work. It *had* to work.

Those soldiers were following me. Abraham's gun had a grenade launcher underneath. Any ammunition? Those were meant to be fired before exploding, but I could use my remote detonator pen and an eraser tab to make one go off.

No luck. The gun was out of grenades. I cursed, but then saw the remote fire switch on the gun. I grinned, then stopped, spun, and put the gun on the ground, wedged back against a chunk of steel. I flipped the switch and ran.

It started firing like crazy, spraying the corridor behind me with bullets. It probably wouldn't do much damage, but all I needed was a short breather. I heard soldiers yelling at one another to take cover.

That would do. I reached another opening and left the hallway, dashing out onto the playing field.

Smoke curled in patches from the ground. Steelheart's blasts seemed to smolder after they hit, starting fires on things that shouldn't burn. I raised the pistol, and in a fleeting moment I wondered what Abraham would say when he learned that I'd lost his gun. Again.

I spotted Steelheart, who was turned away from me, distracted by Prof. I ran for all I was worth, passing through clouds of smoke, leaping over rubble.

Steelheart started to turn as I approached. I could see his eyes, imperious and arrogant. His hands seemed to burn with energy. I pulled to a halt in the whipping smoke, arms shaking as I raised the gun. The gun that had killed my father. The only weapon that had ever wounded this monster in front of me.

I fired three shots.

40

EACH one hit . . . and each one bounced free of Steelheart, like pebbles thrown at a tank.

I lowered the gun. Steelheart raised a hand toward me, energy glowing around his palm, but I didn't care.

That's it, I thought. *We've tried everything.* I didn't know his secret. I never had.

I had failed.

He released a blast of energy, and some primal part of me wouldn't just stand there. I threw myself to the side, and the blast hit the ground beside me, spraying up a shower of molten metal. The ground shook and the blast threw my roll out of control. I tumbled hard on the unyielding ground.

I came to a stop and lay there, dazed. Steelheart stepped forward. His cape had been torn in places from Prof's attacks, but he didn't seem to be anything more than inconvenienced. He loomed above me, hand forward.

He was majestic. I could recognize that, even as I readied myself for death at his hands. Silver and black cape flapping, the rips making it look more *real* somehow. Classically square face, a jaw that any linebacker would have envied, a body that was toned and muscled—but not in the way of a bodybuilder. This wasn't exaggeration; it was perfection.

He studied me, his hand glowing. "Ah yes," he said. "The child in the bank."

I blinked, shocked.

"I remember everyone and everything," he said to me. "You needn't be surprised. I am divine, child. I do not forget. I thought you well and dead. A loose end. I *hate* loose ends."

"You killed my father," I whispered. A stupid thing to say, but it was what came out.

"I've killed a lot of fathers," Steelheart said. "And mothers, sons, daughters. It is my right."

The glow of his hand grew brighter. I braced myself for what was coming.

Prof tackled Steelheart from behind.

I rolled to the side by reflex as the two hit the ground nearby. Prof came up on top. His clothing was burned, ripped, and bloodied. He had his sword, and began slamming it down in Steelheart's face.

Steelheart laughed as the weapon hit; his face actually *dented* the sword.

He was talking to me to draw Prof out, I realized in a daze. *He . . .*

Steelheart reached up and shoved Prof, throwing him backward. What seemed like a tiny bit of effort from Steelheart tossed Prof a good ten feet. He hit and grunted.

The winds picked up, and Steelheart floated up to a standing position. Then he leaped, soaring into the air. He came down on one knee, slamming a fist into Prof's face.

Red blood splashed out around him.

I screamed, scrambling to my feet and running for Prof. My ankle wasn't working properly though, and I fell hard, hitting the ground. Through tears of pain, I saw Steelheart punch down again.

Red. So much red.

The High Epic stood up, shaking his bloodied hand. "You have a distinction, little Epic," he said to the fallen Prof. "I believe you agitated me more than any before you."

I crawled forward, reaching Prof's side. His skull was crushed in on the left, his eyes bulging out the front, staring sightlessly. Dead.

"David!" Tia said in my ear. There was gunfire on her side of the line. Enforcement had found the copter.

"Go," I whispered.

"But—"

"Prof is dead," I said. "I am too. Go."

Silence.

From my pocket, I took the detonator pen. We were in the middle of the field. Cody had placed my blasting cap on the dump of explosives, and it was just beneath us. Well, I'd blow Steelheart into the sky, for what good it would do.

Several Enforcement soldiers rushed up to Steelheart, reporting on the perimeter. I heard the copter thumping as it ascended to leave. I also heard Tia weeping on the line.

I pulled myself up to a kneeling position beside Prof's corpse.

My father dying before me. Kneeling at his side. Go . . . run . . .

At least this time I hadn't been a coward. I raised the pen, fingering the button on the top. The blast would kill me, but it wouldn't harm Steelheart. He'd survived explosions before. I might take a few soldiers with me, though. That was worth it.

"No," Steelheart said to his troops. "I'll deal with him. This one is . . . special."

I looked over at him, blinking dazed eyes. He'd raised his arm to ward away the Enforcement officers.

There was something strange in the distance behind him, over the stadium rim, above the luxury suites. I frowned. Light? But . . . that wasn't the right direction. I wasn't facing the city. Besides, the city had never produced a light that grand. Reds, oranges, yellows. The very sky seemed on fire.

I blinked through the haze of smoke. Sunlight. Nightwielder was dead. The *sun* was rising.

Steelheart spun about. Then he stumbled back, raising an arm against the light. His mouth opened in awe; then he shut it, grinding his teeth.

He turned back on me, eyes wide with anger. "Nightwielder will be difficult to replace," he growled.

Kneeling in the middle of the field, I stared at the light. That beautiful glow, that powerful *something* beyond.

There are *things greater than the Epics*, I thought. *There is life, and love, and nature herself.*

Steelheart strode toward me.

Where there are villains, there will be heroes. My father's voice. *Just wait. They* will *come.*

Steelheart raised a glowing hand.

Sometimes, son, you have to help the heroes along. . . .

And suddenly, I knew.

An awareness opened my mind, like the burning radiance of the sun itself. I knew. I understood.

Not looking down, I gathered up my father's gun. I fiddled with it a moment, then raised it directly at Steelheart.

Steelheart sniffed and stared it down. "Well?"

My hand quivered, wavering, my arm trembling. The sun backlit Steelheart.

"Idiot," Steelheart said, and reached forward, grabbing my hand and crushing the bones. I barely felt the pain. The gun dropped to the ground with a clank. Steelheart held out a hand and the air spun around on the ground, forming a little whirlwind underneath the gun that raised it into his fingers. He turned it on me.

I looked up at him. A murderer outlined in brilliant light. Seen like that, he was just a shadow. Darkness. A nothingness before *real* power.

The men in this world, Epics included, would pass from time. I might be a worm to him, but he was a worm himself in the grand scheme of the universe.

His cheek bore a tiny sliver of a scar. The only imperfection on his body. A gift from a man who had believed in him. A gift from a better man than Steelheart would ever be, or ever understand.

"I should have been more careful that day," Steelheart said.

"My father didn't fear you," I whispered.

Steelheart stiffened, gun pointed to my head as I knelt, bloodied, before him. He always liked to use his enemy's own weapon against him. That was part of the pattern. The wind stirred the smoke rising around us.

"That's the secret," I said. "You keep us in darkness. You show off your terrible powers. You kill, you allow the Epics to kill, you turn men's own weapons against them. You even spread false rumors about how horrible you are, as if you can't be bothered to be as evil as you want to be. You want us to be afraid . . ."

Steelheart's eyes widened.

". . . because you can only be hurt by someone who doesn't fear you," I said. "But such a person doesn't really exist, do they? You make sure of it. Even the Reckoners, even Prof himself. Even me. We are all afraid of you. Fortunately I know someone who isn't afraid of you, and never has been."

"You know nothing," he growled.

"I know everything," I whispered. Then I smiled.

Steelheart pulled the trigger.

Inside the gun, the hammer struck the back of the bullet's

casing. Gunpowder exploded, and the bullet sprang forward, summoned to kill.

In the barrel, it struck the thing I had lodged there. A slender pen, with a button you can click on the top. It was just small enough to fit into the gun. A detonator. Connected to explosives beneath our feet.

The bullet hit the trigger and pushed it in.

I swore I could watch the explosion unfold. Each beat of my heart seemed to take an eternity. Fire channeled upward, steel ground ripping apart like paper. Terrible redness to match the peaceful beauty of the sunrise.

The fire consumed Steelheart and all around him; it ripped his body apart as he opened his mouth to scream. Skin flayed, muscles burned, organs shredded. He turned eyes toward the heavens, consumed by a volcano of fire and fury that opened at his feet. In that fraction of a sliver of a moment, Steelheart—greatest of all Epics—died.

He could only be killed by someone who didn't fear him.

He had pulled the trigger himself.

He had caused the detonation himself.

And as that arrogant, self-confident sneer implied, Steelheart did *not* fear himself. He was, perhaps, the only person alive who did not.

I didn't really have time to smile in that frozen moment, but I was feeling it nonetheless as the fire came for me.

41

I watched the shifting pattern of red, orange, and black. A wall of fire and destruction. I watched it until it vanished. It left a black scar on the ground in front of me, surrounding a hole five paces wide— the blast crater of the explosion.

I watched it all, and found myself still alive. I'll admit, it was the most baffling moment in my life.

Someone groaned behind me. I spun to see Prof sitting up. His clothing was covered in blood and he had a few scratches on his skin, but his skull was whole. Had I mistaken the extent of his injuries?

Prof had his hand forward, palm out. The tensor he'd been wearing was in tatters. "Sparks," he said. "Another inch or so and I wouldn't have been able to stop it." He coughed into his fist. "You're a lucky little slontze."

Even as he spoke, the scratches on his skin pulled together, healing. *Prof's an Epic,* I thought. *Prof's an* Epic. *That was an energy shield he created to block the explosion!*

He stumbled to his feet, looking around the stadium. A few Enforcement soldiers were running away, fleeing as they saw him rise. They seemed to want no part of whatever was happening in the center of the field.

"How . . . ," I said. "How long?"

"Since Calamity," Prof said, cracking his neck. "You think an ordinary person could have stood against Steelheart as long as I did tonight?"

Of course not. "The inventions are all fakes, aren't they?" I said, realization dawning. "You're a gifter! You *gave* us your abilities. Shielding abilities in the form of jackets, healing ability in the form of the harmsway, and destructive powers in the form of the tensors."

"Don't know why I did it," Prof said. "You pathetic little . . ." He groaned, raising his hand to his head, then gritted his teeth and roared.

I scrambled back, startled.

"It's so hard to fight," he said through clenched teeth. "The more you use it, the . . . Arrrrr!" He knelt down, holding his head. He was quiet for a few minutes, and I let him be, not knowing what to say. When he raised his head, he seemed more in control. "I give it away," he said, "because if I use it . . . it does this to me."

"You can fight it, Prof," I said. It felt right. "I've seen you do it. You're a good man. Don't let it consume you."

He nodded, breathing in and out deeply. "Take it." He reached out his hand.

I hesitantly took his hand with my good one—the other was crushed. I should have felt pain from that. I was too much in shock.

I didn't feel any different, but Prof seemed to grow more in control. My wounded hand re-formed, bones pulling together. In seconds I could flex it again, and it worked perfectly.

"I have to split it up among you," he said. "It doesn't seem to . . .

seep into you as quickly as it does me. But if I give it all to one person, they'll change."

"That's why Megan couldn't use the tensors," I said. "Or the harmsway."

"What?"

"Oh, sorry. You don't know. Megan's an Epic too."

"*What?*"

"She's Firefight," I said, cringing back a bit. "She used her illusion powers to fool the dowser. Wait, the dowser—"

"Tia and I programmed it to exclude me," Prof said. "It gives a false negative on me."

"Oh. Well, I think Steelheart must have sent Megan to infiltrate the Reckoners. But Edmund said that he couldn't gift his powers to other Epics, so . . . yeah. That's why she couldn't ever use the tensors."

Prof shook his head. "When he said that, in the hideout, it made me wonder. I'd never tried to give mine to another Epic. I should have seen . . . Megan . . ."

"You couldn't have known," I said.

Prof breathed in and out, then nodded. He looked at me. "It's okay, son. You don't need to be afraid. It's passing quickly this time." He hesitated. "I think."

"Good enough for me," I said, climbing to my feet.

The air smelled of explosives—of gunpowder, smoke, and burned flesh. The growing sunlight was reflecting off the steel surfaces around us. I found it almost blinding, and the sun wasn't even fully up yet.

Prof looked at the sunlight as if he hadn't noticed it before. He actually smiled, and seemed more and more like his old self. He strode out across the field, walking toward something in the rubble.

Megan's personality changed when she used her powers too, I thought. *In the elevator shaft, on the cycle . . . she changed. Became brasher, more arrogant, even more hateful.* It had passed quickly each time, but she'd barely used her powers, so maybe the effects on her had been weaker.

If that was true, then spending time with the Reckoners—when she needed to be careful not to use her abilities lest she give herself away—had served to keep her from being affected. The people she was meant to have infiltrated had instead turned her more human.

Prof came walking back with something in his hand. A skull, blackened and charred. Metal glinted through the soot. A steel skull. He turned it toward me. There was a groove in the right cheekbone, like the trail left by a bullet.

"Huh," I said, taking the skull. "If the bullet could hurt his bones, why couldn't the blast?"

"I wouldn't be surprised if his death triggered his tranfersion abilities," Prof said. "Turning what was left of him as he died—his bones, or some of them—into steel."

Seemed like a stretch to me. But then, strange things happened around Epics. There were oddities, especially when they died.

As I regarded the skull, Prof called Tia. I distractedly caught the sounds of weeping, exclamations of joy, and an exchange that ended with her turning the copter back for us. I looked up, then found myself walking toward the tunnel entrance into the stadium innards.

"David?" Prof called.

"I'll be right back," I said. "I want to get something."

"The copter will be here in a few minutes. I suggest we *not* be here when Enforcement comes in earnest to see what happened."

I started running, but he didn't object further. As I entered the darkness, I turned my mobile's light up to full, illuminating the tall, cavernous corridors. I ran past Nightwielder's body suspended in steel. Past the place where Abraham had detonated the explosion.

I slowed, peeking into concession stands and restrooms. I didn't have long to look, and I soon felt like a fool. What did I expect to find? She'd left. She was . . .

Voices.

I froze, then turned about in the dim corridor. There. I walked forward, eventually finding a steel door frozen open and leading into what appeared to be a janitorial chamber. I could almost make out the voice. It was familiar. Not Megan's voice, but . . .

". . . deserved to live through this, even if I didn't," the voice said. Gunfire followed, sounding distant. "You know, I think I fell for you that first day. Stupid, huh? Love at first sight. What a cliché."

Yes, I knew that voice. It was mine. I stopped at the doorway, feeling like I was in a dream as I listened to my own words. Words spoken as I defended Megan's dying body. I continued listening as the entire scene played out. Right up until the end. "I don't know if I love you," my voice said. "But whatever the emotion is, it's the strongest one I've felt in years. Thank you."

The recording stopped. Then it started playing again from the beginning.

I stepped into the small room. Megan sat on the floor in the corner, staring at the mobile in her hands. She turned down the volume when I entered, but she didn't stop looking at the screen.

"I keep a secret video and audio feed," she whispered. "The camera's embedded in my skin, above my eye. It starts up if I close my eyes for too long, or if my heart rate goes too high or too low. It sends the data to one of my caches in the city. I started doing that after I died the first few times. It's always disorienting to reincarnate. It helps if I can watch what happened leading up to my death."

"Megan, I . . ." What could I say?

"Megan is my real name," she said. "Isn't that funny? I felt I could give it to the Reckoners because that person, the person I was, is dead. Megan Tarash. She's never had any connection to Firefight. She was just another ordinary human."

She looked up at me, and in the light of her mobile screen I could see tears in her eyes. "You carried me all that way," she whispered. "I watched it, when I was first reborn this time. Your actions didn't make sense to me. I thought you must have needed something from me. Now I see something different in what you did."

"We've got to go, Megan," I said, stepping forward. "Prof can explain better than I can. But right now, just come with me."

"My mind *changes,*" she whispered. "When I die, I am reborn out of light a day later. Somewhere random, not where my body was, not where I died, but nearby. Different each time. I . . . I don't feel like myself, now that that's happened. Not the self I want to be. It doesn't make sense. What do you trust, David? What do you trust when your own thoughts and emotions seem to hate you?"

"Prof can—"

"Stop," she said, raising a hand. "Don't . . . don't come closer. Just leave me. I need to think."

I stepped forward.

"Stop!" The walls faded, and fires seemed to flame up around us. The floor warped beneath me, making me nauseous. I stumbled.

"You've *got* to come with me, Megan."

"Take another step and I'll shoot myself," she said, reaching for a gun on the floor beside her. "I'll do it, David. Death is nothing to me. Not anymore."

I backed away, hands up.

"I need to think about this," she mumbled again, looking back at her mobile.

"David." A voice in my ear. Prof's voice. "David, we're leaving *now.*"

"Don't use your powers, Megan," I said to her. "Please. You *have* to understand. They're what change you. Don't use them for a few days. Hide, and your mind will get clearer."

She kept staring at the screen. The recording started over.

"Megan . . ."

She raised the gun toward me without shifting her gaze. The tears dripped down her cheeks.

"David!" Prof yelled.

I turned and ran for the copter. I didn't know what else to do.

Epilogue

I'VE seen Steelheart bleed.

I've seen him scream. I've seen him burn. I've seen him die in an inferno, and I was the one who killed him. Yes, the hand that pushed the detonator was his own, but I don't care—and have never cared—which hand actually took his life. I made it happen. I've got his skull to prove it.

I sat strapped in the copter's chair, looking out the open door to the side, my hair blowing as we lifted off. Cody was stabilizing quickly in the back seat, much to Abraham's amazement. I knew Prof had given the man a large portion of his healing power. From what I knew of Epic regeneration abilities, that would be able to heal Cody from practically anything, so long as he was still breathing when the power was transferred.

We soared up into the air before a blazing yellow sun, leaving the stadium scorched, burned, blasted, but with the scent of triumph. My father told me that Soldier Field had been named in honor of the military men and women who had fallen in battle. Now it had hosted the most important battle since Calamity. The field's name had never seemed more appropriate to me.

We rose above a city that was seeing real light for the first time in a decade. People were in the streets, looking upward.

Tia piloted the copter, one hand reaching over to hold Prof's arm, as if she were unable to believe he was really there with us. He looked out his window, and I wondered if he saw what I did. We hadn't rescued this city. Not yet. We'd killed Steelheart, but other Epics would come.

I didn't accept that we just had to abandon the people now. We'd removed Newcago's source of authority; we'd have to take responsibility for that. I wouldn't abandon my home to chaos, not now, not even for the Reckoners.

Fighting back had to be about more than just killing Epics. It had to be about something greater. Something, perhaps, that had to do with Prof and Megan.

The Epics *can* be beaten. Some, maybe, can even be rescued. I don't know how to manage it exactly. But I intend to keep trying until either we find an answer or I'm dead.

I smiled as we turned out of the city. *The heroes will come . . . we might just have to help them along.*

I always assumed that my father's death would be the most transformative event of my life. Only now, with Steelheart's skull in my hand, did I realize that I hadn't been fighting for vengeance, and hadn't been fighting for redemption. I hadn't been fighting because of my father's death.

I fought because of his dreams.

ACKNOWLEDGMENTS

THIS one has been a long time brewing. I had the first idea for it while on book tour in . . . oh, 2007? With a long ride like that involved in getting the book finished, a *lot* of people have given me feedback over the years. I hope I don't miss any of you!

Notably, thanks go out to my delightful editor, Krista Marino, for her extremely capable direction of this project. She's been a wonderful resource, and her editing was top-notch, taking this book from plucky upstart to polished product. Also, we should make note of that rascal James Dashner, who was kind enough to call her up and get me an introduction.

Others who deserve a cheer are: Michael Trudeau (who did a superb copyedit); and at Random House, Paul Samuelson, Rachel Weinick, Beverly Horowitz, Judith Haut, Dominique Cimina, and Barbara Marcus. Also, Christopher Paolini, for his feedback and help on the book.

As always, I wish to give big thanks to my agents, Joshua Bilmes, who didn't laugh too hard when I told him I had this book I wanted to write instead of working on the twenty other projects I needed to do at the time, and Eddie Schneider, whose jobs include dressing better than the rest of us and having a name I have to look up every time I want to put it in acknowledgments. On the *Steelheart* film front (we're trying hard), thanks go to Joel Gotler, Brian Lipson, Navid McIlhargey, and the superhuman Donald Mustard.

A big thumbs-up goes to the incandescent Peter Ahlstrom, my editorial assistant, who was part of this book's cheering section from the get-go. He was, editorially, the first one who got his hands on this project—and much of its success is due to him.

I also don't want to forget my UK/Ireland/Australia publishing team, including John Berlyne and John Parker of the Zeno Agency, and Simon Spanton and my publicist/mother-in-the-UK, Jonathan Weir of Gollancz.

Others with Epic-level powers in reading and giving feedback (or just great support) include: Dominique Nolan (Dragonsteel's official Gun-Nut super-reference man), Brian McGinley, David West, Peter (again) and Karen Ahlstrom, Benjamin Rodriguez and Danielle Olsen, Alan Layton, Kaylynn ZoBell, Dan "I Wrote Postapocalyptic Before You" Wells, Kathleen Sanderson Dorsey, Brian Hill, Brian "By Now You Owe Me Royalties, Brandon" Delambre, Jason Denzel, Kalyani Poluri, Kyle Mills, Adam Hussey, Austin Hussey, Paul Christopher, Mi'chelle Walker, and Josh Walker. You're all awesome.

Finally, as always, I wish to thank my lovely wife, Emily, and my three destructive little boys, who are constant inspiration for how an Epic might go about blowing up a city. (Or the living room.)

Brandon Sanderson

The battle for mankind continues in

FIREFIGHT

Fall 2014

BRANDON SANDERSON is the author of the internationally bestselling Mistborn trilogy, and he was chosen to complete Robert Jordan's The Wheel of Time series. His books have been published in more than twenty-five languages and have sold millions of copies worldwide. He lives and writes in Utah. To learn more about Brandon and his books, visit him at brandonsanderson.com.

A HISTORY OF SHAKESPEARE ON SCREEN
A CENTURY OF FILM AND TELEVISION

A History of Shakespeare on Screen: A Century of Film and Television chronicles how film makers have re-imagined Shakespeare's plays in moving images from their earliest exhibition in nickelodeons to today's multi-million dollar productions shown in multiplexes. Topics covered include the silent era, Hollywood in the 1930s, the films of Laurence Olivier and Orson Welles, the transgressive cinema of Jarman and Greenaway, and the renaissance of the Shakespeare film with Kenneth Branagh in the 1990s. The book is truly international in scope, looking not only at screen adaptations in the UK and the US but also at the films of Kozintsev, Kurosawa, Zeffirelli and others. A filmography, bibliography and index of names make it invaluable as a one-volume reference work for specialists, while its accessible style will ensure that it appeals to enthusiasts and film-goers as well as to a more academic audience.

KENNETH S. ROTHWELL is Professor of English Emeritus at the University of Vermont, Burlington. He was the co-founder and co-editor with Bernice W. Kliman of the *Shakespeare on Film Newsletter*. He co-chaired the Shakespeare on Film Seminar at the Tokyo 1991 World Shakespeare Congress, and he produced the Shakespeare on Film Festival at the Los Angeles 1996 World Shakespeare Congress. He edited *Shakespeare on Film IV: Papers From the World Shakespeare Congress* (1981) and with Annabelle Henkin Melzer he edited *Shakespeare on Screen: An International Filmography and Videography* (1990).

A History of
Shakespeare on Screen

A CENTURY OF FILM AND TELEVISION

Kenneth S. Rothwell

CAMBRIDGE
UNIVERSITY PRESS

PUBLISHED BY THE PRESS SYNDICATE OF THE UNIVERSITY OF CAMBRIDGE
The Pitt Building, Trumpington Street, Cambridge CB2 1RP, United Kingdom

CAMBRIDGE UNIVERSITY PRESS
The Edinburgh Building, Cambridge, CB2 2RU, UK http://www.cup.cam.ac.uk
40 West 20th Street, New York, NY 10011-4211, USA http://www.cup.org
10 Stamford Road, Oakleigh, Melbourne 3166, Australia

First published 1999

Printed in the United Kingdom at the University Press, Cambridge

Typeset in Palatino

A catalogue record for this book is available from the British Library

Library of Congress Cataloguing in Publication data

Rothwell, Kenneth S. (Kenneth Sprague)
  A history of Shakespeare on screen: a century of film and
television / Kenneth S. Rothwell.
  p. cm
Includes bibliographical references and index.
ISBN 0 521 59404 9 (hardback)
  1. Shakespeare, William, 1564–1616 – Film and video adaptations.
2. English drama – Film and video adaptations.   3. Motion picture
plays – Technique.   I. Title.
PR3093.R67 1999
791.43'6–dc21   98–50547
                                                                        CIP

ISBN 0521 59404 9 hardback

For my grandchildren,
Rosalind Springs Rothwell
Sara Mei-Ping Davis
James Waddell Rothwell

— CONTENTS —

– ILLUSTRATIONS –

This book has been at least a quarter of the century in the making and along the way I have accumulated staggering debts from many generous and wonderful people. At the top of the list are the veteran members of the Shakespeare on Film Seminar at the meetings of the Shakespeare Association of America and the International Shakespeare Association who from Tokyo to Cleveland and Los Angeles to Stratford-upon-Avon have patiently read and critiqued my annual contributions. They include H.R. Coursen, Samuel Crowl, Anthony Davies, Peter S. Donaldson, Lawrence Guntner, Russell Jackson, Jack J. Jorgens, James H. Lake, R. Thomas Simone, Robert F. Willson, Jr., and many others whose friendship and collegiality have become especially meaningful to me.

To Dr. Bernice W. Kliman I owe a special debt for having co-founded and co-edited with me from 1976 to 1992 the *Shakespeare on Film Newsletter*. Dr. Nancy Hodge, formerly executive director of the Shakespeare Association of America, underwrote my three-day Shakespeare Film Festival at the 1996 World Shakespeare Congress in Los Angeles, which became the launching pad for this long-delayed book. Sarah Stanton of the Cambridge University Press added another incentive when in Los Angeles she encouraged me to submit an outline for evaluation. An anonymous reader for the Cambridge University press did me an enormous favor by ferreting out errors of fact and judgment in an earlier draft and his/her industry has been matched by Jocelyn Pye's meticulous copy editing.

The Research Committee of the University of Vermont Graduate College generously contributed toward underwriting the book's movie stills, and other permissions fees. Many on the staff of the University of Vermont Library aided me, among them James T. Barickman, Nancy Crane, Martha T. Day, Barbara T. Lambert, and Roger F. Wiberg. I also have debts to the staff of the British Film Institute Library and National Film and Television Archive, especially Luke McKernan and Olwen Terris. Helpful persons like Rosemary Hanes at the Library of Congress Motion Picture Division, and Terry Geesken of the Museum of Modern Art went out of their way for me. In the pre-videocassette era, Barry M. Parker, Joseph G. Empsucha, and

Candace Bothwell initiated me into the mysteries of the Steenbeck at the Folger Shakespeare Library film archive. Ken Wlaschin of the American Film Institute made some rare silent film materials available. I'm grateful to the lively film department at Burlington College, Chairman Ken Peck, and my Orson Welles teacher, Susan Henry, for helping me to make the crossover from Shakespeare to movies.

Among others who either advertently or inadvertently have helped along the way are the late Robert Hamilton Ball, Thomas Berger, Lynda E. Boose, Richard Burt, Mary Courtney, José Ramón Díaz-Fernández, Christina Egloff, Barbara Freedman, Kathy Grant, Kirk Hendershott-Kraetzer, Kathy Howlett, Michael Klossner, Patricia J. Lennox, Andrew M. McLean, Frank Manchel, Michael Manheim, the late Roger Manvell, Marjorie Meyer, Michael Mullin, Laurie Osborne, the late Ed Ruhe, Lisa S. Starks, Steve Toth, the late Sam Wanamaker, Stanley Wells, and Sara Woods. If I have overlooked anyone, I am truly sorry. Any errors in the pages that follow are of course entirely my responsibility.

Not least, I am grateful to my faithful and loving wife, Lyn, who put up with my becoming a grouchy recluse for two years.

− ACKNOWLEDGMENTS −

On behalf of Neal-Schuman Publishers, Michelle Rivera Rodriguez has granted permission to quote from, and/or paraphrase and rework sections (particularly in chapter five, on television) of my previously published commentaries in *Shakespeare on Screen: An International Filmography and Videography* (New York: Neal-Schuman, 1990). I owe thanks to James Welsh, editor of *Literature/Film Quarterly* for permission to draw on my "Zeffirelli's *Romeo and Juliet*: Words into Picture and Music," *LFQ* 5.4. (Fall 1977), 326–32; Bege K. Bowers, co-editor of CEA Publications, for use of excerpts from my "Roman Polanski's *Macbeth*: the 'Privileging' of Ross," *CEA Critic* 46, 1&2 (1983–84), 50–55; Luis Gámaz for permitting some use of my review essay, "Kenneth Branagh's *Henry V*," in *Comparative Drama* 24.2 (1990), 173–78; and Jason Arthur of Routledge for authorizing borrowings from my "In Search of Nothing: Mapping *King Lear*," in Lynda E. Boose and Richard Burt (eds.), *Shakespeare, The Movie* (London and New York: Routledge, 1997), pp. 135–47. Frequently I have also relied on the *Shakespeare on Film Newsletter* for relevant data. Jacqueline Kavanagh of the BBC Written Archives Centre, Caversham Park, Reading, allowed access to materials stored there and has given me helpful advice.

Excerpts from film reviews in *The New York Times* are: Copyright © 1896, 1921, 1922, 1927, 1929, 1947, 1949, 1950, 1952, 1954, 1960, 1966, 1967, 1971, 1974, 1980, 1983, 1985, 1990, 1991, 1993, 1996, by the New York Times Company. Reprinted by permission. In addition, Brian Whittaker, publishing director of *Sight and Sound* and *Monthly Film Bulletin*, has kindly consented to my quoting from film reviews.

Shakespeare quotations are from: G. Blakemore Evans (ed.), *The Riverside Shakespeare*. Copyright ©1974 by Houghton Mifflin Company. Used with permission.

— ABBREVIATIONS —

BBC	British Broadcasting Company
BFI	British Film Institute
BUFVC	British Universities Film & Video Council
CD	*Comparative Drama*
CSM	*Christian Science Monitor*
ETJ	*Educational Theatre Journal*
FM	*Film Music*
FQ	*Film Quarterly*
FR	*Films in Review*
LFQ	*Literature/Film Quarterly*
MFB	*Monthly Film Bulletin*
MG	*Manchester Guardian*
MPW	*Moving Picture World and View Photographer*
NFTVA	National Film and Television Archive
NYHT	*New York Herald Tribune*
NYO	*The New York Observer*
NYRB	*New York Review of Books*
NYT	*The New York Times*
QFRT	*Quarterly Film, Radio and Television*
RSC	Royal Shakespeare Company
SB	*Shakespeare Bulletin*
SFNL	*Shakespeare on Film Newsletter*
SN	*Shakespeare Newsletter*
SQ	*Shakespeare Quarterly*
S&S	*Sight and Sound*
TA	*Theatre Arts* (previously *Theatre Arts Monthly*)
TN	*The Nation*
TNY	*The New Yorker*
TRS	*The Riverside Shakespeare*
TS	*Theatre Survey*
VV	Village Voice
WAC	BBC Written Archives Centre
WP	*Washington Post*

- 1 -

Shakespeare in silence: from stage to screen

Nickelodeons, penny gaffs, and fair grounds

How best to imagine Shakespeare's words in moving images? The challenge to auteurial ingenuity began in September 1899 when William Kennedy-Laurie Dickson, an early collaborator with Thomas Edison, teamed up with actor/director Sir Herbert Beerbohm Tree to film excerpts from *King John*, then playing at Her Majesty's Theatre in London.[1] Sir Herbert might have hesitated if he had realized how Dickson's technology would one day make waiters out of thousands of unemployed actors. The mechanical reproduction of art was in the air, however. Over the next three decades, film makers would grind out an estimated 150,000 silent movies, though but a tiny fraction, fewer than one percent, perhaps 500, would draw on Shakespeare. With their newly patented Cinématographe, the Lumière brothers had already projected on a screen at a Parisian café one-minute "actualities" of workers leaving a factory.[2] After a rival Edison movie exhibition on April 23, 1896, at New York City's Koster & Bial's Music Hall, Charles Frohman magisterially declared that "when art can make us believe that we see actual living nature, the dead things of the stage must go."[3]

Photographed in widescreen 68 mm at the Thames embankment open-air studio of Dickson's British Mutoscope and Biograph Company, Tree played the dying King John in act five, scene seven, against a studio backdrop for Swinstead Abbey. He was flanked by Prince Henry (Dora Senior) and the Earl of Pembroke (James Fisher), and by Robert Bigot (F.M. Paget), all in period costumes. As the poisoned king, Tree's writhing and clutching and gyrating and swiveling and squirming mime the agony of a human being whose "bowels [are crumbling] up to dust" and whose inner torment is akin to "hell" (5.7.30–45).[4] In King John's death, however, Tree breathed life into an upstart rival to Shakespeare on stage – Shakespeare on screen in moving images. Ironically Shakespeare's *King John* also proleptically deals with the economic forces that would drive this fledgling art from its very beginnings – the curse of "tickling commodity," that "smooth-fac'd gentleman," which Philip the Bastard describes as "this bawd, this broker" that forces even kings

1   In *King John* (UK 1899), Sir Herbert Beerbohm Tree as the dying monarch writhes in agony at Swinstead Abbey, while Pembroke (James Fisher), Prince Henry (Dora Senior), and Bigot (F.M. Paget) look on.

to "break faith" (2.1.573–85). The most cash-driven art form in history, film from the beginning has been enslaved to "tickling commodity." Marx's insight that capitalism's gains for humanity's material comfort often come at the price of its soul needs no better illustration. The iron rule of profit or perish has commodified Shakespeare, dictating the scope, size, frequency, and even the artistry of filmed plays, and at the same time forced the Shakespeare director into an inevitable synergy with popular culture.

At the start of this century, however, no one envisioned the revolutionary potential of the movie industry. Movies were working-class entertainment at England's penny gaffs and music halls, American vaudeville, sideshows at European country fairs, and entr'acte diversions. Since by 1905, France controlled 60 percent of the world's film business, not surprisingly the next Shakespeare "movie," produced by the Phono-Cinéma-Théâtre, emerged, complete with "sound," at the 1900 Paris Exhibition. It photographed Sarah Bernhardt in moving images energetically fighting Laertes (Pierre Magnier) in the duel scene from *Hamlet*, with synchronized Edison cylinders providing the sound of clashing epées.[5] Having played Hamlet on stage thirty-two times in 1899 alone, as well as performing in other earlier Shakespearean roles, and with an extraordinary flair for publicity,[6] Sarah Bernhardt was a natural choice to star in this second ever Shakespeare movie. In her career, frustrated by the dearth of first-rate female parts and encouraged by the French stage tradition for cross-dressing, she acted in over two dozen *travesti* ranging from minor (a page boy) in *Phèdre* to a truly *grand premier travesti rôle* as in *Hamlet*.[7] Moreover, contrary to prevailing ideas about "Hamletism" that stressed the prince's inward femininity, "revenge permeated the production of the Bernhardt *Hamlet*."[8] In silent movies, Bernhardt's famous silvery voice was stilled but on the other hand the French accent that prevented her from playing Romeo against Ellen Terry's Juliet became irrelevant, for by substituting images for words her personality crossed international language barriers. As Carl Laemmle proclaimed in a trade journal advertisement, "Universal pictures speak the Universal language." The spectacle of Shakespeare performed in a déclassé venue at a fairground may have shocked the bourgeois, who probably felt as did Oscar Wilde's Dorian Gray at a cheap London theatre that "I must admit I was rather annoyed at the idea of seeing Shakespeare done in such a wretched hole of a place." Bernhardt's *Hamlet*, like Tree's *King John,* as the extant frame enlargements show, went no further than being a record of a theatrical performance on a conventional stage set, a first step in the evolution of the Shakespeare movie from theatre into film.[9]

The sound effects for a fencing duel in Bernhardt's *Hamlet* remind us that "silent" films were really never silent. As David A. Cook has noted, silent

[3]

film was an "aberration," and "movies were intended to talk from their inception."[10] Thomas Edison's plan for a "coin-operated entertainment machine" envisioned motion pictures illustrating sound from a phonograph, not the other way around. Live musicians quickly showed up in theatres to fill out the awful silences, and typically theatre owner Lyman H. Howe of New York City advertised in a trade journal for "an imitator to create sound effects back of the screen . . . a man [with the] natural ability to produce animal and mechanical sounds."[11] A manager in Clear Lake, Iowa, needed a "singer and piano player combined," to whom he would pay "a good salary,"[12] for he subscribed to the universal belief that "a good piano player is essential to the success of . . . electric theatre."[13] Female pianists could now use their previously unmarketable talents "by earning an honest living playing in a public place."[14] Audiences soon became so accustomed to sound that when the unfortunate John Riker, a projectionist isolated in his booth, mistakenly grabbed a live wire, his shrieks of agony as 1,000 volts surged through him were interpreted as splendid sound effects and wildly applauded. Rescued by the piano player, Riker's roasted hand had "to be pried loose from the wire."[15]

By 1908 the Kleine Optical Company was advertising its "remarkable consignment of film subjects" showing "famous French actors."[16] Like everyone else, the French rejoiced in finding literary properties by famous authors like Shakespeare whose "public domain" status meant freedom from any unpleasantness about royalties. Mesmerized by the prestige of the Comédie Française, French film makers developed the Film d'Art movement to glorify French theatrical tradition, which nurtured high culture but inhibited the growth of film art. In America, some companies like Adolph Zukor's Famous Players, anxious to earn the cachet of high art, imitated the French, their movies often being lower-cased as "film d'art," and the creation in Italy of the Film d'Arte Italiana added further confusion for filmographers. The assumption was that movies were not themselves an art but had to have art put into them with literary classics. Jean Mounet-Sully, "the greatest French actor of the period," who played Hamlet at the Comédie Française, as well as Othello opposite Bernhardt's Desdemona, soon followed, or even preceded Bernhardt, with a vignette from the *Hamlet* graveyard scene;[17] and Georges Méliès, the inventor of trick photography, who put flying machines into space and showed people floating on air, performed the title role in a *Hamlet* segment (1907), as well as a cameo William Shakespeare in *Shakespeare Writing Julius Caesar* (1907), a portrayal of the assassination.[18] Paul Mounet, younger brother of Mounet-Sully, was cast in the lead of *Macbeth* (c.1909). A Pathé semi-Shakespearean *Cleopatra* (1910) starring Madeleine Roch anticipated a long line of films about the Egyptian witch that had little to do with

Shakespeare's tragedy, culminating in the mega-budget 20th-Century Fox *Cleopatra* (1963) with superstars Elizabeth Taylor and Richard Burton. A derivative *Romeo Turns Bandit* (1910), which though only marginally indebted to Shakespeare, broke with and moved away from the merely presentational by employing a rudimentary film grammar. In general, however, the Film d'Art obsession with theatrical models distracted continental cinéastes from the main challenge of envisioning Shakespeare in cinematic tropes. The history of Shakespeare in the movies has, after all, been the search for the best available means to replace the verbal with the visual imagination, an inevitable development deplored by some but interpreted by others as not so much a limitation on, as an extension of, Shakespeare's genius into uncharted seas. In the United States, on the other hand, the trek westward to Hollywood sufficiently disconnected the movies from Broadway theatre to make possible by 1929 the thoroughly liberated Pickford/Fairbanks *The Taming of the Shrew*.

The economic engine in North America driving the production of cheap, one-reel movies was the "nickelodeon," a term coined by John P. Harris of McKeesport, Pennsylvania, by cleverly merging his admission price with the Greek word for music hall.[19] There were no cinemas and then suddenly there were hundreds, and thousands. Like the 1576 opening of Richard Burbage's professional theatre in Shoreditch, the new movie theatres revolutionized the entertainment industry. An editorial writer in the trade journal *Moving Picture World* observed that "there is a new thing under the sun . . . It is the 5-cent theatre . . . it came unobtrusively in the still of the night," and had multiplied "faster then guinea pigs."[20] By 1907 North America alone could tally 2,500 to 3,000 "nickelodeons," or "5-cent theatres," or "electric theatres," as they were variously labeled. It did not take much to get a 5-cent theatre started – an empty store with enough space to cram in 200 to 500 chairs; phonographs; a cashier; a "cinematograph" with a reliable non-smoking operator; a canvas for a screen; a piano; a leather-lunged barker; and of course a manager to oversee all this. Predictably the respectable classes sniffed at the honky-tonk flavor and spurned the upstart.

Such heady success did not go unchallenged. In the midst of its severe growing pains, the movie industry became a lightning rod for hostility. It threatened the praetorians of culture and morality who intuited how these new "site[s] of cultural contagion associated with the 'lower orders'"[21] would one day destroy the iron control of church and school over the masses. The Reverend E. L. Goodell stopped a showing of the Edison *Nero and the Burning of Rome* (1908) because the school children were worked into "a frenzy of fear when they saw men seized, choked, stabbed and their limbs twisted by their torturers."[22] Some little girls covered their faces with their hats to shut out the sight. An Episcopal bishop deplored the "demoralizing influence" of the nickelodeons.[23] Harassing fly-by-night theatre operators, many of whom were eastern European Jewish immigrants, for showing movies on Sunday became a favorite pastime of New York's Finest, but then also it might be a charge of "imperiling the morals of young boys," as in the lamentable case of George Watson who allowed juveniles to watch the drugging of Evelyn Nesbitt in *The Great Thaw Trial*.[24]

With Machiavellian cunning, the vaudevillians and other theatre people who were at risk of redundancy, calculating that politicians would more gladly listen to men of the cloth than to men of the motley, manipulated the clergy into lobbying against 5-cent theatres. In a last-ditch effort they also undercut the scruffy nickelodeons by incorporating movies into their vaudeville programs in real theatres.[25] The actors' clandestine scheming achieved dizzy success on Christmas Eve, 1908, when in a spasm of self-righteousness New York City's Mayor George B. McClellan shut down 500 nickelodeons, ostensibly because they were fire traps, which they indubitably were, but also possibly to appease those who saw them as dens of iniquity. An editorial in *Moving Picture World* accused the actors of chicanery and sarcastically thanked the Mayor for his "unexpected Christmas present."[26] In Los Angeles saloon keepers complained that the nickelodeons were stealing customers away.[27] In London, the penny gaffs competed with the public houses.

In the first decade of film, however, for a brief shining hour the Vitagraph Company's Brooklyn, New York studio emerged as a world hub for Shakespeare films. In 1908, J. Stuart Blackton's Vitagraph Company[28] entered into this rough-and-tumble marketplace with a series of one-reel Shakespeare movies. The cultural politics of turn-of-the-century America made this marriage of elitist Shakespeare with the populist nickelodeons inevitable. Seeing a compelling need for "quality" motion pictures to attract "classier" audiences, and perhaps inspired by France's Film d'Art movement, Blackton made public domain Shakespeare a pawn in a bid for higher social status. "Class," "classy," and "classier" became the mantras of the early film makers as they fought to gain respectability, envisioning a mythical audience for high-mimetic Shakespeare made up of Margaret Dumont types out of the Marx Brothers movies. Shakespeare movies were a small part of the campaign to obliterate socially aware films sympathizing with the plight of the exploited workers.[29] Movies became the sites of contestation for nothing more or less than the American soul. The Vitagraph line of "quality" products included films about George Washington, Dante's Francesca da Rimini, and biblical tales, though its trade journal puffs also listed low-brow material like *The Cook Makes Madeira Sauce* right alongside its "high art" *Midsummer Night's Dream*.[30] Another ideological agenda behind all this do-goodism was the need to civilize the hordes of eastern and southern Europeans disembarking at Ellis Island by exposure to solid Anglo-American values. Through beatifying George Washington, who was after all only transplanted English country gentry, and showcasing Shakespeare, the tired and huddled masses who jammed the nickelodeons could more quickly be melted into the pot.

Vitagraph's Shakespeare movies were highly compressed one-reelers of ten to fifteen minutes in duration that privileged tableaux, such as the assassination of Julius Caesar, or the balcony scene from *Romeo and Juliet*, which were familiar even to the unscrubbed masses. Vitagraph Shakespeare titles, all released between about 1908 and 1912, in addition to *A Midsummer Night's Dream* included *Antony and Cleopatra, As You Like It, Henry VIII [Cardinal Wolsey], Julius Caesar, King Lear, Merchant of Venice, Othello, Richard III, Romeo and Juliet*, and *Twelfth Night*. *A Comedy of Errors* used only the title, and *Hamlet* was planned but never completed. Often directed by William V. Ranous, a veteran stage actor, or Charles Kent, they were mass produced in a row of rooftop stalls, or in glass-roofed indoor studios in Flatbush. Sometimes the company went out on location in New York City's Central and Prospect Parks, or, in one instance on the beach at Bay Shore, Long Island, for Viola's emergence from the sea.[31] By all accounts there was a wonderful, almost amateurish atmosphere. Scenery and costumes were likely to have been borrowed from Broadway or slapped together by a makeshift crew, including the actors, who weren't yet high-paid superstars.[32] They also moonlighted from theatrical jobs on Broadway, a powerful and inhibiting influence on the new art that weakened when the studios moved west to Hollywood.

The Shakespeare and other "high art" films demanded a story-telling grammar that went far beyond the filmic strategies of the earlier "actualities." Film scholars disagree over which film to credit as the "first" to tell a story but Edwin S. Porter's *The Great Train Robbery* (1903) is generally held up as a milestone event,[33] along with D. W. Griffith's subsequent *The Lonedale Operator* (1911) that carried editing to new heights. Porter's railway thriller may not have been the first to do everything but it pointed the way to a rhetoric that would eventually include all the tricks of the trade, such as shifting camera angles, editing in the cutting room, dramatic lighting, full shots, close-ups, intercutting of sequences, slow motion, rhythm in editing, and so forth.

Like the other Vitagraph Shakespeare films, Blackton's *Romeo and Juliet* (1908), starring Florence Lawrence and Paul Panzer, went beyond the primitive "actualities" by using the camera not just as a recorder of but as a participant in the cinematic story telling. The struggle of these early movies was to break out of the prison house of the proscenium stage on nearby

Broadway and make a film that did not look as if it had been photographed with a camera nailed to the floor in the sixth-row orchestra. The camera needed to be released to close in on the action. The two principals, Lawrence and Panzer, later became big stars, Lawrence as a D.W. Griffith favorite, and then as the famed "Biograph Girl" and "IMP girl," the first beneficiary of the new star system that allowed actors to cash in on their fame. After her breakthrough, by 1916 Sir Herbert Beerbohm Tree commanded $100,000 for six weeks' work, and by 1919 Mary Pickford was demanding $675,000 a year plus 50 percent of the gross.[34] Paul Panzer subsequently flourished as the villain in the Saturday-morning thriller serial, *The Perils of Pauline* (1914).

Seventeen different camera set-ups, or shots, thirteen title cards, and noticeable editing off camera make up Vitagraph's 15-minute compression of *Romeo and Juliet.* There is occasional cross-cutting, movement from indoor to outdoor settings, and a minimum of obviously fraudulent painted canvas backdrops. A long shot may interrupt the monotony of mid-shots, or actors are filmed from varied angles, but the close shot is not yet in the vocabulary. Title cards with dialogue and bridging explanations help out in the losing battle to make the aural entirely visual. The movie opens with the sonnet-prologue on a card reading "Two households, both alike in dignity, In fair Verona, where we lay our scene," and so forth. Other bridging cards offer helpful but slightly misleading comments such as "Capulet introduces his daughter, Juliet, to Paris, her future husband." For the Capulet ball and balcony scene, the laconic words "Love at First Sight" suffice, following which Romeo mimes his love for Juliet, while Tybalt's ever-widening mouth signals outrage. Another card reads "The Secret Marriage of Romeo and Juliet in Friar Laurence's Cell" just prior to a sequence showing the Friar, who resembles George Bernard Shaw, joining the couple in matrimony. The camera completely broke with theatre when the crew went out on location for the balcony scene at a house near Fort Hamilton, Brooklyn; for the duel between Romeo and Tybalt to the Boat Lake in Central Park; and for Verona's streets to Central Park's Bethesda Fountain.[35] Even without sound-recording equipment, to stay in character old-time Shakespeareans of the stature of Forbes-Robertson and Frederick Warde scrupulously spoke the lines but some of the lesser sort of actors may have been uttering gibberish.

Interiors were more likely to be thrift-shop stage sets with curtains and cardboard for doors and walls. Harsh lighting was a problem, as when Juliet emotes before drinking off the vial of potion and collapses too heavily on the bed. "Tickling commodity" intrudes in Juliet's bedroom, and elsewhere, with the Vitagraph logo, "V," inscribed over her bed. A precursor to today's FBI warnings on videocassettes against illegal copying, the logo was a relic of the rancorous patent wars that pitted the "Edison group," which included

Vitagraph, against such upstarts as Carl Laemmle of the IMP group (Independent Motion Picture Company of America). The movie industry's endless law suits must have made many attorneys rich and happy.[36] A more satisfactorily realistic scene in *Romeo and Juliet* is the apothecary shop, which boasts a window apparently stocked with a skull, bat, alembic, and beakers, though they may only be good *trompes-l'oeil*. The director himself, William Ranous, played the apothecary.

The Vitagraph *Julius Caesar* (1908) shows no striking advance in film grammar over the *Romeo and Juliet*. It breaks with theatricality by moving outdoors. There is much *Aida*-like parading around of Roman soldiers in papier-mâché helmets who brandish wooden swords and carry placards reading "SPQR," but the "Forum" looks suspiciously like the steps of a Carnegie public library. Almost without exception the movie's fifteen set-ups are in mid-shot, without changing camera angles or using close-ups and long shots. Freed from the spatial and temporal restrictions of the stage, the camera shows events that are only reported in the play, such as the proffering of the crown to Caesar three times. The assassination of Caesar, a plausibly mimed Antony's funeral oration, and an out-of-doors funeral pyre for Brutus create familiar tableaux for a mass audience. Truly cinematic in its early use of special effects is the Méliès-like materializing of Caesar's ghost from thin air in Brutus' tent before Philippi. The battle field at Philippi is something of a disappointment, a flat arid landscape, boring even as the site of carnage. Brutus and Cassius stomp around followed by tiny detachments of soldiers. Costuming is rudimentary. When Brutus' Portia pledges fidelity to her husband, she is only vaguely Roman, being swathed in the yards of material thought chic for ladies traveling first class on liners like the *Titanic*. This cover-up was necessary because a "reverend gentleman" actually objected to costumes showing the men's legs. Ball also quotes a story of actors' bare legs being disastrously painted to avoid the expense of tights.[37]

Julius Caesar failed to impress Mr. W. Stephen Bush, America's earliest critic of filmed Shakespeare, who often waxed ecstatic over other Vitagraph movies. Bush, a frequent correspondent for *Moving Picture World* and its British counterpart, *Bioscope*,[38] regularly advertised his services as a lecturer to supplement "high art" films,[39] and in that way, like the pianists, he compensated for a film's unbearable silence. He uncharitably noted that the funeral pyre at the end of *Julius Caesar* "had a fatal resemblance to a Rhode Island clambake"; neither did he miss out on the opportunity to plug his own profession by pointing out that these plays on screen "are [little] more than a bewildering mass of moving figures to the majority of the patrons of electric theatres, but none stands more emphatically in need of a good lecture than *Julius Caesar*."[40]

The seeds of filmic greatness lie deeply buried in the Vitagraph *King Lear* (1909),[41] which strives for a realism that can only be achieved with enormously expensive sets. Actualities showing the Household Brigade on parade are one thing, but underfunded actualities of a Shakespearean play only succeed in becoming non-actualities. The movie begins innovatively by identifying the characters (but not the players) with their names superimposed below them. About thirteen different set-ups show events from the old king's testing of his daughters to his dying lamentations over the body of Cordelia. The parallel Gloucester plot and the scandalous love triangle among Goneril, Regan, and Edmund collapse under the weight of compression and would require W. Stephen Bush's lecturing service to sort out the story line for the bewildered audience. Exterior shots are non-existent. The white cliffs of Dover are painted on canvas and the storm scenes take place inside a studio with a fake hollowed-out tree for mad Tom to hide in. To spare the audience, and appease the enemies of nickelodeons, when Cornwall gouges out the old man's eyes, "Lest it see more, prevent it. Out vild jelly!" (3.7.83), Gloucester's back is to the camera. In the foreground, the indignant servant stabs the wicked Cornwall, and in a magical flash of pure film, Oswald breaks loose from an irate Kent, runs directly toward the camera, and with a wild look on his face almost invades the audience's space.

The festive *Midsummer Night's Dream* (1909) and *Twelfth Night* (1910) forced Vitagraph's director Charles Kent out of the studio and into the parks with happy results. Not only is the lighting cheerful but also then and future famous actors like Maurice Costello as Lysander and his two little daughters, Dolores and Helene, project high spirits, immensely enjoying themselves. Like all the Vitagraph one-reelers, *Midsummer Night's Dream* moves at the pace of a fast-forwarded videocassette, or as if the Reduced Shakespeare Company had made a movie for Vitagraph, an outcome that sometimes happens when a silent film is projected at the wrong speed. Notwithstanding technical glitches, certain scenes capture the spirit of the play. William V. Ranous, about whom little seems to be known except that he was a journeyman actor, makes a hilarious Bottom as he mimes the weaver's blustering attempts to show how he can roar or play any role in the Pyramus/Thisby skit better than anyone else. The antics of Puck and the emplacement of an ass's head on Bottom are made to order for tricky visuals. There's quite a charming scene by a pond as Puck (Gladys Hulette) is suddenly lifted up into the air to search for the magic flower. An unaccountable switch in casting occurs when a young woman called Penelope replaces Oberon. It's Penelope, not Oberon, that Titania quarrels with and Penelope who sends Puck out to look for the potion. Perhaps the director feared that the pedophile subtext about the Indian boy might upset the censorious classes.

The same story gets told twice, once in pictures when the rude mechanicals come to the forest and again with explanatory cards: "The tradesmen come to the forest to rehearse their play. Puck changes the weaver into an ass. Titania awakens and falls in love with him." Later, at the peak of the silent era, F.W. Murnau's famous *The Last Laugh* (1924) eschewed title cards in favor of telling the story only in pictures, a virtuoso feat wildly acclaimed by purists. A *Moving Picture World* reviewer congratulated Vitagraph on its success with *Midsummer Night's Dream*: "We wondered . . . who amongst the American filmmakers would be the first to strike into the rich preserve of material which Shakespeare offers the producer." He praised the Vitagraph director for his skill in compressing the scenes into "a continuous and intelligible story which does not destroy the narrative."[42]

Vitagraph's *Twelfth Night* (1910) showed increasing cinematic sophistication. Florence Turner, "The Vitagraph Girl," plays a saucy little Viola who, as the first explanatory card tells us, is "separated from her twin brother Sebastian by a shipwreck [and] finds herself in the realm of Duke Orsino." Cross-dressed as Cesario, Turner contrasts nicely with Julia Swayne Gordon's Olivia, who is muffled under the layers of garments that turned Victorian actresses into Volumnia lookalikes. Something close to a deep-focus shot occurs when in Olivia's mansion, courtiers retreat and exit in the background even as in the foreground Viola woos Olivia: "Make me a willow cabin at your gate, / And call upon my soul within the house" (1.5.268). Charles Kent's miming of Malvolio's pomposity when he intercepts the forged letter captures the essence of the dialogue. The audience sees the letter in close-up on a title card: "be not afraid of greatness. Some are [born] great, some [achieve] greatness, and some have greatness thrust upon 'em" (2.5.144). Then as the gulled Malvolio in close mid-shot devours the contents of the letter, the conspirators, Maria, Sir Toby and Aguecheek, gleefully hop and skip. The closing sequence accelerates as the twins are reunited, Maria confesses, the duke discovers Cesario is a girl, and Olivia finds solace in the arms of Sebastian. There is a moment allowed for Charles Kent as the abused and rejected Malvolio to vent his spleen on his tormentors. Decades later, Nigel Hawthorne as Malvolio would have a greater opportunity to wring the full poignancy out of Malvolio's downfall in Trevor Nunn's full-length film of *Twelfth Night* (1996).

Disputes about the nature of the audience for these Vitagraph Shakespeare films ironically recapitulate the many studies of the audience at Shakespeare's Globe playhouse. Lower class? Upper class? Both? There is no simple answer. More in the audience hailed from the huddled masses rather than the coddled classes, but the "class" of the audience tended to correlate with the style of neighborhood that the "nick" was situated in. It should not be forgotten, however, that even the most wretched of the earth had heard of and respected Shakespeare. From Mark Twain's rednecks in *Huckleberry Finn*, residents of sad, little towns along the Mississippi, to the eastern European immigrant Jews in New York City who revered the Shakespeare of Yiddish theatre, Shakespeare possessed enormous cultural capital. For America's nouveau riche, there was no more prestigious cultural trophy than a leather-bound complete Shakespeare for display in the parlor, even if the pages were uncut. The people who paid their nickels to see Shakespeare on screen were schoolboys who giggled at the overacting in *Julius Caesar*, outside salesmen resting between their appointed rounds, persons who simply delighted to see something more enlightening than the morning drill of the king's household guards in London, and totally perplexed and confused immigrants glad to be in out of the cold. When a law suit over an unauthorized movie of General Lew Wallace's *Ben Hur* struck fear into the movie industry, Shakespeare's status as public domain intellectual property made him all the more attractive.[43]

Film critic W. Stephen Bush saw through bourgeois pretensions and found hope in the nickelodeons. Bush attacked the "fashion in certain quarters to look upon the electric theatre as chiefly the poor man's amusement."[44] A high-minded foe of elitism, he rhapsodized that the poor woman's nickel at the movie was the equal of the rich woman's gold at the opera, and predicted that one day the carriage trade would be drawn to movies. He was also sensitive to the difficulties involved in "condensation and arrangement" but believed that the Vitagraph films were probably as "good as any that could have been made." Like many after him, he warned that "to condense or in any way to alter Shakespeare is as delicate and dangerous a task as meddling with an overture by Mozart or a painting by Rembrandt."[45] Still, he believed that "there is no play of Shakespeare that cannot be told in moving images," and that "the notion that Shakespeare, as the half-educated put it, is 'too deep' is altogether wrong."[46]

Bush's professional stake in explanatory lectures and recitations at silent Shakespeare movies may have fueled his zeal for the new art. As we have seen, he firmly believed that the solution to the oxymoron of Shakespeare on silent film was to flesh out the title cards with an "epilogue" in a kind of lecture/performance. That way the "best class of people" would flock to the Shakespeare movies, the "banal, the vulgar and the foolish"[47] would stay away, and high culture would be served. Unfortunately a lecturer like Bush was an extra expense and it's not at all clear how many 5-cent theatres bought his lofty services. As for Vitagraph studios, its "high art" Shakespeare films survive today only in archives, more often than not the targets for brainless laughter, though they should be respected not so much for what they did as for doing anything at all. The Vitagraph empire eventually was swallowed up by Warner Brothers, which purchased it in 1924 for $735,000.[48]

From nickelodeon to palace

While Vitagraph cranked out its one-reelers in New York, cinéastes in England, France, and Italy made Shakespeare films until World War I dictated a readjustment in priorities. After the war, the Germany of the Weimar Republic produced ambitious movies of *Hamlet, Othello,* and *The Merchant of Venice*. The movies increasingly expanded in length from one to three and four reels to fit the needs of the emerging "Palace" theatres that were steadily replacing the tacky nickelodeons, penny gaffs, and fair grounds as exhibition sites.[49] The movement from nickelodeon to palace resembled the shift from the "public" Globe to the "private" Blackfriars playhouse in Shakespeare's London, though the new movie palaces unlike the Blackfriars, attracted both the classes and the masses. S.R. Rothafel's ("Roxy") opening in 1916 of the Regent movie theatre in New York City at the corner of 116th Street and 7th Avenue signaled an emerging era in New York,[50] and Rothafel in 1927 followed up with his famous $10-million Roxy Theatre, "a cathedral of the motion picture" near Times Square. Among its wonders were "foyers and lobbies of incomparable size and splendor" as well as "a staff of attendants [ushers] thoroughly organized and drilled under the direction of a retired Colonel of the U.S. Marines."[51] Roxy's ostentatious theatres, temples of dreams, enshrined megalomania, monuments of bad taste, were part of an international movement. By 1914 Paris boasted a Pathé Palace (600 seats), and Gaumont-Palace (6,000 seats) with an 80-piece orchestra pit.[52] In England, the Balham Empire had already opened in 1907, and was unique in being "a theatre devoted entirely to the display of living pictures."[53] The grand opening of the Palace Electric in Mansfield, England, sent Alderman Alcock into raptures as he congratulated all involved for having produced such a fine building, with its "marble-floored vestibule . . . brass-mounted beveled glass entrance and electric blue seats."[54] In Croydon, another palace opened with "a beautiful vestibule, carpets, hangings, etc."[55] With theatre names like Odeon, Bijou, Jewel, Picturedrome, Electroscope, movies were clearly acquiring the "classy" cachet the movie people were dying for. As Dennis Sharp has pointed out, the new theatres often functioned "like Roman Catholic churches," resembling "a bulging whale on the outside and a stomach full of whipped cream on the inside," for the function of church and theatre building alike is to keep the faithful focused on the holy mysteries within, not the superstructure without.[56]

A two-reel, 33-minute *Shylock* (1913), one of the last of the Film d'Art attempts to record classical French theatre, might have been suitable for Paris' grand new Gaumont Palace. Directed by Henri Desfontaines, the Globe Film Company trade journal advertisement declared that it "would be impossible to exaggerate the splendour and attractiveness of this beautiful and compelling picture story adapted from Shakespeare's immortal work, 'The Merchant of Venice.'"[57] The distinguished cast included Harry Baur (Shylock) of the Athénée Theatre, Romuald Joubé (Antonio) of the Odeon, and Mlle. Pépa Bonafé (Portia) of the Apollo – all from leading Paris theatres. Harry Baur first appears on screen in a formal cutaway, as if he, like W. Stephen Bush, would lecture on Shakespeare's play, with Jean Hervé (Bassanio) and Mlle. Pépa Bonafé in Elizabethan dress. Title cards confide that this is "Venice on the Rialto" and that in Belmont nearby there is "a lady richly left . . . her name is Portia." The establishing shot of the Rialto with its pathetic cardboard backdrop disappointed a contemporary critic, who noted that "the film producer by not making the greatest possible use of natural outdoors effects, deprives himself of one of the greatest advantages that he possesses over the regular stage."[58] A crowd scene on the Rialto, a flashback of Bassanio spitting on Shylock as he drafts the bond, and cross-cutting to compress the space between Portia's carefree Belmont and Shylock's careworn Venice reveal a shift from theatricality toward narrative film making. Title cards bridge the episodes as with an announcement about the loss of Antonio's ships just before the opening of a frenetic trial scene. Harry Baur's Shylock is of the pre-Holocaust vintage, an object of mirth and scorn rather than a victim of bigotry. Ironically the Jewish Harry Baur would himself a few years later fall victim to Adolf Hitler's pathological anti-Semitism. In the courtroom, he menacingly whets his knife, and then a mini-second later he is being pursued by a hooting, jeering mob. The deeper point that Belmont, like the golden casket, remains only superficially attractive and that Shylock, like the leaden casket, yet conceals stern virtues, remains unexplored.

To the south, during this pre-war period, the Neapolitan flair for grand opera infiltrated Italian Shakespeare movies, which also in the Film d'Arte Italiana mode displayed the same anxiety as the French to please only the elitist cadres from the theatrical world. While partial toward the Roman history plays, the Italians also drew on *Hamlet, King Lear, Merchant of Venice, Midsummer Night's Dream, Othello, Romeo and Juliet, Taming of the Shrew,* and *Winter's Tale.*[59] A Film d'Arte Italiana *King Lear* (1910) followed the French model of Film d'Art by putting famous actors and great plays into movies. Directed by Gerolamo Lo Savio, the celebrated tragedian Ermete Novelli played the title role with Francesca Bertini as Cordelia. An 11-minute one-reeler, *King Lear* omits the Gloucester plot and focuses on the king, his three daughters and faithful Kent. Even with the Gloucester plot eliminated, the story line still requires heavy use of title cards for coherence. Having the wind actually ruffle the actors' hair and garments shows another step in the movement away from theatricality toward realism.

Francesca Bertini (Portia) and Ermete Novelli (Shylock) appear again in Lo Savio's color-tinted *Il Mercante di Venezia* (1910). The very first title card by proclaiming that "Lorenzo who is in love with Jessica, the daughter of Shylock the Jew, arranges to come for her" privileges Jessica's rebellion against Shylock over the bond, ring, and casket plots. Novelli's interpretation of Shylock as a man primarily distraught over his wayward daughter turns the Jew into a King Lear figure: "How sharper than a serpent's tooth it is / To have a thankless child!" (*Lear* 1.4.288). The ingrate Jessica's betrayal exacerbates Shylock's anguish over the loss of Leah, the wife whose "turkis" ring he would not have sold "for a wilderness of monkeys" (3.1.122). An inter-title announces that "Antonio's ships have been wrecked, and he is ruined ... He is taken before a court of justice," after which in a familiar stage tradition Shylock whets his knife. A title card prints out Portia's reading to Shylock of the law that plainly outlines the penalties for shedding Christian blood. Sadly as Shylock bitterly laments his predicament, the surviving print (from the NFTVA) abruptly ends.

Lo Savio's 25-minute *Romeo and Juliet* (1911) gave the lovely Francesca Bertini, who by 1915 became one of Italy's greatest stars, a chance to display her talents as a silent film actress with Gustavo Serena as her Romeo. Like Lillian Gish, Bertini could convey almost any mood with only a slight change in expression, showing radiance when with her Romeo, and sullenness when told by Father Capulet to marry Paris. Lo Savio's editing included deletions, transpositions, and additions to adapt the play script to the needs of an audience unfamiliar with the play, and to make the verbal visual. In place of the opening brawl, which comes after the Capulet ball, a mounted Romeo dismounts to retrieve Juliet's glove, which Romeo will later rhapsodize over ("O that I were a glove upon that hand, / That I might touch that cheek!" – 2.2.24). The Italian love for operatic spectacle, which survives in Zeffirelli's Shakespeare movies, brightens the *mise-en-scène* for the Capulet garden, which is filled with statuary, handy for concealing eavesdroppers like the Nurse. The ballroom gleams with shimmering candelabra, a vaulted ceiling and elegantly costumed dancers.

A clichéd establishing shot of William Shakespeare reading the play aloud to a circle of friends frames Baldassare Negroni's *Una Tragedia alla Corte di Sicilia* (1913). With its lavish costumes, realistic settings, and relatively sophisticated editing, a movie that begins in bondage to the library escapes into a filmic world. In rewriting for the screen, Negroni keeps major sections of the play intact but combines them with traces from Shakespeare's own source, Robert Greene's *Pandosto, The Triumph of Time*. The Italian flair for the spectacle of grand opera and the nineteenth-century taste for extravagant stagings of *The Winter's Tale*, like the revivals of Mary Anderson (1887) and Beerbohm Tree (1906), are reflected in the opulence of the banquet at Leontes' palace, as well as with the crowds of extras for the trial of Hermione. The fluid camera work embraces a variety of shots from mid to long, and then some tight framing to show Leontes' inner torment over Hermione's friendliness with Polixenes. If there were sound he would be muttering, "Too hot, too hot! / To mingle friendship far is mingling bloods" (1.2.108). The ostensive acting style of silents, carried over from theatre, allows the sharp-tongued Paulina, whose nagging tongue almost comes alive even in the silence of the screen, to plead eloquently for her mistress, until interrupted by the arrival of the oracles. A title card relays the news that "The two messengers return with the oracle," and we are told that the queen remains distraught. Paulina administers a sleeping potion to Hermione, tells Leontes that the queen is dead, and excoriates him again for his cruelty. Antigonus arriving with little Perdita at Bohemia, for inexplicable reasons is not pursued and eaten by a bear (thus throwing away Shakespeare's most memorable stage direction, *Exit pursued by a bear* – 3.3.58). He is instead captured by thieves and thrown alive into a volcano crater, reminiscent of Vesuvius or Etna. The statue scene goes in a whole new direction when Paulina displays a supine Hermione, who shows no signs of awakening, not even a twinge, despite the title card's contrary "the wakening of Hermione." The film ends with a return to the framing device of Shakespeare and his friends, who like the Hermione of his play have been miraculously revived.

Another Italian film, Paulo Azzuri's *Midsummer Night's Dream* (1913), shows a film rhetoric so highly developed that some historians have challenged the accuracy of its release date. The iris-outs, the dissolves, the cross-cutting, the story-telling powers, clearly go far beyond the Vitagraph *Midsummer Night's Dream* (1909). While starring Socrate Tommasi (Lysander), and Bianca Hübner (Helena), an adorable Puck's flagrant scene-stealing validates the proverbial warning against acting with dogs or children. Chiaroscuro lighting makes the wood at night intensely plausible, and the excessive use of inter-titles notwithstanding, this unpretentious movie leaves the audience as cheerful as the fairies happily skipping down the road in the closing fade. The day of Jan Kott and the dark wood had not yet arrived.

The scope and grandeur of Shakespeare's Roman plays make fine scenarios for lush Italian epics like Enrico Guazzoni's *Quo Vadis* (1912), and Giovanni Pastrone's *Cabiria* (1914), which paved the way for D. W. Griffith's colossal

Intolerance (1916),[60] and ultimately the Cecil B. De Mille Hollywood extravaganza "with a cast of thousands in living Technicolor." Enrico Guazzoni's eight-minute *Brutus* (1910) drew on Shakespeare's sources in Plutarch but without much reference to the way that Shakespeare imagined them. More realistic than the Vitagraph *Julius Caesar*, it shows a triumphal march through Rome with hundreds of gawking and cheering extras, double exposures of the dream "recounted" to Calphurnia, Calphurnia begging Caesar not to go to the senate, and Caesar's ghost appearing magically in Brutus' tent at Philippi. After his triumph with *Quo Vadis*, Guazzoni's ambitious multi-reel Cines *Marcantonio e Cleopatra (1913)*[61] and *Giulio Cesare* (1914) inevitably privileged spectacle over Shakespeare and showcased leading Italian actors Gianna Terribili-Gonzales and Amleto Novelli as Cleopatra and Caesar. Marching Roman legions, unruly mobs, sea fights, catapults, and arrows provide the spectacle of a real movie in contrast with the British Will Barker *Julius Caesar* (1911) that uneventfully recorded a stage production at the Stratford Memorial Theatre. Vestiges of Shakespeare's play survive in *Giulo Cesare* in the plot against Caesar with title cards proclaiming "Beware O Caesar of the Ides of March," "And thou too, Brutus," and "Friends, Romans, countrymen." Guazzoni's energies did not go unappreciated. Eight years later in 1922, the film was brought to New York for a showing at Bim's Standard Theatre in "revised and re-edited" form, possibly with spliced-in clips of mob scenes from the very similar *Marcantonio e Cleopatra*. One critic thought it of "relatively ancient manufacture" with "its harsh, ungraded lighting ... episodic rather than continuous story and its dependence upon mass as opposed to individual action." The audience of teenagers "accorded Antony [*sic*] Novelli (as Caesar) the same honor they customarily give to Tom Mix, Harry Carey and William S. Hart."[62]

In England, just before the outbreak of the war, at London's New Gallery Kinema in Regent St., Gaumont premiered an important feature-length *Hamlet* (1913) in E. Hay Plumb's film produced by Cecil Hepworth using the Drury Lane stage company. This most complete (59-minute) film of *Hamlet* yet then made allows a glimpse into late Victorian theatrical codes as interpreted by an actor many considered the greatest Hamlet of the century, Sir Johnston Forbes-Robertson. With the help of supporting players like Gertrude Elliott (Ophelia), Percy Rhodes (Ghost), and Robert Atkins (First Player), Forbes-Robertson, though at sixty in one sense hopelessly miscast, with his cadaverous and melancholy face nevertheless embodied the establishment's image of a lofty and unendurably sensitive Hamlet, an English variation on a Jules Laforgue's Franco-romantic idea of "Hamletism." Modern audiences, sated on post-Freudian readings, will find such restraint as Hamlet *not* putting his head on Ophelia's lap at the play scene refresh-

2   The versatile Frederick B. Warde, the Yorkist duke of Gloucester in M.B. Dudley's recently discovered *The Life and Death of King Richard III* (USA 1912), exults over the demise of his victim, King Henry VI of the House of Lancaster.

ing. Just as if he were at Drury Lane, Sir Johnston actually recites his lines while on camera. At the same time, there is an unmistakable escalation in cinematic adeptness, Hepworth having insisted on translating "the words of the play into action in the film"[63] as shown with the exterior shots at Lulworth Cove in Dorset, with the Méliès-like dissolve in the Ghost scene, and with the intercutting between Ophelia walking by a stream and of Claudius and Laertes conspiring to poison Hamlet.[64] Hepworth and Plumb's attention to cinema art challenges the dogma that London's West End theatre always suffocated the British film industry's initiative.

With war clouds gathering over Europe, four feature-length Shakespeare movies appeared in the United States between 1912 and 1916 ("feature" being defined as a film lasting at least 40 minutes). M. B. Dudley's "lost" five-reel *Richard III* (1912) besides being one of America's earliest feature-length movies also went beyond merely recording Shakespeare's play and moved toward an independent cinematic art. In 1996, it miraculously surfaced in the Oregon basement of William Buffum, a former projectionist and amateur collector, who had carefully preserved the highly flammable and wickedly unstable old-fashioned nitrate print. The title role of the malevolent Richard duke of Gloucester belonged to an itinerant British-born actor, Frederick B. Warde (1851–1935), whose stage career took him into every backwater in America, as well as to the major cities, where he played an amazing variety of characters, everything from Brutus to Hamlet to King Lear.[65] Directed in part at least by James Keane, the 61-year-old Warde eagerly adapted to the new medium, speaking of what "a great thing moving pictures had become," and how the French Film d'Art had embraced "the services of real artists."[66] As a practical man of the theatre, Warde, a regular on the prestigious North American Chautauqua Assembly lecture circuit and the recipient of an honorary doctorate of letters from the University of Southern California, discovered that he could tour with a film more economically than with an entire acting company, especially if he single-handedly furnished the commentary and the recitations during the reel changes, as advocated by the industrious W. Stephen Bush. Like a Japanese *benshi,* he could explain to his fans what they had already seen to make the silent movie's inscrutability scrutable.

Despite Warde's stage background, the filmed *Richard III* is not a stagy movie, unlike F.R. Benson's contemporaneous British *Richard III* (1911) whose firm attachment to the Stratford Memorial Theatre moved film historian Rachel Low to pronounce anathema on it as typical of "pre-1914 stage adaptations at their worst."[67] Playing the prototypical medieval vice figure and serio-comical villain, Richard duke of Gloucester, Warde's homicidal antics prefigured Hollywood's enormously popular gangster film genre of the 1930s. Marching armies and mounted knights, and bevies of lavishly dressed ladies-in-waiting fill the *mise-en-scène* in various locales of Westchester, New York. A real three-masted warship arrives at "Milford-Haven" (actually City Island on Long Island Sound) with the rebellious Lancastrian forces of Henry earl of Richmond, the future King Henry VII. James Keane, who is thought to have composed the screenplay, was caught up in a whirl of adding, deleting, and switching seventy-seven separate scenes around to make the play into a movie. He followed in the Colley Cibber stage tradition going back to at least 1700 by opening with Richard's vicious murders in *King Henry VI, Part Three* of the Lancastrian Prince Edward and King Henry VI to whip the audience into a froth of indignation over the abominations of Richard, this "bottled spider," this "boar," this "toad." There are scenes added: Edward signing the death warrant for Clarence, Richard wooing Princess Elizabeth, and Richard's hapless Anne drinking poison. Characters are deleted: the acid-tongued Queen Margaret, "she-wolf of France," and the Woodville faction of Rivers, Dorset, and Grey. Events are transposed to explain the strange death of Clarence in the Tower. Visual metonymy translates Shakespeare's words into sharp visual equivalents, as when Machiavellian Richard, following Colly Cibber's 1784 emendations at Drury Lane ("See how my sword weeps for the poor king's death"), wipes the blood off his sword after the assassination of King Henry, or thrusts his ring at the helpless Lady Anne in the first wooing scene, or fawns before the two little princes. These illusions then turn back into reality as the film ends by showing Frederick Warde himself, now in the mufti of a tweed jacket, as he appeared long ago live in the theatre, bowing and smiling graciously to his adoring fans. The film falls short of the contemporary Italian epics like Guazzoni's *Quo Vadis* but compares favorably with the techniques of most American movies of the period.

In a Warde Shakespeare movie, the page and stage always hover in the background. The opening of Edwin Thanhouser's ambitious art film of *King Lear* (1916) looks back nostalgically to the library. Again the star is Frederick B. Warde, this time with cigar smoke curling around him, and perusing a volume of Shakespeare. Suddenly he dissolves from a Victorian gentleman actor/scholar, the "Irving of America," into a hirsute King Lear. Page, stage and screen, the triad of Shakespearean incarnations, have momentarily interfaced, but book and stage must literally be dissolved to make way for the movie. As a special effect, the dissolve seems tame by comparison with today's John Woo, Hong Kong exploding action movies but for Edwardian audiences it may have stirred up a sense of "wonder" like that which Jacobean audiences at the Whitehall court masques felt after the sudden and abrupt disclosure of masked figures in grottos and caves.

Ernest Warde, the director and Frederick's son as well as the Fool in the movie, employs a film rhetoric of long and close shots, as well as sporadic close-ups. Nevertheless a 30-second framing card outlines the plot, and more title cards list names with images of the leading actors, as, for example, "Goneril, eldest daughter of King (Ina Hammer)," and "Her husband duke of Albany (Wayne Arey)." A contemptuous Goneril and Regan with headbands around their brunette hair and glowering expressions embody pure malignancy, while Cordelia (Lorraine Huling) in white radiates schoolgirl innocence. In mid-shot the entire assemblage, some ten persons in the crowded *mise-en-scène,* cluster around the royal throne for the division of the kingdom. Additional intercut title cards thread the narrative together with comments such as "Which of you doth love us most?" though cards do not always literally reflect the Shakespearean text, as when Kent says "Check this hideous rashness, O king, thy youngest daughter does not love thee least." Warde energetically exploits the ostensive acting techniques of the nineteenth-century stage with semaphore-like arm waving, much stalking about, considerable writhing, shaking of the head, finger wagging, and grimacing at the camera. Perhaps as Robert Ball has said, so much has been crammed into the movie, that the directors only succeeded in confusing matters.[68] On the other hand, the visual story-telling devices of a silent movie manage this archetypal conflict between father and daughters fairly well. Extraordinary horn wine goblets convey the primitive life style at the court, and a great battle scene shot somewhere in New Rochelle, New York, contains almost as much cavalry as D.W. Griffith's *The Birth of a Nation* (1915). Given the heavy, immobile cameras, the results are impressive as dozens of extras in costume armor carry out a cavalry charge while foot soldiers murder one another with wicked-looking swords, or throw rocks at the helpless wounded. Reaction shots record Regan and Goneril's gloating over this dreadful carnage while an angelic Cordelia recoils in horror. The very end of the movie, whether through accident or design, leaves an indelible memory of the heartbroken, dying king gradually sliding out of the frame, as if the world were too small to contain his massive anguish. It's a trope that is revived in Peter Brook's *King Lear* (1971), where it becomes a metaphor for post-modernist alienation.

The American Shakespeare boom continued in 1916 with two competing feature-length productions of *Romeo and Juliet*, a Metro release with matinee idol Francis X. Bushman opposite Beverly Bayne, and a Fox studio version with Theda Bara, celebrated as "The Vamp," opposite Harry Hilliard. Except for a few surviving stills, both have been lost, but there is always the bright hope of their being rediscovered, like the 1912 *Richard III*, in some secluded archive.

Growing out of the rich decadence of the "golden age" in German film making's post-war Weimar period, Svend Gade's *Hamlet: The Drama of Vengeance* (1920), starring Danish film actress Asta Nielsen, struck a great blow in liberating the Shakespeare movie from theatrical and textual dependency and moving toward the filmic. As Dudley Andrew succinctly puts it, "during the cinema's first twenty-five years of existence, art was conceived of not as something cinematic, but as something one put into a film: famous actors, a serious drama."[69] In the Weimar phase, a paramount motif was the expressionism that derived from the anti-naturalistic stagings of Max Reinhardt,[70] who in turn had been influenced by the British director Gordon Craig. Max Reinhardt's influence on Shakespeare film had already occurred before the war with Hanns Heinz Ewers' eccentric adaptation of *A*

Midsummer Night's Dream (1913),[71] and it was to continue straight through to the Hollywood career of German emigré director F.W. Murnau, whose prodigious indoor urban sets for *Sunrise* (1927) nearly bankrupted Fox studios, and most importantly to the Reinhardt/Dieterle Hollywood film of *A Midsummer Night's Dream* (1935).

Unlike her Hamlet predecessors, Bernhardt and Forbes-Robertson, Nielsen spent more of her career in film than on stage, which may account for her avoidance of an ostensive acting style, such as Emil Jannings' in a silent *Othello* (1922). Even though she was the greatest screen actress of Europe, celebrated for her Hedda Gabler and Miss Julie, and often compared with Greta Garbo, with whom she actually appeared, along with Marlene Dietrich, in *The Street of Sorrow* (*Die Freudlose Gasse*) (1925), her sex made her Hamlet's claim to reputability shaky. Unlike Bernhardt, however, she played Hamlet as a hybrid somewhere between a *travesti* and a "breeches" part; a *travesti* in the Comédie Française mold totally conceals his/her gender in usurping the guise of the opposite sex, while the English "breeches" part like Viola or Rosalind integrates cross-dressing directly into the role. Later, Judith Anderson (1970), Diane Venora (1982), Marnie Penning (1998) and others, out of "Hamlet-envy," have challenged the monopoly of male actors on the greatest role in theatre. They could legitimately ask if Shakespeare's Hamlet does not have a "feminine" sensibility that can best be captured by a woman.[72] Moreover as Bernhardt argued, "A boy of twenty cannot understand the philosophy of *Hamlet* . . . without understanding there is no delineation of character. . . . the woman more readily looks the part, yet has the maturity of mind to grasp it."[73] As Lawrence Danson has said, however, "a critic who seriously proposes that *Hamlet* is a woman will seem either mad or, with the right theory behind him, very modern."[74] On the other hand, the nineteenth-century concept of "Hamletism" allowed for a considerable streak of femininity in the character of the prince. Hostile to the *travesti* code, Edward Weitzel thought it was "a sacrilege to couple it [the movie] with the name of Shakespeare,"[75] which did not deter *The New York Times* from listing it as one of the "Ten Best Films of the Year," along with *The Cabinet of Dr. Caligari.*

Even more than the Warde *Richard III* and *King Lear*, Nielsen's *Hamlet* draws for its artistry as much on filmic as on literary models. Its record number of iris fades encircling Asta Nielsen's ethereal face alone would qualify it as the ultimate "Iris-out *Hamlet*," though it also abounds in other cinematic tropes after the style of the D.W. Griffith silents. Principally, it becomes unabashedly cinematic in its spatializing of the text through allowing the camera freedom to record not only the text but the subtext, paratext, prototext, crypto-text, and meta-text of Quarto, Folio, and even narrative legends from Saxo Grammaticus. Being silent, what it lacks in sound it does not make up for in sense, but in its surreal redeployment of the *Hamlet* story. Its scenario mines, however, an obscure 1881 monograph by "Dr. Edward P. Vining (Yale-Hon. M.A.)," a reliance on fanciful scholarship matching Roman Polanski's dependency on M.F. Libby's equally recherché "Some New Notes on *Macbeth*" (1893) for his privileging of Rosse in that remarkable 1971 movie.[76] The opening title of Gade's film draws heavily on Vining's theory in notifying the audience that

> This screen version of *Hamlet* is based upon the ancient legends from which Shakespeare drew his first conception for his immortal tragedy . . . It also reveals the contention of the eminent American Shakespearian scholar, Dr. Edward P. Vining . . . that Hamlet was a woman, who for reasons of state, was compelled to assume the guise of a man.

For "reasons of state" the daughter born to Gertrude while the king is absent fighting the war against Norway must be raised as a boy to protect the queen from the wrath of the people. She lied to them about the infant's sex because she mistakenly assumed her husband had been killed in battle. A title card amplifies: "The Nurse's crafty scheme. 'Tell the people it is a son. You can save the crown and still be queen'." An iris fade as the queen exults. When the king unexpectedly returns home alive, he will not admit to the people that their queen has fibbed and so the deception continues. From this white lie a whole array of flaccid watches and curious juxtapositions emerges that in a bizarre way represents Prince Hamlet more effectively than *Hamlet* itself. It is *Hamlet* in a bad dream, a step away from a Dada-suffused Buñuel film. The worst and best kind of the character criticism so roundly excoriated after Bradley also surfaces in the shameless but fascinating exploration of Hamlet's student days at Wittenberg, where he/she falls in love with Horatio to set up a titillating homoerotic agenda. The cross-dressed prince embodies all the ambiguity in the play's leitmotif of the interplay between illusion and reality ("Seems, madam? nay, it is, I know not 'seems'." (1.2.76)), and a Hamlet who is inwardly "female" and outwardly "male" plays a variation on the play's obsession with delay, hesitations, and indecisiveness.

Not the least of the perversities is the anxiety brought on at Wittenberg University when Hamlet feels a strong tug of attraction to fellow student, Horatio, in what looks like an exhumation and legitimization of latent homosexuality. When Horatio then disastrously falls in love with Ophelia, Hamlet has even better reasons for putting on an "antic disposition." Using source material from Saxo Grammaticus, when Hamlet returns alone to Elsinore to discover Ophelia's death, he witnesses first-hand a drunken orgy presided

[23]

over by Claudius, locks the doors, and sets the house afire. Gertrude is left widowed to preside alone at the duel scene and to drink from the poisoned cup. At the close when Hamlet lies dying in Horatio's arms, Horatio in groping to locate his friend's chest wound makes a startling discovery, which had hitherto gone unnoticed. He brushes against Hamlet's bosom and a look of wonder comes over his face. Then in what Danson wittily calls "the greatest scene of *anagnorisis* Shakespeare never wrote,"[77] he cries out (on the title card) "Death reveals thy tragic secret. Now I understand what bound me to that matchless form." It is the measure of the film's artistry that for many viewers the line comes across as more poignant than hilarious.

The movie's split vision of a human being divided between an inner female and outer male persona, the *Doppelgänger* effect as it has been called,[78] which is heavily exploited also in the Celestino Coronado film society *Hamlet* (1976), finds support in Gade's array of expressionistic devices – lengthy hallways and corridors, vast assembly rooms, steep flights of stairs, sloping surfaces, chiaroscuro effects of contrasting light and shadows, energetic camera work, a brooding film noir type atmosphere, and ostensive acting styles taken from the stage. After Fortinbras' final entry, much footage is given over to a solemn procession with Hamlet's body borne aloft down the vast hall, past rows of standing soldiers, and out into a thoroughfare, which, though arguably overdone, in its generous spatializing reveals new potentials for elegizing *Hamlet*. John Milton's *Lycidas* comes to mind.

Current interest in "queer theory," with its resistance to dogmatic categorizations of gender and sex, has brought the movie into the spotlight again as the homoerotic flavor of a feminized *Hamlet* carries Goethe's idea of Hamlet as an unbearably sensitive hero to its ultimate polarity. Textual scholars like Ann Thompson have recently delved into Vining's theory that the three texts for *Hamlet* show a gradual evolution from Hamlet's "pangs of despised love" to "dispriz'd love," the latter suggesting the kind of love that has no name. Vining further goes on to characterize Hamlet's apparent love for men and contempt for women as "inverted," which could be taken as code for homosexuality. It is a clever and enticing argument that requires more consideration than I have room for here, but Thompson's interest in the film,[79] as well as that of J. Lawrence Guntner, Lawrence Danson and others, suggests how after nearly eighty years the movie has renewed the idea of Hamlet in an entirely fresh context. Whether *travesti*, "breeches," or simply cross-dressed, this bizarre *Hamlet* moves directly to the play's concern with revenge, with delay, with metaphysical probing, with deep-seated mysteries of the mind and heart. It did not hurt either that Asta Nielsen was a marvelous actress, who "does not just pose before the camera, nor does she rant and tear around violently . . . Her mouth . . . is an organ to express the

3   The internationally celebrated silent movie star, Asta Nielsen, as a cross-dressed prince in Svend Gade's imaginative *Hamlet: The Drama of Vengeance* (1920).

thoughts and feelings of the woman within."[80] Gade's movie may not have been *Hamlet* but in many ways it not only deconstructed Goethe's Hamlet but also in re-imagining the *Hamlet* text foreshadowed new paradigms for the Shakespeare movie. This paradoxical bondage to and liberation from nineteenth-century "Hamletism," as well as the Quarto and Folio texts, paved the way for more probing treatments in the *Hamlet* films of Wirth, Lyth, Kline, Richardson, Zeffirelli, Kozintsev, and Branagh. Above all else, the movie casts a spell ensnaring the viewer in its web of flickering black-and-white images.

After Nielsen's performance, the Dmitri Buchowetski *Othello* (1922) comes as an anticlimax, even though it stars the formidable Emil Jannings, winner of a 1927 Academy Award for *The Way of All Flesh*, but best known today as Professor Rath, the pathetic schoolmaster enslaved by the sultry Marlene

Dietrich in Josef von Sternberg's *The Blue Angel* (1930). Its mammoth sets, exotic lighting, milling crowds, and flamboyant acting identify it with major patterns of expressionism but its streak of realism makes it too literal-minded for greatness. The more grandeur and pomposity the less believable the behavior of the three principals, Othello, Desdemona (Ika von Lenceffy), and Iago (Werner Krauss). As the Moor of Venice, Jannings seems more concerned with self-indulgently playing the role of the great actor than with locating the soul of Othello. His stage technique burdens his acting style, but as a museum display of the lost art of scenery chewing, the movie is superb, a kind of magnificent wreck. A dubbed-in organ accompaniment on the commercially available video version sonically supports the highs and lows of emotion, as Jannings mimes Othello's growing paranoia. He is goaded on by a demonic Iago, played by the famous Werner Krauss, who appeared in dozens of silent movies, the best known being his title role in the classic, *The Cabinet of Dr. Caligari* (1921). Krauss lurks behind every pillar and post of the gingerbread palace, his pasty white face and tiny moustache turning him into an allegory for Adolf Hitler. He plays Othello like a musical instrument until in the movie's benchmark scene, his crafty insinuations drive Othello to madness. The berserk Othello, his eyes popping, beats himself on the head with his fists, twists and folds Desdemona's handkerchief, and then, in the ultimate act of frustration, literally chews on it in a textbook example of the use of an inanimate "expressive object" to convey emotion.[81] If the handkerchief, as has been suggested by psychoanalytical critics, also represents the wedding sheets, then Jannings is externalizing Othello's innermost resentments.[82] Iago tenderly, affectionately cradles Othello while the Moor cries out (on title cards) "Suspicion, doubt, devil!" and then again "Proof. Proof." With the sonic punctuation provided by the organist, Jannings and Krauss bring out the strange chemistry that makes this implausible story plausible. The smothering of Desdemona is orchestrated as a terrible rite of sacrifice in which the Moor acts as a satanic Abraham sacrificing his Isaac at the behest of the devilish Iago. The valiant film ends in the city square with hundreds of extras waving their arms and screaming "O perfidy!" Never have so many extras done so much to accomplish so little, but the bravura performances of Jannings and Krauss make it worthwhile.

The following year, Werner Krauss emerged again in a loose adaptation of a Shakespeare movie playing Shylock opposite Henny Porten's Portia in *Der Kaufmann von Venedig* (1923), released in North America as *The Jew of Mestri*. As much or more in debt to Shakespeare's own source tale, *Il Pecerone*, than to the *Merchant* itself, it focuses more on the woes of Jessica (Rachela) than on Portia, the "Lady of Belmont." This refocusing underscores the shared affliction of Jessica and Portia in being the daughters of overbearing and demanding fathers. Henny Porten, a superstar until the advent of Adolf Hitler, captures Portia's grace and elegance by parading her Russian wolfhounds across the screen. Ambitious attempts at realism include location shots of Venice with analytical close-ups of feeding pigeons, city clocks, market stalls, and canals. The great hall at Belmont and the trial scene offer opportunities for complicated sets and bizarre lighting schemes in the Weimar tradition, and sophisticated intercutting between the extravagance of Belmont and the sterile world of Shylock. The trial scene features the cliché of a sadistic Shylock whetting his knife but an unusual twist has Gianetti (Antonio) fainting in fright. The Freudian ring plot remains as Portia and Nerissa wrangle their rings away from the bewildered Bassanio and Gratiano: "Sweet Portia, / If you did know to whom I gave the ring, / And how unwillingly I left the ring" (5.1.192). The horror just under the surface of *The Merchant of Venice* is summed up in Shylock's anguished expression as the movie cuts away from him and returns to the carefree young people at Belmont, who are the same rich crowd displaced in time from F. Scott Fitzgerald's *The Great Gatsby*.

- 2 -

Hollywood's four seasons of Shakespeare

As early as 1914 a letter writer to *Bioscope* was railing against the "arty" types who would ignore the plain fact that the business of motion pictures is business – profit, the bottom line, "tickling commodity," commodification, not art.[1] Given this Gradgrindian reality, to no one's surprise out of hundreds of Hollywood talking pictures only four have been full-scale studio feature-length treatments of a Shakespearean text, a fifth – Welles's *Macbeth* (1948) – being a special low budget "poverty row" aberration. Coincidentally, though, Hollywood fell over backwards into Northrop Frye's seasonal classifications by providing a springtime comedy (the rollicking *Taming of the Shrew*); summery idyll (a romantic *Midsummer Night's Dream*); autumnal tragedy (a reverential *Romeo and Juliet*); and wintry tragic irony (a remarkable *Julius Caesar*). For a total investment of about $6 million, the four movies' producers tested the iron law of capitalism that art cannot be divorced from entertainment if it is to survive in the free market. They also replaced the problems of making silent Shakespeare films with a new set of problems in producing sound films. Sometimes actors' voices were not nearly so attractive as their silent images, and the need to speak a specific language automatically destroyed the wonderful internationalism of the silent movie era when a Lillian Gish or Mary Pickford was understood everywhere in the world through gesture rather than language.

Taylor's *The Taming of the Shrew*

By 1929 the audience for the American movie industry had safely progressed, as Steven J. Ross has put it, "from working class to middle class,"[2] a sea change either encouraged by, or resulting in, the replacement of the nickelodeons with the new palace theatres that allowed even the poorest folk to be surrounded for just a few hours by unimagined opulence. When Mary Pickford, "America's Sweetheart," and her independent company decided to make *The Taming of the Shrew* (1929), the queen of silent film actresses was only following Al Jolson's famous advice in the first sound picture, *The Jazz*

Singer (1927). "You ain't heard nothin' yet," he rasped, and she gave audiences much more to hear with her talking picture *Coquette* (1929). In it, she abandoned her persona as a golden-haired, sweet, dear little innocent thing for an Academy Award best-actress role as a brunette roaring-twenties flapper. Her success with *Coquette* encouraged Miss Pickford to accept Sam Taylor's proposal for doing William Shakespeare's *The Taming of the Shrew*[3] with her husband, Douglas Fairbanks, devil-may-care hero of *The Thief of Bagdad* (1924), as a swashbuckling Petruchio. By casting themselves in the lead roles, the fabulously popular Fairbanks also guaranteed a huge audience as an antidote to the "box-office poison" of a highbrow movie. The "poison," however, was administered not at the box office – the movie budgeted at $504,000 grossed $1.1 million – but at the hands of a myth. Sam Taylor's credit line, "Written by William Shakespeare with additional dialogue by Sam Taylor," shocked the "purists,"[4] and "the film [was] immediately discounted."[5] Ironically Taylor's infamous and endlessly repeated credit line may never have existed[6] and at its release the film was for the most part favorably received. Professor Ball, who knew Taylor, found "no evidence whatsoever that the credit ever appeared in the film."[7] Even if the line existed on one lost print, the witty and astute Taylor probably meant the whole thing as a joke. After all, Shakespeare's *Shrew* is a farce, not a tragedy. A studio worker provided the *reductio ad absurdum* when he said, "Sure, we're making *The Taming of the Shrew*, but we're turning it into a cah-medy."[8] Perhaps he meant to say, "we're turning it into a movie, whose artistry will depend more on its filmic values than on its literary origins."

Still another misconception is that Pickford's movie was the first Shakespeare talking picture, a myth perpetuated in the explanatory cards for the 1966 re-release. Not so. It is, however, the first *feature-length* talking Shakespeare movie. The first Shakespeare movie that coordinated sound and image on screen came from England, a ten-minute extract from the trial scene in an experimental De Forest Phonofilms' *The Merchant of Venice* (1927).[9] With sound slowly evolving, movie theatres in many smaller towns lacked sound equipment so *Taming of the Shrew* was filmed in both a silent and talking version, though another option in 1929 was to have movies combine sound with title cards. In an ultimate irony, Mary Pickford herself believed the movie an abysmal failure: "I was talked into doing *The Taming of the Shrew* against my better judgment . . . [it was] my finish. My confidence was completely shattered, and I was never again at ease before the camera or microphone."[10] She banished the offending print to the archives but after the success of the Zeffirelli *Taming of the Shrew* (1966), she relented and commissioned Matty Kemp to restore the movie at a cost of $100,000 for wide screen exhibition. A *Variety* reviewer said that the reissue proved that the Fairbanks "richly deserved their long held positions as top artists."[11]

The world premiere in London's Pavilion Theatre should have alleviated Miss Pickford's despair. Even allowing for his being a hired publicist, James Agate's commentary in the gala printed program demonstrated that movies at last had attracted the "best class of people," which was another way of saying that pictures empathetic to working-class consciousness were being safely shunted aside. Agate combs performance history to show how the abridged film stems more from David Garrick's shortened version of *Shrew*, presented at Drury Lane on March 18, 1754, as *Catherine and Petruchio*, than from the tomfoolery of Sam Taylor's notorious gag writers: "It is Garrick's version upon which the present film is based. Hollywood has taken nothing from Shakespeare's play, which Garrick did not take." The film, in his view, had "nothing of Hollywood about it, except the superb lighting."[12] An equally successful November opening at New York's Rivoli led to the film being included in *The New York Times* list of the "Ten Best Films of the Year." A.M. Sherwood, Jr. called it a "grand talking picture" comparable to "the best Shakespearean productions of all time."[13] Mordaunt Hall of *The New York Times* thought Miss Pickford "delightful" in "her fits of fury and also in those moments when she . . . trembles at Petruchio's wrath."[14]

Slapstick rules. With Fairbanks and Pickford brandishing whips like lion tamers, the movie is more whippy than witty, a reminder that *Shrew* ranks with *Comedy of Errors* as one of Shakespeare's least cerebral comedies. Fairbanks and Pickford make Petruchio's servants hop and skip, and the audience jump. Pickford's movie replaces the traces of profundity on the Italianate motif of "supposings" in the Induction, which Shakespeare borrowed from Ludovico Ariosto's *I Suppositi* (1509), with a crude Punch-and-Judy show. "Kiss me, kiss me," says Punch. "I'll kiss you," Judy says and whacks him. After several whacks, he goes off to get his fool's cap, returns, and conks her three times on the head with his fool's staff. "I'll tame you," he says. "Oh, you're wonderful," she says and throws her arms around him in surrender. Stressing the primal battle of the sexes, the impudent film downplays the massive "supposings" that have Tranio pretending to be Lucentio; Lucentio, Cambio; and Hortensio, Litio. The Lord's concern for the proper care of his hunting dogs is gone, with its anticipation of the "taming school" for Kate, when Petruchio discourses on ways to "man [his] haggard" (4.1.193), Shakespeare at some point having forgotten that Kate is a shrew not an adult hawk.

When the camera pulls back from the Punch-and-Judy show, a realistic street scene from Renaissance Padua fills the *mise-en-scène*, designed by William Cameron Menzies, who did the spectacular sets for *The Thief of*

Bagdad (1924), and *Gone with the Wind* (1939), and who learned the "Warner look" from German expressionist Anton Grot,[15] even though the happy glare of California sunshine exposes the expensive studio set as another movie mirage. The ambient music by strolling musicians supports the bustling street scene of stalls, sidewalk cafés, peddlers, and stone archways but the extras look just a little bit too well-scrubbed to be Italian street people.

Marble and hangings and sweeping staircases adorn Kate's sumptuous domicile, which is presided over by Baptista Minola (Edwin Maxwell). Shakespeare's text suffers ruthless deletions not only from the tyranny of time but also from the movie's having been intended originally as a silent, especially in the case of the pruned Bianca subplot, but the story line survives, at least for those who know it, with a clever exploitation of visual metonymy. There's a quick glimpse of an embracing Hortensio and Bianca framed in a doorway, just before they are caught *in flagrante delicto* by the harried Baptista Minola, who declares that his eldest daughter must marry before the younger. Multiple analytical close-ups and reaction shots spliced in from several different camera set-ups clinically document the Minola family's dysfunctionality. There is a great clatter above, a smashed window, people and objects hurtling down the staircase, a shattered mirror, a dog scrambling for cover underneath a chest, a picture falling off the wall, a man with his head sticking through the picture frame, a cat running up on a chest, and a woman cowering in a closet. The camera moves up the stairs to reveal mayhem – furniture, clothing, objets d'art, everything, smashed and tossed about in disarray, and then the camera pans left to reveal the vixen herself, Katherina Minola (Mary Pickford), smoldering with anger and holding the cruel whip, an instrument of oppression. Verily, the woman is a shrew. Not a large shrew, only five feet tall, but shrewish enough, even off camera, to have once bitten the great D.W. Griffith for raising his voice to her. Her scratchy voice aside, she makes a splendid Katherina Minola.

Douglas Fairbanks, not having a great voice for the talkies either, relies on his trademark expression of maddening insolence. His face fixed in a default mode of mockery, he calmly endures Kate's initial assault, even to the point of stoically ignoring vicious whip lashes across his back, which only exacerbates her fury. Fairbanks' supreme moment, however, comes in the wedding scene. As always, Kate is seen fuming on the church steps with her distraught father, both wondering what has become of the tardy bridegroom. In the packed church, spectators buzz with curiosity. In long shot, Petruchio approaches mounted on a sorry-looking nag, and wearing his ridiculous jackboot of a hat. Insolently munching on an apple and demonstrating an "attitude," he saunters up to his enraged bride. The events at the altar, which are merely reported by Gremio in Shakespeare's play, give direc-

4   In the midst of William Cameron Menzies' opulent set, Mary Pickford and Douglas Fairbanks rest between rounds in the battle of the sexes in *The Taming of the Shrew* (USA 1929), directed by Sam Taylor.

tor Taylor a loophole for indulging in a series of silent film gags. The oafish Petruchio hands the core of his apple to the wretched Grumio, who then spends the next few minutes trying to figure out how to dispose of it surreptitiously, even under the baleful stare of a nearby monk. When a thoroughly disgusted Kate shows signs of not responding positively to the priest's query, "Do you take this man for a husband?" the boorish Petruchio stomps on her foot so hard that she cries out "I do."

The physical abuse of little Kate continues after the wedding feast, when Petruchio drags her off to his place in the country, carrying her like a sack of wheat on his horse, and dumping her into the mud, as called for in the play (4.1.57). As she sits inside by the roaring fire, Kate's expression registers exhaustion, cold, hunger, wetness, and an aching desire for warmth, while above on a balcony Petruchio appears dry and warm in a splendid dressing gown, his expression revealing tenderness for Kate. To burnish his image of cruelty, however, he cracks the terrifying whip at the scrambling servants. The charade continues with Kate's attempts to eat being continually thwarted by Petruchio's loutish antics – knocking over a water basin, and roundly cuffing the servants, while Kate enduring the torture of Tantalus must watch the food forever receding away from her. When she picks up the meat, he declares it "burnt," has it thrown away, and then begins hurling objects. A tightly framed shot of a servant's knees knocking together gives a micro-picture of the macro-terror at the Petruchio household. The two squabble until Kate finally hurls one of the whips into the fire. The sequence ends in an embrace. Fade out.

For Kate's admirers, the crux of the play comes at the banquet scene when Kate wins Petruchio's wager with her infamous speech of submission. Rather than seeing it as an abject surrender, most Elizabethans would have interpreted her sentiments as entirely decorous and proper, an act of faith. If Kate can willingly acknowledge that the moon is the sun and the sun the moon, she can also pay fealty to her lord and master, who in return will care for her or earn the parish's opprobrium, or so the doctrine of passive obedience, which seems so repulsive to modernists, was theoretically intended. The pace of the editing neatly builds up toward Kate's "surrender," and also provides for the surprise twist by which she will both yield and not yield. About a dozen different camera set-ups mostly in long shot of the entire banquet table at Minola's mansion, are then followed by a close-up of Petruchio, still clinging to his beloved whip, though with a bandaged head from colliding with Kate's stool. As a dignified Kate utters the words "sea and land" (5.2.149), she's shown in close-up, before a cut to mid-long shot where the guests at the table are arranged clockwise from the left with Bianca, Gremio, Petruchio, Kate (standing), and Baptista Minola, all awaiting Kate's climactic declaration that "Such duty as the subject owes the prince, /Even such a woman oweth to her husband" (5.2.155). That makes Bianca very uncomfortable but Petruchio wears his patented cocksure grin. At line 164, Kate utters the word "obey" and then subverts her own declaration by broadly winking in the direction of Bianca in such a way as to suggest their sisterly bond in the "female subculture,"[16] leaving men out of it. Kate has shown her ability to manage Petruchio, while Mary Pickford has self-reflexively demonstrated for the world how to be the first speaking Shakespearean heroine on screen. She has taken the Shakespeare movie beyond the actualities, the silents, the proscenium stage, and positioned it for a new role among "spirits of a different sort."

The Reinhardt/Dieterle *A Midsummer Night's Dream* (1935)

In the next (and the best) major Hollywood Shakespeare movie, the Teutonic romanticism of Max Reinhardt and William Dieterle's *A Midsummer Night's Dream* (1935) replaced the rollicking farce of *Taming of the Shrew*. After the success of émigré Max Reinhardt's spectacular live production at the Hollywood Bowl, movie mogul Jack Warner courageously gambled on making it into a movie. It became not only Shakespeare filtered through the Hollywood studio system but also the *Dream* as re-imagined after Gothic films like F.W. Murnau's *Nosferatu* (1921), adapted from Bram Stoker's *Dracula*. That is to say, at one level *Dream* is a classic comedy of the green world triumphing over the wintry as young lovers push aside the blocking parental figures of authority and establish their own hegemony; at another, it is a dark vision of disorder and chaos with nature gone awry and the rule of reason threatened by unchained forces. Its four separate but contiguous plots swirl around, and in between, and among one another. There are the putative ruler, Duke Theseus of Athens, with his weird bride, the captured Amazon queen, Hippolyta; the half mad and thoroughly confused young lovers, Lysander and Hermia and Demetrius and Helena; the powerful underworld of fairyland presided over by the quarreling fairy king and queen, Oberon and Titania; and the socially marginalized "crew of patches, rude mechanicals" (3.2.9), comprised of Bottom, Quince, Snug, Flute, Snout, and Starveling. Reinhardt and Dieterle incarnated this fantasy world of mirror and reverse-mirror effects into a swirling electronic Masque of Light and Dark on the theme of the search for certainty in uncertainty. The casting of Hollywood 's effervescent stars by filtering Shakespeare through popular culture made mass audiences comfortable, but the uncomfortable side, the darkness, as subsequently underscored by Jan Kott,[17] remains secreted in the Gothic recesses of Reinhardt's enchanted forest.

Director Max Reinhardt's deep interest in *Midsummer Night's Dream* began with a 1905 production at Berlin's Neues Theatre, and continued at places like Salzburg, Oxford, and finally in 1934 the Hollywood Bowl.[18] The Warner

Brothers poured $1½ million into the production, orchestrating myriad details and filming on a huge sound stage of over 38,000 square feet. Erich Wolfgang Korngold arranged the musical setting based on Mendelssohn's thrilling *Overture to a Midsummer Night's Dream*, as well as later incidental music, and Max Reinhardt ordered a special machine called an "Akron Spider" to manufacture sufficient cobwebs for the set; the donkey's head for Bottom's scene (James Cagney) with Titania (Anita Louise) was constructed at considerable trouble and expense; central casting called on all available dwarves in Los Angeles county to fill up the gnomes in the elfin orchestra. Art director Anton Grot, who had also worked on the seminal *Thief of Bagdad,* designed the sets for the ballet sequences in the dark wood. The fabled Nijinsky's ballerina sister, Bronislawa, choreographed the dances.[19] The cast included rising stars like Olivia de Havilland (Hermia) and eleven-year-old Mickey Rooney (Puck), who earlier had worked with Reinhardt in the Hollywood Bowl outdoor production, as well as household names among the rude mechanicals – Joe E. Brown (Flute), James Cagney (Bottom), Frank McHugh (Quince), Hugh Herbert (Snout), Arthur Treacher (Ninny's Tomb). Dick Powell (Lysander), Jean Muir (Helena), and the incredibly beautiful starlet Anita Louise (Titania) opposite a menacing Victor Jory (Oberon) all epitomized the charisma of Hollywood in the Golden Years before World War II.

The movie begins as a Masque of Night, which is a visual meditation on a surreal forest in charcoal hues like something out of a set for *Nosferatu.* A luminous quarter moon, intermittent clouds, and bright stars echo the play's iterative images of moonlight, and Titania's ominous diagnosis of disturbed nature, "Therefore the moon (the governess of floods), / Pale in her anger, washes all the air"(2.1.103). Generally thought of as sprightly, Mendelssohn's score contains a darker gothic subtext, embodying in its varied strings and horns the contradictory motifs to come – nuptials and feasting, and high hopes, yet poised on the edge of a dark wood harboring acts of unspeakable bestiality. The chiaroscuro lighting after a seventeenth-century Dutch painting of domestic life colors the mechanicals' rehearsal scenes for *Pyramus and Thisby,* where James Cagney's bouncy gait, Frank McHugh's earnestness, Hugh Herbert's silly giggle, and Joe E. Brown's deadpan face bring the full animal vitality of Hollywood creativity to the redeployment of the Shakespearean text. Indeed the play's imagery translates into a feast for the camera's eye, its swirling non-linear patterns of movement made to order for what Lorne Buchman has described as "the multiple perspectives" in "the spatial field of cinema" for "a world of infinite relationships, of images, sounds, textures, and colors in constant motion," resulting in "a spectacle of multiplicity."[20]

After a title card announcing the duke's desire for "masques and plays to be readied against the nuptial day," the spectacular but overblown baroque establishing shot of the Athenian court, which follows well-entrenched Victorian stage traditions, becomes a dumb show for identifying the key characters and hinting at the future complications. Shielded by an ornate canopy and beatified with the ambient music of trumpets and a mass chorale by loyal subjects, Theseus the duke of Athens (Ian Hunter) and his Amazon fiancée Hippolyta (Verree Teasdale) ascend the steps of a pseudo-Greek temple toward their rightful thrones. A variety of splicing and cutting and editing of close-ups and mid-shots reveals Lysander (Dick Powell) singing and mugging and frantically waving to Olivia de Havilland (Hermia), as Hermia's irascible father, Egeus (Grant Mitchell), pounds his staff to remind the distracted girl of her obligation to join in the vocalizing. In a flurry of cross-cutting, Demetrius (Ross Alexander) competes with Lysander in a singing contest to see who can project more loudly, while there is a reaction shot of Helena looking quite lonely and hurt when Demetrius cuts her dead. The choristers fit into discrete clusters: charming young ladies fresh from the daisy chain, a geriatric male choir, a Hollywoodized Vienna boys' choir, and representatives of the deserving poor embodied in Peter Quince's delegation of rude mechanicals. Despite competition from Hollywood's funniest people, Joe E. Brown manages to steal the show with an expression of matchless stupidity as he chews on and spits out litchi seeds while half-heartedly singing, much to Peter Quince's disgust.

The strains of Mendelssohn's Wedding March underscore the play's original role as a celebration for a wedding reception, yet many dusky currents run just beneath the bright surface. Philip C. McGuire has noted that the "opening moments . . . include a silence – Hippolyta's – that has reverberations" throughout the text.[21] Hippolyta's sullen resentment toward Theseus for his rape of the Amazons, which the Coronado *Midsummer Night's Dream* (1984) makes far more explicit, suggests a covert feminist agenda. Her repellent Max Ree snake costume foreshadows Oberon's, "And there the snake throws her enamell'd skin, / Weed wide enough to wrap a fairy in" (2.1.255), and Hermia's nightmare about the "crawling serpent" (2.2.146). For haughty Hippolyta, it would hardly be a calamity if Theseus' longed-for nuptial night never came.

The movie turns most filmic in the orchestration of camera work, editing, and theme music for the dazzling ballet sequence. There are glimpses of owl, deer, frogs, tiny creepy things, and waterfalls. A spunky little Puck rises out of a damp bed of leaves; fairies in gossamer white emerge from the mist; the disputed Indian boy rides a fabulous unicorn through the forest; and an orchestra of gnarled little gnomes with bizarre masks frantically tootle and saw away. Dozens of shots angled in different ways and spliced into a rhythmical pattern correlate with Mendelssohn's theme music and with glimpses of the Athenian lovers scooting through the forest. Mounted on an ominous black horse, Oberon peremptorily orders Puck to fetch the magic flower "love-in-idleness," and like his forebears in the old Vitagraph *Midsummer Night's Dream*, Puck soars through the air, while Oberon, crowned with a magnificent headpiece, is ensconced in a tree staring down at the lovers. The lighting is a miracle, wringing subtleties out of stark black-and-white, and turning the screen to silver. Even the most enthusiastic cinéphile may turn sullen purist, though, when the theme music drowns out Oberon's "I know a bank where the wild thyme blows" (2.1.249), Keatsian in its lyric sublimity. The subsequent Triumph of the Night ballet has Oberon re-entering on a black horse with a huge black cape billowing behind him and gradually enfolding all the white-costumed attendants of Titania, who has been distracted by her affair with Bottom. The squat dwarves resembling Martians, who adumbrate Dieterle's grotesque Quasimodo in his *The Hunchback of Notre Dame* (1939) fiddle away. Meanwhile the prima ballerina (Nini Theilade) ascends toward the stars with her arms and hands gracefully writhing, twining and intertwining until all that can be seen are the exquisite white hands before they slowly dissolve into the blackness. Poignant in the way that it manifests the play's precarious equilibrium teetering between the forces of light and dark, the scene would qualify as another talisman of wonder in the Inigo Jones/Ben Jonson masques at the court of James I.

With time, the movie's critical reputation has recuperated from the pre-release grumblings about Hollywood's impudence in meddling with a classic, which even fomented "indignation meetings" in London over the casting of "vulgar" actors like Brown and Cagney in a Shakespeare production. Following its release, critics better tolerated the "switching of codes" that involved the wrenching of well-known actors out of their stereotypical roles into unexpected new ones, e.g., having gangster James Cagney play Shakespeare's Bottom. One American critic wrote that *"Midsummer Night's Dream* is by no means as bad as it might have been," followed by a candid admission that it compared favorably with any stage production.[22] John Russell Taylor got about half way there when he wrote, "Not, clearly, a 'serious' approach to Shakespeare at all, and yet, strange to relate, a remarkably successful film."[23] The way that the enthusiasm of Taylor's subordinate clauses subverts the clamminess of the main clauses suggests deep ambivalence. Graham Greene disapproved of Reinhardt's directing in general but admired the acting for the very reason that it lacked "proper Shakespearian diction and bearing."[24] A maelstrom of opinions, they reflect the anxieties of confronting not only the transition from stage to screen but the new technology that gave voices to previously silent film actors.

5   In the dark wood near Athens, Mickey Rooney's Puck and Olivia De Havilland's Hermia show how "quick bright things" do indeed "come to confusion" in this episode from *A Midsummer Night's Dream* (USA 1935), directed by Max Reinhardt and William Dieterle.

The Thalberg/Cukor *Romeo and Juliet* (1936)

With their $2-million *Romeo and Juliet*, Irving Thalberg and George Cukor revered Shakespeare so much that they suffocated his play. A British film critic seemed to think so in noting that "the cinema is not yet at ease with Shakespeare; it approaches him with an anxious sense of occasion, not venturing to make a friend of him but determined to do him proud."[25] The timing was good, however. *A Midsummer Night's Dream* and *Romeo and Juliet*, both sonnet plays written at the same stage of the poet's career, ricochet off each other. As everyone knows, the *Pyramus and Thisby* play not only self-referentially spoofs the four young lovers in *Midsummer Night's Dream* but also burlesques the lugubrious tale of *Romeo and Juliet*.

In casting expatriate British actors, the producers made a preemptive strike against more "indignation meetings" over the *lése-majesté* of American actors in Shakespearean roles. A veritable wax works of British upper class snobbery filled the screen: Leslie Howard (Romeo), Basil Rathbone (Tybalt), Edna May Oliver (Nurse), Violet Kemball Cooper (Lady Capulet), and C. Aubrey Smith (Capulet). Somehow 35-year-old American Norma Shearer was allowed to play Juliet, not just because her husband, Irving Thalberg, had status at MGM, but because she was a recognized star of considerable thespian talent. As a business man constantly exposed to "tickling commodity," Thalberg, the youthful genius at Metro Goldwyn Mayer, would never have risked a $2 million investment by indulging in an act of uxorious nepotism. He also still nurtured the old Vitagraph ambition to make movies with "class" for "classier" audiences, and saw the "picturization" of a Shakespeare play "as the fulfillment of a long-cherished dream," since Shakespeare was a playwright whose "dramatic form is practically that of a scenario."[26] His 35-year-old wife was only following a long stage tradition of mature actors playing Juliet and Romeo, the most recent precedent then being Katherine Cornell as a 36-year-old Juliet on Broadway in 1934. Despite the problem that studio lights are harsher than footlights on older actors, Norma Shearer's Juliet and Leslie Howard's 43-year-old Romeo exactly fit the middle-brow stereotype of "sublime" Shakespearean actors, still closer to a lofty Forbes-Robertson than to a cantankerous Nicol Williamson. To add even more "class," the great John Barrymore as a scenery-chewing, over-aged but nevertheless charming Mercutio aroused faint echoes of past glories on the New York stage. Barrymore had already done screened Shakespeare with his solo appearance as a soliloquizing Richard duke of Gloucester in *The Show of Shows* (1929), a cinematic vaudeville show, where his sweeping declamation from *Henry VI Part III* further endorsed the supremacy of Warner Brothers Vitaphone process.[27] As if terrified that youthful actors might desecrate the worshipful rite, they let 44-year-old competent but icy Basil Rathbone try to be a fiery Tybalt.

The dialectical structure of *Romeo and Juliet* with its deeply embedded antitheses between light and dark, womb and tomb, youth and age, love and death lent itself admirably to the cinematic style of George Cukor and the classical Hollywood film. Romeo hints at this rhetorical strategy when listing his oxymorons of "bright smoke," "cold fire," "sick health" (1.1.180), and the "ancient grudge" between Montagues and Capulets sets thesis against antithesis in a clash of opposites. The visual equivalents emerge on screen through parallel editing and montage that reflect the alternate surges of subversion and containment wrenching Verona apart. The geometrical symmetries of parallel shots correlate with a Verona ruled by reason, and the montage and random cuts become metaphors for overwhelming passion. "They stumble that run fast," the Friar reminds us (2.3.94). Echoing Edmund Spenser's *Mutabilitie Cantos*, which strove to make all things irreconcilable reconcilable, the Panglossian Friar Lawrence would have Romeo's misfortunes magically become fortunate: "thy Juliet is alive . . . / There art thou happy" (3.3.135).

The studio spared no expense in the quest for authenticity and realism. Since a plan to film on location in Italy for "real" realism was ruled out,[28] the producers settled for the *faux* realism of Prospero's "insubstantial pageant" by spending $1 million on a back lot Verona in Hollywood, modeled after Hogenberg's *Civitates Orbis Terrarum*. Two underlings had been dispatched to Italy to make 2,769 pictures for conversion into 54 scale models. Carpenters had then constructed on eight acres of the MGM lot, a Disneyland conflation of buildings from Verona. Professor William Strunk, Jr. of Cornell University, the rhetorician who teamed up with E.B. White to inflict the *New Yorker* style on America, dispensed academic reputability like holy water by declaring the grandiose set to be "an ideal Veronese public square . . . such as Shakespeare himself might have imagined from the accounts of returned travelers."[29] Oliver Messel's original costume sketches for the household liveries, the canopies, the drummers, trumpeters, and guards show Juliet in a blue gown, and a "Negro" page to Paris in pink, red, and white livery. Altogether the costumes required hundreds of sketches, and some 38,000 yards of material, which would have been a triumph in Technicolor but muted in black-and-white.[30] Herbert Stothart's musical themes from Tchaikovsky's *Romeo and Juliet* (1871) enhanced the funereal atmosphere, but Stothart until countermanded by Thalberg had originally planned carefully researched fifteenth and sixteenth-century modes. Agnes De Mille, choreographer of the $100,000 Capulet ballroom scene, tells the story that Thalberg suddenly heard Tchaikovksy's music on the radio for the first time and called Stothart, crying out, "Why did no one ever tell me of this?"[31] Instinctively Thalberg wanted something like the incomparable fusion of sight and sound in Bo Widerberg's *Elvira Madigan* (1967) when the slow movement in F major from Mozart Piano Concerto no. 21 in C major (K 467) punctuates the progress of a young woman running in slow motion across a lush meadow. According to Herbert Coursen, Jr., in the late 30s spin-offs from Tchaikovsky cloyed the airwaves with sentimental hits like "Our Love" and "The Night Is Young and You're so Beautiful,"[32] which inevitably infiltrated this conception of *Romeo and Juliet*.

The Thalberg/Cukor movie works symbiotically with Shakespeare's text by taking its cues and camera angles from the thematic implications and rhythms of the play itself. After old-fashioned credits showing the actors in cameo frames, and after John Barrymore as prologue appears on a prosce-nium stage, there is a cut to Verona's cathedral square. The stylized, geo-metrical, movements of the opposing houses of Montague and Capulet as they cross the main square of Verona provide fodder for multiple reaction shots among the gawking citizenry of extras. As Cedric Gibbons, the film's designer, explained, "with the movement of the camera, the audience is per-mitted to look at the settings from the same angle as the people who are actually in them."[33]

The first 36 of the movie's 262 set-ups must suffice to illustrate Cukor's method. Three men and a woman, all muttering apprehensively, stare at the Capulet and Montague retinues, who in a motif inspired by Gozolli's "Procession of the Magi" fresco from Florence,[34] have just entered the piazza from opposite sides and are converging on a collision course toward the cathedral steps. In medium shot, others cry out, "The Capulets!" which pro-vides the visual metonymy for the reactions of the hundreds of other pseudo-Veronese extras. Rich alike in dignity, Lord Capulet (C. Aubrey Smith) and Lady Capulet (Violet Kemble Cooper) lead the way, attended by servants in light livery and black badges. Then from an over-the-shoulder angle, the stately column continues to march toward its inevitable collision with the rival house. The entrance of the Montagues precisely mirrors the Capulet procession, even down to and including the murmured "It's the Montagues" in more reaction shots. Cross-cutting continues with the Montagues glow-ering in the direction of the Capulets, and vice versa. A cutaway to the Capulets reveals a sneering Basil Rathbone, who had raised sneering to a high art, as a vexed Tybalt, who is whispering into Lord Capulet's ear: "The house of Montague, our foe," while C. Aubrey Smith, for once not the colonel of the Queen's Own Royal Regiment of Imperial Horse Dragoons at the Khyber Pass, warns the impetuous lad, "Soft, keep the peace."

As the editing tempo increases, it echoes the escalating anger of the warring houses. There are two seconds (48 frames perhaps) of Tybalt under a canopy glaring at the Montagues; three seconds (72 frames) of Benvolio responding with a match cut in kind. A Montague retainer grabs for the hilt of his sword; and a parallel shot follows of Tybalt reaching for his sword but being restrained by Father Capulet. The fine-tuned match-cutting between Capulets and Montagues culminates in a full-scale riot in the streets. This is highly skilled, technically proficient movie making whose shifting camera angles, splicing and dubbing of bits and pieces of action and sound create a photographic mosaic that mimics actuality. Cukor's classical style offers a polar opposite to the filmic expressionism in Reinhardt's *Midsummer Night's Dream*. The danger is that patently faked realism like a mockup Verona may turn out looking less real than the blatant falsifications of expressionism. Anthony Davies puts the matter this way: "The cinema aims at spatial realism. Nonetheless our collusion with the medium is such that we will tolerate . . . photographic tricks so long as they are wholly convincing; so long as we are given at the visual level what appears to be spatially real, and so long as we can believe in a spatial reality beyond the boundaries of the frame."[35]

For all the movie's high gloss, at some point rigor mortis sets in. To anyone today grown accustomed to the kind of shock editing used in Oliver Stone's *Natural Born Killers* (1994), the pace borders on the tedious. Even the slapstick antics of Andy DeVine as Peter biting his thumb at the Montagues comes across as a dutiful interruption for comic relief, of which Mr. Thalberg wrote that "four of the five acts are lightened with comedy and gags, all aiming at the diversion of the audience."[36] The indomitable Nurse (Edna May Oliver) waggles her finger at the blubbery Peter to the joy of the Montagues, who revel in Peter's humiliation.

Orderly patterns of parallel editing yield to chaotic montage when full-scale street fighting breaks out. "*They Fight*" licenses directors to use the camera unflinchingly. A wild mêlée follows that in forty or so shots from a variety of camera angles shows Capulets rushing toward Montagues; Peter comically struggling to remove his sword from a scabbard; a man under flower pots being brutally clubbed; duelists in single combat; a terrified woman with a baby (in a quotation from Eisenstein); a man being throttled; two other combatants rolling down the church steps; a Capulet skewered by a sword. With the entrance of the prince to restore order, the wild montage gives way to a full framed *mise-en-scène* filled with the chastened and subdued crowd.

The Cukor *Romeo and Juliet* defines the play this way in the context of broadly sketched dialectical tensions through symmetry and asymmetry in framing and editing. The metronome-like cutting shows again with the

6   Super stars Norma Shearer and Leslie Howard meet and dance at the Capulet ball in this multi-million dollar motion picture of *Romeo and Juliet* (USA 1936), directed by George Cukor.

balcony scene where the approach of Leslie Howard through sepulchral gardens to Juliet's fairy-tale balcony proceeds at the stately pace of 90 shots for 205 lines of dialogue, more attuned to forty-year-old actors than to the teenagers of Zeffirelli and Luhrmann. Howard and Shearer speak their lines well, with clarity and conviction but not with the transcendent fire that makes the words burn in the heart. The overly predictable and mechanical editing straitjackets the film in the way that the sonnet imprisons Juliet's language at the Capulet ball, until she breaks out of its rigidities and speaks alone in her own unfettered blank verse (3.2.1). A mild rebellion against textual purity does occur in the omission of the Friar's prolix speech of exculpation, "I will be brief" (5.3.229), which though to a modern audience is unbearably anticlimactic after the tomb scene, yet retains vital components of Elizabethan moralizing. For one thing, it somewhat exculpates Romeo and Juliet's defiance of parental authority. Little of this means anything today with society's moral roots eroding under modernist relativism, and George Cukor was not to be alone in jettisoning this problematic scene from a movie of *Romeo and Juliet*. He would be joined by Zeffirelli and Lurhmann in 1968 and 1996. Even with this deletion, however, the film remains a reverential but not warm and vibrant *Romeo and Juliet*, received respectfully but not lovingly by the critics, and ultimately too wrapped up in a high mimetic bardolatry for either Shakespeare's or Hollywood's own good. Besides, "tickling commodity" proved too much for it, and its malaise at the box office encouraged Hollywood's moratorium on major Shakespeare films for nearly two decades.

The Mankiewicz/Houseman *Julius Caesar* (1953)

Seventeen years after the studio's *Romeo and Juliet*, MGM's vice-president Dore Schary, with the enthusiastic help of Joseph L. Mankiewicz and John Houseman, again ventured into the perilous waters of Shakespeare movies, this time with a remarkable $2-million *Julius Caesar* (1953),[37] packed full with renowned actors. By 1953 the emerging television industry, the impending collapse of the studio monopoly on distribution, and the new practice of allowing stars a percentage of the gross profits was already chipping away at the Golden Age of the major Hollywood studios. *Julius Caesar* barely squeaked in under the wire before the old centralized system gave way to decentralized, individual producers. It borrowed, though, from television's knack for presenting history as a current newsreel event in a "you are there" mode. It was a gambit that Orson Welles stole from "The March of Time" for *Citizen Kane*, though Mankiewicz's picture for all its stark realism lacks the grainy texture of an actual newsreel. While not so extravagant as Giovanni Pastrone's *Cabiria* (1914), or Cecil B. De Mille's *Ten Commandments* (1956) with a cast of thousands, Mankiewicz's Rome shows an array of crowded streets, steep staircases, elevated pulpits, pillars, balconies, statuary, and 1200 toga-clad extras milling around before a painted backdrop of the entire ancient city. Technical adviser P.M. Pasinetti also wanted an authentic "lived-in" look, a Rome not just of the Forum but one that "was also a city of narrow streets, slums, dirty little taverns, peddlars [*sic*], small squares with people yelling across at each other, etc."[38] Rejecting the modern dress approach of Worthington Miner's Studio One television production (1949), John Houseman put the cast in togas and on heroic theatrical sets like Gordon Craig's but of course free of the proscenium arch. He remained sanguine that "the magic power of lens and microphone"[39] would prevent the sheer size of the sets from overwhelming the actors.

To avoid confusion, William Shakespeare should have called his play *The Tragedy of Marcus Brutus* instead of *The Tragedy of Julius Caesar*, for this most rhetorical of his plays mainly focuses on the tragic irony of Brutus' incapacity for self-scrutiny. After Caesar's assassination in the third act, Brutus (James Mason) takes center stage and must deal with Antony (Marlon Brando), Caesar Augustus (Douglas Watson), and Cassius (John Gielgud). First, Caesar (Louis Calhern) experiences the tragedy of a great fall – Caesar suffers from "the falling sickness" (1.2.254), "great Caesar fell" (3.2.189) – but then after Antony's brilliant eulogy he is raised up again as the mob shouts, "Most noble Caesar!" (3.2.243). When he is as yet unfallen, at the apex of his power and arrogance, Caesar remains framed at the center of the film, whether progressing through the crowded streets preceded by Roman legionnaires, or pressed in on the sides by cheering riffraff. As Robert Hapgood has pointed out,[40] the film supports these spatial arrangements with photography and a set design of steep inclines, platforms, and balconies that serve as metaphors for the ups and downs of power in Rome itself and at Philippi, where Brutus stupidly marches straight into an ambush set up by the triumvirate on both flanks of a narrow defile. Brutus there discovers that actually there is no "tide in the affairs of men, / Which taken at the flood, leads on to fortune" (4.3.218), a passage often quoted out of context. Too often insufficiently noticed, Miklos Rozsa's musical score aurally supports the visual codes in the elaborate thematic counterpointing between the rising and falling fortunes of Caesar and Brutus.[41]

This *Julius Caesar* above all remains an actors' film, an unusual decision having been made to give priority to actors over technicians by filming the virtually uncut play[42] in its original sequence and by eliminating distracting reaction shots. The actors even resemble the many busts and statues of important Romans on the vast sets, not only in physiognomy but even in the folds and drapes of the togas. The movie opens with a tight shot of a bust of Caesar before focusing on the two tribunes, puritanical prigs, scolding the crowd for acclaiming Caesar: "Wherefore rejoice? What conquest brings he home?" (1.1.32), and protesting against the city's excessive quantity of statues of Caesar: "Disrobe the images, / If you do find them deck'd with ceremonies," says Flavius (1.1.64). The busts of noble citizens with their hair brushed well forward in the high Roman style represent the lost world that is now embodied in a living world of the movie's beautiful actors, whom Houseman wanted to look like "men wearing clothes, not characters wearing costumes."[43]

As a man whose lofty idealism ironically makes him into a terrorist, James Mason's Brutus strikes exactly the right note. A complex character, Brutus combines Macbeth's ruthlessness with Hamlet's introspection, and convinces himself that what happens to Caesar underneath Pompey's statue is not so much "a savage spectacle" (3.1.223) as a kind of blood sacrifice: "Let's be sacrificers, but not butchers, Caius / . . . Let's carve him as a dish fit for the gods" (2.1.166). Made all the more imperious by a low angle shot, Caesar at the Capitol, surrounded by the conspirators, spurns Metellus Cimber's (Tom Powers) petition asking a pardon for his brother, Publius: "I am constant as the northern star" (3.1.60). Behind him a dark-browed, scowling Casca (Desmond O'Brien) is maneuvering to deliver the first blow. After Casca plunges the first knife into Caesar's back and after Caesar has been cruelly stabbed by the other conspirators, and as a bloodied and suddenly pitiful Caesar lurches toward him, Brutus draws back, retreats, sickened by the spectacle of what he has engineered, but then resolves to honor his oath and stabs Caesar, notoriously, in the groin, though it's been said (even in Plutarch) that Brutus was Caesar's illegitimate son. Louis Calhern speaks Caesar's immortal "*Et tu, Brute?* – Then fall Caesar!" (3.1.77) as the camera probes his unspeakable anguish.

Other high points include a disingenuous Cassius (John Gielgud), who persuades Brutus of Caesar's untrustworthiness even as he stands in the shadow of yet another statue of Caesar: "Why, man, he doth bestride the narrow world / Like a Colossus" (1.2.135). At the gathering of the conspirators in Brutus' garden, Casca's pedantic correction of Decius Brutus (John Hoyt) and Cinna's (William Cottrell) bickering over where the sun rises make a little more sense when Casca points his sword at the approaching Marcus Brutus, who then metaphorically becomes the rising sun: "Here, as I point my sword, the sun arises" (2.1.106). Brutus' vast capacity for *hamartia*, or "the missing of the mark," emerges when he spares Antony's life: "Our course will seem too bloody, Caius Cassius, / To cut the head off, and then hack the limbs" (2.1.162). As Cassius, Gielgud predictably and characteristically stresses verse over sense, tending to "sing" the lines[44] as he mellifluously but futilely protests against Brutus' decision, leaving unanswered the question of how a man who once so dominated Brutus could now be dominated by him. Deborah Kerr (Portia) and Greer Garson (Calphurnia), portray aristocratic Roman women with steel backbones, Portia after all being "Cato's daughter," who could swallow fire. They glitter with jewelry, necklaces and earrings, upswept hairdos, and wear elegant gowns of miraculously intricate tucks, folds, and pleats. Kerr's eloquence and beauty stay unruffled even when defeated by Brutus' obstinacy. In the parallel "mirror" scene between Caesar and Calphurnia, Greer Garson, for all of her power, also loses out to Decius Brutus, who scoffs at her interpretation of the dream ("This dream is all amiss interpreted" – 2.2.83) and flatters her husband into going to his death at the senate. She is last seen standing alone, the doors shut behind her, as Caesar marches off to the Capitol with a claque of his false friends, her private sufferings, as well as those of Portia, offering fertile ground for essays exposing systems of patriarchal subjugation. Another political subtext also hovers just below the surface with covert parallels to the rise and fall of Mussolini and Hitler in World War II, while the terrible fate of Cinna the poet comes close to echoing the feverish witch hunt hysteria of the McCarthy red scare era: "I am not Cinna the conspirator . . . It is no matter, his name's Cinna" (3.3.32).

Marlon Brando's Broadway role as Stanley Kowalski, the Polish redneck with slurred speech in a *Streetcar Named Desire,* had so stereotyped him that there was a visceral denial of his right or ability to play a Shakespearean role. As a method actor, Brando carried his stage persona of a "tough guy," Hells Angels type into his private life.[45] Despite his charismatic Antony, the critics competed to see who could administer the most unkindest cuts of all: "[he is] so far from Shakespeare's image that the lines cannot be made to stretch"; "he needs a bit of speech training"; and "[he is] oddly muscle-bound and speaks as though a wad of gum lurked in his jaws."[46] A few, however, defied the "switched code" taboo and confessed that Brando brilliantly handled Shakespeare's blank verse and that his silences could be even more eloquent.[47] Elocution aside, Brando radiates power with or without words, his splendid physique then not yet ravaged by time and sloth. Grieving over Caesar's bleeding corpse, he builds up to his bloodthirsty call for revenge in the wildness of, "Cry 'Havoc!' and let slip the dogs of war" (3.1.273).

In the great eulogy over Caesar's body in the public arena, Brando energizes Shakespeare's words from deep reservoirs of strength. The Godfather has no need to shout in order to have others listen. He stands like a Roman statue on steeply rising steps with a backdrop of mighty vertical columns.

Fortunately for Brando, Mankiewicz insisted on the actors' completing their lengthy speeches while the cameras were rolling, even if it meant paying the crew overtime. He feared that "looping," or having actors dub in speeches in a post-filming session, could maim Shakespeare's blank verse, as it notoriously did for Orson Welles's patchwork *Macbeth* (1948). In the film's typically realistic way, Antony actually uses the opening lines of the speech, "Friends, Romans, countrymen, lend me your ears!" (3.2.72) to quiet down an unruly mob who are perched on a rude wooden scaffolding in the public square. In contrast with the rabble, whom Shakespeare himself seemed to despise, Antony from a low camera-angle and over the shoulders of the assembled crowd stands high above, gowned in a graceful toga with the Roman eagle icon on a shoulder clasp. As he moves his arms, the drapery of the toga ripples gracefully in rhythm with his speech. In the crisply blocked crowd scenes, the hoi polloi look alternately brutal, mean, stupid, and occasionally intelligent. Now and then in the foreground, three or four men and women turn and glare at the theatre audience warning them (us) to be silent that Antony may be heard. Brando's Antony validates again Cassius' famous prediction that "this our lofty scene [shall] be acted over / In [states] unborn and accents yet unknown!" (3.1.112). The likes of this remarkable performance will rarely be seen again.

- 3 -

Laurence Olivier directs Shakespeare

As talented an *auteur* of Shakespeare film as ever existed, Laurence Olivier at mid-century reclaimed the British role as guardian of its national poet. Merging art with entertainment, he compromised with "tickling commodity"– one might venture to say he tickled commodity rather than allowing it to tickle him – by producing a "commodified" Shakespeare designed to fit the by then well established Palace theatres that attracted both the classes and some of the masses. A virtuoso actor with a thousand faces, he could banter with Rosalind in the Forest of Arden, rally the troops at Agincourt, scold Gertrude at Elsinore, send the little princes to the Tower, smother Desdemona (in blackface), demand the bond from Antonio, and reject Cordelia. On stage and film, he also managed, among other roles, to be Oedipus Rex, a Nazi dentist, a pathetic music hall entertainer, the cantor father of the Jazz Singer, Emily Brontë's Heathcliff, and Jane Austen's Fitzwilliam Darcy. By age twenty-nine he had already established Shakespearean and Shavian credentials with London's Old Vic playing Romeo, and with West End appearances as Captain Stanhope in *Journey's End*. With the exception of a rare brickbat hurled at him by Russell Davies on the 1992 British Channel Four television program "J'accuse/Without Walls," which painted him as performing with more show than substance, he has been universally acclaimed.[1]

Secretly his inner being may have tugged him toward Austen's Fitzwilliam Darcy, who is thinly concealed in the sullen and diffident Orlando of Hungarian-born director Paul Czinner's $1-million *As You Like It* (1936). Olivier looks all the more gloomy and morose, better suited as Oliver than as Orlando, for being paired opposite the effervescent Polish-born actress, Elisabeth Bergner, wife of director Paul Czinner, whose sprightly Rosalind saves the picture from utter ruin.[2] Thirty-six-year-old Elisabeth Bergner's special knack for Peter-Pan giggling and wriggling may have charmed the film's advisory-scenarist, J.M. Barrie, but it irritated some estimable critics, like the late Roger Manvell, who thought her "kittenish" attitude reflected a "self-destructive femininity," and deplored her "habit of turning somersaults."[3] Olivier and Bergner both faced, like Christine Edzard's recent film-festival *As You Like It* (1992), the uphill challenge of making one of Shakespeare's talkiest plays move. Its sparkling language subordinates plot to a labyrinth of mirror effects through which various deceptions and usurpations devolve on Orlando and the disguised and cross-dressed Rosalind, whose exiled father, "Duke Senior" (Henry Ainley), presides over a band of "merry men," who live "like the old Robin Hood of England ... and fleet the time carelessly" (1.1.115). As denizens of the forest of Arden, where "sweet are the uses of adversity" (2.1.12), Duke Senior's honest followers in the tradition of pastoral myth implicitly rebuke the depraved courtiers at Duke Frederick's palace.

Rightly described as too stagy, the film remains firmly rooted in London's West End theatre. By contrast, having left the theatre thousands of miles behind in New York, Hollywood's new sound films like *Taming of the Shrew* evolved directly from the silent into the talking pictures. Typically one critic wrote that "it remains more a photographed version of a stringently cut stage presentation than a comic classic shaped to the cinema."[4] Even the break with expressionism in francophile Lazare Meerson's "poetic realism" of black-and-white fake woodlands, bubbling brooks, and peasant scenes, some inspired by the Flemish painter Pieter Brueghel, disappointed cinéphiles. The stylized *faux* medievalism, however, anticipated the famous scenes based on the 1490 manuscript of *Les très riches heures du Jean, duc de Berri* in Olivier's subsequent *Henry V*. Meerson's sudden release of genuine sheep, rabbits, and squirrels into the *mise-en-scène* shattered the fragile world of his imaginary barnyards and woods.

Despite the staginess, however, Czinner's resourceful camera work and David Lean's editing transform the text into a plausible film narrative. Intimate as two teenagers with a schoolgirl crush, Rosalind and Celia (Sophie Stewart) in the same brief scene are viewed from every angle on the compass, whether in two-shot, close-up, or over-the-shoulder and in a half-dozen camera set-ups. As Rosalind, Elisabeth Bergner with her charmingly accented English, whirls, turns, sparkles, dazzles, giggles, crosses her arms and offers unconditional love to her best friend, Celia, now cross-dressed as Aliena. At the phrase, the "bay of Portugal" (4.1.208), Rosalind executes her famous somersault as a final desperate measure for energizing words with her body. Adding piquancy, she brandishes a scroll of paper for swatting Touchstone, or for playfully tapping Orlando with, indexing her hidden need to dominate. She punctuates the classic line directed at Phebe for not wanting to marry Silvius with an ominous flourish of her switch fetish: "For I must tell you friendly in your ear, / Sell when you can, you are not for all markets" (3.5.59). Even so, contemporary reviewer James Agate thought her "tenderness and gaiety" insufficient to make up for a lack of "wit," which he attributed to her Teutonic sensibility.[5] By contrast, her Orlando (Olivier) seems wooden. His praise for old Adam ("O good old man, how well in thee appears / The constant service of the antique world" (2.3.56)) sounds sing-song and uninflected, like a sullen pupil called on to read aloud in class. It is not just that he is playing Orlando, who is not nearly so witty as Rosalind, indeed is quite dull, it is that he is not playing anyone in particular at all, unless it's Fitzwilliam Darcy.

The supporting cast includes Leon Quartermaine (Jaques) listed in the credits as "dialogue supervisor," who again demonstrates the old adage that "those who can, do; those who can't, teach." His big moment with "All the world's a stage, / And all the men and women merely players" (2.7.139) looks and sounds too theatrical while trying not to be theatrical. Orlando's wrestling match before a jeering mob with the flabby Charles, the wrestler (Lionel Braham), consumes myriad shots from different angles to record the tossing and thumping in the ring. Abundant reaction shots catch the dismayed faces of Celia and Rosalind, the leering countenance of the wicked duke (Felix Aylmer), the absorbed faces of the peasants crammed behind the palace gate, and an ongoing blow-by-blow account as Touchstone (Mackenzie Ward) pantomimes and viscerally reacts to the wrestlers' crunches and grunts. The London Philharmonic Orchestra's arraignment of Walton's score for the wrestling match between Charles and Orlando foreshadows the quickened tempo during the French cavalry charge at Agincourt in *Henry V*. Incongruously dressed as a bunny rabbit, Touchstone's courtship of Audrey (Dorice Fordred) becomes even more unbelievable, though it's only a mirror to the affairs of Orlando-Rosalind and Phebe-Oliver (Joan White and John Laurie). Touchstone's threat to the scapegoated William, "I will kill thee a hundred and fifty ways: therefore tremble and depart" (5.1.56), comes across as more grotesque than funny, in fact downright cruel.

With a running time of only 97 minutes some key moments have vanished: Oliver Martext's mock wedding scene; and Touchstone's set-piece description of seven types of quarrels. The big wedding scene at the end has been squeezed, compressed, truncated, or filleted out of existence, with Hymen's lines being turned over to Rosalind. Jaques de Boys suddenly arrives with news of the totally implausible conversion of Duke Frederick ("meeting with an old religious man, / After some question with him was converted" (5.4.160)), and of the decision to restore all the lands "to his banish'd brother" and "that were with him exil'd" (5.4.164). When Jaques, the melancholy one, is deprived of the gloomy announcement of his intention to join the duke as a "convertite," the dark subtext, the *memento mori,* so typical of every Shakespearean comedy vanishes. The general rejoicing remains unshadowed by encroaching darkness until Elisabeth Bergner steps

[51]

in, oozing charm, to steal the show with a wonderful epilogue in which, cross-dressed as a man, she brandishes her favorite switch while admonishing the women, and then magically dissolves into a white virginal gown as she flatters the men. Bergner's Rosalind and Laurence Olivier's Orlando may not be exactly as you like it, but in the realm of filmed Shakespeare no one has yet succeeded in being more likeable.

Henry V (1944)

Eight years later the sobriety and high seriousness that had made Olivier look miscast in a Shakespearean comedy proved exactly right for the role of an enigmatic 28-year-old soldier-king in the landmark *King Henry V* (1944). The movie not only launched, indeed invented, the modern Shakespeare film, but also showed that the Shakespeare movie could survive in the Palace theatre as well as in the rarified art houses. Olivier created a cinematic equivalent to the tantalizing ambiguities that reside in the Shakespearean vision of *King Henry V*.[6] The movie in recapitulating the most primal dichotomy in film making between the realism of the Lumière brothers and the fantasy of Georges Méliès simultaneously interrogates the quagmire of doubts in Shakespeare's play about the nature of governance, of kingship, and of the hero, young King Hal.

The ingeniously contrived film echoes the structure and themes of *Henry IV Parts One and Two* as through cross-cutting it moves back and forth between the holiday tavern world of Falstaff and the workaday courtly world of the usurping Lancastrian King Henry. It explores the nature of reality in assessing the gap between the authentic vs. the "counterfeit," the usurping King Henry being after all something of a counterfeit monarch – "Counterfeit? I lie, I am no counterfeit," says Falstaff (*1 Henry IV* 5.4.114) –, and draws attention to the "guilt" over the death of King Richard II concealed beneath the "gilt" of the crown: "England shall double gild his treble guilt" (*2 Henry IV* 4.5.128). As a result, the young king who appears on the screen has an emotional pedigree rich enough for several psychoanalysts, and neither Falstaff's tavern people nor the king's courtiers own a monopoly on morality or counterfeiting.

The film's existence on multiple levels renders it liable to exegesis like some medieval text. Simply as an entertainment the movie belongs, as Harry Geduld has said, to the heroic/action genre in which "a thorough-going extrovert, an almost entirely externalized image of a hero"[7] overcomes evil against all odds. Anthony Davies then further identifies *Henry V* with the western genre, citing André Bazin's definition that calls, among other things, for "simplicity of narrative concentration on archetypes rather than on complexity of character."[8] Bazin's displacing of Hal into the type of a strong, silent western hero endorses the traditional view of many critics that *Henry V* lacks nuance, qualifying splendidly as epic but weakly as drama.

There is much more to the story, however. With battle scenes shot on location in Ireland and interiors at Denham studios in England, the movie has been widely viewed as a propaganda film, mostly because of its dedication to the "Commandos and airborne troops of Great Britain." For that to happen, as John Collick shrewdly has pointed out, there needed to be a "mythical ideal of a wholly integrated British literary culture" in which Shakespeare was as meaningful to the masses as "the songs of Vera Lynn." For Tommies and GIs, it seems safe to say, Will Shakespeare took a back seat to Vera Lynn and Betty Grable. To work as good jingoism, the king had to be sanitized by deleting his "war crimes," such as the obscene threats before the French city of Harfleur: "Your naked infants spitted upon pikes, / Whiles the mad mothers with their howls confus'd / Do break the clouds" (*Henry V* 3.3.38), and the notorious order to put the French prisoners to the sword: "Then every soldier kill his prisoners, / Give the word through" (4.6.37). Michael Manheim has also discussed the movie's ideological parallels to E.M.W. Tillyard's celebrated *The Elizabethan World Picture* that reinforced "the order, system, hierarchy, and the demonstrated superiority of Anglo-Saxon values in the Europe of World War II."[9] Far more than a documentary like Leni Riefenstahl's beatification of the Nazi mystique, *The Triumph of the Will* (1935), *Henry V,* if it is propaganda, veers toward what Walter Benjamin called "the aestheticization of politics," as opposed to the "politicization of art."[10] Obviously, Olivier does not "eroticize"[11] Henry V in quite the way that Riefenstahl makes Hitler an object of desire among the masses, but in many isolated shots, as when the king unsheathes his great speech in the tradition of Armada rhetoric before Agincourt – "we few, we happy few, we band of brothers" (4.3.60) –, the camera gazes adoringly on the hero figure. A closer German parallel to *Henry V* lies in a wartime costume drama of nationalistic propaganda, Veit Harlan's *Der Grosse König* (1944), a celebration of the victories of Frederick the Great in the Seven Years War.[12] Despite these political tasks, the movie still finds some room, however tangentially and tentatively, for the young king's ethical quandaries. Although he is on the surface a carefree young man, a Jack Kennedy style leader, prone to tossing his helmet on a post, all the censorship in the world cannot erase the Hamlet-like burden imposed on the king (and his audience) by his having "two bodies," one of an ordinary mortal and another of an incarnate divine sovereign, "the mirror of all Christian kings"(Chorus, 2.6).[13]

Quite rightly, however, Ace G. Pilkington and others feel that the movie's enduring value arises out of its consummate artistry as a film.[14] It consciously bridges the gap between theatre and film, and in the act of interrogating the idea of making a Shakespeare play into a film through a virtuoso display of cinematic codes self-reflexively valorizes it. Shakespeare movies, as Laurence Guntner has stressed, need to be studied not just in the context of their texts but in the realm of film codes, the visual tropes and conceits such as camera angles, movement, focus, lighting, montage, music, etc. that film makers have contrived for communicating meaning to audiences.[15] Film critic Dudley Andrew's astute analysis of the interplay between artifice and realism in Olivier's film of *Henry V* reveals a cunning structure of nested episodes. Borrowing from André Bazin, Andrew calls this pattern a *hyperbola*, whose outer and inner limits converge in a progression toward both Henry's meditation on the eve of battle and the Battle of Agincourt itself.[16] Essentially a play-within-a-play, or movie-within-a-movie with the Globe playhouse as a framing device, the film critiques the differences between stage and screen. When the limitations of the Globe stage become apparent, the camera steps in to make possible the chorus' advice to take the audience across the channel to France: "Work, work your thoughts, and therein see a siege" (Chorus, 3.25).

The initial bracketing of the film begins, however, with a fluttering handbill proclaiming that today's (1 May 1600) performance at the Globe is "The Chronicle History of King Henry the Fift." Resembling a quarto title page, the handbill's realism supports the subsequent "actualities" of an aerial survey (accompanied by a solemn chorale) tracking southwesterly over Elizabethan London, passing over London Bridge, over St. Mary Overy (now Southwark cathedral), hesitating before seeking out the Globe after snubbing the Bear Gardens,[17] showing the house flag ascending the pole on the roof of the Globe and a trumpet call announcing the show, an ensemble entering the music gallery and starting up a lively overture with flutes and soft recorders, the arriving audience, the circulating orange women, the gallants and ladies, the raucous catcalls, the better sort of persons in the galleries, the book-holder taking his place,[18] the boy with a placard announcing the play's title, the sweeping arrival on stage of the chorus (Leslie Banks), the soul-stirring prologue ("O for a Muse of fire, that would ascend / The brightest heaven of invention!"), the boy actors cross-dressing backstage as Mistress Quickly and Katherine of France, the entrance above of the clownish Canterbury (Felix Aylmer) and Ely (Robert Helpman), and the beginning of the play. Canterbury and Ely turn their scene into a comic *shtick* that makes a mockery of the corrupt trade-off by which they will bless Henry's war against France in exchange for church lands, the legalisms behind Canterbury's brain-numbing, 85-line explanation being anything but "as clear as is the summer's day" (1.2.8). The truculent audience lives up to its reputation by loudly hissing and booing and jeering at the unfortunate Bishop of Ely. On the other hand, it's also possible to see their antics as stemming from their incompetence as actors rather than from their putative roles as bishops. After all this realism, though, Olivier's clearing of his throat as he prepares to enter from backstage reminds us that he is an actor not a king, just as the Globe is a playhouse not the vasty fields of France.

These actualities inside the playhouse yield to the stage-set theatricality of the Boar's Head tavern showing Falstaff's demise in melancholy circumstances punctuated by William Walton's dirge-like *passacaglia*, a musical commentary in bass on the inevitability of death. Theatrical reality then yields to a greater but paradoxically non-alienating fantasy when King Henry boards a warship at Southampton that displays the blatant stylization of a medieval tapestry. Then the camera moves to the pure fantasy world in France that designer Roger Furse modeled on *Les très riches heures du Jean, duc de Berri*, a 14th-century illuminated calendar,[19] its creator the Duke Berri himself (Ernest Thesiger) actually appearing as a character at the French court. The Technicolor parade through "realism" to "neo-illusionism" to "illusionism" to "fantastic," ends at Agincourt, the film's epicenter.

The king's secret anxieties about the state of his soul lie here encrypted under the outer wrappings of the film's illusion and fantasy. The soil of Agincourt is Henry's Garden of Gethsemane: "What infinite heart's ease / Must kings neglect, that private men enjoy!" (4.1.236). In the crucible of the following battle, the king begins the spiral upward again toward reconciliation with the world of reality. Called by Harry M. Geduld, "the most glorious display of pageantry ever to grace a motion picture screen,"[20] the 17-minute Agincourt sequence used hundreds of extras recruited from the Irish Home Guard, cost £80,000 out of the film's projected budget of £300,000 (which escalated to a final cost of £475,708), needed a half-mile railway track for the French cavalry charge, survived a whole series of minor delays from weather and technical glitches, and consumed 39 days of shooting time. According to Dallas Bower, the veteran director who played a crucial role in making the film, the Agincourt scenes shot at Powerscourt near Dublin could not have been made without the help of poet John Betjeman, who as press attaché to the British High Commissioner gained Lord Powerscourt's permission to film on the estate.[21] A crowning glory of the battle scene was the integration of movement with William Walton's inspired music, which in turn followed the example of Sergei Prokofiev's collaboration with Sergei Eisenstein in the battle scenes for *Alexander Nevsky* (1938).[22] Eisenstein is said to have re-edited to make the visuals more compatible with Prokofiev's score. The close tolerance between word and image nowhere shows better than in the analytical close-up when the camera echoes the prologue by showing the horses "printing their proud hoofs I' th' receiving earth" (Chorus, 1.27).

After the battle, like a film run backwards, the same transitions from realism to fantasy and then back to realism occur in reverse order. Back at the French court, Burgundy delivers a panegyric about "our fertile France" that is "the best garden in the world" (5.2.36) while the camera scans a diorama-like landscape beyond the tracery windows of the set. Burgundy's prelapsarian world and the postlapsarian world of Agincourt's battlefield parallel the contrast between the world of the film's "actualities" on the stage of the Globe and the fantastical Europe upon which the chorus has urged the audience to "let [their] imaginary forces work." The contrast between what seems and what is emerges again in the wooing scene when King Henry proposes to Katherine of France (Reneé Asherson), France's most precious ornament. The king passes himself off to Katherine as a rough, crude sort of fellow, the character of a "plain dealer," a kind of John Wayne figure: "thou wouldst find me such a plain king that thou wouldst think I had sold a farm to buy my crown" (5.2.124). The actuality is that he is not a plain farmer at all but king of England and a world-class Machiavel. Olivier and Asherson survive only briefly as the fairy tale king and princess in the Paris Louvre before, almost imperceptibly, they are again back in the Globe, like Cinderella figures, having been dissolved into a mere player king and princess, Reneé Asherson transmogrified into the crudely cross-dressed boy player who was earlier glimpsed backstage at the Globe stuffing oranges into his shirt for décolletage. The fantasy world ends but the journeymen actors now playing the roles are in themselves also fantasies, though less polished ones. The fluttering handbill returns to list the credits and the revels are ended. Those credits include besides Dallas Bower, wonderfully talented assistants for design (Paul Sheriff), costuming (Roger and Margaret Furse), photography (Robert Krasker), and film music (William Walton), plus the inestimable help of Italian producer Filippo Del Giudice.[23] Olivier did more than make the Shakespeare movie suitable for "the better classes" of people. He created a great film. Dudley Andrew writes almost sacerdotally of it as having joined "the fragile momentary inner life of every viewer to the continuity of cultural life in history . . . Seldom has cinema participated in a more massive ideological undertaking. Seldom has it seemed . . . more worthwhile."[24]

Hamlet (1948)

After the heady success of *Henry V*, producer Filippo Del Giudice of Two Cities Films gave Olivier a free rein and a budget of £475,000 to do *Hamlet*

(1948) as he wished. To dull the sharp edges of purists' tongues, Olivier let it be known that his film should be regarded "as an 'Essay in *Hamlet*,' and not as a film version of a necessarily abridged classic."[25] From the realistic/fantasy dichotomies of *Henry V* in Technicolor, he turned to a spartan black-and-white, the inspiration for the *mise-en-scène* no longer the Duke of Berri's colorful Calendar but instead Daniel MacLise's nineteenth-century black-and-white engraving of "The Play Scene in *Hamlet*." Olivier informed his staff that "to me Hamlet is an engraving, not an oil painting,"[26] though his biographer has suggested that the use of black-and-white stock grew more out of expediency than artistic goals when Technicolor film proved unavailable.[27] In any case, black-and-white enhances the deep-focus photography, and better suits the atmosphere of a dark and forbidding tragedy. His sets also remain sparse, abstract, and ultimately timeless. Except for the murals and frescoes of warriors, knights, priests, and saints from twelfth-century European and Byzantine works of art painted on the walls and alcoves, the bareness and emptiness – there is a nearly total lack of furniture – make the castle a metaphor for the protagonist's isolation and loneliness. The result is film noir for highbrows, with chiaroscuro effects reminiscent of Rembrandt's *The Night Watch,* as in the opening scene when Marcellus, Barnardo, and Horatio cluster together in unholy terror of the ghost.

Critics have engaged in quasi-theological disputes about whether the film is primarily "theatrical" or "filmic." Shifting from a movie about the "mirror of all Christian kings" to the tale of a prince who bears "the trappings and the suits of woe" inevitably meant a movement away from a centrifugal to a centripetal kind of space. Epic requires space; tragedy, intimacy. Just as *Henry V* was sweeping and open in response to the chorus' plea for "a muse of fire," *Hamlet* is introspective, at times almost claustrophobic, a constant reminder of Hamlet's observation to Rosencrantz and Guildenstern that "Denmark's a prison" (2.2.243). The empty, virtually unfurnished sets are in one sense theatrical but in another filmic in that their size and scope defy the spatial limitations of a proscenium stage. Certainly this is in many ways a stagy film, all forty of the sets but three having been filmed in the studio at Denham. The sole outdoor shot is apparently of Ophelia's drowning and is modeled on Sir John Millais' famous nineteenth-century painting. Bernice Kliman has observed, however, that "Olivier . . . created a hybrid form, not a filmed play, not precisely a film but a film-infused play."[28] In a later study, Dr. Kliman concluded that this *Hamlet* both "suggests and transcends" the stage as Olivier sought through film "to expand theater" and "[open] up space and [move] the audience without losing the theatrical essence of nonrealistic space."[29] Anthony Davies saw the production as

7   An example of Desmond Dickinson's deep-focus cinematography in *Hamlet* (UK 1948), as Hamlet (Laurence Olivier) observes Ophelia (Jean Simmons) framed in an arch of the castle at Elsinore.

ultimately one of filmic design: "the film is radiant with its essential cine-matic conception."[30] Olivier's art director, Carmen Dillon, anticipated this academic debate when she observed that the *Hamlet* sets at Alexander Korda's Denham studio "defy outright classification into [the] cinematic or theatrical." On the one hand, they are filmic in that they have been envisioned for photography not as stage sets, and on the other they are theatrical in that they neither support a roof nor have "any geographical relationship with one another."[31]

The film's credits appear against an establishing shot of the angry sea that besieges Elsinore, the very "sea of troubles" (3.1.58) from Hamlet's flagship "To be or not to be" soliloquy. Desmond Dickinson's cinematography remains a masterpiece of consistent texture, nearly always in control of the pictorial design. A rare discontinuity occurs when Hamlet, facing a foggy storm-tossed sea, begins his soliloquy from atop the battlements. In a tracking shot from behind, the camera seems literally to move inside his skull and show not only his actual brain but also, as N. L. Alkire has argued, subliminal representations of the masks of comedy and tragedy.[32] A reversal then shows the prince facing the camera in mid-shot and suddenly posed as if for a studio photograph with not a trace of foul weather in the clear skies behind him. Meantime his soliloquy is heard in voice-over.

Olivier liked to bracket his films, this time the framing device being the windswept battlements of Elsinore, where the movie begins and where it will end with four captains bearing Hamlet's body aloft. The castle's dizzy height at the apex imposes the spatial boundary for the multiple levels and planes of the sets as well as serving as the point of departure and arrival for the roving camera on a crane that peers everywhere into the huge sets. As a part of the establishing sequence, the camera begins at the turret and then obligingly guides the audience down the circular stone stairway, passes Ophelia's bedchamber with its window looking out at the sea, peeks into Claudius' "closet," pauses for a brief inspection of the chamber that contains the polluted "royal bed of Denmark," moves down into the king's great hall, and lingers on Hamlet's special armchair. For critics like Peter S. Donaldson, the staircase has subliminal Freudian overtones in echoing a harrowing incident on a stairwell in Olivier's school days.[33]

Olivier's movie is not just film-infused and play-infused but sex-infused. Elsinore holds no greater horror for Hamlet than the recurring icon of the king-sized "enseamed" bed where his mother slept with her own brother-in-law, the "bloat king" Claudius, in "rank sweat . . . / Stew'd in corruption, honeying and making love / Over the nasty sty" (3.4.93). Sexuality, or old-fashioned lust, one of the seven deadly sins, precipitates the "disasters in the sun" at Elsinore. The visual and the aural work against each other. Visually with the symbolic bed Olivier places Hamlet's horror of sexuality, of women, of penetration into the female body, at the core of the action. Aurally, the opening of the film signals quite a different intention with the recital in voice-over of Hamlet's musings on the "stamp of one defect" that may cause a man to "take corruption / From that particular fault" (1.4.31–38). When Olivier's voice then gratuitously announces that this is the tale "of a man who could not make up his mind," he invites assault by Peter Alexander, whose book interrogates this painfully reductive statement.[34] Ironically the movie is not about a man who couldn't make up his mind but about a man who couldn't relate to women, since the political aspect has been shut out by the banishment of Fortinbras. Hamlet's ruin stems from his

Oedipal complex and corollary total inadequacy for dealing with Ophelia. "Frailty, thy name is woman!" (1.2.146) he says, but ironically that very frailty carries a deadly capacity for destroying unwary males, as perhaps Olivier's own recent stage appearance as Oedipus had warned him. Prince Hamlet as misogynist is but one of the prince's multiple masks that include avenger, wit, actor, manager, director, philosopher, murderer, duelist, soldier, courtier, "glass of fashion," and almost every other imaginable human trait. Hamlet is to an amazing degree Everyman and Everywoman, as Asta Nielsen and Sarah Bernhardt so aptly demonstrated, yet in this movie a good deal of Fitzwilliam Darcy's misogyny lurks behind the Hamlet mask.

Of course everything about Hamlet is enigmatic, Mona-Lisa like, as T.S. Eliot said, and the camera's endless peering and probing implies a restless desire to pluck out the heart of the mystery. Like Orson Welles who famously used deep-focus photography in *Citizen Kane* (1941), Olivier employed an identical technique in *Hamlet*, though his immediate inspiration may well have been a pioneering BBC production of *Hamlet* (1947) transmitted from Alexandra Palace. Michael Barry claims that George More O'Ferrall's ambitious television drama (he cast some 70 persons) inspired the tracking shots in Olivier's movie.[35] And tracking shots there are. A labyrinth of hallways, stairways, chambers, inner chambers. Hamlet climbs up the stairway toward the ghost of his father, an analytical close-up showing only his feet. The father's ghost emerges from a mist. At "Alas, poor ghost!" (1.5.4), there's an interpolated flashback to the actual poisoning in the garden, though unlike in the Branagh *Hamlet* (1996) the perpetrator remains appropriately unidentified. In one interchange made possible by deep focus, Hamlet is seated in a chair and watches Ophelia approaching him through a long series of archways blocking his view of Polonius, who is hiding behind a pillar and in a position to warn Ophelia away. When she turns away from him, Hamlet mistakenly concludes that it is of Ophelia's own free will.[36] The castle is filled with balconies, stairwells, ledges, so that high and low angle shots can be employed for empowering and disempowering characters, as when Hamlet looms on a ledge above Polonius to lecture him on the sad state of old men's "most weak hams" (2.2.200), or when in long shot the entourage arriving for the play of the "Murther of Gonzago" grandly progresses down the sweeping staircase. Indeed the horizontal and vertical spatial arrangements unify the entire movie, as Anthony Davies has so effectively pointed out.[37] William Walton's music functions as an integral part of the film's emotional texture. For the players, a consort performs a period piece with violins, cello, oboe, cor anglais, bassoon, and harpsichord, which is immediately followed again by the full symphonic orchestra of some 50 players on the soundtrack. When "the King can stand it no longer, the full power of the big orchestra rises up . . . and [ends] in a tremendous 'crash chord' as the King roars, 'Give me some light. Away!'" (3.2.269).[38]

Deletions from Quarto and Folio eliminate Rosencrantz and Guildenstern and Fortinbras' world beyond Denmark, which makes the movie seem all the more centripetal and claustrophobic. "The Murther of Gonzago" has been combined with the preceding dumb show, and scenarist Alan Dent liberally transposed episodes to clarify the narrative, so that the "To be or not to be" soliloquy comes after rather than before Hamlet's quarrel with Ophelia. The acting is superb. In Gertrude's chamber, the mistaken slaughter of Polonius and the visibly erotic bond between son and mother grotesquely restate the primal love and death motif so pervasive in Elizabethan verse, but played on a different key from the thematic treatment in *Romeo and Juliet,* or in *Antony and Cleopatra.* On the heinous bed, a distraught Gertrude (Eileen Herlie) recoils from her ranting self-righteous son who threatens her with a wicked looking phallic knife. Felix Aylmer again shows his versatility, having been Duke Frederick in *As You Like It,* Canterbury in *Henry V,* and now a garrulous Polonius. Stanley Holloway, later famous as Eliza Doolittle's father in *My Fair Lady*, makes a superb gravedigger. Jean Simmons in her blonde wig looks too sweet and virginal to even think about copulating with Hamlet. Once again the specter of Fitzwilliam Darcy looms as Hamlet shows only coldness without a trace of tenderness for the poor, beleaguered young woman, who remains the ultimate female victim.

At the close of a sequence that actually took several days to film, after the wild duel between Hamlet and Laertes, after the fearful moment when Gertrude stares as if hypnotized at the poisoned cup, after Hamlet's famous fifteen-foot leap on Claudius, Hamlet stands bolt upright in a theatrical pose to deliver his last words, omitting any reference to the missing Fortinbras: "Horatio, I am dead, / Thou livest. Report me and my cause aright / To the unsatisfied" (5.2.338). The soldiers shoot and the framing device that began the movie repeats as if someone had hit the reverse button on a VCR. The camera pulls back from the great hall, takes us up the stairs, the four captains bearing Hamlet's body aloft, up and up, past the chapel where Claudius prayed, past the bed chamber of the king and queen where the camera briefly pauses, glances in at the "nasty sty," and then moves on until Hamlet's body has been borne to the castle's turret and the pallbearers with their burden are etched against the gloomy and melancholy sky. Olivier, like many others, has done his best with a camera to report Hamlet's "cause aright," though like the prince himself no stage production, no scholar, no critic will ever plumb the mystery of how best to tell that story "aright."

Richard III (1955)

With *Richard III* (1955), Olivier returned to the Technicolor that he had employed so effectively in *Henry V*, this time supplemented with a spectacular widescreen process known as VistaVision. In a pioneering film and television crossover, the movie was transmitted on North American television on the afternoon of March 11, 1956 by 146 NBC stations in 45 states on the same day that it was released in movie theatres. Estimates put the television audience at 25 million, though most saw it in black-and-white and a handful, perhaps 25,000, in color. Even if inflated, these statistics imply that more people saw a Shakespeare play on that winter afternoon than in all the previous centuries of Shakespeare performances combined. The producers pocketed a $500,000 fee to offset their multi-million investment but the experiment was never repeated because the television exposure ate drastically into later box office receipts.[39]

Olivier, the actor of a thousand faces, after portraying King Henry V, "the mirror of Christian princes," as a kind of Eagle Scout, yearned to play the villain. When plans for *Macbeth* disintegrated, he settled on the most outrageous usurper of all, Richard duke of Gloucester, the anti-Christ himself. Anthony Davies has also pointed out how *Henry V* and *Richard III* act as reverse mirrors by enacting first the culmination of medieval values, and then their collapse in emerging amoral capitalism. Hamlet, for whom "the time is out of joint," is caught indecisively between these two world views, the old emblemized by the father figure King Hamlet and the new by the corrupt stepfather Claudius.[40] In this sense, *Richard III* completes a master design.

This remarkable movie, which lacks the cinematic complexity of *Henry V* but deserves a separate trophy for sustained acting brilliance, won Olivier an Oscar nomination. Olivier assembled an outstanding cast to include such perennials in his retinue as text advisor Alan Dent, designer Roger Furse, art director Carmen Dillon, editor Helga Cranston, and actors Norman Wooland (Catesby), Esmond Knight (Ratcliffe), John Laurie (Lovel). New on board were notables like Sir John Gielgud (Clarence), Ralph Richardson (Buckingham), Claire Bloom (Lady Anne), and the femme fatale figure, Pamela Brown (Jane Shore). Returning also was composer William Walton, whose score provided stirring descriptive music as the little princes ride toward London, the reinforcing sound of a lute just as Richard in his opening monologue speaks of "the lascivious pleasing of a lute" (1.1.13), or the recurring themes that sonically characterize the despair of Lady Anne.

As a film maker and hostage to "tickling commodity," Olivier also again had the problem of making sense for an unschooled audience out of a segment from a longer saga. As is well known, *Richard III* is the last of the four plays of the "minor tetralogy" that depict the feuding baronial houses of York (the white rose) and Lancaster (the red rose) during the ugly fifteenth-century Wars of the Roses. Shakespeare's *Three Parts of Henry VI* ends with the Yorkist victory over the Lancastrians at the 1471 Battle of Tewkesbury, following which the Yorkist Richard duke of Gloucester allegedly murdered both the Lancastrian King Henry VI, the feeble-minded son of King Henry V, and his son, Edward Prince of Wales. When Shakespeare's *Richard III* begins, the Yorkist King Edward has already ascended the throne and his younger brother, the misshapen Richard duke of Gloucester – "Then since the heavens have shap'd my body so, / Let hell make crook'd my mind to answer it" (*3 Henry VI* 5.6.78) – is scheming to usurp his brother's crown. To make these machinations plain to the audience, Olivier, like Frederick B. Warde in the 1912 version and other directors, adapted Colley Cibber's eigh-teenth-century strategy of grafting lines from *Henry VI Part Three* onto *Richard III*. That way at once the most dastardly side of Richard's character emerges as he confides to the audience that he can "murther" while he smiles and set "the murtherous Machevil to school" (*3 Henry VI* 3.2.180, 193). Acting as his own chorus, Richard then revels in his plans for destroying all who stand between him and the crown, including his brother Clarence, as well as Hastings, Buckingham, his two little nephews, and so forth. They all parade before him in ghastly retribution during the nightmare in the tent on the eve of battle at Bosworth: "O coward conscience, how dost thou afflict me!" (*Richard III* 5.3.179).

The royal crown of England functions this time as Olivier's framing device, appearing in the beginning and then at key stages during the movie, when Richard is himself crowned as king of England and again when at Bosworth Field he has lost his horse and his army and the crown, which falls off his head, and rolls berserkly through the field. It is picked up from a bramble bush by Lord Stanley. In a great moment, supported by Walton's stirring music on the soundtrack, Stanley triumphantly bears the crown aloft as he ceremonially approaches Henry Tudor earl of Richmond, about to be King Henry VII. The expressionistic imaging of the crown as dreamlike obsession reifies Richard's soliloquy in *Henry VI Part Three* when he says "I'll make my heaven to dream upon the crown" (*3 Henry VI* 3.2.168). After the silent-screen cards explaining English history, the crown appears as a large coro-net suspended directly over the throne of Edward of York who is about to be ceremonially crowned king of England. Simultaneously with his older brother's coronation, Richard duke of Gloucester in black velvet with his back to the camera has a coronet emplaced on his head. He turns and stares at the camera as if ready to address the theatre audience (us) in an aside but then, as Dale Silviria points out, "the camera cuts to the full figure of Buckingham, then pans to Clarence, then on to a tight knot of figures – the Queen, the princes, the old Duchess of York, the Queen's relatives."[41] In one sweep the camera tracks Richard's future victims like so many skittles waiting to be bowled over.

As emblematic as the crown, iterative shadows providing visible evidence of Richard's poisonous miasma fall on the walls, on the floors, and even on the Lady Anne's white gown. It's as if the "glorious son" of York, Richard's brother Edward, must inevitably be eclipsed by this younger "sun/son" of York. A crucifix on the wall of Clarence's cell in the Tower, after he has been sequestered there partly through Richard's lies and insinuations, identifies Clarence (John Gielgud) as a sacrificial figure. There is no hint here of Clarence's prior treasonous activities, summed up in Shakespeare's text with the inculpatory words, "thou, perjur'd George" (3 *Henry VI* 5.5.34). Gielgud's mellifluous voice elevates Clarence to sainthood in contrast to his demonized younger brother, who blasphemously thirsts for the blood of his victims as an unholy sacrament for a black mass. After Hastings' execution, Richard snappily says "I will not dine until I see the same [Hastings' head]" (*Richard III* 3.4.77). At the end of the play the proto-angelic Richmond with rapt and holy prayer – "O Thou whose captain I account myself, / Look on my forces with a gracious eye" (5.3.108) – makes England safe again for the true decencies of the Holy Eucharist. Old Queen Margaret, the she-wolf of France, widow of Henry VI, has been banished from the movie, most unfortunately because she, Queen Elizabeth, and the Duchess of York constitute a doleful Senecan chorus for ritually excoriating Richard as "that bottled spider, that foul bunch-back'd toad!" (4.4.81). Among those not banished, however, is Jane Shore (Pamela Brown), the mistress of King Edward, a non-character merely alluded to in Shakespeare's play. Appropriately she remains beautiful, mysterious, ubiquitous but mute, and only appears silently framed in doorways or inscrutably smiling in the background, a classic object for the camera's "male gaze." After his coronation, King Edward, known as "lascivious Edward," speaks to her in public while his queen resolutely ignores her husband's wandering eye.

In Shakespeare's second longest play, and arguably the most sprawling, the character of Richard duke of Gloucester must hold center stage. Without his dynamism, the audience would soon be coughing, shuffling, and wriggling. Olivier plays the role brilliantly, almost as if he had abandoned Fitzwilliam Darcy in favor of a far darker incarnation. A cartoon figure, with his humped back, false oversized nose, beetle brows, lurching limp, and withered arm he resembles a Halloween or Guy Fawkes prankster. The pendent sleeves on his tunic make him look spidery, and his tone of voice hints of unimaginable malice. Olivier's impression seems to have come straight out of Edward Hall's *Union of the Two Noble Famelies of Lancastre and Yorke* (1548), which says of Richard, that

> he was litle of stature, eivill featured of limnes, croke backed, the left shulder muche higher than the righte, harde favoured of visage ... malicious, wrothfull and envious, and ... he came into the world the fete forwarde ... not untothed ... He was close and secrete, a depe dissimuler, ... outwardely familier where he inwardely hated ... despiteous and cruell ... he spared no mannes deathe whose life withstode his purpose. He slewe in the towre kynge Henry the sixte, saiynge now is there no heire male of kynge Edward the thirde, but wee of the house of Yorke.[42]

Vocally, Olivier's magical cadences and rhythms also capture the serio-comical villainy that allows Richard to say the vilest things with a touch of wit, and that in asides to the audience may make him seem downright like-able, scoundrel that he is. Except for the fringe "Friends of Richard III" society, who claim that his reputation was sullied by the House of Tudor official propagandists, Richard is invariably thought of not just as a deep-dyed villain, a Machiavellian, or even a vestige of the medieval Vice like Iago, but as the embodiment of that dread figure, the anti-Christ. In Shakespeare's time, the Protestant reformer, Bishop Jewel, warned that the "anti-Christ shall procure himself credit under the name of Christ" and that "the devil hath devised a new kind of policy, under the very name of Christ to deceive the simple ... Christ [we are warned] is the truth itself; anti-Christ is the truth counterfeit."[43] Olivier out-demonizes the demonizers of Richard III, like the anti-Christ capable of seeming genial, friendly, persuasive, in order to deceive the simple. Buckingham's spin-doctor advice to Richard could have come out of a handbook on the anti-Christ: "Look you get a prayer-book in your hand, / And stand between two churchmen" (3.7.46), who then before the assembled multitude will become "two props of virtue for a Christian prince" (3.7.96). In the first wooing scene, the way that he overwhelms the Lady Anne (Claire Bloom), widow of the man he has murdered, shows his fatal sexual attraction despite his twisted body. Some differences have arisen over whether this gifted villain qualifies as a modern tyrant, along the lines of Adolf Hitler,[44] or whether his engaging charm does not exempt him from this kind of calumny.[45] As the anti-Christ he embodies all these elements, tyrant and charmer, and other gifts for mischief as well. Richard has a dazzling way, like so many complex Shakespeare characters, of evading all the handy labels – Vice figure, Machiavellian, and in modern psycho-babble, a sociopath. Deeper more diabolical energies drive the twisted body and soul that Olivier portrays so stunningly.

8   Laurence Olivier's cartoon-like Richard duke of Gloucester in *King Richard III* (UK 1955), directed by Olivier, makes it impossible to forget that Shakespeare's villain is not only "serio" but "comic."

If the overall impression left by Olivier's *Henry V* is one of grandeur, and by *Hamlet* one of waste, this *Richard III* shocks the audience into seeing not so much the banality as the grandeur of evil. From the outset, the insolent Richard radiates more poison than Chernobyl, embodying the Marlovian overreacher and aspiring to the *Übermensch*. The editing further energizes Richard's swift judgments with segues and quick cuts such as when the beheading block for Buckingham jump cuts to a washerwoman with a sopping cloth; the way that Olivier's camera tracks the gliding movements of the mute but enigmatic Jane Shore; or the cut from the bright palace to the dark horror of Clarence's Tower cell. The parade of ghosts on the eve of Bosworth precedes the final act of retributive justice as Richard lies dying orgasmically on the battlefield, twitching and jerking like an impaled boar, ringed by spears. At the close the morality play message is there for every-one to see, "Crime does not pay," and yet, even knowing he is the anti-Christ, there is a sneaking admiration for the scoundrel, a subversive tug, a shameful desire to be a member of that old Miltonic circle called "the devil's party." Without Elizabeth Bennet, Fitzwilliam Darcy himself might have fallen to this low estate.

Othello (1965)

Olivier bid farewell to the Shakespeare movie, as distinguished from televi-sion, with his title role in Stuart Burge's recording of John Dexter's National Theatre production of *Othello* (1965). F. R. Leavis' famous anti-Bradleyian essay that toppled Othello from his lofty perch and painted him as filled with "an insane and self-deceiving passion" powerfully influenced the orig-inal stage production. Olivier's Othello rather than being a dupe to Iago was, in Dexter's words, "a pompous, word-spinning, arrogant, black general," while Olivier himself conceived of Iago (Frank Finlay) not as a "witty, Machiavellian" but rather as a "solid, honest-to-God NCO."[46] Despite this theoretical bias, Olivier's innate dignity transcends any attempts to make him look "word-spinning" and "arrogant" and Finlay's insinuating lower-class accent endows him with an animal cunning more sinister than Machiavellian intrigue. A recording of a stage play more than a full-scale movie, the hasty filming at Shepperton studios took less time than the bat-tle scenes for *Henry V* or *Richard III*, to the distress of director Burge.[47] Stagy it may have been but this *Othello* was still a masterpiece of its own kind – the record essentially of a great theatre experience that would otherwise have been forever lost. The term "theatrical" should be thought of as merely descriptive, not prescriptive, not in any way prima facie evidence of inferi-ority. The acting makes or breaks the experience.

True, *Othello* lacks outdoor scenes, pitched battles, massive sets, but it shows assorted filmic resources that set it apart from a stage production. Filmed with three Panavision cameras,[48] the various takes have been edited to allow for multiple reaction shots and analytical close-ups. For some scenes, as when Othello debarks at Cyprus (2.1), the *mise-en-scène* is so patently theatrical that, as someone once said, the actors might as well have been talking to an empty auditorium. Elsewhere the multiple cameras and edit-ing permit cutaways from one character to another that would be impossi-ble on stage. Frank Finlay's rugged "honest NCO" profile benefits the most, when, for example, he is foregrounded in profile observing Cassio (Derek Jacobi) and Desdemona (Maggie Smith) on the waterfront at Cyprus as they await Othello's arrival from Venice (2.1.103). A crane shot of Iago's demonic seduction of Othello as the dialogue peaks with Othello's Faustian "Now art thou my lieutenant," and Iago's fervid "I am your own for ever" (3.3.479) qualifies as the most "cinematic" shot in the film.

Olivier, the most versatile of actors, eagerly embraced the challenge of playing a black man, which even before the age of political correctness stirred up a tempest. He is said to even have lowered his voice an octave to qualify for the role. Bosley Crowther complained that Olivier looked "like Rastus or an end man in an American minstrel show";[49] Judith Crist, that Olivier played Othello as "a manic depressive skirting the edges of paranoia";[50] and Brendan Gill, that Olivier's reading of the title role was "utterly daft."[51] A more general condemnation of the production as being insufficiently "cinematic" came from Nathan Kallet: "[the] film is dragged by bloat" because the director "did not seek a cinematic equivalent to Shakespeare's play."[52] Only a unique performance could draw such scathing fire and Olivier's Othello achieves not just technical perfection but genuine passion. From his first appearance at the Venetian court, languidly sniffing a long-stemmed red rose and speaking in a low-pitched West Indian accent, Olivier's Moor radiates primal energy. He taps Iago on the chest with the rose as if to warn him that softer measures will be needed in the weeks to come. The same love of disguise that turned him into a menacing anti-Christ in *Richard III* serves to make him an imposing black warrior.

Wicked, evil, malicious Iago (Frank Finlay) always threatens to upstage Othello and without the formidable presence of Olivier, Frank Finlay may well have succeeded. He conjures up whole new reservoirs of malice and obscenity as he plays the voyeur, "He takes her by the palm; ay, well said, whisper . . . Yet again, your fingers to your lips? Would they were clyster-pipes for your sake!" (2.1.167 ff). Finlay's Iago is a sinister, leering, foul-minded, lower-class East London type, whose drive to control and manipulate is underscored by this camera work that consistently foregrounds him in profile to give the impression of the master puppeteer manipulating a creature ripe for exploitation. From all accounts, he came through more powerfully on camera than on stage in the National Theatre production.

Other cast members turn in equally striking performances. As Michael Cassio, Derek Jacobi, addled with drink by perfidious Iago, foreshadows his future brilliance in major screen and television Shakespeare productions. As Desdemona, Maggie Smith radiates a clear-eyed decency and innocence rooted in an innate strength and dignity worthy of the daughter of Brabantio, a pillar of the Venetian establishment. Her white skin against the coal-black flesh of Olivier points to the play's pervasive subtext of miscegenation. Burge's *Othello* then remains an actor-centered rather than a director-centered production, primarily preserving a record of a first-rate stage performance. A major share of Shakespeare's text remains. With more time to rehearse and a larger budget, Stuart Burge might have made his recorded stage play into a great movie as well. The world would be richer now if, for example, someone had recorded the *Othello* (1959) starring Paul Robeson as Othello with Sam Wanamaker as his Iago.

The Merchant of Venice (1969) and *King Lear* (1983): TV Appearances

Olivier's entry into Shakespeare on television began as early as 1937 when he acted with Judith Anderson in a 30-minute BBC excerpt from the Old Vic *Macbeth*.[53] Many years later, he appeared in two wonderfully skillful tele- vised Shakespeare plays as first Shylock and then in his old age, appropri- ately, as King Lear. In Jonathan Miller's and John Sichel's Precision Video adaptation of the National Theatre Edwardian dress production of *The Merchant of Venice* (1969), he re-invented Shylock with the help of director Jonathan Miller as a Baron Rothschild figure,[54] elegantly turned out in a frock coat, with only a skullcap to identify him as an outsider. The Edwardian milieu is urbane, polished, Miller having even thought of Bassanio and Antonio as mirroring the love between Oscar Wilde and his Bosie. The sleek and well coifed youthful friends of Antonio and Bassanio indolently lounge in waterside cafés. Their infuriating insouciance and glossy façades subvert their own self-images by exposing an intrinsic shallowness of spirit. If the Belmont crowd had lived in Nazi Germany they "would not have known about Hitler's concentration camps," nor would they have cared to know. Although the usual cries of "anti-Semitism" swirled around the show,[55] Miller presented a sympathetic Shylock, more victim than villain.

As a supremely self-confident Portia, Joan Plowright, comfortably tucked away in suburban Belmont with Nerissa (Anna Carteret), gets the first glimpse of her suitors by means of a period-piece stereo-opticon. In an aston- ishing *tour de force*, a perfect Miller touch, two spinsterish looking ladies (Clare Walmesley and Laura Sarti) suddenly appear on screen and erupt into the wildest but most compelling rendition in history of "Tell me where is fancy bred [?]" (3.2.63). The singing sardonically reflects on the patriarchal tyranny that has enmeshed Portia in the absurd casket scheme. Their obvi- ous prompting of Bassanio toward the lead casket, however, somewhat justifies June Schlueter's objection to the "trivializing" of the casket plot into a "sideshow."[56] After the harsh disposal of Shylock in the trial scene and after the sadistic teasing about the lost rings of Bassanio and Gratiano by

Portia and Nerissa, Jessica, Shylock's ingrate of a daughter, is left standing alone, while the Jewish requiem, the "Kaddish" (sung by Heinz Danziger), reverberates on the soundtrack. In Miller's hands and with Laurence Olivier's miraculous contributions, *The Merchant of Venice* surely becomes the woefullest but most complicated comedy ever written.

When nearly twenty years later, Olivier agreed to play the title role in *King Lear* (1983), he was not in good health and at 75 nearly a match for the age of Shakespeare's irascible old king, whom he had played on stage at the Old Vic with Alec Guinness as Fool in 1946. Taped in three weeks at the Manchester TV Centre studios on a set with a polystyrene mock-up of Salisbury Plain's mysterious Stonehenge, the $2-million Granada TV production featured an Olivier not only playing King Lear but also his aged self, a real life embodiment of Shakespeare's geriatric hero. To spare Olivier from excessive strain and to save time, the original idea of a taped stage play was jettisoned in favor of television.[57] Director Michael Elliott could the more easily then edit the action from an elevated central vantage point.

As television host Peter Ustinov said with little hyperbole, it "featured the best Shakespearean cast ever assembled." Not exactly "stunt casting," as Kenneth Branagh's Shakespeare movies have been uncharitably charged with, the director did recruit prominent BBC and RSC regulars, though no Hollywood superstars: Leo McKern (Gloucester), Dorothy Tutin (Goneril), Diana Rigg (Regan), Anna Calder-Marshall (Cordelia), Jeremy Kemp (Cornwall), Colin Blakely (Kent), and John Hurt (Fool). As is often true of televised Shakespeare (see chapter 5), the performance is actor-centered, but Elliott encoded visual signposts expressive of the spiritual turmoil in this epic clash between a father and his three daughters. Stonehenge itself, mysterious druid relic from Britain's ancient times, frames the teleplay. At the beginning to the sound of primitive horns, Lear enters with Cordelia, laughing and chatting and agreeably at ease with himself and his daughters. The decision to tape in color instead of in black-and-white, as is usually the case with screen versions of *King Lear*, makes the sequence almost lighthearted, until the king's initial outburst of choleric rage when Cordelia snubs him. Olivier's prodigious acting skills remain intact, as shown, for example, in the uncanny gift for rolling vowels, and in the body language with his hands when reacting to Cordelia's blunt "Nothing, my lord" (1.1.87).[58] The approach to the play favors the old king over his daughters as the wronged one, disprivileging any post-modernist victimization scenarios of patriarchal oppression. In the last frames, the return to Stonehenge allows Lear and Cordelia to be seen as sacrificial victims stretched out on the temple's slaughtering stone.

A gigantic, rug-sized map, unfolded before Lear to calibrate the division of the kingdom, then becomes the site of the hypocritical obeisance of Regan and Goneril and the arena for the king's petulance when he hurls the crown away. To counterpoint the harshness of stone, the greenery of an oak tree[59] suggests harmony and reconciliation when the chastened old king meets with the blinded Gloucester. The king returns to the basics of nature with his crown of wild flowers and in one very potent episode consumes a freshly slaughtered rabbit, raw and uncooked. With these talismans, he renews his pact with himself in the loneliness of the heath, where in the exposure of his pathetically withered, aged body, he embodies the loathsome appearance of a Swiftian Struldbrug. Except in the notorious Tate eighteenth-century version, the play brooks no happy ending, yet in the last moments when Olivier appears in full color, close-shaven, pink-cheeked, cherubic, robed in white, in his new cleanliness ready to be reborn, he takes the Lear figure close to heavenly enthronement. This is anthropology's sacrificial king, about to be slaughtered that the crops may be renewed, with Anna Calder-Marshall's ethereal Cordelia thrown in for good measure. "Is this the promis'd end?" (5.3.264) asks Kent as the old king dies. A wrenching denouement for Shakespeare's king, no doubt, but for Olivier a noble and dignified exit from the theatre for the man of a thousand faces. The pleasure he has brought to millions might even make Fitzwilliam Darcy smile. Certainly some critics smiled. On a 1998 British Film Institute list of 360 film classics released prior to 1981, only two Shakespeare movies were included and these were both directed by Olivier – *Henry V* and *Richard III*.[60]

- 4 -
Orson Welles: Shakespeare for
the art houses

One of Orson Welles's many, many biographers recently argued that after the legendary film maker's first and greatest success, *Citizen Kane* (1941), "the remaining forty-five years of Welles's life are a sort of sustained falling apart . . . he came increasingly . . . [to be] the legend of the self-destroyed artist."[1] That period when he was "falling apart," however, ironically marks the years when Welles produced the three Shakespeare movies, *Macbeth* (1948), *Othello* (1952), and *Chimes at Midnight* (1966), that showed an admirable resolve not to fall apart. Not that Welles should be beatified as a kind of plaster saint who at all costs put art above "tickling commodity," but his Shakespeare movies were by box office guidelines demonstrably "uncommodified." Scholars and journalists have struggled without great success to pluck out the heart of Orson Welles's mystery.[2] As James Russell Lowell said in *A Fable for Critics* (1848) of another American genius, Edgar Allan Poe, Welles too was perhaps "three-fifths . . . genius and two-fifths sheer fudge." If Laurence Olivier's work is Apollonian, reasonable, comfortably mainstream, and commodified, Welles's is Dionysian and passionate, rough-hewn and unpredictable, and uncommodified. Put reductively, Olivier's work remains theatrical and English; Welles's, cinematic and American.

Orson Welles loved magic. There is a photograph of him on the set of *The Magnificent Ambersons* (1942) gleefully pulling a rabbit out of a hat to the amazement of Joseph Cotten and Dolores Costello;[3] an unfinished movie, *The Magic Show* (1969–85) in which "some of his best acts of prestidigitation [were] done without camera tricks";[4] Suzanne Cloutier's casual remark about how on the *Othello* set in Morocco "he created a magical world for us;"[5] Keith Baxter's saying "Orson was a conjuror, you know," as he described the trick shots for Prince Hal in *Chimes at Midnight*;[6] and Gregg Toland's influence in teaching Welles about wide angle lenses for his trademark deep focus shots.[7] The fascination with magic also extended beyond theatrics into his whole world view. As a child prodigy, he apparently enjoyed playing tricks, in pulling the wool over people's eyes, so to speak.

One of his last films, *F for Fake* (1973), revels in the charms of the art forger, Elmyr de Hory, who could dash off a passable Matisse quicker than Matisse himself. De Hory exemplified to Welles the aphorism attributed to Picasso that "Art is a lie that makes us realize the truth."[8] With Orson Welles blandly announcing that he is himself a "charlatan," the riddle becomes one of figuring out whether Welles really is a charlatan, or is only pretending to be a charlatan. The bewildering search for reality disintegrates into shards like the multiple mirror scene in Welles's *The Lady from Shanghai* (1946). In the ultimate provocation, Welles hints that "profound" symbols, such as the enigmatic "Rosebud" in *Citizen Kane*, may have absolutely no meaning at all. It stands only for a child's sled, like Freud's cigar that only stands for a cigar. The mystery in the movie, or in its ironical director, may be that there is no mystery.

Orson Welles's troubles in Hollywood began when he arrived under contract to RKO at age twenty-three, already heralded as a "boy wonder," and thus inevitably bringing down on his head the wrath of everyone older and less successful than he was. Years later Welles said that all he knew about movies had been learned from viewing John Ford's *Stagecoach* forty-five times and from his cameraman, Gregg Toland, who offered to teach Welles everything about movie making in three hours. Welles was quick to add, however, that "Everything else is if you're any good or not."[9] And as a film maker he was not just "good," he was superb. Whiffs of this youthful condescension toward movie making wafting out into the California sunshine may very well have enraged the unfriendly local cinéastes. His reputation rested on the WPA *Macbeth* (1936) and Mercury Theatre *Julius Caesar* (1937) stage productions in New York, his CBS radio role as the sepulchral voice in "The Shadow" series, and the sensational hoax radio show based on H. G. Wells's "War of the Worlds" (1939) that sent thousands of panicked New Jersey citizens screaming into the streets. Soon, though, after an aborted fling at making Joseph Conrad's *Heart of Darkness*, Welles produced with Herman J. Mankiewicz and John Houseman *Citizen Kane* (1941), which may be America's greatest film but it earned the youthful *auteur* a powerful foe in the William Randolph Hearst publishing empire. After the controversial *Citizen Kane* and production turmoil with *The Magnificent Ambersons* (1942), his situation in Hollywood was precarious. In a *felix culpa*, though, his inability "to eat lunch in that town again," was what eventually made the Shakespeare movies possible.

Macbeth (1948)

Orson Welles's *Macbeth* could have been the first feature-length talking picture of Shakespeare's Scottish play had it not been for David Bradley who, with some help from Charlton Heston, made the first feature-length talkie *Macbeth* at Northwestern University in 1947 on a budget of $5,000.[10] With even a low B-movie budget from Republic Pictures, Welles tapped resources far beyond those available to Bradley and his undergraduate crew. Still, the movie sometimes functions at the amateurish level of provincial theatre, which is where it began when Welles directed the play for the Utah Centennial Festival.[11] The costumes seem tacky, especially the series of ridiculous headgears worn by Macbeth, the first resembling a "beanie"; the second, the crown on the Statue of Liberty; and the third, an inverted kitchen stool. Welles himself complained about the Statue of Liberty crown and explained that it was because the Western Costume company had nothing else to offer. He insulated himself against future critics by describing the hastily made film – the shooting schedule was twenty-three days – as a "violently sketched charcoal drawing of a great play."[12] The hasty filming had been preceded, though, with rehearsals in Utah, four days of performances in May 1947, and Welles's earlier experience at age twenty as director of the famous "Voodoo" *Macbeth* (1936) with an all-black cast at Harlem's Lafayette Theatre. His interest in Shakespeare went back into childhood and continued with an adolescent portrayal of Richard III at the progressive Todd School.[13]

His *Macbeth* then explores the tortured soul of the protagonist through the Wellesian world of skewed camera angles and brilliant découpage. The movie's reception has been almost as fragmented as the film, ranging from Bosley Crowther's denigration of the characters as "half-mad zealots in a Black Mass"[14] to Jean Cocteau's admiring comment that "not a single shot is left to chance."[15] With his hypnotic voice and overwhelming presence, Welles almost literally drowns out all the other characters, his Lady Macbeth, Jeanette Nolan, a competent radio actress, being so upstaged as to be virtually non-existent. The bombast leaves very little room for embodying the nuances and subtleties of a character so complex as Macbeth, who is both gangster and poet. Welles's Macbeth fears evil but he roars about it more than he contemplates it. The great speech in which he ruminates about the murder of Duncan, "If it were done, when 'tis done, then 'twere well / It were done quickly" (1.7.1), sounds more declamatory than meditative.

The scenario includes inspired additions, deletions, and transpositions of all sorts and varieties. With the help of a dialogue overlap, Macbeth is dictating the first part of the letter to Lady Macbeth, who then suddenly is seen at the castle reading the last half aloud (1.5.1); some kind of high priest looking like a character out of *Alexander Nevsky* stands in as a surrogate for Rosse; a Voodoo doll with Macbeth's head sprinkles in pagan elements that are at war with the Christian symbolism so pervasive everywhere else; the Porter

9   Orson Welles as Macbeth and Jeanette Nolan as his Lady filmed in one of
Welles's characteristically bizarre camera angles that suggests the growing schism
between the ambitious couple. *Macbeth* (USA 1948).

loses virtually all of his comic shtick except "Knock, knock, knock!" (2.3.3);
Macbeth shows up first-hand for the murder of Lady MacDuff; and
Lady Macbeth speaks some of Rosse's lines, and so forth.[16] A remnant
from the "Voodoo" stage *Macbeth* lingers on in the execution of Cawdor,
who is lugged around like a sack of flour, until to the eerie thudding of
Haitian tom-toms a giant axe descends on his neck. In the psychomachia
between cinéastes and bardolaters, Welles had no trouble choosing sides.
Shakespeare's play was there to be made into a movie, not the other way
around.

The director's inability to merge his considerable talents for both radio and
film remained a problem. He loved images but he seemed at times to love

voice more, especially his own. Actually in *Macbeth* he was experimenting with the favoring of sound over sight in a style that would be perfected by the time he directed *Othello*. That is to say, in films like Olivier's *Henry V*, William Walton's music supports the cavalry charge at Agincourt, while in Welles's *Macbeth* the execution of Cawdor supports the hypnotic drumbeat of tom-toms. Curiously this reversal of sight/sound for sound/sight replicates Thomas Edison's original goal, which was to develop pictures to support his phonograph, not the other way around.

Even inhibited by the speed of production, Welles's genius peeks through the makeshift papier-mâché sets and the diminutive budget. One of the reasons that the movie, like Welles himself, oscillates between the sublime and the ridiculous lies in the complicated maneuvers in both the pre- and post-production phases. To economize and to show Hollywood how movies "of this importance [could] be made on such a schedule and such a budget,"[17] Welles had the actors pre-record their lines in a Scots burr to slow down their rapid speech and to approximate the sound of Elizabethan actors at the Globe. During the actual shooting of the film, the actors on the set in Hollywood mimed their lines in synch with the speeches that had been pre-recorded in Utah.[18] After the initial release, however, the unhappy producers disliked the soundtrack enough, particularly the Scots burr, to withdraw the print and ask for pruning and relooping (re-recording). They became highly exercised when Welles went abroad, leaving the brunt of the editing to his assistant, Richard Wilson. To the Republic executives, the situation threatened a replay of an earlier fiasco when Welles was filming in South America during the editing phase of *The Magnificent Ambersons*, and RKO's Robert Wise added an unauthorized upbeat ending. The 1950 re-release of *Macbeth* engendered more problems when the original Scots burrs got totally confused with the new unaccented and often unsynched voices. A third restoration in 1979 by the UCLA film archives and Folger Library brought the movie back close to its original form. The Scots burr comes across loud and clear when Macbeth says things like "my soul is too much charrrrged" (5.8.5).

In shot after shot, Welles's radio background results in disembodied dialogue that never really gets into synch with the actors' bodies. The pre-recording created a disjunction between words and images, so that the actors may be speaking off camera, or at times their lips are simply out of synch, or again the words come through in voice-over while lips remain sealed. Jeanette Nolan gives a curiously epicene performance even with "Come, you spirits / That tend on mortal thoughts, unsex me here" (1.5.40),[19] in which the words come mostly in voice-over while she lies first inertly on a bed and then stares out the window at the clouds. She seizes on none of the obvious cues (i.e., "Come to my woman's breasts, / And take my milk for gall" (1.5.47)) for energizing her speech with a writhing body as Jane Lapotaire does so spectacularly in an otherwise pedestrian BBC television version (1983). Similarly with Macbeth's "Out, out, brief candle! / Life's but a walking shadow, a poor player" (5.5.23) there is no Macbeth, only a screen full of ominous clouds. Now and again Welles's dialogue overlaps, which makes one speech slur into another and creates more confusion than artistry. Symbolism oscillates between Christian and pagan with glimpses of a kilt or the skirl of a bagpipe pasted on a weird, Druid background.[20]

On the other hand, the images on screen, while often divorced from the dialogue, show how Welles benefited from his tutoring by cameraman Gregg Toland on *Citizen Kane*. The stylization, surreal effects, and chiaroscuro lighting of German expressionism, along with debts to compositional strategies in Eisenstein's *Alexander Nevsky*, may also have contributed to Welles's filmic grammar. Many low-angle and deep-focus shots resemble the "bravura" effects in *Citizen Kane*. A conversation between Macbeth and Lady Macbeth with the king ensconced high on a throne and Lady Macbeth yards away quotes a blocking of Charles Kane and Susan Alexander in the great hall at Xanadu. The wide-angle lens by distorting the connection between the man and woman underscores their spiritual isolation. Macbeth like Kane is often photographed from a low angle to give him the image of overpowering authority. Instead of the oppressive low ceilings of the *Kane* film, the theatrically inspired sets are vast units that allow the camera to remain stationary while recording the action in the spacious papier-mâché halls, left over from a Republic picture B western. When Lady Macbeth leaps off a precipice, there is a $53.36 special effect[21] in which she falls endlessly, her twisting body gradually receding from view as she hurtles into a bottomless gorge. The banquet scene allows for another deep-focus shot as Banquo's ghost, seen only by a terrified Macbeth, emerges and disappears and re-emerges at the end of an elongated dining table.

His strong theatrical background gave Welles a special interest in lighting effects, especially in the blacking out of one part of the set to shift audience attention to another part of the stage. To the consternation of the studio crew, he tried to take over the lighting on the *Citizen Kane* set from his veteran camera man. The Megahey television interview shows how the lighting for his staged *Julius Caesar* influenced the filmed *Macbeth*. In its expressionistic style, *Macbeth* echoes Robert Wiene's *The Cabinet of Dr. Caligari* (1919) for like other geniuses, William Shakespeare for instance, Welles was fully capable of making inventive use of the work of others. Despite the hostility of many critics, the sheer nerve and energy of the movie in probing for the devil-driven horror at the soul of its tragic hero makes it impossible to ignore.

Welles biographer Joseph McBride completely reversed his negative attitude toward the 1950 release when he saw the 1980 restored version and declared it to be an event of "hypnotic intensity."[22] Like the probing camera that slips past the No Trespassing sign at the opening of *Citizen Kane*, Welles persisted in his epic quest to lift any veil that obscured the truth about others and even about himself.

Othello (1952)

With *Othello*, Welles invented the MTV style decades before it was invented. He abandoned the *mise-en-scène* doctrines that he had learned from Gregg Toland in favor of the opposite school of Sergei Eisenstein's bias toward *découpage*. That is to say, in place of the long take (the classic in the Wellesian *oeuvre* being the kitchen scene between Tim Holt's George and Agnes Moorhead's Aunt Fanny in *Ambersons*), he turned toward montage, which involves the juxtaposition of short scenes. Toland thought that the wide angle lens could permit viewers to select for themselves what to observe on the screen and thus put motion pictures a step closer to reality itself. Instead Welles assembled bits and pieces from Shakespeare's most domestic tragedy, brought together fragments from all corners of the play, reworked them into a mosaic and then shattered them as a talisman to Othello's chaotic search for beauty and love. He played a variation on the jigsaw puzzle trope that he obsessively repeated in *Kane*, and magically in *Othello* it coalesced into a film worthy of a *Palme d'Or*.

The movie of *Othello* opened to a hostile reception. A headline for a London newspaper review sets the tone: "Mr. Welles Murders Shakespeare in the Dark," and the reviewer went on waspishly to note of Welles that "the playwright who has him for a friend does not need any enemies."[23] Another British critic further lambasted the film "made by that big prankish schoolboy Orson Welles" and pontificated that out of this "Wellesian fun fair of angelic, disembodied voices, dizzy camera angles, and shadowy sepulchral scenery [there might be] some small unexpected suggestion which may, one day, help a real director to make *Othello* into a worthy film."[24] Critics back home were no friendlier. Robert Hatch in *Nation* sarcastically observed that "Orson Welles has proved by now that he is too good for Shakespeare; I wish he would start reviving Dion Boucicault."[25] The commentator for *Time* did finally admit, though, after sneering at Welles for several paragraphs, that the work "moves forward with a pulse-quickening stir and bustle."[26] The ultimate insult came with the movie's 1955 release in the United States when box-office receipts amounted to a pathetic $40,000.

With the 1992 re-release, however, a sea change occurred. Some critics saw genius where previously there had only been fudge. After four decades in exile, the film was elevated to "the class of *Citizen Kane*,"[27] and became "a windblown, turbulent, bravura movie."[28] Of course the movie hadn't changed, the times had, though some critics protested that the 1992 release damaged the original soundtrack by electronically altering dialogue so that the film's "restoration" became "a shameful travesty of film history."[29] As Samuel Crowl has suggested, European post-structuralist literary theory paved the way for tolerating narrative discontinuities unfathomable to the rigid mindset of the Fifties.[30] Although not a strident ideologue, Welles was enough of a man of the left to know the penalties for non-conformity in the Eisenhower years when McCarthyism, or Hooverism, turned the American dream into a nightmare for dissident intellectuals. The expectations that made Olivier's *Henry V* acceptable to the critics at mid-century suddenly shifted into the taste for fragmentation that makes Welles's rough-hewn *Othello* the poster child for the chaotic Nineties. In 1952 no one had heard of Roland Barthes' *S/Z* with its painstaking and often tedious explication of the *lexia* or segments that make up a completed narrative.[31] The isolation and decoding of segments in a narrative become an exercise involving the paradox of the hermeneutical circle – the whole cannot be understood without understanding the part, nor the part without understanding the whole.[32] Welles's *Othello* is an exercise in hermeneutics in the way that it takes segments of *Othello* and reconstitutes them spatially to throw fresh light on the machinations of Iago. The segments, like Susan Alexander's jigsaw puzzle in *Citizen Kane,* must be reassembled in the mind of the viewer, preferably with the technical help of a laser disk recording and a Pioneer disk player.

It took Welles three weeks to film *Macbeth*, nearly three years to complete *Othello*. Micheál MacLiammóir's amusing and informative journal[33] chronicles the serio-comic disasters that have made the film's production woes the stuff of folk tales. In June 1949 Welles found himself stranded in Morocco on the Atlantic coast at Mogador, with neither money nor costumes when his Italian backers declared bankruptcy. In the next two years, one financial crisis after another interrupted filming. Actors were "stranded" in remote places and whole scenes had to be re-shot in entirely different locations when the original cast members disappeared. Welles denied that the actors were "marooned" but were left in luxury hotels at Welles's own expense while he undertook an heroic search for money to keep the show alive. He acted in other people's films, playing Harry Lime in *The Third Man* (1949), General Bayan in *The Black Rose* (1950), and himself in *Return to Glennascaul* (1951), borrowed money, ran up huge bills. There were brilliant expedients. When shooting began in French Morocco with no costumes on hand, he hit on staging the murder of Roderigo in a Turkish bath so that bath towels would suffice as costumes. Since actors were forced to abandon the unfinished project to find other work, the move toward montage and away from *mise-en-scène* stemmed not only from artistic design but from the need to cover up defects brought on by the many breaks in the production schedule. Actors who appeared to be in the same scene had actually been photographed in different times and places, perhaps not in Morocco but in Italy, or vice versa. Miraculously, a film eventually emerged from this nerve-wracking ordeal.

Whatever outsiders thought, people who worked with him swore eternal allegiance to Welles. Suzanne Cloutier (Desdemona) testified to the director's enormous powers of invention. "He created all the time," she said, and he left the cast and crew constantly wondering what novel idea he would come up with next. Camera man Obadan Troiano said of Welles's photographic sensibility that "his shots had a language of their own," and facetiously added that working with Welles had "ruined" his career, for ever afterwards if directors "didn't live up to Welles, I couldn't work for them." Composer Francesco Lavagnino was impressed by Welles's musical abilities. He and Welles together conceived of evoking a middle-eastern sound with the mandolin and percussion effects that replaced the original idea for themes from Verdi's *Otello*. Welles liked Lavagnino's work so much that, in an extraordinary reversal of normal expectations, he persuaded him not to cut down on his music but to compose an additional three minutes. Welles then set about to shoot extra footage to go with the music, in yet another demonstration of how his background in radio could make him regard sound as equal to sight. Lavagnino trenchantly said of Welles that "he invented you."[34] Just, one might add, as Welles often invented himself.

According to Welles's own account, the movie's design stemmed from Iago's delight in schemes of entrapment: "With as little a web as this will I ensnare as great a fly as Cassio" (2.1.168), or "And out of her own goodness make the net / That shall enmesh them all" (2.3.361). The resulting foray into entrapment and fear carries the movie into the realm of film noir, the Hollywood B movies that reflected the dark, paranoid side of America obscured by the genial fatuousness of the Eisenhower years. Welles's own film noir masterpiece was *A Touch of Evil* (1958) starring Charlton Heston as a Mexican attorney and Welles as the corrupt and gross police chief with a cameo appearance by *femme fatale* Marlene Dietrich. As Robert Sklar has said, "the hallmark of the film noir is its sense of people trapped . . . trapped in webs of paranoia and fear,"[35] a formula made to order for *Othello*, where there is ample "magic in the web" (3.4.69).

In post-modernist rejection of seamless narrative, *Othello* begins where it should end, with the funeral procession for Othello and Desdemona. In the opening shot, Othello is already not only dead but also upside down as if to stress the unnatural reversal of the moral order in the life of Venice. The funeral procession is cliché Eisenstein, its shadowy black figures silhouetted against the stark unrelieved whiteness of the sky over the roaring sea, with a dirge-like wailing and chanting on the soundtrack. The cortège winds its way along the ramparts of the eighteenth-century Mogador fortress. There are glimpses of the biers of Othello and of Desdemona sometimes seen through the long pikes and spears of armored soldiers, other times in long shot. Then suddenly viewed from a crane shot, there is a wretched man, a rope around his neck, being dragged through the crowd toward a cruel and savage looking cage. He is roughly thrust into it and by the means of a creaking iron wheel and pulley the cage is hoisted skyward to dangle in front of the high stone wall. Framed by the bars of the cage is the bleak, enigmatic face of the arch villain, Iago himself. "I am not what I am," he has said (1.1.65), but now he will have "daws to peck at" him, while his lips remain forever sealed: "Demand me nothing; what you know, you know: / From this time forth I never will speak word" (5.2.303). He stares down at the human wreckage caused by his malice.

Since Welles disliked, or pretended to dislike, ponderous theories, Iago is the ideal Wellesian villain. There is really nothing for him to explain about himself, or others to explain about him. He is simply motivated by pure evil, "unmotivated malignancy," nothing more, or so it is generally believed except by those who take seriously his whining about being passed over for promotion, or his lust for Desdemona. A born actor with a truly magnificent voice, who began listening to Shakespeare read aloud at age three or four, Welles thought formal acting lessons superfluous. Still, Welles apparently allowed Stanislavsky a foot in the door by toying with the idea of Iago being driven by his impotence, as somehow hinted in his remark that Cassio "hath a daily beauty in his life / That makes me ugly" (5.1.19). The skewed camera angles showing people and settings in Venice and Cyprus from every conceivable perspective aid and abet in imagining a dysfunctional world tailored for a sociopath like Iago.

Iago's cage then becomes the *locus classicus* for the rest of the movie. The iron bars that signify entrapment surface everywhere. Othello as he listens to Iago stands under the crisscross of a lattice; Othello overhears Cassio's apparent bantering with Iago about Desdemona from a concealed niche; Desdemona's bedroom contains a leaded glass window through which she is seen as virtually penned in; the sewer in Mogador that serves so usefully for corridors and as a bathhouse is full of cul-de-sacs, arches, corridors, barriers that evoke fantasies of dungeons and torment. When Roderigo is slain by Iago he is entrapped under a barrier of duckboards through which Iago's sword flashes mercilessly. At the very end of the movie, after Othello has smothered Desdemona, he himself stands alone, piteously forlorn, imprisoned behind the bars of an enormous iron door that soars to a lofty ceiling. Like Mister Kurtz in Conrad's *The Heart of Darkness,* which Welles once spent considerable time planning to film, Othello has discovered his own horror. The iron bars imprison him in a private hell exiled from Venice's comfortable bourgeois society. Respectable citizens peer down on him through an open dome as if he were an ape in a cage. As he portrays Othello's remorse and spiritual agony, "Then must you speak / Of one that lov'd not wisely but too well" (5.2.343), Welles does not merely rely on the God-given gift of his hypnotic voice but reaches deep down within himself for the tragic emotion to arouse pity and fear for Othello's unbearable suffering. Iago's net has finally ensnared not only Iago but everyone else as well.

The integration of sight, sound, and music in a baroque scheme of complicated point and counterpoint makes Welles's *Othello* a work of art. No single component stands in isolation from any other but every event on screen counts. The Venetian artist, Vittore Carpaccio (c.1465–1523), inspired Alexandre Trauner's artistic design for the film. The little white dog that follows Iago around derives from Carpaccio's painting of St. Jerome in his study, but the mirror that Othello examines himself in, attributed by Welles to Carpaccio, has not been so easily traced.[36] The setting remains stark and bare rather than crammed with objets d'art as in a Zeffirelli film, an important exception being Desdemona's jumbo-sized bed. When Michael Cassio (Michael Lawrence) reels around during the drinking bout with Iago, walls and crude benches seem to be the only physical details apparent in the kaleidoscopic blur of editing.

Welles's editing at the movieola finally defines the production's value. He immensely enjoyed film editing as shown in his *F for Fake* and again in the television documentary, *Filming Othello* (1978), where he sits at a movieola as he reminisces about *Othello* and how much better it would have been if he could have made it again. Welles matches sound with sight in ingeniously complicated ways as when we see Othello smothering Desdemona with the white handkerchief that then turns into a death mask starkly outlining her features. There is a sighing on the soundtrack, a gong, a beeper, the thud of heartbeats, and then a chilling silence, as Othello says "Cold, cold, my girl?" (5.2.275). Off camera he begins "Blow me about in winds! Roast me in sulphur!" (5.2.279) almost simultaneously with Emilia's transposed "My lord, my lord! / What ho! my lord, my lord!" (5.2.84), accompanied by more pounding and wailing.

Despite Welles's refusal to commodify his work, to make a Faustian bargain by putting commerce above art, *Othello* weathered incredible difficulties. A major difference between it and *Macbeth* is that Welles preserved artistic control of the editing until the film's release date, not wanting to repeat the post-production fiascos with *Macbeth*. After the modest but assured financial underwriting by Republic Pictures for *Macbeth*, he never again had the support of major backers with bundles of cash as Olivier did with producers Filippo Del Giudice and Alexander Korda. In Hollywood he had been virtually blacklisted as an unreliable genius. Yet *Othello,* after receiving a hostile reception, and languishing for decades in the archives of the Library of Congress, phoenix-like, emerged in a controversial resurrection in 1992, which had the effect of renewing interest in his earlier work. Like other great artists, Welles suffered the fate of having his masterworks appreciated only after his death. The suffering, however, contained its own seeds of inspiration for by 1966 he was ready to give his greatest performance as another larger-than-life but vulnerable anti-hero, Sir John Falstaff.

Before that happened, however, Welles enjoyed an opportunity in 1953 to play King Lear on American television. In a rearguard action to rescue the commercial airwaves from the advertising industry, the Sunday afternoon TV Radio-Workshop of the Ford Foundation, known as Omnibus, sponsored *King Lear* in a truncated production directed by Peter Brook that foreshadowed elements of Brook's feature-length *King Lear* (1971) starring Paul Scofield. The tyranny of time demanded the sacrifice of optimistic elements in the Gloucester subplot to compress the performance into 73 minutes, which was framed between commercials for Greyhound buses and bath tissues and embellished with a commentary by a baby-faced Alistair Cooke. An enormous paper map of England inscribed on a theatrical curtain is suddenly ripped open, shredded, and Orson Welles as King Lear steps through, growling and roaring, and bellowing "Give me the map there" (1.1.37), ready to begin the division of the kingdom. When Lear destroys his map, he loses his way, breaking his bond with Cordelia, and falling into a nightmare world of domination and subjugation. This is a "bondage" *King Lear*. Besides the Brechtian and Kottian intellectualization of despair, there is a trace of the obsession with human degradation in Alfred Hitchcock's spy thrillers. It's a sado-masochistic world of iron gates, steel bars, and hempen ropes. As Tony Howard says, "This is the *Marat/Sade* in embryo," as well as a transgressive attack on the smug world of Sunday afternoon cultural television programming.[37] In the windmill where Lear and his party (including longtime Wellesian collaborator Micheál MacLiammóir as poor Tom) take refuge from the storm are hooks, grinding wheels, chains – icons for "the rack of this tough world" (5.3.315) upon which the old king will be figuratively tormented. In the terrible windmill, Gloucester is seized, bound, and has his eyes gouged out with the thumbs, not the spurs, of the venomous Cornwall (Scott Forbes). A wooden-faced Regan (Margaret Phillips) looks on without pity.

The striking camera angles and choreographing of the characters' movements take the production away from naive literalism toward expressionism. In a memorable closing moment, the old king's howls over the death of Cordelia originate in the darkness and dwindle as he moves into the light. Shockingly the rag doll he seems to be dragging turns out to be Cordelia, a bit of business imitated from the Italian tragedian, Tommaso Salvini.[38] The loyal daughter has become a bauble in the hands of a man who has himself reverted to childlike innocence. The primitive studio lighting, probably the "three-point technique" with one key light in front, one back light, and a floodlight in front opposite the key light,[39] correlated darkness with chaos, light with harmony. As might be expected, Welles overacted but with power, verve, and ultimate authenticity. Predictably, critics savaged him, the unkindest cut of all declaring that Welles resembled "a man who had been hauled off a park bench and hastily pressed into service as Macy's Santa Claus."[40] Unhappily Welles never got the opportunity, as we shall see, to make a second attempt at a role that in so many ways intrigued him and suited his volcanic talents.

Chimes at Midnight (1966): The tragedy of Sir John Falstaff (and Orson Welles)

If Orson Welles could not satisfy every actor's ambition of doing Hamlet, in Falstaff he found a role almost as challenging. Using Falstaff as the protagonist, Welles's *Chimes at Midnight* shows the dark side of the youthful monarch whom Laurence Olivier sanctified in *Henry V* as "the mirror of all Christian kings," and "the star of England." In Olivier's movie, King Henry V is the paragon who has defeated Henry Percy (Hotspur) at Shrewsbury, ascended to the throne of England after the death of his father King Henry IV, destroyed the French army at Agincourt, and wooed and won the beautiful princess, Katherine of France. Olivier's movie censors out anything in *Henry V* potentially damaging to the king's candidacy for sainthood. On the other hand, as portrayed by Shakespeare, King Henry V oscillates between heroism as an anointed king and deceit as a mere mortal. What Olivier chose to disregard about the king, Welles chose to regard, but there is something in Shakespeare's sweeping panorama for both those who adore and those who loathe either Falstaff or Hal. A minor character in *All's Well that Ends Well* sums up Shakespeare's gift for articulating the tangled skein of human experience, its daily grubbiness: "The web of our life is of a mingled yarn, good and ill together: our virtues would be proud, if our faults whipt them not, and our crimes would despair, if they were not cherish'd by our virtues" (4.3.71).

For *Chimes,* Orson Welles has ransacked the subtext of the Henriad (*Richard II, 1 Henry IV, 2 Henry IV, Henry V*), as well as shards from *The Merry Wives of Windsor* to show the unintended consequences of Hal's rise to power. The story of Falstaff as victim has been assembled from bits and pieces and scraps scattered throughout the Henriad. His sad tale, which is The Tragedy of Falstaff, has not been fabricated but has been nestling all along within the sprawling historical saga like the core of a Russian doll. Shakespeare's democratic admission into the play of the ordinarily marginalized lower-class tavern characters clustering around Falstaff inspired Welles's foray. While *Richard II* excluded all but the high and mighty, kings and barons, the remaining three plays of the tetralogy beginning with *1 Henry IV* admit the meaner sorts of persons such as Hostess Quickly, Pistol, Nym, Bardolph, hostlers, and tapsters, who might have stepped out of a seventeenth-century Flemish painting of mundane domestic life.

Although Falstaff stands out among the tavern *Lumpen* as socially superior, having been a page to Sir Thomas Mowbray, a student at the Inns of Court, and a knight and officer in the armies of England, he shares in the misery of his forlorn cronies. On the surface only a comic foil to the ambitious young prince, at a deeper level Falstaff becomes the catalyst for exposing society's inner mechanisms of power, greed, and ambition. Falstaff, like one of today's "welfare cheats" in the post-Reagan, post-Thatcher era, is scapegoated as the "disease" infecting all of England, thus distracting from the entrenched hegemony's role in creating the national malaise. As a whipping boy for the diseases of his betters, he plays the role of mock king offered up in sacrifice to propitiate the gods. The tragedy lies in the way that he and Hal alike have been entrapped in the necessity of their own roles as monarch and jester. The king's betrayal of Falstaff ironically rebounds off the king's smug belief on the eve of Agincourt that "the King is not bound to answer the particular endings of his soldiers" (*Henry V* 4.1.155). *Chimes* is about the "particular ending" of one of those soldiers, Falstaff.

It has often been said that *2 Henry IV* repeats the same story as *1 Henry IV* in showing the young prince struggling to come to grips with his frightening responsibilities. In both plays, the young prince serves two fathers: the authentic one, Henry Bolingbroke; and the surrogate one, Falstaff. As has been observed, Hal shows the valour of the lion in arms at Shrewsbury by slaying Hotspur at the close of *Part One*, and the cunning of a fox in statecraft at Westminster by rejecting the destabilizing Falstaff at the close of *Part*

Two.[41] In the Henriad, warning signals about the inevitable schism between Hal and Falstaff appear from the beginning of *Part One*, but in *Part Two* Falstaff's talents as bon vivant and life force noticeably wane. Becoming shriller and meaner, he degenerates from an engaging rogue into a stock *miles gloriosus*, a mere braggart warrior. Welles's adaptation plays up the second Falstaff, the shrunken one of *Part Two* who betrays Mistress Quickly, and becomes the designated buffoon of *The Merry Wives of Windsor*, but just underneath there is the earlier, rollicking jester of *Part One*, the victim of unkind fate and his own bad judgment.

In struggling to pare down Shakespeare's sprawling chronicle of English history, Welles self-referentially identified with the king's rejection of Falstaff, seeing it as a mirror to Hollywood's rejection of him. Jack Jorgens observed that perhaps Welles "saw too much of himself in Falstaff."[42] Keith Baxter from his vantage point of having worked directly with Welles on *Chimes* said much the same thing: "It was his life's ambition to make this film and also to play Falstaff . . . You felt that there was a great deal of him in Falstaff – this sort of trimming one's sails, always short of money, having to lie, perhaps, and to cheat."[43] Behind Falstaff's comic mask, Welles saw the inner desperation. As he said, "the more I studied the part, the less funny he [Falstaff] seemed to be."[44] Ironically as Welles grew older his own "waist" grew in proportion to the apparent "waste" of his career and it was all too easy for people who confuse solemnity with seriousness to misconstrue his irony as a lack of high seriousness. Like Falstaff, a man large of spirit and imagination, Welles forgot he was living among Lilliputians. Given this background, *Chimes*, like *Othello*, had to end up as film noir.

Chimes at Midnight also drew heavily on Welles's theatrical experience, going back to the vast epic of a play called *Five Kings* that opened in Boston in 1939, the script being constructed from about half the major tetralogy. A plan to do the minor tetralogy (*The Three Parts of Henry VI and Richard III*) in tandem was never realized, though the title of *Five Kings* (Richard II, Henry IV, Henry V, Richard III, and Henry VI) vestigially remained. The huge cast included Robert Speaight (Chorus), Burgess Meredith (Prince Hal) and Orson Welles as Falstaff. With Welles interpreting Falstaff as a tragic figure, the play got to Washington, D.C, and then faltered in Philadelphia. Critics complained that it lacked unity and was only a series of "random stage pictures."[45] Welles then subsequently staged a successful *Chimes at Midnight* in Dublin, which put even greater emphasis on Falstaff.[46]

Benefiting from this incubation, the film script for *Chimes* goes beyond mere tinkering with Shakespeare's scenes; it massively reworks, transposes, revises and deletes, indeed deconstructs them. The radical textual surgery that worked so well for *Othello* operates in *Chimes* at an even more intense

10   Orson Welles as Falstaff and Keith Baxter as Prince Hal prepare for one of the ubiquitous partings in *Chimes at Midnight* (*Falstaff*), directed by Welles (Spain/Switzerland 1966).

level. Was Welles on an ego trip bent on destroying Shakespeare's work? Not at all. He told Peter Bogdanovich "no movie that will ever be made is worthy of being discussed in the same breath [with Shakespeare]."[47] He simply intended to re-inscribe a Shakespearean play in the spatial and temporal grammar of cinema, rather than literally inscribing the play itself.

In an exhaustive analysis, Robert Hapgood has located five "hallmarks" in *Chimes* for Welles's style in making complicated textual deletions, transpositions, and additions: (1) expansion/contraction, (2) dynamism, (3) pointing/counterpointing, (4) knitting, and (5) narrative coherence.[48] Sometimes the textual plundering transgresses neat categories, though it always testifies to Welles's ingenuity and scholarship. For example, a conversation between Shallow and Falstaff at the film's opening plunges deep into the

Henriad to hijack twenty-five lines from *2 Henry IV* (3.2.194–219). The language is Shakespeare's but so drastically altered from the original sequence as to be almost a new scenario: "Jesus the days that we have seen. / Ha, Sir John? Said I well?" to which Falstaff replies with the haunting line, "We have heard the chimes at midnight, Master Robert Shallow."[49] "Chimes at midnight" resurfaces in its proper place at Justice Shallow's Cotswolds farm much later in the film (shot 1206, Lyons). One of Welles's most ingenious conflations occurs when Falstaff is substituted for the drunken soldier whom the king orders to be released from the brig just before the fleet sails from Southampton for France: "Uncle of Exeter, / Enlarge the man committed yesterday / That rail'd against our person" (2.2.39). Not only is there a neat pun on "enlarg'd" (which means of course "to set free") in connection with Falstaff's "largeness," but Falstaff has notoriously "railed against [the king's] person." Welles was sparing with additions, only occasionally introducing a word or phrase to clarify the narrative, as in something like Falstaff's "Zounds, this confounded Percy!" (shot 93, Lyons) at the sight of Hotspur's body on the Shrewsbury battlefield.

The movie transcends The Tragedy of Sir John Falstaff,[50] being also as its director thought an elegiac lament for the loss of an older world, "Merrie England," which was "a season of innocence, a dew-bright morning of the world . . . Falstaff . . . its perfect embodiment." As a tavern wit, "he [Falstaff] sings for his supper" but that "isn't really what he's all about."[51] In this nostalgia for a lost world, *Chimes* follows *The Magnificent Ambersons*, which dealt in a Chekhovian kind of way with the demise and decay of an old American family doomed by a new industrialism embodied in the automobile.[52] For the Ambersons, the automobile spelled ruin; for Falstaff, the demise of chivalry deprived him of a life style. When Hal slew Hotspur at Shrewsbury, he also slew Falstaff. On the other hand, Hal's faults are balanced off against Falstaff's, who egregiously cheats poor Hostess Quickly of her tavern receipts and weasels on a £1000 debt to Shallow. As early as *Citizen Kane*, Welles was preoccupied with this theme of loss, of nostalgia for some lost idyll, even when it is symbolized by something so banal as Charles Kane's yearning for the childhood sled, "Rosebud." An instinctive aristocrat, Welles knew as well as Falstaff the sting of impecuniousness among one's inferiors. Worse yet, his art of cinema demanded enormous sums of money to stay alive. Had he been a nineteenth-century painter, he would not have been so enslaved to commodity.

The alternation between court and tavern in the Henriad provides the basis for a textbook scenario with cross-cutting between the two venues, the court being generally identified with austere stone and the tavern with more congenial wood.[53] In making *Chimes*, Welles had the actors on the set for decent periods of time, so that the subsequent editing was not dictated, as was the case with *Othello*, by the need to cover up gaps and inconsistencies brought on by the absence of actors. Sir John Gielgud as the king actually spent two weeks at Cardona, Spain, being filmed, among other sites, in a cathedral, while Margaret Rutherford who is shown in a reaction shot as Hostess Quickly laughing at the play scene in the tavern actually never saw it. She was simply told to laugh at the camera, and the illusion of her spectatorship was edited in later. Keith Baxter as the Prince counted fourteen appearances in the film where he was not playing Hal but was filling in as an extra.[54] Welles wanted this to be an actor's film and the wide-angle lenses and close-ups allow actors to use the camera instead of permitting the camera to use them.

The continuing décor of stone and wood for the settings of court and tavern reflect the character of Hal's real and surrogate fathers. Hal oscillates between the two poles, moving back and forth between the worlds of stone and wood, between workaday duty and holiday festivity, between the restraint of time and the timelessness of festivity, but inevitably he will choose authentic over surrogate father, containment over subversion, and become the chilly monarch his Father had been before him. The King is associated with the stone walls of Cordova cathedral, with vertical planes of light streaming through high windows, with austerity, with loneliness and pitilessness. As Anthony Davies says, "the expansive uncluttered spaces allow the King a slow, majestic fluidity of action . . . The sense of high, open, vertical space above the King affords these shots uninterrupted power, for there is no ceiling to suggest that the King is any way 'contained' or diminished by the world."[55] The King is not contained but he contains others who would challenge his hegemony. The expressionistic lighting streaming through great vertical windows in the vast empty interior of the church, frames him in low-angle shot. Gielgud speaks sepulchrally in his musical but stagy voice, which in giving sound priority over sense perfectly embodies the ethical dilemma of Henry IV. King Henry IV is after all the ultimate hollow man, having usurped the throne from his weak first cousin, Richard Plantagenet. The low-angle perspective stresses the king's enormous power, as well as his isolation and sickness of spirit, the "gilt" that crowns his head being only a cover-up for the "guilt" growing out of his usurpation of the throne from Richard II. His austerity contrasts with Falstaffian cheer, making the "fat guts" all the more attractive.

Falstaff, on the other hand, is associated with horizontal planes of light, squatness, frivolity, and subversion. Falstaff's festive world thrives on wooden structures, either the Boar's Head tavern or the country estate of Master Shallow. Just as the king's stony court remains the barren site of the workaday world, Falstaff's holiday world teems with humanity, with throngs of attractive young women clattering up and down the wooden stairs of the ramshackle inn. If wood is supposed to represent a more organic and softer world than that of stone, then this seedy inn exposes Falstaff's vision of total freedom and generosity as a mirage. Total freedom from restraint only leads to a new kind of bondage. Hal's "fool-born" jester, like all mock kings will be sacrificed on the altar of state and authority. Welles identified with Falstaff's status as a mock king, remarking how as an actor he himself was a "royal bum" with a crown of "tin," and how the biggest sin in the world to him was "betrayal," as "you know from *Chimes at Midnight*."[56]

Close-ups probe for clues about the inner lives of the characters. In what Hapgood might see as "dynamism," Welles has transposed 100 lines to highlight the abyss between Hal and Falstaff. With Falstaff in the background, just outside the tavern entrance, viewed over the Prince's shoulder, Hal utters his cold-blooded intention to betray his tavern cronies: "I know you all, and will a while uphold / The unyok'd humor of your idleness" and ending with "I'll so offend, to make offense a skill, / Redeeming time when men think least I will" (1.2.195ff). As he speaks, he turns away from Falstaff, faces the camera, and seems to be talking to himself. Falstaff who in Shakespeare's Henriad admits to suffering from "the disease of not list'ning, the malady of not marking" (2 *Henry IV* 1.2.120) misses the mark again in trying to turn the somber mood into jocularity by asking, "But I prithee, sweet wag, shall there be gallows standing in England when thou art king?" (1 *Henry IV* 1.2.57). The grim expression on the prince's face makes plain that in his reign gallows will grow like weeds but Falstaff doesn't see that.

The climactic scene in 1 *Henry IV* when Falstaff petitions Hal for understanding calls for close-ups: "but for sweet Jack Falstaff, kind Jack Falstaff, true Jack Falstaff, valiant Jack Falstaff." As Falstaff in low angle begs for exculpation, reaction shots show the women on the balcony waving and derisively laughing: "banish not him thy Harry's company, banish not him thy Harry's company – banish plump Jack, and banish all the world!" (1 *Henry IV* 2.4.476). Oblivious to his inevitable doom from the disease of "not listening," Falstaff's harsh fate as buffoon and scapegoat at the hands of the house wives in the *Merry Wives of Windsor* has been sealed. Then Hal jumps into the frame, pushes Falstaff into the background, and intones the four words "I do, I will." Devastating, they mean death for Falstaff, and for all he stands for – "Merrie England" and the feudal way of life.

As in any other war movie, farewell scenes in *Chimes* accentuate the idea of loss and departure. After his soliloquy about "redeeming time" (shot 81, Lyons), Hal departs from the tavern and Falstaff watches him slowly walking toward the distant stony castle. Hal's sudden break from a walk into a run symbolically increases the gap between him and Falstaff. Falstaff indulgently chuckles and waves, as yet mercifully oblivious to a prince's Machiavellian capacity for jettisoning inconvenient friends. In another farewell, as the sheriff's men pound on the tavern door, the Prince's hiding of Falstaff under a trapdoor foreshadows Falstaff's rejection at Westminster. When Falstaff emerges from hiding (shot 409) mumbling "we must all to the wars," an angry Hostess Quickly exposes him as a deadbeat, sternly saying "You owe me money, Sir John." Doll Tearsheet's (Jeanne Moreau) farewell to Falstaff as he leaves for the wars temporarily restores the old man to grace. Welles patches the dialogue together from lines scattered through act two, scene four of *2 Henry IV*. "[You] whoreson little tidy Bartholomew boar-pig"(2.4.231), says Doll and then holding him close, "Come, I'll be friends with thee, Jack. Thou art going to the wars, and whether I shall ever see thee again or no, there is nobody cares" (shots 411–12; 2.4.63). Welles omits the most poignant words:

> *Doll.* By my troth, I kiss thee with a most constant heart.
> *Fal.* I am old, I am old.
> *Doll.* I love thee better than I love e'er a scurvy young boy of them
> all (2.4.269).

When Falstaff admits to his age and failing strength, he confirms the phallic pun on his name ("Fall-staff"), which the eavesdropping Poins has already observed. "Is it not strange that desire should so many years outlive performance?" (2.4.260).

The farewells over, Falstaff emerges as malingerer, misfit, and outright fraud in the great battle scene at Shrewsbury from *1 Henry IV*, which echoes a similar struggle in *Alexander Nevsky*, as well as contrasting with Olivier's prettified Battle of Agincourt in *Henry V*. Welles once said of Olivier's cavalry charge in *Henry V* that "you see the people riding out of the castle, and suddenly they are on a golf course somewhere charging each other."[57] There is nothing remotely resembling a golf course in Welles's searing Brueghel-like battle that strips "glorious" war of its claim to "pomp and circumstance." And while Eisenstein drew on a cast of thousands for the enormous battle on the ice in *Nevsky*, Welles conjured up the entire battle by magically expanding 200 or so skillfully deployed Spaniards into thousands.

The reliance on *mise-en-scène* so successfully employed in most of the movie for close delineation of character yields in the battle scenes to montage, a tribute to Orson Welles's skill as a film editor, the Battle of Shrewsbury being a collage made up of over 200 separate shots cut from his long takes.[58] This remarkable panorama of the horrors of medieval warfare was recorded in long takes to allow the troops to build up to a plausible rage, and then subsequently cut and spliced and edited. The spectacle becomes a slow death dance for the rites of feudalism. It opens with Hotspur's mindless enthusiasm for violence, "Harry to Harry, shall hot horse to horse, / Meet and ne'er part till one drop down a corse" (4.1.122), though ironically it is Harry Percy, not Harry prince of Wales, who is "to drop down a corse." There is nothing here like the elegant knights in the Olivier film. The soldiers lowering Falstaff from a scaffold to his horse lose their grip on the rope and drop him to the ground like a stone. He lies there encased in his huge armor unable to move. Later, Falstaff appears as a tubby man puffing along well to the rear of the central action, or hiding behind a bush, though in response to Hal's "Why, thou owest God a death" (5.1.126), he is allowed his great commentary on honor (5.1.127), which makes him something more than a mere wastrel and turns him into an existentialist hero. From the brilliant speech on counterfeiting (5.4.111), only the catch phrase, "The better part of valor is discretion" remains. As infantry and cavalry charge toward one another there are the rallying cries of "Percy!" and "St. George for England," with flashes of Falstaff waving his troops forward. Gradually, however, as the fighting becomes increasingly deadly, the martial élan fades. The gallant soldiers are transmogrified into muddy wretches too exhausted even to clobber one another with their axes, clubs, spears, and chains. Against this holocaust backdrop, Hal conquers Hotspur in single combat, copes with Falstaff's ridiculous claim to having slain Hotspur, and then turns Falstaff over to the command of his priggish brother, John.

Like a juggernaut, the movie inexorably rolls toward the newly crowned king's crushing public rejection of Falstaff at Westminster. Falstaff's fatal disease of *hamartia*, or "missing of the mark," nudges him into a calamitous miscalculation when he blunders into the coronation processional to speak to the newly crowned king, thereby setting himself up for scathing public rebuke. Falstaff has trespassed from his own sphere into the forbidden world of stone. In extreme low angle, the king, now entirely his father's man with the vertical light streaming on him, coldly stares down at the expectant Falstaff, who cries out "Speak to me, my heart." The response falls on Falstaff's ears like stones: "I know thee not, old man, fall to thy prayers" and the prince adds the chilling *coup de grâce* of "How ill white hairs becomes a fool and jester!" (2 *Henry IV* 5.5.47). After Falstaff's destruction, the movie quickly moves toward a close, as if to draw a curtain over events too embarrassing to view. Despite Hal's intention to save the old man from poverty, Falstaff finds being humiliated in front of his cronies unendurable. The old insouciance momentarily flares up as he assures them that "he will be sent for [by the king] in private," but that gesture is undercut by Shallow's bluntly demanding that the delinquent Falstaff come up with at least one half of the

£1-thousand debt. This time Falstaff's blustering fails to convince Shallow that "[Falstaff] will be as good as [his] word." The game is up, Falstaff's ignominious bankruptcy crystal clear to everyone. Falstaff is last seen in a deep-focus shot, walking toward a backlit arch, alone, and mumbling to himself that "I shall be sent for soon ... at night." He is sent for, true enough, though not by Hal but by his Creator. Hostess Quickly in yet another farewell, leaning against the wall of the tavern, speaks the haunting eulogy from *Henry V*: "He's in Arthur's bosom, if ever a man went to Arthur's bosom" (2.3.9).

The bitterest irony comes at the end, when as Falstaff's enormous casket is trundled across the bleak winter landscape, the voice of Ralph Richardson praises the young king with encomiums from Holinshed's *Chronicles*:

> This Henry was a captain of such prudence and such policy that he never enterprised anything before it forecast the main chances that it might happen. So humane withal, he left no offense unpunished nor friendship unrewarded. For conclusion, a majesty was he that both lived and died a pattern in princehood, a lodestar in honor, and famous to the world alway. [A drum beats a processional rhythm on the soundtrack.][59]

Falstaff, the holy fool, one of those men Paul spoke of who are foolish in the eyes of men but wise in the eyes of God, is betrayed by his best friend, who is then in turn eulogized as a national hero and a kind of saint. Welles understood this.

Like Falstaff, Welles still hoped to "be sent for," yet fresh betrayals and disappointments lay ahead as he dickered to make more Shakespeare movies. He undertook ambitious plans for feature movies based on two of Shakespeare's other suffering human beings, Shylock and King Lear, but neither project was completed. He was also called to play Brutus in the Burge/Snell *Julius Caesar* (1970), but for obscure reasons had to be replaced at the eleventh hour by Jason Robards, Jr.[60] His film of *The Merchant of Venice*, in which Welles played Shylock and Charles Gray played Antonio, is said to have been completed in 1969. Since then it has been as elusive as Hawthorne's Giant Transcendentalism, various accounts claiming that it never saw the light of day because two reels were stolen from the Rome production office, that a 40-minute segment may be stored in a Hollywood vault, and that excerpts have appeared in a television documentary. In a bold stroke, when Welles's good friend, Oja Kodar, refused to play Portia, the role was eliminated.[61] Footage from the lost *Merchant* is also reported to be contained in Kodar's feature-length movie *Jaded* (1989).[62] Welles's other plans for a major film of *King Lear* were also dashed when much to his disgust the French backers withdrew their support, causing him, he said, more humiliation than "even in the worst days of the old Hollywood." Planning to cast Kodar as Cordelia and Ab Dickson, his magician friend, as the Fool, he envisioned a Shakespeare movie that was to be "not only a new kind of Shakespeare but a new kind of film."[63]

So until 1985 when he died quite unexpectedly, Welles remained the embattled artist besieged by "tickling commodity." In his struggle to find the best available means for putting Shakespeare on screen, he never quite made the transition from art house to mall house. His detractors pursued him relentlessly, mercilessly: "Has he [Falstaff/Welles], deep down, a spirit of rebellion against stuffy authority? Or is he merely what he looks like – a dissolute, bumbling, street-corner Santa Claus?" one reviewer asked of his acting in *Chimes*.[64] Significantly the journalist didn't declare, he interrogated. The element of mystery, of magic, was always there. What Marlene Dietrich as the smoky Tanya memorably said in *A Touch of Evil* about Hank Quinlan, the police chief played by Welles, remains Orson Welles's best epitaph: "He was some kind of a man."

- 5 -

Electronic Shakespeare: from television to the web

Electronic Shakespeare unobtrusively began on Friday afternoon, February 5, 1937, at 3:55 pm, with an 11-minute scene from *As You Like It* transmitted from the BBC's elegantly named "Alexandra Palace," perched on a 400-foot hill in north London. More base than aristocratic in origin, the BBC station was actually a "a derelict resort,"[1] a relic of the "Crystal Palace" left over from an 1861 International Exhibition entertainment center, which could seat 1,000 holiday-makers for luncheon. The scene from *As You Like It*, directed by Robert Atkins, included RADA-trained Margaretta Scott as Rosalind, a West End stage actress who had played Ophelia in a radio *Hamlet*, and Ion Swinlay (or Swinley) as Orlando.[2]

Thanks to pioneers like John Logie Baird,[3] who had by 1930 managed to broadcast Pirandello's *The Man with a Flower in His Mouth* from primitive London laboratories, television, which had been gradually developing over a period of several decades, was beginning to fulfill its multiple inventors' dream of "seeing over the horizon."[4] Some early viewers complained that the image on the screen gave one "the feeling of looking through a cabin keyhole on a rather rough day at sea."[5] No matter that viewers were threatened with seasickness, the march of Shakespeare on television was inevitable, especially when in August 1936 a portrait of William Shakespeare was transmitted during the Radio-Olympia Exhibition.

As was the case with Sir Herbert Tree's 1899 *King John* movie and the Vitagraph silents, the fledgling television industry instinctively exploited Shakespeare's cultural capital to its own ends. Ironically Shakespeare on television arrived on the British scene at exactly the time when the London critics had been happily bashing Hollywood's *Midsummer Night's Dream* (1935) and *Romeo and Juliet* (1936) for the *lèse majesté* of putting Shakespeare in moving images. There remained until late in this century the unshakable conviction of traditionalists that any Shakespeare on screen was bound to be a vulgarization, and of the *avant-garde* that it was indubitably *kitsch*. A flurry of articles in *The Listener*, a BBC house organ, by such luminaries as J. Dover Wilson,[6] G.B. Harrison,[7] and Tyrone Guthrie,[8] demonstrated how Shakespeare on page and stage retained unassailable authority over

Shakespeare on screen, whether on film or television. An occasional seer might object: "It is wholly unreasonable to demand that all productions of Shakespeare should be Elizabethan. The surest proof of the greatness of his plays is their adaptability."[9] Whatever the protests, Shakespeare was bound to be swept up in the "mass distribution and mass consumption of television programs for huge profits."[10] Shakespeare's insight in *King John* about "tickling commodity" again anticipated everyone. Not Britannia but the bottom line would rule the airwaves.

With television's roots in radio, not movies, cinema was by no means the dominant model for its pioneers. As with the early silent films, stage actors from the West End were imported to parade before the pioneering transmission systems in Alexandra Palace. On the same day in February that saw the *As You Like It* segment, a snippet was transmitted from *Henry V*, with actress and pianist Yvonne Arnaud[11] as Katherine of France. It was directed by George More O'Ferrall, who would later play a major role in the BBC's expanded Shakespeare programming. From 1937 to 1939, the BBC scheduled nearly two dozen Shakespeare programs, translating the studio performances into electrical impulses that could then be scanned and reassembled in home receivers. As with early silent film, television favored Lumière-like "actualities" of such news events as the coronation of King George VI, but soon the technology was in place for live transmissions from London's West End playhouses. Through spring 1939, the 11,000 or so owners of London television receivers within a 25-mile vicinity[12] had the opportunity to watch Shakespeare programs based on some fifteen different plays, with three repeats of *A Midsummer Night's Dream,* and *Twelfth Night,* and one repeat of *Julius Caesar* and *Macbeth.* A televised 30-minute segment from the Old Vic *Macbeth*, produced by George More O'Ferrall, with Laurence Olivier and Judith Anderson, on December 3, 1937, moved the *Times* television critic to remark that Olivier and Anderson, were "effective" but they failed "to moderate their voices to television scale, and still spoke to the utmost recesses of an imaginary theatre." In the new medium, the lighting designer held the key to success: "the weird sisters were seen in a series of close-ups, which were rather too brightly lit, so that they appeared grotesque rather than macabre."[13]

Producer/director Dallas Bower's ambitious 141-minute modern dress *Julius Caesar* on July 24, 1938, included a cast of thirty, many of whom doubled in minor roles as Third or Fourth Citizens. Inspired by Orson Welles's Mercury Theatre production, there were special scenic effects by Malcolm Baker-Smith, incidental music by James Hartley, background film of "Riots" from British Movietone, "Gunfire" from the Film Library, an "Explosion Sequence" and "Aeroplanes" from British Movietone. Special disks provided

11　Iago (Stephen Murray), Desdemona (Joan Hopkins), and Emilia (Margaretta Scott) in a tense moment during a "live" BBC transmission of *Othello* from Alexandra Palace in 1950.

the noise of "Angry Crowds," "Cheering Crowd," "Gunfire," "Thunder," the "Internationale," and the Halle Orchestra conducted by Sir Hamilton Harty doing Berlioz's "The Royal Hunt and Storm."[14] A critic praised the "penumbrascope," which added space and depth to the small studio and enhanced the quick change of scenes from "close-up to mid-shot," but he also wondered why "Mr. Bower did not raise one of his cameras to a higher angle after the fashion that the newsreel camera oversees a procession."[15] Another critic expressed surprise that "Ernest Milton as Caesar (dressed like General Franco) was magnificent, but then it is a strange thing that his performance was also good Shakespeare,"[16] while the old bugaboo of Shakespeare in modern dress put a third critic off when "the wife of the modern gangster-politician Brutus smokes cigarettes."[17]

Other major productions included George More O'Ferrall's abridged (67-minute) studio *Othello* (Dec. 15, 1937) with Baliol Holloway in the title role, Celia Johnson as Desdemona and Anthony Quayle as Cassio, initial attempts to cast Ralph Richardson and Jessica Tandy having fizzled. The production's budget at about £300[18] contrasts with the £2,376 cost a decade later for George More O'Ferrall's *Hamlet*, or the £7,000 price tag for a single episode of the 1964 *Spread of the Eagle* series. Although unhappy with the "microscopic screen," the *Times* critic wrote that "Miss Celia Johnson [as] Desdemona . . . made one forget the marvels of science and remember only the beauty of the English language as it should be spoken."[19] Shakespeare's birthday on April 23, 1937, called for a "Mask" arranged from the fairy scenes of *A Midsummer Night's Dream*, which leaned heavily on Felix Mendelssohn for theme music.

The first phase of televised Shakespeare began winding down with Dallas Bower's 100-minute *The Tempest* (1939), with incidental music and dance by Sibelius and the London Ballet. Various BBC internal memos circulated after the performance reveal the perils of live television broadcast with complaints about a lack of rehearsal time resulting in a "prompter standing in the foreground of a long shot," "an actor walking behind the penumbrascope," and "property men entering [a] superimposed shot."[20] Approving of Peggy Ashcroft as Miranda, Grace Wyndham Goldie, the *Listener* critic, reflected on television's increasing maturity declaring that "plays are staggeringly successful on the television screen," and "getting better and better every minute."[21] Things were not always fated to "get better and better," though. On September 1, 1939, at the end of a Mickey Mouse cartoon, with "the lights going out all over Europe," the BBC television also switched off its lights. Its ultra-short waves of seven meters would otherwise have offered handy navigation aids for the Luftwaffe.

When the lights finally came on again all over Europe, the BBC energetically continued to transmit uncommodified Shakespeare, protected from commercialism by the state subsidy but equally protected from any far-out directors. Veteran producer/directors Ian and Robert Atkins and George More O'Ferrall along with Michael Barry, among others, for three decades from 1947 faithfully served the Shakespeare industry with over sixty performances of individual plays in whole or in part, and a complete run of the English and Roman history plays as mini-series. Only such notoriously unpopular titles as *Henry VIII*, *Titus Andronicus*, and *Pericles* got neglected. Until 1978, when the great geyser of the BBC Shakespeare Plays series saturated the market with six plays a year, *Julius Caesar* appeared most frequently with seven productions, followed by *A Midsummer Night's Dream* and *Macbeth* with six each, not including the Roman history saga, *The Spread of the Eagle*.

Prior to that, however, the BBC and independent television, even with competition from boxing and football matches, managed to squeeze out of stingy budgets George More O'Ferrall's full-length, two-part, meticulously planned BBC *Hamlet* (1947) with John Byron as Hamlet and Sebastian Shaw as Claudius, for which the British Television Society awarded O'Ferrall its Silver Medal. Around seventy persons were approached to fill forty-eight roles, with some doubling. Special recordings had to be made for Ophelia's songs and the noise of the ghost. Fittings for costumes at Foxe's ate up considerable time, and Hamlet's customary suits of solemn black had to be made dark green because of lighting problems. The detailed planning included five weeks of rehearsals, all the stage props and scenery of a major theatrical production (a locket for Hamlet, wild flowers for Ophelia, wine goblets for Claudius, etc.), elaborate lighting plots, and the pre-arrangement of angles for cameras one and two and the ubiquitous microphone boom, which hovered menacingly over the whole set.[22] If as Michael Barry has suggested, O'Ferrall's tracking camera inspired the deep-focus cinematography for the filmed Olivier *Hamlet* (1948),[23] then this forgotten 1947 *Hamlet* deserves not to be forgotten. Journalist Drew Middleton became the first American to review a televised Shakespeare play when he reported back to *The New York Times* that John Byron "played the prince for all that it was worth" in a production full of "blood and thunder elements [that gripped the audience] without interruption."[24] The era's lack of kinescope recording makes any reappraisal of these critics' insights impossible.[25]

A cluster of three major mini-series in the 1960s based on the English and Roman history plays resulted in some of Great Britain's most distinguished Shakespeare on television. The first and most ambitious, *An Age of Kings* (including *Richard II, Two Parts of Henry IV, Henry V, Three Parts of Henry VI, and Richard III*) compressed the minor and major tetralogies of the English history plays into a fifteen-week cycle of eight 60-to-90 minute segments. Beginning with "The Hollow Crown" (*Richard II*) on April 28, 1960, and ending with "The Boar Hunt" (*Richard III*) on November 17, 1960, all of them were broadcast nationally on educational television in the United States beginning in October 1961 and were repeated again in 1962. Producer Peter Dews carried out the Herculean casting of some 600 parts for the sprawling, epical dramas, which required thirty weeks of rehearsals, and cost as much as £4,000 an episode. For clarity, the plays were shown in their historical sequence, which meant that the apprentice work of the minor tetralogy covering the years 1422 to 1485 followed the mature artistry of the major tetralogy spanning the years 1399 to 1422. Milton Crane aptly remarked that it was a little bit "like seeing *Titus* after *Hamlet*."[26]

Even on blurry kinescope, the performances hold up extremely well. David William as the feckless King Richard II walks a fine line between vanity and brutality as he exiles Henry Bolingbroke (Tom Fleming) and Mowbray (Noel Johnson) and then heartlessly mocks the dying Gaunt (Edgar Wreford). Gaunt still manages to convey the correct fervor in his set-piece aria of Armada rhetoric: "This blessed plot, this earth, this realm, this England" (2.1.50). As Henry Bolingbroke, Tom Fleming sternly lectures the fettered and cowed "caterpillars of the commonwealth," Bushy and Green, who grovel, weep, and moan before being led away, shrieking, completely terrorized by Bolingbroke's chilling: "See them delivered over / To execution and the hand of death" (3.1.29). You hear off camera the mumbling prayers of a priest, and then the thud of an axe. Silence. Very effective television drama. In another master stroke, a passing courtier's interruption of Northumberland's tangled, and much parodied, order of battle speech makes an unconvincing moment convincing: "receiv'd intelligence / That Harry Duke of Herford, Rainold, Lord Cobham,/ [Thomas, son and heir to th' Earl of Arundel,] / That late broke from the Duke of Exeter" etc., etc. (2.1.278). A "forceful" Sean Connery as Hotspur, en route to being James Bond, and the RSC's Frank Pettingell as Falstaff also convert the bare set into a convincingly mobile territory for the sprawling action. Except for a few disclaimers, the reception was positive, one critic fearing that Falstaff had been buried alive under the relentless pageantry, and that the sense of the "diseased" kingdom (so trenchantly represented a few years later by Orson Welles in *Chimes*) had gotten lost.[27]

Three years later in the nine-part *Spread of the Eagle* (1963), director Peter Dews tried the same formulas, but with somewhat less success, in a miniseries based on *Coriolanus, Julius Caesar,* and *Antony and Cleopatra*. Budgeted at as much as £7,000 per program, the series swallowed up a huge cast of some seventy-six actors. According to Dews, the common denominator was

Plutarch's account of three personal tragedies set against a violent political background. In *Coriolanus* there is a fearless soldier (Robert Hardy), out of his depth in politics; in *Julius Caesar,* a cabal of political moderates out of their depth as terrorists (Barry Jones as Caesar and Keith Michell as Antony); and in *Antony and Cleopatra,* a fabled couple (Keith Michell and Mary Morris) out of control in a middle-aged love affair. A recurring theme echoes a similar concern in *An Age of Kings* – the Tudor obsession with degree and order in government.[28] This Tillyardian view comfortably meshed with the bland bourgeois values of the mid-Sixties in the pre-Vietnam era. To achieve continuity, Dews used the same cast throughout the nine parts, including several veterans from *An Age of Kings.* Robert Hardy traded Prince Hal for the role of Coriolanus, and Frank Pettingell abandoned Falstaff for Junius Brutus. The critic for the *Times* thought that the lack of continuity worked against it since *Antony* is the only character who appears in more than one sequence.[29] In 1965, Michael Barry, BBC's Head of Plays, televised the 1963 RSC Stratford Memorial Theatre production of the *Three Parts of Henry VI* and *Richard III,* which came to be known as *The Wars of the Roses.* Directed principally by Peter Hall and scripted by John Barton, the production rearranged Shakespeare's four plays into three for television – *Henry VI, Edward IV,* and *Richard III.* Twelve cameras taped the resulting pageant of English kings and queens, with a cast of seventy-six, which resourcefully recreated "a theatre production in television terms."[30] The Stratford theatre was converted into a huge television studio by boarding over orchestra seats to extend the stage forty feet outward for a sense of space lacking in the original stage productions, featuring John Bury's influentially realistic metallic settings.[31] Glowing performances offer imaginative visual equivalents to Shakespeare's language, as when, for example, the opening of *Henry VI* seizes on Bedford's lugubrious "Hung be the heavens with black, yield day to night!" (*1 Henry VI* 1.1.1) as a leitmotif by focusing on the corpse of Henry V. When in the Temple Garden the Lancastrians and Yorkists pluck their symbolic red and white roses, tight head shots and rapid cutting, along with banners and music support this most aesthetic of warrior rituals. Still another cut to a close framing of a white rose adumbrates the ascendancy of the Yorkist hegemony. A quicksilver Joan of Arc, Janet Suzman anticipates her later triumphs on television as Lady Macbeth and Cleopatra, by infusing the doggerel verse with fire and beauty. Even the dramatically hopeless scene when Mortimer responds with a prolix narrative of Lancastrian outrages to Richard Plantagenet's disingenuous, "Discover more at large what cause that was, / For I am ignorant and cannot guess" (2.5.59), captures the imagination. The wretched Mortimer, who looks terrible, with lumps all over his face, as if he vaguely understood that his creator, Shakespeare, had confused him with another Mortimer, parses the bewilderingly complicated family tree of the descendants of King Edward III: "Henry the Fourth, grandfather to this king, / Depos'd his nephew Richard, Edward's son," etc. In the critical raves, special praise went to David Warner for his King Henry VI, Ian Holm for Gloucester, Peggy Ashcroft for Margaret, and Donald Sinden for York.[32] Professor Alice Griffin, America's reigning authority on screened Shakespeare, even thought that "these are the best television productions of Shakespeare's plays in the history of television."[33]

In the United States, where major corporations like RCA cautiously studied the possibilities of this strange new creature,[34] the television industry prior to World War II lagged far behind Great Britain's, offering little more than blurry ice hockey games from Madison Square Garden on tiny tavern screens within greater New York City. After World War II, however, US television led the world in quantity with ten million receivers by 1951. As early as 1948 North America's first Shakespeare "event" on television was a transmission of Verdi's *Otello* live from New York's dignified old Metropolitan opera house. During the next decade, Shakespeare indirectly benefited from the Golden Years of pioneering television when commercial networks and sponsors underwrote live drama on Philco Playhouse, Studio One, Kraft Theatre, Omnibus, and the Hallmark Hall of Fame. Quality programming was soon doomed, though, when the working people's perverse willingness to squander hard-earned wages on television sets redirected programming from the classes to the masses. Unlike the films, which started in squalor and yearned for "quality," television began with "quality" and ended with trash. The Madison Avenue advertising industry and its corporate clients now had a clear license for lobotomizing the American mind. "Quality" programming, which publicists for commercial broadcasting cleverly stigmatized as "elitist," suffered another blow when the industry began to "package" programs out to Hollywood producers like Columbia Pictures' teleplay subsidiary, Screen Gems.[35] Uncommodified Shakespeare and drama in general were in serious jeopardy.

Somewhat against the prevailing winds, from 1953 to 1970 Kansas City's Hallmark Greeting Card company underwrote eight televised Shakespeare plays, *Hamlet* (twice), *Macbeth* (twice), *Richard II*, *Taming of the Shrew*, *Tempest*, and *Twelfth Night* – nine if you include *Kiss Me Kate* (1958). Principal director was George Schaefer, a television veteran, who really enjoyed the excitement of the early live transmissions, which carried with them "the hysteria of an opening night performance."[36] A traditionalist, Schaefer fit the greeting card company's profile for a director interested in such "higher forms of entertainment" as Shakespeare. He also as a sergeant in the US Army's troop entertainment program collaborated with Major Maurice Evans in producing wartime Shakespeare for troops overseas.

In the initial Hallmark Shakespeare play, Schaefer directed Maurice Evans, with Sarah Churchill as Ophelia, in *Hamlet* (1953), most memorable for the really stunning Gertrude played by Ruth Chatterton. The $185,000 budget, even allowing for inflation, by today's standards for hit shows like *Seinfeld* is ridiculously low. Maurice Evans' voice resonated exactly the right way for Americans who thought Shakespearean stage diction must inevitably be "RP" British. Moreover his wartime "GI" *Hamlet* had given Evans the requisite "regular guy" image to offset any Shakespearean taint. His admirers mostly failed to notice that the voice, a kind of perpetual quaver, remained pretty much unvaried in every role. Neither did anyone have the poor taste to point out that American soldiers in overseas backwaters made up a world-class captive audience for anything, even a church service, to relieve the boredom. Given her father's record in World War II, Sarah Churchill was well insulated against carping critics.

Evans appeared in the leading role in a 1954 *Richard II* that again featured Sarah Churchill, this time as the unhappy little queen, and then in a pioneering color transmission of *Macbeth* (1954) with Judith Anderson as Lady Macbeth. Professor Alice Griffin caught on to Evans' trick in both *Macbeth* and *Richard II* of "recit[ing] rather than act[ing]."[37] The *Time* critic praised the four cameras for the fluid way they moved "into and out of the scene during each long sequence."[38] In 1956 there was a *Taming of the Shrew* with the very proper Evans badly miscast as Petruchio and Lilli Palmer as Katherine Minola; in 1957, a *Twelfth Night* with Evans as Malvolio and Rosemary Harris as Viola; and in 1960, Hallmark achieved its greatest success in a relaxed *Tempest* with Evans plausibly cast as Prospero, an incredibly beautiful Lee Remick as Miranda, and the gifted Richard Burton as a gruff Caliban. Virginia M. Vaughan compared it to Peter Brook and Derek Jarman's darker visions of *The Tempest*, and said even though it was as "light as a souffle," its lack of pomposity qualified it for a "main course."[39]

With partial funding from Hallmark, Evans and Anderson's second *Macbeth* (1960) was filmed in color on location in Scotland for crossover theatrical and television release, in a collaboration of the arch-rivals: "TV helping the cinema, and the cinema helping TV."[40] Thousands of school children exposed to the 16mm rental version grew up thinking of the Macbeths as looking like Maurice Evans and Judith Anderson, just as in their imaginations Raymond Massey was Abraham Lincoln and Gregory Peck, Captain Ahab. The company sponsored a British *Hamlet* (1970), directed by Peter Wood, with a cluster of well-known actors, including Richard Chamberlain as the Prince, John Gielgud as the Ghost, and Michael Redgrave as Polonius. In turning to England, however, for theatrical talent, Hallmark followed a trend begun as early as 1959 with the Dupont Show of the Month *Hamlet*,

12 Richard Chamberlain as the prince and Ciaran Madden as Ophelia in Regency costumes have Raby Castle as a background in this scene from a Hallmark Hall of Fame *Hamlet* that was imported from Great Britain for transmission on North America's NBC-TV in November 1970.

which gradually eliminated home-brewed serious drama on American television. Commercial programming increasingly was targeted at the plain folk of Middle America, while the cultural elite choked on a diet of public television's British-made Masterpiece Theatre. And "public television" slowly came under the control of major sponsoring corporations to guarantee a blackout of any counter-culture tendencies.

Hallmark Greeting Cards, however, did not entirely monopolize American televised Shakespeare. In the thirty years between 1949 and 1979 (when the BBC Shakespeare Plays series saturated the market), nearly fifty major televised Shakespeare programs appeared in the United States. As early as 1949, NBC made a pilot scene from *Henry V* featuring the late Sam Wanamaker, founder of the Globe replica in London. An amateurish Players Club *Macbeth* (1949) survives on a blurry kinescope with Walter Hampden, described by one critic as looking "uneasy."[41] At CBS, Worthington Miner produced for Studio One a modern dress *Julius Caesar* (1949) starring Robert Keith with the actors costumed in the period's ugly, wide-lapel, padded business suits. A youthful Charlton Heston, who importantly contributed to movie Shakespeare in the years ahead, played Cinna.[42] Television critic Jack Gould praised Miner because he didn't just "take" a picture but "made" one in "the most exciting television yet seen on the home screen."[43] In a pre-feminist, modern dress *Taming of the Shrew* (1950), Charlton Heston manhandled Lisa Kirk's thoroughly subjugated Kate. Starred again in a 1951 *Macbeth*, Charlton Heston's speeches were condemned as "lifeless and meaningless" and the production itself denounced for "too obtrusive" camera work, whatever that time-honored brickbat may mean. In another program that year, Richard Greene played the title role in a *Coriolanus* in the modern dress that Worthington Miner faithfully believed would appeal to a mass audience, optimistically estimated at ten million.

The miracle was not that Shakespeare was done timidly on television but that he was done at all. Producers like Miner fought a rear-guard action against stultifying political conformity and the Madison Avenue ad-agency hegemony. Shakespeare indirectly even became hostage to the holy war against godless communism when at mid-century McCarthyism thoroughly intimidated the moguls of mass entertainment. The rantings of Walter Winchell on national radio, in complicity with his crony, J. Edgar Hoover, and the HUAC Grand Inquisition, effectively silenced politically suspect "reds" and "traitors,"[44] who were blacklisted, jailed, exiled, exposed to the wrath of vigilantes, or bullied by HUAC into ratting on fellow actors. One positive note was that the Hollywood studios' refusal to allow their contracted actors to appear on the feared rival medium of television offered an unparalleled opportunity for younger, unknown actors like George C. Scott, Jack Lemmon, and Charlton Heston (then twenty-three) to win instant reputations.[45]

In a 1956 innovative "crossover," which preceded the Schaefer/Evans *Macbeth* experiment, an audience estimated, perhaps with some exaggeration, at twenty-five million watched a televised Olivier *Richard III* on the same afternoon that the movie was being theatrically released. Imported Shakespeare from Great Britain on television increasingly became a national habit, as, for example, with a 1959 CBS DuPont Show of the Month Old Vic *Hamlet*, starring John Neville as a thin, anxiety-ridden but very effective prince in the "Hamletism" tradition. A handsome illustrated souvenir television script on expensive rag paper testifies to CBS's serious commitment.[46]

Three made-in-the-USA Shakespeare productions, all of them simply recordings of stage performances, surfaced on the national scene. Two came out of the workshops of Joseph Papp's New York Shakespeare Festival: a *King Lear* (1973) and a *Much Ado about Nothing* (1973). James Earl Jones's performance as King Lear when finally televised on public television in 1977 allowed thousands to see a famous black actor cross a color line by impersonating an English king. With his powerful physique, Jones managed to make the old king not so much old and fragile as newly conscious of senescence. Director A.J. Antoon's *Much Ado* with Sam Waterston as Benedick and Kathleen Widdoes as Beatrice, "Americanized" the play by shifting the period from a vaguely medieval Messina to the America of Col. Teddy Roosevelt's Spanish–American War Rough Riders, and by borrowing from film such tropes as slow and accelerated motion and Keystone Kop antics. Regrettably, the exposure on television while the play was still live on Broadway resulted shortly thereafter in the show's demise when box office receipts dried up. In the American Conservatory Theatre's *Taming of the Shrew* (1976), William Ball's San Francisco company displaced *Commedia* tropes into slapstick routines and the Mickey Mouse sound effects of Walt Disney. The presentation, was, however, frankly theatrical, not telegenic, in the sense that even the off-stage audience was made a part of the *mise-en-scène*. By the close of the Seventies, then, there was less studio televising than off-site recording of theatrical productions.

Using the technology of "Electronovision," or alternatively "Theatrofilm," a simultaneous closed-circuit transmission of *Hamlet* (1964), directed by John Gielgud and starring Richard Burton, went out from Broadway's Lunt-Fontanne theatre to 976 American movie theatres in the hinterlands. The idea was to lure provincial folk in Dubuque to the local Bijou at $2.50 a head to enjoy the ritual and glory of a "live" performance on the New York stage. The concept was doomed by alternative, more home-centered, methods of entertainment, which rendered "electronovision" almost immediately obsolete. The "live" performance was actually pieced together from two performances.[47] Nevertheless this experiment managed to gross over £1 million but like Beerbohm Tree's silent movie of *Macbeth* (1916) was to be destroyed after its brief exhibition, particularly because of Richard Burton's dissatisfaction with it, though in fact it has miraculously resurfaced in recent years on voice recordings and widely available videocassettes in the English PAL format.

Richard Burton as the melancholy Dane gives acting lessons to everyone else in the cast, many of whom seem wooden, nervous and uncertain. Even if he was "tired," and "lacked lustre," and the show was "no more than a curiosity," or worse yet, "really dreadful," as various critics remarked after a 1972 revival in London,[48] an actor so richly talented as Burton, with his "animal" vitality, can never be entirely bad, only wonderfully charismatic. Burton's natural gifts included a sturdy Welsh voice, a magnificent head on strong shoulders, and the creativity to energize Shakespeare's language deeply within himself. Perhaps his genius depended in part on the accident that his mellifluous Welsh dialect coincided in mysterious ways with the spoken English heard on the stage of Shakespeare's Globe. At Shakespeare's Globe, the actors' diction would have sounded to modern ears less like a speech by Margaret Thatcher and more like a lilting brogue, perhaps resembling "Ohhh thet thisss tew tew soil-èd flaish would mellt,/ Thawww, and reeesollve itself into a dewww!" (1.2.129). More of the secret of Burton's genius, which he himself apparently understood no more than anyone else,[49] lay in an uncanny knack for perfect timing, pacing, and enunciation – the daring to turn a vowel into a screech. When he says "seems, madam? nay, it is" (1.2.76) to Eileen Herlie as Gertrude (an encore from her same role in the Olivier film), the "seems" crackles throughout the theatre. When he speaks of how "the funeral-bak'd meats / Did coldly furnish forth the marriage tables" (1.2.179), he chuckles at his own witticism and pauses for the audience to share in the joke. When he sends Ophelia to a "nunnery," his last verb, "go" (3.1.149), emerges muted, almost a whisper, magnificently anti-climactic to the way he has just excoriated the poor girl while spinning, whirling, and circling around her in a towering rage. His gifts bring out a side of Hamlet deeply buried in the subtext – the irascible, wilful, petulant, yes, even dangerous, Hamlet, that too easily eludes the grasp of lesser actors. The scene between Hamlet and the Ghost brings Burton together with a shadowy Gielgud as Ghost whose dreadful tale of perfidy and poison emerges in Gielgud's unvaried speaking voice, little different from the voice for King Henry IV in *Chimes at Midnight,* John of Gaunt in the BBC *Richard II* (1979), or Prospero in Greenaway's *Prospero's Books* (1991). Hamlet listens to the voice, interjects, and reacts. Unlike Gielgud's singing voice, Burton as Hamlet rasps and roars.

Except for the visiting players come to Elsinore, it is all done in ordinary street clothes, on a bare stage, pretty much like a first rehearsal off book. Partly because of the poor lighting and partly because of the inept camera work (despite fifteen concealed cameras), Burton's supporting players add very little. Hume Cronyn's Polonius seems bloodless, perhaps miscast; Ophelia (Linda Marsh) is anxious and tentative; and Alfred Drake (Claudius) was better employed on Broadway as Fred Graham (Petruchio) in *Kiss Me Kate* (1958). Without Burton in the cast, no one would have had the consummate gall to offer so little to the trusting folk in the provinces. The offstage audience in the theatre collaborated by applauding wildly at the slightest sign of life from the actors. Is there maybe just a touch of self-referentiality when Burton utters Hamlet's last words to Horatio: "O God, Horatio, what a wounded name" (5.2.344)? Burton felt that preserving the record of this performance could have "wounded" his name, but to make the "rest ... silence" would have robbed posterity of a rare snapshot of a real actor in action.[50]

Prior to the 1978 inauguration of the mammoth BBC Shakespeare Series, much truly first-rate televised Shakespeare came out of England from networks other than the BBC. Several of these appeared within a few years on various alternative television outlets in the United States like Classic Theatre produced by Station WGBN in Boston, PBS offerings from WNET/Thirteen in New York City, or the Bravo Channel. An important rival to the Burton *Hamlet* was the Philip Saville *Hamlet at Elsinore* (1964), which in contrast to the bare-stage Burton *Hamlet* was taped on location in Kronborg Castle at Elsinore in Denmark, where the actual historical events in the play may or may not have taken place. Dr. Bernice Kliman remarks that the result was like Henry James's *The Real Thing*, where the bogus aristocrats look more like aristocrats than the authentic aristocrats. She prefers Kozintsev's made-up sets.[51] A stellar cast and imaginative camera work on the outdoors sets make for a crossover type of production that edges toward the resources of film. Christopher Plummer's Hamlet has been described as "the Hamlet of Goethe and Coleridge, the gentle spirit broken by a burden too heavy for him to bear,"[52] but he can also be cited as a most ingenious and resourceful Hamlet who excels as much with body language as with the spoken word. Michael Caine (Horatio), Robert Shaw (Claudius), Donald Sutherland (Fortinbras), Alec Clunes (Polonius), mime Lindsay Kemp (Player Queen), and Jo Maxwell Muller as a "nastily" crazy Ophelia give him first-rate support.[53]

One of the great successes on Rediffusion Network Television production was Joan Kemp-Welch's 1964 *Midsummer Night's Dream*, which featured England's immensely popular comedian, Benny Hill, as Bottom, though Hill was then virtually unknown to mass North American audiences. The expressionistic influences of the Reinhardt school show just beneath the surface, with Mendelssohn's sprightly incidental music on the soundtrack, risking the condescension of those who prefer to dwell on the play's "darker elements." The woodland *mise-en-scène* showcases shrieking animals, an ubiquitous Puck (Tony Tanner) and a formidable Oberon (Peter Wyngarde) with a pre-punk haircut. The actors' short hair puts Shakespeare's world in the mirror of current fashions.

John Dexter's ATV *Twelfth Night* (1970) can be pleasurably recollected years later, partially because the cast was the best ever for a televised

Shakespeare comedy. As Malvolio, the protean Alec Guinness is a marvel of subtle restraint, a fussy, ridiculous but nevertheless forlorn creature, the embodiment of one of Shakespeare's roster of lost souls. Ralph Richardson's Sir Toby comes across as more sinister than farcical, which makes sense because when all is said and done Sir Toby is really quite a mean fellow, while casting pop star Tommy Steele as Feste turned Shakespeare's clown into a boy with a guitar. Joan Plowright's Viola captures the oscillations between femininity and androgyny accounting for that young woman's confused relationships with both Olivia and Count Orsino. The shifting camera angles embellish the dramatic irony of the letter scene in Olivia's garden when the pathetic, bemused Malvolio discovers the forged letter but cannot overhear his tormentors' cruel japes.

A recording of Trevor Nunn's RSC *Comedy of Errors* (1976) takes imaginative liberties with the Shakespearean original by turning it into a musical comedy, though not quite so wildly divorced from the original source as *The Boys from Syracuse* (1940). Duke Solinus is burlesqued as a kind of Mussolini dictator while Griffith Jones as old Egeon remains wonderfully lost, addlebrained, and unbearably dense. The Antipholus and Dromio pairs of twins function like lab rats in a Skinnerian box blindly responding to rewards and punishments. The most poignant moments come when Judi Dench as Adriana and Francesca Annis as Luciana exchange confidences about their "relationships" with men. Having Barbara Shelley's Courtesan as a flagrant hussy underscores the womens' resentment. Nunn's probing treatment, as with Miller's *Merchant* (1969) and Dexter's *Twelfth Night* (1970) discussed above, shows again how the light-heartedness in Shakespearean drama may conceal monsters from the deep. Shakespearean comedy and tragedy intertwine the carnivalesque and lenten in ways that defy neoclassical yearnings for pure genre.

Surely only by coincidence, *Macbeth* had a minor vogue in the United States after the Kennedy assassination, coming to an apex with the irreverent stage travesty, *MacBird*. A British *Macbeth* (1970), produced by Cedric Messina and directed by John Gorrie for BBC One with US funding, helped to satisfy the unspeakable craving for news about regicides and/or prexicides. A pilot project, as it turned out, for the subsequent BBC Shakespeare Plays series in which Messina and Gorrie were major figures, it features Janet Suzman opposite Eric Porter. Suzman's outward beauty and inner corruption as Lady Macbeth encompasses the play's major theme of the foulness of the fair and the fairness of the foul. That equivocal condition, deeply embedded in the play's language, gets visual support from camera angles forcing the audience to look down, at these two handsome but treacherous creatures. Unfortunately the *faux* realism of the stony castle walls works at cross purposes with the obvious fakery of the crowd scenes. Having Macbeth walk on foot rather than ride into the castle suggests either a low budget or a paralysis of the imagination. Janet Suzman's dynamic readings against Porter's stolid presence show how acting remains the one crucial variable determining success on stage or screen. When she says "We fail? / But screw your courage to the sticking place, / And we'll not fail" (*Macbeth* 1.7.59), she almost manages to break through the glass prison of the television screen and enter alive into our living rooms. Suzman herself felt that the play had special possibilities for television because of its "conspiratorial" nature with the action confined largely "to two or three people."[54] Television expert H.R. Coursen found Suzman's acting "superbly articulated," [55] but some saw the rest of the cast as just "passing through."[56]

Trevor Nunn's 1972 "Roman Plays season" at Stratford resulted ultimately in a televised production of *Antony and Cleopatra*, this time with the help of ATV network director Jon Scoffield. Despite some lukewarm reviews of her Stratford stage performance,[57] Janet Suzman and Richard Johnson's televised version won such accolades as "the finest Shakespearean production on television up to 1975."[58] After the establishing shot of a richly colored Egyptian frieze with superimposed credits and veteran composer Guy Woolfenden's music on the soundtrack, the charismatic Janet Suzman made the legendary queen into a divinity but one sparkling with human wit. In a nod to filmic values, an opening sequence in black-and-white dovetails Enobarbus' description of Antony as "the triple pillars of the world" with a montage symbolic of the Roman empire of orgies, soldiers, faces. Another cut localizes this sweeping panorama to Antony and Cleopatra themselves, who embody Rome and Egypt. Like Orson Welles, the directors were inspired by radio's sonic techniques and introduced a wonderful galaxy of sound for gulls, waves, and so forth; while Patrick Stewart's voice carried the description of Cleopatra's barge by truly describing what he saw, rather than just mechanically grinding out words. Few will forget Suzman's Cleopatra when she utters the words, "I have / Immortal longings in me" and "I am fire and air" (5.2.280, 289). At the end, imperiously erect even at death's door, she becomes an Egyptian icon, who has entered not only into history but into the lives of the audience. Robert Speaight in reviewing the earlier Stratford stage production understandably thought that she had "succeeded [in the role] where Peggy Ashcroft and Edith Evans had both failed."[59]

Arguably one of the greatest successes in the history of televised Shakespeare, Trevor Nunn's *Macbeth* (1976) at Stratford's The Other Place was adapted to television in 1979 without loss to either theatrical or telegenic values. As Michael Mullin observed, "instead of re-conceiving the production for television, the television director Philip Casson seems to have set himself the task of finding ways in which television could re-create the experience of the theatre."[60] With Judi Dench and Ian McKellen, and the rest of the cast in a circle so that they are themselves both actors and audience, the minimalist, starkly bare *mise-en-scène* in a meta-theatrical way virtually puts the audience in the same circle with the actors. Adroit camera angles and tight framing enhance the illusion that the screen is a mirror for ourselves rather than a frame for defining the actors.

Ritual replaces realism. The bizarrely eclectic costumes range from a prissy Rosse in a business suit to Scottish lairds in turtle-neck sweaters, to Macbeth in a black leather-and-boots Nazi outfit, to Lady Macbeth in some kind of black, tent-like garment and black headscarf. Ian McKellen's punk-like hairdo, slicked down and greased, demonizes a face that is egregiously at odds with A.C. Bradley's concept of a romantic/tragic hero, as conceived, for example, by Maurice Evans. Judi Dench, despite the vast folds of her curious garment, exudes a sensuality that makes Macbeth's infatuation with his lady believable. In one close-up, she and Macbeth virtually melt into each other as fervor overwhelms decorum. Ian McKellen makes the tragedy of Macbeth over into the unmasking of Macbeth, the exposure of the man's essential sordidness. Brilliantly, the same actor (Ian McDiarmid) who plays Rosse then turns around and doubles as an astonishing Porter wearing braces over a bare, hairy chest. Unbearable tension grows from such vignettes as Lady Macbeth's sleepwalking when she still wears that horrible black headpiece, and from Ian McKellen's terse spitting out of his "To-morrow, and to-morrow, and to-morrow / Creeps in this petty pace" (5.5.19). The spoken word sustains the chilling atmosphere. Despite many encomiums, a dissenting Richard Ingrams found it strange that the play was "greeted with rapture" by all the critics, thought the costumes, "ridiculous," and lamented that "poor Judi Dench . . . had to wear a duster around her head like a char lady."[61]

More pure video than television, Paul Bosner's plan to record live Shakespeare in performance at London's St. George's theatre produced a *Romeo and Juliet* (1976) starring Sarah Badel and Peter McEnery. In Sarah Badel, Bosner offered "a dreamy-eyed, enchanting Juliet." Nevertheless a stage play recorded on film remains one of the trickier equations to deal with, especially with the fierce competition from the then emerging BBC Shakespeare series.

In 1978 BBC's Cedric Messina, with Dr. John Wilders as literary consultant, began putting all thirty-six plays from the 1623 Folio plus *Pericles* into a six-year series called "The Shakespeare Plays," an epic task that marked a watershed in the history of Shakespeare on screen. The logistics of recruiting actors, designing sets and costumes, and finding creative directors, all within the constraints of a six-year timetable, approached megalomania and inevitably put the BBC production staff under fearful pressure. An unfortunate decision by British Equity to cast only British actors revived the ancient American inferiority complex over things British. Even worse, the decision to ignore American actors meant that American schools and colleges had less interest in spending money on the series. Since the project was heavily funded by US banks and corporations, this protectionism, which has often been reciprocated just as narrowly by Actors Equity on Broadway, sent prominent American theatre people like New York City's Shakespeare impresario, Joseph Papp, into a rage. On the other hand, the series revolutionized the teaching of Shakespeare in the schools. Great numbers of skeptical classroom teachers, taking a leaf from art history lecturers, began exploring the dynamics of screening scenes on the classroom television monitor as a supplement to amateurish readings by teachers and students.

The series got off to a slow start with a lackluster *Julius Caesar*, whose papier-mâché Rome, bedsheet costuming, and rhetorical paralysis signaled a decision to play it safe at all costs, even with estimable acting in Richard Pasco's Brutus, Keith Michell's Antony and especially Elizabeth Spriggs's Calphurnia. An outdoorsy *As You Like It*, filmed on location in May and June at Glamis Castle, Scotland, with Helen Mirren as a somewhat sullen Rosalind, unfortunately clashed with the "icy fang" of winter's wind associated with the Forest of Arden.[62] After that came a dismal *Romeo and Juliet* that was a shadowy replica of the dazzling Zeffirelli film; a king-centered *Richard II* that became a rostrum for the sinewy talents of Derek Jacobi as the narcissistic monarch; a highly successful *Measure for Measure*; and a surprisingly appealing *Henry VIII*. Director Desmond Davis' *Measure for Measure* was the season's hit. Kate Nelligan's Isabella and Tim Pigott-Smith's Angelo with strong support from John McEnery's Lucio (Mercutio in the Zeffirelli *Romeo and Juliet*) and Kenneth Colley's godlike Duke Vincentio, offered a familiar tale of sexual harassment well suited to a medium so congenial to soap opera. The casting of actors familiar to the British on popular programs, e.g., Kenneth Colley who played the blind beggar in *Pennies from Heaven*, was unfortunately lost on American audiences. John Stride, who was the ubiquitous Rosse in the Polanski film version of *Macbeth*, breathed new life into the infrequently performed *King Henry VIII*.

The second season began with John Gorrie's *Twelfth Night*, in which Trevor Peacock played a remarkably "manly and substantial" Feste and Alec McCowen a "deliciously obnoxious" Malvolio.[63] While the sets could not match the extravagant 1955 LenFilm version directed by Y. Fried, sensitive performances by Sinead Cusack as Olivia and Felicity Kendal as Viola conjured up some of the Illyrian magic. A repeat performance of *Richard II* then served as a prologue to the *First and Second Parts of Henry IV and Henry V*. The season ended with an inert *Tempest*, starring Michael Hordern and directed by John Gorrie again, whose gestures toward realism backfired when the plastic island remained dead even to the cry of sea gulls.

The subsequent televising of the major tetralogy of the English history plays allowed viewers a rare opportunity, as with *An Age of Kings*, to see the four plays virtually uncut. As Bolingbroke, Jon Finch suffers from a mysterious skin disease that serves as a metaphor for the diseased body of king and state, but unfortunately begins to make the audience homeopathically itch right along with him. As the "guilt" beneath the "gilt" of the crown surfaces, tension between father and son (Prince Hal is played by David Gwillim) escalates, until catharsis arrives in the great reconciliation scene in *Henry IV Part Two* (4.5.88–240). In the rejection scene during the coronation procession, Anthony Quayle (Falstaff) divulges the inner pathos of Shakespeare's "plump Jack," whose banishment spells the end of the whole world, with at least as much cogency as in Orson Welles's reading (5.5.47). As a Shakespearean actor, Quayle's screen appearances included Cassio in *Othello* (1937) and Marcellus in the Olivier *Hamlet* (1948), while in a lengthy stage career he once directed the RSC at the Stratford Memorial Theatre. The tavern scenes, which as in *Chimes* also suggest the influence of the seventeenth-century Dutch painters, introduce a garrulous Mrs. Quickly (Brenda Bruce) and a sleazy Doll Tearsheet (Frances Cuka), whose middle-aged seediness contrasts with the youthful glow of Jeanne Moreau in Welles's *Chimes*. The earlier plays of the BBC series mostly fell into the trap of assuming that television needed to be realistic even when a milieu such as the lists in Coventry made realism unrealistic. The battle scenes, especially with the gory close-up of Hotspur vomiting blood in his death throes at Shrewsbury, only succeeded in alienating the audience. The tiny television screen shrunk the epical Henriad down in scale so that David Gwillim as King Henry V, the "mirror of Christian princes," seemed to be wearing the borrowed robes of Laurence Olivier.

Nothing revolutionary happened at the beginning of the third season in 1980 with a *Hamlet* starring Derek Jacobi, which suffered from the recurring indecisiveness about whether to be theatrical or telegenic, and succeeding in being neither. The minimalist *mise-en-scène* with a small ramp and a cycloramic curtain looked in its bareness more like a budgetary than an artistic decision, but it did move away from realism toward expressionism. Derek Jacobi delivered his usual brilliant readings, but for those who had recently seen his *Richard II*, it was sometimes hard to tell whether he was Hamlet or a self-pitying "Landlord of England" (*Richard II* 2.1.113).The characters acted but did not interact. It was a Hamlet without *Hamlet*, so to speak, but Claire

Bloom was a memorable Gertrude and Richard Emrys a fine First Player. In a meta-theatrical touch, Hamlet directly enters into the performance of the Mouse Trap as a foil to Lucianus, the nephew of the player king.

In the third year, the versatile and imaginative Dr. Jonathan Miller, sometime member of the satirical Edinburgh Festival group, *Beyond the Fringe*,[64] replaced Cedric Messina, the veteran BBC producer of the project's first perilous years. Miller had the advantage of profiting from his predecessor's mistakes. Most notably he changed the design codes by looking to contemporaneous paintings and architecture as models for costuming and *mise-en-scène*. This same concept had already been explored in the first season with Desmond Davis' intriguing *Measure for Measure*, when designer Odette Barrow built costumes modeled on the clothing of people in seventeenth-century Dutch paintings. By broadening the scope of "Elizabethan" to include all European painting, Miller opened up fresh possibilities for his designers. Shakespeare's own players ignored historical consistency, as illustrated by the famous Longleat sketch of *Titus Andronicus*, in which, except for the principals, all the actors wear Elizabethan attire.

In *Antony and Cleopatra*, Paolo Veronese's paintings inspired the costumes and sets, while Colin Blakely (Antony) and Jane Lapotaire (Cleopatra) compressed the sprawling drama to the size of a geriatric love duet for the television screen. Indeed Richard David feared that "the necessary miniaturization for TV must be more damaging to *Antony and Cleopatra* than to any other play in the canon."[65] In *All's Well that Ends Well*, when Helena is seated at the clavichord with a mirror on the wall above her, she echoes the lady in Emanuel de Witte's "Interior with a Woman at a Clavichord." Beyond that, aided by designer John Summers, Elijah Moshinsky, a television *auteur* equal in talent to Jane Howell and Jonathan Miller, figured out how to enrich Angela Down's eerie Helena with a clever lighting plan. An acerbic Ian Charleson as a grumpy Bertram and the ubiquitous Michael Hordern, who surfaced in so many BBC plays, made the production from a technical point of view as unproblematic as the first season's play, *Measure for Measure,* was problematic. Director Jack Gold's *Merchant of Venice* drew on Tiziano Titian as a backdrop for the stony-faced Portia (Gemma Jones), who in true post-structuralist style subverts her own speech on mercy at the trial of Shylock (Warren Mitchell). Gold's camera also nicely pinpoints the spiritual desolation of both Jessica and Antonio, who at the end are left apart from the other far happier, more integrated, citizens of a waspish society. Despite the ethnic background of the production's director and star, some Jewish groups predictably objected to *Merchant* as anti-Semitic.

While Miller's design policies in drawing on high art drastically improved the series' visual attractiveness, considerable leeway yet remained for the genius of individual directors like Jane Howell, whose *Winter's Tale* experimented with minimalist, expressionistic sets and symbolic costumes (a bearskin hat and cloak for Leontes in prefiguration of the famous bear in the third act). And Miller himself truly ran against the grain of *The Taming of the Shrew* when he reinvented *Fawlty Towers'* comic innkeeper John Cleese as a puritanical and deadly solemn Petruchio. Cleese's prune-faced Petruchio contrasts so vividly with Richard Burton's oafish portrayal in the Zeffirelli movie (1966) as to make them seem altogether different characters. Miller ferreted out a subtext in Petruchio's scorn for the outward trappings of success, and turned him into the dour moralist implicit in his admonishment to Kate that "our purses shall be proud, our garments poor, / For 'tis the mind that makes the body rich" (4.3.171).

The pace slowed somewhat in the fourth season (1981–82) with only four plays: *Othello, Timon of Athens, A Midsummer Night's Dream,* and *Troilus and Cressida.* The two satirical plays, *Timon* and *Troilus,* brought Elizabethan esoterica within the range of mass audiences. Jonathan Pryce as the curmudgeonly and indubitably crazy Timon progressed from the excesses of generosity to the deficiencies of misanthropy. In *Troilus,* director Miller's design theories transported the play about ancient Troy to a world somewhere "between the medieval Gothic of Chaucer and Henryson and the Renaissance of Shakespeare." Theorizing that the Troy story was essentially a medieval legend anyway, Miller looked to woodcuts by Cranach, Dürer, and Altdorfer. Cranach, for example, made Paris over into a Gothic knight in his Judgment of Paris, but Miller also eclectically borrowed from the American television hit MASH for the dreary camp scenes. Charles Gray, a workhorse BBC actor, who in 1979 had played the title role in *Julius Caesar* and the Duke of York in *Richard II,* did Pandarus, while Jack Birkett (The Incredible Orlando [*sic*]) of the Lindsay Kemp company, a blind dancer and mime, whom Miller had seen as Caliban in the Derek Jarman *Tempest* (1980), was the spiteful and "bitchy" Thersites.[66] Director Elijah Moshinsky continued his career as a video *auteur* with a *Midsummer Night's Dream* that followed his earlier *All's Well* in its visual borrowings from the Dutch masters. A shot of the "rude mechanicals" posed on a bench outside a tavern mirrored Hans Bols's "Members of the Wine Merchants Guild," while a touch of whimsy made Cherith Mellor as Helena with her granny glasses and stick figure into an icon for adolescent misery.

The season's most ambitious but not most rewarding production was *Othello.* With Anthony Hopkins as the Moor, Bob Hoskins as Iago and Penelope Wilton as Desdemona, Director Miller's work "represents a noteworthy instance of transferring/transforming Shakespeare to video."[67] Unfazed by the controversy that erupted when British Equity refused permission for black American actor James Earl Jones to accept the role, Miller blithely declared that the play really had little to do with race after all but was focused on the question of jealousy.[68] He then cast Anthony Hopkins as a light-skinned Moor, a decision that was anathema in North America where political correctness makes a white actor playing Othello taboo. Low-keyed, almost humdrum at the beginning, Hopkins' Moor erupts into a manic fit when Hoskins' demonic, insinuating, cackling Iago finally unhinges him in the third act. Even if a mere coincidence, the linkage of the names, "Hopkins," and "Hoskins," hints at the production's stress on the *Doppelgänger* relationship between hero and villain. Like Kenneth Colley in *Measure*, Hoskins also represented for the British audience an unusual casting decision since he had played the pathetic music salesman and rapist in Dennis Potter's wonderful *Pennies from Heaven*, again a code switching that was lost in North America. No one questioned, however, the great power and authority of Hopkins' astounding performance. Costumes and sets showed the influence of a veritable art gallery of Renaissance painters to include Titian, De La Tour, Tintoretto, Brueghel, El Greco, Joos van Wassenhove, and Velasquez! Cyprian settings were modeled on a Renaissance palace in Urbino, Italy.[69]

The frenetic pace continued in the fifth period (1982–83) with six more plays captured on tape. An understated *King Lear* marked the third time, no less, that director Jonathan Miller, and actors Michael Hordern (King Lear) and Frank Middlemass (Fool) had collaborated on Shakespeare's supreme tragedy. Miller and Hordern de-mythologized King Lear by showing how his wicked daughters, with entire logic, might indeed have found the grizzled, somewhat dyspeptic, old king a royal pain in the neck. Instead of the flamboyant, ranting King Lear of a Frederick B. Warde or an Albert Finney as "Sir" in Peter Yates's *The Dresser* (1983), this king looked more like almost anybody's granddad on the verge of Alzheimer's. Through this subversion of the conventional image of the king as Jove-figure, the father–daughter bond became notably more poignant. Since Hordern appeared as King Lear at virtually the same time as the Granada TV Elliott/Olivier *King Lear* (1983), the two visual treatments invite close comparison. Competing with Lord Olivier was hardly anyone's desire, but Hordern's rather cynical old man in dark tones compares favorably with the more romantic image projected by Olivier in bright color. Both actors were self-referentially playing an aged star at the end of lengthy stage and film careers. They chose to interpret King Lear in the same way that they had lived out their professional lives – Hordern as a skilled and reliable journeyman actor, and Olivier as a mercurial and spectacular superstar.

Elijah Moshinsky's *Cymbeline* allowed him to put Claire Bloom back on

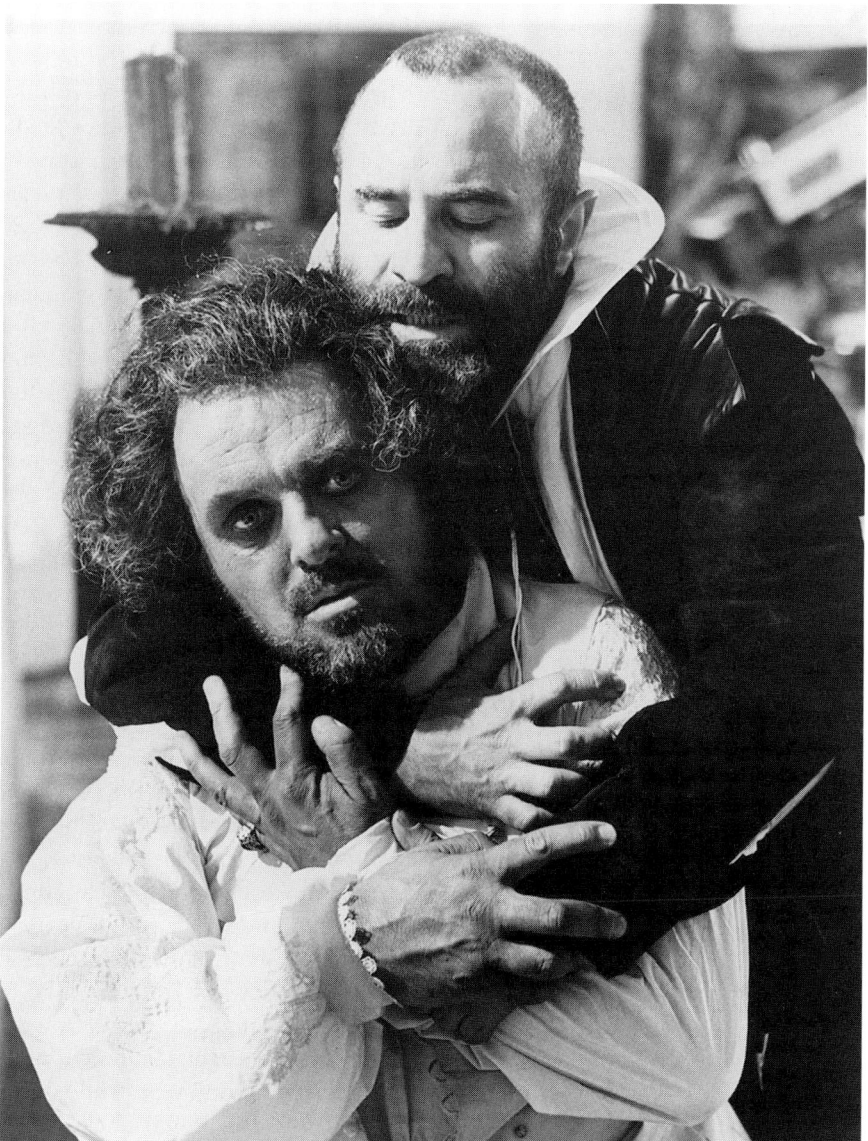

13 In a later televised version of *Othello* (1981), Bob Hoskins as Iago works Anthony Hopkins' Moor into a jealous rage over the alleged infidelity of Desdemona.

the screen as the malevolent queen, while a perfidious Iachimo (Robert Lindsay) schemes against an innocent Imogen (Helen Mirren). The following month saw Ben Kingsley as a paranoid Mr. Ford and Richard Griffiths as the scapegoated Falstaff in *The Merry Wives of Windsor*. The season's greatest achievement, however, was the sleeper of the entire series – Jane Howell's imaginative production of the minor tetralogy of the English history plays, *1–3 Henry VI* and *Richard III*. The BBC plays ripened as the directors began to discover the best means available for presenting them. Thus, Jane Howell junked the stodgy realism that had left audiences yawning in favor of a visually exciting expressionism. With mirrors and with the unlikely help of a children's "adventure playground" in Fulham, Howell's illusory battles became gorier than the real thing. Ron Cook as Richard duke of Gloucester and Julia Foster as Queen Margaret, the "she-wolf of France," portrayed impressively nasty royalty. As the Lady Anne, Zoë Wanamaker deepened and enhanced the role of this tortured but opaque young widow. At the same time, as a person of the twentieth century, Howell condemned warfare while sensationalizing this saga of division and rebellion, as indeed Shakespeare did himself. Howell turns Julia Foster as Queen Margaret into a "kind of death-goddess" as "she sits atop the mound of corpses which have been steadily building up at the end of each play."[70]

The sixth season (1983–84) of *Coriolanus, The Comedy of Errors, Two Gentlemen of Verona, Pericles*, and *Macbeth* was to have brought closure, but in fact four plays had yet not been released. Shaun Sutton had by then replaced Jonathan Miller as producer, and each year the insoluble problems of putting Shakespeare on the small screen seemed more soluble. The way that Alan Howard played Coriolanus opposite Mike Gwilym's Aufidius hinted at a homo-erotic link, while veteran Shakespearean actress, Irene Worth, was Volumnia, exalted mother of the "boy of tears." Both *Comedy of Errors* and *Two Gentlemen of Verona* generated the requisite farce and romance, though the sets for *Errors* with a crane shot of a gigantic map of the Mediterranean right out of Ortelius' atlas, seemed the more cleverly adapted to the medium. Pop singer Roger Daltrey, doubling as the Dromios in *Errors*, went over smashingly with American students, who could identify with him more readily than with actors from the Royal Shakespeare Company. Starring Mike Gwilym in the title role, Director David Jones's *Pericles* with its visual codes of soft Mediterranean lighting caught the flavor of Greek romances like the anonymous *Apollonius of Tyre*. In the brothel scenes, Trevor Peacock as Boult and Amanda Redman as Marina lent credibility to the faraway and exotic mood, while a high frequency of dissolves for Gower's narrative commentary visually corresponded to the rapid reversals of fortune in romance narrative. The season's nominees for best acting, however, were Nicol Williamson and Jane Lapotaire as Macbeth and his Lady, who ransacked the subtext for imaginative readings. Lapotaire's soliloquy, "Come, you spirits / That tend on mortal thoughts, unsex me here" (1.5.40) will surely go down in acting history as anything but unsexed in its steamy nonverbal gestures. Nicol Williamson, as in the Tony Richardson filmed "Roundhouse" *Hamlet* (1969), again brutally assaulted the text until it confessed its innermost secrets. Williamson and Richard Burton, between the two of them, virtually patented a whole new aggressive style for approaching Shakespeare's language, hitherto hostage to the elocution of genteel versifiers.

The years 1984 and 1985 saw the release of Elijah Moshinsky's *Love's Labor's Lost*; Stuart Burge's *Much Ado about Nothing*; David Giles's *King John*, and Jane Howell's *Titus Andronicus*. The first, *Love's Labor's Lost*, broke with the BBC house style when director Moshinsky put his actors in eighteenth-century instead of Elizabethan or Jacobean dress. Burge's rather inhibited *Much Ado* featured a somber Beatrice and Benedick but Susan McCloskey nevertheless praised Burge's spatial sense in arranging the *mise-en-scène* to fit the play's alternating moods of light and dark.[71] David Giles switched codes in *King John* by putting British comic actor Leonard Rossiter in the title role of the unhappy monarch, yet once more the mischief was lost on American audiences ignorant of the funny roles generally associated with Rossiter. By rediscovering the possibilities for Gothic thrills in Shakespeare's strange Senecan tragedy, *Titus Andronicus*, Jane Howell spawned a Rocky Horror Picture Show in minimalist guise. Gripping performances by Trevor Peacock in the title role and Anna Calder-Marshall as the ravished Lavinia make credible the incredibility of the Ovidian/Senecan rhetoric in Shakespeare's grotesque but compelling Roman history play.

Even while the BBC series was unfolding its magisterial design, other notable treatments of Shakespeare on television and/or video were either appearing or waiting in the wings. In New York City, Joseph Papp's *Midsummer Night's Dream* (1982) at the Delacorte Theatre in Central Park cleverly decoded Shakespeare into an idiom understandable to a contemporary audience. The rude mechanicals, for example, are reinvented as hard-hat New York construction workers. Marcel Rosenblatt's antic Puck also confirms the post-modernist understanding of the dream as always on the edge of a nightmare. Far away from Central Park in Johannesburg, South Africa, former RSC actress Janet Suzman, herself a stellar Cleopatra and Joan of Arc, daringly recorded the *Othello* (1988) performed at the Market Place Theatre. "Daringly" because in the context then of South Africa's apartheid policies, the close juxtaposition of a black man and white woman on stage invited brutal reprisals. Barbara Hodgdon reports that some white South

Africans walked out of the theatre at the first embrace between Desdemona and Othello.[72] John Kani as a black actor playing Othello stirs memories of electrifying performances by Paul Robeson and James Earl Jones. Richard Haddon Haines's Iago seems less compelling, but he shows an incomparable gift for mistreating Emilia, while Joanna Weinberg as Desdemona adds to her shimmering whiteness the extra touch of wearing a green gown in anticipation of Othello's jealous fit. The reception was enthusiastic, both in South Africa and after a 1989 telecast from London's Channel Four. Hugh Herbert of *The Guardian* wrote that "John Kani's is a fine and masterful performance that should make every white actor think twice before blacking up for the Moor."[73]

Michael Bogdanov's brilliant seven-part *Wars of the Roses* (1988–89) glitters with bright ideas, but never attracted all the attention and praise that it deserves. The apparent inconsistency of having the characters in the first installment, *King Richard II*, appear in Edwardian costumes and the characters in *Richard III* in modern dress quietly reflects the historical fact that nearly a century elapsed between Bolingbroke's usurpation of Richard II in 1399 and the victory of Lancastrian Henry Tudor at Bosworth Field in 1485. Bogdanov, and his colleague Michael Pennington, supported the recorded performances by the English Theatre Company at the Grand Theatre, Swansea, with a clever mixture of theatre, television, and cinema, and used montages of key figures and events for linking episodes. The haunting, hallucinatory, watery transitions hint at the deadly secrets and horrors that Queen Margaret, the "she-wolf of France," never tires of reciting.

Ever since Colley Cibber's eighteenth-century production, directors have ransacked their ingenuity to clarify the complicated politics behind the opening events of *Richard III*. Here the witty gimmick, in what seems to prefigure the opening scene of the Ian McKellen and Richard Loncraine *Richard III* (1995), lies in having a "Prologue," Barry Stanton, introduce the assembled cast, who have gathered in modern dress for a cocktail party. The tuxedo-clad Chorus, who wears a red-and-white rose boutonniere in sign of the houses of Lancaster and York, genially sorts out the complicated relationships among the characters, introducing each in turn. The doomed Clarence, Rivers, Grey, and Dorset register wonderfully pained facial expressions when they hear Stanton telling the audience that they will die during the play. When Stanton finishes his labyrinthine plot summary, a masterpiece of black humor, he turns to the audience and in a flash of ironic understatement says, "Simple!"

Most unforgettable, however, is Andrew Jarvis' Richard duke of Gloucester. In a drape suit three sizes too big for him, showing a slight hump at the left shoulder, wearing a black glove and heavy orthopedic shoe, his shirt collar unbuttoned, tie askew, and stomping around with an exaggerated limp, Jarvis oozes pure, unadulterated evil. When he woos the Lady Anne over the corpse of her murdered father-in-law, and allows her an opportunity to stab him – "Take up the sword again, or take up me" (1.2.183) – he yanks out a pair of wicked-looking switch-blade knives that give him the look of an Edward Scissorhands. His absolutely bald skull adds yet another repellent feature to this variant on the Beauty and the Beast fable. To rescue him from being a mere caricature of the anti-Christ, though, Richard's response to being spat at by the Lady Anne is an unexpected look of deep hurt and anguish, as if he were truly wounded. Or again, is this just another example of Richard as the "murtherous Machevil," who can "frame [his] face to all occasions" (3 *Henry VI* 3.2.193, 185). Jarvis plays it too cleverly for anyone to be sure.

There was more happening than just on television, though. Shakespeare in moving images has proliferated with the new technology of cheaper, more user-friendly, magnetic taping, hand-held cameras, and portable recording and sound equipment. The residual rights for the sale of home videocassettes transformed the economics of the industry, where theatrical release recoups the cost of a movie and overseas and video sales turn the profit. The commercial exploitation of the entire BBC Shakespeare series on videocassettes by Time Life Inc. opened up a fresh market in the schools with state funds underwriting audio/visual equipment. In addition the possibilities for cheap magnetic recording of Shakespeare on stage, even with camcorders, began to be explored increasingly, as organizations such as the New York City Lincoln Center Library TOFT (Theatre on Film and Tape) collection, the Folger Library, and the embryonic Globe Bankside Centre in London began collecting archival videotapes for study purposes only. Most notably the Royal Shakespeare Company in Stratford-upon-Avon also taped its theatrical productions for storage in the Stratford Shakespeare Centre Library, where one can now view rare footage of Charles Laughton as Bottom in a Peter Hall production from the 50s, and the Royal National Theatre established a performance archive at the British Theatre Museum in Covent Garden. The Canadian Stratford Shakespeare Festival markets videotaped segments of plays like *The Taming of the Shrew* (1981) starring Len Cariou and Sharry Flett, with added commentary for the educational sector. If the Actors' Equity and musicians' unions relax copyright restrictions, future theatre historians will study late twentieth-century Shakespeare performances at video archives.

The growing bifurcation between video as a publication like a book and video for terrestrial transmission has encouraged the recordings of Shakespeare plays on stage primarily for home VCR use rather than for television. With success directly related to the quality of the actors, some notable examples have been R. Thad Taylor's videotaping of a lively *Merry Wives of Windsor* (1979) starring Gloria Grahame as Mistress Page at the Los Angeles Globe Playhouse. Bard Productions, Ltd., with the specific goal of allowing American students to see Shakespeare performed by well-known American daytime soap opera actors, has marketed a *Macbeth, Richard II, Antony and Cleopatra*, and *The Tempest*. The Bard *Macbeth* has received a mixed reception, one critic declaring it "absolutely awful ... a deed without a name,"[74] but the *Richard II*, starring well-known daytime television star David Birney, is impressive. When Bolingbroke interrogates Bushy and Green, the "caterpillars of the commonwealth," he behaves less like the stern English headmaster, as played by Jon Finch in the BBC version, than like a tough cop in a B movie giving a perp the "third degree." Quite a hair-raising scene.

Director Sarah Caldwell's *Macbeth* (1981), a stage production at New York's Lincoln Center available on videocassette, was also televised on a cable channel in 1982. A zany slapstick *Comedy of Errors* (1987) with The Flying Karamazov Brothers circus act and a Kamikaze Ground Crew shown over PBS stations has videotaped a performance from New York's Vivian Beaumont Theatre. An actor costumed as Will Shakespeare occasionally appears to shake his head sadly over what is happening on stage. One of the best of what might be called this video genre is the Cambridgeshire postmodernist *Hamlet* (1987) that, with only four actors, deconstructs and then reconstructs Shakespeare's text in the idiom of a psychedelic rock video. "This is *Hamlet* with an antic disposition,"[75] its re-envisioning of the text springing from an honest drive to use the camera not just for recording a play but for artistry in its own right. Another important televised *Hamlet* was the recording of Kevin Kline's 1990 performance at New York's Public Theatre for WNET/Thirteen's "Great Performances" series. A strong, powerful prince with excellent diction, Kline was helped by a steamy Dana Ivey as Gertrude and a waifish Diane Venora as Ophelia. Meanwhile in Great Britain, the nearly unbroken chain of televised Shakespeare continues, most recently with a *Merchant of Venice* (1995) directed by Alan Horrox for the government-subsidized "schools" programs. With a first-rate professional cast including Bob Peck as Shylock and Haydn Gwynne as Portia, the program examines such contemporary issues as capitalism, feminism, and anti-Semitism.

Yet another thriving sub-species of Shakespeare on television derives from the hijacking of bits and pieces and segments of Shakespeare by scenarists hungry for material. Often not separately listed in *TV Guide,* they are difficult to track down. For example, viewers of ABC's *Moonlighting* enjoyed a radically altered *Taming of the Shrew* (1986) starring Bruce Willis and Cybill Shepherd. Both a broad parody and a feminist revision, the production shrewdly revealed that Kate and Petruchio are "much alike, both shrewish and full of high spirits."[76] British television audiences were regaled with the inspired and sometimes not so inspired nonsense of Rowan Atkinson as Edmund duke of Edinburgh and Brian Blessed as "good King Richard IV" in the BBC sitcom, *The Black Adder* (1983), which sent up costume dramas like Olivier's films of the English history plays. The fabled *Star Trek* in an episode called "The Conscience of the King" has "Riley visit the theater area where the Karidian Players are performing *Hamlet* for the crew,"[77] and the subtitle for *Star Trek VI*, "The Undiscovered Country," does little to conceal its origins. These many, many flash appearances validate how deeply Shakespeare is embedded in popular culture throughout the English-speaking world, the *Star Trek* vein having alone stimulated its own sub-specialty of scholarly commentary.[78] Additionally, keeping track of the myriad videos that come and go in the Shakespeare educational market requires the services of a full-time central archivist like the British Universities Film & Video Council.[79] Instructional videos include everything from "Shakespeare of Stratford and London," to "The Staging of Shakespeare," "Shakespeare's Country," "Reconstructing the Bankside Theatre," "Teaching Shakespeare," and the eleven-part "Playing Shakespeare" series, presided over by John Barton, originally televised in England on the South Bank Show. Even the splendid documentary of the New York Shakespeare Festival *Taming of the Shrew* (1981) with Meryl Streep and Raul Julia falls into some hybrid form of educational program. Several movie versions of the plays (e.g., the Olivier *Hamlet*, the Pickford/Fairbanks *Taming of the Shrew*), and Kenneth Branagh's televised Renaissance Theatre *Twelfth Night* (1988) have found their way into the laser disk market that provides new and highly sophisticated methods for close scanning of the plays with the aid of a Pioneer Disk Player. Shakespeare has emerged on the cutting-edge CD-ROM market with a Voyager Company *Macbeth* (1994), edited by A.R. Braunmuller with commentary by David Rodes, which is a veritable electronic library combining the resources of a variorum with those of a concordance, a map and picture gallery, spoken and screened performances, and even a Karaoke, where a student can play a role in tandem with professional actors. And Shakespeare has entered into the World Wide Web of the computer age where a library of textual and scholarly information can be tapped through Terry Gray's "Mr William Shakespeare & the Internet" at <http://www.palomar.edu/Library/shake.htm>. Most recently the *Encyclopaedia Britannica* has compiled a Web site to celebrate the first season of London's new Globe Theatre (1997) at <http://shakespeare.eb.com/>.

Thus televised Shakespeare that began as a hybrid genre wandering somewhere among the realms of theatre, radio, television studio, and cinema, by the end of the century has evolved into a matrix of crossover potentials. As the century winds down, the differences among television, video, and movies will increasingly narrow with the emergence of high-definition transmission, and the coming digital revolution will also connect in unpredictable ways with personal computers. The need to write a separate chapter on televised Shakespeare may be made obsolete as cutting-edge technology makes Shakespeare on television and film increasingly synergetic. But that is futurist speculation about electronic Shakespeare for the next century to validate.

- 6 -

Spectacle and song in Castellani and Zeffirelli

There is a kind of poetic justice in the way that Shakespeare who filtered Renaissance Italy through the lens of English experience should in the twentieth century have been refiltered through the lens of Italian cinema. A playwright with a European vision, Shakespeare set his plays in all sorts of exotic places, from Verona in Italy to Messina in Sicily to Ephesus in Asia Minor, though it seems likely that he never traveled to any of them. The Italian scholar Mario Praz thought that the quick-witted Shakespeare could have faked his foreign expertise simply by conversing with London's expatriate Italians at the Bankside Elephant Inn.[1] Two Italian directors, Renato Castellani and Franco Zeffirelli, reclaimed the franchise of Italian cinéastes from the silent days of Guazzoni and Lo Savio to resituate Shakespeare's Romeo and Juliet in an ambiance that their creator could only have imagined. A complicated combination of lighter camera equipment, the post-war influence of *cinema verité*, the waning of the once powerful Hollywood studio system, and currency and tax laws affecting American money in European banks made possible the abandonment of the sound stages for the realism of European streets.

Castellani's *Romeo and Juliet*

Renato Castellani's Technicolor *Romeo and Juliet* (1954) inaugurated the vogue for "authentic" Renaissance settings in Shakespeare movies and teleplays. Castellani "recreated works of pictorial art for the camera,"[2] before the idea was discovered by Jonathan Miller and made into a house style for the BBC Shakespeare plays. New portable camera and lighting equipment eliminated the need for a fake Verona on a back lot in Hollywood. Italy itself became the backdrop for *Romeo and Juliet* with filming variously in Siena, Venice, Verona, and Montagana. In a country that remains an outdoor museum immune to bulldozers, Robert Krasker, the cameraman responsible for Olivier's *Henry V*, inscribed Castellani's movie in a world of cobblestone streets, piazzas, and the clustered and shuttered structures of uniquely Italian architecture. Only a few querulous people objected that city streets in Shakespeare's time would have looked less worn than they appear today in the film.

Bardophiles despised Castellani's *Romeo and Juliet* because it put movie making ahead of the text, while the cinéphiles saw it as a work of art independent of its literary source. Outraged "purists" went into the usual feeding frenzy. Castellani's movie was "ineluctably, unforgivably prosaic" for "visual distinction makes a poor substitute for poetry," observed one;[3] another wrote that "never, I imagine, since *Lear* received a happy ending, has any Shakespeare text been so hacked, patched, and insensitively thrown away";[4] and to yet another, the "tragedy collapses and is swept away in a visual flood."[5] Even the detractors, however, confessed that the movie was spectacularly beautiful but, unlike the cinéphiles, they overlooked the nexus between this visual beauty and Shakespeare's lyrical language. Bosley Crowther, on the other hand, saw that Castellani was more interested in making a movie out of the play than in literally reproducing the text on screen: "The lyrical language of Shakespeare . . . was plainly secondary to his concept of a vivid visual build-up of his theme."[6]

Castellani's visual lyricism stands in for Shakespeare's verbal lyricism. The opening prologue ceremonially recited by John Gielgud, costumed rather ridiculously to look like William Shakespeare, identifies the film with the grandest Shakespearean stage traditions. This obligatory concession to Shakespeare's language having been made, Castellani never apologizes for privileging *opsis* over *lexis*, but at the same time he notably strives to transfer Shakespearean themes into vivid images. A medium shot of the city gate of Verona shows the town's name inscribed above it, as people casually stroll in and out past a lone sentry. The highlighting of the city's name in the establishing shot signals that it will not only rival the young lovers for prime billing, but also imprison them within its walls, its alleys, its confused masses of people, its feuds and its anxieties. The city gate exemplifies Romeo's belief that, "There is no world without Verona walls, / But purgatory, torture, hell itself" (3.3.17). All other citizens can pass easily through these walls, but Romeo's misfortune is to be banished, set outside from both the city and his beloved: "The orchard walls are high and hard to climb, / And the place death," says Juliet in the balcony scene, to which Romeo ironically replies "With love's light wings did I o'erperch these walls, / For stony limits cannot hold love out" (2.2.63). His frantic running through the narrow claustrophobic streets also emblemizes Friar Lawrence's warning against Romeo's weakness for "sudden haste": "Wisely and slow, they stumble that run fast" (2.3.94).

Graphic images of confinement, separation, and suffocation replace the

14   Romeo (Laurence Harvey) and Juliet (Susan Shentall) in Renato Castellani's spectacular color movie set in sunny Italy (Italy/UK 1954).

emotional content lost by textual deletions. Castellani's wedding scene (not Shakespeare's, where it takes place off stage) underscores the irony of the forlorn marriage by putting an iron grille between the lovers during the exchange of their wedding vows. In medium shot, Juliet looks through the network of bars, while in low angle Romeo stares down at her from the opposite side of the barrier. A medium shot of Juliet receiving a flower through the bars follows a two-shot of Romeo and the Friar. Off camera, there is the hypnotic sound of Friars' chanting, and then a cut to the Nurse kneeling in medium shot on the stone floor. Romeo and Juliet's sealing of the matrimonial vows with a kiss through the barriers of iron faintly echoes the *Pyramus and Thisby* play in *Midsummer Night's Dream*. Friar Lawrence's, "So smile the heavens upon this holy act" (2.6.1), which is of course transposed from its place *before* the wedding, tinges this pathetic marriage sanctified behind bars with even more irony.

In a tight framing, the "cords," or rope ladder that the Nurse provides for Juliet flop down from the balcony near a stone urn in another trope for imprisonment. As Nurse, Flora Robson brings admirable competence to the role but fails to capture the creature's coarseness of soul. Dread of confinement in the tomb haunts the isolated Juliet: "Shall I not then be stifled in the vault, / To whose foul mouth no healthsome air breathes in [?]" she asks (4.3.33). In her bedchamber, the gold brocaded bridal gown (copied from Botticelli's Flora) draped over a dressmaker's frame ominously prefigures the darkness ahead. Before drinking off the potion, she puts on the wedding dress, which she will wear not for Romeo but for the other bridegroom, Death. In the morning, after a dissolve from the Capulet courtyard to the sleeping Juliet, the camera pulls back to reveal the dress frame tumbled over sideways. Later, Romeo's heroic efforts to crack the seal on Juliet's tomb using a huge metal candlestick for a crowbar encapsulates the tension between the incarcerative city and the ardor of the young lovers. The great door sealing the Church of San Zeno al Maggiore dwarfs the lone figure of Romeo, the star-crossed victim of fate.

Renaissance painting and sculpture, as well as architecture, support the movie's visual splendor. Among the fifteenth-century artists who provided ideas for costumes and props Meredith Lillich catalogs such names as Uccello, Piero della Francesca, Lippi Filippino, Lippo Lippi, and Carpaccio. The Empress Helena in Piero's fresco of the Holy Rood in Arezzo inspired Lady Capulet's hairstyle; the Luca della Robbia sculptured singing gallery in Florence, the five boys singing at the Capulet ball; Raphael's portrait of the Pope, Capulet in his study, and so forth.[7] Among the supporting players, Sebastian Cabot as Capulet wins a lifetime claim to being the best ever Capulet with his ferocious scolding, or scalding, of Juliet for refusing to marry Paris. Juliet remains foregrounded in a hallway while backgrounded in deep focus her father stomps back and forth, appearing and disappearing in an open doorway, raging at her. His adventitiousness supports the discontinuity of his language, and the camera responds rhythmically to the frenetic tempo of his anger. He rants, raves, and roars, indeed "out-Herods Herod," in a temper tantrum only rivaled by Orson Welles's denunciation of his mistress in *Citizen Kane*. Cabot's talent for choleric wrath also adds weight to the ballroom scene when Tybalt's threat to challenge the intruding Romeo stirs Capulet into a froth of alternating geniality and anger. Susan Shentall (Juliet) and Laurence Harvey (Romeo) flourish in these exotic settings that highlight their status as beautiful but fragile young lovers trapped by a star-crossed fate. Several critics noted a certain listlessness or languor in Laurence Harvey's performance but the root cause may actually have been Castellani's intent to make Romeo over into a sacrificial offering, like Juliet. As Paul Jorgenson has said, the chief aim of Castellani was to highlight the "youthfulness and helplessness"[8] of Romeo and Juliet by deliberately imprisoning them in the stony walls of Verona. In both images and words, the film skews the lovers' plight more toward pity than fear to create a "comitragedy," from a play whose comic potential invariably works at cross purposes with the tragic denouement.

Zeffirelli's *Taming of the Shrew*

The Italianate expropriation continued with Franco Zeffirelli's exuberant *Taming of the Shrew* (1966) also filmed in Italy but in Dino de Laurentiis' new studio rather than on location. Zeffirelli said that shooting the film in the studio "gave it an air of unreality which matched the remoteness of the language."[9] A major *auteur* of Shakespeare movies, Zeffirelli was to go on from *Shrew* with a sensational *Romeo and Juliet* (1968), a dazzling Verdi's *Otello* (1986), and a thoughtful *Hamlet* (1990). Bringing his background in opera to the Old Vic, Zeffirelli enjoyed considerable success with his stage *Romeo and Juliet* (1960), starring John Stride and Judi Dench, which wrung from notoriously hard-to-please critic Kenneth Tynan the verdict of a "masterly production." Peter Hall's subsequent invitation to direct *Othello* (1961) at Stratford with John Gielgud as the Moor led, however, in Zeffirelli's own words to an opening night that "must have been one of the most disastrous and ill-fated in the history of the English – and possibly the world – stage."[10] With extensive operatic background, Zeffirelli brought special expertise to a scintillating *Otello* (1987) starring Placido Domingo, which as filmed opera remains outside the scope of this book.

Just as in Castellani's movie, the casting for Zeffirelli's *Taming of the Shrew* favored British and American actors despite the Italian milieu, the stars being Richard Burton and Elizabeth Taylor, then reigning king and queen of the movies. As an assistant to and designer for stage director and film artist

Luchino Visconti, Zeffirelli early in his career developed a trademark passion for meticulous authenticity in costumes and settings. Zeffirelli's vision of *Shrew* nearly matched in splendor Douglas Fairbanks and Mary Pickford's 1929 black-and-white picture, which was designed by William Cameron Menzies, creator of the mammoth sets for *The Thief of Bagdad*. As a serious Shakespearean, Richard Burton wanted to do the film badly enough to underwrite part of its costs, though Elizabeth Taylor, while a brilliant actress as well as a movie star, regarded it as simply another movie.[11] During this same period, she played a devastating Helen of Troy, the ultimate femme fatale, against Burton's Faustus in a film society movie of Christopher Marlowe's *Dr. Faustus* (1968).

Too much has been written about what Zeffirelli's *Shrew* loses from Shakespeare's play and not enough about what it adds. One reviewer began by admonishing his readers: "Don't bother to brush up on your Shakespeare when you go see Elizabeth Taylor and Richard Burton . . . in this totally wild abstraction of the Bard."[12] In fact the movie makes more sense, a lot more sense, if you do bother to "brush up on your Shakespeare." Franco Zeffirelli's movie is by no means a literal-minded adaptation of Shakespeare's text but rather an imaginative filmic reconstruction of the play's essential concerns, which have to do with the ongoing battle of the sexes starting with Adam and Eve and continuing, it would seem, from the medieval Mystery plays about Noah and his wife down to today's feminist animadversions. As with the farcical *Comedy of Errors, Taming of the Shrew* addresses serious concerns behind a façade of absurdity, badinage, and slapstick.

With the help of script writers Paul Dehn and Suso Cecchi d'Amico, as well as genius composer Nino Rota, who had also worked with Visconti, and photographers Oswald Morris and Luciano Trasatti, Zeffirelli happily ignored the play's darker side and turned its sexual warfare into a springtime rite free from any hint of approaching autumn. Much of Shakespeare's text has been slyly (no pun intended) embedded in the movie. Motifs from the Induction scene, centering on the "tinker" Christopher Sly, which sets up the play's major theme of "supposings," the ways in which illusion can distort reality, have been transposed and sprinkled throughout the film. Shakespeare's Induction keeps reappearing almost subliminally throughout the movie as with the arrival in Padua of Lucentio (Michael York) and servant Tranio (Alfred Lynch): they pass under a cage labeled "Drunkard" imprisoning an unhappy wretch, which is a wry reminder of Christopher Sly. Elements of the oafish Sly surface in Burton's boorish portrayal of Petruchio. Of course Petruchio may only be pretending, "supposing," to be a boor just as Sly wonders about his own identity: "Am I a lord, and have I such a lady? / Or do I dream? Or have I dream'd till now?" (Ind. 2.68).

"Supposings" also emerge in the multiple disguisings of Hortensio as Litio, Lucentio as Cambio, Tranio as Lucentio, as well as the "suppos'd Vincentio," the sail maker who tries to pass himself off as Lucentio's father.

Behind this overt disguising, or "supposing," though, is the psychological "supposing" within the minds of Petruchio and Kate as they engage in a duel of wits and egos to discover ways to reach out to, or to reject, or come to terms with, the impossible person that fate has saddled them with. The studio ambiance of the painted backdrop of Padua already implies a "supposing" that this is not really Padua but only a celluloid fantasy. Michael Pursell has carried the idea a step further in showing how the use of an "ochre or sepia-tinted filter" on the camera lens has altered color values to embed the play's theme of "supposings" in the movie's cinematic infra-structure.[13]

A ribald festival of misrule, subversive of hierarchy, in the shape of carnivalesque street revelry after a university semester opening ceremony replaces Shakespeare's Induction in the opening scene. Graham Holderness describes how Zeffirelli (sometimes nicknamed "Shakespirelli") hired eager local *capelloni* ("long-haired ones") as extras.[14] The street festival also cleverly embeds the Bianca/Lucentio subplot into the film's opening. Rota's musical score supports the carnal excitement of the processional, which is reminiscent of a scene in Marcel Carné's *Les Enfants du Paradis* (1944), with a variation at a faster tempo on Petruchio's recurring theme of "What Is a Life?" As a worshipful Lucentio (Michael York) gazes on a lovely blonde Bianca (Natasha Pyne), a prankster with a fish hook on a line raises the veil covering her face, and a cluster of university singers fill the soundtrack with Nino Rota's dulcet ballad "Let me tell, gentle maiden, let me tell." Rota's "Bianca theme" that so eloquently celebrates the outward beauty of Bianca, as if she were Petrarch's Laura, then re-emerges when Kate "surrenders" to Petruchio. The music supports Shakespeare's "chiasmus" motif in which Bianca and Kate gradually exchange roles – Bianca revealing her innate shrewishness; and Kate, her innate generosity. The festive processional with an immense, blowzy blonde framed in the window, a *memento mori* figure carried on a mock bier, masked mummers, and rich costumes, shows Zeffirelli's famous talent for crowd scenes and opulent costumes and sets. Estimating Kate's dowry, Petruchio examines the rich furnishings of Baptista Minola's mansion with all the devotion of a Sotheby's appraiser. As he says, "I come to wive it wealthily in Padua; / If wealthily, then happily in Padua" (1.2.75).

Zeffirelli himself (or was it Dehn's idea?) executes one of the greatest "supposings" of all when he conflates the drunken, lower-class Sly with Petruchio. The real Sly remains the sodden wretch fettered in a cage at the entrance to the city, but the sensuous symbols and images from the Induction, the scented bedchamber and the rose-watered bath, for example, are linked with Petruchio. Unfortunately, Zeffirelli's "supposing" turns Petruchio into a lout rather than the impoverished scion of country gentry, as he is in Shakespeare's play. On the other hand, the idea does not violate the play's mysterious way of casting doubt on people's true identities. Even Petruchio, who might be thought of as the play's "norm" figure, completely reverses himself by turning from a fortune hunter into a true lover. The egregious rough-and-tumble slapstick in the hayloft semiotically matches the indecent exchange about "tales" and "tongues" between Kate and Petruchio ending with Petruchio's outrageous "What, with my tongue in your tail?" (2.1.217).

Petruchio's raucous arrival at the wedding in an "in-your-face" costume seems perverse but actually has the moralizing purpose of teaching Kate (as in Jonathan Miller's 1981 BBC television version) that "Our purses shall be proud, our garments poor, / For 'tis the mind that makes the body rich" (4.3.171). The added farcical scene based on Gremio's (Alan Webb) narrative of the "mad marriage" (3.2.182), which quotes from the 1929 Pickford/Fairbanks movie, achieves its height of sublime impudence when Petruchio drinks off the communion wine, crying out "gogs-wouns" (3.2.160), and stifles Kate's "I will not" in response to the vicar's question by kissing her with "a clamorous smack" (3.2.178). The vicar (Giancaro Cobelli) first steps back in horror from the madcap couple at his altar but then his face is suffused with relief as he hastily pronounces them man and wife. The close-ups of Michael Hordern as Baptista Minola capture his fluttery helplessness over this cranky daughter, as he plays out a father–daughter relationship on a drastically different key from his experience with Cordelia in the 1982 BBC *King Lear*.

Actually the greatest "supposing" or "wonder" of all comes at the end of the film: "Here is a wonder, if you talk of a wonder," says Lucentio (5.2.106). Throughout, Zeffirelli's movie closely follows Shakespeare's play in setting up patterns of wooing and wedding against a backdrop of alternating harmony and discord. Expecting to end on a note of discord rather than harmony, director Zeffirelli was amazed, and apparently so was Richard Burton,[15] when Elizabeth Taylor, hardly a submissive type, delivered Kate's famous speech of surrender in the wager scene without a trace of irony. There was no Mary Pickford wink to her sister Bianca, instead only an eloquent and beautifully spoken tribute to the Elizabethan doctrine of passive obedience, which comes straight out of the Church of England Book of Homilies: "Such duty as the subject owes the prince / Even such a woman oweth to her husband" (5.2.155). So when Burton says, "Why, there's a wench! Come on, and kiss me, Kate" (5.2.179), his words are heartfelt, yet Kate's gesture of suddenly running away from her bewildered bridegroom problematizes the event. Burton and Taylor's Petruchio and Kate are doomed to grow older and turn into the George and Martha of *Who's Afraid of Virginia Woolf* (1966), whom they so brilliantly portray in Mike Nichols' film of Albee's play, but until those shadows encroach they remain in the memory as the irrepressible couple of this sprightly movie.

Zeffirelli's *Romeo and Juliet*

Franco Zeffirelli's *Romeo and Juliet* (1968) showed how "Shakespeare" with some help from a clever movie director can generate an immense profit at the box office. A masterpiece of intricately choreographed music, poetry, and photography, the movie shamelessly plays on the emotions of all but the most stony-hearted critics. From an Anglo-American perspective, the Italian willingness to expose emotions, something that Zeffirelli also saw in Visconti's neo-realist films, turns Shakespeare's play into a "weepy," too low mimetic in sensibility for tragedy. One of its heirs has been the Romeo and Juliet subtext deployed in James Cameron's wildly successful *Titanic* (1998), which packs in teenagers eager to blubber over the fate of Jack (Leonardo DiCaprio) and Rose (Kate Winslet). Inevitably the textual "purists" railed against Zeffirelli's deletions, which were needed to cram the action into two hours and nineteen minutes. The consort in the fifth act has disappeared; the Nurse's neo-Senecan mourning for Juliet, gone; the apothecary scene, jettisoned; Juliet's potion speech, obliterated; and, with some justice, the friar's last-act plot summary, even though it eliminates Shakespeare's important warning against youthful transgressive behavior. Every deletion, however, has been embellished with an addition to show that Shakespeare may legitimately belong to the screen as well as to the stage. Overly sentimentalized or not, the film moves audiences however indirectly toward Aristotle's cryptic notion of "catharsis" through a purging away of emotions. At the fatal climax in the tomb scene, few can resist feeling pity and fear.

To conclude that Zeffirelli sacrificed art on the altar of "tickling commodity" assumes that he might have wanted to handle his movie differently. As one critic wrote, "Zefirelli's [*sic*] aesthetic, in fact, seems funded on a principle of excess for its own sake."[16] Jack J. Jorgens found much to admire but gagged on the "sticky sweet" neo-Petrarchan song, "What Is a Youth?"[17] Yet Zeffirelli, an unabashed populist in art, the prize architect of low mimetic representation, despite his political conservatism, paradoxically thinks that art should be approachable rather than unapproachable, and that elitist cadres, who patronize simple folk, like the Sicilian fishermen in Visconti's *La Terra Trema* (1948), for example, often stray from the primal roots of human experience. Robert Hapgood makes a nice distinction between Olivier's English way "of sharing a family heirloom with outsiders," and Zeffirelli as an outsider, "escorting the uninitiated on the same journey of discovery [of Shakespeare] he himself had made as a youth."[18]

Despite the immense success at the box office of *The Taming of the Shrew*, Zeffirelli's plan to proceed at once with a *Romeo and Juliet* was funded only grudgingly by Paramount Pictures with what he describes as "the derisory sum of $800,000,"[19] though later it was to gross $48 million. Besides the risk of bankrolling a Shakespeare movie, the studio executives were dismayed that Zeffirelli had no plans for big-name stars like Taylor and Burton as box office magnets. Generations of directors had acknowledged the impossibility of finding adolescent actors with the dramatic talent to play Romeo and Juliet and had fallen back, as did George Cukor and Irving Thalberg, on aging matinee idols like Norma Shearer and Leslie Howard. Zeffirelli boldly rejected the superstar route and cast unknown teenagers, Leonard Whiting and Olivia Hussey. As Albert R. Cirillo has observed, "these actors [Hussey and Whiting] have no existence until the film begins, when they *are* simply Romeo and Juliet."[20]

At exhausting auditions, three sets of the company's casting people screened Hussey and some 350 other eager young girls.[21] Hussey won out. Zeffirelli described her as "classically beautiful, with mesmerizing eyes, a certain coarse strength."[22] Even in hiring the extras, Zeffirelli took thousands of photographs for close study and then, as Devlin has noted, made all his extras *do* something – wash, carry, scrub, peddle, or whatever, so that the screen bustles with activity.[23] For locations like Tuscania, Pienza, and Gubbio,[24] he showed the same meticulousness, believing that in these storied old Italian towns, "the whole thing begins to spin, to get nearer to the truth."[25] Finally, even more so than in *The Taming of the Shrew*, Zeffirelli's movie domiciles the neo-realism of his hand-held cameras, professional and non-professional actors, domestic detail, and the splendors of upper-class Renaissance Italy, in the context of lush Renaissance masterworks. He combined the neo-realism of Italian cinema with the unabashed sentimentality of a Puccini opera.[26]

"I want this to be a young people's *Romeo and Juliet*," Zeffirelli said.[27] It has always been a tale *about* but not necessarily *for* young people. Shakespeare's immediate source was Arthur Brooke's moralizing narrative poem, *The Tragicall Historye of Romeus and Juliet* (1562), which loads guilt on the young people rather than on the parents, but the pedigree of the potion motif extends far back in history. Moreover Zeffirelli's admiration of Leonard

Bernstein's Broadway musical, *West Side Story* (1961) shows up in his resolve to make the movie palatable to the rebellious university students of the late sixties, who never doubted for a moment that the guilt was all on the parents.

Like the play, the movie neatly divides into two parts: the comic and the tragic. Except for unfortunate misadventures, particularly Friar John's failure to deliver Friar Lawrence's letter to Romeo in Mantua, it could have ended happily in festivity, like any other respectable comedy, the old people having been shunted aside in favor of the new generation. In London movie theatres, this division was clearly shown with an intermission between the wedding scene and the dueling on the piazza. Part two opens with an establishing shot of Mercutio's white handkerchief ominously covering the screen like a shroud, which plainly defines the division between comedy and tragedy, and their associated imagery of light and dark, and love and death.

In filmic conceits of sight, sound, and music, disparate elements are yoked together to visualize Shakespeare's verbalizations, Shakespeare's fourteen references to the sun being a prime example. In the establishing long shot, the burning sun over Verona, half hidden in a haze, joins with Laurence Olivier's voice-over of the Chorus' sonnet ("Two households, both alike in dignity, / In fair Verona where we lay our scene") and Nino Rota's film music to adumbrate Romeo's "my mind misgives / Some consequence yet hanging in the stars" (1.4.106). While credits roll over, the shrouded sun serves as an emblem of a "fair Verona" that is really not so fair; of a Juliet who according to Romeo is the "sun" (2.2.2) but one he does not yet know will be eclipsed; of lovers whose fate hangs in the "stars"; and of a city that finally must endure in "glooming peace" when "the sun, for sorrow, will not show his head" (5.3.304).

Zeffirelli sets up numerous visual tropes based on Shakespeare's imagery and sometimes on his own inventions. A low medium shot of their codpieces as the Capulet servants swagger down the street in the heat of the day puts a visual spin on the lewd puns, which permeate Shakespeare's bawdiest play: "Draw thy tool, here comes [two] of the house of Montagues" (1.1.31). The frequency of hands in tight framings, for example, reflects a Shakespearean pattern that begins with the prologue's "civil *hands* unclean," and continues at the Capulet ball with Juliet's "For saints have *hands* that pilgrims' *hands* do touch" (1.5.99).[28] Zeffirelli punctuates Juliet's "Parting is such sweet sorrow" (2.2.184) at the close of the balcony scene with a close-up of the lovers' hands clasping and unclasping. At the wedding, the Friar must break up the intense hand holding. In the tomb scene, Romeo grasps Juliet's hand just before he drinks off the poison, and the faint stirrings of her own hand signal her awakening.

Zeffirelli's equivalent to Laurence Olivier's William Walton, composer

Nino Rota, who also did the score for *The Taming of the Shrew*, works multiple variations on themes from festival and liturgical sequences. The leitmotif derives from Glen Weston's on-screen vocalization of "What Is a Youth?" at the Capulet ball. Later a popular hit, the lyrics of this neo-Elizabethan ballad by Eugene Walter mimic the overall two-part design of the film. That most common of Elizabethan devices, a question, "What is a youth?" opens a ten-line statement on the *carpe diem* theme, complete with a fading rose. The closing verses anticipating death in their sobriety and bitter-sweetness speak to the fate of the star-cross'd lovers. Variations of these melodies support the first appearance of Romeo ambling up a street toying with a sprig of blossom, and later at a slower tempo lugubriously comment on the deaths of Tybalt and Mercutio.

A second melody, derived from the Latin hymn *Ave maris stella* ("Ave thou receivest, / Gabriel's word believest / Change to peace and gladness / Eva's name of sadness") defines the mood of both wedding and funeral,[29] love and death, which is implicit in Juliet's "Come, cords, come, nurse, I'll to my wedding-bed, / And death, not Romeo, take my maidenhead!" (3.2.136). The traditional *Magnificat* ("My soul doth magnify the Lord, / And my spirit hath rejoiced in God my Saviour") fills the nave of the Romanesque church during the rendezvous between Romeo and the Nurse.

For the brilliant dance sequence at the Capulet ball, Pasqualino de Santis' subjective camera approaches virtual reality in giving viewers the illusion of their actually participating in choreographer Alberto Testa's "wild Morisco," a dance of Moorish origin mentioned in *Henry VI Part II* (3.1.365) reshaped here to modern taste but cunningly plausible. It immediately follows a *"sinistra tempo giusto* played by a quartet of soprano recorders and a trio of transposed flageolets,"[30] The dizzy whirling of two concentric rings of dancers moving in opposite directions restates Zeffirelli's iterative images of circles, Juliet's desire to be enfolded in them, and Mercutio's bawdy innuendo to Romeo about circles: "'twould anger him / To raise a spirit in his mistress' circle" (2.1.24). A circle on the ballroom floor corresponds to the dancers who exclude Romeo and Juliet from their territory where Juliet wistfully hovers on the fringe, peering in. Mosaics in circular patterns decorate the church floor where Romeo and Juliet kneel for the marriage. Dances and duels spin into rituals of love and hate, acted out in circular motions, suggesting that the headlong love affair has no possibility of doing anything but circling back against itself. During the fight between Tybalt and Mercutio, which is the dance of death, Romeo, like Juliet at the Capulet ball, is barred from the inner circle. The raucous crowds encircling the Nurse and Mercutio in the piazza enact a ritualized fertility dance, and the Duke Escalus joins in the geometrical conceit by speaking from the center of a ring of mounted retainers. Besides quasi-operatic strategies, the film employs more conventional sound effects. The cueing of music to speech, for example, may now and then hint at recitative (e.g., Romeo's sobs in the crypt scene), and a paralanguage of grunts, groans, and gasps lends realism to the duel between the desperate and exhausted Romeo and Tybalt. Then, too, the soundtrack includes a variety of real noises belonging to the diegesis: horses' hooves, church bells, echoes, crickets, clanging swords, barking dogs, and a category that can be summed up as "tumult, confusion, cries, questions." Crowd scenes invite additions: "Did he hurt you?" when John McEnery's Mercutio strikes a bystander while dueling with Michael York's Tybalt. Disguising his voice, Laurence Olivier generously contributed many bits and pieces of random speeches.[31]

John McEnery's powerful manic-depressive Queen Mab speech stands alone, free from musical punctuation. The teenage Romeo and Juliet speak the verse for the balcony scene without major sonic backup, though the short takes probably allowed for editing out imperfections. A zoom shot punctuated with discordant music conveys an unspoken thought when a sour-looking Lady Capulet shuts a window just as Lord Capulet remarks to Paris "and too soon marr'd are those so early made" (1.2.13). Lady Capulet, it would seem, has herself been subjected too soon to a forced marriage. The funeral cortege for Romeo and Juliet needs only eloquent silence, with a tolling bell and murmuring wind for sonic punctuation. Laurence Olivier comes back on the soundtrack to steal the epilogue from the Prince and make even doggerel sound magnificent: "For never was a story of more woe / Than this of Juliet and her Romeo" (5.3.309). The credits roll and in a rite of reconciliation the houses of Montague and Capulet file up the church steps. Albert Cirillo eloquently observes that Zeffirelli "gave us the *Romeo and Juliet* Shakespeare wrote and felt," even more so than the man "who did the definitive edition, or the man who corrected that edition," and thereby he made the play "meaningful here and now," in "a new medium."[32] It is hard to disagree.

Zeffirelli's *Hamlet*

With the exception of the filmed *Otello*, over two decades went by before Zeffirelli undertook another Shakespeare movie, this time not one of the Italian-based plays but the thoroughly English and thoroughly difficult and impenetrable *Hamlet* (1990). By the 1990s, which saw an unprecedented release of big-budget Shakespeare movies, every new film had the specter of a prior huge success peering over its shoulder. By the time that Zeffirelli

15   Silent screen idol Francis X. Bushman and Beverly Bayne in the lost Metro Studio feature-length movie (80 mins.) of *Romeo and Juliet* (1916).

got around to *Hamlet*, Laurence Olivier's *Hamlet* (1948) and Tony Richardson's "Roundhouse" *Hamlet* (1969) were like two more ghosts at Macbeth's banquet, endlessly scowling and defying him to do any better. With a multi-million dollar budget and a cast of famous actors, Franco Zeffirelli's *Hamlet* competed with Hollywood blockbusters in the cineplexes that became the sites of cultural disbursement in late twentieth-century suburban shopping malls. Zeffirelli "switched codes" by daring to reinvent Australian superstar and action hero "Mad Max" Mel Gibson as the melancholy prince. Zeffirelli knew that Gibson's diploma from Australia's NIDA (National Institute of Dramatic Arts) gave him impeccable acting credentials, and that as a wildly popular actor Gibson could also restore Shakespeare's Hamlet to the masses. Besides, there is nothing inherently un-Shakespearean about a Hamlet with a strong masculine presence, for Hamlet as a Renaissance man out of Baldassare Castiglione's *Book of the Courtier* needed to be as skilled with swords, wrestling, and horses as with a fast quip, always with *sprezzatura*, or nonchalance, no matter how daunting the challenge. As mentioned previously, Zeffirelli, an unabashed low mimeticist, unlike Jean-Luc Godard or Peter Greenaway, believes strongly in the popularization of great art. "It irritates me that some people want art to be as 'difficult' as possible, an elitist kind of thing."[33]

The fifth-act duel with broadswords instead of thin epées epitomizes Zeffirelli's conception of a macho Hamlet, equipped to survive in the world of Rambo and the Evil Empire. If Gibson's Hamlet ever delays, it is only momentarily, for much of the text showing indecisiveness has been deleted. The movie's most irresolute character is not Hamlet but Claudius (Alan Bates), who is often caught on camera in moments of hesitation. Hamlet slams poor little Ophelia (Helena Bonham Carter) against a stone wall, assaults Rosencrantz (Michael Maloney) and Guildenstern (Sean Murray) with a recorder, and mocks Laertes (Nathaniel Parker) with a broadsword. Gibson's prince is not weighed down by "conscience," which means in Elizabethan usage "thoughtfulness" rather than moral scruples ("Thus conscience does make cowards [of us all]" – 3.1.82); or what today might be called "guilt." This Hamlet is more the avenger than the thinker, though not merely a brainless gun-toting prince out of Arnold Schwarzenegger's sly meta-cinematic commentary on *Hamlet*, *Last Action Hero* (1993).

Gibson's prince lives in the universe of Foucault's panopticon, a society about spying, about surveillance. Gibson speaks with his cold blue porcelain eyes, as do other talented movie actors, stars of the caliber of Lillian Gish, Buster Keaton, and Robert Mitchum. He can project the demons of a terrifying mad man with a maniacal look as well as play a thoughtful speaker in the "To be or not to be" soliloquy, set in the *memento mori* atmosphere of the crypt where his father is entombed. The eyes of the entire court are more often than not fixed on Hamlet, just as he in turn watches everyone else, something that Gibson was intensely aware of. "Everyone spied on Hamlet, and Hamlet spied on everyone else," he said in an interview.[34] High above on a balcony he is examining Gertrude (Glenn Close) or his stepfather, or he is eavesdropping on Polonius (Ian Holm) lecturing to Laertes and Ophelia, or he is looking down on Claudius engaged in "heavy-headed revel" (1.4.17) at an extravagant feast, or searching on a parapet in the mist from behind the hilt of his sword for a glimpse of his father's spirit (Paul Scofield). He is truly "th'observ'd of all observers" (3.1.154).

This is also a movie that uses Shakespeare's language as a blueprint for the dynamics of motion. The opening scene in the crypt, which is entirely invented by Zeffirelli, establishes the action by triangulating in close-up the film's major characters – Claudius, Gertrude, and Hamlet. To that end fragments from the second scene of act two have been transposed so that in the crypt by his father's body Claudius immediately reassures Hamlet of his rights to succession: "You are the most immediate to our throne" (1.2.109), though the legal claims to succession by "election" in Hamlet's tenth-century Denmark remain murky. Bits and pieces of scene two also drift into the great hall of the castle where Claudius in his oily public-man voice announces the marriage to Gertrude, "With mirth in funeral, and with dirge in marriage" (1.2.12). Still other lines are transposed to Hamlet's library for the king's instructions to Laertes, "What wouldst thou beg, Laertes[?]" (1.2.45), while a fourth setting in Hamlet's study makes a backdrop for the crucial exchange between Hamlet and Gertrude with Hamlet's, "Seems, madam? nay, it is, I know not 'seems'." (1.2.76). Zeffirelli and script collaborator Dyson Lovell have rearranged the text to fit the requirements of a *moving* picture, where spatial barriers can be easily transgressed. To do otherwise is to risk having the static arrangements of, for example, the Kevin Kline televised *Hamlet* where there is virtually no movement as the actors simply stand and rather woodenly deliver their speeches like schoolroom recitations. This is not to say that there are not in Kline's *Hamlet* fine individual performances, Peter James's Horatio being one of the best ever, but they are carried out within the limitations of a television studio set. Limited to two hours by budgetary constraints, Zeffirelli sacrifices Fortinbras, who makes an important mirror foil to both Hamlet and Laertes. This textual loss represents a filmic gain in the way that the opening scene establishes the sense of activity, of motion, characteristic of the entire film. Like Polanski's castle in *Macbeth*, Zeffirelli's is also the locus of a life force, of people moving in and out, people serving on tables, people weaving, cooking, serving, reading, handling horses. There is nothing here of the school of John Cassavetes' counter-cinema *A Woman Under the Influence* (1974) where the characters talk but rarely move.

Claudius' "Give me some light" (3.2.269) after the play-within-the-play points toward the movie's lighting design, which makes extraordinary use of baroque contrasts between light and dark. Designer Dante Ferretti and Zeffirelli copy the rich tones of painters like Vermeer, who provides a model for the library in the castle. Zeffirelli's love for detail, as with the overflowing *objets d'art* in Baptista Minola's villa in *Taming of the Shrew*, has no place in a film set in feudal northern Europe, so David Watkin's lighting and camera work attempts to compensate for that loss. Zeffirelli's style might be called "enhanced realism," which is a variation on Michael Skovmand's preferred description of "picturesque naturalism."[35] The drafty, cold stone walls of Elsinore could not be more "real" than this castle patched together from autochthonous British ruins at Dover, Blackness, and Dunnottar. Deprived of his lush Italian settings, Zeffirelli struggles to make this cold surface appealing by keying the movie to "mostly grays and ash colors, a 'medieval-primitive' look" so that when rich colors do come out "the effect is even more vivid."[36] David Impastato sees the "baroque" influence of the late Renaissance as an encouragement to the obvious fluidity of the actors' movements in and around the castle.[37] He goes a step further, however, in finding metaphorical significance in the interplay between light and dark. In the opening crypt scene, for example, a shaft of light from a window plays over a tightly framed hand holding dirt that is to be scattered over the King's body, after which the camera shows that it is the hand of a deeply hooded Prince Hamlet, whose penetrating eyes glow in the shadows. Again in "O that this too too sallied [solid] flesh would melt" (1.2.129), Hamlet moves in and out of the light until backlit against an enormous window as the soliloquy ends. In the crane shot of the death scene that ends the movie, Hamlet's head recedes into shadows directly after Horatio's "Good night, sweet prince." Michael Skovmand asks if the shadows and light constitute deeply embedded metaphors, like the portentous ones in the Olivier *Richard III*, or if they simply highlight particular moments.[38] Zeffirelli himself describes how the duel scene was deliberately heightened by placing huge white sheets on the walls to bounce the light back on the scene, but says nothing about a symbolical significance.[39]

The musical enhancement (Ennio Morricone) offers a minimalist backdrop score that avoids drawing attention to itself and a flurry of horns and drums for diegetic moments such as toasting during banquets. Film star Glenn Close's sensuous Gertrude turns the modern tradition of a Freudian subtext into hypertext by rarely missing opportunities to kiss fervently both her husband and son full on the mouth. As Edward Quinn has said "you never accept for one moment the notion that Glenn Close's Gertrude and Mel Gibson's Hamlet are mother and son ... there's nothing Oedipal in their straightforward sexuality."[40] On the other hand, Gertrude must be young and attractive enough to justify Claudius' interest in her as a trophy wife. A difficult tightrope. Ian Holm makes a somewhat fatuous but not entirely silly Polonius, who in any event never deserves the harsh fate behind the arras handed to him by Hamlet. As might be expected, Paul Scofield, Peter Brook's King Lear, makes a formidable presence as the ghost, and Helena Bonham Carter scraps the Millais-like romanticism of Jean Simmons' golden-tressed Ophelia in the Olivier version to resituate the role squarely in the context of contemporary feminist militancy. Despite her tiny stature, this Ophelia remains feisty even when driven mad by her men. Framing Gertrude's poignant description of Ophelia's drowning between flashbacks of the actual scene ingeniously preserves both the visual and verbal splendor: "There is a willow grows askaunt the brook / That shows his hoary leaves in the glassy stream" (4.7.166). An aging but familiar face materializes in John McEnery as Osric, the unforgettably manic-depressive Mercutio in Zeffirelli's *Romeo and Juliet* of three decades previously. Emerging personalities include Michael Maloney (Rosencrantz) who will play the Dauphin in the Branagh *Henry V* (1989) and Roderigo in the Parker *Othello* (1995). Pete Postlethwaite (Player King) will turn up as the hip priest in the Luhrmann *Romeo & Juliet* (1996). Ace Pilkington observes that Zeffirelli has produced "a body of work that is always interesting and sometimes splendid, that cuts but does not shirk, rewrites but does not abandon,"[41] and Robert Hapgood thinks that Zeffirelli's work has withstood the test of time even better than Olivier's.[42] High praise, but single-handedly Zeffirelli has probably done more than the entire educational establishment to keep Shakespeare's language alive in an age when images have eclipsed words.

- 7 -

Shakespeare movies in the age of angst

After 1960, the increasing pessimism stemming from the Vietnam war and other deleterious world events inevitably spun off on the Shakespeare movie. The conflict in Southeast Asia had plunged the United States into a cultural revolution pitting youth against age, and in France, Great Britain, and elsewhere university students also rebelled against threadbare conventions. Residual Victorian social codes withered and died as this "youthquake" overturned the restrictive norms of the older generation in favor of an emerging demand for personal liberation. As much as any other book, Jan Kott's discerning *Shakespeare Our Contemporary* (1964) encapsulated the era's nihilistic, despairing, anti-melioristic ethos, which in literature and art emerged as bitter and dark irony. The genteel aspirations for Shakespeare movies of the innocent Vitagraph and Thalberg/Cukor days likewise went up in smoke as the disintegrative political movements and outright anger in the streets escalated.

Two British Shakespeare movies illustrate this ironic drift, which had already surfaced as film noir in mainstream movies: Tony Richardson's *Hamlet* (1969), and Peter Hall's *A Midsummer Night's Dream* (1969). More in the art-house category than in the heavy-hitting commercial world of Zeffirelli's *Romeo and Juliet,* each in its own way enjoyed a critical but not a box-office success. Modestly budgeted (*Hamlet* at only $350,000), today they would be labeled "Indies" or independents to set them apart from the major studio's $40 million plus action blockbusters. By the same token, their limited filmic values and tight framing identified them as crossover films made for television as much as for theatrical release. Richardson's introspective *Hamlet* stretches the limits of interior filming, while Hall's extrovert *Dream* goes outside, and shows what can be done with hand-held cameras and sound looping.

Richardson's *Hamlet*

Richardson's claustrophobic movie was actually filmed at London's Roundhouse Theatre, a recycled railway locomotive shed, in fewer than ten days.[1] The damp stone walls, flickering candles and dark ambience evoke the spirit of gloomy Elsinore. The production had been successfully staged in London, New York, and smaller cities, where the star, Nicol Williamson, developed a reputation for an "attitude," having in Boston actually stalked off in the middle of the play scene, leaving the whole company with "egg on their faces."[2] Nevertheless Williamson's powerful presence, or "being," as an "angry-young-man" Hamlet, recklessly broke with the genteel elocutionary tradition of, say, a John Gielgud. Williamson doesn't just recite but energizes Shakespeare's words with every nerve, fiber, and bone in his body so strenuously that one fears he will self-destruct. He similarly erupts in his BBC *Macbeth* with Jane Lapotaire as Lady Macbeth. Hoping perhaps to capture some of this raw power, Richardson wrote that he wanted "to make a movie of *Hamlet* in which . . . you would *devalue* the power of the image and let the text and performance speak uninterruptedly, scaling the production down and staging it for cameras."[3]

In many ways, Richardson's movie reifies Sir Philip Sidney's definition in *The Defence of Poesie* (1595) of mimesis as "representing, counterfeiting, or figuring forth – to speak metaphorically, a speaking picture." Its system of portraiture – single portraits, double portraits, triple and group portraits – makes it a montage of speaking pictures, or "talking heads." The film so closely depends on close and medium shots that many critics assumed that it was made for the small screen of television rather than for theatrical release.[4] The tight framing inevitably invited comments about its "explosiveness" – a kind of visual tautness. As Bernice Kliman says, "by making the frame a keyhole" there was even a suggestion of a larger world beyond the frame.[5] A *Time* critic saw Williamson as a Hamlet "lit by inner fire" and carrying with him "the smell of smoldering cordite."[6] Louis D. Gianetti thought the Olivier *Hamlet* was "essentially an epic," made up of long shots, while Richardson's offers a psychological study in close-ups in which Hamlet seems to be bursting the confines of the frames, nearly spilling out into "oblivion."[7] The film choreographs not bodies but faces, sometimes singly, sometimes doubly, sometimes triply, like some infinite variation on the figures in Rembrandt's *Night Watch*. The most interesting face is Williamson's, which Alan Brien caricatured as having "eyes like poached eggs, hair like treacle toffee, and a truculent lower lip protruding like a pink front step from the long pale doorway of his face."[8] A deliberate speeding up of the dialogue, breathless at times, enhances the visual tautness. To accelerate the impetuousness, Richardson filleted long speeches or deleted short exchanges to fit into the jumpy montage.[9] Williamson's "rasping, nasal tones . . . liberate him from all the fancy echoes of previous performances," we are told.[10] This madcap behavior creates a Hamlet closer to Kate's Petruchio than to

Ophelia's melancholy prince, not at all indecisive but rather outrageously decisive, equipped to handle a torrent of events that would paralyze a lesser mortal. He cannot "delay" because he lacks the time to delay.

Still, as Brendan Gill acknowledged, Williamson masters the soliloquy.[11] A quick cut from the gloomy ramparts of Elsinore to the brightly lit great hall establishes the gap between the dark world of a murdered king and the superficial world of courtly badinage, where suddenly Hamlet appears lower left in the frame. Now in close-up, a speaking picture, Williamson begins the first soliloquy, his head moving as if "it were thrust from the mouth of a jug."[12] He speaks in staccato bursts, making myriad, small gestures, repeatedly thumping knuckles against his forehead. Toward the end, at "O most wicked speed: to post / With such dexterity to incestious sheets" (1.2.156), the film indulges in one of its rare long shots with the arrival of Horatio (Gordon Jackson), Barnardo (John Trenaman), and Marcellus (John Carney).

The "To be, or not to be" sequence begins with a supine Hamlet, profile facing upward on the frame, to mark his isolation. Part way through, he moves to a posture of resting on his elbow, and then at "fardels bear" (3.1.75) sits straight up, looking back over his shoulder at the camera. He pops up, laughs out loud, and spots Ophelia (Marianne Faithfull) who appears to the right. With Claudius (Anthony Hopkins) and Polonius (Mark Dignam) blatantly eavesdropping, Hamlet and Ophelia are viewed through a hammock netting, their faces criss-crossed, cut up, as if in a Sunday supplement illustration of the ravages of schizophrenia. When the obliging camera, now more of a participant in than a mere recorder of the action, pulls back we observe Hamlet and Ophelia over the shoulders of the eavesdroppers and see the sudden flash of suspicion on Hamlet's face. His mood turns dark as he flies into a tantrum. "Where's your father?" he asks Ophelia (3.1.129), and from then on "nunnery" takes on the bawdy "brothel" insinuation. The motif of the divided self continues as when Ophelia says "O, what a noble mind is here o'erthrown!" (3.1.150), her face is fragmented and cut up by the hammock ropes.

Two-shots handle the hints of incestuousness hovering around Laertes (Michael Pennington) and Ophelia as they bid each other farewell with an intimacy that mirrors the emotional bond between Hamlet and Gertrude (Judy Parfitt). In another two-shot, now in the bed chamber, a looming Hamlet in the upper right corner of the frame dominates his upset mother. Reverse shots capture the wounded looks on the faces of the distraught mother and son – "O Hamlet, speak no more! / Thou turns't [my eyes into my very] soul" (3.4.88). When the ghost reappears, heralded by anguished wailing on the soundtrack, a splash of intense light falls on Hamlet's face –

"Look where he goes, even now, out at the portal!" (3.4.136). Mother and son collapse into each other's arms, weeping and sobbing.

Multiples of three work as well. The faces of Hamlet, Horatio, and Marcellus on the ramparts perpetually change positions, being grouped, separated, exchanged, switched, synchronized, and syncopated. Cinematized portraiture occurs when Hamlet is hemmed in on either side by the king's two spies, Rosencrantz (Ben Aris) and Guildenstern (Clive Graham). "Were you not sent for? is it your own inclining?"(2.2.274), he asks the guilty pair, and then like Edmund Kean before him throws his arms around them, symbolically blocking the two conspirators from uniting against him. By contrast, with the arrival of the players, Hamlet moves freely in and out and among them, more at ease in the world of motley and grease paint than in the prison house of Elsinore. In act one, scene two, the meanness and imbecility in the faces of the sycophantic courtiers at Elsinore achieve toxic levels as they show their eagerness to laugh heartily at any of Claudius' slightest witticisms.

Not that every shot in the film is a close-up. There are some medium shots, but the impression of being in an amputee ward remains powerful. A voyeuristic peek at the royal bed of Denmark shows a depraved Gertrude and Claudius swinishly eating sticky things in bed while dogs snuggle up to them. When Polonius shows up to report on "the very cause of Hamlet's lunacy" (2.2.49), the wanton, bestial behavior of king and queen robs him of any dignity and Gertrude's "more matter with less art" (2.2.95) seems curt, even cruel. The editing and mixing work variations on the basic blocking of one, two, and three, throwing in, as it were, a few sharps and flats, a chord here and there, to transform a simple melody into a complex polyphonic arrangement.

As First Player and Gravedigger, Roger Livesay's hoarse and yet compelling voice, as if he had damaged vocal chords, sears into the memory. In a *tour de force*, Richardson manages to film the complicated duel scene between Hamlet and Laertes without a significant long shot. Richardson's *mise-en-scène* remains sparse and shadowy, in contrast to the elaborate unit sets of Olivier's *Hamlet* with the spacious stairway sweeping down into the throne room. The editing moves backward and forward between the contestants and the queen, whose demise brings about a mini-tragedy with her dying recognition, *anagnorisis*, that "the King's to blame" (5.2.320). Claudius dies horribly, shrieking, vomiting up the wine that Hamlet has forced down his throat. Horatio and Hamlet revert to the two-shot phase, with Hamlet now firmly planted in the dominant position on the right, not on the less assertive left as he had been at the film's outset. In these final moments Williamson's histrionics translate into a sincerity appropriate to the prince.

There is no Fortinbras to carry on, that whole external political angle having been deleted by the exigencies of time. Ultimately, however, Richardson achieved what he set out to do in producing a two-hour *Hamlet* with a major actor in the title role. The synecdoche for the greater whole emerges in turmoil, madness, energy, frenzy, despair, frustration, bitterness, irrationality, and the unadorned nobility of a Danish prince. The rest of the tragedy remains for the audience to piece out for themselves. Richardson's "speaking pictures" suggest but do not flesh out completely "the ripeness [that] is all."

Hall's *Midsummer Night's Dream*

The seeds of Peter Hall's and producer Michael Birkett's film of *Midsummer Night's Dream* were planted at the Stratford Memorial Theatre in 1959 when Hall's cast included Charles Laughton as Bottom, Vanessa Redgrave as Helena, Mary Ure as Titania, and Albert Finney as Lysander. NBC announced that it would eventually televise the stage production in the United States,[13] though the film actually came more directly out of the 1962 Stratford revival, in which the casting had undergone radical changes, and finally was transmitted in 1969 "coast to coast" for some 25 million viewers in North America.[14] Like Richardson's *Hamlet* it emerges straight out of the *Zeitgeist* of the 1960s when a whole phalanx of "angry young men" felt that society had cheated and deprived them of their proper place in the world. Nicol Williamson's raw, hostile, nervous style made him the perfect Hamlet for the times, and in a comic variation on the angry young man, David Warner's Lysander in a Nehru jacket stamps him as a grumpy young man, unlikely to trust anyone over thirty. A crossover film made for both television in the USA and theatrical release in England, it combines the expressionism of the Reinhardt Weimar school with the neo-realism of the post-war Italian school. Like Peter Brook's famous idiosyncratic staged *Midsummer Night's Dream* (1970),[15] it too rejects the Regent's Park style of cute elves and cuddly animals to please the children and their nannies, and stabs at the darker side of the dream, the dream that turns into nightmare in a dark wood. Guy Woolfenden's low-key musical score, which is used very sparingly, replaces the romanticized idyll of Mendelssohn's *Overture* in the Reinhardt version, and a hand-held camera suggests a rawness of experience.

The establishing shot shows an English country house (Compton-Verney in Warwickshire) with the single word "Athens" inscribed over it. The alienating conceit pokes ironic fun at Shakespeare's own whimsy of putting the "duke" of Athens, Hippolyta the Amazon Queen, and a cluster of honest English workingmen like Quince and Bottom all in one time and place in ancient Greece. The English country house setting emphasizes, in Hall's own words, that the play's action takes place during "an English summer in which the seasons have gone wrong ... everywhere is wet and muddy."[16] Judi Dench as Titania, while wearing virtually nothing to shield her nubile body, recites the 40-line speech about the inclement weather. "Therefore the winds, piping to us in vain, / As in revenge, have suck'd up from the sea / Contagious fogs"(2.1.88), she says in medium and close shots from slightly different angles. The English summer that has gone wrong stands for the contemporary England that has "gone wrong," in the eyes of the young, who are busy looking back in anger or anticipating the despair in Derek Jarman's *The Last of England* (1988).

Hall treats the predicament of the four young lovers with disarming wit. The silly infatuations of the young lovers, Helena (Diana Rigg) and Demetrius (Michael Jayston), Hermia (Helen Mirren) and Lysander, take place "on the dank and dirty ground" (2.2.75), their faces even being daubed with mud. At the same time, however, this documentary realism is counterpointed with an expressionistic, or even surrealistic, vision suggested by the peculiar color of the terrain, the lead-green texture of Puck's face (Ian Holm), the array of bright lights in the dark wood, and the weird nature of the fairy world. The wood is both actuality and fantasy, Lumière and Méliès.

For those who like their Shakespeare well spoken, Hall gathered together an ensemble of brilliant actors from a Royal Shakespeare Company then at the peak of its prestige. Jay Halio, who commented favorably on the film's keeping Shakespeare's text virtually intact, unlike the free adapting in the Reinhardt version, thinks also that "this is probably the best spoken of any Shakespeare film that has been made."[17] To insure that outcome, Hall "post-synched" the dialogue to give the actors a friendlier environment for speaking the lines. There has never been a more magnanimous Duke Theseus (Derek Godfrey), who radiates a generosity of spirit toward persons inferior to himself without flipping over into condescension. "If we imagine no worse of them than they of themselves, they may pass for excellent men" (5.1.215). His Hippolyta (Barbara Jeffords) abandons the Reinhardt snake costume for a slightly kinky look of boots and a skin tight mini-skirt, but retains the fiery menace of an Amazon queen underneath the icy exterior. The four young lovers embody the "quick bright things [who] come to confusion" (1.1.148), David Warner's Lysander as a headstrong, truculent young man, and Helen Mirren (Hermia) and Diana Rigg (Helena) as wonderfully befuddled ingenues. At the court during the Pyramus and Thisby play, the two couples expose their own youthful arrogance as rich spoiled darlings by condescending to the earnest but inept actors. The girls' costumes incongruously reflect the swinging London of the late Sixties when Carnaby Street became a household word signifying mini-skirts, rock and roll, and mind-altering drugs. As Michael Mullin has said, the result is to suggest that "Hall has assembled a house party of brilliant people and said 'Let's make a movie'."[18] It is also a house party where they serve Electric Kool-Aid. The fairy world matches the courtly world with a rather sinister Oberon (Ian Richardson), and a hyperactive Puck, whose tongue never stops darting in and out. Judi Dench's voluptuousness stirs up the whiff of bestiality in the nocturnal union between Titania and Bottom (Paul Rogers) with its latent eroticism. As always, the rude mechanicals, led by veteran Shakespearean actor Sebastian Shaw (Quince), steal the show with their Pyramus and Thisby *shtick*. At the very end, the dia-bolical-looking Puck and Oberon return to cast their spell of magical finality on an English country house, whose "constancy" still remains in doubt.

These virtues notwithstanding, the film received mixed reviews, one of the chief protests centering around the alleged amateur photography: "The hand-held camera constantly joggles the image, wearying eyes already repelled by the sheer ugliness of the huge warts-and-all close-ups ... His [Hall's] film is leaden."[19] At times it looks that way, as when Helena laments about Demetrius' preference for Hermia, moving about, or popping and hop-ping about, sometimes standing behind a tree, or again emerging from behind the tree to address the camera directly again. "For ere Demetrius look'd on Hermia's eyne, / He hail'd down oaths that he was only mine" (1.1.242). But rather than being inadequate camera work, the gap between the continuity in the flow of the words and the discontinuity of the images suggests a major theme of the play as articulated by Hippolyta: "But all the story of the night told over, / And all their minds transfigur'd so together, / More witnesseth than fancy's images, / And grows to something of great constancy; / But howsoever, strange and admirable" (5.1.23). The jumpy camera reflects the Elizabethan concern with the interplay between change and constancy, or as Edmund Spenser called it, "mutability" (*Two Cantos of Mutabilitie*, 1596). "New philosophy" had put all in doubt and there was unease about the nature of the universe – what of it was changeable and what unchangeable, what in flow and what in flux. ("Proud Change [not pleasd in mortall things, / Beneath the Moone, to raigne] / Pretends, as well of Gods, as Men, / To be the Soueraine.") In Hippolyta's words it can be had both ways. Things can be changeable but also unchangeable, and Hall's visual trope for this paradox that Frank Occhiogrosso has labeled "cinematic oxymoron"[20] involves continuous and discontinuous employment of picture and word, ringing variations on interchangeability in the relationships of the characters to themselves and to nature.

The Brook/Birkett *King Lear*

Peter Brook's and Michael Lord Birkett's *King Lear* (1971) inflected Shakespeare into a dark and relentlessly ironic vision of the human condition. This uncomfortable tale of an aged and irascible old king who foolishly gives his property away to his ungrateful daughters turned out to be an allegory for the times. Everywhere in the West parents were caught up in daily combat with their children over life-style issues running the gamut from hair styles to pot. They, like Lear, wanted to cry out, "How sharper than a serpent's tooth it is / To have a thankless child!" (1.4.288). Jan Kott was again a powerful influence, his essay, *"King Lear* or *Endgame,"*[21] having identified the analogies between the grotesque elements in Beckett's Theatre of the Absurd and Shakespeare's tragedy. This malaise was already apparent in Brook's earlier "bondage" *King Lear* (1953) with Orson Welles on North American television. Despite protests to the contrary, Brook did not so much drain *King Lear* of its "Christian" elements (if it ever had any) as displace seventeenth-century Christian stoicism into the contemporary idiom of the Theatre of Cruelty, in which Good Friday overwhelms Easter Sunday and the Book of Job replaces the New Testament. A key difference of course is that Christian stoicism was rooted in absolute notions of divine order, and Theatre of Cruelty reflects the existentialist view of the world as absurdity, "absurdity" in Ionesco's terms meaning simply "life without purpose." While the Medieval schoolmen shadowed forth Christian values in pagan terms (*prisca theologia*), Brook embodied Christian stoicism in absurdist symbols. The redemptive elements in Shakespeare's scorching tragedy having been erased in the Birkett/Brook *King Lear*, the movie reflects the ironic, fractured universe poised on the edge of apocalypse after Hiroshima.

Such a dark view inevitably brought the full wrath of the critics down on Brook's head. Even though he had originally staged *King Lear* at Stratford (1962), and producer Birkett had thought the actors in the stage version were far too valuable not to use again in the movie,[22] these fine credentials did not spare Brook from the venting of spleen. The movie was "depoeticized";[23] inept "in handling the film medium . . . a travesty";[24] "an image, not of regeneration, but of moribundity and sad decay";[25] "look[ed] like an overexposed 8mm home movie which [had] been smuggled out of a disaster area";[26] and "murder[ed] [the play] altogether," making it resemble "a telecast of moon landings . . . an electronic blizzard," which is "impossible to follow . . . a pogrom on poetry."[27] A rival player, Orson Welles, was reported as "wildly furious" over Scofield's playing the part as if he were still doing Sir Thomas More in *A Man for All Seasons*.[28] Reigning American film critic Pauline Kael summed it all up. She did not just "dislike" it; she "hated it."[29] On the other hand, a few understood that the camera was *deliberately* out of focus, and acknowledged that though the film may have been "flawed," it also possessed a "wonderful" quality of imagination.[30] Some even found that it "made big demands on the audience, but [that it] is very impressive."[31] The late Lillian Wilds saw the film's defects as artistic triumphs,[32] and Frank Kermode declared, though with some qualifications, that Brook had made "the best of all Shakespeare movies."[33]

Yet Brook's movie is more than a movie about *King Lear*, it is a movie about making movies, deeply post-modernist in its meta-cinematic posture. State-of-the-art technology – hand-held cameras, lighter sound equipment, and superior film stock – liberated the director to re-envision Shakespeare's play spatially. Its grainy texture and deliberately out-of-focus frames shot in black-and-white show a winter world in North Jutland of unrelieved grimness. Aggressively cinematic, it discards Hollywood seamlessness in favor of deliberate strategies of alienation. It is not designed to make audiences comfortable but uncomfortable. Like Jean-Luc Godard, Brook employs discontinuities, zoom-fades, accelerated motion, freeze frames, shock editing, complex reverse-angle and over-the-shoulder shots, montage, jump cuts, overhead shots, silent-screen titles, eyes-only close-ups, and hand-held as well as immobile cameras. His camera redirects the Lear story into its own filmic idiom, just as it had once been hoped that Ted Hughes could "translate" Shakespeare's words into his own personal style,[34] though that scheme fell apart when it became apparent that even a poet so gifted as Hughes could hardly improve on Shakespeare's language. Shakespeare's words burn on the page, but smolder on the screen in charcoal grays and blacks.

A few examples of the ironist agenda must suffice. Shakespeare's play is framed by a map – "Give me the map there"(1.1.37) – and a mirror – "Lend me a looking glass"(5.3.262) – emblems for the geriatric king's futile journey and search for identity. In Brook's movie, however, the mirror seems to have been forgotten but the map plays a pivotal role as an expressive object in the division of the kingdom. Before that, however, an establishing shot, which may be a quotation from Fritz Lang's *M* (1931) starring Peter Lorre, pans over the faces of Lear's notorious 100 knights, who so sorely try his daughters' domestic tranquillity. A study in heads, they remain frozen in position, staring into nothingness, silent and enigmatic. They remain outside, barred from access to the presence chamber by an absurdly tiny door, not to be seen again until the old king angrily exits after Cordelia's impudence. From a reverse angle there is a shot of the claustrophobic throne, in which Paul Scofield is ensconced, a talking head that emerges, slowly but powerfully. Speaking oracularly like some kind of *deus absconditus* from deep within the recesses of his phallic-shaped retreat, his gravelly "No" prefigures the play's existentialist fetish, a leitmotif of "nothingness" ("Nothing, my lord"(1.1.87)). Scofield's king never calls directly for the map ("Give me the map, there" (1.1.37)), but it appears in time for distributing Goneril's one third of the kingdom. Holding aloft the symbol of royal power and justice, an orb surmounted by a cross, Goneril (Irene Worth) attests to her loyalty. Her sycophancy done, the king unfolds a fuzzy, blurry map, so shabby it looks as if it had been stored in a fruit cellar. Cords radiating from a small stake at its center indicate boundaries, as Lear himself says, comprised of natural barriers such as "shadowy forests . . . with champains rich'd, / With plenteous rivers and wide-skirted meads" (1.1.64). Tightly framed, wizened scribes record Lear's decrees on parchment.

A smirking Regan (Susan Engel) then sacramentally elevates the ceremonial orb, recites her hymn of adulation and earns her share of the kingdom. The two outwardly compliant but inwardly recalcitrant daughters have triumphed over the outwardly recalcitrant but inwardly compliant Cordelia (Annelise Gabold), though Brook's movie hints at possible excuses for Regan's and Goneril's impatience with the cantakerous old king. Meanwhile Cordelia remains backgrounded, isolated, alone, in medium long shot, awaiting her turn to speak the fatal three words, "Nothing, my lord." The cinematic rhetoric of shot/reverse shot visually punctuates the dialectical cross-purposes of king and daughter, the virtuous daughter resisting the power of the patriarchal oppressor. Cordelia banished, the king fades back into his vast, enclosed seat of power. When he exits, it is through the little door that separates him and his 100 knights from the cheer and company of his daughters. He has no clear map for his future.

The exterior shots emblemize the king's spiritual agony. Even when filmed out of doors, with horses thundering across frozen turf, tumbling and pitching wagons lurching over the landscape, hard-bitten knights moving en masse, pitched battles on bleak terrain, the movie still retains a sense of the claustrophobic. In the strobe-lit scene on the heath near Gloucester's (Alan Webb) castle, the "poor naked wretches," Lear, the Fool (Jack McGowran) and Edgar (Robert Lloyd), play out intricate variations on the theme of Lear's "Thou art the thing itself: unaccommodated man is no more but such a poor, bare, fork'd animal" (3.4.106). Flashes of lightning illuminate Shakespeare's apocalyptic language with glimpses of Edgar as mad Tom, a Christ figure with a crown of thorns, shivering, twitching, and trembling under torrents of icy rain water. The camera rudely surveys the bare chest, nude abdomen, thinly clad groin, of this "bare, fork'd animal." Rodents scurry across the screen. The Fool's Erastian taunting of Lear, which penetrates into the old king's deepest reservoirs of denial, adds wormwood to the sufferings on the heath: "Fathers that wear rags / Do make their children blind / But fathers that bear bags / Shall see their children kind" (2.3.47). No character than the Fool better explores the paradoxes of Pauline Christianity: foolishness in wisdom, wisdom in foolishness; sight in blindness, blindness in sight; life in death, death in life; and victory in defeat, defeat in victory. Lear like God's lowliest handmaiden of the Magnificat falls in the eyes of men and rises in the eyes of God. The Fool guides him in a Dantesque kind of way through the inferno of the wild storm scenes, his aphorisms of cynical prudence always near the surface. Everywhere malignant nature rules in a space closed off to benevolence.

King Lear's crisis of knowledge about the human experience needs more than the services of a holy fool. The transcendent catalyst emerges in the absurdist, Beckett-like play-within-a-play starring the mad old king and the blinded Gloucester. Viewed from a crane shot, they are tiny figures on a bleak landscape, emblems of the dispossessed state of man. They raise insoluble questions about cause-and-effect, good and evil, which ricochet off texts as ancient as the Book of Job, as recent as Friedrich Nietzsche's *Thus Spoke Zarathustra*, and as contemporary as Derrida's *Of Grammatology*. "Hark in thine ear: change places, and handy-dandy, which is the justice, which is the thief?" (4.6.151), says the old king in a typical reversal of cause and effect.

At the close, the images of horror proliferate. The charcoal texture becomes darker and grayer, more gothic. The old king in a bit of tricky editing speaks first on the left and then on the right side of the frame to explore his innermost being within himself. Looking bedraggled and exhausted, Goneril and Regan smolder in two-shot as they wrangle over their sordid claims to Edmund. As if in agony from strychnine poisoning, Regan writhes and thrashes about, her body spastic with pain, and then in a supremely perverse act of will bashes her own head against a boulder. A mini-second later, Cordelia appears for a fleeting moment (perhaps four or five frames) just exactly as her neck audibly snaps inside the hangman's noose. The king staggers across the barren landscape holding Cordelia in his arms and howling like a trapped animal. He hallucinates, thinking that he sees Cordelia alive. Does this last mirage signify that only mad men can live happily in this fallen world? Is the world finally a place where the sighted remain sightless and the sightless sighted? A place where only a blind man, a beggar and a fool really come to grips with the true horror of man's fate? Brook's movie interrogates but doesn't answer the questions. Instead the ravaged king gradually and inexorably simply falls out of the frame and out of the world, very much like Frederick B. Warde in the old silent Thanhouser *King Lear* (1916). Only a blank screen remains, an exercise in white on white. Despite the map, despite Edgar's faith that the gods are just, despite Kent's (Tom Fleming)

[153]

loyalty ("I have a journey, sir, shortly to go" (5.3.322)), there is after all out there in nature – nothing. God is dead.

Polanski's *Macbeth*

Roman Polanski's blood-soaked vision of *Macbeth* (1971) moved into even darker waters than Brook's *King Lear* in its unsparing journey into the heart of darkness.[35] While "purists" were still agitated over the "mistreatment" of Shakespeare by directors like Peter Hall and Peter Brook, Polanski's sensationally publicized film had a sufficient level of violence to make them apoplectic. Yet another of the plays had been taken by a movie director and resituated in the frantic, disoriented world of the early 70s, when youthful war protesters were shot dead by the Ohio National Guard and when Charles Manson's crazed drug addicts murdered Sharon Tate, Polanski's pregnant wife. Lady Macbeth was everybody's favorite paradigm for the scheming wife of a power executive, and having the film bankrolled by Hugh Hefner's outrageous *Playboy* magazine on a budget of $2,400,000 made it all the more scandalous.[36] For Polanski, though, the movie was a dream come true for he had long been hoping to do a Shakespeare movie but could not because of "the money." He said in his own wry commentary on "tickling commodity," that "the money people are always afraid of Shakespeare. Shakespeare is never a good – how do you say it? – product."[37] Filming began in North Wales in November 1970.

With modern mass communications blurring the line between fact and fiction, Polanski's checkout-counter, tabloid-style personal life inevitably got confused with his film. Audiences arrived at the theatre expecting to see a link between the stabbings of Duncan and of Sharon Tate; the witches, and Polanski's earlier blockbuster movie of Ira Levin's *Rosemary's Baby*; and a nude Lady Macbeth (Francesca Annis), and *Playboy* centerfold soft porn. Yet this "expectational text"[38] was already lodged in Shakespeare's tragedy: the multiple recurring images of blood in *Macbeth* were there before Charles Manson cruelly murdered Sharon Tate; the *Macbeth* witches have always exhausted the ingenuity of directors and make-up artists; and Lady Macbeth's *déshabillé* in the sleepwalking scene is almost virginal, an emblem of her pathetic vulnerability more than anything like *Playboy* eroticism. As Bernice Kliman has pointed out, the play's violence has always been there, though a surprising amount of it has been mitigated even in Polanski's grim portrayal. She gives as an example the restraint shown in the bear baiting sequence, and in the off-camera rape of Lady MacDuff.[39] Squeamish directors for genteel audiences have averted their eyes from what Rosse implies as the despoliation of Lady MacDuff, who was "savagely slaughter'd" (4.3.205). The man who wrote *Titus Andronicus* might not himself have been quite so squeamish.

With some exceptions, Polanski's critics spared him the deluge of hostility that greeted Peter Brook's efforts, perhaps a sign that critics had grown more tolerant of filmed Shakespeare. Of course many complained about the film's egregious violence that brought too much attention to itself;[40] another more complicated argument, assuming film is always naturalistic, concluded that "*Macbeth* fails as a film [because] Polanski's appropriation is incomplete or half-hearted, leaving, for instance, an artistically unbridgeable gap between Shakespeare's supernaturalism and the modern director's naturalism";[41] and Frank Kermode liked it but did not like it, equivocating like Macbeth himself in his quandary over prophecies that "cannot be ill; cannot be good" (1.3.131).[42] Kermode's equivocation is understandable. Violence as art invites culture shock.

The Columbia Pictures release script uses only about forty percent of Shakespeare's text but it substitutes for deleted text a glittering array of visual and aural images. As cameraman Gil Taylor remarked, "nothing is ever static."[43] Polanski, like Zeffirelli and the seventeenth-century Flemish painters, crams his *mise-en-scène* with realistic furniture, hangings, goblets, etc., but he is even more resourceful than Zeffirelli at subtly embedding them into the thematic design, being obsessed with promulgating his agenda down to the last tiny detail. In Polanski's conception of Macbeth's castle, things and people are forever moving. Extras push carts, carry pigs, sweep stairs, feed chickens. Animals fill the courtyard – geese, dogs, chained bears, falcons, and so forth. And his sonic punctuation matches Orson Welles's – horses' hooves, wheels squeaking, chains clanking, seagulls squawking, geese honking, bells ringing, cocks crowing, hens clucking, water splashing, soldiers grunting, warriors gasping, dogs barking, doors groaning, etc., etc. The soundtrack penetrates into the heart of the diegesis.

The pre-credit, spectacular long take subliminally gives portents of the events to follow,[44] and predicts what it means for Macbeth to "have supp'd full with horrors" (5.5.13) before he suffers death by beheading at the hands of MacDuff. First, there is a hazy sunrise and seascape of a lonely beach, and then a crooked stick enters the frame from the right followed by two withered crones and a young woman, whose fairness contrasts with the foulness of the older women: "Fair is foul, and foul is fair"(1.1.11). From a squeaky, dilapidated cart, these less than supernatural hags remove an assortment of macabre objects, among them a hangman's noose and a severed arm, into the hand of which they insert a dagger (is that a sufficient portent?). In close-up, the cackling trio bury the arm in the sand and pour a vial of blood over it. A gull squawks, a talisman of a galaxy of birds' cries to follow, all of which echo Shakespeare's own ornithological obsession in *Macbeth*: "Light thickens, and the crow / Makes wing to th' rooky wood" (3.2.50). Fog and mist roll in with superimposed titles fading in and out, while the Third Ear Band provides discordant violin and bagpipe music for the departure of the witches' rickety cart. The soundtrack reverberates with horses hooves, shouting and screaming, clashing of swords, the whinnying of horses, human wailing, coughing, and moaning, while the superimposed credits continue to roll on the now completely fog-bound screen. After the fog dissipates, dead and wounded litter the battlefield at Forres. In mid-shot a soldier stops by an injured man lying face down on the ground, pulls at his boot, and the man stirs. The injured man feebly lifts his head and the soldier shatters his spine with two or three sickening whacks with an iron ball on a chain. The camera moves on to the bleeding sergeant's battle report and then to a bloodied Thane of Cawdor (Vic Abbott) bound and stretched out on a horse-drawn litter.

Polanski husbands his aural and visual images the way a good writer squeezes words. The mist and fog again suggest the play's leitmotif – the equivocal nature of reality – "Is this a dagger which I see before me [?]" (2.1.33). The beauty of nature contrasts with the ugliness of battle. The medallion and ceremonial chain that Duncan (Nicholas Selby) lifts from the defeated Thane of Cawdor foreshadows more chain images, to include the iron collar and chain around the neck of Cawdor at his grisly execution, an episode only reported in the play. A defiant endomorph, Cawdor oozes contempt for his captors, especially the double-dealing Rosse, and leaps off a castle parapet to die brutally at the end of a chain fastened to an iron collar around his size twenty-two neck, "Nothing in his life / Became him like the leaving it" (1.4.7), reports Malcolm (Stephan Chase) to Duncan. Chains hold the bear to the stone column in the baiting scene before the disastrous banquet. Later, Macbeth hands the same medallion and chain to Seyton (Noel Davis) as a payoff for his corrupt services. The chain also stands for Macbeth's self-enchainment, who, as has rightly been said, murdered himself when he murdered Duncan.

Hanged men dangle, slowly twisting in the wind, from a crudely constructed gallows, while below several more of the condemned are queued up awaiting their turns. Those uncooperative with their hangmen are pummeled into submission. A twitching and jerking wretch is hoisted up high by a rope around his neck. Muffled cries, grunts, groans. Off in the distance, a mounted Macbeth (Jon Finch) and Banquo (Martin Shaw) impassively watch the chamber of horrors, a Brueghel-like nightmare. In the words of the bleeding sergeant, "another Golgotha"(1.1.40), the place of the skull. In

Kottian terms, it is the world as the inexorable Grand Mechanism, a crunching power struggle. This is Theatre of Cruelty – a demonic universe of whips, gibbets, and scaffolds. The violence, as Polanski himself would argue, is not gratuitous but necessary: "if you don't show violence the way it is, I think that's immoral and harmful."[45] The suffering is the outward and visible sign for Macbeth's inner agony. In Jack Jorgens' apt phrase, Polanski makes the "inner outer."[46]

Pictures cling to the memory. In a scatological moment, the Porter (Sydney Bromley), after the terrible knocking at the gate, noisily urinates against the castle wall. He obscenely thrusts out his dagger in a show-and-tell for his thesis that drinking both "provokes, and unprovokes: it provokes the desire, but it takes away the performance" (2.3.29). In the light of dawn, the castle is revealed for what it is, a barnyard, where cocks crow and flea-bitten hounds hop in and out of the straw mattresses on the crude beds.

Spirited *découpage* enhances the horror. The murdered Banquo falls into a stream, an axe protruding from his back, and floats on the water, face-down. This time there is no hope of water washing away "the deed without a name" (4.1.49). A split second later, a chained bear materializes, the same bear that had previously been seen being dragged into the castle. Savage dogs snap at the animal, which is fettered to a ring in a stone column. A strange look of half revulsion and half gloating crosses Lady Macbeth's (Francesca Annis) face as if the spectacle of cruelty erotically stimulated her. Once again, "foul is fair, and fair is foul." The bear-baiting becomes associated with another complex of images. As the mangled bears' carcasses are dragged through the corridors, attendants sprinkle the fouled floor with rushes to make it fair again. After Macbeth has been traumatized by the sight of Banquo's ghost, he drops his wine goblet and Lennox in a tight frame wipes up the foul stain to restore the floor to fairness. This obsession with wiping things clean resonates off Lady Macbeth's vain hope that "a little water clears us of this deed" (2.2.64), which comes full circle in the sleep-walking scene when she discovers that "All the perfumes of Arabia will not sweeten this little hand. O, O, O!" (5.1.50). She herself is of course outwardly fair and inwardly foul, especially in a film that makes her over from the traditional nag/shrew into a fashionable young woman with the style of a super model. As already mentioned, the chain around the neck of Cawdor resonates against the metal collar around the bear's neck, and then at the very end of the film, Macbeth himself falls near the same iron ring in the stone column that had chained the bear. He indeed "bear-like ... must fight the course" (5.7.2). These complex mirror relationships and visual associations deserve enough close exegesis to qualify Roman Polanski as a James Joyce with a camera.

Another Polanski tactic is summed up in his remark that he likes "a realistic situation where things don't quite fit in."[47] Nowhere does this mining of an incongruity for an artistic congruity better show than in the famous banquet scene when Macbeth is confronted by Banquo's ghost. Macbeth enters the dining hall the soul of geniality, like some Mafia godfather. With consummate hypocrisy, concealing the foul with the fair, he remarks on how much happier he would be if "the grac'd person of our Banquo [were] present" (3.4.40). Lennox (Andrew Laurence) and Rosse (John Stride) urge him to be seated at the banquet table, assuring him that a place has been reserved. A quick cut to the table does show a vacant place, but a few seconds later Macbeth glances at the table and says "the table's full" (3.4.45). And indeed it seems so. The camera pans back to reveal an unbroken row of human backs. For a second we are as convinced as Macbeth that all the chairs at the table are occupied but Lennox insists, "Here is a place reserv'd, sir." Again Macbeth peers, looks puzzled. Again he sees only a solid phalanx of human backs. Obviously, though, there is something going on that "doesn't quite fit in." "Where?" says a perplexed Macbeth, echoing the thoughts of the audience as well, who have shared his vision, not Lennox's. Then in a masterstroke of editing, one of the guests turns around, the one at the center, raising his hand to his face, and stares at the king. It is the butchered Banquo (Martin Shaw). Terrified, the king drops his wine goblet and cries out, "Which of you have done this?" and then "never shake / Thy gory locks at me" (3.4.49). The barriers between the king and the off-screen audience evaporate. There is a magical convergence so that Macbeth's and the audience's consciousnesses merge. The thing that "doesn't quite fit in" has been fitted into an artistic coup.

A great oddity is that this hyper-trendy film actually drew for its scenario, which was co-authored by the brilliant but astringent Kenneth Tynan, on M. F. Libby's obscure Victorian essay, "Some New Notes on *Macbeth*" (1893). In it, Libby imaginatively fictionalized that Rosse to curry favor with Macbeth had Cawdor "framed" and executed on the hasty command of the king. Rosse then busily went on to serve Macbeth, grew jealous over Macbeth's intimacy with Banquo, took on the job of the elusive Third Murderer of Banquo, assisted in covering up for Macbeth at the banquet, and became a key agent in the murder of Lady Macduff and her children. After deserting to Malcolm, he finally "as a reward of endless treachery [was] made an earl."[48] Played by John Stride as a smirking sociopath, Rosse's complicity with Macbeth is insinuated by almost every camera angle from his early assistance in Cawdor's destruction, to his iterative, almost subliminal appearances, when he hovers in the background. A murderers' murderer he pushes Banquo's two inept assassins down a castle well with a makeshift crutch that resembles the witches' ragged bough at the beginning of the

16 John Stride as Rosse in *Macbeth* (UK 1971), directed by Roman Polanski, already at the beginning of the film contemplates his dark scenario for rivaling Macbeth himself in villainy.

movie. His fortunes rise further when he orchestrates the heartless slaughter of Macduff's family, which begins with Ian Hogg contemptuously sweeping trinkets off the fireplace mantle in a terrified Lady MacDuff's private quarters. (A Nazi bully apparently once subjected Polanski to a similar treatment when he was a child.) At the end of the film, Rosse, the tireless opportunist, picks up the crown and proffers it to Malcolm, crying "Hail, King of Scotland!" (5.9.25). Off camera, almost lost, Macduff utters his traditional line "The time is free" (5.9.21). The silent movie about Rosse remains nested within the framework of the talking movie about Macbeth.

The last thing that Macbeth sees in his life is a subjective whirl of jeering and catcalling soldiers as his head is swished about on a pole. Only later do we realize that Polanski's subjective camera has positioned us, the audience, *inside* the severed head, so that we too are experiencing the terminal spasms of sensory apprehension, the death throes, *after* the beheading. The time may be "free" in Shakespeare's play but the limping Donalbain's return to the witches' cave suggests the "time" is not free in this movie. The cyclical pattern of evil has begun again and presumably usurper will replace usurper in an infinite regression of existential despair as the Grand Mechanism works out its inexorable design. Polanski's vision echoes Macbeth's, but not necessarily Shakespeare's, view of life as "a tale / Told by an idiot, full of sound and fury, / Signifying nothing" (5.5.26), which runs against the tradition in Shakespearean tragedy for a "wraparound" ending with assurances of a return to order and decency. Yet Polanski never pretended to be Shakespeare. He is a gifted film maker with a genius for pointing a camera. He makes magic out of filming rather than filming to make magic. He didn't need to borrow Shakespeare's robes when he had so many of his own.

The Burge/Snell *Julius Caesar*

In roughly the same time frame when Polanski was making *Macbeth*, Peter Snell was working on his *Julius Caesar* (1970) and Charlton Heston on *Antony and Cleopatra* (1972). Neither film was sealed of the tribe of Kott, being "straight Shakespeare" innocent of any transgressive impulses. Peter Snell, a youthful Canadian producer working for Great Britain's Commonwealth United, was joined by Stuart Burge, an experienced television director, who had directed a BBC *Julius Caesar* (1959) that cost over £8,000 with ninety-nine in the cast. Snell's Anglo-American cast almost matched the distinction of the actors in Mankiewicz's 1953 film. They included John Gielgud, Jason Robards, Jr., and Charlton Heston. Heston's willingness to play Antony for a modest $100,000 plus fifteen percent of the world gross was precisely the leverage that a hard-pressed Peter Snell needed to entice financial backers.[49]

Heston's passion for Antony had begun in a 1950 *Julius Caesar* filmed in and around the environs of Northwestern University, which cleverly exploited the abandoned University of Chicago football stadium as a Roman setting. Made on a tiny budget of $15,000 and directed by David Bradley, the film, though amateurish in many ways, still won good press notices. Critics like Bosley Crowther were sympathetic to *Julius Caesar* but not dazzled, acknowledging the ambitiousness of a 16mm film produced by undergraduates but that ultimately betrayed "its amateur origins and its 'little theatre' bounds."[50] David Bradley, who had also directed a *Macbeth* (1947), that time on a budget of $5,000 at the University of Chicago, played Brutus himself, but never achieved the enormous success in film making of his friend, Heston.

The Burge/Snell *Julius Caesar* remains one of the great mysteries in the history of filmed Shakespeare. Presumably it had everything going for it – professional direction, an excellent cast, intelligent script, and yet somehow it remained dead in the water. As *Variety* said, "it is difficult to pinpoint just what is lacking in Commonwealth's *Julius Caesar*. It has most of its "i's" dotted and its "t's" crossed, but its fire seems manufactured rather than inspired."[51] Other critics were downright hostile: "The new picture is as flat and juiceless as a dead haddock," wrote Howard Thompson;[52] "Robards appears to be receiving his lines by concealed radio transmitter, and delivering them as part of the responsive reading in a Sunday sermon," said Tom Castner.[53]

Filmed in Technicolor instead of black-and-white like the Mankiewicz version, Burge's movie achieves plausibility but not inspiration. With a limited budget of $1,600,000, which needed to cover major battle scenes in Spain, its cast included one star from the Mankiewicz film, John Gielgud, now Caesar not Cassius. Gielgud as Julius Caesar is Gielgud as Gielgud all over again, the singer's voice disconnecting from the character's innermost being. Insufficiently grubby-looking for backdoor politics, Gielgud seems less made-to-order for Caesar than Mankiewicz's phlegmatic Louis Calhern, who fit the stereotype of the ambitious public man so perfectly. With his virile physique and voice, Charlton Heston once again turns Antony into one of the triple pillars of the world. The director hit on the happy idea of having him deliver part of the soliloquy over Caesar's body at the base of Pompey's statue in voice-over, which toned down Heston's histrionics: "O, pardon me, thou bleeding piece of earth, / That I am meek and gentle" (3.1.254).

Where Brando's eulogy at the Forum over Caesar's body reflects the inner writhing of the Stanislavsky school of acting, then a dominant trend in New York theatre circles, Heston speaks with the big voice and authoritative manner of an old-fashioned Shakespearean actor of the Frederick B. Warde school. Richard Johnson makes a more satisfactory Cassius than Gielgud's effete young man in the Mankiewicz movie. With a dark moustache and smoldering expression, he has the Iago-like sneakiness that can justify Caesar's fears: "Yond Cassius has a lean and hungry look, / He thinks too much; such men are dangerous" (1.2.194). Unlike Gielgud, Johnson can plausibly manipulate Brutus to his will, though neither actor's performance sheds light on how by the end of the play the two reverse roles, Brutus being empowered and Cassius disempowered. Both Diana Rigg (Portia) and Jill Bennett (Calphurnia) had the misfortune to repeat the roles played so expertly by Deborah Kerr and Greer Garson. Rigg shows a charming, almost cuddly, appeal but it works against the concept of a high Roman aristocrat who is "Cato's daughter" with the capability to "swallow fire." Bennett, hard put to it to match Greer Garson's formidable earlier cool portrayal of Caesar's wronged wife, is beautiful and appealing, almost a "trophy wife" to the aging Caesar, but lacks the requisite imperial bearing for the spouse of Rome's greatest man. There are grand montage effects in splashy color of swirling crowds, processions, battles, with Michael Lewis' stirring music to enliven the action. Not least are the battle scenes made in Spain with hundreds of extras costumed as Roman soldiers at Philippi. As the horses rear up and fall to the dust and the soldiers hammer away at one another, the battle increasingly quotes from the fighting on the ice in Eisenstein's *Alexander Nevsky*, or even its derivative in Welles's *Chimes at Midnight*. Man against man, horse against horse, hacking away in blind rage.

Sharmini Tiruchelvam's film diary of the daily activities in Spain throws some light on why this otherwise promising venture somehow fell short of expectations. Apparently Jason Robards' low-key performance stemmed from his interpretation of Brutus as an intellectual suppressing his emotions after being traumatized by his entanglement in a political assassination. When James Mason played Brutus in the Mankiewicz film, he spoke Brutus' Hamlet-like soliloquy in a meditative, thoughtful, introspective way: "Th' abuse of greatness is when it disjoins / Remorse from power; and to speak truth of Caesar, / I have not known when his affections sway'd / More than his reason" (2.1.18). By contrast, Robards speaks the lines as if he "lacked affect" (in the psychological sense), totally flat and uninflected. Besides covering up any sign of emotion, Robards also conceived in some high-minded way that "rehearsing in movies should be done just before takes. Then those small spontaneous things can be retained." He grew "restive" on the set, even disappeared, so that "there was talk of recasting."[54] If this is so, in an ironically self-referential way, Robards' lofty scruples about how to interpret Brutus and his idealistic view that rehearsing violated artistic fidelity, sabotaged the film in much the same way that Brutus' lofty idealism virtually destroyed Rome.

Heston's *Antony and Cleopatra*

Charlton Heston's ambitious *Antony and Cleopatra* (1972) reconfirmed his self-less devotion to Shakespeare, particularly for the role of Antony, whom, as we have seen, he had twice previously done on screen. In the 1950s when still a recently discharged Army Air Corps veteran from the Aleutian campaign, he had played Petruchio and Macbeth on television, Macbeth and Proculeius (with Katherine Cornell as Cleopatra) on stage, and most recently he has been a powerful First Player in the Kenneth Branagh *Hamlet* (1996). No two Shakespeare film directors could be more opposite in temperament than Heston and Polanski, the former a sturdy Midwesterner,[55] and the other a decidedly hippy Polish Jew. Heston approaches Shakespeare deferentially, taking the high road, without a jot of Brook's or Polanski's bitter irony. His commitment to the National Rifle Association agenda has made him *persona non grata* to the politically correct in Hollywood. In his commitment to Shakespeare, however, Heston defies stereotypes. He invested time and money to film *Antony and Cleopatra* with its understated but evocative language because he thought it had been neglected, which is hardly indicative of a man with a shriveled soul. Like Plutarch's Antony, perhaps Heston had also been caught up in Cleopatra's "strong toil of grace."[56]

After Orson Welles's warning that without a Cleopatra there was no play,[57] Heston at considerable travail found Hildegard Neil, a stunningly beautiful South African, who possessed the "infinite variety" to survive three weeks of rehearsals in dingy quarters near Covent Garden. Once filming began on location in Spain, Heston's careful preparation allowed him to shoot the scenes in almost any order.[58] As Moses in Cecil B. De Mille's *Ten Commandments* (1956), he had learned first-hand about the logistics of a super-extravaganza in Technicolor with a cast of thousands. Unfortunately his budget pointed him in another direction and he had to cut corners by, for example, intercutting out-takes from MGM's war-galley scenes in *Ben Hur* (1959) for his sea battle of Actium. Borrowed or not, they still capture the horror of ancient naval warfare. In tight frames, battering rams penetrate deep into an enemy ship's hull. Galley slaves chained to their oars shriek in terror as sea water pours in. Images of Octavius (John Castle) and Antony appear superimposed on the screen against the backdrop of battle. The land warfare, though not at the level of Olivier's French cavalry charge at Agincourt in *Henry V*, pieces out the imperfections of stage presentation with an Egyptian army uniformed as Muslims perfidiously stepping aside to allow Octavius' cavalry charge to fall heavily on Antony's infantry.

As Heston himself said, by reason of its wide-ranging geographical scope, *Antony and Cleopatra* cries out for a camera. From the establishing helicopter shot of a trireme at sea to the closing when the camera pulls up and back to show Cleopatra's monument gradually diminishing, the movie shifts venues from Rome to Egypt and from Egypt to Rome. Unlike the battered lovers in Jonathan Miller's television version, Heston's Antony and Cleopatra project the mythical aura of godlike creatures. Heston smoothly shifts from the soldierly Antony in *Julius Caesar* to the lover in midlife crisis of *Antony and Cleopatra*, who makes an attractive bauble for the sensuous and danger-ous Cleopatra. From the beginning while symbolically tearing away at an encircling necklace of pearls and proclaiming, "Let Rome in Tiber melt, and the wide arch / Of the rang'd empire fall! Here is my space" (1.1.33), Antony has unconsciously set himself up to be seduced, betrayed, and ruined by Cleopatra. Hildegard Neil as Cleopatra, though less smoldering than Janet Suzman in the Nunn television version, embodies the wildness of the "Egyptian dish," as Enobarbus (Eric Porter) calls her. A striking brunette with ivory skin and dark eyes, her hair piled high and carefully coifed, she is the femme fatale, or *la belle dame sans merci*, the beautiful woman without pity, seductive enough to make any man throw away an empire. She appears in a variety of sybaritic poses, lounging on a luxurious bed, painting her own or Antony's face, calling for her claque of "women" to wait on her, or displaying total petulance toward anyone unlucky enough to interrupt her crowded agenda of self-indulgence. The hapless messenger who brings the news that Antony has married Octavia feels the full brunt: "I'll spurn thine eyes / Like balls before me; I'll unhair thy head / [*She hales him up and down*] Thou shalt be whipt with wire, and stew'd in brine, / Smarting in ling'ring pickle" (2.5.62). Her delight in inflicting pain rivals that of Antony when he catches Octavius' messenger Phidias kissing Cleopatra's hand: "Whip him, fellows, / Till like a boy you see him cringe his face, / And whine aloud for mercy" (3.13.99). Still, what would seem sordid and cruel in others, some-how with Antony and Cleopatra acquires a measure of grace.

Cleopatra includes in her "strong toil of grace" not only the enchanted Antony but also her faithful retinue of Charmian (Jane Lapotaire), Iras (Monica Peterson), and the eunuch, Mardian (Emiliano Redondo). As Charmian, Jane Lapotaire understudies Neil's Cleopatra, a role that she finally won for herself with Colin Blakely as her Antony in the Jonathan Miller 1981 BBC version. Lapotaire and Peterson make up a pathetic little feminist phalanx protecting Cleopatra from the disastrous consequences of her meddling in Antony's military campaigns. When she blunders into the naval battle and seals her own doom, a soldier protests "trust not to rotten planks" (3.7.62) and Canidius despairs for Antony's cause, "We are women's men" (3.7.69).

In Rome, Antony appears at Octavius' box at the arena, where gladiators train to fight to the death. The chilling spectacle of two exhausted men fighting in the arena for their lives with swords and tridents and shields (2.2) is intercut with Antony's negotiations with Octavius for marriage to Octavius' sister. As if to epitomize Roman cruelty, Octavius Caesar heartlessly ignores the gladiators while he bargains with Antony for power. As Enobarbus, Eric Porter colorfully describes Cleopatra's barge, which may have been inspired by the royal vessel of Queen Elizabeth, depicted on the Thames in Visscher's 1616 engraving of London: "The poop was beaten gold, / Purple the sails, and so perfumed that / The winds were love-sick with them; the oars were silver" (2.2.192), and he also pays the greatest tribute of all to Cleopatra: "Age cannot wither her, nor custom stale / Her infinite variety" (2.2.234). After Enobarbus' appalling desertion of Antony for Octavius, the mean-spirited Octavius places Enobarbus in the vanguard of his attacking troops: "Go charge Agrippa / Plant those that have revolted in the vant" (4.6.7), while Antony fills him with guilt and self-loathing by generously returning his personal property to him. The spiritually desolate Enobarbus laments that "I am alone the villain of the earth, / And feel I am so most" (4.6.28), and vows to "seek / Some ditch wherein to die" (4.6.36). Heston ratchets the "ditch" up several notches into a cliff from which the fallen and wretched Enobarbus hurls himself into the sea.

The crucial death scenes of Antony and Cleopatra have rarely been done any better. Critics tended to be rather harsh, one declaring Heston's Antony to be lacking in "sensual drive,"[59] while another opining of Neil's Egyptian queen that she was "disastrous" with neither "presence . . . nor sexuality."[60] On the other hand, a *Variety* reviewer said that the "film is a neat balance of close-up portraiture and panoramic action" and that "Hildegard Neil proves one of Cleo's more convincing screen incarnations."[61] In the monument, betrayed by Cleopatra, but nevertheless bound to her in a common passion, Antony, for the first time perhaps, shows a sense of loss and humility: "I am dying, Egypt, dying. / Give me some wine" (4.15.41). With Antony's body in front of her, Cleopatra courageously chooses death over certain dishonor in Rome. She shrewdly sees through the sham offers of Octavius and his messenger Proculeius (Julian Glover). Her unbearable fate would be to be shown to "the shouting varlotry / Of censuring Rome" (5.2.55), or to see "some squeaking Cleopatra boy [her] greatness" (5.2.220) in a public playhouse. Cleopatra accepts the notorious basket of asps "I wish you joy o' th' worm" (5.2.279) from a ubiquitous soothsayer who thriftily

17   Paul Scofield in an unforgettable performance as the tyrannical old king in Peter Brook's bleak vision of *King Lear* (UK 1971).

doubles for Shakespeare's grotesque little clown. Plutarch says that she experimented on prisoners to determine what the least painful mode of death would be: "She hath pursu'd conclusions infinite / Of easy ways to die" (5.2.355). Her faithful ladies-in-waiting, Charmian and Alexa, respond to her last request: "Give me my robe, put on my crown, I have / Immortal longings in me" (5.2.280). She then says the ineffable, "I am fire and air" (5.2.289), and manages in her last gestures to perfume the air with sensuous imagery: "Now no more / The juice of Egypt's grape shall moist this lip" (5.2.281); and death itself becomes erotic: "the stroke of death is as a lover's pinch, / Which hurts, and is desir'd" (5.2.295). When Octavius enters and says that "she looks like sleep, / As she would catch another Antony / In her strong toil of grace" (5.2.346), the movie matches the play's largeness of soul. In another costly helicopter shot, the camera pulls back and up and away from the monument, leaving Antony and Cleopatra in another time and place but somehow appropriating their lost world into our own as well.

- 8 -

Other Shakespeares: translation and expropriation

Movie makers from non-Anglophone countries all over the world have resituated Shakespeare's plays in the idiom of their own language and film culture. Not needing to record in English on the soundtrack, they enjoyed the luxury of reinventing the plays in purely cinematic terms, as if they were silent movies. Sometimes the results have met with wide acclaim, as with Akira Kurosawa's famous 1957 *Macbeth* adaptation, *Throne of Blood* (*Kumonosu-Jo*), sometimes with hostility, as with an Indian *Hamlet* (1955), but in all instances these non-Anglophone films show the universal appeal of Shakespeare as a cultural trophy. Few other English writers, if any, have attracted admirers in places so remote as, say, sub-Saharan or East Asian nations. Once removed from the original Anglophone context, the plays have often been converted into "other Shakespeares, Shakespeares not dependent on English and often at odds with it,"[1] so that the shadow of cultural imperialism gradually diminishes.

The vast Indian film industry, which in North Africa, the Middle and Far East has rivaled Hollywood in productivity and influence, in 1979 alone produced more than 700 feature-length movies.[2] The Indian upper middle classes have traditionally been nurtured on Shakespeare in the school curriculum, and, significantly, scholars in New Delhi edit an important English language Shakespeare journal, *Hamlet Studies*. The Merchant/Ivory film *Shakespeare Wallah* (1965) captures the flavor of Anglo/Indian culture with scenarist Ruth Prawer Jhabvala's loose adaptation of actor Geoffrey Kendal's real-life diary of a Shakespeare troupe touring India in 1947. Jhabvala's treatment turns the story of the strolling Anglo players, led by a fictional Mr. and Mrs. Buckingham, into a "metaphor for the end of the British Raj."[3] The talented actors superbly perform scenes from *Antony and Cleopatra*, *Othello, Hamlet,* and *Twelfth Night* in settings ranging from a Maharajah's palace to a boys' school, the smothering scene from *Othello* being particularly exemplary. British cultural as well as economic imperialism is waning, however, and the audiences' growing impatience with the vestiges of the Raj evoke a compelling, almost Chekhovian, nostalgia for a lost Anglo/Indian culture that might rightly be entitled "A Passage *from* India." A sterner critic has said "Good riddance" to the poor Buckinghams, whom she views as agents of oppressive colonialism, and "slightly ridiculous" at that.[4] Chekhov's people are, it is true, often also "slightly ridiculous" but also touchingly and ineffably glorious in sensibility. Banish them and, as with Falstaff, banish the whole world. As Lizzie Buckingham, popular British television actress Felicity Kendal (Viola in the BBC *Twelfth Night*) plays the daughter of the troupe's director (Geoffrey Kendal), a man forced to watch the demise of a lifetime's work. Although in love with a young Indian suitor of means, Lizzie sails off to England, a country that she has in fact never known. With its soft-textured black-and-white photography and deep sensitivity to the nuances of the Anglo-Indian love/hate affair, the low-budget film is a treasure. And it helps to explain why Shakespeare movies were made in the native dialects of India as well.

In India there have been at least two films of *Hamlet* in native languages, probably more. Peter Morris reports on a *Khoon ka Khoon* (1935) directed by Sohrab Modi as a recording of a stage production. If so, this is one of the earliest Shakespeare talkies ever made anywhere.[5] More is known in the West about the earnest 1955 *Hamlet* produced and directed by Kishore Sahu, who for his pains was rewarded after a gala premiere at the Metro Bombay Theatre with unparalleled vituperation by a hostile review in *Filmindia*, "Sahu's *Hamlet* Flops at the Met." Not only does the film "slander" Shakespeare's memory but also "Hiralel who plays the king was made a drunken clown," and Laertes, we are told, had "a callow and silly face." The picture itself is "stupid" and displays "stinking selfishness." An accompanying photograph shows Dame Sybil Thorndike on the opening night posing with a proud and beaming theatre manager, Mr. Butani.[6] In unpublished comments, film archivist Luke McKernan agrees that Sahu's Hamlet left much to be desired, for "a Hamlet who has no idea of what he is doing is not the same as one who simply cannot make up his mind." McKernan was also troubled by some textual changes involving the play-within-the-play and the duel scene; on the other hand, Ophelia was about "as good as you will ever see," being "perky, impassioned, human." Gertrude too was fine, and the film worked hard at imitating the *mise-en-scène* for the Olivier *Hamlet* with castle battlements, poses (Hamlet in his chair), and stair imagery. The two gravediggers unforgettably dance while singing a bizarre comic song. The film's "lack of Indian-ness" disappointed McKernan but he thought its technical side far better than the *Filmindia* reviewer's assessment.[7]

In Ghana, where Anglo influence remains powerful, there was another version of *Hamlet* released in 1964, *Hamile: The Tongo Hamlet*, in which the play's action had been transferred to Tongo, the home of the Frafra people in northern Ghana. The strongest cinema in sub-Saharan Africa has emerged from Francophone rather than Anglophone zones of influence mainly because the French were more inclined than the British to encourage native cinema production. Even so the students at the University of Ghana School of Music and Drama managed to produce this adaptation based on their stage production,[8] which was entered in the 1965 London Commonwealth Film Festival. A few years later, Brazilian Director Ozualdo R. Candeias released an 87-minute Portuguese-language *Hamlet, a Heranca* (1970), which was "based on Shakespeare's play."[9]

The universality of *Romeo and Juliet* with its young lovers frustrated by the older generation cuts so easily across national boundaries that it may be safe from trendy theories of social construction. Thus Peter Morris reports an Egyptian version, *Shuhaddaa El Gharam* (1942) and a Hindi language film *Anjuman* (1948), both with debts to *Romeo and Juliet*.[10] Out of the mideast comes word of a fairly recent variant in *Torn Apart* (1990), the melancholy tale of an Israeli Romeo (Adrian Pasdar) and Arab Juliet (Cecilia Peck), though the soundtrack seems to be in English, not Hebrew.[11] The Indian film industry delved into Shakespeare again with a hit film *Henna* (1992) that retold the story of the star-crossed lovers in both Hindi (the language of India) and Urdu (the Pakistani language), with Zeba Bakhtiar (Juliet) as a Pakistani Muslim and Rishi Kapoor (Romeo) as an Indian Hindu playing the title roles.[12]

A Portuguese-language *Romeu e Julieta* (1980), directed by Paulo Afonso Grisolli for Brazil's Globo TV, and starring Fabio Junior and Lucelia Santos, though strictly speaking a television production, has the "crossover" potential for theatrical release. Freely adapted from Shakespeare's tragedy, it has been removed, according to the narrator, to Ouro Preto, "like Verona . . . a perfect setting for a tragedy of love," a mining town in Brazil reminiscent with its slanted hillsides, red tile rooftops, and cobbled streets of the fragile beauty of the Italian Riviera. It combines the spectacle of Renato Castellani's *Romeo and Juliet*, the operatic flavor of Zeffirelli's, and the topicality of Leonard Bernstein's *West Side Story*. It recontextualizes the play in a Brazilian Portuguese culture, vibrant, topical, and yet, as with all good non-English screen treatments of Shakespeare, paradoxically faithful to its source.

The family Christopher, who are the Capulets, worship at a private chapel along with Juliet's future groom, Paul Rogerto, known in his fraternity as "Skull." Heavy moralizing about the dire consequences of young people disobeying parental authority bypasses Shakespeare and reverts to Arthur Brooke's long-winded narrative poem. The camera travels across the city to a university cafeteria where Romeo studies pharmacy, when not at wild fraternity parties so notorious that Juliet's father has forbidden her to attend them. During a raucous street processional, Juliet falls in love with Romeo and rescues him from the scorn of the entire community as he does a parody of a bull fighter not ritually arraying but disarraying himself for work in the arena. A police commissioner (Prince Escalus) admonishes the boys for their rowdy behavior. Masquerading in drag, the fraternity brothers crash a sorority party that stands in for the Capulet ball, which vibrates to disco rather than to the stately Morisco of the Zeffirelli movie. At the ball, Juliet and Romeo exchange vows, though in English subtitles remote from Shakespeare: "*J.:* 'I'm ignorant, retarded and boring'; *R.:* 'Me, too, I'm neurotic, conceited, ungrateful'." After that, however, the language turns lyrical again and closer to its source with Juliet's impassioned declaration that her love is as "boundless as the sea" (2.2.133). While in Latinate style, baroque funeral rites for Tybalt (Tides) celebrate the cult of death, and Juliet's Nurse becomes a black woman, the potion scene remains, though in displaced form, as does the mourning at the mock death of Juliet. In the altered tomb scene Juliet whispers "O sinister divine peace," as haunting guitar music fills the soundtrack and a high-angle shot reveals the still bodies of the lovers artfully posed in the cellar of a ruin. The production exhibits a clarity and sharpness rarely seen on North American television. A good example of "other Shakespeare," it is unpretentious but serious drama, well done.

Another Portuguese-language production, Grisolli's *Otelo De Oliveira* (1984), re-appropriates *Othello* for the tale of Otelo and Denise, residents in a shanty town in Rio de Janeiro. Otelo leads a sambo band that is rife with jealousies, somewhat like the jazz band in the British *All Night Long* (1962) with Johnny Dankworth and Dave Brubeck (see chapter 9). A charismatically forceful black man plays a Iago with a deceptively soft face that twists on demand into terrifying malevolence. The rich soundtrack provides such special effects as the whirr of a rattlesnake to punctuate Iago's dialogue, while radical alterations accommodate the text to the *mise-en-scène* of a poverty-stricken Rio neighborhood. Otelo is a convincingly graceful and handsome, light-skinned man, married to a very fair Desdemona, who manages to be both virtuous and sexy, a tricky feat. Both Emilia, an agreeable black woman, and Cassio, a white man and a guitar player, make excellent quarry for the predatory Iago. A mysterious ring, which Otelo is of course inordinately fond of, replaces the most celebrated stage prop in history, the handkerchief. Like *Romeu e Julieta*, the movie has been thoroughly Latinized, as, for example, in its fascination with voodoo. A mysterious woman in white periodically appears to sacrifice tiny animals in front of a spooky altar ringed with leering, devilish creatures. As a pagan outsider obsessed with the "magic in the web" of his mother's handkerchief, Otelo seems to fit nicely into this ambience. Like Shakespeare's formula at the Globe, the film offers complexity in the guise of simplicity.

Wirth's *Hamlet*

Germany and Sweden have also invested in major television Hamlets, whose scale has given them a crossover potential for theatrical release. Among these was *Der Rest Ist Schweigen* (1959), a modernized *Hamlet* directed by Helmut Käutner. Of greater interest internationally is Franz Wirth's *Hamlet* (1960), which was originally made for German television but which achieved such success that Hollywood director Edward Dmytryk bought it and arranged to dub in English dialogue, which sometimes created an egregious gap between the aural and the visual. The forthright star, Maximilian Schell, could easily have been cast in a Hollywood wartime propaganda movie as the "good" Wehrmacht officer, secretly opposed to the Nazi regime, who spares little French orphans, while Claudius (Hans Caninenberg) would qualify as the central-casting U-Boat commander especially keen on torpedoing Red Cross hospital ships. From all accounts, the producers rejected Maximilian Schell's request for subtitles, and instead went for the rather awkward dubbing.

Despite this technical problem, the movie contributes a fresh chapter to the history of filmed *Hamlet*s in presenting, if nothing else, a thoroughly unneurotic, emotionally stable, prince, who indeed can be envisioned as Ophelia's "glass of fashion and the mould of form" (3.1.153). On the surface, Schell's prince shows none of the emotional problems of Nicol Williamson's troubled, edgy Hamlet. Where Williamson parades his inner anxieties in outer histrionics, Schell conceals the inner turmoil with a controlled façade. Also original is Franz Schafheitlin's foolish Polonius who must consult a notebook to finish his famous advice to Laertes: "This above all: to thine own self be true, / And it must follow, as the night the day, / Thou canst not then be false to any man" (1.3.78).

The establishing shot showing two vacant thrones immediately underscores the director's concept of Hamlet as a play about politics, about the Grand Mechanism of power and struggle, an allegory easily connected to the post-war hostility between East and West Germany. As the camera pans around two vacant thrones set against a dark background, Rosencrantz's sycophantic speech to Claudius from the third act can be heard in voice-over: "The cess of majesty / Dies not alone, but like a gulf doth draw / What's near it with it" (3.3.15). According to Bernice Kliman, this speech on the Fall of Kings juxtaposed to the two thrones underscores the vulnerability of both Claudius and Hamlet, who will each fall victim to Elsinore's internal power struggle.[13] The camera will return to them again and again as symbols of political turmoil, until in the film's closing moments the dying Claudius strains unsuccessfully to remount the throne. A minimalist *mise-en-scène*, spartan in understatement, employs a symbolist style that Jane Howell used admirably in her BBC *The Winter's Tale* (1980). The late Lillian Wilds thought that the set becomes "unremittingly claustrophobic" and "there is perhaps no daylight, no world outside. Hamlet's world is completely circumscribed by blackness."[14] On the other hand, the set equally liberates by projecting oceans of implications beyond the narrow confines of its catwalks, stairs, and blocks. With superb lighting, the tightly framed faces of the characters in one and two and three shot endow the movie with the patina of a fine lithograph, virtually an exercise in portrait photography.

Director Wirth wrings miracles out of this unadorned set with Rolf Unkel's harsh, discordant musical score, and with such deft strategies as having Hamlet do the "To be or not to be" soliloquy with a close-up of his face cramped under a stairwell, as if confined behind bars: "Denmark's a prison" (2.2.243). At "Ay, there's the rub," Schell leaps up, symbolically unleashed from his bondage and prepared for action. The arrival of the players at Elsinore, when Hamlet openly admires the First Player (Adolf Gerstung), remains a memorable vignette in the film. When later, seated quietly, Hamlet speaks his "O, what a rogue and peasant slave am I!" (2.2.550), the contrast between his lack of a "cue for passion" and the player's passion born of trivia has never been better explicated. The tight framing has the effect of speeding up the action to diminish the sense of Hamlet's delaying in his quest for revenge. A "decisive prince" is a kind of oxymoron but Schell's Hamlet comes close to it, even in his callous treatment of a terrified Ophelia (Dunja Movar). Of course Schell's very certainty leaves the audience in uncertainty over whether he has missed out on the complicated emotional agenda locked away in Hamlet, or simply allowed it to simmer just below the surface. To answer that question, however, would be to demand the impossible, which is to pluck out the heart of Hamlet's mystery.

Lyth's *Hamlet*

Although made for Swedish television and shown with subtitles in North America on Station WYNC-TV, the Ragnar Lyth *Den tragiska historien om Hamlet, prinz av Danmark* (1984) also qualifies as a "crossover" film not only because it was originally made on 16mm but because, as Bernice Kliman says, "it aspires to the more varied life of a moving image on the large screen."[15] It is a truly bizarre *Hamlet*, not quite like any other and yet too close to the essence of Shakespeare's play for summary dismissal, throwing out an aura of being but not being *Hamlet*, as if all the characters had been filtered through some kind of a gauzy lens and emerged only partially recognizable but nevertheless certifiably themselves. By restating *Hamlet* in visual rather than aural terms, Lyth sets up a paradigm for the paradoxical destruction and reconstruction of a Shakespearean work in a foreign language and uncovers subtexts that might be lost to an Anglophone director.

For his filmic strategy, Lyth adroitly combines *mise-en-scène*, montage, and eccentric characterization. Instead of an establishing shot of a remote castle, the film opens with an elaborate montage showing routine domestic life at Elsinore. It is a shadowy, subdued world of labyrinthine corridors, flaring torches, and tolling bells, with intercutting between the watchmen and chefs who are preparing a feast for the wedding celebration of Gertrude and Claudius: "Thrift, thrift, Horatio, the funeral bak'd meats / Did coldly furnish forth the marriage tables" (1.2.179). To a sighing of wind and clanking of iron wheels, the shadowy, barely glimpsed, ghost terrifies Horatio, Marcellus and Barnardo on the battlements. A moon-faced Horatio rightly shivers at this dreadful spectacle, and three scenes before its proper place Marcellus utters the seminal line, "Something is rotten in the state of Denmark" (1.4.89), which is a verbal surrogate for the skipped establishing shot.

The opening montage quickly yields to the *mise-en-scène* of a great but decaying hall, an abandoned warehouse that once belonged to the Nobel dynamite factory.[16] Only unlike the emptiness of Tony Richardson's Roundhouse *Hamlet* or Franz Wirth's minimalist version, this set pulses with activity. A great fire flickers cheerfully at one end of the hall to enhance the convivial, house-party atmosphere. Claudius' courtiers dance, bowl, play chess, fence, or energetically chatter, perhaps exchanging court gossip. Children run happily about and a genial Claudius picks up one child and hugs him. Throughout the film, children serve as innocent foils to the corruption around them and rays of hope against a dark Kottian vision of despair. Claudius himself perpetually grins and smiles and chuckles, almost idiotically, as if Lyth had decided to build his whole character around Hamlet's observation that "one may smile, and smile, and be a villain!" (1.5.108). In this way, Frej Lindquist's Claudius projects the image of a man desperately reaching out to ingratiate himself with other human beings because he harbors deep within a searing guilt. He embodies Hamlet's original "guilty creature[s] sitting at a play" (2.2.589).

Way off by a window with his back turned to the camera lurks a painfully grumpy young man, who, of course, turns out to be Hamlet (Stellan Skarsgård). His costume and demeanor are pure grunge – a soiled white shirt, baggy black breeches, a woeful expression on his face and a shock of very long, unkempt hair badly in need of a shampoo. If Richardson's Hamlet is the angry young man of the Sixties, Lyth's is the heir apparent to the age of punk and grunge and crack. He only lacks a pierced nose. Cleverly, though, this is not the real Hamlet but the Hamlet of the antic disposition who is only masquerading as a lunatic to confound his mother and step-father. He is a Hamlet who is capable of extreme violence, a "crazy" young man not to be trifled with. Meanwhile Claudius briefs Voltemand (Tomas Laustiola) and Laertes (Dan Ekborg) for their mission, while the courtiers, silenced by the tinkling of a little bell, momentarily pause from their enter-tainments to listen. In a portent of imminent disaster, a little boy knocks over his chess set. A plump, buttoned-up Gertrude (Mona Malm) moves toward Hamlet to console him, while Claudius lectures his nephew on the foolish-ness of excessively grieving over his father's death: "'tis unmanly grief, / It shows a will most incorrect to heaven" (1.2.94). A sweet demure Ophelia (Pernilla Wallgren) hastens toward Hamlet's side and hands him a letter dec-orated with her trademark, a flower, transient in beauty and easily crushed by a cruel world. Later, she plays a flute while reclining on her bed in a plain unadorned room in the style of a Vermeer. Among all the bric-à-brac, a caged raven ominously reinforces the image of Denmark as a prison. By the end of the movie, Hamlet and Laertes thrust and parry in this same cavernous, all-purpose room, where the raven still presides, its hovering cage a reminder of man's fate.

Like any film maker into shock editing, Lyth makes bizarre juxtapositions. The virginal Ophelia accidentally opens a door to catch a sinful priest and servant *in flagrante delicto*; Ophelia's sacrificial drowning is intercut by pan-ning over stacks of meats, breads, fruits, and stoups of wine set out for Laertes and Claudius' festive banquet, while a singer entertains with snatches of old lays; and a guileless little boy in pointing out the murderer in the play-within-the-play exposes the king's guilt. Other motifs range from the disgusting to the grotesque. When Claudius grasps the point of the play-within-a-play, he abruptly vomits all over everybody in sight, while shrill atonal wind instruments and percussion effects punctuate the panic and dis-order in the court. A tight close-up of a swaying shred of clothing turns out to be the remnant of a garment worn by the drowned Ophelia, which Gertrude is bringing in to show to a stunned Laertes. Yorick's skull is no smoothly polished stage prop but a muddy horror that Hamlet spears through the eye socket with a twig. Ophelia's funeral drives home the full meaning of "maimed rites" (5.1.219), when Lyth unsparingly shows the dreadful outcome of the feud between Hamlet and Laertes. Ophelia's plain wooden coffin, followed by hooded, black-robed figures, out of some macabre *Totentanz*, is trundled on an ugly cart and dumped beside the open grave. The removal of the coffin lid exposes the corpse's eerily still body and bluish face. The priest and all mourners quickly turn away to flee when

Laertes cries out "Must there no more be done?" Enraged by the priest's response that to do more would "profane the service of the dead," Laertes spits at the cleric. When Hamlet emerges and begins fighting with Laertes, they upset the open coffin and send Ophelia's body lurching out of it and gruesomely sprawling in the grave.

Lyth makes a major point over the change in Hamlet's personality after his return from the aborted trip to England. As everyone knows, the Hamlet of this last part of the play is 30 years old in contrast to the student prince of the earlier scenes, a puzzle that has never really been resolved. Back in Elsinore, the prince has discarded the long, stringy hair of a squalid hippie and reinvented himself as a crew-cut nordic avenger. The crazy Hamlet has metamorphosed into the killer Hamlet. Like the funeral scene, the duel scene again displays Lyth's gifts for imaginative staging. A grotesque mix of brutality and farce terminating in horror replaces the stately grandeur of the duel scene in Olivier's or Branagh's *Hamlet*. Gertrude voluntarily drinks from the poisoned cup to save her son from what she suspects is a murderous plot. Hamlet "moons" Laertes by turning his [clothed] bottom up at him and suggesting that he attack him there. The insulted Laertes lashes Hamlet across the buttocks with the poisoned sword and inflicts the fatal wound. Aware of his approaching death, Hamlet then slowly wriggles his sword through Claudius' neck until in close-up the point emerges on the other side. Blood spatters from the dying Claudius but his silly giggling never stops. Even knowing that he is a dead man, the king pathetically continues his childish efforts to charm people into loving him and implores his stony-faced courtiers for help. The expiring Hamlet ruthlessly pours the poisoned wine over the king's corpse and dies. In the background, the caged raven implacably observes all these lamentable events. When Horatio reads a letter implicating the king, the stony-faced courtiers walk away, having lost interest in the whole affair. It remains, one suspects, for men like Lyth to try to tell the tale "aright" and in doing so conjure up myriad fascinating details that the rest of us, who think we know the play, might never have thought of.

France: Cayette and Chabrol

The French film industry, which once led the world in film making until Hollywood usurped its hegemony, has never made a feature length "conventional" Shakespeare movie. Notwithstanding, in the silent era the French were among the very first, as we have seen, to film Shakespeare, and two French movies from the 1950s and 1960s, which are movies about making Shakespeare movies, interrogate with Gallic wit the unanswerable question,

"But is it Shakespeare?" *Les amants de Verone* [*The Lovers of Verona*] (1949) was made in the Paris Studios-Cinema at Brillancourt and in the glass factory of Pauly & Co. in Venice. Directed by André Cayatte, the movie places *Romeo and Juliet* under a French gaze, while at the same time it creates one of those ironic structures where a "real" story unfolds within the "fictional" story. Like *West Side Story* essentially a modernization, it begins at a Venetian glass factory where location scouts from a company about to film *Romeo and Juliet* inspect the premises. Angelo, a handsome young glassblower, impudently makes a heart-shaped piece of glass for the voluptuous actress, Bettina. A foreshadowing mirror shot frames Bettina and Angelo in the same glass. The director explains to a friend, Maglia, that he will film only interior shots in Venice; the rest of the film will be made in Verona on location. "Poor Shakespeare," says Maglia.

Increasingly then the movie self-referentially deals with movie making and the aesthetics of Shakespeare adaptation. On the movie set, the sissy actor cast as Romeo is too "giddy" to climb the balcony. Angelo (Serge Reggiani), hired as an extra, comes out of the ranks to stand in for the pusillanimous thespian, while the stand-in for Juliet is Georgia Maglia (Nanouk Aimée), a daughter of the proud and haughty Maglia family, quite disdainful of simple glassblowers. From then on the plot thickens and curdles, as the head of the Maglia family is exposed as an ex-fascist judge with underworld connections, and in a wild shootout, Angelo is fatally wounded. The real-life dying lovers act out their tomb scene in the artificial world of a movie set, while Shakespeare's lines are spoken in voice-over and a stagehand closes the door to leave the set in darkness. Despite the inane plot, *Les amants* has powerful redeeming episodes in its *film noir* brooding, atmospheric representation of Venice and Verona. Romeo and Juliet have been displaced to a movie set, as if their myth could only be inscribed on the celluloid frames of film. There are splendid close-ups, one thinks of Carl Dreyer's *Passion of Joan of Arc* (1928), which reinforce the commentary on the destruction of youthful love and innocence in a corrupt and decaying European city.

New Wave film maker and *auteur,* Claude Chabrol, acclaimed in *Cahiers du Cinema*, directed yet another meta-cinematic French Shakespeare film, *Ophelia* (1962). Chabrol's admiration for Alfred Hitchcock once led him away from the film d'art movement and into making suspense movies, which may account for the frisson in *Ophelia*. Like Cayatte's *Les amants*, Chabrol's postmodernist, film-society movie critiques our unexamined assumptions about reality. The protagonist, Yvan, whose mother has recently remarried with his uncle, sees a poster for the Olivier *Hamlet* in a theatre lobby that undermines his ability to distinguish between Shakespeare's prince and Olivier's portrayal. The journalistic critics of the Sixties had little sympathy for this quirky film that gave no quarter to philistines. Surveying at least three planes of reality – the world of the village, the world of Yvan, and the world of a fabled Hamlet – there are multiple perspectives within each category. *Ophelia* therefore, while not itself literally Shakespeare's *Hamlet*, explores how versions of the play intersect with reality and resist clarification. The LeSurfs (Claudius and Gertrude) and LaGrange all inscribe their understanding of the village of "Erneeles" (Elsinore) into their own subtexts in protean and impenetrable ways. As a disciple of Jacques Derrida might say, "there is no outside" to their texts. Karen Newman has pointed out how *Ophelia* is primarily an exercise in perception, "a whimsical and half-heartedly frightening parody of the entire enterprise of adaptation, for Shakespeare himself repeated his *Hamlet* from some unknown ur-*Hamlet*."[17] Chabrol's movie not only explores the complicated patterns of intertextuality that lie behind the making of any Shakespeare movie but also reconfirms the elusiveness of the Shakespearean text.

The Soviet Union: Fried, Yutkevich, and Kozintsev

The most important European Shakespeare movies came, however, from the former USSR. Under socialism the Russian film industry flourished with the VGIK (All-Union State Institute of Film Making) training cadres of technicians, scenarists, and directors, who churned out hundreds of feature-length movies for the state-owned theatres. The downside was a demand for ideological conformity to doctrines of "socialist realism" (which film makers often subverted), but the upside was the liberation of the artists from "tickling commodity's" obsession with "the bottom line." An unrealistic and puritanical goal of "socialist realism" was to entertain the masses without resorting to the sex and violence of western film and television. For these films, the state apparently never sent a bill. One expert has even suggested that "reform" (i.e., counter-revolution) with its return to "tickling commodity," has done more than the old state-controlled apparatus to damage the film industry.[18] Shakespeare had always appealed to Russians on stage because of some innate need in the Russian soul for romanticism and depth of feeling. In the golden era for post-World-War Soviet film known as the "Thaw" after the death of Stalin, four major Shakespeare movies spoke to this need: Yakov Fried's *Twelfth Night* (1955), Sergei Yutkevitch's *Othello* (1955), Grigori Kozintsev's *Hamlet* (1964), and Kozintsev's *King Lear* (1971). There was also Yuli Raizman's *And What If It's Love?* (1962), which spun off from *Romeo and Juliet* as a film subversive of socialist realism.

Whatever its defects, Yakov Fried's rather stodgy *Twelfth Night* (1955)

18 A powerful Sergei Bondarchuk and elegant Irina Skobtseva in Sergei Yutkevich's "slavicized" version of *Othello* (USSR 1955).

triumphs as spectacle with its vigor, enthusiasm, bounce, and extravagance. The sweeping vistas of the coast line, the elaborate interiors for Olivia's palace, the hunting scenes, the sumptuous costumes, the glittering cast, all recorded in lavish Sovcolor reflect the generosity of the old Soviet studio system. In the first indication of culture shock to come, as the credits roll, a troubadour jauntily perched in a window frame energetically sings a thoroughly Slavicized Elizabethan ballad. Throughout, singers like Feste and Sir Toby resolutely bellow away in Russian while stand-in English actors speak the dialogue in RP accents. The tolerably authentic storm at sea that strands Viola and Sebastian in Illyria erupts in a studio tank, but cinematically surpasses the Vitagraph silent that had Viola demurely wading ashore from the placid waters of Long Island's Great South Bay. This is a fantasy Illyria of great white marble palaces, sweeping lawns, colorful hunting scenes, with actors of a quintessentially Russian temperament notable for openness and generosity of spirit. The costumes remain conventionally Elizabethan and the outdoor settings make room for a noticeable equestrian influence, with Orsino (V. Medvediev) mounted like some statue of a condottiere in an Italian renaissance piazza.

If English-speaking audiences find the cultural codes embedded in Elizabethan comedy perplexing, there is no reason to expect less difficulty for non-English speaking cadres. Esoteric puns are edited out, such as Feste's on "hanging" and "colors": "He that is well hang'd in this world needs to fear no colors" (1.5.5); or Maria's reference to "the new map, with the augmentation of the Indies" (3.2.79); or Sir Toby's "passy-measures" (5.1.200). Malvolio's "cross-garters" have no more contemporary relevance than arcane tavern jokes about "we three" (2.3.17). Doubly afflicted because he is dealing with a foreign language, Fried understandably elected to glide along the surface of the text and focus on familiar scenes that come across to audiences visually rather than linguistically. Thus his charming Viola (Katya Luchko), who doubles as Sebastian, eloquently pleads to a gorgeous blonde Olivia (Anna Larionova), "Make me a willow cabin at your gate . . . / Write loyal cantons of contemned love" (1.5.268). A robust Sir Toby (M. Yanshin) with a fierce guardsman's moustache thoroughly manipulates the ectomorphic Sir Andrew (G.Vipin) who is an imbecile of spectacular dimensions; Malvolio (V. Merkuriev) makes a complete ass of himself wooing Olivia in his cross-garters and yellow stockings; and a plump Maria (A. Lisyanskava) presides over her little entourage of Fabian, Sir Toby, and Sir Andrew. All these sketches follow in the play's stage tradition, especially since roguish Sir Toby, a diminished Falstaff who is the type of one of Lear's one hundred knights, shows traces of the underlying streak of meanness in a professional sponge and free-loader. As one reviewer remarked, however, despite the challenges of translation, "it is surprising how much of the spirit of the piece has survived."[19] To which it might be added that while the festive side, "What You Will," is undeniably present, the pre-Lenten side, the hidden liturgical codes for "Twelfth Night," which Feste sums up in his closing ballad of "With hey ho, the wind and the rain" (5.1.390), have been obscured in translation.

Sergei Yutkevich, the director of *Othello* (1955), possessed an extraordinary knowledge of Shakespeare film that ultimately led in 1973 to his scholarly *Shekspir I Kino* (*Shakespeare on Film*), which includes in-depth studies of work by Olivier, Welles, and Kozintsev. As reviewer Mark Pomar wrote, Yutkevich rejects the argument of "purists" that Shakespeare belongs entirely to the theatre and instead maintained that "Shakespeare's drama reveals its artistic richness when presented in different media: theatre, film, television," and insisted that "film is an heir to the Elizabethan theater."[20] With a score by Aram Khachaturian and translation by Boris Pasternak, the opulence of this romantic, virtually operatic, *Othello*, a sweeping costume drama, originally in SovColor but released in the west in Technicolor, reflects again the abundant budgets of the post-war VGIK era. The actor playing Othello (Sergei Bondarchuk), a stern-looking young man whose hair turns white after the smothering scene, had been designated an artist of the Soviet Union, and his Desdemona (Irina Skobtseva) had studied at Moscow's Art Theatre. Regrettably the dubbed-in, and badly out of synch, voices of English actors deprive western audiences of the rich Slavic timbre except for the songs that remain anachronistically but delightfully in Russian.[21] As A.H. Weiler wrote of the movie's virtues and defects: "Although it is beautifully housed and caparisoned, this Russian *Othello* is embarrassed by the gifts [*sic*] of tongues."[22]

Anthony Davies felt that Yutkevich gives us an *Othello* of "blue skies, open sea and spaciousness,"[23] far removed from the play's innate claustrophobia. Before the credits even roll, an establishing montage shows the beautiful Desdemona day dreaming. Standing beside a globe, she imagines Othello's "battles," "sieges," "moving accidents by flood and field,". and life as a galley slave (1.3.130). Sea fights, land battles, and wretched galley slaves chained to their benches fill the screen. Reminiscent at times of the Orson Welles sea-infused *Othello* at Mogador, long shots of clouds, sunsets, and crashing seas act as metaphors for the turmoil within the hearts of Othello and Desdemona, and reminders that in *Othello* the sea is always present, beginning with the tension when the Turkish fleet indulges in feinting tactics to confuse the Venetians, and continuing with the 1,400-mile voyage from Venice to Cyprus: "Tempests themselves, high seas, and howling winds" (2.1.68). The sense of space persists when Cassio takes on the entire watch in the drunken brawl scene with a swashbuckling sword fight on sweeping stone staircases: "Why, very well then; you must not think then that I am drunk" (2.3.118), or when the camera tracks Othello debarking at Cyprus and trotting up a dizzy flight of stairs to the top parapet, where he breathlessly cries out to Desdemona, "O my fair warrior!" (2.1.182).

For all this virtuoso skill with macro effects, Yutkevich shows equal competence with the micro shot. Tightly framed close-ups during Othello's defense against Brabantio's charges at the palace inspect the sculptured faces of the Duke of Venice, Brabantio, Lodovico, and Iago (Andrei Popov), as well as the blonde Slavic beauty of Desdemona. The editing includes rhythmical cross-cutting and reaction shots, like one of wide-eyed Venetian children staring up at the charismatic Moor in awe. A well with a reflecting pool of water becomes a focal point when Iago plots his diabolical schemes: "I'll have our Michael Cassio on the hip" (2.1.305). First clearly reflected in the still water, his face suddenly dissipates in a swirl of ripples. At a decisive moment for Othello, the same pool of well water mirrors his face until the moment of extreme distress when the rippling water disrupts his image "Confess? Handkerchief? O devil!" (4.1.43). Along the sea shore, Iago tempts Othello in the midst of a tangle of fishing nets, metaphors for the villainous scheme to ensnare Othello in his web. As a micro-study, the handkerchief scene excels in ingenuity with the right side of the frame showing only Desdemona's fair white profile and the empty space on the left being occupied by the Moor's contrasting black hand. The black hand punctuates his terse demands for "The handkerchief!" (3.4.92), while his bewildered wife unwittingly fuels the fire by blithering on about the virtues of Michael Cassio. Feminists will object to Yutkevich's omission of Emilia's low opinion of men: "They eat us hungerly, and when they are full / They belch us" (3.4.165), though with a Iago for a husband she must have often seen the darker side. Again, in the smothering scene, in an over-the-shoulder shot showing only Othello's broad back, Desdemona lies terrified on the bed framed between Othello's two black hands while he menacingly advances on her.

As a film made in the shadow of "socialist realism," the play's sub-textual elements rarely surface in this reworking in a tragic key of the old commedia scenario about a January–May marriage. In both appearance and ideology, the production might have qualified for a grand nineteenth-century staging at the Moscow Art Theatre. As with Fried's *Twelfth Night*, there are no hidden agendas, no Freudian innuendoes, no leering hints of homoeroticism between Iago and Othello. In the three-way triangle of Othello, Iago, and Desdemona, Popov's nondescript Iago suffers from comparison with the charismatic Sergei Bondarchuk's Othello, who in low angle towers over his crafty lieutenant, until his perfidious underling in turn emotionally subjugates him. Desdemona remains as Shakespeare envisioned her, pure as the driven snow, innocent and unspotted, free from any kind of nasty suspicions about her relationship with Cassio. Leavisite arguments about whether Othello was destroyed by his own weakness or by Iago's fiendish scheming resemble the old riddle about the distinction between the dancer and the dance, but the vivid portrayals of Othello's epileptic fits suggest that Othello's handicap helped Iago along.

At the end, after Othello utters the hypnotic, "Put out the light, and then put out the light" (5.2.7), and after he smothers the sacrificial Desdemona, Bondarchuk achieves heights of ostensive acting equalled perhaps only by Emil Jannings in the 1922 silent *Othello*. As he approaches the great curtained bed, the lighting further accentuates the fury in his eyes until he seems literally to be flashing fire, his eyeballs electrified. In a compelling interpretation of the "tragic loading of this bed" (5.2.363), Othello then carries Desdemona's limp body in his arms, like King Lear with Cordelia, up winding stone stairs to the castle's battlement. Atop the parapet overlooking the sea and a craggy promontory, he confronts Lodovico and the other Venetians, before ending his life with all the majesty and dignity of a great opera star projecting a glorious aria, like Placido Domingo in Zeffirelli's film of *Otello* (1986). "Then must you speak / Of one that lov'd not wisely but too well" (5.2.343). In a budget-breaking exterior shot, Lodovico sails back to Venice with the enshrined bodies of the two lovers, and with the wretched Iago pinioned to the mast high aloft. The sumptuous *mise-en-scène* of Yutkevich's *Othello* underscores the magnificence of the Othello story but muffles the squalid underside that Orson Welles caught so well with his schizophrenic camera angles. Heroically amplified, this *Othello* aspires to reach some past idealized peak of high mimetic western tragedy.

While Fried and Yutkevich's *Twelfth Night* and *Othello* occupy important niches in the history of Russian Shakespeare movies, Grigori Kozintsev's *Hamlet* (1964) and *King Lear* (1971) have been widely nominated, along with Akira Kurosawa's Japanese adaptations, as the most effective translations of Shakespeare into a foreign language. Preparation for his Shakespeare movies, which were both supplied with Russian translations by Boris Pasternak and epic musical scores by Dmitri Shostakovich, started in 1941 when Kozintsev directed a stage version of *Hamlet* at the Pushkin Academic Theatre in Leningrad, and of *King Lear* at the city's Bolshoi Drama Theatre. Kozintsev has also published two book-length meditations on his Shakespeare movies,[24] in one of which he discusses "Hamletism," the phenomenon by which a whole conglomerate of legends, expectations, myths, conventions accrue to the popular image of Prince Hamlet like barnacles to a ship's hull. Such a "phantom text" emerged in the nineteenth-century when Jules Laforgue popularized Goethe's romantic portrait of Hamlet as a delicate, tender prince, "an oak tree planted in an exquisite vase."[25] The image of this "black plume" Hamlet, so-called because it became a stage convention for Hamlet to wear a black plume on his headpiece,[26] created an "expectational text"[27] for audiences who imagined Hamlet should always look that way. Kozintsev rejected this stereotype of a fragile Danish prince filled with "doubt, vacillation, split personality, and the predominance of reflection over will to action."[28]

Kozintsev's Hamlet (Innokenti Smoktunovsky) consequently emerges as anything but a "black plume" prince; instead he is a throwback to a presumably more activist Elizabethan *Gestalt*. He is so virile and decisive that his struggle against Claudius and Polonius has been allegorized as an Aesopian attack on Stalin,[29] whose death in 1953 had brought about a "thaw" in the film industry. When this Hamlet dies, Fortinbras' celebration of his soldierly qualities is privileged over Horatio's christening of him as "a sweet prince." Kozintsev's interpretation of Hamlet is neither Freudian, like Olivier's; nor absurdist, like Lyth's; nor embittered, like Richardson's, but is rather an existentialist engagement with the world around it. In the dialectic of "to be" or "not to be," Kozintsev's prince chooses the former. Kozintsev's sharply etched black-and-white sets alternate between a subdued expressionism and a dynamic realism. Images of stone, fire, and water provide recurring tropes. The obsession with stone, which is a Kozintsev hallmark derived from his passion for Japanese formal gardens, signifies the obdurate forces arrayed against Hamlet; fire stands for the volatile passions in the court at Elsinore; and the sea figures forth the timeless ebb and flow of the natural order of things. These cosmic images then enclose the puny human action within the prison of the castle. Vistas of the sea, castle walls, black flags of mourning, galloping horses, a huge portcullis with iron teeth, and a tolling bell replace the traditional opening on the battlements. On a realistic note, scene two begins with a herald reading announcements from a scroll to the assembled people outside the castle wall. His words have been transposed from Claudius' speech: "Therefore our sometime sister, now our queen" (1.2.8). It is as if Claudius had hired a public relations agent to mediate between himself and the common people, who play a vital role as silent spectators in Kozintsev's Shakespeare movies. Shakespeare himself shows Claudius' sensitivity to, and fear of, public opinion when he mentions to Laertes how much love "the general gender bear him [Hamlet]" (4.7.18). And this Hamlet is surrounded by prying and snooping courtiers, while poor Ophelia (Anastasia Vertinskaya) can never escape from the surveillance of her clutch of shriveled duennas.

The film's kinetic flow comes out of the rhythmical cutting back and forth between the expressionistic castle exteriors and the relative light and warmth of the realistic interiors. For example, when Hamlet in the blackness encounters the ghost of his father, the ghost remains an ominous, hovering figure with an enormous black cape that swirls and flutters in the darkness against a backdrop of stone and crashing seas. When the stocky, forty-ish Smoktunovsky as Hamlet insists on obeying the ghost's summons despite the frantic protests of his retainers, he breaks away from them saying "My fate cries out . . . I say away" (1.4.81). The actors internalize the words and then energize them by writhing and twisting and turning and gesticulating in their efforts to hold back a Hamlet who is about to be symbolically separated forever from ordinary men. In a terrifying mini-second, Hamlet shows how desperate he is to know his fate, at all costs, and the rhythm of the scene like a flash of lightning illuminates the metaphysics of Hamlet's damnable but wonderful election as the agent of both "heaven and hell" (2.2.584).

[184]

19   Innokenti Smoktunovsky as Hamlet in Grigori Kozintsev's 1964 film ponders over Yorick's skull in a macabre but nostalgic moment in the famous graveyard scene.

Kozintsev resists the temptation to illustrate the ghost's narrative by showing the poisoning but later he interpolates a lengthy sequence about Hamlet's sea voyage to England and his hoisting of Rosencrantz and Guildenstern on their own petards. Somewhere in the midst of all this perturbation, the Grim Reaper appears as a carved figure on an elaborate mechanical clock. A quick cut follows to the raucous festivity inside the castle as Claudius and Gertrude in high spirits celebrate their nuptials, surrounded by candle light and sycophants clad in the ornate finery of the Elizabethan era. The *memento mori* haunts the festivity.

Shostakovich's exalted musical score punctuates Hamlet's second encounter with his father's ghost in the bed chamber, which resists a descent into sexual horseplay. In yet another episode, Hamlet begins his "O, what a rogue and peasant slave am I! / Is it not monstrous that this player here" (2.2.550), while the First Player (A. Chekaerskii) is still passionately reciting his passage from Aeneas' tale to Dido about the fall of Troy ("Now is he total gules, horridly trick'd / With blood of fathers, mothers" (2.2.457). In the very loftiest traditions of the mysterious First Player role, Chekaerskii sets a standard for all the other actors in the play. If there is such a thing as a Russian soul, he embodies it with his flair for expressing the inexpressible sorrows of the human condition. It's a style completely beyond the range of earnest American MFA theatre graduates, and maybe even RSC actors as well. After the king cries out for light, the mouse trap scene ends in catastrophe with a great commotion and swirling of the entire court, which literally falls apart, courtiers rushing this way and that way. At the peak of the hubbub, the symphonic score reinforces the action with a bravura crashing and thudding of strings, horns, and drums. And there is the innovation of having Gertrude (Elza Radzin-Szolkonis) arrive late for the duel so that she can in no way be privy to her husband's nefarious plot with Laertes to poison Hamlet.

The film's most strikingly original contribution to the Hamlet legend, though, may be the probing portrait of Ophelia as an innocent and pathetic victim of both her father and Hamlet. She is first seen dancing like a mechanical doll to the tune of a tinkling child's music box. Later, when being prepared by her swarm of attendants to attend her father's funeral, she is ceremonially encased in an iron corset and farthingale like a bullfighter being prepared to go into the ring, and then draped over like a dressmaker's dummy with a gauzy black gown, both body and soul being symbolically imprisoned. Always elegantly turned out in the tyranically stiff costumes of the Elizabethan era, she wears a pendant with an eastern orthodox cross. A recurring shot of a lone gull flying over the sea sums up the estrangement that she ironically shares with Hamlet. At her burial in the cemetery, silhouetted in the background is a broken cross that parodies the unbroken cross she wore in life. The giggling idiot of a gravedigger (V. Kolpakor) achieves sublimity as a surly lout, his banter with Hamlet sounding gruff and compelling even in the terse subtitles of the American release. As a final insult, the knave insolently hammers nails into the flimsy lid of Ophelia's cheap wooden coffin. Ironically the wronged Ophelia's debasement in death, her "maimed rites," as it were, contrasts with Hamlet's ennoblement as Fortinbras' four captains bear his body aloft up the sweeping stone stairways. This is the man who has helped to destroy Ophelia and whose ineptness as an avenger has caused multiple deaths. Such a bleak interpretation, however, remains unexplored in this movie for it would subvert Kozintsev's central goal, which is to make a film of *Hamlet* that enlarges rather than diminishes the human spirit.

After *Hamlet*, Kozintsev plunged into his exhaustive work on *King Lear* (1969), this despite his sense that as a play with no "ultimate interpretation"[30] it was a text to be wrestled with, like Jacob with the river god. With origins in Marxist meliorism rather than in Kottian pessimism, the movie looks more optimistically on the human condition than its western rival, Peter Brook's *King Lear*, which was made at almost the same time. It rejects political dogma in favor of a generalized humanitarianism (not humanism). Quite reasonably a Soviet critic concluded that it went no further ideologically than denying that "cruelty, violence, and callousness are innate qualities of man" and simply expresses "anger at anything that tramples upon human decency."[31] Like Kozintsev's *Hamlet*, however, it profoundly "Russianizes" Shakespeare's script. By that I mean plot, characters, and *mise-en-scène* are saturated in a Slavic sensibility made up of Boris Pasternak's translation of Shakespeare's language into the sonorities of Russian, Dmitri Shostakovich's powerful musical score, and the cherished acting traditions of the Russian theatre. The huge screen allows the action to flow out into infinity.

Kozintsev thought *Hamlet* almost cheerful by contrast with *King Lear*. He wrote of the latter play that "suffering passes over the whole world like a spasm and even the rocks have split and fallen in ruins . . . It is an unfriendly, ruined and distorted world: there is nothing to eat, nowhere to sit and nowhere to shelter; a mean, cruel and heartless nature."[32] Nevertheless Kozintsev squeezes some hope out of hopelessness by identifying his mad king with the struggles of humanity in general. The cryptic establishing shot wallows in suffering as in close-up hundreds of poorly shod peasant feet clump up a bleak, stark, rock-strewn hillside. The people wear rags. There is a low chanting, more like a moaning, on the soundtrack. Some trundle pathetic belongings on a crude wooden cart. A scrawny child and a legless man on a home-made go-cart appear. The people struggle painfully uphill, and others join them, until a throng of suffering humanity covers the hillside. In long shot is a castle. On a steep staircase leading up to the stone walls of the castle stand Gloucester, Kent, and Edmund, surveying the masses beneath them. The subtitles tell us that the Russian voices are saying, "I thought the king had more affected the Duke of Albany than Cornwall" (1.1.1). The empowered noblemen stand high above the disempowered masses, who stare up at them awe-struck.

The hillside was no accident. Kozintsev painstakingly searched and searched for just the right location, finally discovering it on the Kazantip promontory bordering the Azov Sea, which connects with the larger Black Sea and the Crimean archipelago. "A film landscape," Kozintsev wrote "is concealed, hidden under another sort of covering . . . you do not so much see it as feel it." The landscape that he chose was "the world after the catastrophe."[33] In his remarkable book on the making of *King Lear*, Kozintsev meditates on the mystical experience of contemplating a stone one hot August day in an exquisite Kyoto temple garden. He tells of feelings at the Hiroshima museum, of Noh drama, of the influence of Meyerhold, of Brecht, of Zen, of his own association in the early Twenties with Sergei Yutkevich in FEKS ("The Factory of the Eccentric Actor"), and remarks on the grotesqueries of Gogol and probings of Dostoyevsky.[34] His Shakespeare movies grow out of all these influences, as well as the rich cultural lode nurtured by Russia's temporal and spatial vastness.

The depressing beggars at the beginning of his movie, who replace the surly faces of the 100 knights in the Brook film, embody the wretched of the earth, the "Internationale's" "prisoners of starvation." The landscape, in John Collick's view, becomes "a blank page that can reflect a person's state of consciousness."[35] Brook's movie ignored the disempowered; Kozintsev's serves notice that lowly feet may challenge the hegemony of the arrogant head, which comes very close to the Christian belief that the meek will inherit the earth. As in *Hamlet*, fire is a recurring motif. There is the fireplace near the king during the division of the kingdom scene; the flaming torches in the king's train of carts; the army campfires; the searing tar catapulted at the fort; and a gutted city that resembles Hiroshima. A scribe intones the royal decree, the family enters a cavernous room with light and shadows flickering from the roaring flames in the stone hearth, the women's heels click and pound on the floor. The fire is associated with warfare just as Cordelia is associated with water. As Jack J. Jorgens observes, the fire "seen first in the domestic hearth . . . is soon blazing from the castle walls and in the end destroying the whole kingdom."[36]

The daughters and the courtiers move decisively, rapidly. Heralded by the tinkling of the Fool's tiny bell, the frail old king (Yuri Yarvet) comes through the door light-heartedly, laughing over a joke, and he removes a Noh-like mask from his face before warming his hands over the fire. The mask, a talisman of Kozintsev's interest in Japanese drama, foreshadows the unmasking of the king's pretensions to power and authority, as he progresses in Aristotelian terms from a self-deceived *alazon* to a painfully aware *eiron*. He initially stands high on the castle parapet denouncing his own daughter before the assembled populace, and at the end he returns to the same pinnacle, only this time heartbroken, grieving over the loss of his daughter and appealing forlornly to his subjects for support: "O, [you] are men of stones!" (5.3.258). A harrowing wail satisfies Shakespeare's, "Howl, howl, howl!," a line Marvin Rosenberg describes as a projection of "suffering too fierce for verbalizing" that has been interpreted by various actors as "an anguished cry," "a quiet sobbing," "a deep baying," "the wail of a wolf," a "mourning dog, and even an indignant demand for response from the men of stone."[37]

Not even a native speaker of Russian, Estonian Yuri Yarvet's casting as King Lear came about almost by accident when he was originally auditioned for the role of Fool. A most unlikely looking King Lear, grizzled and withered, not at all a majestic Frederick B. Warde type, Yarvet's repressed power boils over when it is finally released. The opening scene records the intensity and anxiety in the faces of Regan, Goneril, Albany, over the impending division of Lear's kingdom. The old king remains near the fire, warming his aged bones, and Goneril (E. Radzins) speaks first, flattering the king: "Sir, I love you more than [words] can wield the matter" (1.1.54). Next comes Regan (G. Volchek) her head muffled, for her ritual speech of obeisance. Only Cordelia's (Valentina Shendrikova) face is serene, untroubled. Her aside is on the soundtrack, "What shall Cordelia speak? Love and be silent" (1.1.62). She stands alone, a figure in white surrounded by black. Nothing prepares anybody for the king's sudden explosion of rage. "Thy truth then be thy dow'r!" he says (1.1.108), which somehow sounds more menacing for having emerged from the mouth of such a gaunt human being. The helpless map becomes the target of the king's wrath. He snatches it up, rends it, twists it this way and that way, moves it back and forth, shakes it and rattles it so fiercely that it sounds like distant thunder. He tosses it away, a spoiled and shriveled symbol of his lost hopes. Crying out, "Call France. Who stirs? / Call Burgundy" (1.1.126), he aims yet another kick at it. Ironically the map disorients rather than orientates the king. To ward off the disaster, Kent (V. Emelyanov) clings to the map but the king spits at him. In Russian, his scolding sounds especially ferocious: "Hear me, recreant" (1.1.165). The very earth trembles.

The aural dissonance upsets the imperturbability of the human figures,

20   Yuri Yarvet as her remorseful and devastated father cradles the hanged Cordelia in his arms in *King Lear*, directed by Grigori Kozintsev (USSR 1969).

who have until now looked like the subjects in an engraving, faces chiseled from stone. The rapid movement begins again. The king vigorously marches off. A complicated tracking shot follows him through the palace, into the stables, his retinue skipping along behind him, past magnificent horses, beautiful hounds, setters, greyhounds, and falcons. He ascends stairs, shows himself to the people, who look up. The people kneel in low angle. Lear stands above on the parapet. Music comes up and achieves a crescendo. This king having achieved the apex of his power stands at the edge of a precipice for the inevitable fall. The editing reinforces the severing of the bond between father and daughter with a cut to Cordelia and France being blessed by a priest before setting off for the continent with their retinue of cavalry and carriages.

There are startling vignettes. Regan in a white heat to possess Edmund tears off his clothing, only shortly later to plant an erotic kiss full on the lips of Cornwall's corpse. Kozintsev's *découpage*, the quick cuts, display the hanged Cordelia dangling obscenely high above the castle walls. Murky pools of fetid water suggest both everything and nothing. Kozintsev's Fool does not disappear at the end of the third act ("And I'll go to bed at noon" (3.6.85)) but reappears to help comment on the desperate condition of humanity. A funeral cortège bears the bodies of the fallen while the Fool (now transformed into a Russian village idiot) sits amidst the rubble grieving over the loss of his master and of his own identity. And just as the film begins with the sense of a social order, of people relating to a king, it ends with the old king not isolated and alone, not falling out of the frame with a blank nothingness behind him, as in the Frederick Warde and Peter Brook *King Lears*, but rather with the king surrounded by friends. He calls out *"Nyet! Nyet! Nyet!"* over and over again. A man douses a fire. The camera tracks back to reveal that the forlorn weeping comes from the Fool, who plays his flute among the ashes, the same shrill flute featured at the beginning. The cortège winds through the ruined villages, where there are signs of restoration as a man attempts to raise the joist on a ruined house. Edgar (L. Merzin) moves forward but there is silence. A fertile field is superimposed on the carnage. A sign of hope? Images have conveyed meanings that words cannot express. Kozintsev has shared with Shakespeare "the image of that horror." Years ago a reviewer hit the mark when he wrote that the film "reconstructs [a] hellish vision not in the easy, fashionably austere styles of today but in visual terms one imagines would have been acceptable to the author. Is there any higher praise?"[38]

Japan: Akira Kurosawa

Among makers of "foreign" Shakespeare movies, Japan's late Akira Kurosawa has been as much acclaimed as Russia's Grigori Kozintsev, particularly for *Throne of Blood* (or *The Castle of the Spider's Web*) (1957), and *Ran* (1985). *Throne of Blood* has been aptly described as a transformation rather than an adaptation of *Macbeth*; and *Ran*, though it draws less directly than *Throne of Blood* on its Shakespearean prototype, clearly adapts motifs and situations from *King Lear*. Since the 1853 arrival of Commodore Perry, the Japanese, despite the inherent difficulties of translation, have experimented with a variety of Shakespearean productions ranging from Kabuki and Noh-style adaptations to *shingeki*, "translations of European plays staged in western style."[39] Director Yukio Ninagawa's recent Japanese language *Hamlet* (1998), staged at London's Barbican Centre, exhibited a verve and boldness that made most western productions of the tragedy seem pale and timid by comparison. A third Kurosawa movie, less well-known in the West, *The Bad Sleep Well* (1960), a modernized *Hamlet*, very loosely adapts the Hamlet story but nevertheless usefully serves as a springboard for looking at the synergy joining Shakespeare and Kurosawa. As James Goodwin has shown, Kurosawa's "intertextual cinema"[40] ransacks Western and Japanese culture for its music and art, as well as for the existentialism and absurdism of Dostoevsky and Gorki, all of which affects his Shakespearean adaptations. Kurosawa, while intensely Japanese, is therefore paradoxically not solely a Japanese film maker. On the other hand important Japanese scholars like Professor Yoshio Arai see all three of Kurosawa's Shakespeare films as having been "entirely acceptable and comprehensible to the Japanese audience as Japanese films."[41]

The Bad Sleep Well turns out to be a film noir thriller about big business and corruption in postwar Japan in the tradition of *gendai-mono* ("modern-story films")[42] with overtones from *Hamlet*, though Kurosawa has himself denied any particular influence from Shakespeare. The intricate plot is of less importance here than the thematic parallels to Shakespeare, but, briefly, what happens is that a young business man, Nishi (Toshiro Mifune), sets out to avenge the death of his father, Furuya, who was forced into a staged suicide. To achieve his goal by craft, Nishi plays a variation on Hamlet's "antic disposition" by assuming the identity of a friend, Itakura (who loosely corresponds to Horatio). The scenario veers wildly away from Hamlet when Nishi marries Kieko (Ophelia), the daughter of Vice-President Iwabuchi (Claudius/ Polonius). Kieko's brother, Tatsuo, resembles Laertes; Wada and Shirai, subordinate executives who come between the "mighty opposites" of Nishi and Iwabuchi, correspond to Rosencrantz and Guildenstern; and the obliging Moriyama, always available to spy for his boss, resembles Reynaldo. In a space as claustrophobic as Elsinore, they are constantly under surveillance or lost in a maze of deceptions or foundering in a sea of self-doubt. The nexus between Kurosawa's and Shakespeare's artistry lies in a common vision of reality as a fugue-like interplay between conflicting and inexorable forces.

A case could be made that even if Akira Kurosawa had never heard of *Hamlet*, *Macbeth*, or *King Lear*, he would still have made movies that seemed to echo them in their indeterminacy, their tantalizing interplay between illusion and reality, their focus on usurped authority. From *Rashomon* (1950) to *Throne of Blood* (1957), *The Bad Sleep Well* (1960), *The Shadow Warrior* (*Kagemusha*) (1980), and the more recent *Dreams* (1990), Kurosawa plays variations on the theme of the equivocal nature of reality, the gap between seen and unseen, between the false and the real. "Seems, madam? nay, it is, I know not 'seems'" (1.2.76), says Hamlet to Gertrude in the quintessential assertion of what is not just Hamlet's but his creator's *modus operandi*. Kurosawa, as Donald Richie notes,[43] is more of a social observer than an activist. Shakespeare likewise, as John Keats realized, is by his temperament blessed, or afflicted, with *Negative Capability*, which allowed him to live with "uncertainties, mysteries, doubts without any irritable reaching after fact and reason."[44] This willingness to describe rather than prescribe the way of the world links the two men even over centuries.

The Japanese are second to none in their willingness to spend a fortune on a wedding. The elaborate wedding reception in a luxury hotel for Nishi and Kieko (Kyoko Kagawa) at the opening has been cited as a triumph of cinematic narration. In twenty-three minutes of screen time, it compresses Nishi's relationship with his new father-in-law, the deep corruption in the business community, and the strange death of Nishi's father. Every frame reflects motifs of confinement, surveillance, and claustrophobia, all reminiscent of the "prison," which is Hamlet's Denmark. Characters are framed between, or through, the configurations of right angles in windows, doorways, shop display-windows, stairwells. In an instance of Kurosawa's frequent use of western music, the powerful wedding march from *Lohengrin* heralds the arrival of Nishi's bride, who is hemmed in by the formally attired guests. An intrusive tight framing exposes how the bride's *zori* (slipper) is raised to compensate for her lameness. The bride's stumble foreshadows disasters to come, yet ironically the non-diegetic theme music abruptly shifts to the light-hearted Strauss piece, "The Voices of Spring." A gaggle of newspaper reporters peering at the wedding reception through the frame of the wide entrance hall can hardly wait to sensationalize a scandal involving a corporation executive who will soon be arrested and dragged out of the party in disgrace. They constitute an "onstage" audience watching another audience, the wedding guests, who are about to be treated to a play-within-a-play, a "dumb show" as Marion Perret has called it.[45] The "dumb show," it develops, is a wedding cake molded in the shape of the building from which Nishi's father was forced through a window. The reporters also vestigially act as the Japanese *benshi*, an all-purpose narrator who explained events onstage to any in the audience fearful of missing out on details.[46]

As Nishi, the ubiquitous Toshiro Mifune, Kurosawa's favorite actor, wears spectacles and western morning attire in contrast to his usual action-hero roles in costume dramas, such as the bandit Tajomaru in *Rashomon* (1950), the gruff Kikuchiyo in *The Seven Samurai* (1954), the beleaguered Washizu in *Throne of Blood* (1957), and the samurai bodyguard in *Yojimbo* (1961). The eyeglasses serve the double function of converting the samurai-like Mifune into a corporate bureaucrat and underscoring the underlying motif of surveillance. Richie comments on Kurosawa's iteration of this bias toward glasses, mirrors, etc., in *Ikuru* (1952): "Enormous use is made of mirrors, reflecting surfaces, the shiny tops of automobiles, prisms – all those things which reflect (distort) reality."[47] Fog and mist mask reality in *Throne of Blood*;

the Noh-like mask of Kaede's face in *Ran* conceals her fiendish desire for revenge on her husband's Ichimonji clan. Cigarettes often swathe the characters in smoke, all of whom seem hopelessly addicted. Nishi smokes, Nonaka smokes, Iwabuchi smokes, Itakura smokes. Smoke turns to fog and mist when Wada attempts suicide at the crater of a live volcano. The clouds and mist suggest the battlements at Elsinore when Nishi appears, ghost-like, out of the fog to implicate Wada in the revenge plot.

In a trope echoing Hamlet's confrontation with Gertrude, Nishi forces Shirai to examine a picture of his late father as a way of clarifying the enormity of his crime. Nishi like Hamlet then discovers that "conscience [i.e., "reflection"] does make cowards [of us all]" (3.1.82). As a "thoughtful avenger," Nishi turns into a walking oxymoron. His father-in-law Iwabuchi reacts to Nishi's non-action by murdering him in a staged automobile accident. Itakura's hysterical description of how Nishi was set up for the faked car wreck by being injected with alcohol corresponds to Horatio's last words about Hamlet. To complicate things, Nishi's friend, Itakura, turns out to be the real Nishi. The labyrinthine plot keeps returning, though, to the epistemological issue of the equivocal nature of truth. At the end the bad, the wicked, still flourish, for in a world of smoke and mirrors few can see through pretense into the world's inherent evil. The rest of us may squirm and turn at night, but the bad still sleep well.

Identical motifs to those found in *The Bad Sleep Well* also surface in the far better known *Throne of Blood*. Forty years ago, J. Blumenthal declared that "Akira Kurosawa's *Throne of Blood* (1957) is the only work . . . that has ever completely succeeded in transforming a play of Shakespeare's into a film."[48] Blumenthal's bold thesis has been a mantra ever since for eminent persons like Roger Manvell,[49] Peter Brook,[50] Peter Hall,[51] and Robert Hapgood.[52] Without in any way denigrating Kurosawa's achievement, the anti-Anglophone bias here should be warily inspected. It's like the snobbish preference for foreign imports over domestic cars, or it smacks of an Ahab-like search for the white whale of the pure film, the invention of sound having in some Luddite way been declared a disaster for movies. Yet movie makers, as we have seen, have always yearned for spoken dialogue, have struggled for it, and Edison only dabbled with films to find an accompaniment for his phonograph invention, not the other way around. As dissident John Gerlach has asserted, the problem of graphically expressing Shakespeare's language actually eludes *Throne of Blood*. It ignores the iterative images of blood in *Macbeth*, and diminishes Macbeth's stature (Washizu) because of his over-dependency on Lady Macbeth (Asaji).[53]

In *Throne of Blood*, as in *The Seven Samurai*, Kurosawa not only draws on the same unique perspectives that informed *The Bad Sleep Well* but also nests traces of the classic western movie inside the cultural codes of Japan's Noh drama. Unlike *The Bad Sleep Well, Throne of Blood* as a costume drama belongs to the genre of *jidai-geki* ("period pictures"). As Anthony Davies has said, the graphics of the movie oscillate between the vertical lines of the forest and the horizontal lines of the rooms within the castle.[54] Geometrical patterns of circles and angles function metaphorically for the ways in which the worlds of man and nature interact to destroy the overreaching Washizu. Kurosawa frames his film with the forest at the beginning and ending. The film opens in the fogbound forest with a lugubrious off-camera Noh-style chanting about the folly of ambition, which translates as: "men are vain and death is long." A wounded soldier (Bleeding Sergeant) reports to Kuniharu (Duncan) on the heroism of Washizu (Macbeth) and Miki (Banquo) in defeating the rebels. Kuniharu orders the execution of the rebel leader (Thane of Cawdor). The action moves to the deep forest where in a famous scene, thoroughly analyzed by Jack J. Jorgens,[55] Washizu and Miki have become hopelessly lost in the tangled undergrowth and mist. An occasional shaft of sunlight illuminates how what is fair can also be foul. Their frenetic galloping back and forth from left to right and then from right to left illustrates what Stephen Prince sees as an example of another Kurosawa signature, fascination with "the dynamics of motion," in this instance embodied in "lateral motion across the frame."[56] Marsha Kinder further points out how motion is then set off intermittently against its opposite, stasis, in such immobile figures as Asaji (Lady Macbeth), who in Noh style barely breathes.[57] The two samurai encounter a ghostly white figure hunched over a spinning wheel (the Witches) inside a ramshackle hut. Some kind of arbiter of fate, like the Greek Clotho, the old crone equivocally predicts both success and failure, namely that Washizu will rule the Forest Castle but that one day Miki's son, Yoshiteru (Fleance), not Washizu's, will inherit the dominion. The witch's makeshift hut ironically counterpoints the brazen strength of the fortress that Washizu will rule over. In a further irony, it is the forest that will finally win out over the fortress when Birnan wood comes to Dunsinane.

After Kuniharu installs Washizu as Master of the Fort, events unfold very much along the lines of Shakespeare's play, though they have been displaced from tenth-century Scotland to Japan's "Sengoku period of civil wars (1467–1568) when there were frequent incidents of *gekokujo*, the overthrow of a superior by his own retainers."[58] No Scots noblewoman like Lady Macbeth, Asaji (Isuzu Yamada) has been thoroughly made over by the Noh mask of *Shamkumi*, which in representing a beautiful young woman about to go mad was eminently suitable for Lady Macbeth. Because in the Noh tradition, actors study the mask and then adapt themselves to its attributes, Kurosawa exposed Toshiro Mifune (Washizu/Macbeth) to a warrior mask named *Heida*.

When Asaji urges Washizu to assassinate Kuniharu, she rebukes him for his cowardice, takes the bloody spear from his hands, and displays no more emotion than a robot, but she is after all nursing a ferocious grudge. Unlike Macbeth, Washizu actually plans to proclaim Miki's son (Fleance) as heir but Asaji stops him by announcing her own pregnancy. As Miki (Banquo) prepares for the fatal ride through the forest, his horse panics, an ominous prophecy that he unwisely ignores, but that gives Kurosawa, a horse lover, an excuse for alluding to the equine imagery in *Macbeth*: "And Duncan's horses (a thing most strange and certain), / Beauteous and swift, the minions of their race, / Turn'd wild in nature, broke their stalls, flung out" (2.4.14). In the legendary banquet scene that follows, Asaji as a loyal but perplexed hostess explains away her husband's embarrassing behavior. Washizu hallucinates that he is seeing Miki's ghost, panics, silences an innocent entertainer, and lashes out at the specter with a sword. Unlike the Macbeth in the Polanski version, who has Rosse push the assassins down a well, Washizu handles his own bloody work. When a soldier brings Miki's head wrapped in a cloth, Washizu is so shocked over the news of Miki's son still being alive, that he instantly puts the man to death. Like Macbeth, he has then become "in blood / Stepp'd in so far" (3.4.135) that there is no turning back.

As calamities multiply for Washizu, including a report that Asaji's child has been "stillborn," he distils the apocalyptic "to-morrow, and to-morrow" (5.5.19) lamentation into a single word, "Fool!" The film's "materiality," its relentless quest for images as powerful as Shakespeare's language, renders "all our yesterdays have lighted fools / The way to dusty death" (5.5.22) partially redundant. Washizu becomes increasingly restless, moving back and forth and around with a rapidity that contrasts with Asaji's stillness.

In another Kurosawa trademark, characters are given unique behavior traits like Washizu's scornful, nearly hysterical, laughter. In *The Bad Sleep Well*, for example, Nishi is constantly adjusting his eyeglasses on the bridge of his nose, or flicking away cigarette ashes. Asaji's eerie stillness continues even in the hand-washing scene, which finds her crazily trying to purge the blood stains. With enemy forces of Noriyasu approaching the castle, Washizu's defiance escalates. He irrationally boasts of the castle's impregnability: "I bear a charmed life, which must not yield / To one of woman born" (5.8.12), and insists that an ominous flock of birds (inspired by Shakespeare's ornithological imagery) means nothing. "Light thickens, and the crow / Makes wing to th' rooky wood" (3.2.50). The birds also herald the ultimate triumph of the forest over the fortress. Next he is seen peering through the castle's parapets anxiously observing the moving wood, and then maniacally appealing to his sullen troops for support. They respond with a hail of arrows that turn him into a veritable porcupine, as arrow after arrow skewers him, leaving him staggering wildly, crying out in pain, and horribly suffering. A final arrow pierces the side of his neck and he reels toward his troops, the tip and butt of the arrow grotesquely protruding from each side of his neck, eyes glazed, still living and breathing, until after a moment of piquant stasis, he abruptly drops dead. The mist returns, the Noh chanting about a warrior murdered by his own ambition comes up on the soundtrack, but there is no redemptive movement, no Malcolm, for example, to restore order to the gored state. The forest has won out over the fortress. Only remaining are fog, mystery, and the pitiful condition of humanity, always unequivocally doomed by an equivocal fate.

Serge Silberman, a generous patron of the art movie and producer of Luis Buñuel's films, made possible Kurosawa's *Ran* (*Chaos*), a bold re-appropriation of the King Lear tale. With a $10.5-million budget, *Ran* stands as that rare thing, a reasonably well-funded art movie. Still, thrift was required. Instead of expensive studio sets, two of Japan's historical castles, Himeji and Kumamoto, were requisitioned for the First and Second Forts, while the Third Fort, the one belonging to Saburo that is burned to the ground in the middle of the movie, was constructed out of plywood on the slopes of Mount Fuji. The extras needed 1,400 suits of armor, and the samurai's fifty-two horses were flown in from Colorado.[59] The spectacular torching of the castle during the assault by the forces of Taro and Jiro required a risky and nerve-wracking but nevertheless successful single take with all cameras running. A single glitch would have meant financial ruin.

For *Ran*, Kurosawa synthesizes the cultural codes of East and West to unify a marvelous grab-bag of bits and pieces from *King Lear*. Like *Throne of Blood*, *Ran* is a period-piece costume drama, not in fog-shrouded black-and-white, but in bold and vibrant color reflecting sunshine that even at the cataclysmic end tinges the image of the Buddhist Amithab with a golden sheen. The sumptuous costumes of the ancient samurai set against the green hills make for a visual feast at odds with the grim realities of Lear's fate, though the greenery underscores the ironic gap between the glory of nature and the wretchedness of man. The multiple alterations in plot and character mainly stem from a desire to blend Japanese with western cultural codes. The characterization of seventy-year-old Hidetora (King Lear) aligns him more with sadistic Cornwall than with doddering Lear, a version of the old king who is plainly not "More sinn'd against than sinning" (3.2.59). His atrocities include sacking the castles of the families of future daughters-in-law, Sué and Kaede, and gouging out the eyes of Sué's brother, Tsurumaru. In rebuke, Tsurumaru's plaintive Noh flute haunts the old man. The patriarchal biases of Japanese society dictate having the kingdom divided among three sons,

Taro, Jiro, and Saburo, rather than to three daughters. In fact, Kurosawa originally planned a movie about the legendary Motonari Mori, a sixteenth-
century warlord whose three sons in a reversal of the Lear story were
admired as models of virtue. Kurosawa rewrote that script so he could spec-
ulate about what would happen if the sons turned out to be wicked rather
than virtuous![60]

Ran also reflects Kurosawa's fascination with the samurai warrior codes
and their swashbuckling love affair with cavalry and swordplay, which survived well into World War II when Japanese soldiers committed mass suicide with hand grenades on remote north Pacific islands like Attu rather than
dishonorably surrender to US Seventh Division infantry, and when American
soldiers prized more than anything else an officer's samurai sword as booty.
The deep-rooted Japanese conception of *giri,* which deals with the duty owed
by a child to his parents, a wife to a husband, sounds remarkably like the
Elizabethan doctrine of passive obedience. The unspoken "bond" sets up a
tension between apparent presence and actual absence of a moral order that
lends itself to philosophical exploration. In a famous mixed metaphor,
Samuel Goldwyn summed up litigious American attitudes toward the
unspoken "bond," or covenant, if indeed he ever said that "an oral contract
isn't worth the paper it's written on."

The boar hunt at the opening of the film at once establishes the grandeur
of nature and the pettiness of man. Against the big sky and green hills,
Hidetora draws his bow and aims at the prey, his "hawkish eyes [shining]
in his tan face."[61] As he pulls the arrow back, the image dissolves into the
blood red title, *Ran,* and suddenly it becomes apparent that Kurosawa has
materialized King Lear's "The bow is bent and drawn, make from the shaft"
(1.1.143).[62] At the family camp of Ichimonji, the patriarchal Hidetora sits
cross-legged in stiff formality with his three sons, Taro, Jiro, and Saburo,
who are respectively costumed in dazzling yellow, red, and blue kimonos
so that it is possible for westerners to keep them all sorted out. Hidetora
explains his plan for retirement and the division of the fiefdom. The eldest
son, Taro, will receive the First Fort; Jiro, the Second; and Saburo, the Third.
As is to be expected, Taro and Jiro outrageously flatter their father but faithful Saburo (Cordelia) bluntly tells him that he is either senile or mad to pro-
pose such a scheme. Loyal retainer Tango (Kent), who would never consider
violating the "bond," agrees with Saburo, his honesty earning him a curt dismissal. Meanwhile another loyalist, the effeminate Kyoami (Fool), who was
played by "Peitah," a famous Japanese transvestite, dances and sings satirical songs and as "an all-licensed fool" is the only person in the frame with
the freedom to violate the rigid protocols for sitting and standing. Instead
of the map found in *King Lear,* Hidetora uses an arrow to point out the forts

that will be given away. When he also moralizes to the sons that a single arrow can be easily broken but three together cannot, he is stunned when Saburo symbolically breaks three arrows apart at once, in sign of the forthcoming divisiveness in the kingdom. Jiro's deep resentment of his older brother's ascendancy combines elements of the Edmund/Edgar plot and Regan/ Goneril rivalry.

Predictably, when Hidetora sets out with a retinue of thirty retainers to visit his son's castles, he sets himself up for disrespect. Taro's wife, Lady Kaede, humiliates her father-in-law by occupying the seat nearest the wall traditionally reserved for the senior person in the room. When second son, Jiro, insultingly notifies Hidetora that he has no need for retainers, the father's retort that only the birds and beasts can live by themselves echoes "O, reason not the need! our basest beggars / Are in the poorest thing superfluous" (2.4.264). Old Hidetora undergoes his darkest moment when Taro forces him to sign in blood a contract acknowledging that he no longer heads the house of Ichimonji. In a magnified displacement of Kent's striking of Oswald, Hidetora kills one of his son's impudent retainers at the Castle of Taro with a well aimed arrow. After the terrible battle at Third Fort in a wild storm, the Fool shouts that "in this mad world it is the sane who are mad!" paraphrasing Lear's "What, art mad? A man may see how this world goes with no eyes . . . change places, and handy-dandy, which is the justice, which is the thief?" (4.6.150). Again when Kyaomo cries out "All human beings cry when they are born," he borrows from Lear's "When we are born, we cry that we are come" (4.6.182). During the battle at the Third Fort, which occupies the middle of the film, the apocalyptic scenes of warfare peak in the torching of the castle. The brightly uniformed cavalry and infantry advance in a blood bath that is conceived as the "terrible scroll of hell," the only sound being "the wailing of countless Buddhas" as horror piles on horror. There are bodies hurled into the air by explosions, horses running madly, a forest of spears, a man pierced with arrows, a stream of blood with "islands" of severed arms and legs, soldiers raping chambermaids, and so forth. When a single shot rings out and kills Taro at the instigation of his younger brother, Jiro, authentic battle sounds of screams, roaring of fire, hoofbeats, shouting, and gunfire replace the low chanting on the soundtrack. Hidetora trapped high in the burning tower frantically searches for his dagger to commit the honorable act of harakiri. Ignominiously, with his aides committing suicide, the women taking one another's lives to avoid a fate worse than death, he cannot find the dagger and instead must endure the insolent stares of enemy soldiers. After that he goes quite mad in the open fields, his face having deteriorated from the mask of a high-born patrician to a desperate and lonely old man.

Lady Kaede (Mieko Harada) is first Taro's wife, then Jiro's. A lady of exquisite sensibility with a cold-blooded talent for manipulating men, she strongly resembles Asaji, the Lady Macbeth of *The Throne of Blood*. Virtually immobile in the ritualized style of Noh, Lady Kaede, expressionless, stone-faced, inscrutable, barely moves her lips, but she projects a miasma of evil prodigious enough to suffocate the entire castle. After the melée at Saburo's Third Fort, where Jiro dispatches Taro, the widowed Kaede accepts Jiro as a husband but for a price. She demands the head of Jiro's first wife, the gentle Sué. The intoxicating leap from absolute stillness to unchecked ferocity, from subjugation to domination, unleashes a disturbingly erotic scene. With Jiro's own sword, dressed in her widow's white mourning robes, and showing the physical agility of a gymnast, she throws Jiro to the floor, holds the point of his own sword against his throat until the blood runs, and terrorizes him into revealing the identity of Taro's murderers. Jiro, at her nagging, then agrees to the assassination of Sué, his first wife, so that Kaede's relationship with him can be legitimized. Kaede displays her fastidiousness and concern for others by ordering the designated assassin, Kurogane, to wrap Sué's severed head in salt to prevent decomposition in the heat, which she thinks would be a shame. Kurogane instead infuriates the dangerous Kaede by returning with the head of a fox and hinting that the fox's cunning traits are like Kaede's. Kaede's main motive all along has been not to marry into the Iwajimi clan but to avenge the death of her father, slain by Hidetora.

Sué is then saved momentarily for a subsequent meeting with her blind brother, Tsurumaru, also a victim of Hidetora, though by the end of the film she will suffer death by order of Kaede anyway. The faithful son, Saburo, dies in his father's arms, victim of enemy fire, and Hidetora grieves inconsolably over him, like Lear over Cordelia. Kyoami, the Fool, spits toward heaven and cries out against an indifferent Buddha and God. Tango retorts that it is not God or Buddha at fault but the evil of human beings. The blind man, Tsurumaru, still playing his reedy Noh flute, taps with his stick toward the edge of an abyss. It has been a journey through hell, an allegory of the hopeless condition of man. The apostle of existentialist despair, Jan Kott, saw the ending of the film as an expression of complete emptiness: "The blind man feels his way to the edge of the abyss. The parchment falls from his hands ... The blue sky is completely empty."[63] As Lear himself said, "Nothing will come of nothing." Kurosawa's *tour de force* has been to use Shakespeare's Anglophone texts as blueprints for performance and imagine his words recycled in the cultural iconology of Japan. What he has created is truly in the category of "other Shakespeares."

- 9 -

Shakespeare in the cinema of
transgression, and beyond

While prior to the 1960s irony and *film noir* provided the main conduit for covert resentment of the social order, by the Sixties the underlying tensions among the new generation erupted into an overt cinema of transgression. As confrontation replaced irony, progressive cadres rebelled against the policing of art, and broke the stranglehold of the Catholic Legion of Decency and the House Committee on Un-American Activities. England's angry young men and America's hippies beatified avant-garde directors like Italy's Pier Paolo Pasolini who flouted Vatican values with the blasphemous *La ricotta* (1962) that parodied the Deposition from the Cross. In the United States, Andy Warhol's underground *Blowjob* (1963) and *Blue Movie/Fuck* (1968) were roundly denounced as pornographic but were actually too boring to be erotic. In the political arena, Stanley Kubrick's *Dr. Strangelove, or How I Learned to Stop Worrying and Love the Bomb* (1963) exposed the stupidity of HUAC's persecution of the anti-nuclear movement. Commercial movies had already begun to change. Film historian Linda Williams cites Alfred Hitchcock's *Psycho* (1960) as the first film to bring sex and violence into mainstream cinema,[1] where it has been firmly entrenched ever since. More recently the gay rights movement has created a climate for what has been labeled "Shakesqueer" movies, like *My Own Private Idaho* (1991), which even a decade ago would have been taboo.[2]

Celestino Coronado

Celestino Coronado's transgressive *Hamlet* (1976) and *Midsummer Night's Dream* (1984) in their insouciance embody the sort of underground or film society "Shakespeare" movie that makes many critics very uneasy. Coronado's dedication of his misogynist *Hamlet* to Pasolini, *auteur* of *The 120 Days of Sodom* (1975), reflects his artistic and intellectual proclivities. Made on video by the Royal College of Art at North London Polytechnic on a tiny budget of £2,500, but then transferred to 16mm film for screening at the 1976 London Film Festival, this highly experimental student production has enough "crossover" potential to justify its being designated a Shakespeare film.

Beginning students of *Hamlet* looking for a handy visual aid should not consult Coronado's post-modernist movie. It demands a sophisticated audience to appreciate how using a methodology like Roland Barthes' in *S/Z*, Coronado has both de-segmented and then re-segmented the play to privilege Hamlet's dysfunctional connections with Gertrude and Ophelia. Graham Holderness believes it to be "a film treatment attuned to the intellectual sophistication and imaginative complexity of the post-structuralist, post-modern Shakespeare text."[3] The surrealism of "expressionistic, garishly-colored images"[4] includes tightly framed eyeballs belonging to Polonius, a frontally nude ghost of Hamlet's father, twin Hamlets, a Gertrude who also doubles as Ophelia (Helen Mirren), a monocled Polonius (Quentin Crisp), a Laertes and Hamlet "duel" as a wrestling match with the antagonists wearing only athletic supporters, and a soundtrack filled with whistles, bells, flutes, and chimes. These destabilizations coalesce around a central theme of Hamlet's misogyny as the driving force behind his dysfunctionality at Elsinore.

The framing device of a dream/nightmare, punctuated with thunder and lightning, depicts a sleeping Hamlet tormented by the soliloquies, beginning with "To be or not to be." Two Hamlets, played by Anthony and David Meyer, who also both double as the Ghost, represent his split personality. Piercing screams, a howling wind, and gongs accompany close-ups of Hamlet's restless slumber with his head grotesquely distorted by being photographed upside down. A frontally nude ghost, who is also Hamlet's *Doppelgänger*, materializes in a titillating spectacle for patrons who enjoy viewing male bodies, but it is more likely intended as shorthand for the play's labyrinthine but mostly occult sexual politics. The speaking of the verse, however, is wonderfully well done, and the rearrangement and redistribution of segments of the play to get at the mystery of Hamlet stays honest and often witty. David Meyer, who played Hamlet and designed the sets, recently spoke of how the whole project grew out of the youthful exuberance of the times more than from any solemn artistic goal,[5] which apparently went unnoticed by a stern *Time Out* critic who denounced the movie as "at worst, offensive; at best, joyless."[6] Coronado was employing a new paradigm for interrogating the play's mysteries, which have kept themselves inviolate for centuries. A very young Helen Mirren, who doubles as Ophelia and Gertrude, speaks her lines with the conviction and élan that later insured her international success, and Vladek Sheybal invents a uniquely villainous look for the First Player and Lucianus. The movie ends as it begins in thunder and lightning with Hamlet stretched out on a white pallet, his face a death mask. In the struggle against evil, the passive inner Hamlet, the old "black plume" prince of the romantic era, becomes a tortured and tormented reverse mirror to the aggressive, New Age outer Hamlet. In a favorable review, Tim Pulleine rightly points out that Coronado was interested not so much in holding a mirror up to nature as in holding "a mirror up to artifice."[7] Viewed that way the jumble of images, the phallic *Hamlet*, emerges not irrelevantly but imaginatively from the maelstrom of the play's linguistic entanglements.

A few years later, Coronado teamed up with Lindsay Kemp's counter-culture theatrical company to film *A Midsummer Night's Dream* (1984). The play has been variously envisioned on screen as romance (Reinhardt-Dieterle, 1935), as Carnaby Street (Hall, 1968), as fantasy (Moshinsky, BBC-TV, 1981), as pop (Noble, 1996), and in the hands of Coronado and Kemp's "in-your-face" company as "gay." Coronado's film combined "the disparate elements of high camp and low burlesque, aesthetic courtliness and bawdy vaudeville . . . interlaced with snatches from Shakespeare's text and bound together by Carlos Miranda's haunting original musical score."[8] Opera, ballet, and pantomime replace Shakespeare's text in this near travesty, which began as a Sadler's Wells stage production in Islington, then was filmed in Spain for television as *Sueno de Noche de Veran,* and shown in 1984 at the London Film Festival, where a reviewer described it as having "plenty of uninhibited nudity" and "a fairy king and queen [who] are splendidly campy characters."[9] It is indisputably joyful in the zany spirit of its progenitor, Lindsay Kemp, a self-described "ancient Jewish fairy," who is also a "Negro and homosexual."[10] The cast includes not only David Meyer as Lysander, who played one of the two Hamlets in the Coronado *Hamlet*, but also The Incredible Orlando (Jack Birkett), a blind drag queen, as Titania; François Testory as the Indian Boy, of whom much is made by a prurient Oberon; Lindsay Kemp as a sinister voyeur of a Puck with a greenish pallor, who engorges on grapes and approaches orgasm as he spies on young lovers; and a *Pyramus and Thisby* play that turns into a version of *Romeo and Juliet* on stilts. It all adds up to completely irreverent "nose-thumbing" but exuberant entertainment. As Kemp himself said, "What I want to do with the theatre is to restore the glamour of the Folies Bergères, the danger of the circus, the eroticism of Rock 'n' Roll, and the shiver of death."[11] Shakespeare's storehouse of verbal images sorely tempted Kemp to whip up a feast of visual images, and to explore any subterranean homoeroticism.

A ballet prologue shows Theseus' soldiers raping the Amazons against a backdrop of an enormous moon, a talisman of the play's status as "moon-drenched." There then follow the blindfolded four young lovers, snatches of mechanical music, a Helena who moves like a dancing doll, and raucous

wood sprites who mock the romantic creatures of more decorous productions. Watery visions fabricate a dreamy rain forest of Freudian displace-
ments, substitutions, fusions, and overlaps. For example, the crossed lovers
awaken under the spell of Oberon's enchanted "love-in-idleness" (2.1.168)
not to fall in love as Hermia with Lysander or Helena with Demetrius but
as Hermia with Helena and Lysander with Demetrius, though all show versatility by sorting out their "queerness" in time to return to safe heterosexuality. At this point, Puck is amply entitled to his famous line, "Lord, what
fools these mortals be!" (3.2.115). When Bottom awakens from his "dream"
with Titania, the obscene grin on his face signals that he remembers very
well what events have transpired during the night. Love in this *Dream* transcends gender to include all creatures willy nilly and to validate Hippolyta's
observation that "This is the silliest stuff that ever I heard" (5.1.210). What
saves the day, though, is recollection of Theseus' urbane warning against
rushing to judgment: "If we imagine no worse of them than they of themselves, they may pass for excellent men" (5.1.215).

Derek Jarman

The late Derek Jarman's disdain for the cultural norms of a "repressive"
British society suffused his prolific work, which heroically but forlornly ran
against the grain of commercial movie making. He never allowed establishment standards of good taste to stand in the way of the search for the holy
grail of "a new cinema," while bringing an activist gay/punk sensibility to
subversive films like *Sebastiane* (1975), *Jubilee* (1978), and *The Tempest* (1980),
which sometimes were underwritten by grants from the British Film
Institute. Early in his career a set designer for Ken Russell's *The Devils*, among
Jarman's other artistic idols were Italian renaissance painter Michelangelo
Caravaggio (1573–1610) and film director Pier Paolo Pasolini, both patron
saints of the gay movement. Caravaggio's stormy life inspired Jarman to film
the semi-documentary *Caravaggio* (1986),[12] and of Pasolini, he wrote "had
Caravaggio been reincarnated in this century it would have been as a filmmaker, Pasolini."[13] Throughout his short but energetic lifetime, Jarman struggled like a displaced Oscar Wilde to defang "heterosoc" prejudice against
"queers" that he saw as the lynchpin for ideological, racist, and gender policing.[14] Like Wilde, he was a pure aesthete, and except for an occasional political foray with left-leaning fellow actors, did not seem to have much interest
in the plight of exploited workers under capitalism.

His transgressive *Tempest* was an art-house movie first screened at the 1979
Edinburgh Festival. Much to Jarman's distress,[15] who had hoped for main-

stream acceptance, at the New York Film Festival it was torpedoed and sunk without a trace by *New York Times* critic Vincent Canby,[16] but it did invade new turf by imposing a gay/camp vision on a Shakespearean play. Budgeted at £150,000, it was filmed in seven weeks on location mostly at Stoneleigh Abbey, an eighteenth-century Italianate mansion built around the remains of a fourteenth-century monastery in Warwickshire near Coventry. After Jarman's even naughtier *Sebastiane* and *Jubilee*, his *Tempest* seems understated, but insufficiently so to prevent some critics from pronouncing anathema with adjectives like "perverse," or "ugly." Most recently, though, Diana Harris and MacDonald Jackson have energetically defended it: "Jarman's movie, though often bizarre, engages the feelings; it is genuinely moving, and the emotions it arouses are essentially those aroused by Shakespeare's play."[17] In an early draft of his plans, Jarman himself anticipated that "stylistically the film will take great freedom" and it will be "in black-and-white, shot like a German expressionist horror film (*Nosferatu*)," but at the end it "will burst into radiant color," though he must have changed his mind because the final cut emerged in color throughout.[18] The exterior scenes with a blue filtered lighting may possibly have been inspired by Caravaggio's hallmark *tenebrism*, that is to say, muted contrasts between white and black. Jarman saw the enigmatic Prospero as more smug than tyrannical, perhaps a Colonel Blimp figure, "unable to see his exploitation of Caliban and Ariel," while Ariel is essentially "a projection of Prospero's mind which [is struggling] to free itself and escape." As for Caliban, Jarman followed modernist critics in thinking that he is "the exploited servant of Sycorax [who] was beautiful before Prospero introduced the language that enabled Caliban to curse him and exploit his innocence." A benevolent despot, Prospero always suffers from the impossibility of reasonably governing the unreasonable. In Ferdinand, however, he has a subject that Jarman thinks is the embodiment of "youth and innocence," and Stephano and Trinculo remain "simple and ordinary people,"[19] in fact filmed as characters from *The Wizard of Oz* happily skipping along a beach.

Predictably, the establishing shot is a tempest. Alonso's (Peter Bull) ship, a modern vessel, labors through a wild storm with angry waves crashing over the bow, and a gasping and panting on the soundtrack. The panting seems to emit both from the imperiled mariners and from Prospero (Heathcote Williams) restlessly turning and tossing in bed, tormented in his dream by Gonzalo's (Ken Campbell) cries of "We split, we split!" (1.1.62). The "split" acts as metaphor for Prospero's own desperate struggle against the alienation of self from self and society, as well as self-referentially Jarman's own split from conventional movie making. "We are such stuff / As dreams are made on" (4.1.156), says Prospero but his dream becomes a nightmare, after the style of Jan Kott's *Shakespeare Our Contemporary*, which redefined *The Tempest* as a play about power rather than forgiveness. This is a major "split" from the light and airy "soufflé"[20] of George Schaefer's Hallmark *Tempest* (1960) with Richard Burton as Caliban, or the BBC-TV soporific version (1980) with Michael Hordern as Prospero. Prospero cruelly grinding his foot on Caliban's fingers works as visual metonomy for this dark vision. His study in tumble-down Stoneleigh Abbey bursts at the seams with the exotic bric-à-brac of a magus – astrological charts, a model of the zodiac, *The Occult Philosophy* of Agrippa, crystal balls, and so forth. The dialogue is transposed, pushed around, pruned, and yet idiosyncratically intact. What remains is delivered in decidedly non-transgressive establishment RP accents, while the plot follows Shakespeare's with considerable fidelity.

The characters have been audaciously displaced into a contemporary mold, the boldest stroke being the re-invention of Miranda (Toyah Willcox) as a voluptuous tart, a "nymphomaniac" to use Jarman's own label. Caliban, played by the perennial favorite of the Lindsay Kemp clique, The Incredible Orlando (Jack Birkett) of Titania fame, is a giggling obnoxious satyr who resembles Lindsay Kemp's Puck in the Coronado *Midsummer Night's Dream*. Unlike Kemp's Puck, he is no passive voyeur but a lecher intent on pawing the nubile and intermittently topless Toyah Willcox, who was also a major player in Jarman's decadent *Jubilee*. Frontal nudity designed to *épater le bourgeois* is a well-worn trope in the films of transgressive cinema; here David Meyer as Ferdinand (Hamlet and Lysander in the Coronado films) emerges shivering, stark naked, from an icy sea but in a modestly remote long shot. Elements of bondage and aggression in Prospero's mistreatment of Ferdinand conveniently merge with Jarman's sado-masochistic fantasies of the martyrdom of St. Sebastian, who is often portrayed looking almost as pierced with arrows as Washizu at the end of *Throne of Blood*.

Campy sequences abound. Miranda playing dress-up in a tattered gown stands on the stairs, while Caliban, "this thing of darkness" (5.1.275), the hidden side of Prospero, grinds away on a hurdy-gurdy, adding diegetic music to the strange off-camera non-melodies of the film's music makers, *Wavemaker*. Almost everyone has agreed that the flashback of a gross, flabby Sycorax nursing a grown-up Caliban is at best "intrusive" and at worst "disgusting," but even that revolting episode has been rationalized as artistically valid. Caliban's portrayal as a "giant baby" makes having him nursed at his dam's breast "strangely appropriate."[21] Despite the boldness of interpretation, the actual filming is confined to conventional masters, mid-shots, and close-ups with very little use of a wandering camera. Jarman, in a rare fit of conservatism, felt that experimental camera work with unconventional subject-matter could easily "push a film over into incoherence."[22]

21   Jack Birkett (The Incredible Orlando) as an incredible Caliban in Derek Jarman's post-modernist vision of *The Tempest* (UK 1979).

A cast of fifteen actors and a chorus of singers and dancers support soloist Elisabeth Welch, a black blues singer who as "Goddess" combines the roles of Iris, Ceres, and Juno, in the closing "Stormy Weather" dance sequence. Perhaps intended as a mild spoof on a Busby Berkeley production number, it rescues the film from any tendency to fall into a solemn apocalyptic mode like Jarman's *The Last of England* (1987). In what may have been a gay in-joke,[23] several dozen men in white sailor suits along with Welch as soloist do a ragged song-and-dance routine of "Stormy Weather." As Samuel Crowl has pointed out, the refrain of "Keeps rainin' all the time," provides a modern equivalent to Feste's "for the rain it raineth every day" in *Twelfth Night* (5.1.392).[24] Jarman transposes "Our revels now are ended" (4.1.148) from act four to the end of the movie, where it works better as a coda anyway, much more compelling than "Now my charms are all o'erthrown" (Epilogue). Behind all the gaiety and frivolity, the brave front, is the dark agenda in Jarman's life, an endless struggle to locate funding for his films, a vision of a western civilization on the edge of apocalypse, and the ultimate calamity of AIDS, which is the subject of his last film, *Blue* (1993). In this nightmare world, Prospero's name might better be changed to Impecunero, a conclusion covert in Shakespeare's play but made overt here. One thing can be said. No one will ever fall asleep watching Jarman's *Tempest*, which has been so rudely wrenched out of the context of any solemn classroom discussion.

Peter Greenaway

Peter Greenaway's *Prospero's Books* (1991), a post-post-modernist adaptation of *The Tempest*, ratchets Jarman's quest for a new cinema up a notch by combining conventional 35mm film with television post-production techniques using high-definition television processes (HDTV). The result moves beyond Walter Benjamin's concept of the mechanical reproduction of art to the post-mechanical workings of digital cinema, or even the electronic reproduction of art.[25] By his own admission, Jarman was hopeless with machinery and could never have utilized so effectively Greenaway's array of electronic gadgetry. Indeed the master magician Georges Méliès himself, stuck with his hand-cranked camera, would have eaten his heart out with envy to have beheld such technological wizardry. Greenaway's own widely acclaimed visual imagination as shown in enigmatic films like *The Draughtsman's Contract* (1982), and *The Belly of an Architect* (1987), made this marriage with new-age technology all the more promising. His transgressive *The Cook, the Thief, his Wife and her Lover* (1990), which survived briefly in the multiplex market, also vaguely echoes the Thyestean feast in *Titus Andronicus* when a freshly roasted human being serves as the center-piece of a restaurant table. Like Shakespeare, Greenaway also understands the magician's trick for making what may be only an accident of juxtapositions, as in *Hamlet*, seem enormously profound. Yet Prince Hamlet warns us that what "seems" "is," and what "is" may "seem," and who is so wise as to tell the difference? For that reason, *Prospero's Books* contains the ingredients for three doctoral dissertations in film studies.

In *Prospero's Books,* Greenaway comes very close to achieving his ideal of making a movie that is, like Alan Resnais' *Last Year at Marienbad* (1961), a "film-film" that cannot be anything else, neither text, painting nor play. He believes that even after a century "we probably haven't seen any cinema yet, only ... a multi-hybrid that has been slow to develop an autonomous character." Greenaway admired the structure of Resnais' film in the way that it could "manipulate chronology ... repeat and reprise ... take multiple views of the same phenomena, and ... do it with elegant and witty self-reflexion."[26] Resnais' co-scenarist, avant-garde writer Alain Robbe-Grillet, insists that what we see on screen, as compared with written fictional narrative, is always in the present tense, "*in the act of happening,*" the audience receiving the "gesture itself, not an account of it."[27] This anti-linear agenda infiltrates *Prospero's Books,* where John Gielgud as Prospero, Peter Greenaway and William Shakespeare all rolled into one is self-reflexively writing *The Tempest* as we watch him in his writing room modeled on the cell in Da Messina's St. Jerome.[28] The grammar of *Prospero's Books* also resembles Resnais' more accessible *Mon Oncle d'Amérique* with its flow of discontinuous images connected by a voice-over commentary. In *Mon Oncle,* the medical researcher's clinical observations on the behavior of laboratory rats establishes a parallel to the lives of the characters in the movie, just as in Greenaway's film Prospero comments on the action of *The Tempest.* Despite these cinematic biases, Greenaway paradoxically shows great "respect for the literality of Shakespeare's text ... [his film] being as it were a literal rewriting of *The Tempest.*"[29]

Few will deny that Greenaway makes intimidating movies. The easy way out is to announce, like Vincent Canby, that *Prospero's Books* will probably make "some people run boldly for the exits,"[30] which it doubtlessly will, my own daughter among them. Yet as Canby also implies, there is a numinous sense of being in the presence of a masterpiece that makes glib dismissals egregiously philistine. Like Jarman, Godard, and other avant-gardists, Greenaway takes no prisoners when it comes to mediating between his art and his audience. Not just a superb technician, he is also a scholar and an artist who uses film to present a modern version of a dazzling Jacobean court masque. The whole of it is too mannerist, too rich, too impossible, for consumption by any but the most dedicated specialists, but there is much pleasure in dissecting and examining the parts. Greenaway's work is a *Finnegans Wake* of visual art.

Greenaway reconstructs the library of fourteen books that old Gonzalo presumably loaded into Prospero's "rotten carcass of a butt" (1.2.146) when he was exiled from Milan with little Miranda. Even if the movie had never been made, Greenaway's talent for capturing the essence of the "Elizabethan lumber room," as Virginia Woolf called it, would deserve a separate museum exhibit. His *Flying Out of this World* (University of Chicago Press, 1992), which traces the history of flight through images, demonstrates his skill as a collector and editor of, and commentator on, exotic sketches and paintings. For *Prospero's Books*, Greenaway imagines and creates a series of majestically illustrated volumes with titles such as "The Book of Water" (1), "A Book of Mirrors" (2), "A Book of Mythologies" (3), "A Harsh Book of Geometry" (6), "The Vesalius Anatomy of Birth" (8), "The Ninety-Two Conceits of the Minotaur" (13), "The Book of Languages" (14), and finally "Thirty Six Plays" (24). The last book is Shakespeare's 1623 First Folio but with the first nineteen pages left blank for Gielgud as Prospero to insert *The Tempest* into them at the end of the movie when he has finished writing it. In a supreme irony, this play, *The Tempest*, thought to be Shakespeare's "last," was printed first in the Folio. Greenaway works with the imagination of a painter, the meticulousness of a draughtsman, and the eye of a master film maker. In the present context, it is impossible to do justice to even a single one of the books, which have been prepared with the help of a "digital, electronic Graphic Paintbox" that Greenaway sees as the "newest Gutenberg technology."[31]

As Prospero, the magus and creator of the characters, inscribes the words of the play in elegant Elizabethan secretary hand (calligraphy by Brody Neuenschwander), he eventually draws on all of the books, which are stored in compartments around his study. As Donaldson points out, Prospero becomes a magus for our time who gives a "technological inflection" to the white magic of the Renaissance.[32] For example, as Prospero/Greenaway conceives of *The Tempest* and its opening storm, "The Book of Water" lies on his desk along with a model of a galleon. "The Book of Mythology" helps in the first twenty minutes or so of screen time to flesh out the story of his exile from Milan as told to Miranda, with allusions to Hades, Vulcan, Juno, Venus, Hercules, and Ariadne, and attendant nymphs. In the "Bath-house," where water flows so copiously that the audience can easily grasp why Gonzalo would "fain die a dry death" (1.1.67), nude nymphs swim like phantoms underwater. A young boy (Ariel) with a bladder the size of a dirigible holds his "small penis like an ornamental water-spout" and pees torrents into the pool, which drollery may have been inspired by a similar fountain statue in Brussels. It has also aroused murmurs of "kiddy-porn" in some circles. The book of a "Primer of the Small Stars" shows maps for the voyager, constellations, meteors, night skies, while "The Book of the Mirror" includes mirror images for a three-year-old Miranda surrounded by her doting attendants. There are glimpses, for example, of Prospero proceeding through arcades modeled on Bernini's in St. Peter's Square. In Prospero's study, a brisk west wind scatters his papers around, which is yet another quotation, this time from Botticelli's "Birth of Venus." Later, when Antonio gathers his conspirators around him, the visual quotation is from Veronese, though the participants are in Dutch costumes. "Vesalius' Anatomy of Birth" contributes a horrifying cutaway in full color of a woman's womb, in which psychoanalytical critics have mined a rich lode for speculation about Prospero's terror of the female body and his efforts to exert control over its reproductive powers.[33] Colors play a key role in exposing the animal nature of Caliban, who as the paradigm for the ultimate redneck reinforces Alexander Hamilton's belief that "Your people, sir, is a great beast." As prologue to Caliban's entrance, and as totem for his illiteracy, close-ups of dripping urine and glops of vomit stain the pages of books. The rich mosaic of Greenaway's varied images defies description and makes writing about them an exercise in describing the indescribable, which valorizes Greenaway's belief that images should not be surrogates for words but independent of them. To put it another way, the film is a "cultural caprice" that forces the viewer/auditor "to move around among [its] sights, sounds, and accidentals . . . assembling and disassembling meanings as they fleetingly present themselves."[34]

Drawbacks appear, despite the profound reworking of Shakespeare's images and Greenaway's acknowledged genius at film making. For one thing, the choreography often seems disconnected from everything else, as an inordinate number of young, and not so young, men and women prance around nude, seemingly for the sake of prancing around nude, to the rhythms of Michael Nyman's band. A telling point, however, rests in the costuming of Antonio, Alonso, and others in an outlandish travesty of Jacobean clothing with prodigious Milanese ruffs as if to acknowledge the superiority of man's natural to his unnaturally clothed state. Allowed to play every male role in the play, Sir John Gielgud outdoes himself as a singer of verse, his already mellifluous but stagy voice being unnaturally amplified and resonated through the sophisticated electronic recording equipment. Finally, the last word may be that of a reviewer who thought that "by presenting too much to take in at a glance, Greenaway tests to the limits his ideal of a painterly cinema."[35] Notably humorless, the movie leaves you intellectually gorged but emotionally starved.

Jean-Luc Godard

With Jean-Luc Godard's "twisted fairy tale" of a *King Lear* (1987), the cinema of transgression vents its anti-establishment spleen less in the private realm of sexual identity than in the public arena of politics. It was conceived in a legendary way on a table napkin at the Cannes Film Festival with the promise of big name stars, Orson Welles even, and with a $1.4 million budget from Cannon Films. The deal somehow went awry and resulted in the film being partly about how the director was allegedly "stabbed in the back" by his colleagues' breaking of a bond.[36] Godard was playing Cordelia to Cannon Films' King Lear, as it were. As a post-modernist, Godard does not so much give the audience a movie as invite the audience to make a movie out of a kaleidoscope of segments. Peter Donaldson's extended analysis demonstrates that the film is more of a "dissemination," or even a deconstruction in the Derridean sense, than a representation of *King Lear*.[37] By the time he made *King Lear*, Godard had turned his back on the Hollywood movies he once admired in his earlier "bourgeois" films like *Breathless* (1960), and devoted himself entirely to working for the revolution. His *King Lear* takes the spectator on a journey (maybe "three journeys" as one alienating inter-title suggests). His movie is an anti-movie that meta-cinematically shows the impossibility of making movies, of finding visual equivalents for any verbal structures. It is, as a persistent inter-title insists, about "No-thing." Since *Two or Three Things I Know about Her* (1967) Godard has spurned filmic grammar that promotes viewer passivity. He scorns the seamless Hollywood narrative as an instrument of oppression for suppressing independent thought in a mindless consumerist society. Like television, mainstream film lobotomizes the masses and neutralizes them politically. David Impastato puts it succinctly when he says, "Godard himself dispenses with all the basic courtesies of story-telling."[38] Philosopher Gilles Deleuze thinks that Godard's films raise "questions which silence answers."[39] In short, it is up to the viewer not only to look but to see, "See better, Lear" (1.1.157), and, as with Greenaway's work, to construct a personal narratology out of the galaxy of images.

Most critics despised it. Brickbats flew. "Tedious convolutions." "[Shakespeare] doubtless rotating in his grave." "A massively perverse farrago." "A vulgar contrivance." David Nokes thought that "not the least of the privations of a nuclear winter would be the threat that its culture might be comprised of films like this."[40] Others saw things differently. Sheila Johnston found "integrity and conviction,"[41] and J. Hoberman thought it was "deft, funny, and intermittently exhilarating . . . as stylized a reading as Kurosawa's *Ran*."[42] There is little point, however, in looking for linearity in a deliberately non-linear work that turns what is fragmented, segmented, and disjointed into a celebration of apocalypse. Syntax crumbles like Mad Tom's gibberish about the "foul fiend." This thing of shreds and patches struggles with the insane condition of man after Chernobyl, after the Death of God, after the old king's calamitous fall into misery. Artful segmentations, however, often give more truth than inept full-scale dramatizations. Like a metaphysical poem that yokes together disparate images, Godard's *King Lear* offers an academic feast for explication of the way it juxtaposes apparently irrelevant images.

Godard sets his cryptic movie in the Hotel Beau-Rivage at Nyon, Switzerland, on the shores of Lake Léman, though there are vague references to its being also located in America. The casting includes Norman Mailer as The Great Writer and his daughter Kate. After one day's shooting, Mailer departed in a rage for the States ("first class for himself and daughter, economy for his daughter's boy friend," we are snidely told), his role as Don Learo being taken over by Burgess Meredith, a versatile and skilful actor. Mailer's disaffection becomes a leitmotif in the movie as Godard explores the alleged breach of trust between him and the film's backers, and the recurring inter-title, "Stabbed in the Back," raises connotations of perfidy, treachery, and villainy, if not paranoia. The opening scene, however, remains The Great Writer's, who declares that "the Mafia's the only way to do *King Lear*." His perplexed daughter anxiously asks "Why are you so interested in the Mafia?" Later, we find out why. Burgess Meredith, by now cast as Don Learo, reads from Albert Fried's book on Jewish gangsters about how Bugsy Siegel's efforts ultimately "Las Vegasized" the entire United States. In a passage lifted verbatim from Fried, we hear Don Learo quoting Meyer Lansky sounding like Michael Cassio: "When you lose your money you lose nothing; when you lose your character, you lose everything."[43] The nexus is suddenly clear. This moralizing gangster fits into Lear's own vision of a world as morally bankrupt, a predatory jungle:

> What, art mad? A man may see how this world goes with no eyes. Look with thine ears; see how yond justice rails upon yond simple thief. Hark in thine ear: change places, and handy-dandy, which is the justice, which is the thief? (4.6.150ff)

Molly Ringwald as Cordelia contributes a pretty but petulant face that reflects the thinly disguised impatience of an adolescent girl with a tiresome father. When she stands alone in a white dress on the hotel balcony while her father reads letters from her sisters, "Gloria," and "Regina," she embodies the recurring Godardian image of women entrapped by language and customs. Only her disjunctive voice on the soundtrack reciting sonnet 47 ("Betwixt mine eye and heart a league is took") tips off the audience to her inner estimate of herself. Like all Cordelias a holy mystery, she is an object to gaze at while she is gazing at herself, in a role that takes her back to her equally appealing Miranda in Paul Mazursky's *The Tempest* (1981).

As William Shakespeare, Jr. The Fifth, Peter Sellars plays the role of an editor in search of the unrecoverable text of his ancestor. At first he is struggling for the title of *As You Like It,* which initially emerges as *As You Wish It.* Later he begins transcribing passages from *King Lear* that gradually are transferred over to Don Learo himself, who pathetically becomes dependent on young William for his lines. The search for the text becomes an icon for the artist's impotence in a post-modernist world, "after Chernobyl," when art is dead.

In a paroxysm of self-referentiality, Godard plays himself playfully in a ridiculous get-up with dreadlocks and dogtags streaming from his head, his redeeming ability not to take himself too seriously having even led to his casting the inimitable Woody Allen in the movie. As Professor Pluggy, Godard affects some kind of a speech defect, talking out of the corner of his mouth in a maddeningly garbled way, again to show the inadequacy of language for expressing ideas. As well as being Lear's Fool, Professor Pluggy conveniently serves as the philosopher-commentator, a stock figure in many of Godard's movies who discourses learnedly on the action. Questions directed at Professor Pluggy, "Just what are you aiming at, Professor?" really sum up the audience's collective resentment over being so thoroughly bamboozled. There are no answers, only alienating title cards with enigmatic messages like "No-thing," "Power and Virtue," "An Approach to Lear," and "Fear and Loathing."

All the clutter from the family attic crops up in the movie. There is Albert Fried's *The Rise and Fall of the Jewish Gangster in America* with its mythmaking about Meyer Lansky and Bugsy Siegel; a page out of the technical history of film making; iterative images of the Angel Raphael, who may have been "shot in the back" (see this identical motif at the close of *Breathless*); photo albums with tributes to great film directors like Welles and Renoir; frequent disjunctions of sound and image; many squawking gulls; and now and then Burgess Meredith's great voice enunciating majestic passages from *King Lear.* Standard Godardian tropes, like the covers of books being incorporated into the narrative and outdoor advertising billboards, show up in close-ups of a copy of Virginia Woolf's *The Waves* washed up on the beach, and the neon-lit sign of the Hotel Beau-Rivage at night. Other memorable images include a galloping white horse from the stirring last paragraph of Virginia Woolf's novel; Godard as the Professor striving for closure in untangling his hopelessly snarled film; a beautiful Cordelia in white robes lying as a sacrifice on a large boulder.

All of this chaotic material might be suspected of being mere gibberish – or clinically speaking, "image salad," the cinematic equivalent to the pathology of "word salad," which is defined as the brilliant images in muddled syntax characteristic of schizophrenia[44] – if it were not for the movie's denseness of texture. It all adds up to a radiant nothingness of the variety that threatens to turn back into a something too profound to capture in any known language. In these ways, Godard "spectates" the sight of his own film's impossibility for closure to illustrate, as he puts it, that "cinema plays with itself." At the end of the movie, Alien (Woody Allen), perhaps in a quote from Orson Welles's *F for Fake*, sits at a Movieola ineptly trying to splice together the flawed film with needle and thread. In voice-over, he recites Shakespeare's sonnet 60 ("Like as the waves make towards the pebbled shore / So do our minutes hasten to their end").

Contrary to what has often been claimed, Godard's alienating images – aggressive *découpage*, rapid editing, discontinuities, fractured images – do not detract from the language of *King Lear* but frame it. The raucous, mocking cries of the gulls over the lake sonically underscore Shakespeare's exposure of the horror of the human condition. Cordelia is displaced into the teenage surliness of Molly Ringwald. Burgess Meredith's splendid American voice turns sacerdotal with the devastating, "She's gone forever! / I know when one is dead" (5.3.260). The pale white horse moves like a phantom across the screen, and the waves beat on the shore. The images dazzle but even in this strange new world of pure images, Shakespeare's language still holds center stage, as the work of an Academy Award nominee for scenarist should.

Independent film makers

Perhaps less "transgressive" than "quixotic" are the independent Shakespeare movies that emerge as a labor of love without any hope of financial reward in the cruel world of "tickling commodity." Of three that appeared in the late 80s and early 90s, two versions of *Othello* came from minority American film makers, and one of *As You Like It* from British film maker Christine Edzard. For the same reasons that Janet Suzman chose it as her Market Theatre statement against South African apartheid, minority film makers have shown special interest in *Othello*. On a tiny budget of $200,000 she financed herself, Liz White's all-black *Othello* (1980) with Yaphet Kotto in the lead and Audrey Dixon as Desdemona added a heroic marker to the history of filmed Shakespeare. The challenges faced by independent film makers entitle them to their own modern singer of epic tales of the hero/artist in formidable combat against the tyranny of the distribution system. The artist manqué descends into the Hades of Heartbreak House but unlike Odysseus never re-ascends. Originally a 1966 summer theatre production at Martha's Vineyard, where the director's family had long been established in the island's elite black summer resort community, the 16mm movie had award-winning Charles Dorkins as cinematographer and Jonas Gwangwa as composer of the Afro-American jazz score. Peter Donaldson has praised it not just for White's ethnically subtle casting of a black actor to play the role of Othello among lighter-skinned blacks, but also for how "the social context of the production becomes part of the meaning of the film."[45] Director White had apparently disliked seeing Caucasian actors like Olivier and Sergei Bondarchuk playing Othello in blackface. She interprets Iago's malice toward Othello as stemming from the psychological damage caused by his subconscious displacement of himself into the role of a rejected son. Regrettably the film remains sequestered in archives, having never been distributed commercially, as it deserves comparison with the recently released Oliver Parker *Othello* (1996), starring Laurence Fishburne and Irene Jacob.

Yet another example of minority film making is Ted Lange's Rockbottom Productions *Othello* (1989), which began as a stage production at the Inner City Cultural Center in Los Angeles. Aimed at American audiences in an MTV and "Miami Vice" style with generous use of music and shock editing, Lange, an experienced commercial television director, cast a black Othello (Ted Lange) and Iago (Hawthorne James) against a white, blonde Desdemona (Mary Otis). The result privileged Iago's envy over Othello's jealousy with a subsequent diminishment of the other characters.[46] One mainstream reviewer praised the movie, especially for Hawthorne James's performance as Iago and thought its "novelty elements . . . could generate theatrical and video interest."[47]

So far mostly exhibited only at film festivals, Christine Edzard's *As You Like It* (1992) has created quite a stir among academics. Edzard, director of the award-winning *Little Dorrit* (1988), has also worked with Franco Zeffirelli and has played a key role in establishing the independent Sands Film Studio in London. Her film's low budget, technical glitches, and impenetrable British diction, however, condemned it to a short life even though the cast includes some well-known British actors. Because its displacement of the Forest of Arden into a starkly realistic urban jungle runs against the grain of Shakespeare's festive language and was widely misunderstood, most viewers would agree with Derek Elley's judgment that it "sacrifices sylvan whimsy for social edge."[48] Her *As You Like It* takes exactly the opposite approach from the 1936 film with Laurence Olivier and Elisabeth Bergner. Instead of studio opulence designed by the prestigious Lazare Meerson, the movie's sets look as if they had been thriftily recycled from Derek Jarman's *The Last of England* (1987), which wallows in urban grime. The Forest of Arden has been transmogrified into a vacant lot on the East London waterfront, and Duke Senior and his merry crew are making sweet the uses of adversity by living out of packing cases. The pastoral myth at the core of Shakespeare's play that contrasts the edenic countryside with the fallen world of the city and court has been stood on its head. Now it is the wretched of the earth within the city itself that implicitly condemn the callous Thatcherites. Appropriately for this reading, the court of the bad Duke Frederick seems to have been constructed out of an abandoned bank lobby, and he and his friends cavort in splendid clothing vastly superior to the rags of his good brother's cohorts. A shivering Duke Senior and the melancholy Jaques huddle around an oil drum brazier, and Orlando dwells in a polyurethane shack.

An imaginative decision to use Jaques' Seven Ages of Man speech as a prologue to the movie goes astray when in his subdued reading James Fox, dressed in a shabby black hat and overcoat, confuses somnambulism with understatement. Some clever doubling reinforces the split between city and urban pastoral by having Andrew Tiernan play both Orlando and Oliver, Don Henderson both of the dukes, and Roger Hammond both LeBeau and Corin. In an apparent bid for the youth market, Edzard cast the very young Emma Croft as Rosalind against Tiernan's youthful Orlando. The contrast between Tiernan as Orlando and the aged Cyril Cusack, who did Aegeon in the BBC *Comedy of Errors*, as old Adam almost self-reflexively underscores the past and present in British theatre. Emma Croft brings energy, youth, bounce to the demanding role but there is so much bounce as she leaps and swirls and cavorts that it distracts from the bouncy language. "Wherein went he? What makes he here? Did he ask for me? Where remains he? How parted he with thee? And when shalt thou see him again? Answer me in one word." (3.2.221). This interrogative torrent pours out of a Rosalind costumed in jeans, a work jacket and watch cap which to the literal-minded makes the references to her "doublet and hose" seem odd, but on the other hand the modern unisex style blends nicely with the play's androgynous politics.[49] Orlando's love poems that normally get tacked up on trees turn up as graffiti on the fence around the vacant lot. For American audiences ignorant of Griff Rhys Jones's work as a British television comic, his thick dialect as Touchstone raises formidable barriers. No one nowadays expects RP (BBC Received Pronunciation) but for overseas English-speaking audiences Jones's character might as well be speaking in Swahili. As snobbish and painful as RP may be, it has the virtue of being easily understood by speakers of any other English dialect. The surface and air traffic noises on the uneven soundtrack suggest that filming took place directly under the main flight path to Heathrow. This unfiltered rumble either enhances the urban atmosphere, as Samuel Crowl thinks,[50] or is intrusive and points to the need for better technical work in the sound department. Sonic support in an interesting avant-garde Godardian kind of way is one thing, but faulty recording is something else. Two actresses nicely catch the spirit of the production: Celia [*sic*] Bannerman as a pert Celia, and Valerie Gogan as a mini-skirted, punk-style Phebe, with a sassy attitude. The closing Masque of Hymen successfully integrates the mystery of the past with the ugly realities of the present by having a mist roll in from the river just as the wedding preparations begin. "Pray you no more of this, 'tis like the howling of Irish wolves against the moon [*To Silvius.*] I will help you if I can. [*To Phebe.*] I would love you if I could" (5.2.109), though the singing of "It was a lover and his lass" might have worked better if it had been entrusted to some passing street urchins rather than to the two elderly actors who are allowed to make spectacles of themselves cavorting around the "palace" of Duke Frederick. Edzard's movie is certainly fresher and livelier, if less polished, than the wooden 1936 version with Laurence Olivier but the first truly successful film of this challenging play has yet to be seen.

Shakespeare derivatives of seven kinds: beyond the fringe

The Shakespeare movie that drifts far away from "Shakespeare" raises uncomfortable questions about taxonomy. Roger Manvell's system of six stages of adaptation, which categorizes films by their distance from stage productions, has not really been improved upon very much.[51] Jack J. Jorgens' scheme complements it, however, through sorting out Shakespeare movies in three-step pigeonholes such as "theatrical, realist, and filmic," or by criteria of "presentation, interpretation, and adaptation."[52] The drawback is that the six categories sometimes overlap and cross one another like Polonius' infamous "tragedy, comedy, history, pastoral, pastoral-comical, historical-pastoral, [tragical-historical, tragical-comical-historical-pastoral,] scene individable, or poem unlimited" (*Ham.* 2.2.396). For example, the Stuart Burge *Othello* is "theatrical-presentational-interpretative" but probably not very "realistic" or "adaptational," while the RADA *Romeo and Juliet* (1966) as a plain record of a stage performance remains purely theatrical and perhaps only mildly interpretative – in short, embalmed theatre. It should be understood that these labels are not to be construed as either pejorative or honorific, but simply descriptive and in no way prescriptive. In its own way, a "theatrical" *Romeo and Juliet* may equal in merit a "realist" Mankiewicz *Julius Caesar*, or a "filmic" Kurosawa's *Throne of Blood*. Ultimately all Shakespeare movies, like stage productions, are adaptations in that they mediate between Shakespeare and the director, but they take so many forms as to make rigorous taxonomy elusive.[53] As Orson Welles said, sooner or later "we all betray Shakespeare."[54]

If there were an imaginary scale from one to ten, then a movie faithful to stage tradition or textual authority (e.g., the Burge *Othello*) could be labeled "conservative" or "closed," and rated a "one"; another more realistic as cinema but conservative with textual changes (e.g., the Mankiewicz *Julius Caesar*), would be a "five"; while a film that massively rearranges the text and embellishes the *mise-en-scène* could be called "radical" or "open," and rated as a "ten" (e.g., Greenaway's *Prospero's Books*). Mainline Shakespeare movies mostly fit into this scale of one to ten, as they go up and down the scale from "closed" to "open," "conservative" to "radical," "presentational" to "filmic," or "theatrical" to "adaptational," but others as yet unconsidered elude these categories. Sometimes bizarre or eccentric, these films do not so much *adapt* as *derive* from Shakespeare. The major difference between the adaptation and the derivative is that adaptations in English (foreign adaptations represent another issue: see chapter 8) rely heavily on Shakespeare's actual words, and derivatives abandon his language altogether. For textual scholars, the remoteness of derivatives from Folio and Quarto relegates them to the fringe, but for cultural historians they may offer a gold mine for speculation about mass consciousness. Like unwanted illegitimate children, no matter how emphatic the protests that they are "not Shakespeare," they have the impudence to lurk on the fringe of the family circle.

There are seven kinds of Shakespeare derivatives, which take protean shapes in plot, theme, language, design, purpose, and camera work. Those of the first kind (recontextualizations) will keep the plot but move Shakespeare's play into a wholly new era and jettison the Elizabethan language (*Joe Macbeth*); the second kind (mirror movies) will meta-cinematically make the movie's backstage plot about the troubled lives of actors run parallel to the plot of the Shakespearean play that the actors are appearing in (*A Double Life*); the third kind (music/dance) will turn the plays into musicals (*West Side Story*), or ballets and operas such as Zeffirelli's *Otello* (1986), the latter of which lie outside the range of this book; the fourth kind (revues) will use the excuse of a biography (*Prince of Players*), or of a documentary (*Looking for Richard*), or even a horror show (*Theatre of Blood*) to showcase scenes from Shakespeare's plays; the fifth (parasitical) will exploit Shakespeare for embellishment, and/or graft brief visual or verbal quotations onto an otherwise unrelated scenario (Katharine Hepburn in *Morning Glory*); the sixth kind (animations) – at this point the scheme does begin sounding like Polonius' – will put Shakespeare into cartoon images (*The Lion King*); and finally the seventh kind (documentaries and educational films) will make a variety of pedagogical films that in turn may overlap with any of the permutations and combinations in the previous categories. Howsoever labeled, this catalog of hundreds of titles, not so much "Shakespeare" as "Shakespearean," testifies to Shakespeare's prodigious cultural capital.

Briefly, examples of the first kind of derivatives include the American *Strange Illusion* (1945), which retells the Hamlet legend in modern guise. Starring James Lydon, who later made a career out of playing Henry Aldrich, and directed by Edgar G. Ulmer who began as a director of European Yiddish films, the movie is a prime specimen of the film noir B movie, whose trademark dark lighting may have come more from the accident of stingy budgets than from any artistic genius. The movie begins with Paul Cartwight's nightmare about the problematic death of his father, and resentment of his widowed mother's infatuation with Brett Curtis (Claudius). A sullen young man with a taste for wide-lapel suits, Paul mopes about in the baronial family mansion and occasionally shows interest in Lydia (Ophelia). His experiments with real and pretended madness in an effort to block his mother's marriage to Curtis especially link this strangely disturbing film to *Hamlet.*

Like other derivatives of its type, *Joe Macbeth* (1955) makes no pretensions to representing Shakespeare's text on screen but instead recontextualizes the play, again in film noir, by moving the Scottish tragedy into the underworld of Chicago's gangland. The parallels are pervasive. Joe Macbeth (Paul Douglas) after rubbing out the Mob Boss's Lieutenant (Cawdor), learns from Rosie, a fortune teller (the witches), that he is destined to be Lord of Lakeview Drive, and ultimately King of the City. A hackneyed cops-and-robbers chase yields to a quick shot of a bawling baby, "And pity, like a naked new-born babe" (1.7.21), and Joe's wife, Lili (Ruth Roman), to advance her husband's career, invites the Duke (Duncan) to be an overnight guest at her home, where he is terminated, or rubbed out. The moment when Lili hands the knife to Joe becomes prime film noir as the somber lighting and *mise-en-scène* reflect the anguish in Joe's eyes over his coming act of betrayal. The metaphysics of the witches' prophecies in *Macbeth* are summed up in a single remark to Joe: "Maybe it didn't happen because Rosie said it would but because you did what she said."

Men of Respect (1990), directed by William Reilly and starring John Turturro and Rod Steiger, plays a variation on *Joe Macbeth* in modernizing the play as a gangster movie but the title itself suggests the further influence of Francis Ford Coppola's trilogy based on Mario Puzo's Mafia novels. *Godfather III* (1990) also fits into the category Shakespeare derivative of the fifth kind with a plot that vaguely echoes *King Lear* as well as a direct quotation from it. No Shakespearean playing King Lear has ever surpassed Al Pacino as Don Corleone when on the steps of the opera house he cradles the body of his beloved daughter, a Cordelia figure, and lets loose with a heart-rending

"Howl, howl, howl!" (5.3.258). Director Fred Wilcox's *Forbidden Planet* (1956) takes the Shakespeare movie into the realm of science fiction with the story of the mad scientist Dr. Morbius (Walter Pidgeon). Dwelling with Dr. Morbius (Prospero) on Planet Alain-4 is Altaira (Miranda and Ariel), whose equanimity is upset by the arrival of a space ship with a Ferdinand figure aboard. There is a robot who vaguely corresponds to Caliban and enlisted crew members who are surrogates for Trinculo and Stephano. A great scary, amorphous creature dredged up from Dr. Morbius' Id terrifies everyone. A reviewer called "the Freudian monster from the Id . . . a finely outrageous conception, a King Kong of space."[55]

Another farfetched derivative is Peter Ustinov's *Romanoff and Juliet* (1961), which uses Shakespeare's plot and themes but displaces the Capulet/Montague feud into Cold War politics. Igor Romanoff of Concordia, an imaginary obscure East European country, falls in love with Juliet Moulsworth (Sandra Dee), the daughter of the US ambassador. Her parents, surrogates of course for the Capulets, prefer her ex-boy friend, the vapid Freddie (Paris) as a suitor. Tybalt appears in the guise of a KGB agent, and the president of Concordia (Escalus, the prince of Verona) mediates between the warring factions. In the midst of this star-crossed love affair a little boy with a 98-cent chemistry set manages to build an A-bomb, throwing the movie right back in the maw of Cold War hysteria. Unlike Shakespeare's tragedy, the springtime world of youth triumphs over the winter world of the elderly with the marriage of Lt. and Mrs. Igor Romanoff. Behind its surface frivolity, the movie subverts McCarthyism by condemning the stupidity of the Cold War era.

Hollywood director Paul Mazursky, an associate of maverick film maker John Cassavetes, has been responsible for two first-kind derivatives in *Harry and Tonto* (1974), in which a retired New York school teacher reenacts the agony of *King Lear*,[56] and *Tempest* (1982). Filmed on a budget of $13 million at several locations from New York to Atlantic City to Rome and Greece,[57] this modernized *Tempest*, starring John Cassavetes as a New York architect in mid-life crisis, shows again how Shakespeare's play covers the entire history of humanity. Mazursky's cast of Gena Rowlands (Antonia), Susan Sarandon (Aretha/Ariel), Molly Ringwald (Miranda), Raul Julia (Caliban), and Cassavetes (Philip/Prospero), play out variations on Shakespeare's themes as the troubled Philip summons up tempests as ferocious as his own inner demons. On a desolate island in Greece, Philip recognizes like Prospero the intractability of human relationships. Even though "The rarer action is / In virtue than in vengeance" (5.1.27), there yet remains the problem of equitably distributing forgiveness and power among the Calibans and Antonios of the world. Raul Julia's Caliban rivals Jarman's The Incredible

22   Michael Matou as Oberon and Lindsay Kemp as Puck suggest some of the wild charm of this transgressive *A Midsummer Night's Dream* (Spain/UK 1984), directed by Celestino Coronado.

Orlando for leering prurience. Molly Ringwald as an innocent but scarily invulnerable Miranda contrasts with Toyah Willcox's minx-like but appealingly vulnerable characterization.

Derivatives of the second kind almost invariably involve a meta-cinematic scenario in which a backstage intrigue mirrors the plot of a Shakespearean play. Perhaps because on the surface *Othello* shares in such major motifs of soap opera as jealousy and misunderstanding, it has inspired several mirror-like derivatives, not the least being the real-life O.J. Simpson case. A silent era movie, *Carnival* (1921), serves up the standard plot in which actors playing *Othello* on stage find the Othello story mirrored in their personal lives. Silvio Steno, the great Italian Shakespearean actor, goes mad with jealousy and on stage, egged on by Lelio (Iago), almost strangles his wife, Simonetta, to death while she is playing Desdemona.

Two British movies, *Men Are Not Gods* (1936) and *All Night Long* (1962) mine the same material, again to show how an actor can easily lose his grip on reality. A scene in a pre-war London theatre frames *Men Are Not Gods* when, as was then the custom, the audience rises just before the curtain goes up to sing "God Save the Queen." The wife and leading lady (Gertrude Lawrence) of the actor playing Othello, Edmund Davey (Sebastian Shaw), rescues her egocentric husband from a cruel review of his opening performance by persuading the critic's little secretary, Ann Williams (Miriam Hopkins), to alter it. For her trouble, Ann is fired by her waspish employer (Skeates), but she remains so smitten with Davey that she attends *Othello* night after night to admire the man whom she sacrificed her job for. One night by screaming from the balcony, she just manages to prevent Othello from smothering Desdemona (Gertrude Lawrence) for real on stage. Meanwhile she is courted by obituary reporter Tommy Stapleton, played by a very young and amiable Rex Harrison. This gem of a movie never falters.

Compelling in a different kind of way is *All Night Long* (1962), which uses a jazz band as the core for the machinations and plots that drive Aurelius Rex (Paul Harris/Othello) nearly to strangle his Delia (Marti Stevens/Desdemona) because of the nefarious plotting of Johnny Cousin (Patrick McGoohan/Iago). In a flagrant modernization, a cigarette case substitutes for Othello's handkerchief and Iago uses a tape recorder to entrap people. The *mise-en-scène* is a renovated luxury flat in London's East End, or Bankside, maybe the Liberty of the Clink before it was gentrified, filled with famous musicians like Johnny Dankworth and Dave Brubeck, all sartorially qualified to be J. Edgar Hoover FBI agents with their short Fifties-style haircuts, narrow ties, and dark suits. Jazz lovers will find the movie intriguing even when it wanders away from Shakespeare, though I personally find reaction shots of grown people at jam sessions tapping, clapping, and nodding to the beat embarrassing. Still another mirror plot based on *Othello* turns up in the Academy-Award-winning *A Double Life* (1947), directed by George Cukor. Ronald Colman plays John Anthony, a great British matinee idol on Broadway, who with good reason fears taking on the role of Othello. His inability to separate his stage and real-life persona deludes him into strangling a pathetic waitress (Shelley Winters), whom he mistakes for an unfaithful Desdemona. Wonderfully acted snippets from *Othello* occur during the on-stage sequences in a movie about the agonies and doubts of the actor's trade that Shakespeare himself knew so well ("As an unperfect actor on the stage, / Who with his fear is put besides his part," sonnet 23).

A movie that fits this rubric, though farcical rather than serious, is *To Be or Not to Be* (1942), Ernst Lubitsch's clever exploitation of *Hamlet* in which Jack Benny's rendering of Hamlet's soliloquy becomes the signal for a Polish airman in the audience (Robert Stack) to go backstage for an assignation with the actor's wife, who plays Ophelia (Carole Lombard). Unfortunately, as Robert F. Willson, Jr., has pointed out, Ophelia should be on stage at this point with Hamlet for the "nunnery" scene, making the dressing room assignation impossible, but Willson admits that only the most dyspeptic purist would object to this bit of whimsy.[58] Also in the mirror/backstage genre is *The Goodbye Girl* (1977), an amusing tale by Neil Simon about a struggling actor (Richard Dreyfuss) who is cast as Richard duke of Gloucester in an off-off-Broadway *Richard III*. The play's pompous ass of a director insists on a ludicrous interpretation of Richard as a homosexual cripple in lavender, but there are also some parallels between the wooing of Lady Anne by Richard in the play and the pursuit of Marsha Mason by Richard Dreyfuss in the movie.[59]

Most recently Kenneth Branagh's *In the Bleak Midwinter/A Midwinter's Tale* (1995) has depicted impoverished British actors putting on *Hamlet* at Christmas time in the abandoned church of a village ironically called Hope. Although Branagh has said that he was influenced by the old Judy Garland/Mickey Rooney movies when the youngsters decide to put on a show in the barn, his movie stirs up much deeper emotional waters. This backstage serio-comic drama happens to deal with actors who are losers, not glamorous stars, making pathetic efforts to interest the world in their Shakespearean tragedy. Essentially Luddites, the actors' obsolete but precious literary values are threatened by the whole mega-entertainment complex of mass communications, just as the abandoned church represents the triumph of consumerism over Christian values. The enchantment of assuming the identities of fabled persons like Hamlet, Gertrude, and Ophelia casts its spell and their play turns into a Christmas miracle in which wretchedness is transfigured into sublimity. As an aspiring actor says in auditions, *Hamlet* is not just a play but his whole life. One critic has faulted the movie for its "cloying sentiment,"[60] but I see it instead, like the Merchant/Ivory *Shakespeare Wallah*, as a poignant defense of a lost world of the imagination. The presence of sleek Joan Collins as the actor's agent in the midst of all this genteel decay adds further interest.

The film adaptation of Jane Smiley's best-selling novel, *A Thousand Acres* (1997), which in turn reappropriated *King Lear*, brings a third-hand Shakespearean derivative to the screen. Smiley's, or perhaps more accurately, director Moorhouse's King Lear (Jason Robards, Jr.) has been updated into a mean-spirited midwestern farmer and child-molester whose daughters rightly despise him. Even the best efforts of talented actresses like Jessica Lange and Michelle Pfeiffer cannot save the movie from degenerating into a weepy. Another derivative, whose special status springs from a gay orientation, is Gus Van Sant's art-house/mainstream *My Own Private Idaho* (1991), starring the late River Phoenix and Keanu Reeves. With overt textual appropriations from the Henriad and the redeployment of the Prince Hal prodigal-son story in Scott Favor's (Keanu Reeves) role as a street hustler and the ne'er-do-well son of Portland's mayor, the movie makes heavy Shakespeare claims. Scott's surrogate father is a beery Falstaff figure, who guzzles from bottles of Falstaff beer, and his friend Mike Waters' (River Phoenix) forlorn search for home in Idaho implicitly comments on American family values. The big question, raised by the film's leading critic, is where in all this is Shakespeare?[61] If Shakespeare is only window dressing, the movie belongs more to Shakespeare movies of the fifth kind (parasitical) than to those of the second kind, where I have tentatively assigned it.

A third kind, the musical, is also doubly derivative in that it usually arrives on screen as the filming of a successful theatrical event rather than as direct inspiration from Shakespeare. Examples include *The Boys from Syracuse* (1940), *Kiss Me Kate* (1953), *West Side Story* (1961), and *Catch My Soul: Santa Fe Satan* (1973). In *The Boys from Syracuse*, based on the Abbott/Rodgers/Hart Broadway musical, director A. Edward Sutherland never hesitates to turn a farce into a travesty as *Comedy of Errors* becomes grist for campy jokes and absurd sight gags. The taxi taking one of the Antipholuses to the "Wooden Horse Inn" is a metered chariot, and the Hollywood star system provided a cast of stereotyped comics like Joe ("Wanna buy a duck?") Penner and Martha ("Big Mouth") Ray. Singer Allan Jones warbles away as Antipholus of Ephesus. Newspapers in Ephesus blare out headlines with faded allusions in need of glossing for today's audiences: "Ephesus Blitzkriegs Syracuse." Only the terminally stuffy will be offended by this good-natured hilarity.

The celebrated Cole Porter *Kiss Me Kate*, which remains a perennial stage hit famous for such witty lyrics as "Brush up your Shakespeare," represents another backstage story. Except for its being a musical, it could as logically be classified with derivatives of the second kind. Squabbling actors Fred Graham (Howard Keel) and Killi Vanessa (Kathryn Grayson) mirror the stormy behavior of Kate and Petruchio in *The Taming of the Shrew*. Similarly the movie of *West Side Story* evolves from previous stage incarnations. With music and lyrics by Leonard Bernstein and Stephen Sondheim, and extensive choreography by Jerome Robbins, it transforms Romeo Montague and Juliet Capulet into Tony and Maria, pawns in a struggle between warring street gangs in a New York City slum. Compared to today's hip-hop street thugs and punks, the gang members in *West Side Story* look like choir boys, but the movie's powerful linkage of Shakespeare's play with modern youth culture has been copied since then in Franco Zeffirelli's *Romeo and Juliet* and Baz Luhrmann's recent *Romeo & Juliet* (1996). Yet another musical treatment of Shakespeare that came to film via the stage is *Catch My Soul: Santa Fe Satan* (1973), a musical of *Othello* that first played in London as a rock opera in the voguish style of *Jesus Christ Superstar* and *Hair*. Later, Patrick McGoohan, who also appeared in *All Night Long*, made it into a movie, which is set a long way from Piccadilly in the New Mexico desert. In this derivative, Othello is a black cult leader (Richie Havens), while Desdemona (Season Hubley) is a round-faced white girl with granny glasses. Emilia turns into a raffish looking hippie, and Iago fits all negative stereotypes for dropouts with his scruffy beard and unwashed look. The plot follows Shakespeare's quite closely with the scene when the church burns down standing in for Cassio's drunken brawl, and Iago tormenting Othello with innuendoes about Desdemona's interest in Cassio (Tony Joe White). Iago's immortal ploy for generating paranoia, "Hah? I like not that" (3.3.35), remains intact. As the evil Santa Fe Satan, Iago manipulates Othello into smothering Desdemona while the Moor's "Put out the light, and then put out the light" (5.2.7) pulsates in electronic rock rhythms.

The fourth kind uses a biography or a documentary as the rationale for doing scenes from the plays. *The Royal Box* (1930), where Alexander Moissi as Edmund Kean plays a scene from Hamlet with Camilla Horn as Ophelia, furnishes an early example. As Edwin Booth in *Prince of Players* (1954), Richard Burton performs as Romeo, Hamlet, and Richard duke of Gloucester. His strong personality, especially as Richard III, reminds everyone that in Shakespeare movies all the talk about technical problems, camera angles, *découpage*, and so forth, is so much rubbish without a gifted actor of Burton's caliber. An all-time favorite must be Vincent Price's *Theatre of Blood* (1973), which ingeniously mines the canon for horrible murders. An aging Shakespeare actor, Edward Lionheart (Vincent Price), embittered by hostile reviews, sets out with the help of his balmy daughter (Diana Rigg) to avenge himself on the critics who have made his life miserable. He chooses to murder them with the methods used in Shakespeare's plays, which turns the movie into a veritable quiz show as the audience guesses which Shakespearean play is being quoted. One arrogant critic is stabbed like Julius Caesar; another, drowned in wine like Clarence in *Richard III*; yet another finds himself eating his pet poodles in a baked pie like Tamora in *Titus Andronicus*, and so forth. Sometimes this category may take the shape of a documentary such as Al Pacino's imaginative *Looking for Richard* (1996) in which Pacino constructs a documentary about Shakespeare's Richard duke of Gloucester and unifies the different interviews with actors, with scholars, and people on the street by means of powerfully acted segments from the play. As an actor who has played Richard twice on stage and who, as noted above, clearly quoted from *King Lear* at the ending of *Godfather III*, Pacino wants to share his bardolatry with others. His purity of motive in rendering a votive offering to Shakespeare suffuses the whole film and makes it utterly delightful. Never talking down to the audience, Pacino adopts a Socratic pose of ignorance to win it over. His street interviews with surprised New Yorkers "stand as an engaging documentary about the relevance of Shakespeare to 90s culture."[62] As the actors sit around a table rehearsing in a Manhattan office, the casual situation develops its own dynamic, with glorious moments when one actress gives an extraordinary reading of Queen Elizabeth's lines. Pacino shows his own skills in the first wooing scene as he pursues Lady Anne (Winona Ryder) over the corpse of her deceased father-in-law at New York City's The Cloisters. Janet Maslin rightly thought that no major Shakespeare film could match this low-budget endeavor for "irresistible zeal."[63]

As for the fifth kind, derivatives that use only fragments of Shakespeare that are not deeply embedded in the film's main plot, the canon is lengthy and overwhelming. In the silent era, for example, Buster Keaton in *Day Dreams* (1922) imagined himself in Walter Mitty style as an actor playing Hamlet.[64] Two early revue-type talkies used Shakespeare. A charismatic John Barrymore performed Gloucester's soliloquy from *King Henry Sixth Part Three* in the early talkie revue, *Show of Shows* (1929), which critics felt was the stand-out performance from among "76 stars, a chorus of 500, 18 songs and fifteen specialty acts";[65] John Gilbert and Norma Shearer played the balcony scene from *Romeo and Juliet* in *The Hollywood Revue of 1929*. Later, Katharine Hepburn as a tipsy ingénue recited the "To be or not to be" soliloquy and fragments of Juliet's balcony speech at a stuffy party in *Morning Glory* (1933);[66] the drunken actor (Alan Mowbray) in an Arizona saloon spoke a soliloquy from *Hamlet* under duress by the Clanton gang in the John Ford western *My Darling Clementine* (1946); Karidian Players do *Hamlet* for the crew in an episode of *Star Trek*, called *The Conscience of the King* (1966); try-outs for a show in *Fame* (1980) feature Shakespeare recitations; Robin Williams directs the school play of *Midsummer Night's Dream* for his entranced pupils in *The Dead Poets Society* (1989); Steve Martin wittily spoofs the *Hamlet* graveyard scene in *L.A. Story* (1991); and Danny DeVito teaches an unlikely class of army recruits about the glories of *Hamlet* in *Renaissance Man* (1994). A thorough treatment of the unwieldy subject would need a book far lengthier than this one.[67]

The derivative of the sixth kind appears in the animations of Shakespeare's plays, which began as early as 1920 with Anson Dyer's black-and-white cartoon of *Othello* for Cecil Hepworth. In what is for the times a technical *tour de force*, a black-faced Minstrel falls in love with Mona, the daughter of a bath house proprietor. Richard Burton and Alec McCowen supplied voices for Czech animator Jir' Trnka's feature-length *Midsummer Night's Dream* (*Sen noci svatojánské*, 1959). The recent Disney *The Lion King* (1994) with its overtones from *Hamlet* took in millions at the box office despite fears that its "sexist, racist, [and] homophobic" overtones might upset the very young.[68] A recent series, aimed at schools, "Shakespeare: The Animated Tales," scripted in Wales and animated in Moscow, with scenarios by Leon Garfield and the advice of Shakespeare scholar Stanley Wells, offer brilliantly executed thirty-minute versions of the plays with voices by well-known British actors. Laurie Osborne's definitive essay likens their cultural impact today to the *Tales from Shakespeare* (1807) by Charles and Mary Lamb that gripped the imaginations of Victorian children. Osborne explores in depth the technical challenges underlying the creation of the cartoons, cites their allusions to more conventional Shakespeare movies, and comments on how animations of Shakespeare's plays "can and should be culturally positioned."[69]

The derivative of the seventh kind, mainly educational and documentary and more often than not made for television, again represents too vast a landscape for consideration here, ranging everywhere from *Discovering Hamlet* (1990) with Derek Jacobi directing Branagh in rehearsal as the prince, to John Barton's *Playing Shakespeare* series (1984) on acting the plays.[70] Needless to say, they often egregiously overlap with all of the above categories, particularly the fifth, the "revue" picture. They also satisfy "tickling commodity" by generating considerable income from the insatiable demand of schools and universities for the products of the Shakespeare industry.

Beyond all classifications, way beyond the fringe, lie Shakespeare movies of no kind, which are a sub-class of hard-core pornography. To say they are beyond the pale is only to risk offending marginalized deviants, or looking priggish twenty years from now when western civilization may have completely collapsed. The borderline between the cinema of transgression (art) and pornography (smut) has eluded definition even by the United States Supreme Court. A few Shakespeare movies dwell in the suburbs. *Playboy* magazine produced a soft-core *Twelfth Night* (1972), directed by Ron Wertheim for its television program, "Playboy at Night." There have also been a "hard-core" *Romeo and Juliet* (1987), directed by Paul Thomas, in which Juliet and Romeo "end up having sex on stage," as well as a sequel, *Romeo and Juliet 2*. Other risqué titles include *Hamlet: For the Love of Ophelia* (1996) featuring porn star Sarah Young as the object of Hamlet's lust, *A Mid-Slumber Night's Dream* and reportedly a *Much Ado about Humping*.[71] Most recently commercial theatres in London saw a widely released *Tromeo and Juliet* (1996) made by Troma Pictures, which specializes in not just transgressive but outrageously transgressive films. Kim Newman has acidly observed that "Lloyd Kaufman's Troma pictures (essentially a one-man outfit) works so hard at degeneracy and self-delighted crassness that it's a miracle they have never made a good film."[72] Supposedly a redeeming element is that Shakespeare's dialogue is firmly separated from its grossest episodes, but even that hope is blasted with such inanities as "What light from yonder plexiglass shines?" At this point the distance from the Shakespearean vision is so vast that the label must be something like Shakespeare movies of no kind whatsoever. And yet no kind may turn out to be some kind, after all.

- 10 -

The renaissance of Shakespeare
in moving images

Towards the end of the century, beginning with Kenneth Branagh's *Henry V* (1989), the multi-million-dollar Shakespeare movie underwent a powerful resurgence. The 1990s renaissance had deeper roots of course than in the commendable energies of Kenneth Branagh alone. He and others benefited from the movie industry's rising fortunes, whose shrinking box-office receipts were reversed by the development of the multiplex. Theatre owners followed the customers out of the cities and into the suburbs with multi-screen theatres in shopping malls, sometimes on the same acreage that had once been taken up with drive-in movies. Unlike the old single-screen picture palaces, the multi-screened cineplex offered a wide variety of choices congenial to both highbrow and lowbrow tastes, and it also made movie going almost as easy as sitting at home slumped in front of the VCR. The dress protocols and uniformed ushers of the old Palace theatres no longer existed, and in North America T-shirts, jeans and baseball caps became the fashion statement for movie going. A Shakespeare film stood a better chance of securing a niche in this open market, especially if it was packaged with big-name stars and state-of-the-art sight and sound.

The Loncraine/McKellen *Richard III*

Investors were courageous enough to put up $8.5 million for Ian McKellen's brilliant modernization of *Richard III* (1996). Like Zeffirelli, McKellen was determined to make Shakespeare entertaining without concessions to either *hoi polloi* or the elite.[1] His Richard does not quite capture the sly wit in the serio-comic medieval vice figure, which Olivier mastered in the 1955 version, but McKellen is otherwise in a reptilian kind of way as certifiably diabolic. Like Olivier's movie a costume drama, its milieu has been reset from the corrupt, late medieval world of the Yorkists and Lancastrians into the age of the Duke of Windsor and Wallace Warfield Simpson. British upper middle-class 1930s society with its mannequin women, opulent surroundings, and ruthless politics have been recreated in a style that McKellen described as "heightened reality."[2] It might also be thought of as "enhanced but ironic realism." As James N. Loehlin suggests, the irony seeps through in a self-mockery nested away in the standard visual codes for upper-class "Englishness,"[3] often labeled the "heritage" look. While the gap between England as it is and as it is represented in this romanticized view may induce cognitive dissonance in British intellectuals, Americans who watch Sunday-night mini-series like *The Jewel in the Crown* on public television see it as the fulfillment of all their cherished stereotypes about the English upper classes, whom they secretly admire. While the ballroom scene is quintessentially "heritage," the movie also quotes from the John Woo action movie, documentary newsreels, traces of the gangster movie, tropes from Dennis Potter's television scripts, and in some sequences, a destabilizing mix of realism and surrealism reminiscent of a Luis Buñuel movie like *The Discreet Charm of the Bourgeoisie* (1972). That is to say, there are elements of nightmare and the grotesque, as in the dream when Richard sees himself with a boar's head, or the parade of ghosts on the eve of Bosworth. Most macabre, though, is a low-angle shot of Hastings' body as it hurtles down from the gallows, the sickening jerk as the rope catches his neck, his body spinning and twisting just above the audience's heads. The Dennis Potter trick from *The Singing Detective* of backing up Michael Gambon's serious moments with contra-puntal popular music surfaces in the grim mortuary after the battle, where Richard skips and hops to a jazzy off-camera tune. At the end of the movie when the satanic Richard tumbles downward into the fiery pit, and Al Jolson's voice is overlaid singing "I'm sitting on top of the world," the enhanced realism turns bitterly ironic.

McKellen and director Richard Loncraine, forced to economize on settings, ingeniously made a virtue out of necessity with brilliant use of ready-made locations in Greater London, though Samuel Crowl preferred the symbolic and suggestive settings of the 1990 National Theatre stage play to Loncraine's "relentlessly realistic" film.[4] The exterior of Bankside Power Station near the site of the New Globe Theatre becomes a convincing Tower of London, redesignated as simply "The Tower"; the vast decaying Victorian railway hotel at St. Pancras station on Euston Road, Buckingham Palace; the basement of a vacant insurance building in Holborn, a mortuary for the body of Prince Edward; the Long Gallery at Brighton Pavilion, a drawing room; the abandoned Battersea Power station, the battlefield at Bosworth, and so forth. Happily sound mixer David Stephenson[5] managed to filter out the traffic noises that plagued the Edzard *As You Like It* on its urban wasteland.

To displace Shakespeare's controversial King Richard into a twentieth-century social and political context, McKellen hit on the year 1936 as being neither too remote from, nor too close to, contemporary concerns. McKellen's

23   Kenneth Branagh as the beleaguered young warrior/monarch in *King Henry V* (UK 1989), directed by Kenneth Branagh.

duke of Gloucester combines the ferocity of Adolf Hitler with the suaveness of Juan Peron, as imagined in *Evita*. He sports smartly tailored uniforms with the boar's head insignia and addresses the hypnotized masses from a lofty podium festooned with banners. The deep circles under his eyes and the pencil-thin moustache emblemize his dual persona of a great lover like Clark Gable in fantasy and a loathsome creep in reality. McKellen explains Lady Anne's abrupt capitulation to Richard in the first wooing scene as purely mercenary, a necessary step to shore up her income, analogous to the widowed Jacqueline Kennedy's marriage to Aristotle Onassis.[6]

No Shakespearean play has a more confusing story line than *Richard III* and only one (*Hamlet*) is lengthier. Few but specialists can readily untangle the tangle of relationships among the warring factions in the play. Like many other directors, McKellen has generally followed Colley Cibber's formula of employing bridging materials from *The Third Part of Henry VI* to sort out the power struggle among the unpleasant descendants of King Edward III (1312–77). Because the play is impossibly lengthy, Queen Margaret, the Lancastrian "she-wolf of France," mother of the murdered Henry VI, had to be cut to keep the audience on the edge of their seats. With Margaret went the choric diatribes against Richard, though McKellen gives some of them to the Duchess of York (Maggie Smith), who closely resembles Queen Mary in scratchy 1930s newsreels.

In the opening scene, a Yorkist tank smashes into the headquarters of Edward Prince of Wales's Lancastrian army. Richard duke of Gloucester, disguised by a gas mask, calmly executes the young prince, who wears the well-tailored uniform of a British army officer, and then cold-bloodedly shoots King Henry VI in his bedroom. Soon after, Richard triumphantly returns to London to a glittering ballroom filled with kings and queens, princes and princesses, and lesser aristocracy, where he delivers the famous opening soliloquy, "Now is the winter of our discontent / Made glorious summer by this son of York" (1.1.1). After the harrowing gangster-style executions of the Lancastrians, the sumptuous Victory Ball comes as a culture shock and furnishes the "gilt" to cover up the "guilt" of what is now Yorkist, but once had been Lancastrian, villainy: "England shall double gild his treble guilt" (2 *Henry IV* 4.5.128). A twenty-piece band led by a Glen Miller lookalike plays on the dais behind music stands emblazoned with the letters "WS." A female vocalist (Stacey Kent) warbles Trevor Jones's "Come live with me and be my love" so slickly arranged that the anachronism of the Christopher Marlowe lyrics set to a catchy 30s tune goes unnoticed. On the ballroom floor, the king (John Wood) and his American queen (Annette Bening) foxtrot to the applause and admiration of the exquisitely gowned ladies and their white-tie-and-tails, or baroquely uniformed, escorts. This sophisticated, worldly, elegant but heartless society would not be unhappy with a monarch, or an Adolf Hitler, who kept the labor unions and undeserving poor in their places.

Subliminal references to Shakespeare's play flash across the screen. Preparing for the ball, the notoriously lecherous but now sickly King Edward gropes at the thigh of the nurse attending on him. ("Lascivious Edward, and thou perjur'd George, / And thou misshapen Dick" says Prince Edward of Lancaster just before being stabbed by Edward, George [Clarence], and Dick [Richard] (3 *Henry VI* 5.5.37).) The Princess Elizabeth (Kate Steavenson-Payne), who is a non-speaking character in Shakespeare's play, shows her pleasure in being introduced to her future husband, Henry Richmond (Dominic West), a young naval officer and future Tudor King Henry VII. McKellen's clue for the concept of Richmond as a naval officer came from

Lord Stanley's unsettling news that "Richmond is on the seas" (4.4.462).[7] In another astute move, Queen Elizabeth's Woodville brother, Earl Rivers (Robert Downey, Jr.), is imagined as an American playboy, who appears at the ball after arriving on PanAm from New York. Later Tyrell (Adrian Dunbar) stabs him with a phallic knife while he is performing an X-rated sex scene in bed with the airline hostess (Tres Hanley). In Shakespeare's play the outsider Woodville relatives of the widowed queen, by supporting the succession to the crown of her son, the older of the two little princes, earn the hostility of wily Richard, who schemes for the crown himself. As an American, McKellen's Queen Elizabeth shows what might have happened in England if Wallis Warfield Simpson, perish the thought, had become King Edward's queen, and brought her relatives to the court.

To keep things moving (as Zeffirelli did with Claudius' first speech in his *Hamlet*), McKellen divides the opening soliloquy up and resituates the segments. He announces from the bandstand that this is "Now . . . the winter of our discontent," to the applause of the champagne-sipping audience, and he continues in the men's room, where he admires himself in the mirror on the wall near the urinals. The face in the mirror is a triumph of make-up artistry with enormous circles under the eyes, a thin moustache, and a slightly puffy cheek. He walks with a limp and has a noticeable hump on his shoulder in the stage tradition of a Richard "crook-back" (*3 Henry VI* 2.2.96), a "foul misshapen stigmatic" (2.2.136), whose physical deformity outwardly and visibly indexes a malignant soul. Then he addresses both himself in the mirror and the theatre audience with the chilling words transposed from *Henry VI Part Three*, "Why, I can smile, and murther whiles I smile" (3.2.182), before returning to the glitzy ballroom, which is now exposed as an elaborate stage set for Richard's power trip.

To further capture the flavor of the 1930s, Ian McKellen chainsmokes "Abdullas" in a virtuoso performance that adds yet another chapter to movie "cigarette semiology,"[8] almost at the level of world-class nicotine addicts like Bette Davis and Humphrey Bogart. His cigarettes become expressive objects, surrogates to his need for human affection, as he caresses, pats, taps, and puffs on them. When, after Hastings' execution, he gloats over obscene pictures of the hanging he is also mimicking one of Adolf Hitler's less agreeable pastimes, except that *der Führer*, the better to enjoy his victims' writhings from slow strangulation, preferred motion to still pictures. In a tell-tale moment, Lady Anne in the privacy of her limousine injects a needle into her thigh, which signals her own addiction, brought on by her fatal relationship with Richard. She dies horribly with a spider crossing her motionless face, presumably the victim of some dastardly intervention by Richard, though Shakespeare never clarifies this point.

Loncraine's *Richard III* met with the wildly varied reception that seems to be the fate of most Shakespeare films, Shakespeare purists having been joined by film purists, who are equally elitist and impossible to please. Two intelligent and knowledgeable critics writing in the same newspaper concluded that the film was (a) "a pathetic pastiche of transplantations," and (b) "opulent and hypnotic."[9] The *New Yorker* critic put the film down with clever sound bites about a "time-travel experiment gone wrong."[10] Most reactions, however, were more like that of Brian Gilbey, who even after complaining that the film is "more concerned with visuals than with verse" also confessed that not "any of this really matters."[11] As James Cameron-Wilson put it, "The film's terrific . . . McKellen has taken us by the scruff of the neck and shaken it into a cinematic context,"[12] and David Gritten thought it was "a piece of cinema in its own right, emphatically not a filmed version of a stage play."[13] Critics heaped scorn on Richard's uttering "A horse, a horse! My kingdom for a horse!" (5.4.13) while anachronistically riding in a jeep. Yet omitting the best-known line in the play would have stirred up even more of a tempest. In truth, old army types, World War II cavalrymen like General George Patton, an avid polo player, often nostalgically yearned for a horse while seated in a jeep. If, as has been argued, McKellen and Loncraine have done nothing original with the play, they have most certainly made an original *movie* out of it, one of the best of its kind.

Parker's *Othello*

While critics accused the Loncraine/McKellen *Richard III* of being too cinematic and insufficiently Shakespearean, the Oliver Parker *Othello* of the same year (1995) was indicted for the opposite crime. It was too theatrical and insufficiently cinematic.[14] Although not so "filmic" as Orson Welles's *Othello*, only a step away from theatre actually, it nevertheless goes beyond the merely presentational. While Parker's lighting and camera angles, his *mise-en-scène*, seem cautiously theatrical, his editing shows a talent for telling a story visually. The opening montage clarifies the vague pronoun reference, "this," in the first line of *Othello*, when Roderigo says to Iago "[Tush,] never tell me! I take it much unkindly / That thou Iago, who hast had my purse / As if the strings were thine, shouldst know of *this*" [italics mine] (1.1.1). This what? Parker replies in pictures. The clichéd establishing shot of a gondola in Venice actually shows Desdemona en route to her elopement with Othello. Then, in another invented scene, Desdemona steps out of the gondola and runs down a long piazza, while in the foreground a concealed Iago and Roderigo peer at her. She stops wide-eyed in a doorway greeting someone, who later turns out to be Othello.

The film jumps ahead to scene three at the palace where the duke and his counselors are evaluating the threat from the Turkish fleet and examining a map of the Mediterranean showing the enemy fleet deployment: "The Turkish preparation makes for Rhodes" (1.3.14), and it is decided that Othello must lead the Venetians against the enemy. In tight framing, two hands clasp, one black and one white, and one hand places a ring on the other, after which the camera pulls back to show a priest officiating over the marriage of Othello and Desdemona. The camera pulls even further back to reveal Roderigo peering through the window and spying on the marriage between Desdemona and Othello. A cut back to Shakespeare's opening lines has Iago (Kenneth Branagh) and Roderigo (Michael Maloney) reviling Othello with racist epithets ("the thick-lips," "lascivious moor"), and tormenting Brabantio with the news that "an old black ram / Is tupping your white ewe" (1.1.98). A glimpse of Cassio (Nathaniel Parker), throws kerosene on Iago's fiery contempt for "One Michael Cassio a Florentine" (1.1.20).[15] Next, there is Desdemona's irate father, Brabantio, leading a posse of angry citizens toward the ducal palace to lodge a complaint against the Moor. This intricate montage has explained much of what is behind the single pronoun, "this." Desdemona has eloped with Othello; Iago is a hate-filled malcontent; Roderigo is Iago's puppet; Brabantio is outraged by his daughter's marriage; Venice is at risk from an approaching Turkish fleet; and Othello's services as a *condottiero* are needed in Cyprus.

Not untidy like *Richard III*, *Othello* has the focused plot and characters of a classical tragedy. Parker's aim was to foreground the love affair of Othello (Laurence Fishburne) and Desdemona (Irène Jacob) and to downplay Iago (Kenneth Branagh). Critics nevertheless found the movie "Iago-centric," as if the talented Branagh had totally stolen the show, even though Fishburne[16] contributes a massive dignity and physical presence. Egg bald and covered with bracelets and earrings, he most resembles Sergei Bondarchuk in the Yutkevich *Othello*. His Desdemona projects a wonderful innocence and sweetness, which her slight Swiss accent makes all the more endearing. In the movie's boldest stroke, it pries into the connubial activities of Othello and Desdemona, a topic that Shakespeare avoids and that scholars have mostly averted their eyes from. When, if ever, the literal-minded have asked, did the happy pair consummate their marriage? There was little time for dalliance since they were abruptly dispatched to Cyprus on separate vessels, and Cassio's drunken brawl egregiously interrupted their first night together. Steamy boudoir footage of Othello and Desdemona resolves the mystery when in close-up Othello removes the leather belt from around his waist, and in a long shot Desdemona opposite him provocatively disrobes. Elements of "heteroc," as Derek Jarman might call them, include a paranoid Othello's porn fantasies about Desdemona and Cassio frolicking in bed; and a Iago discoursing to Roderigo on the subject of "Lechery, by this hand; an index and obscure prologue to the history of lust and foul thoughts" (2.1.257), while they sit under a wagon occupied by two copulating Cyprians. A very nice touch has Iago observing Cassio through the reflected image from a knife blade as "He takes her by the palm" (2.1.167) immediately after disembarkation in Cyprus.

Fishburne's and Jacob's success by no means detracts from Branagh's skilful Iago that demands an actor capable of simultaneously projecting overt bonhomie and covert malice. Olivier's Iago, Frank Finlay, mastered the difficult trick, but most actors tend to be too genial for serious villainy. Kenneth Branagh juggles this Janus-like stance mainly by a knack for timing that suggests he is speaking very reluctantly even when he is actually falling all over himself to slander Cassio and Desdemona. He adds to that a gift for facial expressions, often in collusion with the audience, that clearly signal his innate vileness. Parker's tight shots and deft camera movements support the acting talents of the principals by, for example, zooming in on Iago's moving lips as they telegraph his perfidious intentions. More interested in interpreting Shakespeare's play than in indulging in cinematic rhetoric, Parker pays no attention to the fashionable vogue for a homoerotic attraction between Iago and Othello. On the other hand, the camera dutifully records the progress of the play's most famous expressive object, the handkerchief, as it is passed along from Emilia to Iago to Bianca. Covered with the strawberry marks that also appear on Desdemona's wedding sheets, the fetish handkerchief floats aloft as a surrealistic image of its terrible powers. Michael Maloney, who even threatens Iago with a knife, plays Roderigo as surprisingly truculent, not at all the gullible wimp. After his particularly nasty murder, blood spills out of his mouth just before a jump cut to Othello extinguishing a row of candles firmly connects the two masques of death. All the more dreadful in its cold-blooded moralizing, Othello's self-righteous "It is the cause, it is the cause, my soul" (5.2.1) initiates the ritual of Desdemona's demise. Surprisingly, the angelic Desdemona does not go quietly into the night, but fiercely resists the bullying Othello, and fights desperately for her life. Once exposed by Emilia, Iago invokes his obstinate silence: "Demand me nothing; what you know, you know: / From this time forth I never will speak word" (5.2.303). The bodies of Iago's victims, Emilia, Othello, and Desdemona, lie side by side on display, bathed in sunlight from an opened window, literally illustrating "the tragic loading of [the] bed" (5.2.363). A somber burial at sea replaces the grand funeral cortège in the Welles *Othello,* or the mob scene in the piazza in the silent Emil Jannings *Othello.* Perhaps Lodovico who has gone "straight aboard" to return to Venice, has arranged for this consummation of a marriage in death even if not in life. Parker has used his license as a movie maker to embellish the Othello story with one more vignette.

Nunn's *Twelfth Night*

Trevor Nunn's $5-million *Twelfth Night* (1996) added yet another mainstream Shakespeare movie to the glittering array of late twentieth-century offerings. By far the best screen treatment since the John Sichel 1970 British television version starring Alec Guinness (Malvolio), Joan Plowright (Viola), and Ralph Richardson (Sir Toby Belch), in its world-weariness and rather fashionable despair it ironically replicates the *fin-de-siècle* mood of the late nineteenth century. Kenneth Branagh's description of his own Renaissance Theatre *Twelfth Night* as "close[r] to Chekhov"[17] applies equally well to Trevor Nunn's, which shares a bitter-sweet melancholy and nostalgia with *Uncle Vanya* and *The Cherry Orchard.* Just as *Twelfth Night, or What You Will,* first performed around 1600, probably either at the court or at one of the Inns of Court, marks the end of Shakespeare's festive comedies and the beginning of the darker period of city comedies and tragedies, so the Christian feast day of "Twelfth Night" (January 6) terminates the Twelve Days of Christmas, and shadows forth Lent.

Nunn does not allow any of the potentially serious subtext to spoil the fun of a good movie, which is about "what you will," though as a veteran stage director he admits to having expected an "imminent thunderbolt" as he "tampered" with Shakespeare's language to convert it into a film scenario.[18] The fashionably melancholy Illyrians in their desire for love, and frustration in not being loved, reflect various stages of order and disorder, with little Viola/Cesario at the still center of a whirligig of emotions. Nunn fleshes out Shakespeare's plot with two major additions. The first, a *Titanic* trope, imagines Viola (Imogen Stubbs) and Sebastian (Stephen Mackintosh) in the dining salon of a nineteenth-century passenger vessel on the edge of doom. It is the last night out and at the captain's party the brother and sister, costumed as Moslem women with yashmaks, are entertaining the first-class passengers with a duet of "O mistress mine." When they remove their veils, Viola is sporting a moustache like Sebastian's. The full implications of this cross-dressing are suspended when the ship founders in a wild storm, and pandemonium erupts. Convincing special effects spill Viola into the briny sea and show her struggling for survival under water. The second addition occurs when she comes out of the ocean to crawl ashore on the seacoast of Illyria, and asks "And what should I do in Illyria?" (1.2.3). The answer must be that she should keep a very low profile, for Nunn has added the twist that her native Messaline and Illyria have long been at war, a motif copied from contentious ancient cities of Syracuse and Ephesus in *The Comedy of Errors*. Unfortunately this added plot element also robs Viola of some of the mystery that Shakespeare surrounded her with, and turns Illyria into a police state. Much later, in a touch of whimsy when Sebastian comes ashore in this now hostile territory, he carries a copy of the *Baedeker Guidebook to Illyria*.

Nunn's cross-cutting supports the cross-dressing that is so much a part of the play, and undercuts beliefs that the movie favors the theatrical over the filmic. Viola and Olivia (Helena Bonham Carter) mirror each other in their grief for lost brothers and in their quest to find substitute males.The camera explores the gender anxieties brought on by Orsino's falling in love with a boy, and Olivia's infatuation with the same man/woman. As Nunn has said, this is "the most fundamental Shakespearean play about sexuality and gender,"[19] featuring as it does identical twins of opposite gender. As the cross-dressed Viola/Cesario, Imogen Stubbs interrogates the feminist fantasy that being male can resolve all female problems. Under the watchful eye of the sea captain, she wraps herself like a mummy to flatten her bosom, and stuffs cloth into her trousers to conceal how much she "lack[s] of a man" (3.4.303). Putting on a brave front for Orsino, as the newly invented Cesario she takes up horseback riding, billiards, fencing, learns to walk like a man with hands in pockets, and, hilariously, to puff on a cigar in a macho kind of way, though the latter rite almost finishes her off. The fencing lessons pay off when, for possibly the first time in the play's performance history, she manages a respectable sword fight against the terrified Sir Andrew Aguecheek. When Viola delivers the poignant set-piece to Olivia beginning, "Make me a willow cabin at your gate" (1.5.268), she really does make Olivia's name "reverberate [into the] hills." Helena Bonham Carter in her regal black Victorian mourning dress, and then later when she swoons over Cesario, in a pre-Raphaelite turquoise gown, brings high fashion to the P.G. Wodehouse country-house setting. Meanwhile little Viola must be content with a pert but unadorned military tunic. The sea is never far away. As Samuel Crowl has pointed out,[20] Nunn integrates the play's water imagery by having the world-weary Orsino (Toby Stephens) compare the capacity of love with the sea (1.1.10), by placing Orsino's home directly at the sea, in Cornwall actually, and then by having Viola miraculously come out of the sea. Later on Viola says cryptically, "Tempests are kind and salt waves fresh in love" (3.4.384).

Like Falstaff in *The Merry Wives of Windsor*, the merry pranksters, Sir Toby Belch (Mel Smith), Maria (Imelda Staunton), Fabian (Peter Gunn), and Sir Andrew Aguecheek (Richard E. Grant), end up looking somewhat more boorish than funny. When the grumpy Malvolio (Nigel Hawthorne) attempts to break up the midnight revelry, Sir Toby scathingly puts him down with his famous one-liner, "Art any more than a steward? Dost thou think because thou art virtuous there shall be no more cakes and ale?" (2.3.114). Wholesale deletions of the badinage, punning, quibbling, and bawdry from this lin-guistically rich play work against Sir Toby, but no modern audience could possibly decode, for example, the labyrinthine puns on "hang," "colors," and "none" in act one, scene five. A tight frame of Maria's yellow stockings dur-ing Malvolio's row with Sir Toby hints at a major element in Malvolio's future martyrdom.

Nigel Hawthorne masterfully plays the scapegoated Malvolio with an air of "injured majesty,"[21] reminiscent of his film role as King George III. At the end of the play, having escaped the dark house, but having been further rejected and humiliated in front of the entire household staff, Feste mali-ciously baits him, "And thus the whirligig of time brings in his revenges" (5.1.376). Olivia says that Malvolio has been "most notoriously abus'd" but he remains unmollified and stomps out of the house carrying a pathetic suit-case. Hawthorne energetically ferrets out the hidden speck of humanity in Malvolio's shriveled soul, yet the film leaves little doubt that Malvolio will one day have his revenge "on the whole pack" of them. While some critics have deplored his sobriety, Feste (Ben Kingsley) frames the film with his "hey ho, the wind and the rain" (5.1.389), whose haunting words, which also become the Fool's in *King Lear* (3.2.74), warn against the consequences of folly, indeed, of doing "what you will." At the height of the fraternity house roistering with Sir Toby and Maria, an aloof Feste renders a heartfelt solo of "O mistress mine, where are you roaming?" (2.3.39), which is all the more compelling for its rugged amateurism. When he reaches "Then come kiss me, sweet and twenty; / Youth's a stuff will not endure," Maria senses the deep pathos and her face crumbles almost into tears. Kingsley's somber tone reflects a major streak of sobriety in *Twelfth Night,* which the late Harry Levin once encapsulated in the remark that "the cakes and ale of Illyria are con-sumed in a house of mourning."[22] In *Twelfth Night*, Shakespeare created a verbal structure that probes the sadness and sweetness in the mystery of life, and Nunn has gracefully and wittily put that daunting challenge into mov-ing images.

Luhrmann's *Romeo & Juliet*

Baz Luhrmann's Generation-X *William Shakespeare's Romeo & Juliet* (1996) makes Franco Zeffirelli's *Romeo and Juliet* (1968) look stodgy by comparison. The film rhetoric in Luhrmann's screenplay introduces terms undreamt of thirty years ago, like "Whip Pan," "Super Macro Slam Zoom," "Chopper P.O.V.," "Window Cam," "Distorted Out-of-Control Close-up," and even a "Slow Motion: Washing Machine Tumble Shot."[23] This is watching Shakespeare's *Romeo and Juliet* under strobe lights. It has been filtered through John Woo's Hong Kong action movies, and the hiphop and gangsta rap of MTV, yet the characters speak in Elizabethan English. The verbal runs against the grain of the visual semiotics. Yes, it is odd to hear Romeo say "O me! what fray was here?" (1.1.173) after a violent explosion in a gasoline station, but once the ear adjusts, it becomes a probable improbability. The flat American voices lack the stagy sonorities of John Gielgud but carry fierce conviction. There is absolutely nothing new about putting Shakespeare in modern dress but dressing him in the jeans and T-shirts and pierced bodies of the MTV generation ratchets the transgressiveness up a notch. It was Lurhmann's intention "to make this movie rambunctious, sexy, violent, and entertaining the way Shakespeare might have if he had been a filmmaker."[24] Janet Maslin summed up a general critical attitude of dismay combined with admiration: "This is headache Shakespeare, but there's method to its madness."[25]

For music, Luhrmann scraps Zeffirelli's variations on a single theme from Nino Rota's "What Is a Youth?" in favor of a mélange of pop singers and bands to include Garbage, Everclear, One Inch Punch, Butthole Surfers, The Wannadies, almost everybody, one might say, except the Screaming Headless Torsos. And yet the soundtrack can no more be stereotyped than the scenario for at pivotal intervals when Romeo is first introduced, or in the tomb scene, a graceful passage from Mozart or Wagner's *Liebestod* captures the mood. Luhrmann's movie also eschews Zeffirelli's heightened realism in an Italian hill town for the constructed world of a never-never land of Verona, partly filmed in Mexico City but as placeless in many ways as the set for a sci-fi movie. The great statue of Jesus looms over the action, a rebuke to the city's warring factions and a surrogate for the golden statue that in a variation on the Midas myth one day will memorialize the martyred Juliet.

In a major conceit, Luhrmann inserts the sonnet prologue within the frame of a television screen, giving the speech to the anchorwoman on the evening news. The anchorwoman's formulaic reading of the evening news replaces the formal three-quatrains-and-a-couplet Elizabethan sonnet as a symbol of oppression. When Romeo says "O me, what fray was here?" he is actually witnessing a derivative replay of the rioting between Capulets and Montagues on a television monitor. The new challenge for the young is not to break out of the formal restraints of the sonnet into blank verse as Juliet does with "Gallop apace, you fiery-footed steeds" (3.2.1), and her equally compelling but horrifying potion speech, "What if it be poison which the friar / Subtilly hath minist'red to have me dead [?]" (4.3.24), but to escape from television's straitjacket of mass conformity. Like nothing else in history, the tube has the power to manipulate ordinary people into confusing reality with fantasy to the extent of having them emotionally identify with celebrities that they have never laid eyes on, nor ever will. The film's blurring together of the multiple planes of perception in the world of the audience, the world of the movie, of the illusory television newscast, which is so easily confused with an actual newscast, gets as bewildering as Shakespeare's own meta-dramatic taste for putting plays within plays within plays.

The interplay between the crude actualities of television newscasts and MTV fantasies generates the film's *raison d'être*, which is the displacement into contemporary idiom of the oxymorons of Shakespeare's oppositions of womb and tomb, love and death, youth and age, and so forth. The gap between profane and sacred love is everywhere. The Verona sea shore, as littered as a Sicilian beach, is a showcase of tawdriness, a hangout for prostitutes, where a decaying theatrical stage with a Globe theatre marquee underscores the gap between the majesty of the sea and the tackiness of the polluted beach. The machine has invaded the garden in the shape of sleek automobiles, beatup jalopies, and roaring motorcycles.

The sacred love of the teenagers, Leonardo DiCaprio and Claire Danes, counterpoints this profane disease and corruption. Like all youthful Romeos and Juliets, they are accused of not being up to the challenge. Rex Reed thought that neither "has a clue to what they are saying, or what Shakespeare is all about," moreover DiCaprio has "raw talent, no discipline or training, and a spectacular stupidity."[26] The young stars of the Zeffirelli movie, Olivia Hussey and Leonard Whiting, in their day were maligned no less vitriolically. The course of their true love unfolds from the episode when to the strains of Mozart, Romeo is first seen musing alone by Benvolio, to the arrival at the Capulet ball when Romeo must douse his head in a basin to shake off the mind-altering effects of Mercutio's pill, to the strangely displaced balcony scene that immerses Romeo and Juliet in the Capulet swimming pool (presumably to emerge reborn from the sacred waters), to the violent duel with Tybalt using "Sword 9mm series S" pistols to slide around an awkward anachronism, to the candle-lit tomb scene (following a cops-and-robbers chase sequence) when Juliet awakens before Romeo dies and each is made aware of the terrible irony in the way their "stars" have cheated them.

Actually Luhrmann did not invent this searing piece of business, its origins having been traced back at the least to eighteenth-century staging, though a more recent film precedent is the Theda Bara and Harry Hilliard silent *Romeo and Juliet* (1916). Wagner's *Liebestod* rather than Rota's sentimental score more appropriately colors Luhrmann's anti-romantic dénouement.

The lovers use almost all of Shakespeare's sonnet sequence in the Capulet ballroom, and some of the verse from the truncated aubade scene. When Father [*sic*] Laurence instructs Juliet on how to take the sleeping potion, realism gives way to filmic tactics as in the background the screen fills with an envelope addressed to Romeo in Mantua. The "Post Post Haste" delivery van misses Romeo in Mantua when the headphones of his Walkman radio deafen him to the knocking on the door of his grungy house trailer. A "We Called" card is shoved under his door, just before the dissolve to Juliet's bed chamber where she is about to imbibe the sleeping potion.

The movie tears off the façade of bourgeois respectability from Juliet's parents and turns [Lady] Gloria Capulet (Diane Venora) into a shallow, pill-popping fashion plate and Father Fulgencio Capulet (Paul Sorvino) into a monstrous tyrant. Sorvino's scolding of Juliet for her unwillingness to marry Paris nearly matches the volcanic eruption of Sebastian Cabot in the Castellani *Romeo and Juliet*. In the service of diversity and multi-culturalism, the film includes a black actor, Harold Perrineau, as a splendid Mercutio, who performs a virtuoso Queen Mab speech and whose friendship with Romeo hints at a streak of homoeroticism. For the Capulet ball, Mercutio cross-dresses in a mini-skirt, Romeo wears the armor of a young King Arthur, Gregory and Sampson are Vikings, and Benvolio wears a monk's habit. Perrineau's "A plague a' both your houses!" (3.1.106), after the disastrous duel with Tybalt, takes on a special edge in view of the lily-white status of both Montagues and Capulets. The English actress, Miriam Margolyes, also adds to political correctness by becoming a Hispanic Nurse, though she is denied her great monologue about Susan, "Well, Susan is with God, / She was too good for me" (1.3.19), and her betrayal of Juliet, "Romeo's a dish-clout to him" (3.5.219), is weakly orchestrated.

As "Father," not "Friar," Laurence, Pete Postlethwaite, who also turns up as the Player King in the Zeffirelli *Hamlet*, incarnates the contemporary type of the troubled clergyman, close to a public scandal over charges of pedophilia, or worse. With a kinky look, a Runic cross emblazoned on his back like a tattoo, or the back of a Gianni Versace dress, he is not the sort to be entrusted with choir boys. A victim as much as anyone else of the media tyranny, he is shown fantasizing, like Walter Mitty, about newspaper headlines that will proclaim his genius in mediating the feud between Montagues and Capulets. His tiresome fifth-act plot summary telling the fidgety audience what it already knows, though admittedly the on-stage persons may not know it, suffers an unkind cut, but his craven desertion in the tomb of Juliet, "the watch is coming / Come go, good Juliet [*noise again*], I dare no longer stay" (5.3.158) partly survives.

The candle-lit, acid-trip atmosphere of the ornate tomb-scene then yields to footage on the evening news of the young lovers' bodies being hauled off in an ambulance. The confident tones of the oracular anchorwoman reporting terrible events in the tomb redefine reality as sound bites and isolated segments. From actualities to fantasies to actualities, the lines separating the one from the other recede into the electronic time warp. Romance has given way to actuality. And to make the question of reality all the more elusive, the television screen gradually fades away into a pinpoint of blackness. All may be "punished," as Captain Prince (Vondie Curtis-Hall) proclaims, but all will most certainly end by disappearing into the black hole of the television screen. Romeo and Juliet are lost like the rest of us in the empty spaces of electronic media, but not before this perversely beautiful movie employs Shakespeare's text as a kind of surrogate to "inspect the place of Shakespeare ... in contemporary culture."[27] In a stunning reversal of the normal stage to screen formula, a 1998 touring RSC production of *Hamlet* directed by Matthew Warchus and starring Alex Jennings has "clearly been inspired by Baz Luhrmann's inventive 1996 film version of *Romeo and Juliet*."[28]

Another of the ambitious films of the 1990s was Adrian Noble's made-for-television *Midsummer Night's Dream* (1996), which was theatrically released in England. It makes all the right gestures but never quite comes up with a protocol believable enough to attract the widespread interest generated by competing productions. The idea of having the audience experience the action through the eyes of a small boy (Osheen Jones), who dreams the events in the play, comes close to Jane Howell's use of a similar point of view in her successful BBC *Titus Andronicus*. The boy/spectator entering and re-entering the computerized *mise-en-scène* possibly is designed to enchant the children in the audience, along with the quotations from Mary Poppins, Beatrix Potter, Victorian cut-out theatres, and country music for the rude mechanicals. Today's over-stimulated children, however, may find all of this just a bit too much department-store Christmas decorations for acceptance. At the other end of the spectrum, the movie contains adult material involving sexual innuendoes that almost qualify the film as a chapter nine event in this book alongside the Coronado gay/punk *Dream*. For instance, a languid Puck kisses a limp-wristed Oberon full on the mouth, and Hippolyta is shown supine on a pink couch resembling the "medlar" fruit that Mercutio bawdily describes to Romeo (2.1.36). The actors vary in quality, the men sometimes veering toward the prissy, particularly Theseus/Oberon (Alex

24   Ian McKellen as the villainous Richard duke of Gloucester in the 1990 Richard
Eyre stage production at the National Theatre, which preceded the making of
Richard Loncraine's 1996 movie, also starring McKellen.

Jennings), the women sometimes first-rate as in the happy case of Hippolyta/Titania (Lindsay Duncan). The impeccable RSC diction carries more polish than feeling. The choreography and costumes are like a box of overly rich cream-filled chocolates, so sweet as to be slightly nauseating. Putting the rude mechanicals on a motorcycle is a good idea but somehow out of synch with the decadent style of the rest of the production. Critic Mark Sinker put it well when he wrote that it is "fitfully engaging at best, [but] ends up implicating no one.[29]

The age of Kenneth Branagh

By a shrewd merger of art and commerce, Kenneth Branagh magically resuscitated the Shakespeare movie just when everyone was announcing its death at the hands of television. He was a young man of working-class origins from Belfast and Reading, who attended the Royal Academy of Dramatic Art and who against all odds swiftly rose to the pinnacle of the acting profession.[30] At twenty-six, he founded his own repertory company, the Renaissance Theatre Company, and talked major stars like Judi Dench and Derek Jacobi into being directors. He directed the RTC version of *Twelfth Night* (1987), which was subsequently taped for video release,[31] played the lead in Adrian Noble's *Henry V* at Stratford (1984), did *Hamlet* with the Renaissance Theatre Company (1988), and again for Adrian Noble at the RSC's Barbican (1992), and took the leading role in *Coriolanus* at the Chichester Festival Theatre (1992). So by 1989 when he produced his film of *Henry V*, which heralded a fresh parade of Shakespeare movies in the 1990s, his career was already in fast forward. Besides supervising three large-screen Shakespeare movies, he has, as we have seen, also played Iago in the Oliver Parker *Othello* (1996), and produced his *Hamlet* derivative, *A Midwinter's Tale* (1995). Most recently he has even successfully impersonated Woody Allen's voice and manner in *Celebrity* (1998), and he has been planning a film of *Love's Labor's Lost*. With his $9-million *Henry V*, he boldly moved from stage to screen to create what has been widely acclaimed as "an audacious, resonant, passionate film,[32] "a Henry for a decade,"[33] and one "masterfully adapted,"[34] especially in North America where the politics of British theatre lose velocity. For many of his countrymen, however, Branagh had not only sold out to the Thatcherites and the feel-good Shakespeareans[35] but also committed the unpardonable sin of being too successful too young. Branagh's movie was self-reflexively the equivalent of Hal's invasion of France. When this novice director's work then turned a handsome profit for its plucky backers, his success became unbearable.

[246]

While his King Henry inevitably triggered comparisons with Laurence Olivier's performance in the famous 1944 movie, as well as suggestions of influence, it was Branagh's stage experience in Adrian Noble's RSC *Henry V* (1984) that mainly inspired the movie.[36] He kept saying that he did not want to be the "new Olivier" but to create a film that was special and unique in its own right.[37] Olivier's film reflected the wartime ideologies of 1944, while Branagh's grew out of the late-80s post-Falkland era, though there were efforts to transcend any particular topicality. Olivier's king was an invulnerable matinee idol; Branagh's king, vulnerable and plain-spoken, outwardly a warrior king but inwardly a Hamlet figure, torn between duty and compassion. Branagh speaks of trying "to realise the qualities of introspection, fear, doubt and anger"[38] which he saw in the character and which dictated more close-ups than long shots. With some justification, critic Jill Forbes, besides disliking the soundtrack, thought that Branagh's down-home monarch sacrificed "the notion of ceremony" among kings which Olivier's anti-naturalistic acting reinforced.[39] And where Olivier censored out images damaging to the "mirror of all Christian kings," like ordering the deaths of the Cambridge conspirators, Branagh not only arrests but assaults Cambridge, Gray, and Scroop, though he also scraps the notorious order for genocide at Agincourt: "Then every soldier kill his prisoners, / Give the word through" (4.6.37). Olivier's camera tended to pull back and up so that the actors' voices grew and flourished in rhetorical splendor as the bodies diminished; Branagh's movie often begins a sequence in mid-shot and then moves in tighter and tighter to peer more and more closely at faces. When Hostess Quickly (Judi Dench) poignantly eulogizes Falstaff, the camera bores in on her stricken countenance as if it would wrest the truth out of her innermost secret being.

Branagh's gift is in knowing how to combine the theatrical with the filmic. He brought with him to film making none of the prejudices of stage against screen, nor does he particularly worry about the opposite dilemma of privileging screen over theatre. What is mostly a realistic film ironically begins with a touch of Brechtian alienation in its meta-cinematic concern with the mechanics of making the movie. The Chorus (Derek Jacobi), who dresses as and acts the role of a CNN war correspondent in the midst of Elizabethan warfare, recites the prologue in a deserted Shepperton sound stage, strewn about with the props for the filming of *Henry V*. When he lights a match to locate the giant studio switchboard, the sudden spluttering and flare gives "Muse of fire" a clever spin. And the glare of the studio arc lights suggests "the brightest heaven of invention!" The Olivier Globe has given way to the motion picture studio. Jacobi continues the Chorus' lines, until, shouting as he reaches the last word in "kindly to judge our *play*," he flings open gigantic wooden doors to enter the world of the film. The avant-garde film making ends here as Canterbury and Ely loom out of the darkness and, with the exception of the Chorus' occasional appearances, some flashbacks to the Boar's head tavern, and decelerated motion in the battle sequences, the picture settles back into the realism of a seamless narrative.[40] A pragmatic Branagh uses whatever film grammar works to his advantage.

Like the play, the film carries a heavy freightage of ambiguity about the true nature of the young king. As often said, King Henry embodies the type of the "king's two bodies," one human, the other virtually divine. Shakespeare often leaves unresolved the question of when his hero is plain old Prince Hal and when God's deputy on earth. Critics of Branagh's film, like Donald K. Hedrick and Dympna Callaghan, have cogently argued that the movie is even more ambiguous than its Shakespearean source in its ability to appear anti-war while employing pro-war codes. As Hedrick says, if "war has a necessary dark or muddy side," then the king's character is "exonerated"; if the king has a "dark side" then war is "exonerated."[41] This "knotted ambiguity" also crops up in Callaghan's noting of the interplay between "resistance and recuperation"[42] by which the king can be all things to all men. To put it reductively, and not do full justice to Hedrick's and Callaghan's subtle analyses, Branagh has the ability to have his cake and eat it too. He can make an anti-war movie that also glorifies war.

The Archbishop's Rube Goldberg explanation of the Law Salique – "No woman shall succeed in Salique land" (1.2.39) – is only one of many ambiguous cruxes. Hooded and muffled, a proto-conspirator against man and the commonwealth, the archbishop (Charles Kay) takes a brain-numbingly boring passage on the legitimacy of the French monarchy and actually makes it engrossing, without resorting to the clowning of the two clergymen in the Olivier movie. The panning camera tracks the faces of his auditors during his labyrinthine recitation, a masterpiece of legalese, of learned double talk, which justifies an immoral invasion of France. When he ends by saying that all this is "as clear as is the summer's sun" (1.2.86), the nervous barons catch the irony and relax into sniggers. Meanwhile Exeter and Westmoreland exchange meaningful glances, hinting at some kind of collusion between them to manipulate their sovereign into the invasion.[43] Young Henry, however, is apparently not fooled. Sensing furtiveness in the archbishop's demeanor, he yet ignores his doubts and embarks for France. The son now carries the guilt of genocide just as his father before him endured the guilt of regicide for the slaying of his cousin Richard II. Heavy is the "guilt" behind the "gilt" of the crown.

In his dissolute youth, King Henry has also accumulated his own inventory of guilt. To survive as king, he has needed to reject his tavern crony,

Falstaff, at his Westminster coronation, which is shown in flashback: "I know thee not, old man, fall to thy prayers. / How ill white hairs becomes a fool and jester!"(2 *Henry IV*, 5.5.47). The gruesome hanging of Bardolph for the theft of a "pax" (*Henry V* 3.6.40) also calls for a flashback to the cronyism of the good-old-boy Boar's Head tavern days. As a leader, the king cannot afford the self indulgence of compassion, but must hang his friend in order to remain credible to an army that has been put on notice that looters and rapists will be put to death. Another poignant reminder of Hal's wild youth occurs at the end of the battle of Agincourt when Pistol, in language transposed from act five, contemplates a bleak future in England after the wars: "Doth fortune play the huswife with me now? / News have I that my Doll is dead i' th' spittle" (5.2.80). Both play and movie are haunted by the Faustian question of "What shall it profit a man to gain the whole world and lose his own immortal soul?" When in an interpolated flashback, Falstaff turns to the king and says, "We have heard the chimes at midnight, / [Master Harry]" (3.2.214), a line actually addressed to Master Shallow in *Henry IV Part Two,* even those unfamiliar with the entire tetralogy can sense the king's spiritual torment. Somehow he is made to look good even when he is betraying the companions of his youth.

Minor characters like Nym, Pistol, Bardolph, and Hostess Quickly have tired, worn, defeated faces. When they go off to war they slouch and crawl rather than move in quick step to fife and drum. Perpetual tavern cronies, they have never managed to sort out workaday from holiday, so time wastes them as they waste time. Paul Scofield as the French king is sober and thoughtful unlike his scatter-brained predecessor in the Olivier film, though his son the Dauphin (Michael Maloney) remains mindless. The French Princess Katherine (Emma Thompson) offers a counterweight to her light-headed brother, appearing especially delightful in the dazzling English lesson episode with the lady-in-waiting, Alice (Geraldine McEwan). Gallic fastidiousness and Anglo bluffness are contrasted when squat, burly Exeter (Brian Blessed), the king's chief aide, shows up as an envoy at the French court looking like a cement mixer in a rose garden.

Olivier's picture-book romanticizing of Agincourt on a sunny green field is replaced with a surrealistic tapestry of slow-motion medieval horror reminiscent of the butchery in the battle scenes of Welles's *Chimes at Midnight.* Olivier's English archers with the devastating long bows that destroyed the overly armored mounted French knights do reappear, but the magnificent French cavalry charge with prancing steeds "printing their proud hoofs I' th' receiving earth" (Pro. 27) and with royal pennants are replaced with hacking and groaning and thieving and wretched deaths in a muddy field. When it is all over, a mammoth tracking shot, filmed in Shepperton, follows the king, cradling the body of a slain baggage boy, as he wearily traverses the battlefield carnage. Thieves plunder bodies and angry French women scream at the man responsible for their new widowhood, this spectacle all having been managed with "150 extras, thirty horses, numerous carts, actors, and stuntmen," even while coping with the "the sonic horrors of the Heathrow flight path."[44] Patrick Doyle's stirring vocal and orchestral "Non Nobis" swells and builds to a crescendo, so climactic that some in the New York audience thought it was the end of the movie and began to put on their coats. Well worth waiting for, Henry's wooing of Princess Katherine is carried out charmingly enough to suggest it is more than just a dynastic marriage. Even the cultural materialists who loathe Branagh's politics might concede that this *Henry V*, while not so breathtaking as Olivier's film, far overshadows any televised version, including the recent transmission of *Henry V* for the inaugural program at the new Globe Bankside.

While Kenneth Branagh's next Shakespeare film, *Much Ado about Nothing* (1993), offers striking cinematic moments, especially in the opening quotation from *The Magnificent Seven*, its strength lies in the style and elocution of Emma Thompson as the petulant but brilliant Beatrice, who was born to play the role. When Don Pedro (Denzel Washington) says "You were born in a merry hour," and she replies, "No, sure, my lord, my mother cried, but then there was a star danc'd, and under that was I born" (2.1.332), Thompson's eloquent eyes certify that Beatrice is vulnerable after all, an *eiron* aware of her own limitations. Outwardly "merry," engaged in a "merry war" and "skirmish of wit" (1.1.62) with Benedick, she is yet like other mortals inwardly subject to doubt, and ultimately "star-cross'd" in some arcane way. After she exits, Denzel Washington in a tightly framed shot, his face aglow with admiration, reacts to her presence with "By my troth, a pleasant-spirited lady" (2.1.341). Alternating camera angles and close shots, of course, involve filmic as well as theatrical resources but the effect comes mainly from the power of Shakespeare's language and the charisma of the actors. While the bravura but irrelevant opening shot of the horsemen grabs the attention of the audience, Thompson's studied readings traverse back to the essence of Shakespeare's play about the serio-farcical battle of the sexes.

Despite Thompson's extraordinary performance, which correctly privileges the play's wit over its sentimentality, British critics uncovered flaws where Americans were more likely to find virtues.[45] Vincent Canby called it a "ravishing entertainment ";[46] Stuart Klawans said that it "neatly balanc[ed] the demands of the box office with those of the script";[47] and Todd McCarthy called it a "spirited, winningly acted rendition."[48] A critic in an American magazine under British editorship, however, could hardly contain his scorn: "Rarely has the title [*Much Ado about Nothing*] rung so true."[49] There were other non-believers as well, again British, such as Leslie Felperin Sharman, whose complaint about Branagh's "imaginative banality" and "cinematic bardology" echoes the mantra of British cultural materialists that Kenneth Branagh is somehow darkly complicit with agents of capitalist imperialism. Shaman while deploring this side of Branagh also acknowledges that it is his "biggest asset as a purveyor of lucrative filmic commodities for a specialized middle-brow market with upwardly mobile tastes."[50] Branagh's concern for pleasing the suburban cineplexes may have led to his shrewd casting of American film stars, Keanu Reeves and Michael Keaton, as well as acknowledging multi-culturalism by casting Denzel Washington as Don Pedro.

Cinematic rather than theatrical elements dominate three parts of the movie – the establishing shots, the garden scene, and the grand finale – while elsewhere the movie lapses into theatricality. The production opens almost clandestinely like a prelude to a silent film with the words from Balthasar's song, "Sigh no more, ladies, sigh no more / Men were deceivers ever" (2.3.62), inscribed in white against a dark screen, but instead of a bouncing ball inviting an old-fashioned sing-along, the words are spoken in impeccable "RP" by Beatrice. Then there is a dissolve to a full frame of an impressionistic watercolor of the fourteenth-century Villa Vignamaggio in Tuscany's Chianti wine region, where Branagh elected to film for better light instead of in Messina, Sicily, the locale for Shakespeare's play.[51] Soon the camera pulls back to reveal the ancient villa itself where Mona Lisa once resided, a verdant hillside, the painter Leonato (Richard Briers), the fashionable picnickers, and finally red-haired Beatrice herself perched in a tree reading the poem aloud to her doting friends. There is a glimpse of Brian Blessed, once the formidable Exeter in *Henry V*, now transformed into Antonio, Leonato's brother, and a presence, though mainly silent, throughout the film. This is the green world of comedy that always ends in the victory of the young over the old, and in feasting and matrimony.

The stasis of the watercolor gives way to a kinetic screen alive with motion as a messenger brings news of the approach of Don Pedro, prince of Arragon with a retinue that includes Benedick (Kenneth Branagh), Don John bastard brother of Don Pedro (Keanu Reeves), and Claudio (Robert Sean Leonard). A stirring proto-symphonic score by Patrick Doyle fills the soundtrack as in a mix of real time and slow motion the women scurry to the showers to prepare for the men's arrival, the horsemen hoot and holler and gallop over the hill in a quotation from *The Magnificent Seven*, a steadicam pursues the women into the shower for a melée of scrubbing, washing, shrieking, and titillating split-second exposures of bare bosoms and backs, the men gallop into the villa grounds and tumble and splash into an outdoor wash area for their own ritual of cleansing and scrubbing, the women climb into nearly identical flowing white dresses of which there seems to be an endless supply, and the men emerge from their cleansing uniformed in breeches and white tunics. The camera lifts up high for a crane shot and far down below through an opened gate, the gentlemen in a V-shaped formation spearheaded by Don Pedro approach the ladies, and the ladies in turn approach the men, as if this were a ritual prelude to the Battle of the Sexes.

The camera next most actively participates in the garden scene with the release of Benedick and Beatrice from the thralldom of their own wit by means of what Northrop Frye calls a "benevolent practical joke."[52] The business in the garden that makes Benedick into a bumbler as he struggles in Robert Benchley fashion with a recalcitrant lawn chair and eavesdrops on the staged conversation about Beatrice's feelings, momentarily tips the balance of power toward Beatrice. She herself would not be caught dead in so awkward a performance. Benedick's ridiculous Cary Grant imitation by the fountain as she approaches further exposes his deep-seated insecurity. In rapid intercutting, alternating between real time and slow motion, Beatrice ecstatically soars through the air on her swing, and Benedick dances and sloshes around the fountain, but the intercutting segues into a double exposure that superimposes the one overjoyed person on the other. The nondiegetic music reprises "Sigh no more, ladies," and the moving images of soaring and splashing manifest the spiritual rebirth of two previously self-repressed people. As Frye also points out, the parallel practical joke, this time malevolent not benevolent, is carried out by Don John in tricking the gullible, and very young, Claudio into thinking that his Hero is a strumpet.

To remain accessible and popular, Branagh resists any transgressive temptation to deconstruct the psychology of the Benedick–Beatrice relationship, which unravels under the cloud of an egregious Elizabethan pun involving "no-thing," bawdry for a lack of sexual parts. Is the wit of Beatrice and Benedick really a cover-up for closeted lesbianism and homosexuality? "Middlebrow" film goers with "upwardly mobile tastes" out for popcorn and a good time at the mall do not want to hear about such destabilizing matters, which are best left to the seminar room. Nor does Branagh exploit the parallel between Claudio/Hero/Don John and Othello/Desdemona /Iago. Hero (Kate Beckinsale) and her Claudio, though principals in the main plot, pretty much remain marionettes as the sentimental lovers who play off against the usurping witty pair of Beatrice and Benedick in the minor plot. The third major cinematic moment involves the steadicam shots of the dancing and singing at the end of the movie, and the crane shots high above filming the entire ensemble skipping and hopping and laughing and dancing through the lush courtyards of the villa grounds. The theme of "Sigh no more" swells on the soundtrack again and off in one corner is the figure of Don Pedro, alone, made doubly compelling by Washington's status as the sole black actor in the cast.

Keanu Reeves as Don John and Michael Keaton as Dogberry bore the brunt of critical disapproval, again for unfathomable reasons. The complaint that Reeves did little but scowl ignores the fact that Shakespeare gave his Don John very little to do but scowl, he not being a full-fledged Shakespearean villain or vice in the tradition of Aaron the Moor, Richard Crookback, or Iago. While the other Shakespeare villains are serio-comic, Reeves was stuck with being merely serious. In short, Reeves was doing what the script called for. Purist rage against movie Shakespeare rose to a crescendo, however, in the attacks on Michael Keaton's lunatic Dogberry. Keaton became the movie's designated scapegoat, yet his bizarre mugging, staring, grimacing, and clenched teeth delivery, his zany entrances and exits on a non-existent horse, his sadistic tormenting of the "opinion'd" Conrade and Borachio, and his Three Stooges routine with Verges (Ben Elton) derive, it can be said, not from sheer perversity but from both textual and cinematic considerations. In Dogberry, Shakespeare created another minor character, like Hostess Quickly, whose mysterious past is hinted at in the wistful remark that he is "a fellow that hath had losses, and one that hath two gowns" (4.2.84). Keaton's Dogberry recreates the type of the frustrated, minor bureaucrat, in a role of petty authority, an incipient Adolf Hitler as adept at making life miserable for his inferiors as he is at toadying to his superiors. Ironically he lacks control over what he most prizes, which is his language, and has a repertory of malapropisms rivaling Hostess Quickly's or even Lady Teazle's: "O villain! Thou wilt be condemn'd into everlasting redemption for this" (4.2.56). Branagh reified the malapropisms by making Dogberry both physically and verbally inept.[53] When granny-glassed Ben Elton peers closely into Dogberry's face, and when they prance off on imaginary horses, mirroring the *Magnificent Seven* quotation at the beginning of the film, the approach becomes hilariously funny. Yet when he asks the unrepentant Conrade (who has called him an "ass"), "Dost thou not suspect my place?" (4.2.74), Dogberry's primal despair peeps through. Thousands and thousands in the multiplexes, who would otherwise have yawned through Dogberry's mostly obscure homonyms and quibbles, must have been touched by the "switching of codes" in Keaton's "whacko-manic conception," as Samuel Crowl characterizes it. Crowl also wittily concludes of Branagh's "screwball comedy" that he "gives us the most successful translation we have of a Shakespearean comedy onto film and converts all our potential critical sounds of woe 'Into Hey nonny nonny'."[54]

Kenneth Branagh next accomplished what everyone had always said couldn't be accomplished – a four-hour, uncut *Hamlet* (1996) on widescreen in full color, based on the First Folio and Second Quarto texts, whose scenario by Shakespeare, in a great irony, was thought well enough of to be nominated for an Academy Award. Despite its 240-minute duration, many ordinary citizens said that they had found it anything but unendurable. Quite the contrary: it was gripping. Branagh's precedent for the uncut version was of course Adrian Noble's RSC production that ran fifteen minutes over four hours. Praise and condemnation for Branagh's work were this time distributed more or less evenly on both sides of the Atlantic. Few if any denied the movie's visual splendor, its Masterpiece Theatre lushness of sets, costumes and good-looking people. Critics variously thought it "relentless and overpowering and devastating";[55] praiseworthy for "the quality and elegance of its treatment of Shakespeare's verse";[56] and "often inspired, bringing new life to scenes that were regularly drawing unintentional laughter."[57] Others found the very Masterpiece Theatre look too conservative, too middlebrow, and Branagh unconvincing as the prince. Stuart Klawans dismissed it as "a certifiable mess,"[58] and John Mullan while still reserving high praise for Derek Jacobi's Claudius labeled it a *folie de grandeur*.[59] The dread v-word, "vulgar," popped up at least once.[60]

Again as in *Much Ado*, Branagh had continued his astute policies of casting internationally, of using a realistic speaking style, of choosing a setting consistent with the heightened language, and above all of making the work "accessible . . . to modern life."[61] The same perspicacity by the producers of the BBC Shakespeare series in reaching out worldwide for actors would have made their work instantly more popular. As Marcellus, veteran movie star Jack Lemmon, like Michael Keaton in *Much Ado*, became the designated scapegoat, feeling the sting of "age-ism" from critics, who thought him "too old" for the role. Actually except for throwing away the gem, "Something is rotten in the state of Denmark" (1.4.89), Lemmon performed tolerably well and even that lapse may have been more an editing fumble than his. Imperturbable French superstar Gerard Depardieu as Reynaldo made a foxy spy for a hypocritical old Polonius (Richard Briers), who after moralizing to his own children conceals a prostitute (Melanie Ramsey) in his chambers. Although made to order for the role, right out of central casting, Robin Williams to his credit understates the role of Osric, an inept and insecure dandy. As Player King, Charlton Heston cannot help sounding like Moses in a meticulous recitation of Aeneas' tale to Dido, while Rosemary Harris' Player Queen supports him in the "mouse trap." Stand-up comic Billy Crystal as the impudent First Gravedigger knew exactly how to bandy with Hamlet about Yorick's skull, and Richard Attenborough lends a special dignity to the tiny role of English Ambassador. In tribute to their honorific status, dur-

25   In two-shot, a cross-dressed Imogen Stubbs as Viola/Cesario attracts the attention of a bemused Olivia, played by Helena Bonham Carter in the 1996 film of *Twelfth Night*, directed by Trevor Nunn.

ing the Player King's speech Judi Dench and John Gielgud mime Hecuba and Priam. For all these pains in signing up unsignable actors, Branagh was immediately attacked for "stunt casting." Famous faces, it was said, distracted the audience from the text. No one would admit that these big stars also woke the audience up and breathed new life into obscure roles. Who ever paid any attention to Marcellus until Jack Lemmon came along? Branagh's plight illustrates again the wisdom of Machiavelli's famous dictum that a man is more obliged for those favors he confers than those he accepts.

As for the principals he did as well. Derek Jacobi turned out to be one of the greatest ever players of Claudius with a real knack for being a charming cad and bounder. If Zeffirelli's *Hamlet* was Gertrude-centered then this *Hamlet* is Claudius-centered. When first viewed in the opulent interior set at Shepperton with sensuous Julie Christie in her bridal gown, happily skipping by Claudius' side, the couple take on the aura of a fun-loving Scott and

Zelda Fitzgerald. Their effervescence squashes any thought that Claudius could commit a dastardly deed like kill a king and then marry his widowed sister-in-law. The handsome king with a trim beard and athletic figure speaks confidently, intelligently, in measured tones, savoring the antithetical clauses in his opening speech and demonstrating his superb self-confidence by ripping up the insolent letter about the disputed lands from a scowling young Fortinbras (Rufus Sewell). The camera, which is restlessly peering, circling (often dizzyingly), probing, zooming in and out, and analyzing, then moves right to reveal Hamlet in the customary suits of solemn black sulking under the bleachers. The effect of seeing this petulant young man after witnessing the polished and urbane uncle is to undermine confidence in Hamlet. How can anyone be so sullen in such jovial surroundings? When shown later, the monarch-sized royal bed of Denmark that is "a couch for luxury and damned incest" (1.5.83) resembles a lush advertisement for Laura Ashley sheets, at times suggestively rumpled from marital activity. Kate Winslet brought a fresh-faced vulnerability to her Ophelia, who in her madness is cruelly incarcerated in a padded cell and hosed down. Horatio (Nicholas Farrell) handles the jargon-riddled legalistic speech about the covenant between Norway and Denmark with the help of flashbacks to workers in a gun factory, making in Marcellus' words "the night joint-laborer with the day" (1.1.78).

The large and reliable Brian Blessed turns up again, this time not as Exeter nor Antonio, but as the Ghost of Hamlet's father. To Hamlet, he oozes contempt for his younger brother, Claudius, "that incestuous, that adulterate beast" (1.5.41), while a tight framing shows his beautiful teeth and serpent's eyes. The flashback showing dear little Prince Hamlet playing with his father helps to explain Hamlet's Electra complex but the flashback to the poisoning in the garden makes Claudius' culpability as the sneaky bearer of "juice of cursed hebona in a vial" (1.5.62) far more obvious than it was probably intended. Despite jeers about "sensationalism" and imitating Stephen Spielberg, the special effects of exploding ground in the cellarage scene derive from Hamlet's expletive, "a worthy pioner!"(1.5.163). Hamlet is referring to the military's "pioneer," or "sapper," a kind of glorified ditch-digger, now called "engineers," who tunnel under enemy lines to implant explosives for blowing the enemy to smithereens as in *Henry V* (3.2.87). These same base fellows, "pioners," were the knaves that the paranoid Othello feared had tasted of Desdemona's "sweet body" (3.3.346). Helping out with *memento mori* motifs is Ken Dodd, British stand-up comic little known in the United States, who in flashback displays teeth identical to those in the skull tossed up by the Gravedigger. Finally, versatile Richard Briers, Malvolio in the Branagh *Twelfth Night*, Leonato in the Branagh *Much Ado*, plays Polonius as crafty, lecherous, dangerous, cruel, doting, and even inept. He delivers his farewell advice to Laertes, however, sincerely and poignantly, as if sub-consciously aware of the dramatic irony – the whole family is doomed, like the Tsarist Romanoffs, Polonius to be stabbed behind the arras, Ophelia drowned, and eventually Laertes slain in a duel.

Naturally all eyes are on "th' observ'd of all observers" (3.1.154), Prince Hamlet. Many years ago, S.F. Johnson argued that the Hamlet of the first act is "the student prince," while the Hamlet of the fifth act is "the ordained minister of providence."[62] In Kenneth Branagh's hands, Hamlet embodies Johnson's "student prince," who at the end can swing on a rope like Douglas Fairbanks to kill Claudius, but who comes up short as "the ordained minister of providence." The lavish Shepperton studio set for Elsinore could be thriftily recycled for Sigmund Romberg's *The Student Prince* (1924). Its grand chandeliers and balconies and mirrored walls serve as backdrop for bevies of elegant women in flattering hour-glass gowns, and platoons of handsome men in comic opera uniforms. The ladies look as if they will momentarily join their dashing men for a Strauss waltz on the checkered ballroom floor, if the men have not gone off for a rousing songfest at the beer garden, or maybe a little gentlemanly fencing at the dueling society. These Technicolor fantasies, a far cry from the ominous unit set of Laurence Olivier, the brick basement of Tony Richardson, or the clammy stone walls of Franco Zeffirelli, correlate with a Hamlet who turns into one of the more affable princes in performance history, not stern like Smoktunovsky, solemn like Olivier, nor neurotic like Williamson but plain spoken and direct, almost pleasant. The long rows of gnostic mirrors on the walls of the throne room into which Hamlet addresses his "To be or not to be" warn, though, that all that glisters may not be gold. Behind the outward festivity of this glittering Elsinore lurks inwardly the corrupt and dissolute court in which that which "seems" conceals that which "is." The mirrors also signify how every character in this most baroque of verbal structures mirrors every other, like infinite reflections in the contiguous mirrors of an old-fashioned barber shop. This is particularly so with Hamlet, Laertes, and Fortinbras, all sons of wronged fathers. Hamlet has returned from Wittenberg University to a "prison" of spying, corruption, scheming, and incest. Fortinbras sums it up pithily when he says, "For he was likely, had he been put on, / To have prov'd most royal" (5.2.397). Hamlet never gets a chance to prove himself "most royal" but instead shows a potential for performing in a circus high-wire act.

It is not what Branagh omitted (very little) but what he added that further reinforced this image of an undergraduate Hamlet. In the extraordinary flashbacks, for example, of an angry, surly Fortinbras haranguing his officers and viciously stabbing at military maps, the Norwegian plays Adolf Hitler invading Poland to Hamlet's Neville Chamberlain. None of Fortinbras' ravings fits very well with Hamlet's subsequent description of him as a "delicate and tender prince" (4.4.48). Branagh's Hamlet, not Sewell's Fortinbras, turns out to be the "delicate and tender" one, a description Goethe might have endorsed. Branagh's tendency to shout out the soliloquies, as if he were still on the Stratford stage instead of in a movie annoyed some reviewers. An egregious example occurs at the climactic end of Part One, just before the interval, when Fortinbras' army is passing through a valley in the remote background and Branagh is shrieking at the top of his lungs to drown out Patrick Doyle's theme music, "My thoughts be bloody, or be nothing worth!" (4.4.65). Not only an unfortunate reprise of a Julie Andrews' *shtick* in *The Sound of Music*, it also makes Hamlet seem less antic than hysterical. In short, a Student Prince.

As a consequence, when Fortinbras' menacing gray wool army crashes into the palace, even wounding the harmless "water-fly" Osric, no one, least of all Fortinbras, seems terribly interested in what Hamlet's views are on his successor, "I do prophesy th' election lights / On Fortinbras, he has my dying voice" (5.2.355). The steamy sex between Hamlet and Ophelia reaffirms Hamlet's heterosexuality but compromises the priest at Ophelia's burial who, despite her "doubtful" death, will "yet here [allow] her virgin crants, / Her maiden strewments" (5.1.232). Since "virgin crants" and "maiden strewments" were reserved for virtuous young maids, the good doctor must have been ignorant of Ophelia's dalliance with Hamlet.

For too many in the audience, majestic Blenheim Palace, ancestral home of the Duke of Marlborough (who appears fleetingly in the film) and birthplace of Winston Churchill, looked less like Elsinore and more like a mecca for tourist buses. Branagh's company filmed in the winter, however, and the snowy grounds lend credibility to Francisco's "'Tis bitter cold" (1.1.8), but make incredible King Hamlet's afternoon naps outdoors in the snow-covered garden with a charcoal brazier fire to keep him warm. The winter set also causes the literal-minded to fret that Ophelia's drowning in mid-winter might wreck her plans for assembling "fantastic garlands" of "crow flowers, nettles, daisies, and long purples" (4.7.169). Maybe because of this inconsistency, Branagh scraps the conventional movie flashback to Ophelia's drowning, and instead has Gertrude deliver her famous aria-like description without visual aides, which Julie Christie admirably accomplishes. The movie ends as it begins with a framing shot of the statue of old King Hamlet, except that at the end it has been toppled over like some forlorn bust of Lenin in the former Soviet Union. With his epic film, Kenneth Branagh also toppled over the taboo against making movies of an uncut *Hamlet*. For this heroic effort, he deserves much thanks.

In conclusion, I would add that despite the great variety of successful screen adaptations, there remain pockets of resistance to Shakespeare movies among bardolaters who see them as endangering the word, and among cinéastes who find them unsuitable for images.[63] The ongoing revolution in communications technology makes speculation about the shape of twenty-first-century Shakespeare movies idle. The eye of man cannot see nor the ear of man hear what is to come, but Peter Geenaway's belief that film is still in its infancy applies with special force to the Shakespeare movie. Whatever new paradigms the future holds for Shakespeare cinema, Shakespeare will remain on the page for the bibliophile, on stage for the theatre lover, and on the screen for the cinéphile. These are not gated communities, though; they remain eminently synergetic. To echo Paul, "there is one glory of the page [the sun]; and another glory of the stage [the moon]; and another glory of the screen [the stars]; for one star differeth from another star in glory" (1 Cor. 15:41). True, the unanswerable questions will never stop. "Is it Shakespeare?" "What is the best available means for putting Shakespeare on screen?" "How best to imagine his words in moving images?" "How to attract the 'best class of people'?" Nor should they. As has been wisely said, art is never completed, only interrupted.

— NOTES —

1 SHAKESPEARE IN SILENCE: FROM STAGE TO SCREEN

1. *King John* was only recently discovered in the Netherlands Film Museum after having been lost for decades, a remarkable story in the annals of film scholarship too lengthy for full discussion here. Years ago Professor Robert Hamilton Ball, the leading expert on Shakespeare silent film, hypothesized from available data that the then lost *King John* was comprised of the "Magna Carta" interpolation in Tree's stage play. See his *Shakespeare on Silent Film: A Strange Eventful History* (London: George Allen & Unwin Ltd., 1968), pp. 21–23; 303–04; and "Tree's *King John* Film: An Addendum," *SQ* 24.4 (1973), 455. Later discoveries by B.A. Kachur pointed to other scenes in the lost film. See her "The First Shakespeare Film: A Reconsideration and Reconstruction of Tree's *King John*," *TS* 32 (May 1991), 43–63. Finally, there was the definitive work establishing the original plan for the filming by Luke McKernan, "Beerbohm Tree's *King John* Rediscovered: The First Shakespeare Film, September 1899," *SB* 11.1 (1993), 35–36; and "Further News on Beerbohm Tree's *King John*," *SB* 11.2 (1993), 49–50.

2. John Wyver, *The Moving Image: An International History of Film, Television and Video* (Oxford and New York: Blackwell/BFI, 1989), p. 17.

3. *NYT* 24 Apr. 1896, 5; 26 Apr. 1896, 10.

4. All Shakespeare quotations are from G. Blakemore Evans, *et al.* (eds.), *The Riverside Shakespeare* (Boston: Houghton Mifflin, 1974).

5. Gerda Taranow, *Sarah Bernhardt: The Art within the Legend* (Princeton University Press, 1972), pp. 265–66. Ball in *Silent Film* (p. 305) raises the possibility of live sound effects, though he then rejects the idea.

6. Sarah Bernhardt, *Memoirs of My Life* (1908, repr. New York: Benjamin Blom, 1968). Among other things, she engaged in balloon ascensions and memorizing her lines in a coffin.

7. Taranow, *Bernhardt: The Art*, pp. 210–11.

8. Gerda Taranow, *The Bernhardt "Hamlet": Culture and Context* (New York: Peter Lang. 1996) p. 129. I am much indebted to Taranow's thorough study of Bernhardt's acting career. See also the thirteen frame enlargements from the Bernhardt *Hamlet* film, pp. 231–34.

9. See Roger Manvell, *Theater and Film: A Comparative Study* (Cranbury, NJ: Associated University Presses, 1979), p. 36. The late Dr. Manvell's six-step progression from "undisguised recordings of a production" in a theatre (e.g., the Burton *Hamlet*), to complete transformations (e.g., Kurosawa's *Throne of Blood*) remains a starting point for any taxonomy of screened Shakespeare.

10. David A. Cook, *A History of Narrative Film*, 3rd edn (New York: Norton, 1996), p. 5.

11. *MPW* 6 Feb. 1907, 147.

12. *Ibid.*, 2 May 1907, 154.

13. *Ibid.*, 24 Oct. 1908, 317.

14. *Ibid.*, 25 May 1907, 180.

15. "Audience Applauds His Shrieks of Agony," *MPW* 22 Feb. 1908, 138.

16. *MPW* 31 Oct. 1908, 348.

17. Ball, *Silent Film*, p. 108.

18. *Ibid.*, p. 35.

19. Ben M. Hall, *The Best Remaining Seats: The Story of the Golden Age of the Movie Palace* (New York: Clarkson N. Potter, 1961), p. 13.

20. *MPW* 4 May 1907, 140.

21. William Uricchio and Roberta E. Pearson, *Reframing Culture: The Case of the Vitagraph Quality Films* (Princeton University Press, 1993), p. 25.

22. *MPW* 5 Dec. 1908, 444.

23. Uricchio and Pearson, *Reframing Culture*, p. 33.

24. *MPW* 11 May 1907, 153.

25. Robert C. Allen, *Vaudeville and Film 1895–1915: A Study in Media Interaction* (New York: Arno Press, 1980), pp. 220–30.

26. *MPW* 2 Jan. 1909, 3.

27. *Ibid.*, 4 July 1908, 5.

28. See the biography by his daughter, which contains one or two vignettes about his work with Shakespeare, particularly the aging Rose Coghlan's attempt to play a svelte Rosalind in *As You Like It*. Marion Blackton Trimble, *J. Stuart Blackton, A Personal Biography* (Metuchen and London: Scarecrow Press, 1985), pp. 40–41.

29. See Steven J. Ross, *Working-Class Hollywood: Silent Film and the Shaping of Class in America* (Princeton University Press, 1998). Ross's study shows how popular entertainment redefines and reinvents reality for mass audiences. His conclusion is eloquent: "Vision is a gift, a gift held by the best writers, the best orators, and the best filmmakers. Committed filmmakers could help replace the current politics of despair with the politics of hope . . . [cinema] can take a politically blind population and offer them the gift of sight" (p. 257).

30. *MPW* 18 Dec. 1909, 870.

31. Ball, *Silent Film*, p. 314.

32. Kevin Brownlow, *Hollywood: The Pioneers* (New York: Knopf, 1979), p. 28 and *passim*.

33. William K. Everson, *American Silent Film* (Oxford University Press, 1978), p. 36. Everson says that of 525 silents released in 1921 only 50 remained in 1978 (p. 14). Ball indexes over 500 titles of alleged Shakespeare films, of which only a tiny fraction survive. Classics scholars have the same problem in generalizing about Greek drama from a skimpy data base.

34. Brownlow, *Hollywood*, p. 156.

35. Ball, *Silent Film*, p. 43.

36. See Charles Musser, *The Emergence of Cinema: The American Screen to 1907* (New York: Charles Scribner's Sons, 1990), vol. I in *History of American Cinema*, gen. ed. Charles Harpole (New York: Charles Scribner's Sons, 1990–), especially pp. 239–40, 305–06, 540–42.

37. Ball, *Silent Film*, p. 48.

38. Bush, "Our American Letter," *Bioscope* 16 Apr. 1914, 287.

39. *MPW* 4 July 1908, 12. Bush offered to accompany screenings of *Othello* and *Romeo and Juliet* with lectures and recitals as a way of attracting "the best class of people" to the movies.

40. *MPW* 5 Dec. 1908, 446–47.

41. Archival prints of Vitagraph movies often have title cards in languages other than English, e.g., the opening of the NFTVA copy of *King Lear*: "Der Herzog von Kent /

Wird Verbannt / Weil er Cordelia / Verteidict." Liberated from spoken language, silent movies ignored national boundaries in favor of a universal system of non-verbal communication. Charlie Chaplin and Lillian Gish worked as well in Berlin as in Peoria. Theatre owners could very cheaply splice in translated cards, or requests for ladies to remove their majestic hats, a practice that may account for the demise of the millinery industry. A trade journal advertisement reads: "Film titles made to order. Five feet for ¢50. No delay. Toledo, Ohio." (*MPW* 9 Jan. 1909, 46).

42. *MPW* 8 Jan. 1910, 101.

43. Everson, *American Silent Film*, p. 102.

44. Bush's remarks do not support the revisionist film scholars who have recently argued that nickelodeon audiences included upper as well as lower-income persons. There is a parallel here in Shakespeare studies with the debates over the make-up of the audiences at the Globe and Blackfriars playhouses. See Sumiko Higashi, "Dialogue; Manhattan's Nickelodeons"; Robert C. Allen, "Manhattan Myopia, or Oh! Iowa!"; and reply by Ben Singer, "New York, Just Like I Pictured It," in *Cinema Journal* 35.3 (1996), 72–128. I personally tend to side with Singer's view of a correlation between neighborhood and audience demography. In Shakespeare's time, the Globe patrons more or less reflected the seediness of Southwark, just as the grander folk at Blackfriars carried with them the whiff of prosperity from their "classier" neighborhood. For details, see my "The Audience for the Blackfriars Playhouse in Shakespeare's London," *The Yearbook of the American Philosophical Society* (Philadelphia, 1969), pp. 649–50.

45. *MPW* 5 Sept. 1908, 234.

46. *Ibid.*, 5 Dec. 1908, 446–47.

47. "Editorial," *Bioscope* 25 June 1914, 1289. The writer was an unrepentant elitist of the pre-politically correct era.

48. Anthony Slide, *The American Film Industry* (New York: Greenwood Press, 1986), p. 372.

49. Richard Abel, *The Cine Goes to Town: French Cinema 1896–1914* (Berkeley: University of California Press, 1994), p. 59.

50. Hall, *Best Remaining Seats*, p. 30.

51. Advertisement, *NYT* 6 March 1927, VIII 9.

52. Richard Abel, *French Cinema: The First Wave 1915–1929* (Princeton University Press, 1984), p. 52.

53. Quoted in Rachel Low, *History of British Film 1906–1914* (London: George Allen & Unwin, 1949), p. 14.

54. *Bioscope* 5 Jan. 1911, 55.

55. "Another Palace Opens," *Bioscope* 12 Jan. 1911, 15; see also David Atwell, *Cathedrals of the Movies: A History of British Cinema and Their Audiences* (London: The Architectural Press, 1980), for descriptions of these early theatres.

56. Quoted in Nathan Silver's review of Dennis Sharp's *The Picture Palace* (London (?): Hugh Evelyn, 1969) in *S&S* 38.3 (Summer 1969), 160 and *passim*.

57. *Bioscope* 12 June 1913, suppl. xxvi.

58. *Ibid.*, p. 835.

59. My data base comes from four principal sources: R.H. Ball's *Shakespeare on Silent Film*; K.S. Rothwell and Annabelle Henkin Melzer, *Shakespeare on Screen: An International Filmography and Videography* (New York and London: Neal-Schuman,1990), which I have collated with the more recent SIFT data base in the British Film Institute Library, and with Luke McKernan and Olwen Terris, *Walking Shadows: Shakespeare in the National Film and Television Archive* (London: BFI, 1994).

60. Brownlow, *Hollywood the Pioneers*, p. 70.

61. The film received a full-page advertisement in *Bioscope* 10 July 1913, 107.

62. *NYT* 12 Feb. 1922, II.3.

63. "The Filming of *Hamlet*: Interview with Mr. Cecil Hepworth," *Bioscope* 24 July 1913, 275.

64. For detailed analysis, see Bernice W. Kliman, *Hamlet: Film, Television, and Audio Performance* (London and Toronto: Assoc. University Presses, 1988), pp. 247–74.

65. See Frederick B. Warde, *Fifty Years of Make-Believe* (New York: International Press Syndicate, 1920) for a full account.

66. Quoted in American Film Institute Souvenir Program, 29 Oct. 1996.

67. *History of British Film*, p. 224.

68. *Shakespeare on Silent Film*, p. 243.

69. "*Broken Blossoms:* The Vulnerable Text and the Marketing of Masochism," in *Film in The Aura of Art* (Princeton University Press, 1984), pp. 16–17.

70. For background, see Siegfried Kracauer, *From Caligari to Hitler: A Psychological History of the German Film* (Princeton University Press, 1947).

71. Ball, *Silent Film*, p. 176.

72. See Ann Thompson, "Asta Nielsen and the Mystery of *Hamlet*," in *Shakespeare, The Movie*, ed. Lynda E. Boose and Richard Burt (London and New York: Routledge, 1997), pp. 215–24.

73. Quoted in Taranow, *Bernhardt*, pp. 212–13.

74. "Gazing at Hamlet, or the Danish Cabaret," *SS* 45 (1993), 40.

75. *MPW* 19 Nov. 1921, 336.

76. See K.S. Rothwell, "Roman Polanski's *Macbeth*: The 'Privileging' of Ross," *The CEA Critic* 46, 1&2 (Fall & Winter 1983–84), 50–55.

77. Danson, "Gazing at Hamlet," p. 48.

78. J. Lawrence Guntner, "Expressionist Shakespeare: The Gade/Nielsen *Hamlet* (1920) and the History of Shakespeare on Film," *Post Script: Essays in Film and the Humanities*, 17.2 (Winter/Spring 1998), 97. Dr. Guntner is a pioneering student of this film.

79. Ann Thompson, "Asta Nielsen and the Mystery of *Hamlet*," in Boose and Burt (eds.), *Shakespeare, The Movie*, pp. 220–21.

80. *NYT* 9 Nov. 1921, 20.

81. See V.I. Pudovkin, *Film Technique, Film Acting*, trans. Ivor Montagu (1929; repr. Hackensack NJ: Wehman Brothers, 1968), p. 143.

82. Karen Newman, *Fashioning Femininity and English Renaissance Drama* (University of Chicago Press, 1991), p. 91. Newman cites this theory as having been Lynda Boose's.

2 HOLLYWOOD'S FOUR SEASONS OF SHAKESPEARE

1. "Letter," 15 March 1914, quoted in Low, *History of British Film*, p. 29.

2. Ross, *Working-Class Hollywood*, p. 113.

3. Essay on dust jacket, Mirage Corp. laser disk, *The Taming of the Shrew*. The Mary Pickford Co. © 1966; 1990.

4. Russell Jackson points out that the "purists" are essentially bogey men, figments of the imagination of journalists, rarely encountered in real life. See his "Shakespeare's Comedies on Film," in Anthony Davies and Stanley Wells (eds.), *Shakespeare and the Moving Image: The Plays on Film and Television* (Cambridge University Press, 1994).

5. Roger Manvell, *Shakespeare and the Film* (repr. Cranbury, NJ: A.S. Barnes, 1979), p. 23.

6. See, for example, *The Motion Picture Guide, 1927–1983*, ed. Jay Robert Nash and Stanley Ralph Ross (Chicago: Cinebooks, 1987), p. 3274.

7. James M. Welsh, "Shakespeare, With – and Without – Words," *LFQ* 1.1 (Jan. 1973), 88.

8. Manvell, *Shakespeare and the Film*, p. 24.

9. See the British Film Institute's computer-based SIFT catalog, which lists Widgey R. Newman's *Merchant of Venice* as the first attempt at a Shakespeare talkie. Luke McKernan and Olwen Terris cite an extract from Gounod's *Romeo E Giulietta* (c. 1927) as a candidate for first-time honors, *Walking Shadows: Shakespeare in the National Film and Television Archive* (London: BFI, 1994), p. 106.

10. Mary Pickford, *Sunshine and Shadow* (New York: Doubleday, 1955), pp. 311–12.

11. *Variety* 2 Nov. 1966.

12. James Agate, "Notes," *The Magazine Programme*, London Pavilion, 14 Nov. 1929.

13. "The Movies," *Outlook* 153 (18 Dec. 1929), 633–34.

14. *NYT* 30 Nov. 1929, 23.

15. John Wyver, *The Moving Image: An International History of Film, Television and Video* (London: Blackwell/BFI, 1989), p. 84.

16. Diana E. Henderson, "A Shrew for the Times," in Boose and Burt, *Shakespeare, The Movie*, p. 154. Henderson's point is well taken since so many have thought the wink was directed at the audience rather than at the sister. She also surveys virtually every screened *Shrew*.

17. "Titania and the Ass's Head," in *Shakespeare Our Contemporary* (New York: Anchor Books, 1966), pp. 213–36.

18. Jay L. Halio, *"A Midsummer Night's Dream": Shakespeare in Performance* (Manchester University Press, 1994), pp. 36–38.

19. Public relations kit, Warner Brothers, at British Film Institute.

20. *Still in Movement: Shakespeare on Screen* (New York: Oxford University Press, 1991), p. 12.

21. *Speechless Dialect: Shakespeare's Open Silences* (Berkeley: University of California Press, 1985), p. 1.

22. *Time* 26 (21 Oct. 1935), 44–45.

23. Quoted in Manvell, *Shakespeare and the Film*, p. 27 from *Shakespeare, A Celebration*, ed. T.J.B. Spencer, pp. 109–10.

24. *The Graham Greene Film Reader: Reviews, Essays, Interviews and Film Stories*, ed. David Parkinson (New York: Applause Theatre Book Publishers, 1993), p. 38.

25. "Films," *The London Mercury* 35 (Nov. 1936), 57.

26. "Picturizing *Romeo and Juliet*," in *"Romeo and Juliet" by William Shakespeare. A Motion Picture Edition* (New York: Random House, 1936), p. 13.

27. A still of Barrymore in this role appears in James Kotsilibas-Davis, *The Barrymores, the Royal Family in Hollywood* (New York: Crown Publishers, 1981), p. 89. (Reference thanks to Craig Toth.)

28. Patrick McGilligan, *George Cukor: A Double Life* (New York: St. Martin's Press, 1991), p. 105.

29. *Motion Picture Edition*, p. 24.

30. Romeo and Juliet. *With Designs by Oliver Messel* (London: B.T. Batsford, 1936).

31. *Dance to the Piper* (Boston: Little, Brown, and Company 1952), pp. 233–34.

32. *Shakespeare in Production. Whose History?* (Athens: Ohio University Press, 1996), p. 49.

33. *Motion Picture Edition*, p. 256.

34. Meredith Lillich, "Shakespeare on the Screen: A Survey of How His Plays Have Been Made Into Movies," *FR* (June 1956), 251.

35. *Filming Shakespeare's Plays: The Adaptations of Laurence Olivier, Orson Welles, Peter Brook and Akira Kurosawa* (Cambridge University Press, 1988), p. 7.

36. *A Motion Picture Edition*, p. 14.

37. "M.G.M. Proudly Brings to the Screen," *Souvenir Book* (n.d.), p. 3.

38. "The Role of the Technical Adviser," from *QFRT* 8.2 (1953), 131–38, as quoted in Eckert, *Focus on Shakespearean Films*, p. 104.

39. John Houseman, "Filming *Julius Caesar*," *S&S* 23 (July/Sept. 1953), 25.

40. "Shakespeare and the Included Spectator," in *Reinterpretations of Elizabethan Drama*, ed. Norman Rabkin (New York: Columbia University Press, 1969), p. 123.

41. Miklos Rozsa, "*Julius Caesar*," *Film Music* 13 (Sept./Oct. 1953), 9.

42. See the outline in the film's companion volume, *Julius Caesar and the Life of William Shakespeare*, introduction by Sir John Gielgud (London: The Gawthorn Press, 1953).

43. "Filming *Julius Caesar*," *S&S* 23 (July/Sept. 1953), 25.

44. See Murray Biggs, "'He's Going to His Mother's Closet': Hamlet and Gertrude on Screen," *SS* 45 (1993), 56. Biggs sees 1960 as the year when actors began turning verse into prose, and Gielgud's favoring of song over sense, his "ample vibrato to boot," identifies him with the older era.

45. Linda Costanzo Cahir, "The Artful Rerouting of *A Streetcar Named Desire*," *LFQ* 22.2 (1994), 73.

46. Quoted in Meredith Lillich, "Shakespeare on the Screen," p. 258.

47. Original Film Trailer on MGM/UA Home Video laser disk. Side three.

3 LAURENCE OLIVIER DIRECTS SHAKESPEARE

1. *Walking Shadows*, p. 199.

2. Others do not see it this way. See Donald Spoto, *Laurence Olivier: A Biography* (New York: HarperCollins, 1992), p. 97: "But the direst liability of *As You Like It* was the star [Elisabeth Bergner]."

3. *Shakespeare and the Film*, p. 31. By my count she only turns one somersault, and that not of Olympic gymnastics quality.

4. Howard Barnes, "*As You Like It*," *NYHT* 6 Nov. 1936, n.p.; for similar views, see also W.F., "*As You Like It*," *MFB* 3.33 (Sept. 1936), 147, 519.

5. "Bergner as Rosalind," in *Around Cinemas* (London: Home & Van Thal, 1946; repr. New York: Arno Press, 1972), p. 176.

6. See the frequently cited essay by Norman Rabkin, "Rabbits, Ducks and *Henry V*," *SQ* 28 (1977), 279–96.

7. Harry M. Geduld, *Filmguide to Henry V* (Bloomington: Indiana University Press, 1973), p. 55.

8. *Filming Shakespeare's Plays: The Adaptations of Laurence Olivier, Orson Welles, Peter Brook and Akira Kurosawa* (Cambridge University Press, 1988), p. 36.

9. "Olivier's *Henry V* and the Elizabethan World Picture," *LFQ* 11.3 (1983: Special issue of papers from Seminar 16, World Shakespeare Congress; guest ed. Kenneth S. Rothwell), 179.

10. Quoted in Charles Musser, "Engaging with Reality," in *The Oxford History of World Cinema*, ed. Geoffrey Nowell-Smith (Oxford University Press, 1996), p. 326.

11. *Ibid.*

12. Peter Drexler, "Laurence Olivier's *Henry V* and Veit Harlan's *Der Grosse König*: Two Versions of the National Hero on Film," in *Negotiations with Hal: Multi-Media Perceptions of [Shakespeare's] Henry the Fifth*, ed. Peter Drexler and Lawrence Guntner (Technische Universität Braunschweig: Braunschweiger Anglistische Arbeiten, 1995), p. 129.

13. See Ernest Kantorowicz, *The King's Two Bodies: A Study in Medieval Political Theology* (Princeton University Press, 1957). This well-known concept is touched on by Nicole Weigel and Stefanie Schreiner in "England's Glory, or 'Bildungsroman': A Comparison of Olivier's and Branagh's *Henry V* Films," in Drexler and Guntner, *Negotiations with Hal*, p. 68.

14. *Screening Shakespeare from* Richard II *to* Henry V (Newark: University of Delaware Press, 1991), p. 101.

15. "Recycled Film Codes and 'The Great Tradition of Shakespeare on Film'," in Drexler and Guntner, *Negotiations with Hal*, p. 51.

16. *Film in the Aura of Art* (Princeton University Press, 1984), p. 132. This is the most searching essay on the film that I have found.

17. Robert F. Willson, Jr., "The Opening of *Henry V*: Olivier's Visual Pun," *SFNL* 5.2 (May 1981), 1ff.

18. My colleague R. Thomas Simone in an unpublished paper has made a compelling case that the prompter is actually intended to be William Shakespeare.

19. Spoto, *Olivier*, p. 166. Apparently Olivier himself may have been the one to find the illuminated manuscript.

20. *Filmguide*, p. 42.

21. Brian McFarlane, *An Autobiography of British Cinema* (London: Methuen, 1997), p. 82. I am obliged to Dr. Russell Jackson for drawing this book to my attention.

22. Martin Marks, "The Sound of Music," in *The Oxford History of World Cinema* (Oxford University Press, 1996), p. 257.

23. Manvell, *Shakespeare and the Film*, p. 46.

24. *Film in the Aura*, p. 151.

25. Laurence Olivier, "An Essay in *Hamlet*," in Brenda Cross (ed.), *The Film "Hamlet". A Record of Its Production* (New York: Saturn Press, 1948), p. 12.

26. Souvenir Program, Theatre Guild, n.p.

27. Spoto, *Olivier*, p. 207.

28. "Olivier's *Hamlet*: A Film-Infused Play," in *LFQ* 5.4 (Fall 1977, guest ed. Michael Mullin), 305.

29. "*Hamlet.*" *Film, Television and Audio Performance* (London and Toronto: Associated University Presses, 1988), pp. 23–25.

30. Davies, *Filming Shakespeare's Plays*, p. 64.

31. "Building the Sets," in Cross, *The Film* Hamlet, p. 44.

32. "Subliminal Masks in Olivier's *Hamlet*," *SFNL* 16.1 (Dec. 1991), 5.

33. "Olivier, Hamlet, and Freud," in *Shakespearean Films/Shakespearean Directors* (Boston: Unwin Hyman, 1990), p. 39 and *passim*.

34. *Hamlet Father and Son* (Oxford: Clarendon Press, 1955), p. 115 and *passim*. Alexander thinks that *arete* is of greater consequence to the tragic hero than *hamartia*. The stress in the Olivier film on "flaw" distorts Hamlet's character.

35. "Shakespeare on TV," *BBC Quarterly* 9.3 (Autumn 1954), 146.

36. Olivier, "An Essay in *Hamlet*," in Cross, *The Film*, p. 12.

37. *Filming Shakespeare's Plays*, pp. 49, 55. Two stills from *Hamlet* effectively illustrate the vertical and horizontal strategies used in the movie.

38. "Note on *Hamlet*," *FM* 13 (Jan./Feb. 1954), 19.

39. A similar debacle occurred in 1973 when Joseph Papp's Broadway hit version of *Much Ado* was forced to close down only nine days after IBM sponsored its transmission on television.

40. Davies, *Filming Shakespeare's Plays*, p. 66.

41. *Laurence Olivier and the Art of Film Making* (London and Toronto: Associated University Presses, 1985), p. 229.

42. Quoted in Geoffrey Bullough (ed.), *Narrative and Dramatic Sources of Shakespeare*, III (New York: Columbia University Press, 1975), p. 253.

43. "A Defence of the Apologie of the Church of England," in *Works of John Jewel*, III, ed. John Eyre (Cambridge University Press, 1848), p. 152.

44. See Constance A. Brown's unrivalled essay, "Olivier's *Richard III* – A Re-evaluation," *FQ* 20 (1967), 25.

45. Silviria, *Olivier and Film Making*, p. 237.

46. F.R. Leavis, "Diabolic Intellect and the Noble Hero," in *Shakespeare "Othello." A Casebook*, ed. John Wain (London, 1971), p. 135; Kenneth Tynan, *The Sound of Two Hands Clapping* (London: Jonathan Cape, 1975), pp. 130–31. Tynan's essay offers deep insight into Olivier's approach to this role.

47. Spoto, *Olivier*, p. 334.

48. Jorgens, *Shakespeare on Film*, p. 191.

49. "Minstrel Show *Othello*," *NYT* 2 Feb. 1966, 24.

50. "Olivier Paints Othello Ridden by Neuroses," *NYHT* 2 Feb. 1966.

51. "Black and White," *TNY*, 19 Feb. 1966, 145.

52. "Olivier and the Moor," *Holiday*, 26 Apr. 1966, 143 and *passim*.

53. *The Times* 13 Dec. 1937, 18.

54. Jonathan Miller, *Subsequent Performances* (New York: Elisabeth Sifton Books/ Viking, 1986), pp. 104–08.

55. John O'Connor, "Olivier as the Controversial Shylock in 1880s," *NYT* 15 March 1974, 67.

56. "Trivial Pursuit: The Casket plot in the Miller/Olivier *Merchant of Venice*," *SFNL* 10.1 (Dec. 1985), 7 and *passim*.

57. Peter Cowie, "Olivier at 75 Returns to Lear," *NYT* 1 May 1983, II. 1.

58. Frank Occhiogrosso, "'Give Me Thy Hand': Manual Gesture in the Elliott/Olivier *King Lear*," *SB* 2.9 (May–June 1984), 16–19.

59. Tucker Orbison, "The Stone and the Oak: Olivier's TV Film of *King Lear*," *CEA Critic* 47 (Fall–Winter 1984), 67–77.

60. *360 Film Classics* (supplement to *Sight and Sound*), ed. Nick James (London: NFTVA and BFI, 1998). Ernst Lubitsch's Shakespeare derivative, *To Be or Not to Be*, also made the list.

4 ORSON WELLES: SHAKESPEARE FOR THE ART HOUSES

1. Simon Callow, *Orson Welles: The Road to Xanadu* (London: Jonathan Cape, 1995), p. 576. Among other biographies consulted for this section are: Frank Brady, *Citizen Welles: A Biography of Orson Welles* (New York: Charles Scribner's Sons, 1989); Barbara Leaming, *Orson Welles* (New York: Viking, 1985); Joseph McBride, *Orson Welles*, rev. ed. (New York: Da Capo, 1996); James Naremore, *The Magic World of Orson Welles* (Dallas: Southern Methodist University Press, 1989); Jonathan Rosenbaum (ed.), *This Is Orson Welles: Orson Welles and Peter Bogdanovich* (New York: HarperCollins, 1992); David Thomson, *Rosebud: The Story of Orson Welles* (New York: Alfred Knopf, 1996).

2. For an overview of this complicated subject, which is beyond the scope of the present study, see Ronald Gottesman (ed.), *Focus on Orson Welles* (Englewood Cliffs: Prentice Hall, 1976).

3. Brady, *Welles*, p. 432.

4. Jonathan Rosenbaum, "The Invisible Orson Welles: A First Inventory," *S&S* 55.3 (Summer 1986), 168.

5. "Interview," from Italian Documentary, *Rosabella*, appendix no. 51, *Othello* [1952] The Voyager Company laser disk, 1995.

6. "Interview with Keith Baxter," in *"Chimes at Midnight": Orson Welles, director*, ed. Bridget Gellert Lyons (New Brunswick and London: Rutgers University Press, 1988), p. 279.

7. See "The Magician," in James Naremore's aptly named *The Magic World of Orson Welles*, pp. 30–51.

8. *Ibid.*, p. 250.

9. "With Orson Welles: Stories from a Life in Film," television interview in 1980 by Leslie Megahey, with Jeanne Moreau, John Huston, Charlton Heston, Anthony Perkins, and Peter Bogdanovich, transmitted on Channel TNT, Monday, 5 Feb. 1990.

10. David Bradley, "Shakespeare on a Shoestring," *Movie Makers* (April 1947), 146ff.

11. Richard Wilson, "*Macbeth* on Film," *TA* 33.5 (June 1949), 53–55.

12. Quoted in Manvell, *Shakespeare and the Film*, p. 59.

13. Richard France (ed.), *Orson Welles on Shakespeare: The W.P.A. and Mercury Theatre Playscripts* (New York: The Greenwood Press, 1990), p. 5 and *passim*.

14. *NYT* 28 Dec. 1950, 22.

15. Quoted in Rosenbaum, *This Is Orson Welles*, p. 203.

16. For analysis of the textual changes, see Michael Mullin, "Orson Welles' *Macbeth*: Script and Screen," in Gottesman (ed.), *Focus on Orson Welles*, pp. 136–45.

17. Harold Leonard, "Hollywood: Notes on *Macbeth*," *S&S* 19.1 (March 1950), 17.

18. Mullin, 136–45. With three different versions in existence, any opinions about the movie are contingent on the incarnation that the critic has screened. Commentary here has been based on re-screenings of the 1979 release available on videocassette from Republic Pictures.

19. The reader is entitled to know that David Thomson sees Lady Macbeth in exactly opposite terms, as "very erotic." *Rosebud,* p. 286.

20. For a superb account of production details, see Bernice W. Kliman, "Welles's *Macbeth*, A Textual Parable," in Michael Skovmand (ed.), *Screen Shakespeare* (Aarhus University Press, 1994), pp. 25–38. See also Kliman's "Orson Welles's 1936 'Voodoo' *Macbeth* and Its Reincarnation on Film," in Macbeth, *Shakespeare in Performance Series* (Manchester University Press, 1992), pp. 86–99.

21. Kliman, "Welles's *Macbeth*," in Skovmand (ed.), *Screen Shakespeare*, p. 28.

22. *Welles*, p. 118.

23. Alan Brien, *The Evening Standard* 23 Feb. 1956.

24. Anon., "The 'Othello' of Mr. Orson Welles," *MG* 25 Feb. 1956.

25. "Films," *TN* 1 Oct. 1955, 81.

26. "The New Pictures," *Time* 6 June 1955, 106.

27. W.J. Weatherby, "Forgotten Heir of *Citizen Kane*," *Guardian* 28 April 1992, 38.

28. J. Hoberman, "Moor Better Blues," *VV* 31 March 1992, 5.

29. McBride, *Welles*, pp. 124–25. McBride points out that a 1995 Criterion Collection laser disk uses the 1955 US release version.

30. *Shakespeare Observed: Studies in Performance on Stage and Screen* (Athens: Ohio University Press, 1992), pp. 51–53.

31. Roland Barthes, *S/Z. An Essay*, trans. Richard Miller (New York: Hill & Wang, 1972).

32. Richard Palmer, *Hermeneutics: Interpretation Theory in Schleiermacher, Dilthey, Heidegger, and Gadamer* (Evanston: Northwestern University Press, 1969), p. 87.

33. *Put Money in Thy Purse: A Diary of the Film of* Othello (London: Methuen, 1952).

34. Interviews from Italian Documentary *Rosabella*, appendices nos. 51, 49, and 50.

35. *Movie Made America* (New York: Vintage, 1975), p. 253; repr. in *The Book of Film Noir*, ed. Ian Cameron (New York: Continuum, 1992), p. 89.

36. Crowl, *Shakespeare Observed*, p. 181, f.n. 9. Crowl failed to find the mirror in any of the reprints of Carpaccio's work that he surveyed but he did find a mirror that is put to a similar reflective purpose in Jan van Eyck's "The Marriage of Arnolfini."

37. "When Peter Met Orson: The 1953 CBS *King Lear*," In Boose and Burt (eds.), *Shakespeare, The Movie*, p. 129. Howard's interesting essay also comments on "how oddly uncomfortable" Welles's films were with "women's sexuality" (p. 131), a provocative point that deserves to be considered at greater length.

38. Marvin Rosenberg, *The Masks of* King Lear (Berkeley: University of California Press, 1972), p. 312.

39. Nikos Metallinos, *Television Aesthetics*, pp. 237–40. A large topic, but Metallinos' chapter on "Applied Rules for Composition of Television Pictures" (pp. 197–283) offers a useful summary.

40. Quoted in Robert A. Hetherington, "The *Lears* of Peter Brook," *SFNL* 6.1 (1982), 7.

41. "Introduction," *King Henry IV Part Two, The Arden Shakespeare* (London: Methuen,1966), p. xxvii.

42. *Shakespeare on Film*, p. 111.

43. "Interview," in Lyons, *Chimes at Midnight*, p. 282.

44. Juan Cobos and Miguel Rubio, "Welles and Falstaff: An Interview by Juan Cobos and Miguel Rubio," *S&S* 35.4 (Autumn 1966), 159.

45. France (ed.), *Orson Welles on Shakespeare*, p. 172.

46. Robert Hapgood, "*Chimes at Midnight* From Stage to Screen: The Art of Adaptation," in *Shakespeare Survey* 39, ed. Stanley Wells (Cambridge University Press, 1987), p. 40.

47. Rosenbaum, *This Is Orson Welles*, p. 217.

48. Hapgood, "*Chimes at Midnight*," pp. 44–47.

49. See Lyons (ed.), *Chimes at Midnight*, for the film's continuity script. Scene and shot numbers in the text refer to Lyons.

50. Pilkington, *Screening Shakespeare*, p. 137, warns about the "difficulty in identifying Falstaff too closely with Welles." The difficulty granted, there still seem to be many reasons for identifying him with Welles.

51. Quoted in Rosenbaum, *This is Orson Welles*, p. 100.

52. "The Magnificent Ambersons," in Gottesmann (ed.), *Focus on Orson Welles*, p. 123.

53. Davies, *Filming Shakespeare's Plays*, pp. 124–28.

54. Baxter, "Interview," Lyons (ed.), *Chimes at Midnight*, pp. 280–81.

55. Davies, *Filming Shakespeare's Plays*, p. 125.

56. Rosenbaum, *This Is Orson Welles*, pp. 294; 297–98.

57. Cobos and Rubio, "Interview," 158.

58. Lyons (ed.), *Chimes at Midnight*. See "Continuity Script," pp. 142–67.

59. *Ibid.*, p. 254.

60. Sharmini Tiruchelvam, "Encounter on the Field of Philippi," *The Daily Telegraph Magazine*, 6 Feb. 1970, 17.

61. Jonathan Rosenbaum, "The Invisible Orson Welles," pp. 167–68.

62. BFI "SIFT" catalog, entry A02M005.

63. Rosenbaum, "The Invisible Orson Welles," p. 170.

64. Bosley Crowther, "Review," *NYT* 20 March 1967, 26.

5 ELECTRONIC SHAKESPEARE: FROM TELEVISION TO THE WEB

1. Ashley Dukes, "Televised Drama So Far: The English Scene," *TAM* (1939), 259.

2. Transmission data from mimeographed *Television Programme as Broadcast* (*TPAB*) 1937. BBC WAC, Caversham Park, Reading. Susan Willis, *The BBC Shakespeare Plays: Making the Televised Canon* (Chapel Hill: University of North Carolina Press, 1991) correctly puts the BBC 1937 *As You Like It* as falling on February 5 rather than 6. A blurry mimeographed program caused the incorrect February 6 date in Rothwell & Melzer.

3. Gordon Ross, *Television Jubilee: The Story of 25 Years of BBC Television* (London: W.H. Allen, 1961), p. 13.

4. Albert Abramson, "The Invention of Television," in *Television: An International History*, ed. Anthony Smith (Oxford University Press, 1995), p. 13.

5. Ross, *Television Jubilee*, p. 20. Quotation of a review from *The Guardian*.

6. "Shakespeare: The Scholar's Contribution," *The Listener* 17 March 1937, 498 and *passim*.

7. "Shakespeare in His Theatre," *The Listener* 20 Jan. 1937, 116–18.

8. "Shakespeare on the Modern Stage," *The Listener* 3 Feb. 1937, 207.

9. Allwyn Tibbenham, "Shakespeare Today," in "Points from Letters," *The Listener* 17 March 1937, 521.

10. Nikos Metallinos, *Television Aesthetics: Perceptual, Cognitive and Compositional Bases* (Mahwah, NJ: Lawrence Erlbaum Associates, 1996), p. 1.

11. *Radio and TV Who's Who*, 3rd edn, ed. Cyrus Andrews (London: George Young, 1954).

12. Ross, *Television Jubilee*, p. 59.

13. "Review," *The Times* 13 Dec. 1937, 18.

14. BBC, *TPAB* Sunday, 24 July 1938.

15. Anon., "Review," *World Film News* 30 Aug. 1938.

16. "*Julius Caesar* in Modern Dress," *News Chronicle* 25 July 1938.

17. "*Julius Caesar* in Modern dress: Television Version," *Sunday Times* 24 July 1938.

18. Correspondence about *Othello*, BBC WAC T5/379 *Othello* 1937–50.

19. "Televised Drama," *The Times* 15 Dec. 1937, 14.

20. "Floor Mistakes," internal circulating memo, BBC WAC T5/508, 6 Feb. 1939.

21. "Critic on the Hearth," *The Listener* 29 Dec. 1938, 1428.

22. WAC T5/220, 4 March 1948.

23. "Shakespeare on Television," *BBC Quarterly* 9.3 (Autumn 1954), 146.

24. "Televised *Hamlet*," *NYT* 14 Dec. 1947, X 11.

25. For more production details about televised Shakespeare from 1937 to 1990, see Rothwell and Melzer, *Shakespeare on Screen*. Also useful is the appended checklist in Willis, *The BBC Shakespeare Plays*.

26. "Shakespeare on Television," *SQ* 12.3 (Summer 1961), 323–27.

27. "Uneasy Lies the Head," *The Times* 8 July 1960, 4.

28. Peter Dews, "The Spread of the Eagle," *Radio Times* 25 Apr. 1963, 49.

29. "Continuity Problem of New B.B.C. Shakespeare Series," *The Times* 4 May 1963, 5d.

30. Elspeth Parker, "*The Wars of the Roses*: Space, Shape, and Flow," *SB* 13.2 (Spring 1995), 40–41.

31. David Addenbrooke, *The Royal Shakespeare Company. The Peter Hall Years* (London: William Kimber, 1974), p. 126.

32. "A Shakespearian Experience on TV," *The Times* 21 April 1965, 13d.

33. "Shakespeare Through the Camera's Eye," *SQ* 17.4 (1966), 385.

34. The ins and outs of this complicated battle for control of the airwaves, and of the consciousness of the masses, are spelled out in William Boddy, "The Beginnings of American Television," in Smith (ed.), *Television: An International History*, pp. 35–61.

35. Boddy, "The Beginnings," p. 48.

36. "An Interview with George Schaefer," *Hallmark Hall of Fame: A Tradition of Excellence* (New York: Museum of Broadcasting, 1984), pp. 29, 30.

37. "Shakespeare through the Camera's Eye," *SQ* VI.1 (Winter 1955), 65.

38. "*Macbeth* in Color," *Time* 13 Dec. 1954, 36.

39. "The Forgotten Television *Tempest*," *SFNL* 9.1 (Dec. 1984), 3.

40. Clayton Hutton, Macbeth: *The Making of the Film* (London: Max Parrish, n.d.), preface.

41. Jack Gould, *NYT* 22 May 1949, II.9.

42. Charlton Heston, *In the Arena*: An Autobiography (New York: Simon & Schuster, 1995), p. 89.

43. "Worthington Miner's Version [of *Julius Caesar*] in Modern Dress Proves Spectacular TV," *NYT* 13 March 1949, II.11.

44. For a fascinating survey of these political questions, see Neal Gabler, *Winchell: Gossip, Power and the Culture of Celebrity* (New York: Knopf, 1994).

45. Heston, *In the Arena*, p. 87.

46. Ralph Nelson (ed.), Hamlet. *A Television Script* (New York: CBS, 1976).

47. BFI Microjacket Cuttings. Arthur Knight, "Review," *Saturday Review*, 17 Oct. 1964, n.p.

48. BFI Microjacket Cuttings. John Russell Taylor, *The Times* 7 July 1972; David Robinson, *Financial Times* 7 July 1972; and Margaret Hinxman, *Sunday Telegraph* 9 July 1972.

49. See Melvyn Bragg, *Richard Burton, A Life* (Boston: Little, Brown, and Company, 1988), for a remarkable chronicle of Burton's stormy career.

50. For the details surrounding this production, see Richard L. Sterne, *John Gielgud Directs Richard Burton in* Hamlet: *A Journal of Rehearsals* (New York: Random House, 1967).

51. Hamlet: *Film, Television*, p. 154. Kliman's essay covers the production in depth, pp. 154–66.

52. *The Times* 20 April 1964, 16.

53. *Ibid.*

54. "Interview," *Radio Times* 188 (17 Sept. 1970), 6–7.

55. "The Classic Theatre *Macbeth*," *Pulse* (Oct. 1976), repr. in *Shakespeare on Television: An Anthology of Essays and Review*, eds. J.C. Bulman and H.R. Coursen (Hanover and London: University Press of New England, 1988), p. 247.

56. McKernan and Terris, *Walking Shadows*, p. 97.

57. Addenbrooke, *Royal Shakespeare Company*, p. 175.

58. H.R. Coursen, *Shakespearean Performance as Interpretation* (Newark: Associated University Presses, 1992), p. 195.

59. "Shakespeare in Britain," *SQ* 23 (Fall 1972), repr. in Bulman and Coursen, *Shakespeare on Television*, p. 246.

60. "Stage and Screen: The Trevor Nunn *Macbeth*," *SQ* 38.3 (Autumn 1987), 350–59.

61. *The Standard* 13 Jan. 1979 n.p. [Press cutting, BFI].

62. R. Alan Kimbrough, "The First Season," *SFNL* 3.2 (April 1979), 5.

63. Virginia M. Carr [Vaughan], "The Second Season: *Twelfth Night*," *SFNL* 4.2 (April 1980), 5.

64. Willis, *The BBC Shakespeare Plays*, p. 25.

65. "Shakespeare in Miniature: The BBC *Antony and Cleopatra*," in Bulman and Coursen (eds.), *Shakespeare on Television*, p. 144.

66. Henry Fenwick, "The Production," in *"Troilus and Cressida" The BBC TV Shakespeare* (London: BBC, 1981), pp. 18–24.

67. Lynda E. Boose, "Grossly Gaping Viewers and Jonathan Miller's *Othello*," in Boose and Burt (eds.), *Shakespeare, The Movie*, p. 186.

68. Henry Fenwick, "The Production," in *The BBC-TV Shakespeare "Othello"* (London: BBC, 1981), p. 18.

69. *Ibid.*, pp. 19–21.

70. Michael Manheim, "The Shakespeare Plays on TV," *SFNL* 8.2 (April 1984), 4.

71. Susan McCloskey, "The Shakespeare Plays on TV," *SFNL* 9.2 (April 1985), 5.

72. "Race-ing *Othello*, Re-Engendering White-Out," in Boose and Burt (eds.), *Shakespeare, The Movie*, p. 28.

73. Press kit, *Othello*.

74. H.R. Coursen, "Not Fit to Live," *SFNL* 13.1 (Dec. 1988), 4.

75. Samuel Crowl and Mary Z. Maher, "Cambridgeshire *Hamlet*: Two Views," *SFNL* 13.1 (Dec. 1988), 7.

76. Jack Oruch, "Shakespeare for the Millions: Kiss Me, Petruchio," *SFNL* 11.2 (April 1987), 7.

77. See Bjo Trimble, *Star Trek Concordance*, 1990, n.p. I am obliged to Michael J. Klossner of Little Rock, Arkansas, for useful data on this topic.

78. See the special issue on *Star Trek: Extrapolation* 36.1 (Spring 1995), guest editor Susan Hines, published at Kent State University, especially Stephen M. Buhler, "'Who Calls Me Villain?': Blank Verse and the Black Hat," pp. 18–27, which covers Shakespearean allusions in *Star Trek VI*.

79. See *As You Like It: Audio-Visual Shakespeare*, ed. Cathy Grant (London: BUFVC, 1992) for its most recent listings.

6 SPECTACLE AND SONG IN CASTELLANI AND ZEFFIRELLI

1. "Shakespeare's Italy," in *SS* 7 (1954), 104.

2. Willis, *The BBC Shakespeare Plays*, p. 104.

3. "Cinema," *The Spectator* (24 Sept. 1954), 361.

4. William Whitebait, "Romeo and Juliet at the Odeon," *New Statesman and Nation* 48 (2 Oct. 1954), 390.

5. Robert Hatch, "Review," *TN* 8 Jan. 1955, 37.

6. "Review," *NYT* 22 Dec. 1954, 28.

7. "Shakespeare on the Screen," *FR* 7.6 (June/July 1956), 259.

8. "Castellani's *Romeo and Juliet*: Intention and Response," in Eckert (ed.), *Focus on Shakespearean Films*, p. 112.

9 Franco Zeffirelli, *Zeffirelli: The Autobiography of Franco Zeffirelli* (New York: Weidenfeld & Nicolson, 1986), p. 214.

10. *Ibid.*, pp. 164–68.

11. *Ibid.*, p. 212.

12. Bosley Crowther, "Review," *NYT* 9 March 1967, 43.

13. "Zeffirelli's Shakespeare: The Visual Realization of Tone and Theme," *LFQ* 8.4 (1980), 210–18.

14. *The Taming of the Shrew* (Manchester University Press, 1989), pp. 55–58. Holderness' essay offers many interesting insights too numerous to summarize here.

15. Zeffirelli, *Autobiography*, p. 216.

16. Martin S. Dworkin, "'Stay Illusion!' Having Words about Shakespeare on Screen," *The Journal of Aesthetic Education* 11 (Jan. 1977), 59.

17. *Shakespeare on Film*, p. 82.

18. "Popularizing Shakespeare: The Artistry of Franco Zeffirelli," in Boose and Burt (eds.), *Shakespeare, The Movie*, p. 85.

19. Zeffirelli, *Autobiography*, p. 225.

20. "The Art of Franco Zeffirelli and Shakespeare's *Romeo and Juliet*," in Fred Marcus (ed.), *Film and Literature: Contrasts in Media* (Scranton: Chandler, 1971), p. 211.

21. Olivia Hussey (as told to Edwin Miller), "Love is the Sweetest Thing," *Seventeen* 27 (Jan. 1968), 104.

22. Anon., "A New *Romeo and Juliet*," *Look* 31 (17 Oct. 1967), 58.

23. *Ibid.*, p. 34.

24. Zeffirelli, *Autobiography*, p. 227.

25. Polly Devlin, "I Know My Romeo and Juliet," *Vogue* 151 (1 Apr. 1968), 52.

26. Michael Pursell, "Artifice and Authenticity in Zeffirelli's *Romeo and Juliet*," *LFQ* 14.4 (1986), 173–78. If I understand him correctly, Pursell makes much the same point in a

detailed examination of the film's interplay between realism and artifice.

27. Anon., "A New *Romeo*," p. 55.

28. For close scrutiny of the hand imagery in both film and play, see James H. Lake, "Hands in Zeffirelli's *Romeo*," SAA Abstracts, 1990, in *SFNL* 15.1 (Dec. 1990), 4; and Barbara L. Parker, "Review of George W. Williams' videocassette lecture, 'Feuding and Loving in Shakespeare's *Romeo and Juliet*'," in *SFNL* 16.1 (Dec. 1991), 8.

29. "2nd Vesper Services, Masses for the Virgin Mary," *Penguin Book of Latin Verses*, ed. Frederick Brittain (Baltimore: Peter Smith, 1962), p. 129. I'm obliged to Professor Jane Ambrose of the University of Vermont for tracking down this reference.

30. Page Cook, "The Sound Track," *FR* 19 (Nov. 1968), 571.

31. Zeffirelli, *Autobiography*, p. 229.

32. Cirillo, "Art of Zeffirelli," in Marcus (ed.), *Film and Literature*, p. 227.

33. John Tibbetts, "Breaking the Classical Barrier: Franco Zeffirelli Interviewed by John Tibbetts," *LFQ* 22.2 (1994), 138.

34. Michael P. Jensen, "Mel Gibson on *Hamlet*," *SFNL* 15.2 (April 1991), 1 and *passim*.

35. "Mel's Melodramatic Melancholy: Zeffirelli's *Hamlet*," *Screen Shakespeare*, p. 122.

36. Tibbetts, "Zeffirelli Interviewed," p. 139.

37. See "Zeffirelli's *Hamlet*: Sunlight Makes Meaning," *SFNL* 16.1 (Dec. 1991), 1 and *passim*; and "Zeffirelli's *Hamlet* and the Baroque," *SFNL* 16.2 (April 1992), 1 and *passim*.

38. *Screen Shakespeare*, p. 126.

39. Tibbetts, "Zeffirelli Interviewed," p. 139.

40. "Zeffirelli's *Hamlet*," *SFNL* 15.2 (April 1991), 1 and *passim*.

41. "Zeffirelli's Shakespeare," in Davies and Wells (eds.), *Shakespeare and the Moving Image*, p. 176.

42. "Popularizing Shakespeare," in Boose and Burt (eds.), *Shakespeare, The Movie*, p. 85.

7 SHAKESPEARE MOVIES IN THE AGE OF ANGST

1. Tony Richardson, *Long Distance Runner. A Memoir*, intro. by Lindsay Anderson (London: Faber & Faber, 1993), p. 220.

2. *Ibid.*, p. 219.

3. *Ibid.*

4. See Neil Taylor, "The Films of *Hamlet*," in Davies and Wells (eds.), *Shakespeare and the Moving Image*, p. 195. Taylor protests that no evidence has been presented that the film was intended for television; on the other hand, it has never been clear that it was not! Although in his *Memoir* (see above), Richardson throws no light on this question, it would be odd if he and his producers didn't have in mind the profitable residual rights for television that have often underwritten movie production.

5. Kliman, *Hamlet*, p. 169.

6. "Review," *Time* 28 Feb. 1969, 74.

7. *Understanding Movies*, 2nd edn (Englewood Cliffs, NJ: Prentice, Hall, 1976), p. 103.

8. Review in *London Sunday Times* quoted in *Time*, see n. 6, above.

9. Michael Mullin, "Tony Richardson's *Hamlet*: Script and Screen," *LFQ* 4.2 (Spring 1976), 126. Mullin's article exhaustively analyzes Richardson's textual alterations.

10. "Review," *Newsweek* 12 May 1969, 119.

11. "Not Lacking Gall," *TNY* 45, 10 May 1969, 121.

12. Gerald Weales, "I Am Not Prince Hamlet," *Commonweal* 30 May 1969, 319. (Review of stage performance.)

13. Addenbrooke, *The Royal Shakespeare Company*, p. 20.

14. *Ibid.*, p. 282.

15. Crowl, *Shakespeare Observed*, p. 75.

16. Quoted in Manvell, *Shakespeare and the Film*, p. 123.
17. A Midsummer Night's Dream. *Shakespeare in Performance* (Manchester University Press, 1994), p. 93.
18. "Peter Hall's *Midsummer Night's Dream* on Film," *ETJ* 27 (1975), 529–34.
19. Brenda Davies, "Review," *MFB* 36.422 (March 1969), 51.
20. "Cinematic Oxymoron in Peter Hall's *A Midsummer Night's Dream*," *LFQ* 11.3 (1983), 174–78.
21. "*King Lear* or *Endgame*," in *Shakespeare Our Contemporary*, trans. Boleslaw Taborski (New York: Anchor Books, 1966), pp. 127–68.
22. Manvell, *Shakespeare and the Film*, p. 140. Manvell's lengthy interview with Michael Lord Birkett is well worth reading in its entirety.
23. Normand Berlin, "Peter Brook's Interpretation of *King Lear*: 'Nothing Will Come of Nothing'," *LFQ* 5.4 (1977), 303.
24. William Johnson, "*King Lear* and *Macbeth*," *FQ* 25 (1972), 43.
25. Sylvia Millar, "*King Lear*," *MFB* 38 (1971), 183.
26. Jonathan Raban, "Peter Brook's *King Lear*," *New Statesman* 30 July 1971, n.p.
27. John Simon, "Review," *The New Leader* 27 Dec. 1971.
28. Charlton Heston, *In the Arena: An Autobiography* (New York: Simon & Schuster, 1995), p. 302.
29. "Peter Brook's Night of the Living Dead," *TNY* 11 Dec. 1971, 136.
30. Alexander Walker, "Review," *Evening Standard* 22 July 1971.
31. Felix Barker, "Review," *Evening Standard* 23 July 1971.
32. "One *King Lear* for Our Time: A Bleak Film Vision by Peter Brook," *LFQ* 4.2 (1976), 159–64.
33. "Shakespeare in the Movies," *NYRB* 18 (4 May 1972), 19.
34. Manvell, *Shakespeare and the Film*, p. 137.
35. For discussion of Shakespeare movies influenced by Kott, see Samuel Crowl, "Chain Reaction: A Study of Roman Polanski's *Macbeth*," *Soundings* LIX.2 (Summer 1976), 226–33.
36. Tynan, *The Sound of Two Hands Clapping*, p. 87.
37. Bernard Weinraub, "Interview with Polanski," *NYT Magazine* 12 Dec. 1971, 36.
38. I owe the phrase to Dr. Barbara Hodgdon's "Two *King Lears*: Uncovering the Filmtext," *LFQ* 11.3 (1983), 143.
39. Macbeth: *Shakespeare in Performance* (Manchester University Press, 1992), p. 121.
40. William P. Shaw, "Violence and Vision in Polanski's *Macbeth* and Brook's *King Lear*," *LFQ* 14.4 (1986), 211.
41. Per Serritslev Petersen, "The 'Bloody Business' of Roman Polanski's *Macbeth*: A Case Study of the Dynamics of Modern Shakespeare [Reception] Appropriation," in Skovmand (ed.), *Screen Shakespeare*, p. 52.
42. "Shakespeare in the Movies," *NYRB* 18 May 1972, 18.
43. Weinraub, "Interview with Polanski," p. 68.
44. The opening "long take" has been much discussed. See Norman Silverstein, "The Opening Shot of Roman Polanski's *Macbeth*," *LFQ* 2.1 (1974), 88–90, which incorrectly corrects my "Roman Polanski's *Macbeth*: Golgotha Triumphant," *LFQ* 1.1 (1973), 71–75, and Jack J. Jorgens' note that correctly corrects everybody, "The Opening Scene of Polanski's *Macbeth*," *LFQ* 3.3 (1975), 277–78.
45. Weinraub, "Interview," pp. 36, 64.
46. Jorgens, *Shakespeare and Film*, p. 170.
47. Weinraub, "Interview," p. 68.
48. "Some New Notes on *Macbeth*," in *Vindication of the Reading of the Folio of 1623* (Toronto: The Copp, Clark Co., Ltd., 1893), pp. vii–viii. For a detailed analysis of how

Libby's theory influenced Polanski's film, see my "Roman Polanski's *Macbeth*: The 'Privileging' of Ross," *The CEA Critic* 46 1&2 (1983–84), 50–55.

49. Manvell, *Shakespeare and the Film*, p. 92.
50. "Review," *NYT* 25 Nov. 1952, 33.
51. "Julius Caesar," *Variety* 10 June 1970.
52. "Jason Robards, *et al.*," *NYT* 4 Feb. 1971, 30.
53. "*Et tu*, Charlton," *VV* 25 Feb. 1971, 57.
54. Tiruchelvam, "Encounter on the Field of Philippi," p. 19.
55. Charlton Heston, *In the Arena*, pp. 564–77. These final pages sum up Heston's political and social views, which are difficult to characterize without falling into reductive labels like "libertarian," "conservative," or "liberal."
56. *Ibid.*, p. 445.
57. *Ibid.*, p. 439.
58. Charlton Heston, "Heston Directs Heston," Publicity Booklet, London, 1972, n.p.
59. Sylvia Millar, "Review," *MFB* 39.459 (April 1972), 67.
60. Frank Kermode, "Shakespeare in the Movies," p. 18.
61. "Pit.," *Variety* 8 March 1972.

8 OTHER SHAKESPEARES: TRANSLATION AND EXPROPRIATION

1. Dennis Kennedy (ed.), "Introduction," *Foreign Shakespeare: Contemporary Performance* (Cambridge University Press, 1993), p. 2.
2. See Ashish Rajadhyaksha, "India: Filming the Nation," in *Oxford History of World Cinema*, pp. 678–89.
3. James Ivory, *Savages/Shakespeare Wallah. A Film by James Ivory from a Screenplay by R. Prawer Jhabvala and James Ivory* (New York: Grove Press, 1973), p. 87.
4. Valerie Wayne, "*Shakespeare Wallah* and Colonial Specularity," in Boose and Burt (eds.), *Shakespeare the Movie*, p. 101.
5. Peter Morris, ed., *Shakespeare on Film* (Ottawa: Canadian Film Institute, 1972), p. 8.
6. *Filmindia* (Feb. 1955), 71–75.
7. Luke McKernan, Unpublished private letter, 4 Nov. 1994.
8. See also "Review," *Variety* 20.10 (1965).
9. "Review," *Guia de Filmes* 34 (July/Aug. 1971), 152.
10. Morris, *Shakespeare on Film*, pp. 10, 13. I do not, however, find *Anjuman* listed in the recent *Encyclopedia of Indian Film*, ed. Rajadhyaksha and Willeman (Oxford, 1994).
11. Caryn James, "A Mideast Variation," *NYT* 20 Apr. 1990, C.13.
12. Philip Shenon, "A Hindu Romeo, A Muslim Juliet," *NYT* 5 Sept. 1991, A.4.
13. Kliman, *Hamlet: Film, Television*, p. 139.
14. "On Film: Maximilian Schell's Most Royal *Hamlet*," *LFQ* 4.2 (1976), 139.
15. Kliman, *Hamlet: Film, Television*, p. 206. Kliman's essay is the best close analysis of the film; see pp. 202–24.
16. Bernice W. Kliman, "Swedish *Hamlet* Bursts into View," *SFNL* 11.2 (April 1987), 1 and *passim*.
17. "Chabrol's *Ophelia*," *SFNL* 6.2. (March 1982), 1 and *passim*.
18. Vida Johnson, "Russia After the Thaw," in *Oxford History of World Cinema*, p. 641.
19. J.G., "Review," *MFB* 23.269 (June 1956), 74.
20. "Books in Review," *SFNL* 4.1 (Dec. 1979), 10–11.
21. I have been told by a reliable source that there is an undubbed version available on PAL video in the United Kingdom.
22. "Review," *NYT* 16 May 1960, 39.
23. "Filming *Othello*," in Davies and Wells (eds.), *Shakespeare and the Moving Image*, p. 201.

24. *Shakespeare: Time and Conscience*, trans. Joyce Vining (New York: Hill & Wang, 1966), which deals with *Hamlet*; and King Lear: *The Space of Tragedy: The Diary of a Film Director*, trans. Mary Mackintosh (Berkeley: University of California Press, 1977).

25. Quoted in Taranow, *The Bernhardt "Hamlet"*, p. 10.

26. *Ibid.*, pp. 9–10.

27. See chapter 7, n. 38.

28. Kozintsev, *Shakespeare: Time and Conscience*, pp. 107–8.

29. Bernice W. Kliman, "Kozintsev's *Hamlet*: A Flawed Masterpiece," *Hamlet Studies* 1.2 (Oct. 1979), 127.

30. Kozintsev, *The Space of Tragedy*, p. ix.

31. Alexander Anikst, "Grigori Kozintsev's *King Lear*," *Soviet Literature* 6 (1971), 177.

32. Kozintsev, *The Space of Tragedy*, pp. 130–31.

33. *Ibid.*, pp. 128–29.

34. *Ibid.*, pp. 4, 108, and *passim*.

35. *Shakespeare, Cinema and Society* (Manchester University Press, 1989), p. 145.

36. *Shakespeare on Film*, p. 249. Jorgens' essay is required reading for any student of this film.

37. *The Masks of* King Lear (Berkeley: University of California Press, 1972), p. 312.

38. Howard Kissel, "*King Lear*," *Women's Wear Daily*, 4 Aug. 1975, 24.

39. Andrea J. Nouryeh, "Shakespeare and the Japanese stage," in *Foreign Shakespeare*, pp. 254–55.

40. *Akira Kurosawa and Intertextual Cinema* (Baltimore and London: Johns Hopkins University Press, 1994), p. 233.

41. "Kurosawa's Three Shakespeare Films," in *Journal of the Faculty of Letters, Komazawa University* 55 (March 1977), p. 23.

42. Robert Hapgood, "Kurosawa's Shakespeare Films: *Throne of Blood, The Bad Sleep Well,* and *Ran*," in Davies and Wells (eds.), *Shakespeare and the Moving Image*, p. 235.

43. Donald Richie, *The Films of Akira Kurosawa*, 3rd edn (Berkeley: University of California Press, 1996), pp. 140–46.

44. "Letter 32, To George and Thomas Keats" (21 Dec. 1817), in *The Letters of John Keats*, 2nd edn, ed. Maurice Buxton Forman (Oxford University Press, 1935), p. 72. For a cogent discussion of the Shakespearean ability to live with ambiguities, see Jonathan Bate, "Words in a Quantum World," *TLS* 25 July 1997, 14–15.

45. "Kurosawa's *Hamlet*: Samurai in Business Dress," *SFNL* 15.1 (Fall 1990), 6.

46. During the silent movie era, even in America the house was filled with would-be *benshis*, like my own solicitous father, loudly reading the titles and explaining the movie to wives and children.

47. *Films of Akira Kurosawa*, p. 93.

48. "*Macbeth* into *Throne of Blood*," *S&S* 34.4 (Autumn 1965), 190–95.

49. *Shakespeare and the Film*, p. 106.

50. "Shakespeare and Kurosawa," in James Goodwin (ed.), *Perspectives on Akira Kurosawa* (New York: G.K. Hall & Co., 1994), pp. 31–32.

51. *Ibid.*, p. 33.

52. "Kurosawa's Shakespeare Films," p. 234.

53. "Shakespeare, Kurosawa, and *Macbeth*: A Response to J. Blumenthal," *LFQ* 1.4 (1973), 352–59.

54. *Filming Shakespeare's Plays*, pp. 156–57.

55. "Kurosawa's *Throne of Blood*: Washizu and Miki Meet the Forest Spirit," *LFQ* 11.3 (1983), 167–72.

56. *The Warrior's Camera: The Cinema of Akira Kurosawa* (Princeton University Press, 1991), p. 18.

57. *"Throne of Blood*: A Morality Dance," *LFQ* 5.4 (1977), 340.

58. James Goodwin, *Akira Kurosawa and Intertextual Cinema* (Baltimore and London: Johns Hopkins University Press, 1994), p. 176.

59. See David Kehr, "Samurai *Lear*," *American Film* 10.10 (Sept. 1985), p. 24.

60. Peter Grilli, "Kurosawa Directs a Cinematic 'Lear'," *NYT* 15 Dec. 1985, II. 1 and *passim*.

61. See *Ran*, illus. Akira Kurosawa, screenplay by Akira Kurosawa, Hideo Oguni, and Ide Masato, trans. Tadashi Shishido (Boston and London: Shambhala, 1986), p. 8. Stunningly illustrated by Kurosawa himself, this screenplay is a treasure.

62. Samuel Crowl, "The Bow Is Bent and Drawn: Kurosawa's *Ran* and the Shakespearean Arrow of Desire," *LFQ* 22.2 (1994), 109–16.

63. Jan Kott, "The Edo *Lear*," *NYRB* 32.7 (24 Apr. 1986), 14.

9 SHAKESPEARE IN THE CINEMA OF TRANSGRESSION, AND BEYOND

1. "Sex and Sensation," *Oxford History of World Cinema*, p. 491.

2. See Richard Burt, "The Love that Dare Not Speak Shakespeare's Name: New Shakesqueer Cinema," in Boose and Burt (eds.), *Shakespeare, The Movie*, pp. 240–68. I am obliged to Professor Burt for sharing his unpublished research on this general topic. His recently published book, *Unspeakable ShaXXXspeares: Queer Theory and American Kiddie Culture* (New York: St. Martin's Press, 1998) explores the nuances of "Queer theory," which sees sex and gender as distinct but sometimes overlapping entities.

3. "Shakespeare Rewound," *SS* 45 (1993), 69.

4. "Pit.," "London Fest," *Variety* 1 Dec. 1976.

5. Conversation with David Meyer at London Globe Theatre, October 1996.

6. *Time-Out Film Guide*, ed. Tom Milne, 3rd edn (London: Penguin, 1993), p. 291.

7. "Hamlet," *MFB* 45.529 (Feb. 1978), 24.

8. Michael Griffiths, "Review Gay-Music," *Time Out* 1984, in Ritzy-Brixton Cinema Club notes.

9. "Strat.," *Variety* 11 Nov. 1984.

10. Ritzy-Brixton Cinema Club notes, 1984.

11. Quoted in David Haughton, "Program Notes for the Lindsay Kemp Company," Sadler's Wells Theatre, 15 Apr.–11 May, 1985.

12. See Derek Jarman, *Derek Jarman's* Caravaggio, *The Complete Film Script and Commentaries* (London: Thames and Hudson, 1986).

13. Derek Jarman, *Dancing Ledge*, ed. Shaun Allen (London: Quartet Books, 1984), p. 9.

14. Derek Jarman, *At Your Own Risk: A Saint's Testament*, ed. Michael Christie (London: Vintage, 1993). This autobiographical work that sometimes overlaps with *Dancing Ledge* is largely devoted to Jarman's obsession with homosexuality.

15. Jarman, *Dancing Ledge*, pp. 211–12.

16. "Screen: *The Tempest*," *NYT* 22 Sept. 1980, C20. Canby calls the film "very nearly unbearable."

17. "Stormy Weather: Derek Jarman's *Tempest*," *LFQ* 25.2 (1997), 97.

18. Derek Jarman Special Collection, British Film Institute Library, manuscript, item no. 23.

19. *Ibid.*, item no. 17.

20. Alden T. Vaughan and Virginia Mason Vaughan, *Shakespeare's Caliban: A Cultural History* (Cambridge University Press, 1991), p. 206.

21. Harris and Jackson, "Stormy Weather," p. 93.

22. Jarman, *Dancing Ledge*, p. 194.

23. Harris and Jackson, "Stormy Weather," p. 95.

24. "Stormy Weather: A New *Tempest* on Film," *SFNL* 5.1 (Dec. 1980), 1 and *passim*.

25. See Peter S. Donaldson, "Shakespeare in the Age of Post-Mechanical Production: Sexual and Electronic Magic in *Prospero's Books*," in Boose and Burt (eds.), *Shakespeare, The Movie*, pp. 169–85.

26. Peter Greenaway, in "Movie Memories," *S&S* 6.5. suppl. (May 1996), 15, 16.

27. Alain Robbe-Grillet and Alain Resnais, *Last Year at Marienbad*, trans. Richard Howard (New York: Grove Press, 1962), p. 12.

28. Peter Greenaway, *Prospero's Books: A Film of Shakespeare's* The Tempest (New York: Four Walls Eight Windows, 1991), p. 50. It is hopeless to study this complicated film without the help of Greenaway's lavishly illustrated screen play.

29. Claus Schatz-Jacobsen, "'Knowing I Lov'd My Books': Shakespeare, Greenaway, and the Prosperous Dialectics of Word and Image," in Skovmand (ed.), *Screen Shakespeare*, p. 133.

30. "Reams on the Renaissance," *NYT* 28 Sept. 1991, 9ff.

31. Greenaway, *Prospero's Books*, p. 28.

32. Donaldson, "Shakespeare in the Age of Post-Mechanical Reproduction," in Boose and Burt (eds.), *Shakespeare, The Movie*, p. 169.

33. *Ibid.*, p. 179.

34. Mariacristina Cavecchi, "Peter Greenaway's *Prospero's Books*: A Tempest Between Word and Image," *LFQ* 25.2 (1997), 87.

35. Jonathan Romney, "*Prospero's Books*," *S&S* 1.5 n.s. (Sept. 1991), 45.

36. David Sterritt, "A *King Lear* Launched over Lunch," *CSM*, 22 Jan. 1988.

37. *Shakespearean Films/Shakespearean Directors*, pp. 189–225.

38. "Godard's *Lear* . . . Why Is It So Bad?" *SB* 12.3 (Summer 1994), 41. The author concludes that the film's so-called "badness" stems only from Godard's "radical faithfulness to his own stance."

39. Colin McCabe, *et al.*, *Godard: Images, Sounds, Politics* (Bloomington: Indiana University Press, 1980), p. 211.

40. "Echoes of Godard," *TLS* 29 Jan. 1988, 112.

41. *Independent* 28 Jan. 1988, 14.

42. *VV* 26 Jan. 1988, 53.

43. Albert Fried, *The Rise and Fall of the Jewish Gangster in America* (New York: Holt, Rinehart and Winston, 1980), p. 80.

44. "Brilliant" but incoherent writing as an index to emotional disturbance, is something I explored in "Psychiatry and the Freshman Theme," *College English* 20.7 (April 1959), 338–42.

45. "'Haply for I Am Black': Liz White's *Othello*," *Shakespearean Films/Shakespearean Directors*, p. 130.

46. I'm obliged to Professor Peggy Russo for my information. The film is available on videotape from Rockbottom Productions, 18653 Ventura Blvd, 131B, Tarzana, CA 91356.

47. "Lor.," *Variety* 31 May 1989.

48. "Review," *Variety* 5 Oct. 1992.

49. For commentary, see Coursen, *Shakespeare in Production*, pp. 98–102.

50. "Review," *SB* 11.3 (Summer 1993), 41.

51. *Theater and Film*, pp. 36–37.

52. See Jorgens' succinct discussion of taxonomy in "Modes and Styles," *Shakespeare on Film*, pp. 7–16.

53. For elaboration on and embellishment of Jorgens' useful taxonomy, see also Peter Holland, "Two-Dimensional Shakespeare: *King Lear* on Film," in Davies and Wells (eds.), *Shakespeare and the Moving Image*, pp. 50–68.

54. Quoted in Tony Howard, "When Peter Met Orson," in Boose and Burt (eds.), *Shakespeare, The Movie*, p. 133.

55. [P.H.] "*Forbidden Planet*," *MFB* 23.269 (June 1956), 71.

56. See S. Schoenbaum, "Looking for Shakespeare," in *Shakespeare Craft*, ed. Philip Highfill (Carbondale: Southern Illinois University Press, 1982), pp. 156–72.

57. Geoffrey Taylor (ed.), *Paul Mazursky's* Tempest (New York Zoetrope, 1982). This is a wonderful illustrated book about the making of Mazursky's *Tempest*, which is the next best thing to having been there in person.

58. "Lubitsch's *To Be or Not to Be* or Shakespeare Mangled," *SFNL* 1.1 (Dec. 1976), 2 and *passim*.

59. Robert F. Willson, Jr., "Shakespeare in *The Goodbye Girl*," *SFNL* 2.2 (April 1978) 1 and *passim*.

60. David Jays, "Review," *S&S* 5.12 (Dec. 1995), 47.

61. Susan Wiseman, "The Family Tree Motel: Subliming Shakespeare in *My Own Private Idaho*," in Boose and Burt (eds.), *Shakespeare, The Movie*, pp. 225–39.

62. Geoffrey Macnab, "Looking for Richard," *S&S* 7.2 (Feb. 1997), 49.

63. "Royal Monster, Are You Out There?" *NYT* 11 Oct. 1996, C3.

64. Ball, *Silent Film*, p. 269.

65. Craig Toth, "Letter," personal, n.d.

66. Bernice W. Kliman, "Katharine Hepburn as Hamlet and Juliet," *SFNL* 13.2 (Apr. 1989), 6.

67. An excellent filmography of these elusive moments on screen is the British Film Institute Shakespeare catalog, *Walking Shadows*. A forthcoming study by Robert F. Willson, Jr. will cover much of this ground.

68. See Doug Stenberg, "The Circle of Life and the Chain of Being: Shakespearean Motifs in *The Lion King*," *SB* 14.2 (Spring 1996), 36.

69. "Poetry in Motion. Animating Shakespeare," in Boose and Burt (eds.), *Shakespeare, The Movie*, p. 118.

70. See *As You Like It: Audio Visual Shakespeare*, ed. Cathy Grant (London: British Universities Film & Video Council, 1992) for a good listing of educational films. For older pre-video films, see Andrew M. McLean, *Shakespeare: Annotated Bibliographies and Media Guide for Teachers* (Urbana: NCTE, 1980).

71. Again, I'm obliged to Richard Burt for sharing his unpublished research on transgressive Shakespeare.

72. "Review," *S&S* 6.12 (Dec. 1996), 54.

10 THE RENAISSANCE OF SHAKESPEARE IN MOVING IMAGES

1. Ian McKellen, *William Shakespeare's* Richard III: *A Screenplay* (New York: The Overlook Press, 1996), pp. 24–27. McKellen's fascinating commentary on the screenplay reveals his tireless concern for making the play relevant to modern audiences.

2. *Ibid.*, p. 44.

3. "'Top of the World, Ma': *Richard III* and Cinematic Convention," Boose and Burt (eds.), *Shakespeare, The Movie*, pp. 67–79. Loehlin's perceptive essay also cites the "Heritage" look and stresses the gangster film codes, which are sometimes hard to sort out from Shakespeare's own patterns of violence.

4. "Changing Colors like the Chameleon: Ian McKellen's *Richard III* from Stage to Film," *Post Script* 17.1 (1998), 55.

5. McKellen, *Richard III*, p. 244.

6. *Ibid.*, pp. 72, 80.

7. *Ibid.*, p. 258.

8. Gus Parr, "S for Smoking," *S&S* 7.12 (Dec. 1997), 30–33. A delightful exploration of this neglected topic.

9. Andrew Sarris, "At the Movies," *NYO* 8 Jan. 1996, 17; Rex Reed, "On the Town," *NYO* 8 Jan. 1996, 22.

10. Terence Rafferty, "Time Out of Joint," *TNY* 22 Jan. 1996, 86.

11. "Bard Therapy," *Independent* 2. 25 Apr. 1996, 11.

12. James Cameron-Wilson, "Review," *What's on in London?* 24 Apr. 1996.

13. David Gritten, "Bard with a Vengeance," *Daily Telegraph* 19 Apr. 1996, 21 and *passim*.

14. Geoffrey Macnab, "Review," *S&S* 6.2 (Feb. 1996), 51–52.

15. Parker played Laertes and Maloney, Rosencrantz in the Zeffirelli *Hamlet*.

16. Contrary to some published reports, Fishburne was not the first black actor to play Othello on screen. Although more art house than mall house, Liz White's *Othello* (1980) and Ted Lange's *Othello* (1989) both starred black actors, Yaphet Kotto and Hawthorne Jones. A video/TV version of Janet Suzman's South African *Othello* (1987–89) had a talented black actor, John Kani, as the Moor.

17. "Introduction," *"Much Ado about Nothing" by William Shakespeare* (New York: W.W. Norton & Co., 1993), p. ix.

18. Trevor Nunn (ed.), *"Twelfth Night" by William Shakespeare. A Screenplay* (London: Methuen Drama), 1996, Introduction, n.p.

19. Peter Marks, "So Young, So Fragile ..." *NYT* 20 Oct. 1996, 13.

20. "Review," *SB* 15.1 (Winter 1997), 37.

21. Geoffrey Macnab, "*Twelfth Night*," *S&S* 6.11 (Nov. 1996), 60.

22. "General Introduction," *TRS*, p. 22.

23. See Craig Pearce and Baz Luhrmann, *William Shakespeare's* Romeo & Juliet: *The Contemporary Film, The Classic Play* (New York: Bantam Doubleday Books, 1996). In some publicity materials, the title is given as *Romeo + Juliet*.

24. *Ibid.*, p. i.

25. "Soft! What Light? It's Flash, Romeo," *NYT* 1 Nov. 1996, C.1.

26. "Parting, Like, Sucks! So Does *Romeo*," *NYO* 11 Nov. 1996, 41.

27. W.B. Worthen, "Drama, Performativity, and Performance," *PMLA* 113.5 (Oct. 1998), 1103.

28. Alan Riding, "The Royal Shakespeare: Renewing Itself under Fire," *NYT* 17 May 1998, II.1.

29. "Review," *S&S* 7.1 (Jan. 1997), 41.

30. Kenneth Branagh, *Beginning* (New York: W.W. Norton, 1990), pp. 1–53. To write an *autobiography* at age 28 is also something of an achievement.

31. For commentary, see Peter Holland, *English Shakespeares: Shakespeare on the English Stage in the 1990s* (Cambridge University Press, 1997), pp. 137, 146, 150.

32. Hal Hinson, "The Heart of 'Henry V'," *WP* 15 Dec. 1989.

33. Richard Corliss, "King Ken Comes to Conquer," *Time* 13 Nov. 1989, 119.

34. Joseph Gelmis, "Shakespeare's *Henry V* in Two Incarnations," *Newsday* 7 Dec. 1990, II.153; see also Jonathan Yardley, "The Metamorphosis of 'Henry'," *WP* 26 Feb. 1990, C.2, for more encomiums.

35. See Michael Skovmand, "Introduction," in *Screen Shakespeare*, pp. 10–11, for discussion of the hostile reaction by several Marxist critics to Branagh's work.

36. Crowl, *Shakespeare Observed*, p. 168.

37. Jack Kroll, "A *Henry V* for Our Time," *Newsweek* 20 Nov. 1989, 78. One of many newspaper and magazine interviews in 1989.

38. Kenneth Branagh, Henry V *by William Shakespeare: A Screen Adaptation by Kenneth Branagh* (London: Chatto & Windus, 1989), p. 9.

39. "Henry," *S&S* 58.4 (Autumn 1989), 259.

40. See Peter S. Donaldson, "Taking on Shakespeare: Kenneth Branagh's *Henry V*," *SQ* 42 (Spring 1991), 61.

41. "War Is Mud: Branagh's Dirty Harry V and the types of political ambiguity," in Boose and Burt (eds.), *Shakespeare, The Movie*, p. 47.

42. "Resistance and Recuperation: Branagh's *Henry V*," *SFNL* 15.2 (April 1991), 5.

43. William P. Shaw, "Textual Ambiguities and Cinematic Certainties in *Henry V*," *LFQ* 22.2 (1994), 123. Shaw cites Norman Rabkin's point that *Henry V* is a play about ambiguities, and historical uncertainties. To add to the ambiguity, Shaw disagrees with Donaldson's belief that Exeter, as portrayed in the film, is a surrogate father figure like Falstaff; instead Exeter may be a conspirator against the king! Exeter, it seems to me, behaves like a loyal supporter.

44. Branagh, *Beginning*, p. 234.

45. See Coursen, *Shakespeare in Production*, pp. 102–17, for a detailed survey of the movie's reception.

46. "A House Party of Beatrice, Benedick and Friends," *NYT* 7 May 1993, C.16.

47. "Films," *TN* 256.21 (31 May 1993), 750.

48. "*Much Ado about Nothing*," *Variety* 3 May 1993.

49. Anthony Lane, "Too Much Ado," *TNY* 69.12 (10 May 1993), 99.

50. "*Much Ado about Nothing*," *S&S* 3.9 (Sept. 1993), 50–51.

51. Kenneth Branagh, Much Ado about Nothing *by William Shakespeare. Screenplay, Introduction and Notes on the Making of the Movie by Kenneth Branagh.* Photographs by Clive Foot (New York: W.W. Norton, 1993), p. 5.

52. *A Natural Perspective: The Development of Shakespearean Comedy and Romance* (New York: Harcourt, Brace & World, 1965), p. 81.

53. Branagh, *Much Ado*, p. xiii.

54. "Review," *SB* 11.3 (Summer 1993), 40.

55. Samuel Crowl, "*Hamlet*," *SB* 15.1 (Winter 1997), 35.

56. Gail Paster, quoted in John F. Andrews, "Kenneth Branagh's *Hamlet* Launched . . .," *SN* 46.3 no. 230 (Fall 1996), 53.

57. David Parkinson, "Performance of Epic Proportions," *Oxford Times* 2 May 1997, n.p.

58. "Holiday Celluloid Wrap-Up," *TN* 13/20 Jan. 1997, 36.

59. "Ken, Al and Will, too," *TLS* 21 Feb. 1997, 19.

60. Quoted in Nina da Vinci Nichols, "Branagh's *Hamlet* Redux," *SB* 15.3 (Summer 1997), 39. Nichols' excellent reception study surveys a wide range of critical opinion.

61. Kenneth Branagh, Hamlet *by William Shakespeare* (New York: W.W. Norton & Company, 1996), p. xv.

62. "The Regeneration of Hamlet: A Reply to E.M.W. Tillyard . . .," *SQ* 3 (July 1952), 206.

63. Leslie Felperin, "*Hamlet*," *S&S* 7.2 (Feb. 1997), 46. Felperin says the Branagh *Hamlet* "like so many of these recent adaptations . . . never convinces us why we still need to keep on adapting Shakespeare for the movies."

— BIBLIOGRAPHY —

BOOKS

Abel, Richard, *The Cine Goes to Town: French Cinema 1896–1914*, University of
California Press, 1994.
  French Cinema: The First Wave 1915–1929, Princeton University Press, 1984.
Addenbrooke, David, *The Royal Shakespeare Company. The Peter Hall Years*, London:
William Kimber, 1974.
Alexander, Peter, *Hamlet Father and Son*, Oxford University Press, 1955.
Allen, Robert C., *Vaudeville and Film 1895–1915: A Study in Media Interaction*, New
York: Arno Press, 1980.
Andrew, Dudley, *Film in the Aura of Art*, Princeton University Press, 1984.
Andrews, Cyrus, *Radio and TV Who's Who*, 3rd edn, London: George Young, 1954.
Atwell, David, *Cathedrals of the Movies: A History of British Cinema and Their
Audiences*, London: The Architectural Press, 1980.
Ball, Robert Hamilton, *Shakespeare on Silent Film: A Strange Eventful History*, London:
George Allen & Unwin, 1968.
Barthes, Roland, *S/Z. An Essay*, trans. Richard Miller, New York: Hill & Wang,
1972.
Bernhardt, Sarah, *Memoirs of My Life*, 1908; repr. New York: Benjamin Blom, 1968.
Boose, Lynda E. and Richard Burt (eds.), *Shakespeare, The Movie: Popularizing the
Plays on Film, TV, and Video*, New York and London: Routledge, 1997.
Brady, Frank, *Citizen Welles: A Biography of Orson Welles*, New York: Charles
Scribner's Sons, 1989.
Bragg, Melvyn, *Richard Burton, A Life*, Boston: Little, Brown and Company, 1988.
Branagh, Kenneth, *Beginning*, New York: W.W. Norton, 1989.
  "Hamlet" by William Shakespeare, screenplay and introduction by Kenneth
Branagh, film diary by Russell Jackson, New York: W.W. Norton, 1996.
  "Henry V" by William Shakespeare: A Screen Adaptation by Kenneth Branagh,
London: Chatto & Windus, 1989.
  "Much Ado about Nothing" by William Shakespeare, screenplay, introduction, and
notes on the making of the movie by Kenneth Branagh, photographs by Clive
Coote, New York: W.W. Norton, 1993.
Brownlow, Kevin, *Hollywood the Pioneers*, New York: Knopf, 1979.
Buchman, Lorne, *Still in Movement: Shakespeare on Screen*, Oxford University Press,
1991.
Bullough, Geoffrey (ed.), *Narrative and Dramatic Sources of Shakespeare*, III, New
York: Columbia University Press, 1975.

Bulman, J.C. and H.R. Coursen (eds.), *Shakespeare on Television: An Anthology of Essays and Reviews*, Hanover and London: University Press of New England, 1988.

Burt, Richard, *Unspeakable ShaXXXspeares: Queer Theory and American Kiddie Culture*, New York: St. Martin's Press, 1998.

Callow, Simon, *Orson Welles: The Road to Xanadu*, London: Jonathan Cape, 1995.

Cameron, Ian (ed.), *The Book of Film Noir*, New York: Continuum, 1992.

Collick, John, *Shakespeare, Cinema and Society*, Manchester University Press, 1989.

Cook, David A., *A History of Narrative Film*, 3rd edn, New York: Norton, 1996.

Coursen, H.R., *Shakespeare in Production. Whose History?* Athens: Ohio University Press, 1996.

  Shakespearean Performance as Interpretation, Newark: Associated University Presses, 1992.

Cross, Brenda (ed.), *The Film* Hamlet. *A Record of Its Production*, New York: Saturn Press, 1948.

Crowl, Samuel, *Shakespeare Observed: Studies in Performance on Stage and Screen*, Athens: Ohio University Press, 1992.

Cubitt, Sean, *Videography: Video Media as Art and Culture*, New York: St. Martin's Press, 1993.

Davies, Anthony and Stanley Wells (eds.), *Shakespeare and the Moving Image: The Plays on Film and Television*, Cambridge University Press, 1994.

Davies, Anthony, *Filming Shakespeare's Plays: The Adaptations of Laurence Olivier, Orson Welles, Peter Brook and Akira Kurosawa*, Cambridge University Press, 1988.

De Mille, Agnes, *Dance to the Piper*, Boston: Little, Brown and Company, 1952.

Donaldson, Peter S., *Shakespearean Films/Shakespearean Directors*, Boston: Unwin Hyman, 1990.

Drexler, Peter and Lawrence Guntner (eds.), *Negotiations with Hal: Multi-Media Perceptions of [Shakespeare's] Henry the Fifth*, Technische Universität Braunschweig: Braunschweiger Anglistische Arbeiten, 1995.

Eckert, Charles W. (ed.), *Focus on Shakespearean Films*, Englewood Cliffs: Prentice Hall, 1972.

Evans, G. Blakemore *et al.* (eds.), *The Riverside Shakespeare*, Boston: Houghton Mifflin, 1974.

Everson, William K., *American Silent Film*, Oxford University Press, 1978.

Forman, Maurice Buxton (ed.), *The Letters of John Keats*, 2nd edn, Oxford University Press, 1935.

France, Richard (ed.), *Orson Welles on Shakespeare: The W.P.A. and Mercury Theatre Playscripts*, New York: The Greenwood Press, 1990.

Fried, Albert, *The Rise and Fall of the Jewish Gangster in America*, New York: Holt, Rinehart and Winston, 1980.

Frye, Northrop, *A Natural Perspective: The Development of Shakespearean Comedy and Romance*, New York: Harcourt, Brace & World, 1965.

Gabler, Neal, *Winchell: Gossip, Power and the Culture of Celebrity*, New York: Knopf, 1994.

Geduld, Harry M., *Filmguide to* Henry V, Bloomington: Indiana University Press, 1973.

Giannetti, Louis D., *Understanding Movies*, 2nd edn, Englewood Cliffs, NJ: Prentice Hall, 1972.

Gielgud, Sir John (introduction), *"Julius Caesar" and the Life of William Shakespeare*, London: The Gawthorn Press, 1953.

Goodwin, James, *Akira Kurosawa and Intertextual Cinema*, Baltimore and London: Johns Hopkins University Press, 1994

  (ed.), *Perspectives on Akira Kurosawa*, New York: G.K. Hall, 1994.

Gottesman, Ronald (ed.), *Focus on Orson Welles*, Englewood Cliffs: Prentice Hall, 1976.

Grant, Cathy (ed.), *As You Like It: Audio Visual Shakespeare*, London: British Universities Film & Video Council, 1992.

Greenaway, Peter, *The Belly of an Architect* (Film Script, 1987), London: Faber and Faber, 1988.

  Prospero's Books: A Film of Shakespeare's "The Tempest," New York: Four Walls Eight Windows, 1991.

Halio, Jay L., *"A Midsummer Night's Dream": Shakespeare in Performance*, Manchester University Press, 1994.

Hall, Ben M., *The Best Remaining Seats: The Story of the Golden Age of the Movie Palace,* New York: Clarkson N. Potter, 1961.

Heston, Charlton, *In the Arena: An Autobiography*, New York: Simon & Schuster, 1995.

Holderness, Graham, *"The Taming of the Shrew": Shakespeare in Performance,* Manchester University Press, 1989.

Holland, Peter, *English Shakespeares, Shakespeare on the English Stage in the 1990s*, Cambridge University Press, 1997.

Ivory, James, *Savages/Shakespeare Wallah. A Film by James Ivory from a Screenplay by R. Prawer Jhabvala and James Ivory*, New York: Grove Press, 1973.

James, Nick (ed.), *360 Film Classics* (supplement to *S&S*), London: BFI, 1998.

Jarman, Derek, *At Your Own Risk: A Saint's Testament*, ed. Michael Christie, London: Vintage, 1993.

  Dancing Ledge, ed. Shaun Allen, London: Quartet Books, 1984

  Derek Jarman's Caravaggio, *The Complete Film Script and Commentaries,* London: Thames & Hudson, 1986.

Jorgens, Jack J., *Shakespeare on Film*, Bloomington: Indiana University Press, 1977.

Kantorowicz, Ernest, *The King's Two Bodies: A Study in Medieval Political Theology,* Princeton University Press, 1957.

Katz, Ephraim (ed.), *The Film Encyclopedia*, New York: Putnam, 1979.

Kennedy, Dennis (ed.), *Foreign Shakespeare, Contemporary Performance*, Cambridge University Press, 1993.

Kliman, Bernice W., *"Hamlet": Film, Television, and Audio Performance,* London and Toronto: Associated University Presses, 1988.

  "Macbeth": Shakespeare in Performance, Manchester University Press, 1992.

Kotsilibas-Davis, James, *The Barrymores, the Royal Family in Hollywood,* New York: Crown Publishers, 1981.

Kott, Jan, *Shakespeare Our Contemporary*, New York: Anchor Books, 1966.

Kozintsev, Grigori, King Lear: *The Space of Tragedy: The Diary of a Film Director*, trans. Mary Mackintosh, Berkeley: University of California Press, 1977.
  Shakespeare: Time and Conscience, trans. Joyce Vining, New York: Hill & Wang, 1966.
Kracauer, Siegfried, *From Caligari to Hitler: A Psychological History of the German Film*, Princeton University Press, 1947.
Kurosawa, Akira, *Ran*, illus. by Akira Kurosawa, screenplay by Akira Kurosawa, Hideo Oguni, and Ide Masato, trans. Tadashi Shishido, Boston and London: Shambhala, 1986.
Leaming, Barbara, *Orson Welles*, New York: Viking, 1985.
Low, Rachel, *History of British Film 1906–1914*, London: George Allen & Unwin, 1949.
Lyons, Bridget Gellert (ed.), Chimes at Midnight: *Orson Welles, director*, New Brunswick and London: Rutgers University Press, 1988.
MacLiammóir, Micheál, *Put Money in Thy Purse: A Diary of the Film of* Othello, London: Methuen, 1952.
Manvell, Roger, *Shakespeare and the Film*, repr., Cranbury, NJ: A.S. Barnes, 1979.
  Theater and Film: A Comparative Study of the Two Forms of Dramatic Art, and of the Problems of Adaptation of Stage Plays into Films, Cranbury, NJ: Associated University Presses, 1979.
McBride, Joseph, *Orson Welles*, rev. edn, New York: Da Capo, 1996.
McCabe, Colin, *et al.*, *Godard: Images, Sounds, Politics*, Bloomington: Indiana University Press, 1980.
McFarlane, Brian, *An Autobiography of British Cinema, as told by the filmmakers and actors who made it*, foreword by Julie Christie, London: Methuen, 1997.
McGilligan, Patrick, *George Cukor: A Double Life*, New York: St. Martin's Press, 1991.
McGuire, Philip C., *Speechless Dialect: Shakespeare's Open Silences*, Berkeley: University of California Press, 1985.
McKellen, Ian, *William Shakespeare's* Richard III: *A Screenplay*, New York: The Overlook Press, 1996.
McKernan, Luke and Olwen Terris, *Walking Shadows: Shakespeare in the National Film and Television Archive*, London: BFI, 1994.
McLean, Andrew M., *Shakespeare: Annotated Bibliographies and Media Guide for Teachers*, Urbana: NCTE, 1980.
Metallinos, Nikos, *Television Aesthetics: Perceptual, Cognitive, and Compositional Bases*, Mahwah, NJ: Earlbaum Associates, 1996.
Miller, Jonathan, *Subsequent Performances*, New York: Elisabeth Sifton/Viking, 1986.
Morris, Beja (ed.), *Perspective on Orson Welles*, New York: G.K. Hall, 1995.
Morris, Peter (ed.), *Shakespeare on Film*, Ottawa: Canadian Film Institute, 1972.
Musser, Charles, *The Emergence of Cinema: The American Screen to 1907*, New York: Charles Scribner's Sons, 1990. Vol. I in *History of American Cinema*, gen. ed. Charles Harpole, New York: Charles Scribner's Sons, 1990–.
Naremore, James, *The Magic World of Orson Welles*, rev. edn, Dallas: Southern Methodist University Press, 1989.
Nash, Jay Robert and Stanley Ralph Ross (eds.), *The Motion Picture Guide, 1927–1983*, Chicago: Cinebooks, 1987.

Nelson, Ralph (ed.), *"Hamlet." A Television Script*, New York: CBS, 1976.

Newman, Karen, *Fashioning Femininity and English Renaissance Drama*, University of Chicago Press, 1994.

Nowell-Smith, Geoffrey (ed.), *Oxford History of World Cinema*, Oxford University Press, 1996.

Nunn, Trevor (ed.), *"Twelfth Night" by William Shakespeare. A Screenplay* (London: Methuen Drama, 1996).

Palmer, Richard, *Hermeneutics: Interpretation Theory in Schleiermacher, Dilthey, Heidegger, and Gadamer*, Evanston: Northwestern University Press, 1969.

Parkinson, David (ed.), *The Graham Greene Film Reader: Reviews, Essays, Interviews and Film Stories*, New York: Applause Theatre Book Publishers, 1993.

Pearce, Craig and Baz Luhrmann, *William Shakespeare's* Romeo & Juliet: *The Contemporary Film, The Classic Play*, New York: Bantam Doubleday Books, 1996.

Pickford, Mary, *Sunshine and Shadow*, New York: Doubleday, 1955.

Pilkington, Ace G., *Screening Shakespeare from* Richard II *to* Henry V, Newark: University of Delaware Press, 1991.

Prince, Stephen, *The Warrior's Camera: The Cinema of Akira Kurosawa*, Princeton University Press, 1991.

Pudovkin, V.I., *Film Technique, Film Acting*, trans. Ivor Montagu, 1929; repr. Hackensack, NJ: Wehman Brothers, 1968.

Rajadhyaksha, Ashish and Paul Willeman, *Encyclopedia of Indian Cinema*, New Delhi: Oxford University Press, 1994.

Richardson, Tony, *Long Distance Runner. A Memoir*, intro. by Lindsay Anderson, London: Faber & Faber, 1993.

Richie, Donald (with additional material by Joan Mellen), *The Films of Akira Kurosawa*, 3rd edn, Berkeley: University of California Press, 1973.

Robbe-Grillet, Alain and Alain Resnais, *Last Year at Marienbad*, trans. Richard Howard, New York: Grove Press, 1962.

Rosabella, Italian Documentary Film, on *Othello* [1952] Voyager Company laser disk, 1995.

Rosenbaum, Jonathan (ed.), *This Is Orson Welles*: Orson Welles and Peter Bogdanovich, New York: HarperCollins, 1992.

Rosenberg, Marvin, *The Masks of* King Lear, Berkeley: University of California Press, 1972.

Ross, Gordon, *Television Jubilee: The Story of 25 Years of BBC Television*, London: W.H. Allen, 1961.

Ross, Steven J., *Working-Class Hollywood: Silent Film and the Shaping of Class in America*, Princeton University Press, 1998.

Rothwell, Kenneth S. and Annabelle Henkin Melzer, *Shakespeare on Screen: An International Filmography and Videography*, New York and London: Neal Schuman, 1990.

Shakespeare, William, *Romeo and Juliet. With Designs by Oliver Messel* [Cukor *Rom.*], London: B.T. Batsford, 1936.

  A Motion Picture Edition [Cukor *Rom.*], New York: Random House, 1936.

Silviria, Dale, *Laurence Olivier and the Art of Film Making*, London and Toronto: Associated University Presses, 1985.

Sklar, Robert, *Movie Made America*, New York: Vintage, 1975.

Skovmand, Michael (ed.), *Screen Shakespeare*, Aarhus University Press, 1994.

Slide, Anthony, *The American Film Industry*, New York: Greenwood Press, 1986.

Smith, Anthony (ed.), *Television: An International History*, Oxford University Press, 1995.

Spoto, Donald, *Laurence Olivier: A Biography*, New York: HarperCollins, 1992.

Sterne, Richard L., *John Gielgud Directs Richard Burton in* Hamlet*: A Journal of Rehearsals*, New York: Random House, 1967.

Taranow, Gerda, *Sarah Bernhardt: The Art Within the Legend*, Princeton University Press, 1972.

  The Bernhardt "Hamlet": Culture and Context, New York: Peter Lang, 1996.

Taylor, Geoffrey (ed.), *Paul Mazursky's "Tempest,"* New York: Zoetrope, 1982.

Thomson, David, *Rosebud: The Story of Orson Welles*, New York: Alfred Knopf, 1996.

Time Out Film Guide, ed. Tom Milne, 3rd edn, London: Penguin, 1993.

Trimble, Bjo, *Star Trek Concordance*, 1990, unpaged.

Trimble, Marion Blackton, *J. Stuart Blackton, A Personal Biography*, Metuchen & London: The Scarecrow Press, 1985.

Tynan, Kenneth, *The Sound of Two Hands Clapping*, London: Jonathan Cape, 1975.

Uricchio, William and Roberta E. Pearson, *Reframing Culture: The Case of the Vitagraph Quality Films*, Princeton University Press, 1993.

Vaughan, Alden T. and Virginia Mason Vaughan, *Shakespeare's Caliban: A Cultural History*, Cambridge University Press, 1991.

Warde, Frederick B., *Fifty Years of Make-Believe*, New York: International Press Syndicate, 1920.

Wells, Stanley (ed.), *Shakespeare Survey 39*, Cambridge University Press, 1987.

Willis, Susan, *The BBC Shakespeare Plays: Making the Televised Canon*, Chapel Hill: University of North Carolina Press, 1991.

Wyver, John, *The Moving Image: An International History of Film, Television and Video*, Oxford and New York: Basil Blackwell/BFI, 1989.

Zeffirelli, Franco, *Zeffirelli: The Autobiography of Franco Zeffirelli*, New York: Weidenfeld & Nicolson, 1986.

ARTICLES, REVIEWS, AND ESSAYS IN JOURNALS, NEWSPAPERS, AND ANTHOLOGIES

Abramson, Albert, "The Invention of Television," in Smith (ed.), *Television: An International History*, 1995, pp. 13–34.

Agate, James, "Bergner as Rosalind," in *Around Cinemas*, London: Home & Van Thal, 1946; repr. New York: Arno Press, 1972, pp. 73–77.

  "Notes," *The Magazine Programme*, London Pavilion, 14 Nov. 1929.

Alkire, N.L., "Subliminal Masks in Olivier's *Hamlet*," SFNL 16.1 (Dec. 1991), 5.

Allen Robert C., "Manhattan Myopia, or Oh! Iowa!" *Cinema Journal* 35.3 (1996), 75–103.

American Film Institute Souvenir Program, 29 Oct. 1996, for Warde *Richard III* premiere.

Andrews, John F., "Kenneth Branagh's *Hamlet* Launched . . .," SN 46.3 no. 230 (Fall 1996), 61ff.

Anikst, Alexander, "Grigori Kozintsev's *King Lear*," *Soviet Literature* 6 (1971), 176–82.

Arai, Yoshio, "Kurosawa's Three Shakespeare Films," in *Journal of the Faculty of Letters, Komazawa University* 55, March 1977, 23–36.

Ball, Robert Hamilton, "Tree's *King John* Film: An Addendum," *SQ* 24.4 (1973), 455–59.

Barker, Felix, "Review [Brook *Lear*]," *Evening Standard* 23 July 1971.

Barnes, Howard, "*As You Like It*," *NYHT* 6 Nov. 1936.

Barry, Michael, "Shakespeare on Television," *BBC Quarterly* 9.3 (Autumn 1954), 146.

Bate, Jonathan, "Words in a Quantum World," *TLS* 25 July 1997, 14–15.

BBC, "Floor Mistakes," internal circulating memo, WAC T5/508, 6 Feb. 1939.

Berlin, Normand, "Peter Brook's Interpretation of *King Lear*: 'Nothing Will Come of Nothing'," *LFQ* 5.4 (1977), 299–303.

Biggs, Murray, "'He's Going to His Mother's Closet': Hamlet and Gertrude on Screen," *S&S* 45 (1993), 53–62.

Bioscope, "Opening of Palace Electric," 5 Jan. 1911, 55.
  "Another Palace Opens," 12 Jan. 1911, 15.
  "Trade Ad for Globe *MV*," 12 June 1913, suppl. xxvi.
  "The Filming of *Hamlet*: Interview with Mr. Cecil Hepworth," 24 July 1913.
  "Editorial," 25 June 1914, 1289.

Blumenthal, J., "*Macbeth* into *Throne of Blood*," *S&S* 34.4 (1965), 190–95.

Boddy, William, "The Beginnings of American Television," in Smith (ed.), *Television: An International History*, pp. 35–61.

Bradley, David, "Shakespeare on a Shoestring," *Movie Makers* (April 1974), 146ff.

Brien, Alan, "Review [Welles *Othello*]," *The Evening Standard* 23 Feb. 1956.

Brittain, Frederick (ed.), "2nd Vesper Services, Masses for the Virgin Mary," *Penguin Book of Latin Verses*, Baltimore: Peter Smith, 1962.

Brook, Peter, "Shakespeare and Kurosawa," in James Goodwin (ed.), *Perspectives on Akira Kurosawa*, pp. 31–32.

Brown, Constance A., "Olivier's *Richard III* – A Re-evaluation," *FQ* 20 (1967), 23–32.

Buhler, Stephen M., "'Who Calls me Villain?': Blank Verse and the Black Hat," *Extrapolation* 36.1 (Spring 1995), 18–27.

Burt, Richard, "The Love that Dare Not Speak Shakespeare's Name: New Shakesqueer Cinema," in Boose and Burt (eds.), *Shakespeare, The Movie*, pp. 240–68.

Bush, W. Stephen, "Our American Letter," *Bioscope* 16 Apr. 1914.

Cahir, Linda Costanzo, "The Artful Rerouting of *A Streetcar Named Desire*," *LFQ* 22.2 (1994), 72–77.

Callaghan, Dympna, "Resistance and Recuperation: Branagh's *Henry V*," *SFNL* 15.2 (April 1991), 5.

Cameron-Wilson, James, "Review [Loncraine *R3*]," *What's on in London?* 24 Apr. 1996.

Canby, Vincent, "Screen: *The Tempest*," *NYT* 22 Sept. 1980, C.20.
  "Reams on the Renaissance Fill 'Prospero's Books'," *NYT* 28 Sept. 1991, 9ff.
  "A House Party of Beatrice, Benedick and Friends," *NYT* 7 May 1993, C.16.

Carr [Vaughan], Virginia M., "The Second Season: *Twelfth Night*," *SFNL* 4.2 (April 1980), 5.

Castner, Tom, "*Et tu*, Charlton," *VV* 25 Feb. 1971, 57.

Cavecchi, Mariacristina, "Peter Greenaway's *Prospero's Books*: A Tempest Between Word and Image," *LFQ* 25.2 (1997), 83–89.

Cirillo, Albert R., "The Art of Franco Zeffirelli and Shakespeare's *Romeo and Juliet*," in Fred Marcus (ed.), *Film and Literature: Contrasts in Media*, Scranton: Chandler, 1971, 205–27.

Cloutier, Suzanne, "Interview," *Othello* [1952] Voyager Co. laser disk, 1992, appendix no. 51.

Cobos, Juan and Miguel Rubio, "Welles and Falstaff: An Interview by Juan Cobos and Miguel Rubio," *S&S* 35.4 (Autumn 1966), 158–63.

Cook, Page, "The Sound Track," *Films in Review* 19 (Nov. 1968), 570–73.

Corliss, Richard, "King Ken Comes to Conquer," *Time* 13 Nov. 1989, 119.

Coursen, H.R., "Not Fit to Live [Bard *Macbeth*]," *SFNL* 13.1 (Dec. 1988), 4.
  "The Classic Theatre *Macbeth*," *Pulse* (Oct. 1976), repr. in Bulman and Coursen (eds.), *Shakespeare on Television*, pp. 247–48.

Cowie, Peter, "Olivier at 75 Returns to Lear," *NYT* 1 May 1983.

Crane, Milton, "Shakespeare on Television," *SQ* 12.3 (Summer 1961), 323–27.

Crist, Judith, "Olivier Paints Othello Ridden by Neuroses," *NYHT* 2 Feb. 1966.

Crowl, Samuel, "Chain Reaction: A Study of Roman Polanski's *Macbeth*," *Soundings* LIX. 2 (Summer 1976), 226–33.
  "Stormy Weather: A New *Tempest* on Film," *SFNL* 5.1 (Dec. 1980), 1ff.
  "Review [Branagh *Ado*]," *SB* 11.3 (Summer 1993), 39–40.
  "Review [Edzard *AYL*]," *SB* 11.3 (Summer 1993), 41.
  "The Bow Is Bent and Drawn: Kurosawa's *Ran* and the Shakespearean Arrow of Desire," *LFQ* 22. 2 (1994), 109–16.
  "Review [Branagh *Hamlet*]," *SB* 15.1 (Winter 1997), 34–35.
  "Review [Nunn *TN*]," *SB* 15.1 (Winter 1997), 36–37.
  "Changing Colors like the Chameleon: Ian McKellen's *Richard III* from Stage to Film," *Post Script* 17.1 (1998), 53–63.

Crowl, Samuel and Mary Z. Maher, "Cambridgeshire *Hamlet*: Two Views," *SFNL* 13.1 (Dec. 1988), 7.

Crowther, Bosley, "Review [Welles *Macbeth*]," *NYT* 28 Dec. 1950, 22.
  "Review [Bradley *JC*]," *NYT* 25 Nov. 1952, 33.
  "Review [Castellani *Romeo*]," *NYT* 22 Dec. 1954, 28.
  "Minstrel Show *Othello* [Olivier]," *NYT* 2 Feb. 1966, 24.
  "Review [Zeffirelli *Shrew*]," *NYT* 9 March 1967, 43.
  "Review [Welles *Chimes*]," *NYT* 20 March 1967, 26.

Danson, Lawrence, "Gazing at Hamlet, or The Danish Cabaret," *SS* 45 (1993), 37–51.

David, Richard, "Shakespeare in Miniature: The BBC *Antony and Cleopatra*," in Bulman and Coursen (eds.), *Shakespeare on Television*, 139–44.

Davies, Brenda, "Review [Hall *MND*]," *MFB* 36.422 (March 1969), 51.

Davy, Charles, "Films [Cukor *Romeo*]," *The London Mercury* 35 (Nov. 1936), 57–58.

Devlin, Polly, "I Know My Romeo and Juliet," *Vogue* 151 (1 April 1968), 34ff.

Dews, Peter, "The Spread of the Eagle," *Radio Times* 25 Apr 1963, 49.

Donaldson, Peter S., "Shakespeare in the Age of Post-Mechanical Reproduction: Sexual and Electronic Magic in *Prospero's Books*," in Boose and Burt (eds.), *Shakespeare, The Movie*, pp. 169–85.

"Taking on Shakespeare: Kenneth Branagh's *Henry V*," *SQ* 42 (Spring 1991), 60–71.

Dukes, Ashley, "Televised Drama So Far: The English Scene," *TAM* 22.4 (April 1938), 256–62.

Dworkin, Martin S., "'Stay Illusion!' Having Words about Shakespeare on Screen," *The Journal of Aesthetic Education* 11 (Jan. 1977), 51–61.

Edwards, Geoffrey, "*Julius Caesar* in Modern Dress," *News Chronicle* 25 July 1938.

Elley, Derek, "Review of Edzard *AYL*," *Variety* 5 Oct. 1992.

Felperin, Leslie, "*Hamlet*," *S&S* 7.2 (Feb. 1997), 46.

Fenwick, Henry, "The Production," in *The BBC TV Shakespeare* Othello, London: BBC, 1982, pp. 18–28.

"The Production," in *The BBC TV Shakespeare* Troilus and Cressida, London: BBC, 1981, pp. 18–24.

Filmindia, "Hamlet Flops," 21.2 (Feb. 1955), 71–75.

Forbes, Jill, "Henry [Branagh *H5*]," *S&S* 58.4 (Autumn 1989), 258–59.

Gelmis, Joseph, "Shakespeare's *Henry V* in Two Incarnations," *Newsday* 7 Dec. 1990, II. 153.

Gerlach, John, "Shakespeare, Kurosawa, and *Macbeth*: A Response to J. Blumenthal," *LFQ* 1.4 (Fall 1973), 352–59.

Gilbey, Brian, "Bard Therapy [Review of McKellen *R3*]," *Independent* 25 Apr. 1996, 2.11.

Gill, Brendan, "Black and White [Olivier *Othello*]," *TNY* 19 Feb. 1966, 145.

"Not Lacking Gall [Richardson *Hamlet*]," *TNY* 10 May 1969, 121–22.

Goldie, Grace Wyndham, "Critic on the Hearth," *The Listener* 29 Dec. 1938, 1428.

Gould, Jack, "Worthington Miner's Version [of *Julius Caesar*] in Modern Dress Proves Spectacular," *NYT* 13 March 1949, II.11.

"Review: *Macbeth*," *NYT* 22 May 1949, II.9.

Greenaway, Peter, "Movie Memories," *S&S* 6.5 suppl. (May 1996), 15, 16.

Griffin, Alice, "Shakespeare through the Camera's Eye," *SQ* 6.1 (1955), 63–66.

"Shakespeare Through the Camera's Eye," *SQ* 17.4 (1966), 383–87.

Griffiths, Michael, "Review Gay-Music [Coronado *MND*]," *Time Out*, 1984, in Ritzy-Brixton Cinema Club notes.

Grilli, Peter, "Kurosawa Directs a Cinematic 'Lear'," *NYT* 15 Dec. 1985, sec. 2, 1ff.

Gritten, David, "Bard with a Vengeance [McKellen *R3*]," *Daily Telegraph* 19 Apr. 1996, 21ff.

Guia de Filmes, "Review [Brazilian *a Heranca*]," 34 (July/Aug. 1971), 152–53.

Guntner, J. Lawrence, "Expressionist Shakespeare: the Gade/Nielsen *Hamlet* (1920) and the History of Shakespeare on Film," *Postscript: Essays in Film and the Humanities* 17.2 (Winter/Spring 1988), 90–104.

Guthrie, Tyrone, "Shakespeare on the Modern Stage," *The Listener* 3 Feb. 1937, 207.

Hall, Mordaunt, "Review [Taylor *Shr.*]," *NYT* 29 Nov. 1929, 23.

Hapgood, Robert, "*Chimes at Midnight* From Stage to Screen: The Art of Adaptation," in Wells (ed.), *Shakespeare Survey 39*, pp. 39–52.

"Shakespeare and the Included Spectator," in Norman Rabkin (ed.), *Reinterpretations of Elizabethan Drama*, New York: Columbia University Press, 1969, pp. 117–36.

"Kurosawa's Shakespeare Films: *Throne of Blood, The Bad Sleep Well*, and *Ran*," in Davies and Wells (eds.), *Shakespeare and the Moving Image*, pp. 234–49.

"Popularizing Shakespeare: The Artistry of Franco Zeffirelli," in Boose and Burt (eds.), *Shakespeare, The Movie*, pp. 80–94.

Harris, Diana and MacDonald Jackson, "Stormy Weather: Derek Jarman's *The Tempest*," *LFQ* 25.2 (1997), 90–98.

Harrison, G.B., "Shakespeare in His Theatre," *The Listener* 20 Jan. 1937, 116–18.

Hatch, Robert, "Films [Review Welles *Othello*]," *TN* 1 Oct. 1955, 81.

"Films [Review Castellani *Romeo*]," *TN* 8 Jan. 1955, 37.

Haughton, David, "Program Notes for the Lindsay Kemp Company," Sadler's Wells Theatre, 15 Apr.–11 May 1985.

Hedrick, Donald K., "War Is Mud: Branagh's Dirty Harry V and the Types of Political Ambiguity," in Boose and Burt (eds.), *Shakespeare, The Movie*, pp. 45–66.

Henderson, Diana E., "A Shrew for the Times," in Boose and Burt (eds.), *Shakespeare, The Movie*, pp. 148–68.

Heston, Charlton, "Heston Directs Heston," Publicity Booklet, London, 1972, unpaged.

Hetherington, Robert A., "*The Lears* of Peter Brook," *SFNL* 6.1 (1982), 7.

Higashi, Sumiko, "Dialogue: Manhattan's Nickelodeons," *Cinema Journal* 35.3 (1996), 72–74.

Hinson, Hal, "The Heart of 'Henry V'," *WP* 15 Dec. 1989, D.1.

Hinxman, Margaret, "Review [of Burton *Hamlet*]," *Sunday Telegraph* 9 July 1972.

Hoberman, J., "Review of Godard *Lear*," *VV* 26 Jan. 1988, 53.

"Moor Better Blues [Review of Welles *Othello* Re-release]," *VV* 31 March 1992, 5.

Hodgdon, Barbara, "Race-ing *Othello*, Re-Engendering White-Out," in Boose and Burt (eds.), *Shakespeare, The Movie*," pp. 23–44.

"Two *King Lears*: Uncovering the Filmtext," *LFQ* 11.3 (1983), 143–51.

Holderness, Graham, "Shakespeare Rewound," *SS* 45 (1993), 63–74.

Holland, Peter, "Two-Dimensional Shakespeare, *King Lear* on Film," in Davies and Wells (eds.), *Shakespeare and the Moving Image*, pp. 50–68.

Houseman, John, "Filming *Julius Caesar*," *S&S* 23 (July/Sept. 1953), 24–27.

Howard, Tony, "When Peter Met Orson: The 1953 CBS *King Lear*," in Boose and Burt (eds.), *Shakespeare, The Movie*, pp. 121–34.

Humphrey, A.R., "Introduction," *King Henry IV Part Two*, *The Arden Shakespeare*, London: Methuen, 1966.

Impastato, David, "Zeffirelli's *Hamlet*: Sunlight Makes Meaning" *SFNL* 16.1 (Dec. 1991), 1ff.

"Zeffirelli's *Hamlet* and the Baroque," *SFNL* 16.2 (April 1992), 1ff.

"Godard's *Lear* . . . Why Is It So Bad?" *SB* 12.3 (Summer 1994), 38–41.

Ingrams, Richard, "Review [Nunn *Mac.*]," *The Standard* 13 Jan. 1979.

Jackson, Russell, "Shakespeare's Comedies on Film," in Davies and Wells (eds.), *Shakespeare and the Moving Image*, pp. 99–120.

James, Caryn, "A Mideast Variation," *NYT* 20 Apr. 1999, C.13.

Jarman, Derek, Derek Jarman Special Collection, British Film Institute Library, Ms., Item no. 23.

Jays, David, "Review," *S&S* 5.12 (Dec. 1995), 47.

Jensen, Michael P., "Mel Gibson on *Hamlet*," *SFNL* 15.2 (April 1991), 1ff.

Jewel, John, "A Defence of the Apologie of the Church of England, conteining an Answer to a Certain Book lately set forth by Mr. Harding . . ." in John Eyre (ed.), *Works of John Jewel*, III, The Parker Society, XXV, Cambridge University Press, 1848.

Johnson, William, "*King Lear* and *Macbeth*," *FQ* 25.3 (1972), 41–48.

Johnson, S.F., "The Regeneration of Hamlet: A Reply to E.M.W. Tillyard . . .," *SQ* 3 (July 1952), 187–207.

Johnson, Vida, "Russia After the Thaw," in Nowell-Smith (ed.), *Oxford History of World Cinema*, pp. 641–51.

Johnston, Sheila, "Review of Godard *Lear*," *Independent* 28 Jan. 1988, 14.

Jorgens, Jack J., "Kurosawa's *Throne of Blood*: Washizu and Miki Meet the Forest Spirit," *LFQ* 11.3 (1983), 167–72.

"The Opening Scene of Polanski's *Macbeth*," *LFQ* 3.3 (1975), 277–78.

Jorgenson, Paul A., "Castellani's *Romeo and Juliet*: Intention and Response," in Eckert (ed.), *Focus on Shakespearean Films*, pp. 108–15.

Kachur, B. A., "The First Shakespeare Film: A Reconsideration and Reconstruction of Tree's *King John*," *TS* 32 (May 1991), 43–63.

Kael, Pauline, "Peter Brook's Night of the Living Dead," *TNY* 11 Dec. 1971, 135–37.

Kallet, Nathan, "Olivier and the Moor," *Holiday* 26 Apr. 1966, 143ff.

Kehr, David, "Samurai *Lear*," *American Film* 10 (Sept. 1985), 21–26.

Kermode, Frank, "Shakespeare in the Movies," *NYRB* 18 (4 May 1972), 18–21.

Kimbrough, R. Alan, "The First Season [BBC Series]," *SFNL* 3.2 (April 1979), 5.

Kinder, Marsha, "*Throne of Blood*: A Morality Dance," *LFQ* 5.4 (1977), 339–45.

Kissel, Howard, "*King Lear*," *Women's Wear Daily*, 4 Aug. 1975, 24.

Klawans, Stuart, "Films [Branagh *Ado*]," *TN* 31 May 1993, 750–52.

"Holiday Celluloid Wrap-Up [Branagh *Ham.*]," *TN* 13/20 Jan. 1997, 36.

Kliman, Bernice W., "Katharine Hepburn as Hamlet and Juliet," *SFNL* 13.2 (April 1989), 6.

"Kozintsev's *Hamlet*: A Flawed Masterpiece," *Hamlet Studies* 1.2 (Oct. 1979), 117–28.

"Olivier's *Hamlet*: A Film-Infused Play," in *LFQ*, Michael Mullin (ed.), 5.4 (Fall 1977), 305–14.

"Swedish *Hamlet* Bursts into View," *SFNL* 11.2 (April 1987), 1ff.

"Welles's *Macbeth*, A Textual Parable," in Skovmand (ed.), *Screen Shakespeare*, 25–38.

Knight, Arthur, "Review [Burton *Hamlet*]," *Saturday Review* 17 Oct. 1964.

Kott, Jan, "The Edo *Lear*," *NYRB* 32.7 (24 Apr. 1986), 13–15.

Kroll, Jack, "A *Henry V* for Our Time," *Newsweek* 20 Nov. 1989, 78.

Lake, James H., "Hands in Zeffirelli's *Romeo*," SAA Abstracts, 1990, in *SFNL* 15.1 (Dec. 1990), 4.

Lane, Anthony, "Too Much Ado," *TNY* 69.12 (10 May 1993), 97–99.

Leavis, F.R., "Diabolic Intellect and the Noble Hero," in John Wain (ed.), *Shakespeare "Othello." A Casebook*, London: MacMillan, 1971, pp. 123–46.

Leonard, Harold, "Hollywood: Notes on *Macbeth*," *S&S* 19.1 (March 1950), 15–17.

Levin, Harry, "General Introduction," *TRS*, pp. 1–25.

Libby, M.F., "Some New Notes on *Macbeth*," in *Vindication of the Reading of the Folio of 1623*, Toronto: The Copp, Clark Co., 1893.

Lillich, Meredith, "Shakespeare on the Screen: A Survey of How His Plays Have Been Made Into Movies," *FR* (June/July 1956), 247–60.

Loehlin, James N., "'Top of the World, Ma': *Richard III* and Cinematic Convention," in Boose and Burt, (eds.), *Shakespeare, The Movie*, pp. 67–79.

London Mercury, The, "Films [Review of Cukor *Romeo*]," *The London Mercury* 35 (Nov. 1936), 57.

Look, "A New *Romeo and Juliet*," 31 (17 Oct. 1967), 58ff.

MGM, "MGM Proudly Brings to the Screen [1953 *JC*]," Souvenir Book, n.d., p. 3.

MacArthur, Colin, "Review of Freeston *Macbeth*," *S&S* 7.6 (June 1997), 56–57.

Macnab, Geoffrey, "Review: Parker *Othello*," *S&S* 6.2 (Feb. 1996), 51–52.

"Review: Nunn *Twelfth Night*," *S&S* 6.11 (Nov. 1996), 60.

"Review: *Looking for Richard*," *S&S* 7.2 (Feb. 1997), 48–49.

Manheim, Michael, "Olivier's *Henry V* and the Elizabethan World Picture," *LFQ* (Kenneth S. Rothwell (ed.), special issue of papers from Seminar 16, World Shakespeare Congress), 11.3 (1983), 179–84.

"The Shakespeare Plays on TV," *SFNL* 8.2 (April 1984), 4.

Marks, Martin, "The Sound of Music," in Nowell-Smith (ed.) *The Oxford History of World Cinema*, pp. 248–59.

Marks, Peter, "So Young, So Fragile . . . [Nunn *TN*]," *NYT* 20 Oct. 1996, II. 13.

Maslin, Janet, "Royal Monster, Are You Out There?" *NYT* 11 Oct. 1996, C.3.

"Soft! What Light? It's Flash, Romeo," *NYT* 1 Nov. 1996, C.1.

Mathieson, Muir, "Note on *Hamlet*," *Film Music* 13 (Jan./Feb. 1954), 19.

McCarthy, Todd, "*Much Ado about Nothing*," *Variety* 3 May 1993.

McCloskey, Susan, "The Shakespeare Plays on TV [*Much Ado*]," *SFNL* 9.2 (Apr. 1985), 5.

McKernan, Luke, "Beerbohm Tree's *King John* Rediscovered: The First Shakespeare Film, September 1899," *SB* 11.1 (1993), 35–36.

"Further News on Beerbohm Tree's *King John*," *SB* 11.2 (1993), 49–50.

Private letter, 4 Nov. 1994.

Megahey, Leslie (Interviewer), "With Orson Welles: Stories from a Life in Film," Television interview in 1980, Channel TNT, Monday, 5 Feb. 1990.

Meyer, David, Conversation at London Globe Theatre, October 1996.

MFB, "[J.G.] Review of Fried *TN*," 23.269 (June 1956), 74.

MFB, "[P.H.] Review of *Forbidden Planet*," 23.269 (June 1956), 71.

MFB, "[W.F.] *As You Like It* [Czinner]," 3.33 (Sept. 1936), 147.

MG, "The 'Othello' of Mr. Orson Welles," 25 Feb. 1956.

Middleton, Drew, "Review of Televised *Hamlet*," *NYT* 14 Dec. 1947, X. 11.

Millar, Sylvia, *"King Lear,"* MFB 38 (1971), 182–83.

"Review [Heston *Ant.*]," *MFB* 39.459 (April 1972), 67.

Miller, Edwin, "Love is the Sweetest Thing," *Seventeen* 27 (Jan. 1968), 82ff.

Mirage Corp., "Essay on Dust Jacket," laser disk, *The Taming of the Shrew*. The
   Mary Pickford Co.© 1966; 1990.

MPW, "Audience Applauds His Shrieks of Agony," 22 Feb. 1908.

Mullan, John, "Ken, Al and Will, too," *TLS* 21 Feb. 1997, 19.

Mullin, Michael, "Peter Hall's *Midsummer Night's Dream* on Film," *ETJ* 27 (1975),
   529–34.

"Stage and Screen: The Trevor Nunn *Macbeth*," *SQ* 38.3 (Autumn 1987),
   350–59.

"Tony Richardson's *Hamlet*: Script and Screen," *LFQ* 4.2 (Spring 1976), 123–33.

"Orson Welles' *Macbeth*: Script and Screen," in Gottesman (ed.), *Focus on Orson
   Welles*, 136–145.

Newman, Karen, "Chabrol's *Ophelia*," *SFNL* 6.2 (March 1982), 1ff.

Newman, Kim, "Review of *Tromeo and Juliet*," *S&S* 6.12 (Dec. 1996), 54–55.

Nichols, Nina da Vinci, "Branagh's *Hamlet* Redux," *SB* 15.3 (Summer 1997), 38–41.

Nokes, David, "Echoes of Godard," *TLS* 29 Jan. 1988, 112.

Nouryeh, Andrea J., "Shakespeare and the Japanese Stage," in Dennis Kennedy
   (ed.), *Foreign Shakespeare*, 254–69.

NYT, "Edison's Film at Koster & Bial," 24 and 26 Apr. 1896, 5, 19.

"Review of Asta Nielsen *Hamlet*," 9 Nov. 1921, 20.

"Review of Guazzoni's *JC*," 12 Feb. 1922, II. 3.

Advertisement for Roxy Theatre, 6 March 1927, VIII.9.

O'Connor, John, "Olivier as the Controversial Shylock in 1880s," *NYT* 15 March
   1974, 67.

Occhiogrosso, Frank, "Cinematic Oxymoron in Peter Hall's *A Midsummer Night's
   Dream*," *LFQ* 11.3 (1983), 174–78.

"'Give Me Thy Hand': Manual Gesture in the Elliott/Olivier *King Lear*," *SB* 2.9
   (May–June 1984), 16–19.

Olivier, Laurence, "An Essay in *Hamlet*," in Cross (ed.), *The Film* Hamlet,
   pp. 11–15.

Orbison, Tucker, "The Stone and the Oak: Olivier's TV Film of *King Lear*," *CEA
   Critic* 47 (Fall-Winter 1984), 67–77.

Oruch, Jack, "Shakespeare for the Millions: Kiss Me, Petruchio," *SFNL* 11.2 (April
   1987), 7.

Osborne, Laurie E., "Poetry in Motion. Animating Shakespeare," in Boose and Burt
   (eds.), *Shakespeare, The Movie*, pp. 103–20.

Parker, Barbara L., "Review of George W. Williams' Videocassette Lecture,
   'Feuding and Loving in Shakespeare's *Romeo and Juliet*'," in *SFNL* 16.1 (Dec.
   1991), 8.

Parker, Elspeth, *"The Wars of the Roses*: Space, Shape, and Flow," *SB* 13.2 (Spring
   1995), 40–41.

"Performance of Epic Proportions [Branagh *Hamlet*]," *Oxford Times* 2 May 1997.

Parr, Gus, "S for Smoking," *S&S* 7. 12 (Dec. 1997), 30–33.

Pasinetti, P.M., "The Role of the Technical Adviser," *QFRT* 8.2 (1953), 131–38.

Perret, Marion, "Kurosawa's *Hamlet*: Samurai in Business Dress," *SFNL* 15.1 (Fall 1990), 6.

Petersen, Per Serritslev, "The 'Bloody Business' of Roman Polanski's *Macbeth*: A Case Study of the Dynamics of Modern Shakespeare [Reception] Appropriation," in Skovmand (ed.), *Screen Shakespeare*, pp. 38–53.

Pilkington, Ace G., "Zeffirelli's Shakespeare," in Davies and Wells (eds.), *Shakespeare and the Moving Image*, 163–79.

Pomar, Mark, "Books in Review," *SFNL* 4.1 (Dec. 1979), 10ff.

Praz, Mario, "Shakespeare's Italy," in *SS* 7 (1954), 95–106.

Pulleine, Tim, "Review of Coronado *Hamlet*," *MFB* 45.529 (Feb. 1978), 24.

Pursell, Michael, "Artifice and Authenticity in Zeffirelli's *Romeo and Juliet*," *LFQ* 14.4 (1986), 173–78.

"Zeffirelli's Shakespeare: The Visual Realization of Tone and Theme," *LFQ* 8.4 (1980), 210–18.

Quinn, Edward, "Zeffirelli's *Hamlet*," *SFNL* 15.2 (April 1991), 1ff.

Raban, Jonathan, "Peter Brook's *King Lear*," *New Statesman* 30 July 1971.

Rabkin, Norman, "Rabbits, Ducks and *Henry V*," *SQ* 28 (1977), 279–96.

Radio Times, "Interview with Janet Suzman," 188 (17 Sept. 1970), 6–7.

Rafferty, Terence, "Time Out of Joint [Review of McKellen *R3*]," *TNY* 22 Jan. 1996, 86.

Rajadhyaksha, Ashish, "India: Filming TN," in Nowell-Smith, (ed.), *Oxford History of World Cinema*, pp. 678–89.

Reed, Rex, "On the Town [Loncraine *R3*]," *NYO* 8 Jan. 1996, 22.

"Parting, Like, Sucks! So Does *Romeo*," *NYO* 11 Nov. 1996, 41.

Riding, Alan, "The Royal Shakespeare: Renewing Itself under Fire," *NYT* 17 May 1998, II.1ff.

Robinson, David, "Review [of Burton *Hamlet*]," *Financial Times* 7 July 1972.

Romney, Jonathan, "*Prospero's Books*," *S&S* 1.5 (Sept. 1991), 44–45.

Rosenbaum, Jonathan, "The Invisible Orson Welles: A First Inventory," *S&S* 55.3 (Summer 1986), 164–71.

Rothwell, Kenneth S., "Psychiatry and the Freshman Theme," *College English* 20.7 (April 1959), 338–42.

"The Audience for the Blackfriars Playhouse in Shakespeare's London," *The Yearbook of the American Philosophical Society*, Philadelphia, 1969: 649–50.

"Roman Polanski's *Macbeth*: Golgotha Triumphant," *LFQ* 1.4 (1973), 71–75.

"Zeffirelli's *Romeo and Juliet*: Words into Picture and Music," *LFQ* 5.4 (1977), 326–31.

"Roman Polanski's *Macbeth*: The 'Privileging' of Ross," *The CEA Critic*, 46 1&2 (1983–84), 50–55.

"Kenneth Branagh's *Henry V*: The Gilt [Guilt] in the Crown Re-Examined," *CD* 24.2 (Summer 1990), 173–78.

"In Search of Nothing: Mapping King Lear," in Boose and Burt (eds.), *Shakespeare, The Movie*, pp. 135–47.

Rozsa, Miklos "*Julius Caesar*," *FM* 13 (Sept./Oct. 1953), 7–13.

Sarris, Andrew, "At the Movies [Loncraine *R3*]," *NYO* 8 Jan. 1996, 17.

Schatz-Jacobsen, Claus, "'Knowing I Lov'd My Books': Shakespeare, Greenaway, and the Prosperous Dialectics of Word and Image," in Skovmand (ed.), *Screen Shakespeare*, pp. 132–47.

Schlueter, June, "Trivial Pursuit: The Casket plot in the Miller/Olivier *Merchant of Venice*," *SFNL* 10.1 (Dec. 1985), 7ff.

Schoenbaum, S., "Looking for Shakespeare," in Philip Highfill (ed.), *Shakespeare Craft*, Carbondale: Southern Illinois University Press, 1982, pp. 156–72.

Sharman, Leslie Felperin, "*Much Ado about Nothing*," *S&S* 3.9 (Sept. 1993), 50–51.

Shaw, William P., "Textual Ambiguities and Cinematic Certainties in *Henry V*," *LFQ* 22.2 (1994), 117–28.

"Violence and Vision in Polanski's *Macbeth* and Brook's *King Lear*," *LFQ* 14.4 (1986), 211–13.

Shenon, Philip, "A Hindu Romeo, A Muslim Juliet," *NYT* 5 Sept. 1991, A.4.

Sherwood, A. M. Jr., "The Movies [Taylor *Shr.*]," *Outlook* 153 (18 Dec. 1929), 633–34.

Silver, Nathan, [Review of Dennis Sharp's, *The Picture Palace* (London (?): Hugh Evelyn, 1969)] in *S&S* 38.3 (Summer 1969), 160ff.

Silverstein, Norman, "The Opening Shot of Roman Polanski's *Macbeth*," *LFQ* 2.1 (1974), 88–90.

Simon, John, "Review [Brook *Lear*]," *The New Leader* 27 Dec. 1971.

Simon, Ronald, "An Interview with George Schaefer," *Hallmark Hall of Fame: A Tradition of Excellence*, New York: Museum of Broadcasting, 1984: 23–30.

Singer, Ben, "New York, Just Like I Pictured It," *Cinema Journal* 35.3 (1996), 104–28.

Sinker, Mark, "Review [Noble *MND*]," *S&S* 7.1 (Jan. 1997), 41.

Sokolov, Raymond A., "Angry Young Hamlet [Richardson *Hamlet*]," *Newsweek* 73, 12 May 1969, 119.

Speaight, Robert, "Shakespeare in Britain," *SQ* 23 (Fall 1972) in Bulman and Coursen (eds.), *Shakespeare on Television*, pp. 246–47.

Stenberg, Doug, "The Circle of Life and the Chain of Being: Shakespearean Motifs in *The Lion King*," *SB* 14.2 (Spring 1996), 36–37.

Sterritt, David, "A *King Lear* Launched over Lunch," *CSM* 22 Jan. 1988.

Sunday Times, "*Julius Caesar* in Modern dress: Television Version," 24 July 1938.

Taylor, John Russell, "Review [Burton *Hamlet*]," *Times* 7 July 1972.

"Shakespeare in Film, Radio and Television," in T.J.B. Spencer (ed.), *Shakespeare: A Celebration, 1564–1616*, Penguin: Baltimore, 1964, 97–113.

Taylor, Neil, "The Films of *Hamlet*," in Davies and Wells (eds.), *Shakespeare and the Moving Image*, pp. 180–95.

Thalberg, Irving, "Picturizing *Romeo and Juliet*," in Romeo and Juliet *by William Shakespeare. A Motion Picture Edition*, New York: Random House, 1936, pp. 13–15.

The Spectator, "Cinema [Castellani *Romeo*]," no. 6587 (24 Sept. 1954), 361.

Thompson, Ann, "Asta Nielsen and the Mystery of *Hamlet*," in Boose and Burt (eds.), *Shakespeare, The Movie*, pp. 215–24.

Thompson, Howard, "Jason Robards, *et al.* [Burge/Snell *JC*]," *NYT* 4 Feb. 1971, 30.

Tibbenham, Allwyn, "Shakespeare Today," in "Points from Letters," *The Listener* 17 March 1937, 521.

Tibbetts, John, "Breaking the Classical Barrier [An Interview with Zeffirelli]," *LFQ* 22.2 (1994), 136–40.

Time, "Review [Dieterle/Reinhardt *MND*]," 26 (21 Oct. 1935), 44–45.

"*Macbeth* in Color," 13 Dec. 1954, 36.

"The New Pictures [Review of Welles *Othello*]," 6 June 1955, 106.

"Review [Richardson *Hamlet*]," 93, 28 Feb. 1969, 74.

Times, The, "Review of BBC Old Vic *Macbeth*," 13 Dec. 1937.

"Televised Drama [Review of BBC *Othello*]," 15 Dec. 1937.

"Uneasy Lies the Head [Review of *An Age of Kings*]," 8 July 1960.

"Continuity Problem of New BBC Shakespeare Series," 4 May 1963, 5d.

"Review [*Hamlet* at Elsinore]," 20 April 1964, 16.

"A Shakespearian Experience on TV," 21 April 1965, 13d.

Tiruchelvam, Sharmini, "Encounter on the Field of Philippi," *The Daily Telegraph Magazine* 6 Feb. 1970, 14–22.

Variety, "Review [of Ghana *Hamile*]," 20 Oct. 1965.

"[Whit.] Review of Re-Release Taylor *Shrew*," 2 Nov. 1966.

"[Rich.] Starry Cast . . . Review of Snell *JC*," 10 June 1970.

"[Pit.] Review of Heston *Antony*," 8 March 1972.

"[Pit.] Review of Coronado *Hamlet* at London Fest," 1 Dec. 1976.

"[Strat.] Review of Kemp *MND*," 11 Nov. 1984.

"[Lor.] Review of Lange *Othello*," 31 May 1989.

Vaughan, Virginia Mason, "The Forgotten Television *Tempest*," *SFNL* 9.1 (Dec. 1984), 3.

Walker, Alexander, "Review [Brook *Lr.*]," *Evening Standard*, 22 July 1971.

Warner Brothers, Public relations kit at British Film Institute.

Wayne, Valerie, "*Shakespeare Wallah* and Colonial Specularity," in Boose and Burt (eds.), *Shakespeare, The Movie*, 95–101.

Weales, Gerald, "I Am Not Prince Hamlet [review of stage performance]," *Commonweal* 90, 30 May 1969, 319–20.

Weatherby, W.J., "Forgotten Heir of *Citizen Kane*," *Guardian* 28 April 1992, 38.

Weiler, A.H., "Review [Yutkevich *Othello*]," *NYT* 16 May 1960, 39.

Weinraub, Bernard, "Interview with Polanski," *NYT Magazine* 12 Dec. 1971, 36 and *passim*.

Welles, Orson, "Interview," 1992 Voyager laser disk, appendix no. 49.

Welsh, James M., "Shakespeare, With – and Without – Words," *LFQ* 1.1 (1973), 84–88.

Whitebait, William, "Romeo and Juliet at the Odeon," *New Statesman and Nation* (2 Oct. 1954), 390.

Wilds, Lillian, "On Film: Maximilian Schell's Most Royal *Hamlet*," *LFQ* 4.2 (1976), 134–40;

"One *King Lear* for Our Time: A Bleak Film Vision by Peter Brook," *LFQ* 4.2 (1976), 159–64.

Williams, Linda, "Sex and Sensation," in Nowell-Smith (ed.), *Oxford History of World Cinema*, pp. 490–96.

Willson, Robert F. Jr., "Lubitsch's *To Be or Not to Be*," *SFNL* 1.1 (Dec. 1976), 2 and *passim*.

"Shakespeare in *The Goodbye Girl*," *SFNL* 2.2 (April 1978), 1 and *passim*.

"The Opening of *Henry V*: Olivier's Visual Pun," *SFNL* 5.2 (May 1981), 1 and *passim*.

"Disarming Scenes in *Richard III* & *Casablanca*," *SFNL* 10.1 (Dec. 1985), 4.

Wilson, Richard, "*Macbeth* on Film [Welles]," *TA* 33.5 (June 1949), 53–55.

Wilson, J. Dover, "Shakespeare: The Scholar's Contribution," *The Listener*, 17 March 1937, 498 and *passim*.

Wiseman, Susan, "The Family Tree Motel: Subliming Shakespeare in *My Own Private Idaho*," in Boose and Burt (eds.), *Shakespeare, The Movie*, 225–39.

World Film News, "Review of BBC *Julius Caesar*," 30 Aug. 1938.

Worthen, W.B., "Drama, Performativity, and Performance," *PMLA* 113.5 (Oct. 1998), 1093–1107.

Yardley, Jonathan, "The Metamorphosis of 'Henry'," *WP* 26 Feb. 1990, C2.

— CHRONOLOGICAL LIST OF FILMS —

Year	Title	Country	Director
1899	*Jn.*	UK	Dickson
1900	*Hamlet*	France	Maurice
1903	*Great Train Robbery*	USA	Porter
1907	*Ben Hur*	USA	X
1907	*Great Thaw Trial, The*	USA	X
1907	*Hamlet*	France	Méliès
1907	*Shakespeare Writing Julius Caesar*	France	Méliès
1908	*Ant.*	USA	Kent
1908	*JC*	USA	Ranous
1908	*MV*	USA	Ranous
1908	*Nero and the Burning of Rome*	USA	Porter
1908	*Othello*	USA	Ranous
1908	*R3*	USA	Ranous
1908	*Rom.*	USA	Ranous
1909	*Cook Makes Madeira Sauce, The*	USA	X
1909	*Lr.*	USA	Ranous
1909	*Macbeth*	France	Calmettes
1909	*MND*	USA	Kent
1909	*Othello*	Italy	Savio
1910	*Brutus* [JC]	Italy	Guazzoni
1910	*Cleopatra*	France	Zecca
1910	*Il Mercante di Venezia* [MV]	Italy	Savio
1910	*Lr.*	Italy	Savio
1910	*Romeo Turns Bandit*	France	X
1910	*TN*	USA	Kent
1911	*JC*	UK	Benson/Barker
1911	*Lonedale Operator, The*	USA	Griffith
1911	*R3*	UK	Barker
1911	*Rom.*	Italy	Savio
1912	*AYL*	USA	Kent
1912	*Cardinal Wolsey* [H8]	USA	Trimble
1912	*Quo Vadis*	Italy	Guazzoni
1912	*R3*	USA	Keane
1913	*Bisbetica Domata, La* [Shr.]	Italy	Ambrosio
1913	*Hamlet*	UK	Hepworth
1913	*Marcantonio e Cleopatra*	Italy	Guazzoni
1913	*MND*	Italy	Azzuri

Year	Title	Country	Director
1913	*MND*	Germany	Ewer
1913	*Shylock* [MV]	France	Desfontaines
1913	*Tragedie alla Corte di Sicilia, Una* [WT]	Italy	Negroni
1914	*Cabiria*	Italy	Pastrone
1914	*Giulio Caesar* [JC]	Italy	Guazzoni
1914	*Perils of Pauline, The*	USA	Gaznier/ MacKenzie
1915	*Birth of a Nation, The*	USA	Griffith
1916	*Intolerance*	USA	Griffith
1916	*Lr.*	USA	Warde, E.
1916	*Macbeth*	USA	Griffith/ Emerson
1916	*Rom.*	USA	Noble, J.
1916	*Rom.*	USA	Edwards
1917	*Hamlet*	Italy	Rodolfi
1919	*Cabinet of Dr. Caligari, The*	Germany	Wiene
1920	*Hamlet, The Drama of Vengeance*	Germany	Gade
1920	*Othello*	UK	Dyer
1921	*Carnival*	Uk	Knoles
1921	*Kid, The*	USA	Chaplin
1922	*Day Dreams*	USA	Keaton
1922	*Nosferatu*	Germany	Murnau
1922	*Othello*	Germany	Buchowetski
1923	*Kaufmann von Venedig, Der*	Germany	Felner
1924	*Last Laugh, The*	Germany	Murnau
1924	*Thief of Bagdad, The*	USA	Walsh
1925	*Street of Sorrow (Die freudlose Gasse)*	Germany	Pabst
1927	*Jazz Singer, The*	USA	Crosland
1927	*MV*	UK	Newman
1927	*Sunrise*	USA	Murnau
1927	*Way of All Flesh, The*	USA	Fleming
1928	*Passion of Joan of Arc*	France	Dreyer
1929	*Coquette*	USA	Taylor
1929	*Hollywood Revue of 1929*	USA	Reisner
1929	*Show of Shows* [Excerpt]	USA	Adolfi
1929	*Shr.*	USA	Taylor
1930	*Blue Angel, The*	Germany	von Sternberg
1930	*Man with Flower in Mouth*	UK	Baird
1930	*Royal Box, The*	USA	Foy
1931	*M*	Germany	Lang
1933	*Morning Glory*	USA	Sherman
1935	*Khoon Ka Khoon* [Hamlet]	India	Modi
1935	*MND*	USA	Dieterle/ Reinhardt
1935	*Triumph of the Will*	Germany	Reifenstahl
1936	*AYL*	UK	Czinner
1936	*Men Are Not Gods*	UK	Reisch
1936	*Rom.*	USA	Cukor/ Thalberg

Year	Title	Country	Director
1937	*AYL*	UK	Atkins
1937	*H5*	UK	O'Ferrall
1937	*Macbeth*	UK	O'Ferrall
1937	*Othello*	UK	O'Ferrall
1938	*Alexander Nevsky*	Russia	Eisenstein
1938	*JC*	UK	Bower
1939	*Gone with the Wind*	USA	Fleming
1939	*Stagecoach*	USA	Ford
1939	*Tmp.*	UK	Bower
1939	*Wizard of Oz*	USA	Fleming
1939	*Hunchback of Notre Dame*		Dieterle
1940	*Boys from Syracuse, The*	USA	Sutherland
1941	*Citizen Kane*	USA	Welles
1942	*Magnificent Ambersons, The*	USA	Welles
1942	*Shuhaddaa el Gharam* [Rom.]	Egypt	Selim
1942	*To Be or Not to Be*	USA	Lubitsch
1944	*Enfants du paradis, Les*	France	Carné
1944	*Grosse König, Der*	Germany	Harlan
1944	*H5*	UK	Olivier
1945	*Strange Illusion*	USA	Ulmer
1946	*Lady from Shanghai, The*	USA	Welles
1946	*My Darling Clementine*	USA	Ford
1947	*Double Life, A*	USA	Cukor
1947	*Hamlet*	UK	O'Ferrall
1947	*Macbeth*	USA	Bradley
1948	*Anjuman*	India	Hussain
1948	*Hamlet*	UK	Olivier
1948	*Macbeth*	USA	Welles
1948	*Otello*	USA	Crotty
1948	*Terra trema, La*	Italy	Visconti
1949	*H5* [scene]	USA	Demonstration for affiliates
1949	*JC*	USA	Miner/Nickell
1949	*Les amants de Verone*	France	Cayatte
1949	*Macbeth*	USA	Simpson/ Brown
1949	*Third Man, The*	UK	Reed
1950	*Black Rose, The*	USA	Hathaway
1950	*JC*	USA	Bradley
1950	*Rashomon*	Japan	Kurosawa
1950	*Shr.*	USA	Miner/Nickell
1951	*Coriolanus*	USA	Miner/Nickell
1951	*Macbeth*	USA	Miner/ Schaffner
1951	*Return to Glennascaul*	UK	Edwards
1952	*Othello*	Morocco Italy	Welles
1953	*Hamlet*	USA	Schaefer
1953	*JC*	USA	Mankiewicz/ Houseman

Year	Title	Country	Director
1953	*Kiss Me Kate* [Shr.]	USA	Sidney
1953	*Lr.*	USA	Brook
1954	*Macbeth*	USA	Schaefer
1954	*Prince of Players*	USA	Dunne
1954	*R2*	USA	Schaefer
1954	*Rom.*	UK/Italy	Castellani
1954	*Seven Samurai*	Japan	Kurosawa
1955	*Hamlet*	India	Sahu
1955	*Joe Macbeth*	UK	Hughes
1955	*Othello*	Russia	Yutkevitch
1955	*R3*	UK	Olivier
1955	*TN*	Russia	Fried
1956	*Forbidden Planet*	USA	Wilcox
1956	*Shr.*	USA	Schaefer
1956	*Ten Commandments, The*	USA	DeMille
1957	*Throne of Blood*	Japan	Kurosawa
1957	*Throne of Blood, The*	Japan	Kurosawa
1957	*TN*	USA	Greene
1958	*Kiss Me Kate* [Shr.]	USA	Schaefer
1958	*Touch of Evil, A*	USA	Welles
1959	*Ben-Hur*	USA	Wyler
1959	*Der Rest ist Schweigen*	Germany	Käutner
1959	*Hamlet*	USA	Nelson/ Benthall
1959	*JC*	UK	Burge
1959	*MND*	Czechoslovakia	Trnka
1960	*Bad Sleep Well, The* [Hamlet]	Japan	Kurosawa
1960	*Breathless*	France	Godard
1960	*Hamlet*	Germany	Wirth/Dmytryk
1960	*Macbeth*	USA	Schaefer
1960	*Magnificent Seven, The*	USA	Sturges
1960	*Tmp.*	USA	Schaefer
1961	*Age of Kings, An*	UK	Dews/Hayes
1961	*Last Year at Marienbad*	France	Resnais
1961	*Romanoff and Juliet*	USA	Ustinov
1961	*West Side Story*	USA	Wise/Robbins
1961	*Yojimbo*	Japan	Kurosawa
1962	*All Night Long*	UK	Dearden
1962	*And What If It's Love?* [Rom.]	Russia	Raizman
1962	*Ophelia*	France	Chabrol
1963	*Blowjob*	USA	Warhol
1963	*Cleopatra*	USA	Mankiewicz
1963	*Rricotta, La* [Curd-cheese]	Italy	Pasolini
1963	*Spread of the Eagle*	UK	Dews
1964	*Dr. Strangelove*	USA	Kubrick
1964	*Hamile: The Tongo Hamlet*	Ghana	Bishop
1964	*Hamlet*	Russia	Kozintsev
1964	*Hamlet*	USA	Gielgud
1964	*Hamlet at Elsinore*	UK/Denmark	Luke/Saville

Year	Title	Country	Director
1964	*MND*	UK	Kemp-Welch
1964	*My Fair Lady*	USA	Cukor
1965	*Othello*	UK	Burge
1965	*Shakespeare Wallah*	India	Ivory
1965	*Sound of Music, The*	USA	Wise
1965	*Wars of the Roses*	UK	Bakewell/ Barton/Hall
1966	*Chimes at Midnight*	Spain/ Switzerland	Welles
1966	*Conscience of the King*	USA	Oswald
1966	*Rom.*	UK	Drum
1966	*Shr.*	USA/Italy	Zeffirelli
1967	*Dr. Faustus*	UK	Coghill, B. & N.
1967	*Elvira Madigan*	Sweden	Widerberg
1967	*Two or Three Things I Know about Her*	France	Godard
1968	*Blue Movie*	USA	Warhol
1968	*Rom.*	Italy/UK	Zeffirelli
1968	*Rosemary's Baby*	USA	Polanski
1969	*Hamlet*	UK	Richardson
1969	*Lr.*	Russia	Kozintsev
1969	*Magic Show, The*	USA	Welles
1969	*MND*	UK	Birkett/Hall
1969	*MV*	UK	Miller
1969	*MV*	X	Welles
1970	*Hamlet*	UK	Wood
1970	*Hamlet, a Heranca*	Brazil	Candelas
1970	*JC*	UK	Burge
1970	*JC*	UK	Snell/Burge
1970 (1975)	*Macbeth*	UK	Messina/Gorrie
1970	*TN*	UK	Dexter/Sichel
1971	*Devils, The*	UK	Russell
1971	*Lr.*	UK	Brook
1971	*Macbeth*	UK	Polanski
1972 (1974)	*Ant.*	UK	Nunn/Scoffield
1972	*Ant.*	Spain/ Switzerland/UK	Heston
1972	*Discreet Charm of the Bourgeoisie*	France	Buñuel
1972	*TN*	USA	Wertheim
1973	*Ado*	USA	Papp/Antoon
1973	*Catch My Soul: Santa Fe Satan*	USA	McGoohan
1973	*F for Fake*	France	Welles
1973 (1977)	*Lr.*	USA	Papp/Sherin
1973	*Theatre of Blood*	UK	Hickox
974	*Harry and Tonto* [Lr.]	USA	Mazurzky
1974	*Woman Under the Influence, A*	USA	Cassavetes
1975	*One Hundred Twenty Days of Sodom*	Italy	Pasolini

Year	Title	Country	Director
11975	*Sebastiane*	UK	Jarman/ Humfress
1976 (1978)	*Err.*	UK	Nunn/Casson
1976	*Hamlet*	Spain/UK	Coronado
1976 (1979)	*Macbeth*	UK	Nunn/Casson
1976	*Rom.*	UK	Bosner
1976	*Shr.*	USA	Ball
1977	*Goodbye Girl, The*	USA	Ross
1978 (1979)	*AYL*	UK	Messina/ Coleman
1978	*Pennies from Heaven*	UK	Haggard
1978	*Filming Othello*	Germany	Welles
1978	*Jubilee*	UK	Jarman
1978 (1979)	*R2*	UK	Messina/Giles
1978 (1979)	*Rom.*	UK	Messina/Rakoff
1979 (1980)	*H41*	UK	Messina/Giles
1979 (1980)	*H42*	UK	Messina/Giles
1979 (1980)	*H5*	UK	Messina/Giles
1979	*H8*	UK	Messina/ Billington
1979	*JC*	UK	Messina/Wise
1979	*MM*	UK	Messina/Davis
1979	*Wiv.*	USA	Taylor
1980	*Fame*	USA	Parker
1980	*Hamlet*	UK	Messina/Bennett
1980	*Mon Oncle d'Amerique*	France	Resnais
1980 (1981)	*MV*	UK	Miller/Gold
1980	*Othello*	USA	White
1980	*Romeu e Julieta*	Brazil	Grisolli
1980	*Shadow Warrior, The*	Japan	Kurosawa
1980 1981	*Shr.*	UK	Miller
1980	*Tempest, The*	UK	Jarman
1980	*Tmp.*	UK	Messina/Gorrie
1980	*TN*	UK	Messina/Gorrie
1981	*Ant.*	UK	Miller
1981	*AWW*	UK	Miller/ Moshinsky
1981	*Kiss Me, Petruchio (Shr.)*	USA	Papp/Leach
1981	*Macbeth*	USA	Caldwell
1981	*Macbeth*	USA	Seidelman

Year	Title	Country	Director
1981 (1982)	*MND*	UK	Miller/ Moshinsky
1981	*Othello*	UK	Miller
1981	*Shr.*	Canada	Dews
1981	*Tempest*	USA	Mazursky
1981	*Tim.*	UK	Miller
1981 (1982)	*Tro.*	UK	Miller
1981	*WT*	UK	Miller/Howell
1982	*Draughtsman's Contract, The*	UK	Greenaway
1982	*Lr.*	UK	Sutton/Miller
1982	*MND*	USA	Papp/Lapine
1982	*R2*	USA	Woodman
1982 (1983)	*Wiv.*	UK	Sutton/Jones
1983 (1982)	*Cymbeline*	UK	Sutton/ Moshinsky
1983	*Dresser, The*	USA	Yates
1983 (1984)	*Err.*	UK	Sutton/ Cellan-Jones
1983	*The Black Adder*	UK	Atkinson
1983	*H6 1–3*	UK	Sutton/Howell
1983	*Lr.*	UK	Elliott
1983	*Macbeth*	UK	Sutton/Gold
1983	*R3*	UK	Sutton/Howell
1983 (1984)	*TGV*	UK	Sutton/Taylor
1984	*Ado*	UK	Sutton/Burge
1984	*Coriolanus*	UK	Sutton/ Moshinsky
1984	*Den tragiska historien om Hamlet, prinz av Danmark*	Sweden	Lyth
1984	*Jewel in the Crown, The*	UK	Monahan/ O'Brien
1984 (1985)	*Jn.*	UK	Sutton/Giles
1984	*MND*	Spain/UK	Coronado
1984	*Otelo de Oliveira*	Brazil	Grisolli
1984	*Per.*	UK	Sutton/Jones
1984	*Playing Shakespeare*	UK	Barton
1985	*Ant.*	USA	Carra
1985	*LLL*	UK	Sutton/ Moshinsky
1985	*Ran*	Japan	Kurosawa
1985	*Tit.*	UK	Sutton/Howell
1985	*Tmp.*	USA	Woodman
1986	*Carravagio*	UK	Jarman
1986	*Otello*	USA/Italy	Zeffirelli
1986	*Shr.*	USA	MacKenzie

Year	Title	Country	Director
1986	*Singing Detective, The*	UK	Amiel
1987	*Belly of an Architect, The*	UK	Greenaway
1987	*Err.*	USA	Mosher/ Woodruff
1987	*Hamlet*	UK	Kenyon/ MacDonald
1987	*Lr.*	USA/ Switzerland	Godard
1987	*Rom.*	USA	Thomas
1988	*Last of England, The*	UK	Jarman
1988	*Little Dorrit*	UK	Edzard
1988	*Othello*	UK/ South Africa	Suzman
1988	*TN*	UK	Branagh/ Kafno
1988 (1989)	*Wars of the Roses, The*	UK	Bogdanov
1989	*Dead Poets Society, The*	USA	Weir
1989	*H5*	UK	Branagh
1989	*Jaded*	USA	Kodar
1989	*Othello*	USA	Lange
1990	*Cook, the Thief, his Wife and Her Lover, The*	Netherlands/ France	Greenaway
1990	*Discovering Hamlet*	UK	Olshaker
1990	*Dreams*	Japan	Kurosawa
1990	*Godfather III*	USA	Coppola
1990	*Hamlet*	USA	Kline/ Browning
1990	*Hamlet*	USA	Zeffirelli
1990	*Men of Respect*	USA	Reilly
1990	*Torn Apart* [Rom.]	USA	Fisher
1991	*Henna*	India/Pakistan	Kapoor
1991	*L.A. Story*	USA	Jackson
1991	*My Own Private Idaho*	USA	Van Sant
1991	*Prospero's Books*	Netherlands/ France/Italy	Greenaway
1992	*AYL*	UK	Edzard
1992	*Shakespeare: The Animated Tales*	UK/Russia	Serebryakov/ Edwards
1993	*Ado*	UK/USA	Branagh
1993	*Blue*	UK	Jarman
1993	*Last Action Hero, The*	USA	McTiernan
1990s	*Seinfeld*	USA	Seinfeld
1994	*Lion King, The*	USA	Disney
1994	*Macbeth*	USA	Braunmuller/ Rodes
1994	*Natural Born Killers*	USA	Stone
1994	*Renaissance Man*	USA	Marshall
1995	*Hamlet: For the Love of Ophelia*	USA (?)	Damiano

Year	Title	Country	Director
1995	*In the Bleak Midwinter* [A Midwinter's Tale]	UK	Branagh
1995	*MV*	UK	Horrox
1995	*Othello*	UK	Parker
1995	*R3*	UK	Loncraine
1996	*Evita*	USA	Parker
1996	*Hamlet*	UK	Branagh
1996	*Looking for Richard*	USA	Pacino
1996	*MND*	UK	Noble
1996	*Romeo & Juliet*	USA	Luhrmann
1996	*TN*	UK	Nunn
1996	*Tromeo and Juliet*	USA	Kaufman
1997	*Thousand Acres, A*	USA	Moorhouse
1998	*Celebrity*	USA	Allen
X	*Mid-Slumber Night's Dream*	X	X
X	*Much Ado about Humping*	X	X

— FILMOGRAPHY AND TITLE INDEX —

Abbreviations for multi-word Shakespeare titles follow the standard MLA format, e.g., *MND=A Midsummer Night's Dream*, but single word titles like *Othello* are not abbreviated. For several reasons, release dates may vary slightly from one country to another but an attempt has been made to select a plausible one when reliable sources are in conflict. When two dates appear, as with the BBC The Shakespeare Plays series, the first is the UK release date, the second the US date. Surnames only of directors and key actors are given to help identify the film or television program. Early silent films, some sound films, and early television prior to the invention of the Kinescope may be permanently lost or archived in remote places so full information cannot be given.

Other abbreviations are as follows:

Fsibw	Film silent black-and-white
Fsit	Film silent tinted
Fsdbw	Film sound black-and-white
Fsdc	Film sound color
Tvbw	Television black-and-white
Tvc	Television color. Tvbw and Tvc are also used for black-and-white or color videos that have never been transmitted on the air.
Prod. Co/Dist.	Denotes one or two, of what may be several, companies involved with either making or marketing the film.
Mins.	Duration, though running times will vary depending on the condition of the print and the speed of projection. Allow for some leeway, especially for older films.
X	Information unavailable.

Title	Country	Year	Director	Actor(s)	Type	Prod. Co./Dist.	Mins.	Pages
Ado	USA	1973	Papp/ Antoon	Waterston, Widdoes, Watson	Tvc	NY Shakespeare Fest./CBS	120	106
Ado	UK	1984	Sutton/ Burge	Lunghi/ Lindsay	Tvc	BBC Shakespeare Plays	150	119
Ado	UK/USA	1993	Branagh	Branagh/ Thompson	Fsdc	Goldwyn	111	250–53, 254, 256
Age of Kings, An	UK	1961	Dews/ Hayes	Atkins/ Warner	Tvbw	BBC	Serial	99–100 101, 113
Alexander Nevsky	Russia	1938	Eisenstein	Cherkassov	Fsdbw	Mosfilm	112	55, 74, 77, 80, 91 162
All Night Long	UK	1962	Dearden	McGoohan/ Michell	Fsdbw	Rank	82	171, 223, 226
And What If It's Love? [Rom.]	Russia	1962	Raizman	X	Fsdc (?)	USSR	X	178
Anjuman	India	1948	Hussain	Nargis/Jaraj	Fsdbw	Nargis Art	140	170
Amants de Verone, Les	France	1949	Cayatte	Reggiani/ Aimée	Fsdbw	Films de France	110	177
Ant.	USA	1908	Kent	Chapman	Fsibw	Vitagraph	10	7

Title	Country	Year	Director	Actor(s)	Type	Prod. Co./Dist.	Mins.	Pages
Ant.	UK	1972 (1974)	Nunn/ Scoffield	Suzman/ Johnson	Tvc	ATV	162	110
Ant.	Spain/ Switzerland/ UK	1972	Heston	Heston/Neil	Fsdc	Folio Films	160	160, 163–67
Ant.	UK	1981	Miller	Blakely/ Lapotaire	Tvc	BBC Shakespeare Plays	177	114, 164
Ant.	USA	1985	Carra	Redgrave/ Dalton	Tvc	Bard Prod.	183	122
AWW	UK	1981	Miller/ Moshinsky	Johnson/ Charleson	Tvc	BBC Shakespeare Plays	160	114–15
AYL	USA	1912	Kent	Coghlan	Fsibw	Vitagraph	30	7
AYL	UK	1936	Czinner	Olivier	Fsdbw	20th-Century Fox	97	49–52, 61 216
AYL	UK	1937	Atkins	Scott/Swinlay	Tvbw	BBC	11	95
AYL	UK	1978 (1979)	Messina/ Coleman	Mirren/ Pasco	Tvc	BBC Shakespeare Plays	150	112
AYL	UK	1992	Edzard	Cusack/Fox/ Croft	Fsdc	Sands Films	117	50, 215–16, 231

Title	Country	Year	Director	Actor(s)	Type	Prod. Co./Dist.	Mins.	Pages
Bad Sleep Well, The [Hamlet]	Japan	1960	Kurosawa	Mifune	Fsdbw	Toho	135	191–94, 196
Belly of an Architect, The	UK	1987	Greenaway	Dennehy	Fsdc	Hemdale Releasing	118	208
Ben Hur	USA	1907	X	X	Fsibw	Kalem	10	12
Birth of a Nation, The	USA	1915	Griffith	Gish	Fsit	Mutual Film	120	21
Bisbetica Domata, La [Shr.]	Italy	1913	Ambrosio	Rodolfi	Fsibw	Ambrosio.	40	14
Black Adder, The	UK	1983	BBC	Atkinson	Tv	BBC	Series	123
Black Rose, The	USA	1950	Hathaway	Welles	Fsdbw	20th-Cent. Fox	120	79
Blowjob	USA	1963	Warhol	X	Fsdbw	The Factory	30	201
Blue	UK	1993	Jarman	Jarman	Fsdc	Basilisk Communications	76	208
Blue Angel, The	Germany	1930	von Sternberg	Dietrich/ Jannings	Fsdbw	UFA	98	26
Blue Movie	USA	1968	Warhol	Waldron, V & L.	Fsdbw	The Factory	133	201
Boys from Syracuse, The	USA	1940	Sutherland	Jones/Penner/ Raye	Fsdbw	Universal	73	109, 225

Title	Country	Year	Director	Actor(s)	Type	Prod. Co./Dist.	Mins.	Pages
Breathless	France	1960	Godard	Belmondo/Seberg	Fsdbw	Imperia Films	89	212
Brutus [JC]	Italy	1910	Guazzoni	Novelli	Fsibw	Cines	8	17
Cabinet of Dr. Caligari, The	Germany	1919	Wiene	Krauss	Fsibw	Decla-Bioskop	60	22, 26, 77
Cabiria	Italy	1914	Pastrone	Pagano	Fsibw	Itala Film	140	16, 45
Cardinal Wolsey [H8]	USA	1912	Trimble	Young	Fsibw	Vitagraph	10	7
Carnival	UK	1921	Knoles	Lang/Bayley	Fsibw	Alliance Films	54	222
Caravaggio	UK	1986	Jarman	Terry/Cooper	Fsdc	BFI	97	204
Celebrity	USA	1998	Allen	Branagh	Fsdbw	Sweetland/Miramax	113	246
Catch My Soul: Santa Fe Satan	USA	1973	McGoohan	Havens/LeGault	Fsdc	Metromedia	100	225–26
Chimes at Midnight	Spain/Switzerland	1966	Welles	Welles	Fsdbw	Internacionale/Peppercorn (US)	119	72, 84–89, 107, 113, 249
Citizen Kane	USA	1941	Welles	Welles	Fsdbw	RKO Mercury	119	44, 60, 72, 73, 77, 79, 129

Title	Country	Year	Director	Actor(s)	Type	Prod. Co./Dist.	Mins.	Pages
Cleopatra	France	1910	Zecca	Roche	Fsibw	Pathé	12	4
Cleopatra	USA	1963	Mankie-wicz	Burton/Taylor	Fsdc	20th-Century Fox	243	5
Conscience of the King	USA	1966	Oswald	Adams/Moss	Tvc	Star Trek	30	227
Cook Makes Madeira Sauce, The	USA	1909	X	X	Fsibw	X	X	6
Cook, the Thief, his Wife and Her Lover, The	Netherlands/France	1990	Greenaway	Gambon/Mirren	Fsdc	Allarts/Cook/Erato	123	208
Coquette	USA	1929	Taylor	Pickford	Fsdbw	United Artists	75	29
Coriolanus	USA	1951	Miner/Nickell	Greene/Evelyn	Tvbw	Westinghouse Studio One, CBS	60	105
Coriolanus	UK	1984	Sutton/Moshinsky	Howard/Worth	Tvc	BBC Shakespeare Plays	150	118
Cymbeline	UK	1983 1982	Sutton/Moshinsky	Sutton/Bloom/Mirren	Tvc	BBC Shakespeare Plays	175	116–17
Day Dreams	USA	1922	Keaton	Keaton	Fsibw	Buster Keaton Prod.	30	227
Dead Poets Society, The	USA	1989	Weir	Williams	Fsdc	Touchstone	129	227
Devils, The	UK	1971	Russell	Reed/Redgrave	Fsdc	Warner Bros.	109	204

Title	Country	Year	Director	Actor(s)	Type	Prod. Co./Dist.	Mins.	Pages
Discovering Hamlet	UK	1990	Olshaker	Branagh/Jacobi	Tvc	Renaissance Theatre Co.	53	228
Discreet Charm of the Bourgeoisie	France	1972	Buñuel	Rey	Fsdc	20th-Century Fox	120	231
Double Life, A	USA	1947	Cukor	Colman	Fsdbw	Universal	103	219, 223
Dr. Faustus	UK	1967	Coghill B. & N.	Taylor/Burton	Fsdc	Oxford Drama/Columbia	92	130
Dr. Strangelove	USA	1963	Kubrick	Sellers	Fsdbw	Columbia	102	201
Draughtsman's Contract, The	UK	1982	Greenaway	Higgins/Suzman	Fsdc	BFI/Channel Four	108	208
Dreams	Japan	1990	Kurosawa	Terao/Scorsese	Fsdc	Warner/Spielberg	120	192
Dresser, The	USA	1983	Yates	Finney/Courtenay	Fsdc	Columbia	118	116
Elvira Madigan	Sweden	1967	Widerberg	Degermark	Fsdc	Jance Film	95	41
Enfants du paradis, Les	France	1944	Carné	Barrault	Fsdbw	Tricolore Films	144	131
Err.	UK	1976 (1978)	Nunn/Casson	Dench/Annis	Tvc	ATV/RSC	130	109
Err.	UK	1983 1984	Sutton/Cellan-Jones	Gray/Cusack/Daltrey	Tvc	BBC Shakespeare Plays	110	118, 217

Title	Country	Year	Director	Actor(s)	Type	Prod. Co./Dist.	Mins.	Pages
Err.	USA	1987	Mosher/ Woodruff	Karamazov Brothers	Tvc	Lincoln Center/PBS	120	122
Evita	USA	1996	Parker	Madonna	Fsdc	Cinergi Pictures	134	232
F for Fake	France	1973	Welles	Kodar	Fsdbw	Films de l'Astrophore	85	72, 82, 215
Fame	USA	1980	Parker	Cara	Fsdc	MGM/United Artists	130	227
Filming Othello	Germany	1978	Welles	Welles	Tvbw	Hellwig	84	82
Forbidden Planet	USA	1956	Wilcox	Pidgeon	Fsdc	MGM	96	221
Giulio Cesare (JC)	Italy	1914	Guazzoni	Gonzales	Fsibw	Cines	60	17
Godfather III	USA	1990	Coppola	Pacino	Fsdc	Paramount	163	220, 226
Gone with the Wind	USA	1939	Fleming	Gable/Leigh	Fsdc	Selznick International	222	31
Goodbye Girl, The	USA	1977	Ross	Dreyfuss	Fsdc	Rastar	110	224
Great Thaw Trial, The	USA	1907	X	X	Fsibw	X	X	6
Great Train Robbery	USA	1903	Porter	Anderson	Fsibw	Edison	10	7
Grosse König, Der	Germany	1944	Harlan	X	Fsdbw	X	X	53

Title	Country	Year	Director	Actor(s)	Type	Prod. Co./Dist.	Mins.	Pages
H41	UK	*1979 (1980)*	Messina/ Giles	Finch/Gwillim	Tvc	BBC Shakespeare Plays	155	113
H42	UK	*1979 (1980)*	Messina/ Giles	Finch/Gwillim	Tvc	BBC Shakespeare Plays	155	113
H5	UK	*1937*	O'Ferrall	Arnaud	Tvbw	BBC	16	96
H5	UK	*1944*	Olivier	Olivier	Fsdc	Two Cities	137	50–56, 61, 71, 79, 84, 91, 125, 163
H5	UK	*1979 (1980)*	Messina/ Giles	McCowen Gwillim	Tvc	BBC Shakespeare Plays	170	113
H5	UK	*1989*	Branagh	Branagh/ Thompson	Fsdc	Sam Goldwyn	135	142, 230 246–50
H5 [scene]	USA	*1949*	Demon-stration for affiliates	Wanamaker	Tvbw	NBC	X	104
H6 1–3	UK	*1983*	Sutton/ Howell	Benson/Cook/ Foster	Tvc	BBC Shakespeare Plays	1–185 2–201 3–200	118
H8	UK	*1979*	Messina/ Billington	Stride/Bloom	Tvc	BBC Shakespeare Plays	145	112

Title	Country	Year	Director	Actor(s)	Type	Prod. Co./Dist.	Mins.	Pages
Hamile: The Tongo Hamlet	Ghana	1964	Bishop	Kofi/Yirenki	Fsdbw	Ghana Film	120	169–70
Hamlet	France	1900	Maurice	Bernhardt	Fsibw	Maurice	3	3
Hamlet	France	1907	Méliès	Méliès	Fsibw	Méliès	5	4
Hamlet	UK	1913	Hepworth	Forbes-Robertson	Fsibw	Gaumont	59	17–18
Hamlet	Italy	1917	Rodolfi	Ruggeri	Fsibw	Rodolfi-Film	40	14
Hamlet	UK	1947	O'Ferrall	Byron/Shaw	Tvbw	BBC	180	60, 98–99
Hamlet	UK	1948	Olivier	Olivier	Fsdbw	Two Cities	155	56–61, 99, 113, 144, 146, 177
Hamlet	USA	1953	Schaefer	Evans/Churchill	Tvbw	Hallmark	98	103
Hamlet	India	1955	Sahu	Sahu/Sinha	Fsdbw	Hindustan Chitra	X	168–69

Title	Country	Year	Director	Actor(s)	Type	Prod. Co./Dist.	Mins.	Pages
Hamlet	USA	1959	Nelson/ Benthall	Neville/ Jefford	Tvbw	DuPont Show of Month	90	103, 105
Hamlet	Germany	1960	Wirth/ Dmytryk	Schell/ Movar	Tvbw/ Fsdbw	Bavaria Attelier	127	172–73
Hamlet	Russia	1964	Kozintsev	Smoktunovsky/ Vertinskaya	Fsdbw	LenFilm	148	178, 183–87
Hamlet	USA	1964	Gielgud	Burton/ Cronan/Drake/ Herlie	Electrono-vision	Classic Cinemas	199	106–08
Hamlet	UK	1969	Richardson	Williamson/ Parfitt/ Hopkins	Fsdc	Woodfall	117	119, 139, 143–45 174
Hamlet	UK	1970	Wood	Chamberlain/ Redgrave	Tvc	Hallmark	115	102, 103
Hamlet	Spain/UK	1976	Coronado	Meyer/Mirren	Tvc	Cabochon	67	24, 201–03
Hamlet	UK	1980	Messina/ Bennett	Jacobi/Bloom/ Porter/Stewart	Tvc	BBC Shakespeare Plays	210	113
Hamlet	UK	1987	Kenyon/ MacDonald	Hitchcock/ Spaul	Tvc	Cambridge CCAT	96	122

Title	Country	Year	Director	Actor(s)	Type	Prod. Co./Dist.	Mins.	Pages
Hamlet	USA	1990	Kline/ Browning	Kline/ Venora	Tvc	WNET/ Great Performances	150	122, 140
Hamlet	USA	1990	Zeffirelli	Gibson/Close	Fsdc	Warner Bros.	135	137–42, 234, 255
Hamlet	UK	1996	Branagh	Branagh	Fsdc	Castle Rock/Columbia	242	60, 163, 254–58
Hamlet at Elsinore	UK/Denmark	1964	Luke/ Saville	Plummer/ Shaw/Caine	Tvc	BBC/Danmark Radio	80	108
Hamlet, The Drama of Vengeance	Germany	1920	Gade	Nielsen	Fsibw	Art-Film	117	21–25
Hamlet, a Heranca	Brazil	1970	Candelas	Cardoso/Fazio	Fsdc	Longfilm	87	170
Hamlet: For the Love of Ophelia	USA (?)	1995	Damiano	Young	Tvc	X	X	228
Harry and Tonto [Lr.]	USA	1974	Mazurzky	Carney	Fsdc	20th-Century Fox	115	221
Henna	India/Pakistan	1991	Kapoor	Bakhtiar/Kapoor	Fsdc	X	X	170
Hollywood Revue of 1929	USA	1929	Reisner	Gilbert/Shearer	Fsdbw	MGM	113	227
Hunchback of Notre Dame	USA	1939	Dieterle	Laughton	Fsdbw	RKO	117	37

Title	Country	Year	Director	Actor(s)	Type	Prod. Co./Dist.	Mins.	Pages
Intolerance	USA	1916	Griffith	Gish	Fsibw	Griffith	123	17
Jaded	USA	1989	Kodar	Brady	Fsdc	Olpal Prod.	93	93
Jazz Singer, The	USA	1927	Crosland	Jolson	Fsdbw	Warner Bros.	89	28
JC	USA	1908	Ranous	Kent	Fsibw	Vitagraph	13	7, 9, 17
JC	UK	1911	Benson/ Barker	Benson	Fsibw	Co-op Cine-matographer	10	17
JC	UK	1938	Bower	Milton	Tvbw	BBC	141	96
JC	USA	1949	Miner/ Nickell	Keith/Heston	Tvbw	CBS Studio One	60	105
JC	USA	1950	Bradley	Heston	Fsdbw	Avon Prod.	90	161
JC	USA	1953	Mankie-wicz/ Houseman	Brando/ Gielgud	Fsdbw	MGM	121	28, 44–48, 218, 219
JC	UK	1959	Burge	Sylvester/Porter	Tvbw	BBC	115	160
JC	UK	1970	Snell/ Burge	Heston/Rigg/ Robards/Gielgud	Fsdc	Common Wealth United	117	93, 160–63
JC	UK	1979	Messina/ Wise	Pasco/ Michell/Gray	Tvc	BBC Shakespeare Plays	180	112, 115

Title	Country	Year	Director	Actor(s)	Type	Prod. Co./Dist.	Mins.	Pages
Jewel in the Crown, The	UK	1984	Monahan/ O'Brien	Pigott-Smith/ Ashcroft	Tvc	BBC	700 (14 Episodes)	231
Jn	UK	1899	Dickson	Tree	Fsibw	British Mutoscope	1	1
Jn.	UK	1984 1985	Sutton/ Giles	Rossiter/ Bloom	Tvc	BBC Shakespeare Plays	155	119
Joe Macbeth	UK	1955	Hughes	Douglas/ Roman	Fsdbw	Columbia	107	219–20
Jubilee	UK	1978	Jarman	Runacre	Fsdc	Cinegate	103	204, 205
Kaufmann von Venedig, Der	Germany	1923	Felner	Krauss/Porten	Fsibw	Felner	64	26
Khoon Ka Khoon [Hamlet]	India	1935	Modi	Banu	Fsdbw	Stage Film	122	169
Kiss Me Kate [Shr.]	USA	1953	Sidney	Keel/Grayson	Fsdc	MGM	109	225
Kiss Me Kate [Shr.]	USA	1958	Schaefer	Drake/ Morrison	Tvbw	Hallmark	90	102
Kiss Me, Petruchio [Shr.]	USA	1981	Papp/ Leach	Streep/Julia	Tvc	NY Shakespeare Fest.	58	123
L.A. Story	USA	1991	Jackson	Martin	Fsdc	Rastar Prod.	95	227

Title	Country	Year	Director	Actor(s)	Type	Prod. Co./Dist.	Mins.	Pages
Lady from Shanghai, The	USA	1946	Welles	Hayworth	Fsdbw	Columbia	155/86	73
Last Action Hero, The	USA	1993	McTiernan	Schwarzenegger	Fsdc	Columbia Tristar	131	139
Last Laugh, The	Germany	1924	Murnau	Jannings	Fsibw	UFA.	91	11
Last of England, The	UK	1988	Jarman	Swinton	Fsdbw/c	BFI (?)	87	148, 207, 216
Last Year at Marienbad	France	1961	Resnais	Seyrig	Fsdbw	Astor Pictures	93	209
Lion King, The	USA	1994	Disney	Goldberg, Whoopi (Voice)	Animation	Disney	87	219, 228
Little Dorrit	UK	1988	Edzard	Guinness/Jacobi	Fsdc	Sands Film	Series	216
LLL	UK	1985	Sutton/ Moshinsky	Gwilym/ Warner	Tvc	BBC Shakespeare Plays	120	119
Lonedale Operator, The	USA	1911	Griffith	Sweet	Fsibw	Biograph	10	7
Looking for Richard	USA	1996	Pacino	Pacino/Baldwin	Fsdc	20th-Century Fox	109	219, 226–27
Lr.	USA	1909	Ranous	Ranous	Fsibw	Vitagraph	15	7, 10
Lr.	Italy	1910	Savio	Novelli	Fsibw	Film d'Arte Italiana	11	14
Lr.	USA	1916	Warde, E.	Warde, F.	Fsibw	Thanhouser	43	22, 153, 189, 191

Title	Country	Year	Director	Actor(s)	Type	Prod. Co./Dist.	Mins.	Pages
Lr.	USA	*1953*	Brook	Welles	Tvbw	Omnibus	73	21, 83–84, 150, 191
Lr.	Russia	*1969*	Kozintsev	Yarvet/ Shendrikova	Fsdbw	USSR	140	178, 183, 187–91
Lr.	UK	*1971*	Brook	Scofield	Fsdbw	Filmways/Athene	137	83, 150–54, 187
Lr.	USA	*1973 (1977)*	Papp/ Sherin	Jones/Julia/ Watson	Tvbw	Theatre in America NY Shakespeare Fest.	120	106
Lr.	UK	*1982*	Sutton/ Miller	Hordern/ Blethyn	Tvc	BBC Shakespeare Plays	180	116, 132
Lr.	UK	*1983*	Elliott	Olivier	Tvc	Granada TV	158	70–71, 116
Lr.	USA/ Switzerland	*1987*	Godard	Meredith	Fsdc	Cannon	95	211–15
M	Germany	*1931*	Lang	Lorre	Fsdbw	A.G.Ver/Star Film	89	151
Macbeth	France	*1909*	Calmettes	Mounet	Fsibw	Film d'Art	10	4
Macbeth	USA	*1916*	Griffith/ Emerson	Tree	Fsibw	Triangle	45 (?)	106

Title	Country	Year	Director	Actor(s)	Type	Prod. Co./Dist.	Mins.	Pages
Macbeth	UK	*1937*	O'Ferrall	Olivier/ Anderson	Tvbw	BBC/Old Vic	30	69, 96
Macbeth	USA	*1947*	Bradley	Bradley	Fsdbw	Willow Prod.	73	73, 161
Macbeth	USA	*1948*	Welles	Welles	Fsdbw	Republic	89	28, 48, 72, 73–78, 83
Macbeth	USA	*1949*	Simpson/ Brown	Hampden, Bellamy	Tvbw	NBC TV	60	105
Macbeth	USA	*1951*	Miner/ Schaffner	Heston/ Evelyn	Tvbw	Westinghouse Studio One, CBS	60	105
Macbeth	USA	*1954*	Schaefer	Evans/ Anderson	Tvc	Hallmark	103	102, 103
Macbeth	USA	*1960*	Schaefer	Evans/ Anderson	Fsdc/ For TV	Hallmark	107	102, 103
Macbeth	UK	*1970 (1975)*	Messina/ Gorrie	Porter/ Suzman	Tvc	PBS Classic Theatre	137	109
Macbeth	UK	*1971*	Polanski	Finch/Annis	Fsdc	Playboy	140	112, 140, 154–60, 196

Title	Country	Year	Director	Actor(s)	Type	Prod. Co./Dist.	Mins.	Pages
Macbeth	UK	1976 (1979)	Nunn/ Casson	Dench/ McKellen	Tvc	Thames TV	120	110–11
Macbeth	USA	1981	Caldwell	Anglim/ Anderman	Tvc	Lincoln Center	148	122
Macbeth	USA	1981	Seidelman	Brett/Piper	Tvc	Bard Prod.	150	122
Macbeth	UK	1983	Sutton/ Gold	Williamson/ Lapotaire	Tvc	BBC Shakespeare Plays	150	77, 118–19, 144
Macbeth	USA	1994	Braun-muller/ Rodes	Rodes	CD/ ROM	Voyager	X	123
Magic Show, The	USA	1969	Welles	X	X	X	Un-finished	72
Magnificent Ambersons, The	USA	1942	Welles	Welles/Cotten/ Costello	Fsdbw	Republic/RKO	131/ 88	72, 73, 76, 78, 88
Magnificent Seven, The	USA	1960	Sturges	Brynner/ McQueen	Fsdc	Alpha/Mirisch	126	250, 251, 253
Man with Flower in Mouth	UK	1930	Baird	Pirandello	Tvbw	Baird	X	95
Marcantonio e Cleopatra	Italy	1913	Guazzoni	Novelli/ Gonzales	Fsibw	Kleine	63	17

Title	Country	Year	Director	Actor(s)	Type	Prod. Co./Dist.	Mins.	Pages
Men Are Not Gods	UK	1936	Reisch	Hopkins/ Harrison	Fsdbw	United Artists	110	223
Men of Respect	USA	1990	Reilly	Turturro/ Steiger	Fsdc	Central City/Columbia	107	220
Mercante di Venezia, [MV]	Italy	1910	Savio	Bertini	Fsit	Film d'Arte Italiana	10	15
Mid-Slumber Night's Dream	X	X	X	X	X	X	X	228
In the Bleak Midwinter [Midwinter's Tale, A]	UK	1995	Branagh	Briers	Fsdbw	Rank	98	224, 246
MM	UK	1979	Messina/ Davis	Nelligan/ Pigott-Smith	Tvc	BBC Shakespeare Plays	150	112, 114
MND	USA	1909	Kent	Costello	Fsibw	Vitagraph	11	6, 10
MND	Italy	1913	Azzuri	Tommasi	Fsibw	Artistic Cinema Negatives	22	14, 16
MND	Germany	1913	Ewer	Berger	Fsibw	Deutsche Bioscop	45	22
MND	USA	1935	Dieterle/ Reinhardt	Cagney/ Rooney	Fsdbw	Warner Bros.	132	22, 28, 34–38, 147, 203

Title	Country	Year	Director	Actor(s)	Type	Prod. Co./Dist.	Mins.	Pages
MND	Czecho-slovakia	1959	Trnka	Burton (Voice)	Fsibw	Cescoslovensky	74	228
MND	UK	1964	Kemp-Welch	Hill	Tvbw	Rediffusion	111	108
MND	UK	1969	Birkett/Hall	Warner/Rigg/Mirren	Fsdc	RSC Ent./Alan Clore	124	143, 147–49,
MND	UK	1981 1982	Miller/Moshinsky	Mirren/Davenport	Tvc	BBC Shakespeare Plays	120	115, 206
MND	USA	1982	Papp/Lapine	Venora/DeMunn	Tvc	ABC Video	165	119
MND	Spain/UK	1984	Coronado	Kemp/Testory/Meyer	Fsdc	Cabochon	72	36, 201, 203–04
MND	UK	1996	Noble	Jennings/Duncan	Fsdc	Channel Four Films	103	244–46
Mon Oncle d'Amerique	France	1980	Resnais	Depardieu	Fsdc	Home Film Festival	123	209
Morning Glory	USA	1933	Sherman	Hepburn	Fsdbw	RKO	74	219, 227
Much Ado about Humping	X	X	X	X	X	X	X	228
MV	USA	1908	Ranous	Turner	Fsibw	Vitagraph	10	7

Title	Country	Year	Director	Actor(s)	Type	Prod. Co./Dist.	Mins.	Pages
MV	UK	1927	Newman	Casson	Fsdbw	DeForest Phonofilms	10	29
MV	UK	1969	Miller	Olivier	Tvc	Precision Video	120	69, 109
MV	X	1969	Welles	Gray	Fsd	Never completed	-0-	93
MV	UK	1980 (1981)	Miller/ Gold	Mitchell/ Jones	Tvc	BBC Shakespeare Plays	160	114
MV	UK	1995	Horrox	Peck/Gwynne	Tvc	Tetra Films	81	122
My Darling Clementine	USA	1946	Ford	Fonda/ Mowbray	Fsdbw	20th-Century Fox	97	227
My Fair Lady	USA	1964	Cukor	Harrison/ Hepburn	Fsdc	MGM	170	61
My Own Private Idaho	USA	1991	Van Sant	Phoenix/Reeves	Fsdc	Fine Line Features	102	201, 225
Natural Born Killers	USA	1994	Stone	Harrelson/Lewis	Fsdc	Warner Bros.	119	42
Nero and the Burning of Rome	USA	1908	Porter	X	Fsibw	Edison	10	5
Nosferatu	Germany	1922	Murnau	Schreck	Fsibw	Prana-Film	63	34, 205
One Hundred Twenty Days of Sodom	Italy	1975	Pasolini	Bonacelli/ Cataldi	Fsdc	Peppercorn/Wormser	117	201

Title	Country	Year	Director	Actor(s)	Type	Prod. Co./Dist.	Mins.	Pages
Ophelia	France	1962	Chabrol	Valli/Jocelyn	Fsdbw	Boreal Pictures	105	177
Otello	USA	1948	Crotty	Albanese/ Warren	Tvbw	ABC TV	240	102
Otello	USA/Italy	1987	Zeffirelli	Domingo	Fsdc	Cannon Group	123	129, 219
Otelo de Oliveira	Brazil	1984	Grisolli	Bonfim/ Lemmertz	Tvc	TV Globo	120	171
Othello	USA	1908	Ranous	Ranous	Fsibw	Vitagraph	10	7
Othello	Italy	1909	Savio	Garavaglia	Fsibw	Film d'Arte Italiana	16	14
Othello	UK	1920	Dyer	Animation	Fsibw	Hepworth	10	227
Othello	Germany	1922	Bucho- wetski	Jannings	Fsibw	Wörner-Film	98	22, 25, 238
Othello	UK	1937	O'Ferrall	Johnson/ Holloway	TVbw	BBC	67	98
Othello	Morocco/Italy	1952	Welles	Welles	Fsdbw	Mogador/Mercury	91	72, 76, 78–84, 181, 183, 235, 238
Othello	Russia	1955	Yutkevitch	Bondarchuk/ Skobtseva	Fsdc	MosFilm	108	178, 180–83

Title	Country	Year	Director	Actor(s)	Type	Prod. Co./Dist.	Mins.	Pages
Othello	UK	1965	Burge	Olivier	Fsdc	BHE/Eagle	166	67–69, 218–19
Othello	USA	1980	White	Kotto/Dixon	Fsdc	Howard University	115	215–16
Othello	UK	1981	Miller	Hopkins/ Hoskins	Tvc	BBC Shakespeare Plays	210	115–16
Othello	UK/ South Africa	1988	Suzman	Kani/Haines	Tvc	Focus/Portobello	199	119–20, 215
Othello	USA	1989	Lange	Lange/James	Fsdc	Rockbottom Productions	120	216
Othello	UK	1995	Parker	Fishburne/ Jacob/Branagh	Fsdc	Rank/Castle Rock	123	142, 235–38, 246
Passion of Joan of Arc	France	1928	Dreyer	Falconetti	Fsibw	Société Générale de Film	114	177
Pennies from Heaven	UK	1978	Haggard	Hoskins	Tvc	BBC	Series	116
Per.	UK	1984	Sutton/ Jones	Gwilym/ Peacock	Tvc	BBC Shakespeare Plays	180	118
Perils of Pauline, The	USA	1914	Gaznier/ MacKenzie	Panzer/ White	Fsibw	Pathé	Series	8
Playing Shakespeare	UK	1984	Barton	Multiple actors	Tvc	Channel Four	Series	123, 228

Title	Country	Year	Director	Actor(s)	Type	Prod. Co./Dist.	Mins.	Pages
Prince of Players	USA	1954	Dunne	Burton	Fsdc	20th-Century Fox	105	219, 226
Prospero's Books	Netherlands/ France/Italy	1991	Greenaway	Gielgud	Fsdc	Allarts/Cine/Camera One		107, 208–11, 219
Quo Vadis	Italy	1912	Guazzoni	X	Fsibw	X	X	17, 20
R2	USA	1954	Schaefer	Evans/ Churchill	Tvbw	Hallmark	120	120, 103
R2	UK	1978 (1979)	Messina/ Giles	Jacobi/ Gielgud	Tvc	BBC Shakespeare Plays	180	107, 112, 113, 115
R2	USA	1982	Woodman	Birney/ Hammond	Tvc	Bard Prod.	172	122
R3	USA	1908	Ranous	Turner	Fsibw	Vitagraph	10	7
R3	UK	1911	Barker	Benson	Fsibw	Cooperative Cinematographer	15	19
R3	USA	1912	Keane	Warde	Fsibw	Dudley	55	18–22
R3	UK	1955	Olivier	Olivier	Fsdc	London Film Prod.	158	62–67, 71, 105, 141

Title	Country	Year	Director	Actor(s)	Type	Prod. Co./Dist.	Mins.	Pages
R3	UK	*1983*	Sutton/ Howell	Cook/ Wanamaker	Tvc	BBC Shakespeare Plays	230	118
R3	UK	*1995*	Loncraine	McKellen/ Smith	Fsdc	United Artists	104	120, 191, 230–35
Ran	Japan	*1985*	Kurosawa	Nakadai	Fsdc	Greenway Film/ Nippon	160	197–200, 212
Rashomon	Japan	*1950*	Kurosawa	Mifune	Fsdbw	Daiei Prod.	88	192
Renaissance Man	USA	*1994*	Marshall	DeVito	Fsdc	Cinergi Pictures	128	277
Rest ist Schweigen, Der	Germany	*1959*	Käutner	Kruger/Andree	Fsdbw	Frele Film	106	172
Return to Glennascaul	UK	*1951*	Edwards	Welles	Fsdbw	X	X	79
Ricotta, La [Curd-cheese]	Italy	*1963*	Pasolini	X	Fsdbw	X	15 (?)	201
Rom.	USA	*1908*	Ranous	Panzer/ Lawrence	Fsibw	Vitagraph	15	7, 8
Rom.	Italy	*1911*	Savio	Bertini	Fsibw	Film d'Arte Italiana	25	14
Rom.	USA	*1916*	Noble, J.	Bushman/ Bayne	Fsibw	Metro	80	21
Rom.	USA	*1916*	Edwards	Hilliard/Bara	Fsibw	Fox	50	21, 243

Title	Country	Year	Director	Actor(s)	Type	Prod. Co./Dist.	Mins.	Pages
Rom.	USA	*1936*	Cukor/Thalberg	Shearer/Howard	Fsdbw	MGM	126	28, 39–44, 134, 143
Rom.	UK/Italy	*1954*	Castellani	Harvey/Shentall	Fsdc	Verona Productions	138	125–29, 170, 243
Rom.	UK	*1966*	Drum	Francis/Scoular	Fsdbw	RADA	107	218
Rom.	Italy/UK	*1968*	Zeffirelli	Hussey/Whiting	Fsdc	BHE/Dino De Laurentiis	152	112, 133–37, 142, 143, 170, 225, 241, 243
Rom.	UK	*1976*	Bosner	McEnery/Badel	Tvc	St. George's Playhouse	170	111
Rom.	UK	*1978 (1979)*	Messina/Rakoff	Ryecarft/Saire/Johnson	Tvc	BBC Shakespeare Plays	170	112
Rom.	USA	*1987*	Thomas	X	Tvc	X	X	228
Romanoff and Juliet	USA	*1961*	Ustinov	Ustinov/Dee	Fsdc	Universal/International	112	221
Romeo & Juliet	USA	*1996*	Luhrmann	DiCaprio/Danes	Fsdc	20th-Century Fox	120	142, 225, 241–44
Romeo Turns Bandit	France	*1910*	X	X	Fsibw	Pathé	6	5

Title	Country	Year	Director	Actor(s)	Type	Prod. Co./Dist.	Mins.	Pages
Romeu e Julieta	Brazil	1980	Grisolli	Junior/Santos	Tvc	TV Globo	94	170–71
Rosemary's Baby	USA	1968	Polanski	Farrow/Cassa-vetes/Gordon	Fsdc	Paramount	136	154
Royal Box, The	USA	1930	Foy	Moissi	Fsibw	Warner Bros.	89	226
Sebastiane	UK	1975	Jarman/Humfress	Treviglio	Fsdc	Discopat	85	204–5
Seinfeld	USA	1990's	NBC	Seinfeld	Tv	NBC	Series	103
Seven Samurai	Japan	1954	Kurosawa	Mifune	Fsdbw	Toho	207	193, 194
Shadow Warrior, The	Japan	1980	Kurosawa	Nakadai	Fsdbw	Kurosawa/Toho	162	192
Shakespeare Wallah	India	1965	Ivory	Kendal/Kapoor	Fsdc	Merchant/Ivory	124	168–69, 224
Shakespeare Writing "Julius Caesar"	France	1907	Méliès	Méliès	Fsibw	Méliès	10	4
Shakespeare: The Animated Tales	UK/Russia	1992	Serebry-akov/Edwards	Animations	Tvc	Island World Video	Series	228
Show of Shows [Excerpt]	USA	1929	Adolfi	Barrymore	Fsdbw	Warner Bros.	120	39, 227

Title	Country	Year	Director	Actor(s)	Type	Prod. Co./Dist.	Mins.	Pages
Shr.	USA	1929	Taylor	Pickford/Fairbanks	Fsdbw	United Artists	68	5, 28–34 50
Shr.	USA	1950	Miner/Nickell	Heston/Kirk	Tvbw	Westinghouse Studio One, CBS	60	105
Shr.	USA	1956	Schaefer	Evans/Palmer	Tvc	Hallmark	90	102, 103
Shr.	USA/Italy	1966	Zeffirelli	Taylor/Burton	Fsdc	Royal Films	121	29, 35, 129–33, 136, 141
Shr.	USA	1976	Ball	Singer/Olster	Tvc	Am. Cons. Theatre	82	106
Shr.	UK	1980 1981	Miller	Cleese/Badel	Tvc	BBC Shakespeare Plays	125	115, 132
Shr.	Canada	1981	Dews	Cariou/Flett	Tvc	Stratford Fest.	153	121
Shr.	USA	1986	MacKenzie	Willis/Shepherd	Tvc	ABC-TV, "Moonlighting"	X	123
Shuhaddaa el Gharam [Rom.]	Egypt	1942	Selim	Mourad	Fsdbw	Films el Nil	90	170
Shylock [MV]	France	1913	Desfontaines	Baur	Fsibw	Film d'Art	33	14
Singing Detective, The	UK	1986	Amiel	Gambon	Tvc	BBC	Series	231

Title	Country	Year	Director	Actor(s)	Type	Prod. Co./Dist.	Mins.	Pages
Sound of Music, The	USA	1965	Wise	Andrews	Fsdc	20th-Century Fox	172	258
Spread of the Eagle	UK	1963	Dews	Pettingell	Tvbw	BBC	Series	98, 99, 100–01
Stagecoach	USA	1939	Ford	Wayne	Fsdbw	United Artists	99	73
Strange Illusion	USA	1945	Ulmer	Lydon	Fsdbw	PRC Pictures	80	220
Street of Sorrow (Die freudlose Gasse)	Germany	1925	Pabst	Garbo/Nielsen	Fsibw	X	X	22
Sunrise	USA	1927	Murnau	Gaynor	Fsibw	Fox	90	22
Ten Commandments	USA	1956	De Mille	Heston/ Brynner	Fsdbw	MGM	219	45 ,163
Terra trema, La	Italy	1948	Visconti	Non-professionals	Fsdbw	Universalis	160	134
TGV	UK	1983 1984	Sutton/ Taylor	Hudson/ Butterworth	Tvc	BBC Shakespeare Plays	135	118
Theatre of Blood	UK	1973	Hickox	Price	Tvc	United Artists	104	219, 226
Thief of Bagdad, The	USA	1924	Walsh	Fairbanks	Fsibw	United Artists	140	29, 30, 130
Third Man, The	UK	1949	Reed	Welles	Fsdbw	London Films	104	79

Title	Country	Year	Director	Actor(s)	Type	Prod. Co./Dist.	Mins.	Pages
Thousand Acres, A	USA	1997	Moorhouse	Lange	Fsdc	Beacon Comm.	105	224
Throne of Blood	Japan	1957	Kurosawa	Mifune	Fsdbw	Toho	109	168, 191, 193–97, 200, 206, 218
Tim.	UK	1981	Miller	Price/Shrapnel	Tvc	BBC Shakespeare Plays	130	115
Tit.	UK	1985	Sutton/ Howell	Peacock/ Calder-Marshall	Tvc	BBC Shakespeare Plays	150	119
Tmp.	UK	1939	Bower	Ashcroft	Tvbw	BBC	100	98
Tmp.	USA	1960	Schaefer	Remick/Burton	Tvc	Hallmark	90	102, 103, 206
Tmp.	UK	1980	Messina/ Gorrie	Hordern/ Guard	Tvc	BBC Shakespeare Plays	125	113, 206
Tmp.	UK	1980	Jarman	Wilcox/Birkett	Fsdc	World Northal	90	103, 204–08
Tmp.	USA	1981	Mazursky	Cassavetes	Fsdc	Columbia	140	213, 221–22
Tmp.	USA	1985	Woodman	Zimbalist/ Taylor	Tvc	Bard Prod.	126	122

Title	Country	Year	Director	Actor(s)	Type	Prod. Co./Dist.	Mins.	Pages
TN	USA	1910	Kent	Gordon	Fsibw	Vitagraph	12	7, 10, 179
TN	Russia	1955	Fried	Luchko/Larionova	Fsdc	LenFilm	90	112, 178–80, 182, 183
TN	USA	1957	Greene	Evans/Harris	Tvbw	Hallmark	90	102, 103
TN	UK	1970	Dexter/Sichel	Guinness/Richardson/Plowright	Tvc	ATV TV	105	108, 109 238
TN	USA	1972	Wertheim	X	Tvc	Playboy	X	228
TN	UK	1980	Messina/Gorrie	McCowen/Peacock/Kendal	Tvc	BBC Shakespeare Plays	130	112, 169
TN	UK	1988	Branagh/Kafno	Barber/Lesser	Tvc/Disk	Renaissance Theatre Co.	165	123, 246, 256
TN	UK	1996	Nunn	Carter	Fsdc	Fine Line Features	105	238–40
To Be or Not to Be	USA	1942	Lubitsch	Benny	Fsdbw	United Artists	99	223–24
Torn Apart [Rom.]	USA	1990	Fisher	Pasdar/Peck	Fsdc	Castle Hill	95	170
Touch of Evil, A	USA	1958	Welles	Heston	Fsdbw	Universal	108/93	80, 94

Title	Country	Year	Director	Actor(s)	Type	Prod. Co./Dist.	Mins.	Pages
Tragedie alla Corte di Sicilia, Una [WT]	Italy	1913	Negroni	Fabbri	Fsit	Milano-Film	40	15
Tragiska historien om Hamlet, prinz av Danmark, Den	Sweden	1984	Lyth	Skarsgård/ Malm	Tvc	Rundquist	160	173–76
Triumph of the Will	Germany	1935	Reifenstahl	Documentary	Fsdbw	UFA	80	53
Tro.	UK	1981 1982	Miller	Lesser/Burden	Tvc	BBC Shakespeare Plays	180	115
Tromeo and Juliet	USA	1996	Kaufman	Jensen/Keenan	Fsdc	Troma Inc.	107	228–29
Two or Three Things I Know about Her	France	1967	Godard	Vlady	Fsdbw	Anouchka Films	95	212
Wars of the Roses	UK	1965	Bakewell/ Barton/ Hall	Warner Holm Ashcroft	Tvbw	BBC	Series	101–02
Wars of the Roses, The	UK	1988 (1989)	Bogdanov	Jarvis/ Pennington	Tvc	English Shakespeare Co.	194	120–21
Way of All Flesh, The	USA	1927	Fleming	Jannings	Fsibw	Paramount/Lasky	90	25
West Side Story	USA	1961	Wise/ Robbins	Wood	Fsdc	United Artist	151	170, 177, 219, 225

Title	Country	Year	Director	Actor(s)	Type	Prod. Co./Dist.	Mins.	Pages
Wiv.	USA	*1979*	Taylor	Charles/ Grahame	Tvc	Los Angeles Globe	*120*	*122*
Wiv.	UK	*1982 1983*	Sutton/ Jones	Griffiths/ Kingsley	Tvc	BBC Shakespeare Plays	*150*	*118*
Wizard of Oz	USA	*1939*	Fleming	Garland	Fsdc	MGM	*119*	*205*
Woman Under the Influence, A	USA	*1974*	Cassavetes	Rowlands	Fsdc	Faces International	*155*	*141*
WT	UK	*1981*	Miller/ Howell	Kemp/ Calder-Marshall	Tvc	BBC Shakespeare Plays	*185*	*115, 173*
Yojimbo	Japan	*1961*	Kurosawa	Mifune	Fsdbw	Kurosawa/Toho	*110*	*193*

— NAME INDEX —